RANGER'S LAW

Forge Books by Elmer Kelton

SONS OF TEXAS TRILOGY

Sons of Texas

The Raiders

The Rebels

Badger Boy

Bitter Trail

The Buckskin Line

Buffalo Wagons

Cloudy in the West

Hot Iron

Jericho's Road

The Pumpkin Rollers

Ranger's Trail

Six Bits a Day

The Smiling Country

Texas Rifles

Texas Vendetta

The Way of the Coyote

Lone Star Rising

(comprising *The Buckskin Line, Badger Boy,*
and *The Way of the Coyote*)

NONFICTION

Sandhills Boy: The Winding Trail of a Texas Writer

RANGER'S LAW

A LONE STAR SAGA

ELMER KELTON

FORGE® A Tom Doherty
Associates Book
New York

RANGER'S LAW: A LONE STAR SAGA

Copyright © 2006 by Elmer Kelton

Ranger's Trail copyright © 2002 by Elmer Kelton
Texas Vendetta copyright © 2004 by Elmer Kelton
Jericho's Road copyright © 2004 by Elmer Kelton

A Forge Book
Published by Tom Doherty Associates, LLC
175 Fifth Avenue
New York, NY 10010

www.tor-forge.com

Forge® is a registered trademark of Tom Doherty Associates, LLC.

Library of Congress Cataloging-in-Publication Data

Kelton, Elmer.
    Ranger's law : a Lone Star saga / Elmer Kelton.
        p. cm.
    Contents: Ranger's trail—Texas vendetta—Jericho's road.
    "A Tom Doherty Associates Book."
    ISBN-13: 978-0-7653-1520-5
    ISBN-10: 0-7653-1520-3
    I. Title.

PS3561.E3975 R357 2006
813'.54—dc22

                                                                2007270839

First Hardcover Edition: November 2006
First Trade Paperback Edition: November 2007

Printed in the United States of America

0 9 8 7 6 5 4 3 2 1

CONTENTS

RANGER'S
Trail

Dedicated to Nat Sobel, agent, friend, and a good judge of a story

CHAPTER

ONE

AUSTIN, TEXAS, JANUARY 1874

The election had gone smoothly except for certain extralegal shenanigans perpetrated by both sides. Those were a normal feature of Texas politics and came as no surprise. By contrast the aftermath was chaotic enough to try the patience of saints, if there had been any. Rusty Shannon had encountered few saints in reconstruction Texas.

He slow-trotted his dun horse westward along a rutted wagon road skirting the edge of the Colorado River and wished he were back home on the farm where he belonged. On one side of him rode Sheriff Tom Blessing, in his sixties but still blacksmith-strong, solid as a block of oak timber. On the other, Andy Pickard whistled in a country boy's youthful awe and marveled at the town just ahead. His urban experience had been limited to a few small crossroads settlements.

Andy declared, "I had no idea Austin was this big. Must be three—maybe four—thousand people here. I never saw such a place in my life."

No one knew exactly how long a life that had been. Andy had been orphaned before he was old enough to retain clear memories. Rusty's best judgment was that he might be eighteen or nineteen, allowing some leeway on one side or the other. Strenuous outdoor labor and the excesses of Texas weather had given him a mature appearance beyond his years. He had a young man's seasoned face but had not lost the questing eyes of a boy eager to ride over the hill and see the other side. Girls seemed to consider him handsome. Andy seemed to have no objection to their thinking so.

Rusty turned up his frayed old coat collar against a cold wind coming off of the river. He had been wearing that coat for more than ten years, always intending to buy a new one someday when he felt he had a few dollars to spare but always "making do" for one more winter. He said, "San Antonio's bigger. I was there once."

His face, browned and chiseled with premature lines, was that of a man forty or more. Actually he was in his mid-thirties, but most had been hard years spent in sun and wind, riding with frontier rangers or walking behind mules and a plow. He said, "Got no use for San Antonio, though. It's overrun with gamblers and whiskey peddlers and pickpockets."

Tom Blessing declared, "Austin's worse. It's overrun with lawyers."

Andy had seen little of gamblers, whiskey peddlers, pickpockets or lawyers, but he was itching to start. He told Rusty, "You always say I need more learnin'. I'll bet I could learn a lot here."

"Mostly stuff you oughtn't to know."

Andy was well schooled in the ways of nature, but Rusty had worried about his limited book education. Andy had caught a little here and a little there as country teachers came, stayed awhile, then drifted on. Rusty, in his time, had had the advantage of coaching by a foster mother. There had been no woman to help teach Andy. At least he could read a newspaper, and he had an aptitude with figures. He was not easily cheated, nor was he a forgiving victim. Most who tried once never cared to do it a second time.

Andy said, "I doubt I'd get bored in a place like this. Bet there's somethin' goin' on all the time."

In Rusty's view, that was the trouble. His idea of a perfect day was a quiet one. He had finally begun having a lot of those, thanks to the farm. "Most of it you wouldn't want any part of. Country folks couldn't abide the crowdin'. You soon get tired of people trompin' on your toes all the time."

He was here against his will and better judgment. He had planned a journey north toward old Fort Belknap to visit the Monahan family and to bring Josie Monahan back with him as his wife. But Tom had asked him to make this trip, and it was against Rusty's nature to refuse a good friend. Tom had ridden often with Daddy Mike Shannon in old times when there was Indian trouble. He had introduced Rusty to the rangers at a crisis point when Rusty had badly needed somewhere to go. Rusty often said he would follow Tom into hell with a bucket of water. He had, once or twice. Austin might not be hell, but Rusty did not consider it heaven, either.

He wished he had not given in to Andy's plea that he be allowed to come along. He dreaded the temptations this town might present to someone no longer a boy but not quite yet a man. Rusty had taken on the responsibility of a foster brother after Andy's nearest known relative, an uncle, had rejected him. At times, like now, it had been an uneasy burden to carry.

He surveyed the town with apprehension. "Tom, reckon how we'll find your friend amongst all those people?"

"Maybe we'll get lucky and stumble into him. Otherwise, he's likely puttin' up at a wagon yard. We'll ask around."

Tom had been a county sheriff before reconstruction authorities threw him out of office for having served the Texas Confederate government. The recent election had restored his badge after the former Confederates finally regained their right to vote. Another sheriff, a friend of his, had sent word that he was badly needed in Austin. He had not explained his reasons. He had just said to hurry and to bring help. Tom had immediately called on Rusty, respecting his law enforcement experience before war's end had caused the ranger companies to disintegrate.

Andy had jumped at a chance to quit the farm a while and see the city. To Rusty he had argued, "You're liable to need somebody to watch your back. You made some enemies while you were a ranger."

Rusty suspected Andy's motivation had less to do with protectiveness than with an urge to see something new and enjoy some excitement.

Because it was the dead of winter, Rusty and Andy had little farmwork that could not be postponed. Last year's crop was long since harvested, and this year's planting had to await warm ground. It would have been a good time for Rusty to get his red hair trimmed, then take a several-days' ride up to the Monahan place and ask Josie a question he had postponed much too long. Instead, he found himself approaching Austin and wondering why.

During ranger service that often took him far from home, Rusty had remained at heart a farmer with a strong tie to land he had known since boyhood. Andy empathized but had never been that dedicated to the soil. A tumultuous boyhood had given him a restless spirit. He welcomed any excuse to saddle Long Red and travel over new ground, to cross rivers he had not previously known.

"It's the Indian in him," Rusty had heard people say. "You never saw an Indian stay in one place long unless he was dead."

Andy was not Indian, at least by blood, but when he was a small boy the Comanches had taken him. They had held him through several of his vital formative years. Rusty had found him injured and helpless and returned him to the white man's world. But Andy had never given up all of his Indian ways.

Rusty hoped youthful curiosity would be satisfied quickly. He doubted that Andy would remain contented for long in a city like Austin any more than he was likely to be content spending all his life on the farm.

A squad of black soldiers drew Rusty's attention. He and Andy and Tom had drawn theirs as well. He murmured, "They're studyin' us like we might be outlaws."

Tom muttered in a deep voice, "They're lookin' at our guns. They're always afraid some old rebel may take a notion to declare war again." A few had, from time to time.

Rusty half expected the soldiers to stop them, but they simply watched in stone-faced silence as the three riders passed by and turned into a long street, which a sign on the corner said was Congress. At the head of it, well to the north, stood an imposing structure larger than any other Rusty could see.

Andy's eyes were wide. "Is that the capitol? The place where they make all the laws?"

Tom said, "That's the place. Fixin' to be a lot of different faces there now that we've elected a new governor. Be a lot of carpetbaggers huntin' new country."

Rusty had mixed feelings about the outsiders who had crowded into Texas after the war, hungry for opportunity. On the positive side they had brought money to a state drained dry after four years of debilitating conflict. On the negative side some had brought a bottomless hunger for anything they could grab and went to any lengths of stealth or violence necessary to satisfy it.

Now thousands of ex-Confederates, disenfranchised after the war, had finally recovered their voting rights. By a margin of two to one they had defeated the Union-backed reconstruction governor, Edmund J. Davis. They had voted in Richard Coke, a former Confederate army officer and one of their own. Perhaps that transition accounted for the large numbers of men standing along the street as if waiting for something to happen, Rusty thought. It did not, however, account for so many being heavily burdened by a variety of firearms.

Andy grinned. "Looks like the war is fixin' to start again." War had been a central fact of life among the Comanches, often sought after when it did not come on its own.

Rusty frowned. "I'm commencin' to wonder what we've ridden into." He reined his dun horse over to a man leaning against a cedar hitching post. "Say, friend, what's the big attraction in town?"

The man straightened, fixing suspicious eyes on Rusty, then on Andy and Tom. "I reckon you know, or you wouldn't be here. Did Governor Davis send for you?"

"I wouldn't know Edmund J. Davis from George Washington."

The man said, "A lot of Davis's friends have come to town includin' his old state police. They're all totin' guns. I see that you are, too."

Rusty kept his right hand away from the pistol on his hip, avoiding any appearance of a threat. "We brought our guns because we came a long ways. We didn't know what we might run into, or who."

"Just so you ain't one of them Davis police."

Mention of the Davis police put a bad taste in Rusty's mouth. "I used to be a ranger, but I never was a state policeman."

The governor's special police force—a mixture of white and black— had been organized as part of the state's reconstruction government, replacing the traditional rangers. Excesses had given the force a reputation for arrogance and brutality, arousing enmity in most Texans. Rusty had always felt that a majority were well intentioned, but a scattering of scoundrels overshadowed the law enforcement achievements of the rest.

A new legislature had recently abolished the state police to the relief of the citizenry and the consternation of Governor Davis.

The man said, "Local folks are naturally stirred up about so many strangers bringin' guns to town. Coke has been sworn in as governor, but Davis won't recognize him. Word has gone around that he has no intention of givin' up the office."

"But the people voted him out."

"He's declared the election unconstitutional."

Tom's face reddened. "He can't. That's not legal."

"He claims he's got the authority to say what's legal and what's not. Thinks he's the king of England, or maybe old Pharaoh."

The occupying Union forces had given their handpicked governor dictatorial power. He had instituted worthwhile improvements, particularly to the educational system, yet Texans resented his issuing punitive executive orders from which they had no recourse. Though Davis was a Southerner and a longtime citizen of the state, most former Confederates felt that he belonged to the enemy. He had fled Texas early in the war, eventually becoming a brigadier general in the Union army. The governor's office had been his reward.

Now it appeared that he did not intend to give it up.

Tom said, "We hold no brief for Davis. We voted for Coke." He glanced questioningly at Rusty. "At least I did."

Rusty nodded. He, too, had voted for Coke because he felt it was time to shed the smothering reconstruction regime so Texas could work its own way back to order and stability.

"Then I'd advise you to either join Coke's militia or take care of your business and move out of town before the roof blows off of the capitol yonder."

Pulling away, Rusty muttered to Tom, "I think I see why your sheriff friend asked you to come and bring help."

"I've known him a long time. I couldn't turn him down."

Tom's loyalty to a friend was such that he had reluctantly left an ailing wife at home to come on this mission. Rusty's loyalty to Tom did not allow him to refuse Tom's request, though he had planned to be marrying Josie Monahan about now. He said, "We're liable to get pulled into a fight that ain't ours. That whole damned war wasn't really ours."

Like the late Sam Houston, Rusty had never favored secession from the Union, nor had he ever developed any allegiance to the Confederacy. One reason he had remained with the frontier rangers throughout the war was to avoid conscription into the rebel army. Even so, he had come to resent the oppressive federal occupation.

Tom frowned. "I wouldn't have asked you to come if I'd known we were ridin' into a situation like this. Maybe you and Andy better turn around and go home."

Disappointed, Andy said, "We ain't hardly seen the city yet."

Rusty said, "We've come this far, so we'll wait and size things up. Then we can go home if we're a mind to."

Initially Tom had harbored reservations about the wisdom of the war, but once it began he had given his loyalty to Texas and the South without looking back. He said, "Davis got beat fair and square. If he was a proper gentleman he'd recognize the will of the people. He'd yield up the office."

Andy said, "The Comanche way is simpler. A chief can't force anybody to do anything. If the people don't like him anymore they just quit payin' attention to him. No election, no fight, no nothin'." He snorted. "And everybody claims white people are smarter."

Andy's sorrel shied to one side, bumping against Rusty's dun. Two men burst off the sidewalk and into the dirt street, wildly swinging their fists. Immediately another man joined the fray, then two more, cursing, wrestling awkwardly. Foot and horse traffic stopped. Onlookers crowded around while the fight escalated.

Andy asked, "Whose side are we on?"

Rusty said, "Nobody's." He saw little difference between the combatants except that some might be drunker than others. He said, "We'd best move on before some fool pulls a gun." He found the way blocked by men rushing to watch the fight.

Faces were bloodied and shirts torn, but nobody drew a pistol or knife. Whatever the quarrel was about, the participants did not seem to consider it worth a killing.

A city policeman strode down the street, gave the situation a quick study, then stepped back to observe from a comfortable distance, hands in his pockets. Shortly a blue-clad army officer trotted his horse up beside the policeman. His sharp voice indicated he was used to people snapping to attention in his presence. "Aren't you going to stop this?"

The policeman did not take his hands from his pockets. "A man can get hurt messin' in where he wasn't asked. Long as they don't kill one another, I say let them have their fun."

"You are paid to enforce the peace."

"Not near enough. Ain't been any peace around here since this governor business came up. You want to stop the fight, go ahead."

"The army is not supposed to interfere. This is a civilian matter."

"And this here civilian is goin' into that grog shop yonder to have himself a drink. If anybody gets killed, come and fetch me." The policeman turned away. The officer watched him in frustration, then turned his attention to the ongoing fight. A couple of the brawlers had had enough and crawled away to sit on the edge of the wooden sidewalk, there to nurse their wounds while the altercation went on. They were not missed.

Andy's eyes danced with excitement as his fists mimicked the movements of the belligerents. He had been in plenty of fights himself, usually instigated by other young men making fun of the ways he had learned from the Indians.

Rusty knew a good scrap when he saw one. This was not a good one. It was slow-footed and clumsy, loud but not likely to produce anything more serious than loose teeth, bruised knuckles, and maybe a flattened nose. He decided the policeman had been right in leaving bad nature to run its course.

Onlookers' comments bore out his assumption that some of the fighters were Davis men. Others supported Coke. The fight slowly staggered to a standstill. The Coke men appeared to carry the victory, such as it was. They moved away in a triumphant group, weaving toward the grog shop the policeman had chosen. Their opponents dragged themselves to the side-walk and slumped there, exhausted.

The fight had energized Andy. He said, "Some folks take their politics serious."

Tom Blessing nodded grimly. "With good reason. Davis's men tromped on everybody that got in their way. Stole half the state of Texas. Now comes the day of reckonin', and they ain't willin' to 'fess up."

The three rode north up the wide street, Rusty warily eyeing the armed men scattered all along. He saw no reason anyone would shoot at him on purpose, but he had learned long ago that the innocent bystander was usually the first one hurt. The more innocent, the more likely.

They reined up short of the capitol building. Several men stood shoulder to shoulder at the front door, holding rifles. They had a military bearing but did not wear uniforms. Rusty surmised they were former Confederate soldiers who had not forgotten the regimens learned in war.

He said, "Looks like they're guardin' the state treasury."

Tom said, "Too late for that. Talk is that Davis's adjutant general slipped away with it and sailed for Europe." He stepped down from the saddle and lifted the reins for Andy to hold. "You-all better stay here so we don't accidentally provoke somebody into somethin' rash. I'll walk up there and see what the game is." He unstrapped his pistol belt and hung it over the saddle horn as an indication that his intentions were benign.

Andy gazed southward back down Congress Avenue, where substantial buildings lined each side. Rusty assumed he was marveling at the variety of merchandise available here for anyone who had the money to buy it. That was the catch. Texas was just emerging from the economic devastation of war and its aftermath. Not many people other than opportunistic outsiders had much money to spend. Most of what Texans needed, they produced for themselves or did without. But Austin had been something of an oasis, money flowing more freely because of the Union soldiers and the state's reconstruction government based here.

It dawned on Rusty that Andy's attention was focused on two young women who stood in front of a nearby saloon. It was obvious they were not Sunday school teachers.

He warned, "Don't let your curiosity get stirred up too much. I don't expect we'll be stayin'." It occurred to him that he had taught Andy a lot about plowing straight rows but not enough about avoiding society's pitfalls.

Tom returned, his jaw set grimly. "Governor Davis has got himself barricaded in the capitol basement with a bunch of his old state police. The Coke men and the legislature have got the upper floor."

"A Mexican standoff," Rusty said.

"Maybe not for long. Davis has sent a wire to President Grant. He's askin' him to order the troops in. Wants them to throw out the Coke crowd and keep him in office."

That news troubled Rusty. "If he does, there's apt to be an awful fight."

Andy had no problem with the notion of a fight. "I wish old Buffalo Caller could've seen this." Buffalo Caller was the Comanche warrior who had first captured him and kept him for his own. "He would've given a hundred horses to watch white men battle one another instead of fightin' the People. And it would've been worth every one of them."

Tom declared, "You're white. That's a scandalous thing to say."

Andy said, "Was it to happen, I'd cheer for the old Texans to win. But not too quick. I'd like to see the fight stretch out a while."

Tom shook his head. "Scandalous." He looked back toward the capitol. "I've offered to do my part and stand with Coke. This ain't none of you-all's fight unless you want it to be."

Rusty said, "We're here now. We wouldn't go off and leave you by yourself."

Tom seemed pleased. "You sound like your old Daddy Mike. But I won't be by myself. There's several of my friends up there from way back. There's a bunch of old rangers, too. Friends of yours, I'd warrant."

Rusty's interest quickened. "Rangers?"

"Yeah, but like I said, it don't have to be your fight. I wouldn't want a young feller like Andy on my conscience. Or you, either."

"We came of our own accord. We're grown men." Rusty glanced at Andy. "*I* am, anyway."

Tom nodded. "There's a wagon yard down yonder. Would you take my horse for me?"

Rusty jerked his head. "Come on, Andy."

Andy led Tom's mount. Rusty guessed there must be a hundred horses in the several corrals to the side of and beyond the large wooden barn. A droop-shouldered liveryman slouched in the big open doorway, waiting for customers. He limped out a few paces and spat a stream of brown tobacco juice at a bedraggled cat, missing by a foot. A bit of the spittle remained in his stubble of gray-and-black beard. He said, "You're supposed to be in there chasin' mice. They're fixin' to carry off the whole shebang, barn and all." He looked up at Rusty. "What can I do for you-all?"

"Got room for three more horses?"

"If there ain't room enough we'll just stack them like cordwood. I expect you-all are in town to see the excitement?" It was a statement, but he made it sound like a question.

"We didn't know about it 'til we got here."

"I ain't takin' sides, you understand, but I hope the Coke people give that Davis crowd a hell of a lickin'. I've had a gutful of them thieves."

Rusty smiled. "Sounds like you *have* taken sides."

"I reckon, but if the shootin' starts I'm keepin' my head down. I taken a Yankee ball in my leg durin' the war. Convinced me I ain't no fightin' man."

"But you're willin' to take money from either side?"

"I take care of horses, and horses don't know nothin' about politics. I do business with any and all, long as the money is genuine." He extended his hand, the palm up. "And paid in advance."

Rusty took his time counting out the coins, for he did not have enough that he could afford to spend them needlessly. "We'll want to bed down here in the wagon yard tonight. We've got no money to waste on a hotel."

"Hotels are all full, anyway. Spread your blankets anywhere you can find an empty space. And be careful with your matches. You don't want to buy no burned-up barn." He dropped Rusty's coins into his pocket. They clinked against silver already there.

The capitol standoff was good for business.

The liveryman looked behind him as if to be certain he would not be overheard. "Couple of fellers were talkin' back of the barn. They're waitin' for Coke to give the word to make a rush against the capitol and put Davis out on the street. Could be a right interestin' show."

Rusty glanced uneasily at Andy. "Tom could get hurt. He's a shade old to be mixin' in a bad fight."

Andy said, "He's never run away from one yet. That's why they made him sheriff again."

"He ought not to've let them put that badge back on him. I've got a notion to try and talk him into goin' home before somethin' happens. That sick wife of his needs him more than anybody here does."

Andy had not seen enough of the town. "Gettin' kind of late in the day. We couldn't go far before dark."

"We could get out of gunshot range."

Andy resigned himself to disappointment. He patted Long Red's neck. "You better eat your oats in a hurry." He followed Rusty out the door.

Rusty told the liveryman, "Don't turn our horses into the lot just yet. We're liable to be leavin'."

The old man shoved his hands into his pockets. The coins jingled like tiny bells. Reluctantly he said, "I guess you'll want your money back. You still want me to feed them some oats?"

"I wish you would." Rusty was more willing to spend on the horses than on himself.

He saw a crowd of nervous-looking men standing around the front of a hotel as if waiting for someone to assert leadership and take them somewhere . . . anywhere, to do something . . . anything. A familiar voice called his name, and a man pushed through the cluster. Len Tanner was tall and lanky, in patched trousers that hung loose around a waist thin as a slab of bacon. He always looked as if he had not eaten a square meal in a month. In truth, he could put away an alarming amount of groceries when the opportunity presented itself.

Rusty exclaimed, "Len! Thought you were back in East Texas, visitin' your kin."

"Ain't much excitement in seein' kinfolks. Here's where the fun is at."

Rusty had ridden with Tanner during his ranger service. Since the war, Tanner had spent much of his time at Rusty's farm when he lacked something better to do. He was not addicted to steady employment. Tanner said, "There's a bunch of our old ranger bunkies here ready to run the carpetbaggers out of town on a rail. But Coke keeps holdin' back, hopin' Davis will cave in without a fight."

"What if he doesn't?"

"After fightin' the damned Comanches, this oughtn't to make us break a sweat." Tanner frowned at Andy. "Sorry, button, I didn't mean nothin' personal."

Andy shrugged. "I take it as a compliment to the Comanches."

"They're honest enemies, at least. They come against you face-to-face. Carpetbaggers sneak up behind you and kill you with affidavits." Tanner's family had lost their farm to confiscatory reconstruction taxes, though he, like Rusty, had never actively supported the Confederacy. He said, "I know why Davis wants to keep that office. There's some of Texas that his cronies ain't stole yet." His momentary dark mood fell away. "Speakin' of old friends, I'll bet it's been a spell since you seen Jim and Johnny Morris."

"Sure has." Rusty looked around eagerly. "Are those rascals here?"

The Morris brothers had served in the same ranger company as Rusty and Tanner until they went into the Confederate army late in the war.

Tanner said, "Me and them are plannin' on a little sortie tonight. Goin' to aggravate some Yankee soldiers."

That did not surprise Rusty. Like Tanner, the brothers had always gloried in a fracas. If they could not find a fight already in progress they had occasionally instigated one.

Rusty and Andy followed Tanner through the crowd. Two men of roughly Rusty's age shouted his name and pushed their way to him. They could be taken for twins, though Jim was a year or so the oldest. He declared, "Glad to see you're still alive." He gripped Rusty's outstretched hand with a force that could crush bones. "Me and Johnny figured you'd worked yourself to death on that wore-out farm."

"I've come awful close."

Jim turned to Andy, his manner jovial. "You'd be the Comanche button Len's been tellin' us about."

The brothers' being friends of Tanner's did not automatically assure Andy's acceptance. He regarded them with an element of doubt. "Len's been known to lie a little, once or twice."

Johnny Morris grinned. "We've caught him abusin' the facts ourselves. But only when he's awake." He jerked his head, beckoning Rusty and the others beyond the edge of the crowd. In a low voice he said, "Rusty, you're just the man to help us do a little job tonight."

Rusty felt misgivings. As much as he liked Tanner and the Morrises, he remembered times when they had acted first and considered the consequences later, if at all. Events had not always worked to their advantage. "I'd want to hear the particulars before I say anything." He already leaned toward saying *no*.

"The army's brought up a cannon from San Antonio."

Rusty's jaw dropped. He had not considered that the dispute would come to this. A cannon could blow a big hole in the capitol building. He thought immediately of Tom Blessing, standing guard somewhere in or around it.

He protested, "Hard to believe the army would fire on the capitol while Davis and some of his people hold the basement floor."

"No," Johnny said, "but they'd fire into the crowd if a bunch was to try and rush the buildin'. We figure they're just waitin' for Grant to wire them the orders."

"But a cannon . . . what could you do against a weapon the size of that?"

Jim said, "Me and Johnny and Len are goin' to spike it."

Andy demanded, "What do you mean, 'spike' it?"

Johnny explained, "You drive an iron spike into the touchhole. They can't fire 'til they get it out, and that can be hell to do if it's pounded in there hard enough."

Rusty said, "Don't you know they'll be guardin' it? You'll get your-selves shot."

"Len'll distract the guards. Won't take us but a minute to fix the can-non and be gone. You could help him."

The idea was much too simple. Rusty could see a dozen holes in it, most of them potentially lethal. "You're crazy, all three of you."

Andy said eagerly, "Let's do it, Rusty. We can run rings around them soldiers."

"*Four* of you are crazy. You're too young to be mixin' into a thing like this."

"How old were you the first time you rode with the rangers?"

"That was a long time ago. Times were different." It struck Rusty that his foster father, Daddy Mike Shannon, had said the same thing to him once, to no effect.

Johnny Morris turned. "Yonder come some of them brunette Yankees." A small squad of black troopers marched up the street, led by a white offi-cer on horseback, the same one Rusty had seen earlier. "At least they ain't brought their cannon with them."

Jim said, "Washington still ain't given them permission to mix in. That's all they're waitin' for."

The presence of black troops had been a thorn in the sides of ex-Confederates during the reconstruction years. Texans were convinced that the victorious Union intended to humiliate them by putting them under the authority of former slaves. The effect had been more of outrage than of humiliation.

Several in the crowd began catcalling, shouting racial and political insults at the soldiers and their officer. One man stepped out past the others and shook his fist, loudly cursing all Yankees and their antecedents from the poorest foot soldier all the way up to President Grant. His slurred speech indicated that he had imbibed a good measure of liquid courage.

The officer unbuttoned his holster and drew a pistol. He pushed his horse up close and brought the barrel down across the heckler's head. The man went down, his hat rolling in the dirt.

The officer turned in the saddle. "Arrest him. Two of you men take him to the bull pen."

Len swore under his breath. "That old boy was too drunk to know what he was sayin'."

"He knew," Rusty said sternly. "But loud talk is no reason to break a man's skull."

A noisy protest arose from the crowd, but no one made a move toward the well-armed soldiers.

Jim Morris said, "Whatever happened to free speech?"

Johnny replied, "It ain't free anymore. And the price keeps goin' up."

Rusty gave way to rising anger as two troopers dragged the half-conscious man away. He looked into the faces of his friends and saw the same reaction.

Andy demanded, "Don't you think we ought to do somethin'?"

Rusty said, "Like what? The South already lost one war."

Tanner said, "At least you can look the situation over with us. Help us figure out how we're goin' to do it."

"I guess I can go that far. But this is a dog fight, and me and Andy have got no dog in it."

CHAPTER
TWO

he liveryman did not get up from his rawhide-bound chair, but he eyed Rusty with regret. "Fixin' to go? I done fed your horses some oats, so I can't give all your money back."

Rusty said, "We're not leavin' town yet."

Cheered, the liveryman pushed away from the chair. "I'll show you where they're at."

Andy lagged behind, nursing his disappointment. Rusty had told him he had to stay at the wagon yard. He saw no need for Andy to take chances by joining Tanner and the Morrises.

The liveryman led Rusty into the barn to a small pen where his horse, Andy's, and Tom's still nuzzled a wooden trough, seeking stray bits of grain stuck in the cracks. Rusty wondered if they had actually been fed as much as he had paid for.

He led his dun out into the fading daylight. As he prepared to mount, Rusty heard a familiar voice. "How's my young Comanche friend?" It was addressed to Andy.

Andy considered his answer, then said firmly, "I don't remember that we was ever friends, Farley Brackett."

Brackett was a large man with a scar from the edge of his eye down to his cheek. War had scarred him even worse on the inside, turning him into an outlaw, at least in the eyes of the state police. As Brackett approached, Andy took half a step back before standing his ground.

Brackett pointed his chin at Long Red. "I see you've still got my sorrel horse."

Andy bristled. "He never was your horse. Your daddy gave him to Rusty, and Rusty gave him to me."

"He wasn't my daddy's to give. He was mine."

Andy stiffened. "So you say, but your daddy's dead. We can't ask him."

Rusty intruded. "You're runnin' a risk, Farley, showin' up in public. The state police don't forget."

"They've had their fangs pulled, but I haven't. Any of them tries to mess with me, he'll get what they gave my old daddy." State police had mistaken the father for Farley and had killed him.

Rusty said, "Anyway, you leave Andy alone. We're not here to fight."

"Everybody else is." Brackett looked back at Andy. "I still say he's my horse. You've just got the loan of him. For now." He walked away, toward the milling crowd that stirred dust along Congress Avenue.

Worriedly Andy asked, "He can't take Long Red back, can he?" Andy thought more of that horse than of any human. Almost any human, at least.

Rusty said, "He's got no claim. His daddy gave me that horse to replace one Farley stole when he was on the run."

"If he tries to take Long Red, I'll shoot him."

Rusty suspected Andy would at least try. But Farley Brackett had shown the reconstruction authorities he was a hard man to kill. "You shouldn't talk loose about killin'. It can lead to more than just talk."

"Just the same, I'm keepin' a close eye on Long Red. Farley had better not so much as look crossways at him."

Rusty met Tanner and the brothers where the three had dropped their blankets near the river. Johnny pointed. "The troops made camp down this-away."

As they rode, Rusty heard a horse loping up from behind. Andy pushed to overtake them.

Rusty turned in anger as Andy pulled in beside him. "I told you to stay behind."

"That Farley kept hangin' around the stable. I decided the best way for me to keep an eye on Long Red was to be ridin' him."

Rusty knew that was more an excuse than a reason. "All right, but don't be gettin' any foolish notions."

He saw several rows of tents lined in military order. Johnny said, "They got the cannon placed back of the tents."

A hundred yards beyond the tent line stood a set of wooden pens. The troops were infantry. Rusty surmised that the few horses he saw were for the officers. He counted four draft mules. Drawing the cannon would be their job.

He shivered at the thought of such a weapon being fired into a crowd. For that purpose artillerymen would probably load it with scraps of metal and pieces of chain. Those would damage more rioters than a single cannonball.

Tanner muttered, "A mean piece of business. And all on account of politics."

Rusty said, "The whole war was because of politics."

He was not surprised to see two black soldiers standing guard on either side of the cannon. He was a little surprised there were not more. "You think they'll stand by idle while you-all drive your spike?"

Tanner said, "When the time comes I'll see to it that they ain't there."

"You wouldn't kill them? The army would run you to the ground and hang you from the tallest tree they can find. If they didn't just shoot you outright."

Johnny said, "We wouldn't hurt a hair on their heads. Len is goin' to draw them away."

"How?"

"We hoped you'd help us figure that out."

Rusty studied the cannon and everything around it. He saw a stack of hay near the horse pens. He said, "I don't see anybody guardin' that hay yonder. If it was to accidentally catch afire . . ."

Jim nodded, his eyes brightening. "That's the same stunt me and Johnny pulled on some Yankees just before the end of the war. Got away with a bunch of their horses. They didn't need that many, anyway, since their hay burned up. They didn't have anything to feed them."

Andy had listened quietly, but excitement built in his eyes. Rusty sought to head him off. "You're not goin' along with them. You're too young, and it's too dangerous."

"I've been in dangerous places before. My Comanche brother Steals the Ponies could tell you that."

"But he's not here. If he was, he'd be welcome to help. But not you. I didn't spend all these years raisin' you to lose you in a fight that's none of your business."

Rusty expected more argument. Andy simply shrugged and said, "Here come some soldiers to see what we're about. You want to talk to them?"

Four troopers and a white officer were marching toward the five Texans. Rusty said, "I don't believe we've got anything to talk about." He reined his horse around and started back toward the brothers' camp, careful not to move faster than a walk. He did not want to arouse suspicion by appearing to run away. The others followed him. The troopers soon stopped.

Tanner asked, "You reckon they suspect us?"

Rusty said, "They suspect everybody, and have since the first day they came into Texas."

Tom Blessing walked to the wagon yard about sundown, tired and burdened with worry. "Hard to guess what's fixin' to happen," he said. "Governor Coke has got a bunch of his old rangers at his side. Governor Davis has called out the Travis Rifles to help him hold the capitol. Some of them have come over to us, but there's enough left to give us a right smart of trouble. And we still don't know what President Grant will do. If he orders the troops in, with their cannon, . . ."

Tanner declared, "Don't you worry yourself about that cannon. It's fixin' to be took care of."

Rusty frowned at Tanner and looked about to see if anyone might have overheard. Most people around here were strangers. He had no way of knowing which side they were on. He said in little more than a whisper, "The Morris boys figure on spikin' that cannon tonight."

Tom was not relieved. "They're liable to get spiked themselves."

Rusty said, "Len Tanner's goin' to help."

"That's no big relief." Tom nodded toward Andy. "Surely you're not lettin' the boy go."

"He's stayin' here with me."

Tom said, "Good. We're dealin' with people who are used to absolute power. If they got him in their sights, they wouldn't take his youth into account."

Andy spoke up. "If I was still with the Comanches I'd be looked at as a warrior now. I sure wouldn't let a bunch of bluecoats scare me."

Tom said, "They scare *me*. I just hope Grant doesn't set them loose. You know they arrested the mayor today."

Rusty said, "I hadn't heard that."

"Roughed him up some, then turned him loose because it looked like a riot was fixin' to break out. They still haven't got their orders from Washington."

Rusty walked to the door and stared out into the street. Everywhere he looked little clusters of armed men stood waiting, watching. The tension was electric, much like the atmosphere before a thunderstorm. "Wouldn't take but one good spark to touch off the powder. I wish we'd gone back home."

Tom said, "For my wife's sake, I wish we'd never been asked to come in the first place. She needs a woman to be with her 'til she gets her feet back under her. I ain't been able to find one who'd stay."

Rusty kept a disturbing thought to himself. What would become of Mrs. Blessing if a bullet brought down her husband? "We could start home right now. It won't be full dark for another hour."

Tom shook his head. "We finally got back the right to vote. It's time to get off of our knees and stand on our feet."

"No matter what it costs?"

"We're at a fork in the road. One way follows the law. The other twists the law to whatever it wants it to be."

Rusty smiled. "First time I ever heard you make a speech."

"I don't often feel the need, especially with you."

Rusty did not intend to go to sleep so early, but it had been a long day. Soon after he lay down on his blankets he dozed off. He awakened suddenly to the squealing of two horses nipping at one another. He saw that Andy's blankets had been thrown back. Andy was gone.

Damn fool kid, he thought. He's gone to help Tanner and the Morrises.

The stableman was asleep on a steel cot in a small office at the front of the barn. Rusty aroused him to ask when Andy had left. The man sat up, blinking rapidly, swinging his bare feet over the side. His voice was sour. "Don't you people know what the night is meant for?"

"That boy who was with me, did you see him leave?"

The man ignored the question. "Night's a time for rest. If you want your horse, you know where he's at. Catch him yourself. And you can put him back for yourself when you come in. If you're too drunk to unlatch the gate, just tie him to the fence."

"How long has it been since the kid left?"

"I didn't look at my watch." The man scratched his backside. "What kind of a critter is that button, anyway?"

"What do you mean?"

"He come stealin' in and got his horse. I wouldn't have knowed he was here if the horse hadn't snorted just as he passed my door. Wouldn't surprise me none if that boy's got Indian blood in him."

"I'll admit he acts like it."

The stableman said, "Probably snuck off to find him a sportin' gal. I did when I was his age. 'Spect you did, too. I got no quarrel with it as long as they let a man sleep."

Rusty saddled his horse while the stableman returned to his blankets, muttering all the way.

The kid's got more nerve than judgment, Rusty thought darkly. As bad as Len Tanner.

He rode in a long trot to the Morris brothers' camp at the edge of town. He found the fire burned low. No one was there. He was sure he knew where they were, and Andy with them.

Damn Len Tanner. He knew I didn't want Andy to be any part of this.

He rode toward the soldier camp under a dark sky, the moon hidden by a heavy cover of clouds. Unable to see much, he almost rode upon two men sitting on horseback. Johnny Morris demanded, "Who the hell are you?"

"It's me, Rusty. Where are Len and Andy?"

"They've snuck off down yonder to set the hay afire. While everybody's runnin' to fight the fire, me and Jim will fix the cannon." He showed Rusty an iron rod. Jim carried a blacksmith's hammer across the pommel of his saddle.

Rusty said, "Why didn't you-all turn the boy back?"

Jim said, "His mind was made up. We couldn't have stopped him if we'd hit him over the head with this hammer."

Rusty knew how stubborn Andy could be. "Maybe I can head him off. You-all be careful. Some Yankees are good shots."

He rode down toward the camp. He could not make out the shape of the haystack, but he knew more or less where it should be. He felt a chilly dampness moving up from the river on the south wind. He shivered and pulled his old coat more tightly around him. A couple of fires flickered in the soldier camp. He envied the men warming themselves there.

The cannon guards had a fire of their own. Rusty took that as a good sign. Glare from the flames would diminish their ability to see through the darkness.

He saw a match flare, then flicker out. Andy and Tanner must be having poor luck getting the hay to catch fire. Both were single-minded enough to keep trying, even if soldiers swarmed over them.

A hostile voice demanded. "Who goes there?"

Rusty realized the challenge was directed at Andy and Tanner. He put spurs to the dun horse, urging him into a long trot.

A rough voice shouted, "Who are you? Speak before I blow your head off!"

Tanner's answer was defiant. "I'm Robert E. Lee and I'm here to whup some Yankee sons of bitches."

Rusty saw a quick movement and heard a thud as a soldier struck Tanner in the stomach with the butt of a rifle. Rusty did not give him a second chance. He rode in, swinging his pistol. He felt the barrel connect with a trooper's head. The trooper fell, firing his rifle by reflex. Tanner wrestled with another soldier but was losing ground. Rusty grabbed a handful of uniform and pulled the man off of him. He swung the pistol but missed.

He heard a shout. "Corporal of the guard! Post number two!" It came from the direction of the cannon. He heard more soldiers running toward him. A rifle cracked. Rusty fired his pistol into the air, hoping to confuse and perhaps discourage the soldiers. "Forget the fire," he shouted. "Get out of here."

The troopers guarding the cannon came on the run, silhouetted against their fire. Rusty aimed a shot in their general direction, slowing them. One discharged his rifle into the darkness but had no clear target. Rusty leaned low to be sure he did not present one.

Andy came riding out, leading Tanner's horse. "Here, Len. Get on him quick."

Rusty heard the whisper of bullets passing much too close. Len staggered. Andy swung around to help lift him into the saddle. The three set their horses into a run.

The firing continued behind them. Rusty said, "You two stirred up the whole Yankee army."

Andy laughed. "Didn't we, though? But we couldn't get the fire started."

Len lamented, "Damned hay was wet. All I burned was my fingers."

Rusty said, "It was a fool notion in the first place."

Andy said, "Only thing wrong with it was that it didn't work."

Rusty did not see the Morris brothers, but he figured they were old enough to take care of themselves. They always had. Andy was young, eager, and still needed watching. Tanner should have known better, but he was inclined to create trouble even where there had been none. He had long maintained that a good fight was more invigorating than a double shot of whiskey.

Rusty led Andy and Tanner along the river until he was sure they had shaken off pursuit by the foot soldiers. Then he circled back in the direction of the Morris brothers' camp. Andy was still laughing.

Rusty decided it was time for the lecture. "Now listen here—"

Andy cut him off. "I know what you're goin' to say, so there ain't no use sayin' it. I didn't have any business bein' out here. But I figured Len needed help. By himself, he was apt to get killed."

"You could've both been killed."

"We weren't, and I had more fun tonight than I ever got followin' a mule across a field. Len, you're lookin' kind of sick."

"Took a rifle butt in my ribs. I'm goin' to be awful sore in the mornin'." He moaned. "Every time a man gets to feelin' smart, somethin' comes along and kicks him in the belly."

Johnny and Jim arrived in camp just ahead of them. "Everybody all right?" Johnny asked worriedly. "What went wrong out there?"

"Damp hay," Rusty said. "Looks like it ruined you-all's plan."

The brothers grinned at one another. "Not really," Johnny said. "Len and the boy set out to draw attention away from us. They sure did that."

"You managed to spike the cannon, after all?"

"The only way it could hurt anybody now would be if it fell on him."

Rusty grunted, surprised but pleased. The troops could do a lot of damage with their rifles if they were called into the dispute, but at least they should not be able to use artillery against the crowd.

He said, "If you-all don't mind a little company, I think me and Andy'll bed down here instead of goin' back to the wagon yard. The stable keeper needs his sleep."

With only their saddle blankets for cover against the night chill, Rusty and Andy lay near the campfire. Rusty poked a little fresh wood among the coals and watched the flames rise up before he stretched out on the ground. He lay awake, replaying the evening's action in his mind.

Tanner was soon snoring. Andy rolled onto one side, then moved to the other, pulling his legs up tightly. Rusty asked, "Can't you sleep?"

"I'm a little cold. And there was too much excitement, I guess. Got my blood all stirred up."

"I'm not havin' much luck myself." Rusty arose to put more wood on the fire. Instead of lying down and rolling up in his saddle blanket, he squatted on his heels and stared into the fire.

"Been doin' some thinkin', too," he said. "How would you like to have a cabin of your own?"

"What do I need a cabin for? There's plenty of room in yours."

"Maybe not for long."

Andy stared at him in puzzlement. "How come?"

"I've been plannin' a trip up to the Monahan farm. Been wantin' to see how everybody's gettin' along."

"Especially Josie?"

"Especially Josie. I'm figurin' on askin' her to marry me."

Andy grunted. "It's about time. She's been askin' *you* long enough."

"Things weren't right before. I never knew what the carpetbaggers might throw at us. They tried once to take the farm, and I was always afraid they might do it again. But things'll settle down now that we've got a new governor."

"We've got two governors. We don't know which one will win out."

"I've got a feelin'. Old Preacher Webb always said if you keep the faith, good things will eventually come to you."

After a campfire breakfast of bacon and black coffee, all five rode up onto Congress Avenue to see if anything had changed overnight. A large group of men had gathered some distance below the capitol building. Rusty recognized several as former rangers with whom he had ridden at one time or another. Tom Blessing walked out from among them and hailed Rusty. He said, "Word has come from Washington. President Grant won't order the troops to help Davis. Told him the election is over, he lost, and he had just as well yield like a gentleman."

Rusty accepted that as good news, but not the ultimate answer. "He hasn't given up though, has he?"

"Not yet, but he must be feelin' like a mule has kicked him in the ribs. He can't call in the army. All he's got backin' him now is a bunch of his old state police and some officeholders who know they're fixin' to be out of a job."

Rusty was still trying to absorb the fact that the troops were not to be involved. That meant they would not have used the cannon even if it had not been spiked. Last night's wild sashay had been unnecessary.

Tanner had waked up with sore ribs and belly from the blow he had taken. He would hurt even more when it soaked in on him that he had taken the punishment for nothing.

Tom said, "We're waitin' for Governor Coke to show up and lead us on a march to the capitol."

"And if Davis won't give up?"

"We'll burn that bridge when we get to it."

Richard Coke was tall and heavyset, his white beard neatly trimmed. He wore a suit well tailored to his bulk and projected a sense of dignity the way a governor of Texas was supposed to, in Rusty's view. In a booming voice he shouted, "Let's go."

Flanked on either side by ex-rangers and Confederate officers Rip Ford and Henry McCulloch, he led the parade of determined men up Congress. In front of the capitol stood a line of well-armed Davis men, appearing just as determined. Coke acted as if he did not see them, never breaking stride. The defenders looked to one another for guidance, for someone to take the initiative and do something. No one did. The Davis men stepped back grudgingly, and the Coke procession marched into the capitol.

A tall, gaunt, defiant Davis awaited them in the hallway outside of his office. The door was closed. He stared sullenly at Coke.

Coke said, "Governor Davis, the new legislature has convened and canvassed the vote. They have declared that I am the rightful holder of this office. I respectfully request that you honor the wishes of the people of Texas."

Davis glared, his gaze sweeping over the men who faced him. "I do not recognize the election as legitimate. But I see that the laws of the state have been trampled underfoot. The rule of the mob has prevailed."

He strode past Coke. His opponents moved aside to let him pass. He did not look to right or left but focused his gaze straight ahead.

An audible sigh of relief arose from the men clustered in the hallway. One of Coke's lieutenants tried the door to the governor's office. "Locked," he said. "Davis did not turn over the key."

Another lieutenant said, "Break it open."

Tanner and a couple of others put their shoulders into the task. The door splintered. Tanner stepped back, gripped his belly, and grimaced in pain.

Inside the office, Davis's secretary of state still sat at his desk. The lieutenant who had tried the door said, "It's over. You can leave."

The man sat in stubborn silence.

The lieutenant said, "Some of you escort him outside."

A momentary clamor arose as several in the crowd suggested throwing the man out the window, but Coke overruled the idea. "That is the way of the old regime. As of today Texas is steering a new course."

Three men lifted the secretary from his chair and hustled him outside. Tanner did not volunteer to join them. He was still holding his stomach.

The people of Austin, and most of the visitors, celebrated far into the night. Rusty thought of the stable keeper. He wouldn't be getting much sleep.

Tom Blessing sat on the ground near the Morris brothers' campfire, chewing a piece of bacon. He told Rusty, "I'm ready to start home come daylight. You and Andy seen enough of the big city?"

Rusty glanced at Andy, who put up no argument. "I was ready before we came. But now that it's over, I'm glad we were here to see it. It'll be somethin' to tell our grandchildren about someday."

"Andy's too young to be thinkin' about grandchildren. And you ain't even married."

"I'm figurin' on fixin' that."

Tom stopped chewing. He seemed a little perturbed. "You sure bein' a ranger is a proper thing for a married man?"

"I'm not a ranger anymore."

"But you could be again. Governor Coke says one of the first things he plans to do is reorganize the rangers. He'll be lookin' for men of experience."

"I've *had* plenty of experience," Rusty said ruefully. "More than I ever looked for. I'm not sure I want any more like it."

"It gets in your blood, like sheriffin' got into mine. You'll want to study on it before you take to double harness."

CHAPTER

THREE

Len Tanner stood with hands in his pockets to keep them warm. He watched as Rusty and Andy lifted blankets, provisions, and Rusty's saddle into the bed of the wagon. The sun was just breaking over the eastern horizon, looking crisp and frosty through a thin blanket of gray winter clouds.

"I don't see why you want to take the wagon," he said. "You'd get there a lot sooner if you rode horseback."

"Josie'll be wantin' to bring all her things," Rusty said.

"How do you know she'll even come? You ain't asked her yet."

"She'll come." Rusty looked toward a new single log cabin standing halfway between the older double cabin and the livestock pens. "I hope you don't mind finishin' the roof on Andy's cabin."

"I got nothin' better to do. And Shanty's comin' over to help me build the chimly." Shanty was a former slave who lived a few miles away. Age had bent his slender frame, but his hands were still those of an artisan. "We'll have the place ready for the button to move in by the time you-all get back."

Andy had been torn about making the trip. He wanted to stay and help finish the cabin, but Rusty had persuaded him that the Monahans would be eager to see him. They had come to look upon him as a member of the family.

Andy saddled Long Red and tied Rusty's dun horse behind the wagon. "Reckon we got it all?"

Rusty said, "If we don't, we'll do without it." He shook Tanner's hand and climbed onto the wagon seat.

Tanner said, "Tell that cute little Alice girl I said howdy."

Rusty grinned. "We'll tell her."

"And watch out for Indians. They may not all know they're Andy's friends."

"I doubt they'll come far enough south for us to see them. They've got their hands full fightin' buffalo hunters."

Rusty had heard talk that large numbers of hide hunters had filtered down onto the Texas high plains from Kansas during the fall and winter. They had decimated the herds farther north in Cheyenne country. Now they were invading the Comanches' best hunting grounds. The Comanches were not feeling generous.

The news had disturbed Andy. His first thought was of his Comanche family and how the buffalo slaughter would affect them. "I thought there was a treaty that said the hunters couldn't come south of the Cimarron River."

Rusty said, "The treaty was with the federal government, on federal land. The federals have no right to make agreements about Texas land."

"I doubt that Steals the Ponies knows where the line is or that he would give a damn. Land is land. The Comanches figure they own all of it they're strong enough to hold."

"That's what counts, bein' strong enough."

Rusty had not tried to argue Texas's case. Andy had strong feelings where Indians were concerned. Trying to alter his views was like trying to stop a flowing river with a leaky bucket.

Andy looked back as they started away. He said, "I like my cabin, but a good tepee would serve me just as well."

"You won't feel that way when you've got a blaze goin' in the fireplace on a cold night. I hear the reservation Indians have started buildin' houses."

"Yes, but a lot of them put up tepees beside their cabins. They like to sleep next to Mother Earth. She gives them their strength."

"I've spent a lot of my life sleepin' on the ground. All I got from Mother Earth was rheumatism and a likin' for an honest-to-God bed."

They crossed the Colorado River at a ford. The water was higher than it would be in spring, when winter-dormant vegetation came back to life and sapped much of the underground moisture before it had a chance to seep into the river. Rusty pushed hard to keep the team moving forward briskly enough that the current would not pick up the wagon and carry it away.

He had ridden this trail many times, going to or from the Monahan farm or in the course of his ranger duties. Andy had ridden it, too, once when he was almost too young to remember. On that first trip he had traveled northward as captive of a Comanche raiding party. He had ridden again as a half-grown boy, this time heading southward to join his adopted brother as a participant in a horse-stealing foray. Fate in the guise of a fallen horse and a broken leg had dropped him back into the white world. There he had remained, though not willingly at first. He had never completely relinquished the heritage of his Comanche years.

Some people considered him unreconstructed, a streak of the savage locked forever in his heart. Andy had found he could use such people's attitude against them, keeping them at arm's length as a measure of self defense. His friends accepted him as he was. He was not troubled by what others thought.

Andy rode alongside the wagon, talking at intervals, then silent for long stretches. He was especially quiet after they made the first night's camp. Rusty recognized the dark moods that came over him now and then and did not push him for conversation. As they hitched the team next morning, Andy asked, "We goin' by the grave?"

Rusty had suspected this had been heavy on Andy's mind. "We can if you want to."

"I reckon I want to."

The grave was above the north bank of a small creek, just off the wagon track. At one end of a stack of stones a wooden cross had fallen to the ground. Rusty moved the wagon a little beyond and stopped. He got down, but he stood back, letting Andy have his time alone.

Andy dismounted and removed his hat, his head bowed. After a while he wiped a sleeve across his eyes, then straightened the cross. He pulled off a small wad of dark hair. "Buffalo," he said. "They knocked it over, scratchin' their itch."

Many of the stones lay scattered. Andy placed them neatly back over the mound. "Someday," he said, "I'm comin' back and puttin' a fence around this." When he was satisfied with the appearance of the grave, he straightened. Rusty joined him, hat in his hand.

Andy said, "I wish we had Preacher Webb with us. He'd know the words to say."

Rusty nodded. "He already said them, when we first buried her here." He shuddered, remembering.

Andy bit his lip. "I can't quite remember what my mother looked like. I sort of remember her voice, but I can't see her face in my mind. I like to think she was pretty."

"I expect she was, but she'd been poorly treated by the time we found her."

The memory chilled Rusty. It had been his first time to ride with the rangers, though they were little more than a loose band of local militia at the time. They had trailed after marauding Comanches who had killed several settlers and swept away all the horses they could find. They had kidnapped a small boy and his mother. The rangers had found the mother here, dead. The boy had disappeared. He was not seen again until Andy turned up years later, left behind in the wake of another Comanche raid.

Andy said, "I guess a lot of folks wouldn't understand. I don't myself, sometimes. The Comanches killed my mother here. Then they took me as one of their own. Some would say I ought to hate them, but they became my people. They're still my people."

"I like to think we're your people, too, me and Len and Shanty, and the Monahans. Tom Blessing, too."

"You are. Guess there ain't many like me with people on both sides of the fence. Not blood kin, but even better." Andy turned toward his horse.

Rusty said, "We don't have to be in any hurry if you'd like to stay a while."

"I've said all I know to say to her. Stayin' and wishin' won't bring her back. It won't even bring back a clear memory." Andy mounted the sorrel and started out.

Rusty remembered the first time he had seen the Monahan farm. Preacher Webb had escorted him there on his way to join the rangers at Fort Belknap. The place had looked like paradise after a long ride up from the Colorado River. Paradise was lost during the strife of war, but fragments had been regained in the years since.

Andy asked, "You nervous?"

Rusty was. The nearer they came to the farm, the less certain he was of what he should say, how he should approach Josie. In his view, one thing had always stood between them. He had once loved her older sister Geneva, but she had married another. For a long time he had feared that his growing feeling for Josie came only because she had begun to resemble her sister so much. The years had gradually erased his doubt, but he was afraid Josie might not be so certain.

He saw two men working with a young horse in a corral, trotting him around and around at the end of a rope. A boy sat on the fence, watching. He raised his arm and pointed, then jumped down and began running toward the two visitors. One of the men called after him. "Billy!"

The boy seemed not to hear. He cried, "Andy! Andy!"

Andy dismounted and swept the boy into his arms, swinging him halfway around. "You derned little Indian, you've grown a foot."

"I ain't no Indian. But I *have* grown. I'm near as big as you are."

He was not, but the point did not merit an argument.

Rusty said, "Howdy, Billy."

The boy replied, "Rusty," and gave his attention back to Andy.

He thinks Andy's the one that hung the moon, Rusty told himself, smiling. Billy was Geneva's son, and Evan Gifford's. While Rusty had been away serving as a frontier ranger, Evan had come back from the war, gravely wounded. Geneva had nursed him, and a strong bond had developed between them. Rusty recognized Evan in the corral, along with his brother-in-law, James Monahan. Evan climbed over the fence and walked out to meet the visitors. He was smiling, but his voice was stern.

"Billy, we've taught you not to go runnin' off by yourself that way. You don't always know who's comin' in."

Billy said, "I could see it was Andy. Couldn't you see it was Andy?"

"My eyes aren't as sharp as yours." Evan grasped Andy's hand as if to crush it. "Good to have you back." He looked up at Rusty. "You, too. Bring your wagon on up and we'll unload it."

Rusty looked toward the main house, hoping to see Josie come out onto the porch. Evidently she did not know he had arrived.

"Is everybody all right?" he asked.

He caught the serious look that came over Evan's face. Evan said, "Didn't anybody write you about Clemmie?"

Clemmie was the family matriarch, mother of Josie, Geneva, and the youngest sister, Alice.

Rusty felt a sharp foreboding. "Our mail goes astray a lot. What's happened to Clemmie?"

Evan jerked his head in the direction of the main house. "Yonder comes Preacher Webb. It's more his place to tell you than mine."

More than thirty years ago, circuit rider Webb and farmer Mike Shannon had found the orphaned Rusty wandering bewildered in the wake of an Indian battle. Mike had become Rusty's foster father. Webb had been like a benevolent uncle, poor in the world's goods but generous in spirit and rich in friends. He had married the widowed Clemmie Monahan three years ago.

He seemed older now than he actually was. He had lived a strenuous life, most of it in the service of others. Rusty felt a rush of sympathy as the tall, gaunt minister walked slowly toward him. Every step seemed to bring pain. Rusty hurried to meet him, to spare him from having to come so far. He was conscious that Andy followed him, eager to hear about Clemmie. She had become like a grandmother to him.

Rusty was careful how he grasped Webb's gnarled hand, knowing arthritis afflicted him. "It's good to see you, sir. What's this about Clemmie?"

Webb's face was grave. "The Bible tells us that even the just must suffer times of tribulation. Clemmie has had a stroke. Her limbs are paralyzed on one side. She cannot so much as leave her bed without someone to support her. She even has trouble in speaking."

Rusty was momentarily speechless. Clemmie Monahan was a little woman, weighing scarcely a hundred pounds, but she had always reminded him of a willow. Ill winds had bent her more times than was her due, but never, it had seemed, could they break her. It always shook him to see infirmities catch up with people he had considered invincible, like Daddy Mike and Preacher Webb and Clemmie. Such occasions forced him to consider his own vulnerability.

He asked, "Can't anything be done?"

"James fetched a doctor out here all the way from Sherman. He gave her some medicine, but I think it was more to bring the family's hopes up than to fix what's wrong with her. I've lost count of how many times I've prayed over this."

"I wish there was somethin' I could do."

"She'll be cheered that you've come." Webb put an arm around Andy's shoulder. "Andy, seein' you will be better medicine than anything a doctor could give her. She looks on you as one of her own."

Andy said, "I wish I was."

Rusty said, "I wonder what brought this on."

Webb frowned. "Just one trouble too many, I reckon. I don't guess you knew that Alice ran off with a cowboy."

Alice was the youngest daughter. Len Tanner had long had eyes for her. This news would be a sad disappointment to him. "Any idea where they went?"

"We had a letter. Said they got married down at Fort Griffin. James swore he'd go and fetch her back whether she wanted to come or not. He was killin' mad. Clemmie had to talk hard to stop him. That's when the stroke hit her."

"How did Josie and Geneva take Alice's runnin' away?"

"Better than their mother did, but that's not sayin' much."

Rusty could not wait longer without asking, "How *is* Josie?"

"Bone tired. Besides bein' nurse, she's takin' on all the work Clemmie used to do. I've been afraid she'd wind up sick herself. You'll be like a dose of tonic to her."

"I'd have come earlier if I'd known."

"Josie wrote to you. I guess you didn't get her letter."

"Never did." He had lost Geneva because of a lack of communication during the last part of his ranger service. She had thought him dead. Evan Gifford had come along, an answer to her loneliness.

Josie heard footsteps on the porch and came to the door. She stared at Rusty in pleased surprise, then self-consciously reached up to check her hair. It needed combing. She said, "I must look a sight." She seemed to consider retreating back into the house, then stepped out onto the porch and into his arms. He held her tightly and said, "You look beautiful."

"You're a terrible liar."

"I'd have come sooner if I'd known about Clemmie."

He stepped back without releasing her. As Webb had said, she looked tired and drawn. Even so, she was still a pretty woman. Josie's blue eyes glistened. "I wrote you a letter," she said.

"I never got it. I ought to've come sooner anyway."

Webb asked, "Is Clemmie asleep?"

Josie shook her head. "She woke up when she heard Billy holler. She'll feel better, seein' who's come." She kissed Rusty again. "So do I." She led him to a bedroom. Andy and Webb followed.

Rusty wanted to say something that might pretend cheerfulness. Seeing Clemmie lying there even thinner than normal, her mouth twisted by the stroke, he could think of nothing that would not sound flippant and false. "I'm sorry, Clemmie." That was all he could say before he choked.

Her left arm was still and useless. She raised her right arm, and he took her hand. She struggled with her words. "The heart . . . ain't quit beatin'." Her eyes cut to Andy. "How's . . . my Indian boy?"

Some people could call him that and he would take it as a compliment. Others said it and he was ready to fight. Clemmie could call him anything she wanted to.

Andy seemed to have as much trouble with his words as Clemmie did. "I'm . . . I'm just fine." He leaned down and kissed her on the forehead. His face was pinched. Rusty sensed that only a strong will held back Andy's tears.

She squeezed Rusty's hand and looked at her daughter. "Take Josie . . . take her out into the sunshine. Make her smile."

Josie protested, "What if you need somethin', Mama?"

"Warren . . . ," she nodded toward her husband . . . "he can get it. Or Andy." She touched the boy's arm. "You stay with me, Andy."

Andy cleared his throat. "Sure. I ain't goin' nowhere. You want somethin', you just tell me."

Josie seemed hesitant, but Clemmie dismissed her with a motion of her hand. Rusty put his arm around Josie and walked her out onto the porch. They seated themselves on a bench. She took a deep breath and expelled it. "The fresh air does feel good. I haven't had much time outdoors since this all happened."

"Preacher Webb is worried about you. I'm sure Clemmie is, too."

"There's nobody else here to care for her in the things it takes a woman to do. Alice is gone. Geneva's got her own family to see after. Preacher Webb and James do what they can, but the rest is up to me."

"You've got your own life to live."

"I wouldn't have a life if it wasn't for Mama. She always took care of me. Papa would turn over in his grave if I didn't take good care of her."

The family had never entirely recovered from Lon Monahan's death early in the war. Radical secessionists had killed him for his Union sympathies, and a young son had died with him. After many hardships and indignities, the surviving Monahans had found shelter and protection at Rusty's farm on the Colorado River. There they had remained until the war ended.

Then, at least, Rusty had known how to help them. He felt useless now.

He said, "I suppose you can guess why I came."

The look she gave him seemed strangely defensive. "I think I might."

"Things are in good shape down at the farm. They came near takin' it away from me once, but that's over now. I'm askin' you to go back down there with me."

The sadness deepened in her eyes. Tears welled before she turned her head and wiped them away. "For years I waited for you to ask me. Even a few weeks ago, I could've said yes. Now I can't. I can't leave here while Mama's in this shape."

Rusty could not have said the answer surprised him, but it shook him nevertheless. He could have come earlier. Once last fall's crops had been gathered he could have made the trip at any time. But he had waited, uncertain of the future, uncertain he would continue to own the farm when others wanted it and were more favored by the reconstruction government.

"We've built a separate cabin for Andy," he said, realizing how feeble an argument that was, how little it must mean to her in the face of hard reality.

She said, "You can see, can't you, why I can't go with you? Even if I'd gone with you before, I'd have had to come back. There's no debt as heavy as one you owe to your blood kin."

Rusty had no blood kin that he knew of. He had been a nameless orphan, left wandering in the wake of an Indian raid. But he understood what she meant by debt, for since boyhood he had felt a deep obligation to those who had given him a home and selflessly cared for him as if he had been their own.

"Clemmie would want you to be happy," he said. He knew that was another weak argument.

"I couldn't be happy knowin' I hadn't done right by her. No, Rusty, we'll have to wait . . . wait 'til Mama gets over this stroke, or 'til . . ." She did not finish.

He tried to keep his voice from betraying the disappointment he felt. "You've got to do what you think is best."

She leaned against him. "I wasn't sure you'd understand."

"I understand."

"I always said you're the best man I ever knew, Rusty, except maybe for Papa and Preacher Webb. I'll just have to wait some more. I hope you can."

He could. He had to. In all his life he had loved only two women. One had been lost to him. He would go to any length to avoid losing this one.

"However long it takes," he said. "I just wish there was somethin' I could do for Clemmie."

"The best medicine she could have would be to see Alice come back. Or at least to know she's all right."

"Why wouldn't Alice be all right?"

"It's that man, Corey Bascom. I never did trust him. I don't think anybody did except Alice. James wouldn't have hired him if he hadn't been desperate for help in breakin' horses. I could see that Alice was taken with him, but I never once suspected they might run off together."

"It's hard sometimes to tell what's in young folks' minds." Rusty often had difficulty in reading Andy's intentions. He could be as inscrutable as an Indian.

Josie said, "Alice got a thrill out of havin' all the young bachelors around here come and pay court to her. That's why I can't figure why she settled for Corey. He had an air about him like he was hidin' somethin'. Maybe it was the mystery that attracted her."

Rusty considered a while before he offered, "What if I was to go and look for her? Maybe I can find out if she's all right and bring her home if she's not."

Josie's eyes flickered with momentary hope that quickly gave way to doubt. "I always felt like there was somethin' a little dangerous about Corey. Nothin' I could put my finger on, nothin' he ever exactly said or did. Just a strong feelin'. He might hurt you."

"There's been others tried."

"What if he doesn't want to be found? What if Alice wants to come home but he doesn't want to let her?"

"I'll just have to persuade him."

Misgivings were strong in her eyes. "It's too much to ask of you, Rusty."

"You're not askin'. I'm offerin'."

"I wouldn't want you to put yourself in harm's way for this family."

"I've been in harm's way most of my life. And you-all and Andy are the nearest thing to family that I've got."

"At least talk to James. And to Evan. They worked with Corey. They'll know the most about him."

"I'll do that. It's best you don't say anything to Clemmie. If I don't find Alice, she'd just be hurt all over again."

Josie remained on the porch while he walked toward the dusty corral where James and Evan were working with a young horse, sliding a saddle blanket along its back, getting it used to the strange new feel. Geneva Gifford stood outside the fence, watching them. Her son, Billy, and a young daughter were beside her. Turning as Rusty approached, she extended her hand. She attempted a smile but could not quite bring it off. She said, "Billy told me you and Andy had come. I guess you've seen Mama."

"I wish I'd known sooner."

He could never look at Geneva without feeling a sense of loss, though he had gradually come to terms with that loss a long time ago. He had taken comfort in the fact that her marriage was a good one. She had a husband who was worthy of her. Childbearing had matured her. She carried more weight than when he had courted her, but she was still handsome.

She said, "I saw you on the porch with Josie. Did you ask her this time?"

Geneva had always been able to read him as if his thoughts were written across his face in block letters. He replied, "She said no. On account of her mother."

"You can't blame her."

"I told her I'd try to find Alice."

"I'm not sure that's a good idea."

"It's the only idea I've got."

James released the horse and walked over to the fence. Geneva told her brother, "Rusty says he's goin' to look for Alice."

Rusty's relationship with James had always been shaky. Ranger service had put him at cross-purposes with Josie's brother more than once. The end of the war had brought them to a truce, but earlier disagreements had left a lingering aftertaste like burned coffee on the tongue.

James demanded, "What's Mama say about this?"

Rusty said, "She doesn't know. It's best to leave it that way."

James frowned. "In other words, you're not sure you can do it."

"All I'm sure of is that I'll try."

James said grimly, "I wanted to go myself, but Mama wouldn't hear of it. She thought I'd more than likely shoot the son of a bitch. And I would've, if he gave me any excuse."

Rusty pointed out, "He did marry her, at least. He is Alice's husband."

"A son of a bitch, just the same. A good rider but rough on horses. Used his spurs too much. A man rough on horses is apt to be rough on a woman, too." He motioned, and Evan came over to the fence, carrying a coiled rope. "Evan worked with him as much as I did. His opinion is the same as mine."

Geneva told her husband what she had told James. Evan said, "I was always uneasy while Corey worked here. I suspicioned that he planned to steal some of our horses. I never thought that he might steal Alice instead."

James said, "I never was plumb sure that Corey Bascom was his real name. Wouldn't surprise me if he borrowed it someplace."

Most of the aliases Rusty had come across seemed to be simple names such as Smith or Jones or Brown, not unusual enough to be memorable. "You have any idea where he came from, or where he might've gone with Alice?"

James and Evan glanced at one another. James said, "All we know for sure is that Alice sent her mother a letter from Fort Griffin sayin' she had got married."

Evan added, "He told me one time that his family had a stock farm over east someplace. I think he mentioned the Clear Fork. But I guess there's several of those in Texas."

Rusty said, "He could've meant the Clear Fork of the Brazos. It flows past Fort Griffin and spills into the main Brazos farther east."

James grunted. "That's a long ways from here. But if it was closer I'd've gone after Alice no matter what Mama said."

Evan asked, "You want somebody to go with you?"

Rusty caught the misgivings in Geneva's face. "There's no need in that. You-all have got enough to worry about right here."

Geneva looked relieved. She reached through the fence and clutched her husband's arm. Evan did not argue the point.

Geneva bit her lip. "One thing, Rusty. If you find Alice, don't give her the notion that she caused Mama's stroke. There were so many things that piled up . . . the stroke might've come even if Alice hadn't run away."

James said, "And maybe it wouldn't. Alice hasn't exactly been a sweet little angel. Maybe she *ought* to feel guilty."

Rusty shook his head. "It's not my place to blame her *or* to forgive her. I'll just see if she wants to come home and bring her if she does."

James added, "And don't kill anybody you don't have to. Mama wouldn't like it."

CHAPTER

FOUR

Rusty tightened the cinch on his dun horse in the frosty light of the winter sunrise. Andy led Long Red to where his saddle rested on the top rail of a fence. The sorrel's breath made a small cloud in the crisp air.

Rusty demanded, "What do you think you're doin'?"

"Fixin' to go with you."

"I want you to stay here. Make yourself useful to the Monahan family."

Andy lifted his saddle from the fence. "You don't know what you may be ridin' into. You're liable to need help."

"I doubt it. If I do I'll go to the local law. You stay here." Rusty mounted and rode away, looking back. Andy stood with the saddle at arm's length, watching him.

"You stay," Rusty hollered back.

He had ridden half a mile when he heard a horse coming up behind him. He stopped and turned the dun around as Andy approached. He said, "I told you I'm goin' by myself."

"And I'm goin' by *my*self. I just happen to be travelin' the same direction you are."

Rusty wanted to be angry with him but couldn't. "As I remember it, you trailed after your Comanche brother once when he told you not to. Got yourself in bad trouble." That had been the time Rusty had found him lying helpless, his leg broken after his horse fell.

"I was just a kid then."

"By my lights, you're still a kid."

"But too big for you to whip. Are we movin' on, or do we just sit here and talk?"

Rusty saw that neither reason nor threat would change Andy's mind. He had a stubbornness that Daddy Mike Shannon would have appreciated. "I guess we can argue and ride at the same time. Come on."

He carried supplies rolled up in a blanket tied behind the cantle of his saddle. Andy had brought nothing but an extra blanket. Rusty knew they would have to be sparing of his coffee and flour and bacon. He said, "Keep a sharp eye out for game or we'll be awful lank by the time we reach Fort Griffin."

"You don't know what hungry is 'til you've ridden with the Comanches. They can go for a week on a chunk of sundried meat the size of your hand."

"I've done it, but I never liked it."

Fortunately Andy's sharp eyes picked up some antelope that afternoon, and his keen marksmanship brought one down. Antelope would never replace beef in Rusty's opinion, but it was better than fat hogback.

Preacher Webb had told him about an army chaplain he had met in Fort Griffin. "When he wasn't ministerin' to the soldiers he was takin' the gospel to others that needed it. The good Lord knows there's a lot of them that need it around Fort Griffin. The ground over there is soaked in whiskey."

Andy asked, "Is Fort Griffin really as bad as Preacher makes out?"

Rusty said, "From what I hear, one minister isn't near enough."

It was not much of a village. Its main clientele was soldiers stationed at the post on a flat-topped hill just to the south. It catered also to ranchers and farmers of the area and to freighters passing through. Whatever resentment the old Confederates might harbor against Union soldiers, they were never averse to profiting from them.

Rusty had found from experience that a saloon was a good place for information, though sometimes it required a modest investment in goods from behind the bar. He tied the dun in front of a crudely constructed frame building and told Andy, "You don't belong in there."

Andy smiled. "Neither one of us does. Looks like a place where you could get your head stove in for two bits."

"Or maybe less," Rusty agreed. "You stay here while I go ask a question or two."

Andy moved his head in a manner that said neither yes nor no. But he took a position out in front, by the door, where he could hear what was said inside.

The saloon keeper reminded Rusty a little of the stableman in Austin, middle-aged, thin, a red-tinged face indicating that he was quite familiar with his stock. He gave Rusty a piercing study as if gauging his ability to pay. "What's your pleasure?"

"Depends on what you've got."

The barman waved his hand toward a row of bottles along the wall behind him. "You see it. Different bottles, same whiskey. Whichever one you take, you'll wish you'd taken somethin' else. But there ain't nothin' else."

Rusty liked a little whiskey when it came handy, but he had never felt any addiction to it. "I'll trust you. Just pour me one."

The whiskey seared his throat as it went down. He almost choked.

The barman said, "Told you."

Rusty had no wish for another drink. When his throat stopped burning he said, "I'm lookin' for a preacher."

"You ain't dyin'. My whiskey ain't *that* bad."

"The preacher I'm lookin' for would've married a young couple a while back. I'm hopin' he can give me an idea where they went."

"Probably the chaplain up on the hill. Regular preachers usually take a look at this town and decide it's beyond salvation. Young couple, you say? Name wouldn't be Bascom, would it?"

Rusty stiffened. "That's right, Corey Bascom. You know somethin' about him?"

"Enough not to be talkin' much. He brought a young lady to town with him and got the chaplain to tie the knot. Spent the night camped on the river. Some of the boys thought about goin' down and givin' them a shivaree but decided against it. Them Bascoms are mean all the time. They get *real* mean when they're riled up."

"Do you have any idea where they went from here?"

"The family claims land to the northeast. I doubt it's recorded at the courthouse, but who with any sense is goin' to challenge them?"

"How would I get there?"

"You know where the settlers forted up against the Indians durin' the war?"

Rusty remembered the place. It had been named Fort Davis in honor of Jefferson Davis, disregarding the fact that a military post by the same name existed in mountains far to the west. It had been populated a relatively short time, affording protection to civilians against the Comanches and Kiowas while so many of their young men were away to war.

The barman frowned. "I hope you ain't got trouble on your mind. Them Bascom boys can give you more of it than you can handle. And old Bessie Bascom . . . she's the devil's stepmother. You a lawman?"

"Used to be a ranger. I'm not anymore."

"You'd better not let them know you ever was. They're a grudge-holdin' bunch, and they got a grudge against any kind of law."

"I'm just lookin' to be sure the girl's all right. She needs to know that her mother has taken down sick."

"Just the same, you tread softly around that bunch. There ain't a preacher amongst them."

The barkeep drew a crude map on the back of an outdated fugitive poster originally circulated by the state police. The description on the poster fitted the man himself. He cautioned, "Now, don't you let them Bascoms know I told you how to find them. I was lucky to live through the war. I don't know how much luck I got left."

Andy was waiting outside. He indicated that he had heard everything so Rusty need not repeat any of it. Rusty said, "I'd ought to leave you here, only this is no place for a green young feller like you."

Andy said, "Maybe those Bascoms aren't as bad as he makes out."

Rusty did not attempt a reply.

He had visited the site of Fort Davis while on ranger patrol, so he had no difficulty in finding it. Old cedar picket buildings, thrown up for temporary shelter, slumped in various stages of ruin. A stockade fence, started but never finished, leaned toward its final rest upon the ground. A hungry-looking coyote slunk away at the far end of the quadrangle, its ribs showing through a rough coat. Winter had not been kind.

Rusty said, "Folks here had a hard life. Carried water up from the river in buckets. The men, what there was of them, did their cow huntin' in bunches. Had to watch for Indians all the time. They took care of their farms the same way. There were more women and children than men."

Andy remarked, "The Comanches had just as hard a time of it. If they had ever really wanted to they could've cut through this place like a knife through butter." He spoke with a touch of pride.

The saloon keeper's map was vague. It showed a wagon road leading away from the ruined fort, but Rusty found there were several. He asked, "Which one do your Indian instincts tell you to take?"

"I'm afraid my guardian spirits stayed back at Fort Griffin. I'm not hearin' anything from them."

Rusty chose one at random. "Let's try this."

A couple of miles proved it to be a bad choice. The road showed no sign of recent use. It disappeared where heavy rain had washed it away, taking a deep cut into the topsoil. Rusty decided to strike due east, hoping he might intersect a trail showing more sign of recent travel. He did, after a time, and followed it until he came upon a farmer breaking sod with two mules and a moldboard plow.

He asked if they were anywhere near the Bascom place.

The farmer eyed him suspiciously. "You a friend of theirs?"

"I don't even know them. I'm just carryin' a message." He saw no need to burden the man with details.

"Well, if you don't know them, and they don't know you, it might be better if you don't find them."

"The message is important."

The farmer hunched his shoulders as if to say he had given fair warning. "You follow this road another mile or so, then take the first wagon trail that forks off to the right. Stay with it 'til you get to a long picket house with dirt coverin' on the roof. Better holler good and loud before you ride in so you don't surprise anybody. Them Bascoms don't like surprises. Don't like neighbors much, either."

Rusty thanked him for the information and the advice. He glanced at Andy as they resumed their journey. "Aren't you glad you came with me?"

Andy smiled. "Beats plowin'. They sound like interestin' folks."

If it had not been for Clemmie, Josie, and Geneva, Rusty would not have undertaken this mission. Alice had made her bed, and it might do her good to lie in it a while. She resembled her two older sisters in appearance but not in personality. If anything she was prettier, and she was filled with fun-loving spirit. This in some respects had been to her detriment. It had brought her more adulation than was healthy from starry-eyed boys and young men of the area. As the baby sister she had been petted, sheltered, and catered to more than the others. Too young during the war years to realize fully what was going on around her, she had not had to develop the toughness and steadiness of purpose that marked Geneva and Josie. Much had come easily for her. Rusty could imagine how the dashing manner of a handsome stranger could have turned her head.

In due time he and Andy came to the picket house the farmer had described. Rusty paused for a long look. "I don't see but one horse in the pen. Maybe most of the family is gone somewhere."

"That's just as well. They sound like the kind of folks you'd want to meet one at a time."

The farmer had said the Bascoms did not like neighbors. To Rusty that meant they were probably into some kind of business that did not welcome observation. The chaotic years that followed the war had spawned much of that kind of industry. The state police, often more involved with politics than with law enforcement, had done relatively little to stem such offenses as bank robbery and horse and cattle theft.

He said, "If we ever get the rangers back, this whole country is due for a big sweepin' up."

Andy asked, "Do you figure on joinin' them?"

"Like Tom Blessing said, the rangers is no place for a married man."

"You ain't married yet." As an afterthought Andy added, "Neither am I."

"You're too young to be a ranger."

"How do you know? *I* don't even know how old I am. If I told them I'm twenty-one they'd never know the difference. For all we know, I may *be* twenty-one."

"You're some short of that."

"We don't have to tell them so."

Rusty had not suspected that joining the rangers had even crossed Andy's mind. "We'll talk about it when and if the time comes. The state's broke. It may not have enough money to reorganize the rangers anyway."

"I'm bettin' it will. You saw Rip Ford and Henry McCulloch with Coke when he marched up to the capitol. He didn't pick old rangers like them for nothin'."

Rusty remembered the farmer's admonition to announce himself before he rode up to the Bascom place. He shouted, "Hello the house."

He saw a movement at a window and had a quick impression of a face, though it was gone so quickly he could not be sure whether it was that of a man or a woman. He shouted again.

The door opened. A tall, raw-boned middle-aged woman stepped outside with a double-barreled shotgun pointed in Rusty's and Andy's general direction. The chill wind toyed with her long, stringy hair that showed no familiarity with comb or brush. "I don't know you," she hollered. "You got no business on this property."

"If this is the Bascom place, we're carryin' a message for Alice."

"You're close enough. I can hear you from where you're at. Deliver your message."

Rusty disliked having to shout, but that shotgun did not invite a closer conversation. "It's kind of private. It's about her mother. Is Alice here?"

Rusty caught a quick glimpse of a girl coming up behind the woman in the doorway. The woman shoved her back inside. "You tell me, and I'll tell her what she needs to know."

"Her mother is worried. Wonders if she's all right."

"Of course she's all right. Why wouldn't she be?"

"Her mother's *not* all right. Alice needs to know that she's awful sick."

Alice pushed her way outside toward Rusty, but the woman grabbed her and pulled her back. Alice struggled to free herself. Momentarily distracted by her effort to control the girl, the woman turned the shotgun away from Rusty. He took the opportunity to spur the dun and close the distance. Without dismounting, he wrenched the weapon from her hand. He pitched it to Andy, who caught it and broke it open to extract the shells.

The woman's face flushed with rage. "Who are you to come bustin' in here like this? You've got no right."

"We just came to see Alice and tell her about her mother."

Alice's eyes said she was afraid of the woman. She pulled away. "What's happened to Mama?"

"She's had a stroke. Paralyzed on one side. It's a struggle for her to talk."

"She was all right when I left."

"It happened afterwards. It'd do her a world of good to see you."

The woman's eyes were the deadly gray of bullet lead. "You got no business goin' anywhere. Your place is here with your husband."

"I want to see my mother."

"And ride off with two strangers? I won't stand for it."

"They're not strangers. Rusty and Andy are friends of my family."

"They're men, and you're a woman. A married woman. It wouldn't be decent."

"Decent?" Growing indignation pushed Alice's fear aside. "You call this family decent? You call robbin' and stealin' decent?"

The woman raised her hand as if to slap Alice. "Shut up, girl. You don't know what you're talkin' about."

"Oh, but I do. You think I don't know where Corey and his brothers have gone?"

Rusty saw murder in the woman's eyes. "You shut your mouth or I'll shut it for you. I told Corey he made a mistake bringin' you here."

Rusty felt a strong apprehension. "Alice, you'd better come with us. I already see that this is no place for you."

She hesitated. "I don't know what Corey might do."

"We'll take you back to the protection of your family. There's nothin' he *can* do."

The woman declared, "The hell there ain't. He'll be comin' after you and draggin' you back by the hair of the head."

The girl wasted no more time considering. She said, "I'll gather my things." She went into the house.

Rusty said, "Andy, go saddle that horse yonder for Alice. I'll keep Mrs. Bascom company."

The woman seethed. Rusty was glad she no longer had the shotgun. She scolded, "It's a mortal sin, comin' between a man and his wife. My son and Alice taken the vows before a minister of the gospel and in the sight of the good Lord Hisself. The Book says what God has joined together . . ."

"You don't talk like somebody who'd know much about the Book."

"I know it says an eye for an eye and a tooth for a tooth. You carry that girl away and I'll see to it that my boys take a lot more than an eye and a tooth."

Rusty saw no point in arguing. He let her continue a malevolent harangue laced with profanities the likes of which he had never heard pass a woman's lips and some he had heard from few men.

Alice brought a cloth bag out of the house. Rusty asked, "Is that all you've got?"

"I didn't come here with much. I haven't picked up anything new except bitter experience."

Mrs. Bascom shook a finger at her. "There'll be hell to pay when the boys fetch you back here. And they will."

Alice murmured, "Hell is all I've had since I came."

"You Jezebel!" The woman slapped Alice so hard that a red splotch arose where the flat of her hand had struck.

Alice made an angry cry and drove her fist into Bessie Bascom's face. The woman rocked back, almost falling.

Rusty watched in pleased surprise. Maybe he had underestimated Alice. He said, "Looks like you're your mother's daughter, after all."

Andy led a brown horse up from the pen, a sidesaddle on its back. He boosted Alice up into place. Mrs. Bascom held one hand to her jaw, her eyes blazing from shock and pain and anger.

Alice said, "I've wanted to hit that woman ever since the day I came here."

Rusty asked, "Why didn't you?"

"She'd have killed me, or made me wish she had."

"Well, she can't do anything to you anymore."

Andy still had the shotgun. He pitched it up on top of the dirt-covered roof, raising a wisp of dust. He said, "I hope the law don't get after us for takin' this horse."

Alice said, "It's the one I came here on. It never belonged to the Bascoms."

Rusty said, "Let's git. I wouldn't put it past that old woman to climb up there after that gun."

They rode at a rapid pace for a mile or so, then slowed. Alice looked back with concern. Rusty said, "She wouldn't chase us afoot, not this far."

Alice was not comforted. "You don't know Bessie Bascom. She's liable to take a broomstick and come flyin' after us."

"How long do you think it'll be before her menfolks come home?"

"Hard to say. They've been gone three days. Corey was talkin' about a nice little Yankee bank over east that he said needed robbin'."

"So that's what they do for a livin', rob banks?"

"Part of it. They burgle stores, steal cattle, horses, whatever comes easy to hand. I'm sure now that's why Corey came to our farm in the first place. He had heard about the Monahan horses. But we took a shine to one another, and he carried me off instead."

"Against your will?"

"Not then. I wanted to come with him. But when I got here I found things weren't like he'd been tellin' me. Nowheres near."

Rusty had noticed a blue mark beneath her left eye. "Corey did that to you, I suppose."

"Not Corey. His mother. She reminds me of the wicked stepmothers I used to read about in fairy tales."

"How long has she been a widow?"

"Several years. From what Corey told me, Old Ansel got surprised by the state police and tried to put up a fight. After that the Bascoms declared war against all authority. The only thing the boys are scared of is that old woman. Anybody who crosses her is fixin' to bleed some."

She plied Rusty with anxious questions about her mother and others of the family. He knew her concern was genuine.

There's hope for her, after all, he thought. Maybe she's smartened up. Perhaps this bitter experience would bring out the strength and will that was her rightful heritage from Clemmie and Lon Monahan.

They rode by Fort Griffin but did not tarry longer than was necessary to pick up a few supplies. Rusty suspected that pursuit would not be long in coming. Bessie Bascom would insist upon it.

They rode by the saloon where he had stopped for information. The barkeeper stood out in front, puffing smoke from an evil-looking black cigar. His eyes lighted with curiosity as he saw Alice riding with Rusty and Andy. He asked no questions, and Rusty did not pause to offer any answers. But he noted that the man looked hard in the direction from which they had come.

He figures like I do, Rusty thought. They'll be coming after her.

"Let's pick up the pace a little," he said. "We can cover a lot of miles before dark."

Rusty did not ride boldly into the Monahan headquarters. He reasoned that Corey Bascom would expect them to head straight for Alice's home. Though it was unlikely, there was a chance that he and his brothers might have pushed hard and gotten here first.

He watched a while to be sure everything looked normal. He saw Evan Gifford riding a hackamored young horse around and around in a corral. Geneva stood on the porch and shouted for Billy to come home. He climbed down reluctantly and trotted toward her.

Rusty eased. "I don't see anything amiss."

"Let's hurry," Alice said. "I want to see Mama."

As they rode in, James Monahan came out of the barn, a bridle in his hand. Seeing Alice, he quickly hung the bridle across the top of a fence, then trotted to meet the three riders. "Alice!" he shouted. "Baby sister!"

He had every right to be angry with her, and some recriminations might come later, but now was not the time. He lifted her down from the saddle and hugged her as if she had come back from the dead.

"Mama is goin' to be tickled to see you. She's liable to get up and come runnin' when you walk in the door."

"How is she?" Alice asked anxiously.

"Fair to middlin'. She'll do better now." He looked up at Rusty and Andy. "Did you have to kill anybody?"

"Not yet."

"Where's Corey?"

Rusty looked behind him. "Back that way, somewhere. We figure he'll be comin' for Alice. We just don't know when."

James gave his sister a searching look. "When he does, will you be wantin' to go with him?"

"I'd rather kill him than go back there."

"We'll try to see that you don't have to do either one." James reached up to shake hands with Rusty, then Andy. "Fellers, I ain't got words enough to thank you."

Rusty said, "It wasn't much trouble to get her away. Keepin' her may be somethin' else."

"We'll keep her. We've fought off rebel hangmen and Comanche Indians and horse thieves. Corey Bascom ought not to be that much of a challenge."

Alice said, "You haven't met the rest of his family. Especially his mother."

James frowned. "I don't see how one old woman could give us much trouble."

Andy said, "You'll think different if you see her. When she dies and goes to hell even the devil is liable to take out a-runnin'."

Geneva saw Alice and hurried down from her house, throwing her arms around her sister. "Thank God you've come back."

"Thank Rusty and Andy. I wouldn't be here if they hadn't come and fetched me."

Geneva turned to express her thanks to Rusty. She held onto his arm long enough to stir old feelings he had hoped he had put behind him. He was almost relieved when Evan came up to join his wife.

Josie stepped out onto the porch in response to the racket. Recognizing Alice, she came running. She embraced her sister with tears in her eyes. "You're the best medicine anybody could've brought for Mama." When she released Alice she hugged Rusty. "And you're the doctor who fetched it." She looked up at the boy. "And you, Andy." She turned back to her sister. "Come on, let's go show you to Mama."

The family trooped into the big house. Andy started to follow, but Rusty raised a hand to stop him. "This is for the family," he said.

Andy nodded, seeing the rightness of it. "But you're one of the family too, just about."

"Not yet, not 'til Josie and me stand up in front of Preacher Webb. Right now there's no tellin' when that is liable to happen."

CHAPTER

FIVE

Corey Bascom was in a dark mood as he and three younger brothers approached the long picket house that had been their home since soon after they had left Arkansas just ahead of some angry horsemen. The bank for which he had held considerable hope had been a disappointment. With the muzzle of a pistol in his face, the bank's president had stammered that local farmers had made only a mediocre crop the previous fall and most of their money had already been spent. The county government should have had some funds on deposit, but the outgoing officeholders had absconded with most of the money. "We've got nothing but a toenail hold," he had said, "and hopes for a better year."

Frustrated, Corey had promised to come back in the fall, after harvest. "You'd better have somethin' here worth the takin'. Otherwise you'd better start learnin' how to play a harp."

His brother Lacey then forced the sweating banker to go to his knees and beg for mercy. It was a bluff, but Lacey took pleasure in his ability to frighten people. He especially enjoyed it when he could make them wet themselves, which the banker did. Corey sometimes worried that Lacey would get carried away and really kill someone. He had come close. So far the Bascom brothers' crimes had stopped short of murder. So far.

Before leaving town the brothers had paused to rob a mercantile store but found its till was as poor as the bank's.

Lacey shot out a window glass as they left. "Somethin' for them to remember us by," he had explained. It was an unnecessary gesture. Nobody ever forgot a visit by the Bascoms.

The only bright spot Corey could see in this whole trip was the prospect of getting back to Alice. He had enjoyed women before, usually with payment involved, but this girl had awakened a hunger in him that never remained satisfied for long. She had been shy and uncertain the first few times, and he had gotten a little rough. He had occasionally been rough with other women but considered that to be his right inasmuch as he had bought and paid for them. He suspected this treatment was the reason Alice had become increasingly reluctant about his attentions as the weeks passed. He had tried to be gentler, but he didn't know how.

This trip had kept him away for four days—and four long, lonely nights. He hoped his absence would have made her more receptive. He would keep working on the gentleness thing and see if it helped.

He saw smoke rising from the chimney and realized he was hungry for more than Alice. Though Ma's cooking wouldn't get her a job even in a hole-in-the-wall chili joint, when a man's belly was empty her beans and cornbread were welcome. Nobody ever complained, at least where she might hear. Though her sons were grown, she felt obliged now and again to take a quirt to one or another of them just as she did when they were little. To Ma they would always be "my boys," to be praised highly or punished severely, whichever the situation called for.

Praise came sparingly. She had come near taking a quirt to Corey when he brought Alice home unannounced. In her view he had no right to get married without her approval, especially to a pampered girl who was obviously a misfit, unlikely ever to find a comfortable place in this close-knit family. Bessie Bascom had tried hard to weld her boys into an insular unit, mutually shielding one another from the rest of the world. To her it had always been "us against them." Anyone outside of the family was a potential enemy, not to be trusted.

She always preached that old Ansel Bascom had died because he trusted others too much. Someone had betrayed him to the damnable state police. He had died with a dozen bulletholes draining his life's blood into the dirt street outside of a two-bit bank that had not been worth the gamble in the first place.

"Never take nobody into your confidence outside of family," she had told her boys again and again. That prohibition included Alice, whom she regarded as a potential Jonah, if not a Judas.

Corey had been reluctant about being away from Alice so long, leaving her in Ma's less than gentle hands, but family needs took precedence over his personal desires. He would make up for lost time tonight. In his mind he was already in bed with her.

He noticed that the Monahans' brown horse was not in the corral where he had been kept penned and fed, handy in case Ma needed to saddle him and go somewhere in a hurry. The gate stood open, which struck him as odd.

Bessie Bascom heard her sons' arrival and came striding out from the picket house. Her long steps and grim face told Corey that something had gone awry. He had expected her to raise hell when she found out how little money they had brought home, but it appeared she was not going to wait for the bad news.

She went immediately on the attack, shaking her finger in his face. "I told you that little hussy didn't belong here. Well, the buttermilk has done been spilt now. She's gone."

Corey swallowed hard. She could not have hit him harder if she had struck him with a club. "Gone? Where?"

She touched her fingers to her chin. "See this bruise? She put it there. Hit me with her fist, she did, then rode off with two men bold as brass. And they wasn't even her brothers. Told you she wasn't no good."

Corey did not care about the bruise. He cared about Alice. "What men? Who were they?"

"She said they were friends of her family. I told her it wasn't fitten for a married women to do such a thing. I told her it was agin the Book."

Corey struggled to absorb what his mother was telling him. Damn it all, how could Alice just up and leave like that? She belonged to him. She had no right to do anything or go anywhere without his say-so.

"Did they tell you where they were goin'?"

"Back to her folks, they said. But from what you've told me, that's at least two days' ride. That means two nights, layin' out with two men. It don't take much imagination . . ."

The image was too ugly for him to contemplate. He clenched a fist. "Stop it, Ma. She wouldn't do that."

"She did it with you, didn't she? I've heard the two of you many a night, and I've seen you slip into the barn with her in the daytime when your brothers was out workin', like *you* was supposed to be. She's a tart."

"Did you hear her call them by name?"

"I heard her call the oldest one Rusty. The other one was just a big boy, but I expect he's old enough to know what to do with a woman like her."

Corey tried to remember. Rusty. He had heard the Monahans mention that name often. Rusty Shannon, it was. Had an understanding with Alice's sister Josie, as he recalled. He had been a ranger for a long time. Had a farm way down south somewhere. Alice had told him the Monahans stayed on that farm during part of the war, getting away from Confederate zealots who had killed Lon Monahan and a young son named Billy for Unionist leanings.

Corey tried to push his conflicting emotions aside and think. If Rusty Shannon was going to marry Josie, it seemed unlikely he would do anything untoward with Alice no matter how many nights it took them to get back to the Monahan farm. As for the boy, though, he must be the one they said had lived with the Comanches. A boy brought up on Indian ways was something to worry about. There was no telling what he might do.

He demanded, "How long they been gone?"

"Left about this time yesterday. They got a long start on you if you're figurin' on goin' after them."

"Damn right I'm goin' after her."

Bessie nodded. "I told her you would. Told her you'd come draggin' her back by the hair of the head."

"Them Monahans may not give her up easy."

"You better get her back, or else shoot her. She knows too much about our business. If she talks to the wrong people it's liable to cause us a lot of trouble."

"I couldn't shoot her, Ma."

"I could. Wouldn't bat an eyelash. And you'd better be ready to do the same thing. You don't need her. You can buy plenty of women better than her for the price of whiskey."

Corey felt sick at his stomach. He had not dreamed the girl would go off and leave him. "Love, honor, and obey," the chaplain had said. *Obey* was the word that stuck in Corey's mind. She had pledged to obey him no matter what. As his wife she was property like his spurs and saddle and guns, like his horses. A man didn't let somebody run off with what belonged to him and not do something about it.

He turned to Lacey. "You boys go rustle us up some fresh horses. Soon as Ma fixes dinner we're goin' after Alice."

Lacey grinned in anticipation. "You goin' to take a quirt to her, Corey? That's what you ought to do, is take a quirt to her." Lacey had been on the receiving end of many a smart whipping from Ma, and deserved most of them. He enjoyed seeing somebody else get it.

Bessie said, "Lacey, you and Newley and little Anse bring up a horse for me, too. I'm goin' along with you boys to make sure you do the right thing."

Corey had rather she didn't go. She was not a good traveler, always finding fault. He said, "It'll be a hard trip, Ma."

"I've made many a hard trip before. I want to see you give little missy what's comin' to her. And if you don't do it, by God I will."

Rusty sat on the front-porch bench with Josie and watched as twilight darkened the fields stretching beyond the barn. She laid her head against his shoulder, her fingers firmly clasping his arm. She said, "I've been thinkin' a lot about that farm of yours."

"Ours," he said.

"I remember how it looked when Mama and us stayed there durin' the war."

"It's nicer now. We've fixed it up a right smart, me and Andy and Len Tanner, when Len would stand hitched long enough to help. You'll like it. I'm anxious to take you down there."

"Maybe it won't be as long as we thought. Mama perked up a lot when you brought Alice home. She's got a stronger look in her eyes, and I do believe her talkin' has improved."

"But you don't want to leave her just yet?"

"Not 'til she's on her feet. Preacher Webb is hopeful this will all pass and by summer she'll be back to the way she was."

"Summer seems like a long time off. Me and Andy will have to go back home and get the plantin' done before that."

"But you're not in a hurry, are you?" Her tone was hopeful. "You *are* goin' to stay with us a while longer?"

"I'm waitin' to see what Corey Bascom does. James and Evan and Preacher Webb will need all the help they can get if he and his brothers come for Alice."

"You've already done a lot. We're all grateful." She kissed him on the cheek. "How many times have I asked you to marry me?"

He smiled. "Lately, or altogether?"

"I guess it's been shameless of me, but you know I wanted you. I've wanted you ever since I was a girl."

"That was when you first asked me."

"I just didn't want to let you get away. I knew I had to speak up because I could see you and Geneva had eyes for one another."

"That was a long time ago. Things change."

"Not my feelin's about you. I love you."

Rusty tried to say what she had said, but the words would not come as he wanted them to. He said, "I . . . I've got the same feelin's."

Geneva came out of her house across the yard, her small daughter at her side. Josie's gaze followed her sister as she seated herself in a rocker on the porch. The girl climbed up into her lap.

Josie said, "Geneva's still a pretty woman."

"Yes, she is." Rusty felt uneasy, talking about her.

"I remember when everybody figured you-all would get married after the war was over."

"That was before Evan came along."

"Some feelin's never die. I can't help but wonder sometimes if you just think you love me because I remind you of her."

Rusty thought hard about his reply, for he did not want to say anything that would reinforce her doubts. Only to himself would he admit that the same question haunted him from time to time. The answer seemed clear as he sat here beside Josie, feeling the pleasant warmth of her cheek, the arousing pressure of her body leaning against him. But away from her, he might wonder again.

He said, "Geneva's got her own family, and she's happy. Whatever was between us once is long gone."

She pulled away far enough to stare into his eyes. "I wouldn't want to find out someday that I'm a substitute for somebody else. Not even my own sister."

"I can't deny that Geneva was the first woman I ever loved. But you'll be the last."

"Show me," she said, and kissed him again. He felt as if the sun was bearing down upon him with all its noonday heat.

She said, "Hold me, Rusty. Hold me like you'll never let me go."

Evan Gifford had been keeping watch and sounded the alarm. "They're comin'," he said, running up from the corrals. "Looks like a bunch of them."

Rusty had seen them from the porch. He squinted. "I count five. You sure it's the Bascoms?"

"That's Corey in the lead. I never saw the rest of his family."

The only rider Rusty could recognize was Bessie Bascom, sitting straight as a fence post on a sidesaddle. She had a determined posture that reminded him of old Captain August Burmeister of the prewar rangers. Rusty was surprised to see her on a mission like this, but after reflection he decided he could have expected it. He had quickly gained the impression that she was mother, father, and supreme commander of her troop.

James and Preacher Webb and Andy came out of the house. James gave the situation a quick study. "I'll stand here and wait for them. I wish the rest of you would scatter the way we talked about." He glanced back at Webb. "Preacher, it might be better if you stayed in yonder with Mama and the girls."

Webb demurred. "Maybe I can talk common sense to them."

"I doubt as they'd pay attention to it. If you're goin' to stay out here with me you'd best fetch a gun. That way maybe they'll be more willin' to listen to the gospel."

Evan trotted to his own house. Geneva came out onto the porch. He waved her back inside and took a position at the corner. Andy moved out to stand beside the woodpile. Checking the load in his rifle, Rusty walked to the corner of the barn and stepped back out of sight. If the Bascoms rode all the way up to the main house they would be covered from all sides.

From his vantage point Rusty studied the faces. He already knew Bessie Bascom's. Her square jaw was firmly set, her eyes fierce like a hawk's. In comparison, her sons looked almost benign. Rusty decided the one riding closest to Bessie must be Corey, for he appeared a little the oldest and had the most serious expression. The others, Rusty guessed, had probably come along mostly because Bessie had ordered it. He doubted the strength of their resolve. Alice was not *their* wife.

One of the Bascoms had an ironic smile as if he found the situation amusing in some off-center way. Instinct told Rusty that this one might bear special watching.

James stepped to the edge of the porch, a rifle across his folded arms. "That's about close enough, Corey."

Rusty had been correct in assuming which was Alice's husband. Corey stopped and leaned on his saddlehorn. He said, "You know what we've come for."

"You can't have her."

"She's mine. We had the knot tied by a sure-enough preacher." He nodded at Preacher Webb, standing beside James, rifle in his hand. "Wasn't no jackleg, neither. Army chaplain, he was. Had the papers and everything."

James argued, "Bein' married don't make her your property, to be branded and treated like a mare. She's still a freeborn American, with the rights God gave us all."

"Her place is with me. How I treat her is between me and her. She ain't your business anymore."

"She's my sister, so she'll always be my business. *Our* business, this family's."

"She belongs to my family now. And I brought them along to see that she goes back where she's supposed to be. There ain't enough of you Monahans to stop us."

James frowned. "Maybe you ain't seen everybody yet. You're just countin' me and Preacher Webb. You're probably thinkin' a preacher ain't any hand with a gun. You'd be wrong. He can knock a coyote's eye out at a hundred yards. And you know my brother-in-law Evan. That's him over on the porch of his house, carryin' that shiny new shotgun."

All the Bascoms turned to look as Evan stepped away from the corner of his house, bringing the shotgun up into both hands.

James went on, "Now, if you'll look out yonder by the woodpile you'll see Andy Pickard. Raised by the Comanches to be mean as hell. Crack shot with pistol or rifle. If he runs out of shells, he can get you with a bow and arrow.

"And finally, I want you to make the acquaintance of Rusty Shannon. That's him beside the barn yonder, with the rifle. A ranger for years. Brought many a bad man and several Indians to heel in his prime, and he still ain't got enough gray hair that you'd notice it much." He shifted his attention back to Corey. "You still got a notion you want to tackle this family?"

Corey sat rigid in the saddle, his face reddening. He said nothing.

Bessie watched him, looked at James a moment, then turned back to her son. "Is that the best you can do, Corey Bascom, sit there and let them run a bluff on us?"

Corey did not look at her. Grittily he said, "You better count the guns, Ma."

She turned in fury toward her other sons. "You-all just goin' to let this stand? They've got a woman in yonder that rightfully belongs to your brother. Carryin' his seed now, more than likely. Ain't there any shame in the lot of you?"

Nobody moved. They could count, even if the old woman couldn't.

She shrilled, "I'm glad your pa ain't here to see his family tuck their tails between their legs like egg-suckin' hounds." She pushed her horse forward. "If you-all won't do anything, I will."

Rusty saw hesitancy in the faces of James and Webb. If one of the Bascom brothers had made this move they would have stopped him. But though they raised their rifles, he knew they would not shoot a woman.

The front door opened, and Alice stepped out holding a pistol in both hands. She aimed it at Bessie and shouted, "They won't shoot you, but I will. I got cause enough."

Rusty's lungs burned. He had been holding his breath. The air was cool, but he sweated as if he were digging post-holes.

Corey said, "Better stop, Ma. She means it." He rode forward far enough to grab her bridle reins. "This ain't worth gettin' killed over."

Bessie's face was flushed with fury. "It ain't her. You can buy better than her in any dancehall from here to Arkansas. But the shame she's brought on this family, that *is* worth killin' for, or even gettin' killed."

"Nothin' is worth gettin' killed for, not money, not pride, not even a woman. Come on, Ma. We're startin' home." He had to pull on the reins and forcibly turn her horse around.

She cursed her son as she had cursed Rusty the day he had taken Alice away.

Not until they were a hundred yards out did Rusty pause to wipe sweat from his hands onto his trousers, then rub a sleeve across his face. Andy came to meet him halfway to the house. He whistled in relief. "The Fort Griffin bartender was right. That old woman is the devil's stepmother."

Rusty nodded. "You're a good judge of character."

The Bascoms stopped a half mile from the Monahan place, all but Corey. He kept riding.

Bessie shouted, "Where you goin'?"

"I'm goin' home, and I'm goin' by myself. You'd bitch at me the whole way, and I don't want to listen to it."

"You come back here. We got talkin' to do."

Corey kept riding. Bessie hollered at him again, more of a screech than a shout. "Damn you, come back here!"

Corey gave no sign that he heard. Bessie turned to her other sons, her mouth puckered with fury, her eyes cutting like a knife. "To hell with him then. It's up to us to do what has to be done."

Lacey was the next oldest to Corey. He said, "We could slip back in there and pick off them Monahans one at a time 'til Alice gives up and comes with us."

"One or two of us might get picked off, too. No, there's just one thing to do. That girl knows a way too much about this family and our business. If she was to testify in a court, ain't no tellin' what the law might do. So if we can't take her home, we have to see that she don't talk to anybody ever again."

Lacey almost grinned. "You mean kill her?" He had had no use for Alice since she had blackened his eye one day when he tried to drag her into the barn.

Bessie said, "This won't set well with Corey. She turned his head real good. But he'll get over it. So we'll find us a place to rest a while. Come full dark, Lacey, me and you will go back and do what Corey didn't have the stomach for."

Little Anse, the youngest, asked, "You ain't takin' me and Newley, Ma?"

"Two's enough. More than that might attract attention."

Newley Bascom had had a crush on Alice ever since Corey had brought her home, but he had had the good judgment not to let Corey see it. He said, "Seems a waste, killin' her. She was a lot of help to you doin' chores around the place. Couldn't we just grab her and drag her away before they can stop us?"

"I know what you want her for, and it ain't the chores. She ain't worth the risk. Come on, boys. Let's find us a good place to wait for dark."

Rusty sat on the porch bench, staring off into the darkness, wondering if the Bascoms were really gone. He was aware that Evan sat on his own porch, doing the same.

Josie came out and seated herself beside him. He asked, "How's Clemmie?"

"A little worried the Bascoms might come back. But I guess everybody's worried some or you wouldn't be sittin' out here watchin'."

"It doesn't seem likely they'd try, but with people like them you never know. Main thing is to keep Alice indoors so they can't grab her and run before we can stop them."

"You figure they really want her that bad?"

"Maybe Corey does, that's hard to say. I feel like the old woman is mostly afraid of what Alice knows and what she might tell the law."

"I don't understand people like that. They could probably make a good livin' for themselves if they'd buckle down to honest work, probably better than they're doin' now with the risks they're takin' and the trouble they cause to others. Maybe it's the times."

"You can't just blame it on the times. We've always had people like them, good times and bad. By what Alice has said, Bessie and her husband brought the boys up to see the rest of the world as their enemy. They always hated the law. Didn't make any difference if it was Union or Confederate. Most people raise their younguns to be whatever *they* were. The Bascoms always had a wide streak of outlaw in their blood. The old man and the old woman taught the boys to make the most of it. Used the whip on them if they showed weakness."

She leaned to him, and he put his arm around her. She said, "We won't have a whip on the place, you and me. We'll raise our children with love, like Mama and Papa did."

Rusty remembered the kindness of Daddy Mike and Mother Dora, treating him as if he were their own. He said, "I can almost feel sorry for the Bascom boys. They weren't raised up, they were just jerked up. Life's too short to do it that way."

From the direction of the barn he heard the snort of a horse, followed by the sound of hooves. He stood up and grabbed the rifle that leaned against the wall. "Stay put," he told Josie.

He walked partway to the barn, pausing to listen. The horses were quiet again. Hearing no more from them, he returned to the porch. He said, "Just a little bitin' match, I suppose. My dun horse never has quite got used to these here."

Josie motioned for him to sit. "I guess even the horses are a little skittish. They seem to sense when things aren't right."

"What you-all need is a couple of real mean dogs to keep watch on this place."

From inside the house he heard a woman's voice. The words were not clear. Josie said, "That's Mama. I guess she needs me."

Rusty grasped her hand for a moment. "I'm hopin' she won't be needin' you too much longer."

She smiled at him. "Don't go away. I'll be back." She kissed him and went into the house.

Moments later he saw a flash from out in the night and heard the crack of a rifle. A windowpane shattered. Josie gave a cry that made Rusty's blood run cold.

He raised the rifle and sent a wild shot in the direction of the flash he had seen. He heard Alice scream. "Josie! Josie!"

Rusty rushed into the house. In the lamplight he saw Alice holding Josie, trying to keep her from falling. Dropping the rifle, Rusty took three long steps and grabbed Josie. His hand against her back felt warm and sticky.

Josie looked up at him with stricken eyes. She gasped for breath. Rusty lifted her up and carried her into the room she shared with Alice. He placed her gently on her bed and found his hands red with her blood. "Josie!" he cried. "Josie!"

She found breath enough to whisper his name once. The light slowly faded from her eyes. He shook her, trying desperately to find life, but there was none.

He heard Alice sobbing. "Rusty, she's gone."

CHAPTER
SIX

Rusty felt numb, kneeling beside the bed where Josie lay. He did not look up as James and Andy rushed into the room. Alice leaned her head against the wall and cried softly, her back turned.

James shouted, "Andy, blow out the light."

The room fell into darkness. From the next room Clemmie called in a desperate voice, barely understandable, wanting to know what was happening.

James bent to touch his sister, then drew his hand away. "My God. They've killed her."

Rusty heard Preacher Webb's quiet voice, offering a prayer. Andy said, "I'd best see after Clemmie." A moment later Clemmie gave a cry of anguish. Her voice seemed clearer then. "Help me, Andy. I've got to . . . got to go to my daughter."

Still in shock, Rusty managed to push to his feet and make room for Clemmie. She limped painfully into the room, her arm around Andy's strong shoulder. Webb moved to help her. She fell across Josie and wept.

James trembled, his voice breaking. "For God's sake, how many more? First Pa and Billy. Now my sister."

Rusty heard heavy footsteps on the porch. Evan rushed in. Though the room was dark, he immediately grasped the sense of tragedy. "They shot Alice?"

Andy was the only one who seemed to find voice. "No, they killed Josie."

Evan sighed, "God help her." He bent down for a look, then straightened. "I heard two horses runnin' away right after the shots. We all expected them to come for Alice, but why Josie?"

Andy said, "They were out yonder a ways. They saw Josie in the lamplight and mistook her for Alice."

Rusty had been too stricken to reason it out, but he judged that Andy was probably right.

Alice saw it, too. She turned, both hands to her mouth as she stared at Josie's still form in the dim reflected light from the moon. "Then she died in my place. Why couldn't it have been me instead?" She seemed about to collapse. James and Webb both grabbed her.

Webb said, "Hold tight, Alice. Some things we are not given to understand. It was not your fault."

"But it was." She made a weak effort to break free of them, then fell back against the gaunt Webb. "If I hadn't been addle brained, if I hadn't run off with Corey, . . ."

Webb said, "You couldn't have known it would lead to this. You couldn't have known what Corey was capable of."

Corey. The name ignited a flame in Rusty's brain. Bessie Bascom had vowed that her sons would take an eye for an eye. The flame built into wildfire. He said, "Corey Bascom will die for this."

Webb said, "You're in shock, Rusty. Wait 'til you have time to think straight."

"I'm thinkin' straight enough. Corey Bascom killed her. I'm goin' after him."

Andy moved to his side. "Not by yourself. I'll go with you."

Webb showed no more inclination to argue. He bowed his head, his voice breaking. "I prayed for Clemmie, and I prayed for Alice. I never thought to pray for Josie."

James placed his hands on Rusty's shoulders. "Josie was my sister. I've got as much interest in Corey as you have. But let's don't go off half cocked. We need to see her buried first, with the proper words said over her."

"And give Corey a long start? No, I know where he'll go first. I'm not givin' him time to go any farther."

Evan said, "You and Andy may not be enough against that bunch. I'll be ridin' with you."

Rusty argued, "You've got a wife and family to think about."

"This family took me in when I was near dead and gave me a life again. Josie was my wife's sister, and like my own. I'm goin'."

Rusty felt too beaten down to protest more.

Evan said, "But first I've got to break this to Geneva. She's at the house with the kids, probably worried to death. Tellin' her will be as about as hard a thing as I ever did."

Andy said, "I'll go catch up our horses."

James relighted the lamp and turned to Rusty. "You've got your mind made up to go. Nothin' I can say will stop you?"

Rusty found it painful to speak. "I can't do anything to help Josie now. But I can do somethin' about Corey."

"Then I'll throw some grub together for the three of you. You'll need it."

Corey Bascom expected his mother and brothers to return home soon, but they did not show up until near noon of the day after his arrival. He walked to the barn to meet them as they rode in. They were dusty and weary, but his mother had a stern look of triumph about her.

He asked, "What kept you-all? You ought to've been home yesterday."

She fastened accusing gray eyes on him. "We stayed around and finished the job you ought to've done for yourself."

Alarm quickly stirred in him. "What do you mean?"

"I mean your sweet little Alice girl ain't goin' to do no talkin' to the law or anybody, not ever again."

He felt as if his skin were afire. "What did you do?"

"Me and your brother Lacey went back and took care of her."

Corey's jaw dropped. For a moment he could not move. He could only look at her in disbelief. But he knew he had to believe. He felt a fool for not having realized she might do it. She was fully capable of killing anyone who stood in the way of her and the family. He remembered that years ago she had stalked and shot a witness in Arkansas just before the grand jury was to convene and bring an indictment against old Ansel for stealing hogs.

He trembled. "But I loved her, Ma."

"Love!" She spat the word. "Love is what you give to your family, not to some calf-eyed little tart. All your thinkin' lately has been below your belt or you'd have seen what had to be done and done it yourself."

Grief and fury rose together, swelling and spilling over. "Damn you, Ma!" He drew back his hand and slapped her, hard. He had never done it before.

She recoiled in disbelief, then brought up her quirt. She lashed him about the face and shoulders until he grabbed the limber leather end and jerked it out of her hands. He flung it aside and strode beneath the shed where his saddle sat astraddle a rough log rack.

"Where are you goin'?" she demanded.

"As far from you as I can get." He turned burning eyes toward his brothers. "From all of you." He took a rawhide reata and cast a loop around the neck of his black horse.

She shouted, "Corey Bascom, you turn that horse a-loose. You ain't goin' nowhere."

"How are you goin' to stop me? You goin' to shoot me, too?"

Bessie made a gesture at Lacey. Lacey came at Corey with clenched fists. Corey did not wait for him to strike the first blow. He hit Lacey first in the stomach, taking his brother's breath away, then a second time to the jaw. Lacey went down on his knees and spat blood.

"That's for Alice," Corey said. "I ought to kill you." He saddled his horse and rode away, not once looking back.

Lacey pushed to his feet, rubbing his aching jaw, wiping blood on his sleeve. Newley, who had been morosely silent since the shooting, watched his older brother's departure with concern. "He ain't fixed for travelin', Ma. He didn't take so much as a blanket, and no grub at all."

Newley was a fool, she thought, concerned only about Corey's comfort. Because he, too, had a weakness for Alice, he could not see or chose not to see the threat she had presented to them all. She said, "He'll come draggin' back when he gets hungry enough."

"Maybe not. He looked awful mad."

"Then he'll have to take care of himself. He chose that girl over family." She spread her fingers against a face still reddened and burning from Corey's slap. "First time one of you boys ever raised a hand against me. I don't know why the Lord has let the world come to this. Folks are losin' all sense of right and wrong, the way it looks to me."

Bessie recognized Rusty Shannon and the boy Andy on sight. She did not remember the name of the third rider, though she recalled that he had backed the Monahans when the Bascoms had made their first try at recovering Alice.

She looked around to be sure her three remaining sons were close by and armed. They were. She had put years of training into preparing them for a hostile world, though they had fallen short of her expectations in many particulars. Especially the weak-willed Newley, and now Corey. She stood waiting, the quirt in her hand.

Rusty Shannon had a look of death about him. He reined his dun horse to a stop. The boy Andy pulled a long-legged sorrel in beside Shannon. The third man drew up on the other side, a shotgun across the pommel of his saddle.

Shannon's furious gaze swept over the Bascoms. "Where's Corey?"

Bessie said, "You can see for yourself, he ain't here."

"You say he's not, but you could be lyin'."

Bessie felt a quick indignation. She never lied except when it seemed expedient. This time she didn't have to. "He's gone away. What do you want him for?"

"For killin' a woman."

Bessie felt gratified. She had been a little concerned over the slight possibility that Alice might have survived the bullet, though Bessie had seen the blood gush when it struck her in the back. Lacey's aim had been true.

She asked as innocently as she could, "And what woman would that be?"

"Josie Monahan."

Bessie felt as if a bullet had struck *her*. She struggled to control herself lest Shannon read the dismay she felt. "*Josie* Monahan?"

"That's what I said."

Bessie began to shake in spite of a determined effort to take a grip on her emotions.

Shannon seemed to read her thoughts. "I guess you thought it was Alice. But Corey shot the wrong woman."

Bessie's mind raced as she considered the implications of the mistake. Shannon was clearly in a killing mood. It was a good thing Corey had left. Shannon was prepared to kill him or die in the effort. But there was another complication. Alice might or might not have talked before, but her sister's death would make her eager to tell everything she knew about the Bascoms.

Shannon stared at her with a severity she could not handle. She looked away from his blazing eyes. He said, "I'm askin' you again, where's Corey?"

Newley said, "Corey didn't—"

Ma cut him off short. "Shut your mouth, Newley."

Andy brought his rifle to bear on the brothers, and Evan followed his lead with the shotgun. Andy said, "We'll keep these boys off of your back if you want to go search the house."

Without answering, Shannon rode close to the picket house and dismounted, keeping the horse between himself and the dwelling. Rifle in hand, he walked to the door and kicked it open. He rushed inside.

Bessie said to the other two, "Told him Corey ain't here. He left, and I doubt he's comin' back. Ever."

Andy said, "Won't do him any good. Rusty'll hunt 'til he finds him."

"Shannon ain't a Monahan, and neither are you. What was that Josie woman to you-all?"

"Rusty and her were fixin' to get married."

Bessie had no time or inclination to feel sorry for people outside of her own, but she recognized that this made Shannon a lethal threat. She had seen with Corey how much store a man could place in a woman whether she deserved it or not. The mood he was in, Shannon was as dangerous as a den of rattlesnakes. She hoped neither Lacey nor little Anse was foolish enough to try a move against him, not right now. Shannon could probably kill them both and not lose a minute's sleep over it. She did not have to worry about Newley. At the first shot he would probably turn and run like a dog.

Shannon remounted his dun and returned, his eyes as threatening as before. "Whichaway was he goin' when he left here?"

She said, "You know we wouldn't tell you. Look for yourself. Maybe you can find his tracks." She had little concern on that score. There were so many horse tracks around here that he could have no idea which were left by Corey's mount.

Shannon said, "I'll find him. Consider him dead, because I'll find him no matter how long it takes." He jerked his head at his two companions. They rode away in the general direction of Fort Griffin. That was the course Corey had been taking when she last saw him.

Newley was the first to speak. He had looked relieved when he found out Alice was still alive. "Ma, you let them go on thinkin' Corey done it when it was really Lacey."

She lashed him with the quirt. "Don't ever let me hear you say that again. They'd have killed Lacey as sure as he's standin' there."

"But they'll kill Corey if they find him."

"Corey can take care of himself better than Lacey. He's a better shot. But we stand together, us Bascoms. We take care of one another, and we don't point a finger at any of our own. Now gather close and listen." She looked around as if she thought some outsider might hear. They had let Alice hear too much. "You boys have got a job of work to do. Lacey, you heard what he said. You shot the wrong woman."

Lacey was immediately defensive, raising his hands as if he expected her to take the quirt to him. "You know we couldn't get real close to the house. She looked like Alice, the best I could see in the lamplight."

"You was in too much of a hurry to get it over with and run. So now you got to do it again."

"They'll have that place guarded better than it was before. I might not come back."

"If you don't kill that girl there ain't no use in you comin' back. Time she gets through tellin' what she knows, Texas won't be big enough for any of us."

Newley said, "Let me go do it, Ma."

Her eyes narrowed in suspicion. "I got other work for you and little Anse." She knew about Newley's infatuation. He had no intention of killing Alice. If he had the chance he might carry her away to protect her. "You heard what Shannon said. The only way to keep him from huntin' down your brother is to kill him before he can."

Newley betrayed strong misgivings, as she expected. Little Anse seemed eager. "How do you want us to do it?"

"Any way you can. Trail after him. First chance you get, bushwhack him."

"What about them two that's with him?"

"Maybe they'll split up. Even if not, they don't have the killin' fever in their eyes like Shannon has. Get him and they'll probably give up the chase."

Without enthusiasm Newley said, "We'll do our best."

Newley's best wouldn't be worth a Confederate dollar, but little Anse would give it a good try. "Get at it then. Saddle your horses. I'll be puttin' some grub together."

In the house she paused in her task to look at a tintype on the mantel over the fireplace. It was of old Ansel. She kept it there as a constant inspiration to her sons and a reminder that they had to keep their guard up because the world was against them as it had been against their father.

"You was always weak, Anse," she said. "I've tried to make your boys stronger than you ever was, but I swear sometimes I have to wonder. Maybe they got too much of your blood and not enough of mine."

Rusty stopped once they were out of the Bascoms' sight. "I'm afraid I just made a bad mistake."

Andy said, "I didn't see you do anything wrong."

"I talked when I ought to've stayed quiet. They thought Corey had killed Alice. I let them know otherwise. Now they're liable to make another try for her."

Evan said gravely, "I hadn't thought of it that way."

Andy said, "We'd better get back to Alice before they have a chance."

Rusty nodded. "You two go. The Monahans may need all the help they can get. I'll keep after Corey. Maybe I can catch him before he finds out Alice is still alive."

Andy frowned. "By yourself?"

"He's by *him*self."

"You don't even know which way he went."

"No matter where he intends to go, I'm bettin' he'll stop at Fort Griffin first for supplies. Maybe I can pick up his trail there."

"How long do you figure on bein' gone?"

"Don't look for me 'til you see me comin'."

Andy gave Rusty a worried study. "You ain't slept, hardly, since Josie died. You're worn out. If you do catch up with him, the shape you're in, you may not be a match for him. You could get yourself killed."

"I lost a lot of sleep in my rangerin' days. Never got killed yet." Rusty stepped down and tightened the cinch. Josie's image came to him suddenly and unbidden. He swallowed hard and turned to Evan. "There's somethin' I want you to do."

"Anything you ask."

"It won't be hard." Rusty's eyes burned. He blinked away the tears that came to cool them. "When you get home, you take Geneva in your arms and hold her like you'll never let her go."

He could hardly expect Corey Bascom to be waiting for him on the street in Griffin Town, but he watched closely just the same. He saw everything that moved. He rode up to the saloon where he had stopped the time he had asked directions to the Bascom place. He found the same dour bartender wiping dust from glasses and placing them on a shelf behind the bar.

The bartender gave him a critical study. "I know you, but you look different."

"I'm huntin' for Corey Bascom."

"I told you the last time where he lives."

"He left there. I thought he might've come this way."

The bartender grunted thoughtfully and went back to dusting glasses. "Any special reason you're lookin' for him?"

"He killed a woman."

The barman stopped what he was doing and studied Rusty with a more critical eye. "*Your* woman?"

"She was."

The man turned to retrieve a bottle from a shelf. He poured a glassful and set it in front of Rusty. "The look on your face tells me you need a drink."

"What I need, I won't find in that bottle."

"But it might help. Drink it."

Rusty took the contents of the glass in two swallows. The initial burn was followed by a healing glow.

The bartender said, "I don't ordinarily mix myself in other people's problems, and I sure don't go around givin' out information on other people's business. But I reckon this case justifies an exception. Corey was in here late yesterday. Bought supplies at a store down the street, then he stopped in here and got him two bottles of whiskey. Said he needed them for the road. Sounded like it was goin' to be a long one."

"Do you know which way he went after he left here?"

"No, swear to God I don't. I never watched him. There's lots of trails out of here. He could've gone south toward the Conchos and Mexico. Could've gone east, toward Arkansas, or even north, toward the Indian nations. There ain't no tellin'. With all the travelers who come and go, I doubt anybody paid him much mind."

The barman poured another drink. "Down this one. For what you been through, you ain't hardly started."

Rusty hesitated, then tipped the glass.

The barman said, "Couldn't nobody blame you if you went and got yourself staggerin' drunk."

"But then I couldn't do what I came for." Rusty paid him for the drinks. "Do you know what kind of horse he was ridin'?"

"It was a black one. That's all I can tell you."

"Thanks for the help."

He went down the street to the general store. The clerk, like the bartender, was meticulous about not minding other people's business. He was evasive until Rusty told him he knew Corey had bought supplies. He admitted, "Yeah, I sold him some stuff . . . coffee, bacon, salt, cartridges, and a wool blanket. I took it he was figurin' on a long trip, but I didn't ask any questions and he didn't offer any information."

"Did you see which direction he went leavin' town?"

"With customers like the Bascoms I make it a point not to see anything they do after they walk out this door. For all I know, he just evaporated."

Rusty recognized the futility of further questions. He walked back out to his horse. He rode around the tall hill on which the army post stood and hit the military road that led southward toward distant Fort Concho. Fresh wagon tracks covered any trail Corey might have made, if he had even ridden this way. Rusty swung back to the Clear Fork and looked at the wagon road that led eastward. It had the same abundance of fresh tracks as the other. The north road toward Forts Richardson and Sill would be no different.

He came upon a pair of heavily laden freight wagons creaking their way down from the north, the hubs badly in need of a greasing. He asked the first teamster if he had come upon anybody riding a black horse. The teamster considered, then said, "A troop of them dark-complected cavalry soldiers is all. Talked like they was lookin' for Indians, but I suspect they wasn't lookin' very hard."

Rusty scouted around until dark but knew his search for tracks was futile. Corey could have put on wings and flown away for all the trace that could be found now. He returned to the saloon, weary and sick at heart.

The bartender knew by the look on his face. "I told you. You ready for another drink?"

Rusty placed two coins on the bar. "A whole bottle."

He rode along the Clear Fork a while until full dark caught him. He unsaddled the dun, staked him on a long rope, then considered fixing a little supper. He had not eaten anything today. He built a fire but decided he was too weary to cook any of the bacon he carried. He opened the bottle and took a couple of long drinks.

He stared into the flames, feeding in dead wood to keep the fire going.

The need for sleep weighted his eyelids and the whiskey churned his empty stomach, but he feared the dreams that might assault him. He concentrated on the flames. They went in and out of focus as he turned to the bottle from time to time. An old arrow wound in his leg began to ache. It often did when he was tired.

He kept seeing Josie's face in the flickering coals. He imagined Josie's voice, assuring him they would not have to wait much longer. He dwelled at length on the plans they had made for a long life together. Gone. Torn away from him in an instant.

After a time, from grief and sleepiness and the whiskey, he became confused. Was it Josie's face he saw, or Geneva's? Somehow they started looking alike.

He had loved two women, and he had lost them both.

Sleep overwhelmed him. He sprawled on the ground and fell away into a troubled darkness.

The bottle tipped over. The whiskey trickled out and soaked into the dry earth.

He boiled a can of coffee and forced himself to broil some bacon on a stick for his breakfast. At least the Clear Fork's water was good. A lot of water in the rolling plains was barely fit to drink. He felt better rested, but his head hurt from the whiskey. He wondered at the weakness that had allowed him to drink it. Normally he seldom drank, and on the rare occasions that he did it was more for sociability than for enjoyment.

Josie's image was much on his mind, and he was less alert than he should have been. At mid-morning he became aware that two riders had fallen in three or four hundred yards behind him. He gave them little thought at first because the trail showed signs of frequent travel. But after a time he noticed that when he slowed, they slowed. They seemed deliberately trying not to catch up to him. He sensed with rising alarm that they were waiting and watching for the right place to overtake and trap him.

He wondered who they might be. He considered the possibility that Corey had doubled back to the family place and brought one of his brothers to help.

Under other circumstances Rusty would be content simply to elude those who followed him. The thought that one might be Corey made this situation different. He began looking for a chance to swap places with his pursuers, to employ a double-back trick Indians sometimes used against those who would trail them. Corey might be too shrewd to fall for it, but the chance was worth taking. All Rusty wanted was to get close enough to place Corey in his sights.

He edged into the timber that lined the creek, trusting that it would hide him from the two riders' view. After a couple of hundred yards he crossed the creek and rode back in the opposite direction. He hid himself in heavy foliage and dismounted, drawing his rifle from its scabbard. He placed his hand on the dun's nostrils to prevent it from nickering at the other horses should it feel moved to do so. The dun was not particularly sociable with its own kind.

Through the heavy leaves he watched the two men on the other side of the creek, one leaning from the saddle to observe Rusty's tracks.

He felt a sharp disappointment as the pair came into clear view. Neither was Corey. But they were Bascoms, a couple of Corey's brothers. When they rode past him, he remounted and brought the rifle up high enough that he could place the stock against his shoulder in an instant. He put the dun across the creek and closed the distance. The murmur of the creek masked the sound of his horse's hooves.

He ordered, "Turn around and raise your hands."

The voice startled the two. One of the brothers complied, carefully reining his horse about, then lifting his arms. The younger hesitated.

Rusty shouted, "I won't say it again."

The youngster made a grab at the pistol on his hip, at the same time jerking on the reins, trying to turn his horse around to give him a clear shot. Rusty did not allow him time to complete the move. He fired the rifle. Dust puffed from little Anse's shirt. The impact drove him backward as the horse took fright and jumped to one side. Anse tumbled from the saddle. The horse turned and ran a short distance before the dangling reins became entangled in the underbrush.

The younger brother lay in an awkward heap, just as he had landed. He hardly quivered. Newley Bascom's face seemed drained of blood. He trembled.

"Please, Shannon, don't shoot."

"I won't unless you give me reason. Fish your six-shooter out of the holster and pitch it into the creek."

Newley complied.

Rusty said, "Now the rifle under your leg." Newley tossed it away, too. It made a splash and quickly sank to the bottom.

Rusty demanded, "Who sent you-all after me? Was it Corey?"

Newley fought to keep his frightened voice under some measure of control. "We ain't seen Corey since he left home. It was Ma sent us."

That did not surprise Rusty. "Corey hasn't been back? You're not lyin' to me?"

"I wouldn't lie, not when you got that rifle in my face. And my baby brother layin' there on the ground."

"There was four of you brothers. Where's the other one at?"

Newley was reluctant but finally replied, "Ma sent Lacey out to do another job."

Rusty knew what that would be: to finish Alice. "All right, get down real careful and go fetch your brother's horse."

Newley freed the bridle reins and led little Anse's mount back. Rusty dismounted and picked up Anse's pistol. He started to pitch it into the creek to join Newley's but reconsidered and shoved it into his waistband. An extra weapon might come in handy.

"Put your brother's body up on his saddle. Tie his hands and feet so he won't slide off."

Tears streamed down Newley's face. In a breaking voice he said, "I don't know how I'm goin' to tell Ma about this. She's goin' to take it mighty hard."

Remembering the woman's ruthless nature, Rusty could muster no sympathy. "Tell her it's her own fault, sendin' you-all out to do a dirty job."

Only as he watched Newley lead away the horse with his brother's body tied on it did Rusty succumb to any sense of remorse, and that only because of little Anse's youth. The boy was a member of an outlaw family. Even with the best of luck he had probably been fated to an early death by bullet or perhaps by hanging. It was likely that Bessie Bascom would live to mourn all her sons unless her machinations somehow resulted in her own death beforehand.

He considered what Newley had said about the third brother, Lacey, being sent to kill Alice. That came as no surprise; Rusty had expected another try. He had warned Andy and Evan to keep a close watch. Now he began to reassess his own mission, the search for Corey Bascom. This endless riding was getting him nowhere. He might travel a thousand miles and get no nearer to Corey than he already was. Even if he found Corey and killed him, that would do nothing for Josie except avenge her death. The best thing he could do for Josie at this point would be to help keep her younger sister alive.

He decided to return to the Monahan place. He would not give up his search for Corey, but he would reluctantly defer it for a while. Vengeance would have to wait.

He approached the farm, his shoulders hunched, his body so tired he held himself in the saddle by force of will. The dun horse seemed to falter in its step. It needed long rest and many generous helpings of grain.

James Monahan walked out from the barn. "My God, Rusty, is that you? You look like hell."

Rusty rubbed a hand over his unshaven face. "I've been through hell and out the far side. I'd swear I've ridden this poor horse a thousand miles."

"He shows it. Find any sign of Corey?"

"Not one. He could be in Mexico or Colorado or California for all I found out. How are things here?"

"Grim."

"Is Alice all right?"

"She's feelin' low. Blames herself. Still wishes it had been her instead of Josie."

So do I, Rusty thought with a rush of bitterness, then felt guilty for it. "The Bascoms made any more effort to get her?"

"One. Somebody tried to sneak up to the house a couple nights ago. Andy challenged him with a shotgun. Whoever it was, he turned and ran. Andy gave him a blast and heard him holler."

"All the Bascoms except Corey know Alice is alive. Far as I can tell, though, he still thinks she's dead." Rusty told about his encounter with the two younger Bascom brothers.

James said, "Maybe losin' that boy will convince the old woman to take what's left of her family and leave the country."

"You ever see a hurt snake get so mad it bites itself? She'll probably be meaner than ever, and more determined. All the way back, I've been thinkin' we need to get Alice away from here."

"Where could she go that they wouldn't find her?"

"My old friend Tom Blessing has a wife who's ailin'. He's been wishin' he could find a woman to help take care of her 'til she's back on her feet. It's a long ways down there. The Bascoms would have no idea how to find her."

"Mama's still in bad shape. I don't know as Alice would want to leave her."

"Clemmie's lost one daughter. What would come of her if she lost another?"

James mulled that over. "Then we'll send Alice away with you whether she wants to go or not."

"Me and Andy can take her out of here after good dark. Even if the Bascoms find out she's gone, they won't have any idea where she went."

"Don't you think you need to rest a day or two first?"

"We don't know how much rest the Bascoms are takin'. I can rest after I get home."

Alice was strongly opposed to leaving, as Rusty had expected her to be. But even Clemmie urged her to go. In a strained but determined voice Clemmie told her, "I don't figure on stayin' in this bed forever. I'll still have Warren and Geneva and James. They'll see after me. You go and see after yourself."

Alice gave in. Clemmie beckoned Rusty to her side and took his hand. Her grip was weak. This woman had been heart and soul of the Monahan family. He hated to leave her now when she was ill.

She said, "I know you're hurtin'. We're all hurtin'. But I've been there before. It passes, with time."

Rusty's eyes burned. "I hope so, because it sure hurts right now. You-all are the nearest thing to family that I've had since my folks died."

"You'll always be family to us."

Preacher Webb walked with him up to the little Monahan cemetery. A bare new mound had appeared beside the grassed-over plots where Lon Monahan and his son Billy had been buried years before.

He felt Webb's comforting arm on his shoulder. As far back as he could remember, Preacher Webb had been around to offer spiritual strength when he needed it.

Webb said, "She's not really here, you know. She's gone on to a better world."

Rusty took no comfort in the words. "I wanted her here, in *this* world. If your God is so merciful, why does He let things like this happen?"

"People have asked that ever since time began. I don't know the answer to it. I just know there is sunlight and there is dark. There is good and there is evil. It's up to those of good heart to try and end the evil."

"I'll put an end to Corey Bascom if I ever find him. And I'll find him!"

"The Bascoms have taken away somethin' precious to you, but don't let them take away your soul. You don't stop evil by doin' more evil. Whatever you do, do it within the law."

"It's been a long time since we've had real law in Texas."

"But we'll have it again. Be a part of it, like you used to be."

"Like in the rangers?"

"Like in the rangers. I hear they're comin' back."

CHAPTER
SEVEN

Bessie Bascom had been preparing to milk the cow when she first saw the oncoming rider. So long as she was outdoors, she missed very little that moved. She had watched the horseman now for half an hour, hoping he would prove to be Corey. Her eldest was the only one she felt was capable of lifting the darkness that had befallen the Bascoms. Sure, he was the one who had brought it upon them in the first place, fetching that girl Alice here, making her privy to the family's doings. And sure, he had taken it badly when he thought his brother Lacey had killed her. But she felt he would come around to his mother's way of thinking eventually. He was family. When the chips were down, the Bascoms always pulled together. Her sons had rallied like troopers when old Anse died at the hands of the state police. They would rally now.

She knew the rider was one of her sons. She knew them by the way they sat in the saddle, the same way their father had done before them. In time she became aware that he led another horse. It appeared to be carrying a pack. That was strange. She had not sent the boys for supplies. She had ordered Newley and little Anse out to trail the man named Shannon. She had dispatched Lacey to finish the job he had botched the first time, killing Josie. He had returned in pain, barely able to sit in the saddle. She had spent more than an hour digging buckshot out of his backside while he howled like a hurt dog.

Not until the horseman was within a hundred yards did she recognize him as Newley. Her heart began to race as she realized that what she had thought was a pack was in reality a body tied across a saddle. She went running, screaming. "Little Anse, my baby. Oh Lord God, my baby."

The horses spooked at the wailing and the flare of Bessie's skirts. Newley had to hold tightly to the reins.

Bessie threw her arms over the body and kissed the still, cold face. She wept bitter tears while Newley dismounted and stood awkwardly, his head down. He rubbed his sleeve over his face.

Bessie turned on him. Accusation overrode the grief in her eyes. "What happened?"

Newley took a step backward in fear of her. "Wasn't no fault of mine, Ma. He oughtn't to've tried to draw on that Shannon. It was over before I could move."

"I'm guessin' you never moved at all. I'm guessin' you just sat there."

"Wasn't nothin' I could do. Shannon come up from behind. He had the drop on us before we even seen him."

"But your little brother drawed on him just the same?"

"He oughtn't to've."

"Why didn't you draw, too? You could at least have shot Shannon while he was busy shootin' your baby brother."

"He'd have shot me, too. You got no idee how fast he is."

"Maybe it would've been better. You'd've been spared the shame of bringin' this innocent baby boy back here dead while you don't appear to have a scratch on you."

Newley turned away, tears running down his cheeks. "I'm sorry, Ma. I done the best I know how."

"I ought to take a quirt to you, but it wouldn't do no good. Wouldn't make you no smarter, nor braver. Wouldn't bring little Anse back to us. I'm just glad old Anse ain't here to see this. One son dead. One son gone off to God knows where. Two other sons dumber than dirt, can't even take care of a simple job. It's a mean world we've come to."

Newley drew himself up with what pride he could muster. "I'll go find that Shannon, and I'll kill him."

Bessie was gratified that Newley had that much pride, but she knew pride would soon give way to fear. "No, we'll give your brother a decent buryin' first. Then I'll want you to go find Corey and bring him back here."

"Ain't no tellin' where he's at."

"He's somewhere. You'll find him."

"What's Lacey goin' to do?"

"When he's able to ride again I'll send him back to watch for another chance at that girl. It's your job to find Corey before Shannon does."

Newley brought himself to look at his mother for only a moment, then he cut his eyes away. "Do we *have* to kill Alice?"

"Get them silly romantic notions out of your mind. You know it's her that's at the root of all our trouble. It's like she's cast a witch's spell over this family. Trouble will keep throwin' its shadow over our door 'til we've got rid of her.

"Now go carry your baby brother into the house. I'll be washin' him while you and Lacey dig a proper grave. We'll send him to glory in style. And when the time comes, we'll send Shannon to hell."

Looking back in the rosy glow of sunup, Rusty saw that the wagon wheels were cutting deep tracks through the winter-brittle grass. The days were warming, but the nights still brought chill enough to delay the green-up. Riding Long Red alongside the wagon, Andy looked back with concern. "Even a blind Apache could follow our trail."

His Comanche upbringing had given him a dim view of the Apache. The Comanche considered himself superior to all other beings, especially the Apache.

Alice sat on the wagon seat beside Rusty. He had not spoken to her and had hardly looked at her since they'd left the Monahan farm about midnight. Dense clouds had hidden the moon. He had counted on darkness to hide their leaving.

He said, "There's other tracks besides ours, freight wagons and such."

He had left his weary dun horse at the Monahans', trading for a bay to take its place. It was tied to the rear of the wagon.

James had said of the horse, "He's a good one. Come to a chase, he's about as fast as anything I've rode in a long time. Got some wild spirit left, though, so you have to stay awake and watch him. Now and then he'll bog his head and pitch for no cause except he wants to throw you off. You'll like him."

Andy kept looking at the back trail, not convinced that no one was following. He glanced at Alice from time to time, his face troubled. Out of her hearing, he had expressed to Rusty his concern that people might question the propriety of her making this long trip with two men. Rusty had said, "You can be her chaperon."

Andy's Indian upbringing had subjected him to a lot of speculative gossip over the years. "I don't care when it's just me," he had said. "I'm used to it. But folks will mean-talk a woman whether she deserves it or not."

"Maybe she does deserve a little of it." Rusty immediately regretted what he said and was glad nobody except Andy had heard. Andy had too much honor to repeat it.

Alice looked back from time to time. "It's goin' to be tough, not knowin' how Mama is gettin' along."

Rusty had fought against his resentment toward Alice and tried to keep it out of his voice. "Your mother isn't much bigger than a banty hen, but she's got a will like iron. If she makes up her mind to get on her feet, that bed won't hold her for long."

He could see some of Clemmie's strength in Alice, though she still had a young woman's voice. He wished she had employed that will against Corey's entreaties and had not gone off with him in the first place.

Perhaps caring for Mrs. Blessing would help keep Alice's mind off of her mother. He remembered a strong nurturing instinct in Clemmie and her two oldest daughters. Geneva had stayed close by Rusty years ago while he recovered from a bad arrow wound incurred in ranger service. Later, Josie had nursed him after he took a bullet in the back. He hoped Alice possessed the same instincts, though he had seen nothing to convince him that she did.

They took a long noon rest. Rusty slept despite pain from the old wound. He was still weary after his long search for Corey Bascom. He suspected that Andy did not even try to sleep, watching their trail for sign of pursuit. Moving on, Rusty felt better for having had a little rest. Andy's shoulders drooped a little.

Rusty said, "You ought to've slept while you had a chance."

Andy's answer was curt. "Somebody had to watch."

"They don't even know we're gone."

"Maybe not. And maybe they do. That old woman has got an evil spirit sittin' on her shoulder. For all we know, it's tellin' her everything."

Rusty frowned. He had tried for years to turn Andy away from notions left over from his life with the Indians. They still cropped out from time to time. "What does an evil spirit look like?"

"It can look like anything. Most of the time you can't see it, but you can feel that it's there. Did you hear the owl last night, just before we left?"

"There's been owls around the Monahan place for years."

"Not like that one."

One owl had always sounded like another to Rusty, but he knew owls were a symbol of ill fortune, sometimes death, to the Comanche people.

Andy said, "For all we know, that owl could've been the old woman herself, watchin' us. There's some people can do that, you know, turn themselves into somethin' else. I knew a medicine man once who could turn himself into a wolf."

"Did you see him do it?"

"No, but I talked to people who said they saw him go into a cave, and a wolf came out. He could howl like one. I've heard him start, and wolves would answer him."

"That doesn't prove anything. I've known a few white people who could do that. It helped them hunt down wolves."

Andy said nothing more for a while, his feelings wounded a little. Argument over such matters was pointless. Neither he nor Rusty would change his mind.

Alice had held quiet for the most part. Finally she said, "This far south, do we need to worry about Indians?"

Rusty suspected Andy's talk about spirits had prompted her to wonder. "You never stop watchin' for Indians, wherever you are. But the odds are that most of them are still in winter camp north of us. The way the country is settlin' up, they're bein' crowded off of a lot of their old stompin' grounds."

Andy broke his silence. "And losin' their buffalo to the hide hunters. Damn shame, people killin' buffalo for the skin and leavin' the meat to rot. What do they expect the Indian to do?"

Rusty said, "I expect most would like to see the Indians all evaporate, like a puddle of water in the sunshine."

Andy's voice became strident. "Well, they won't. They'll take just so much crowdin', then they'll raise up and fight." He sounded as if he wished he could join them. Over the years there had been times when Rusty feared he might do just that. But Andy had left enemies as well as friends in the Comanche camps. Going back would be fraught with risk.

Alice took in a sharp breath and pointed. "If there aren't any Indians around here, what's that yonder?"

Rusty saw a dozen horsemen moving toward them out of the west. He knew at a glance that they were Indians.

Andy said, "Next time I talk to you about owls, maybe you'll listen."

Rusty did not waste time with argument or denial. He said, "We'll head for that buffalo wallow yonder. Maybe they haven't seen us."

Andy said, "They probably saw us before we saw them. Anyway, that hole's not deep enough to hide us."

It would give them a better defensive position, however, if this meeting turned into a fight. Sometimes a good position and a show of weapons would turn away a hunting party that was out mainly for meat and not for scalps. A war party would be something else.

He took the wagon into the dry-bottomed wallow and stopped. "Help Alice down," he told Andy. "She's too good a target up on this wagon." When Andy had done that, Rusty said, "Look in my saddlebag. You'll find that Bascom boy's pistol. Give it to her."

Worriedly Andy said, "We don't want to kill any of them unless we're forced to. Some might be friends of mine."

"Then they'd better act friendly."

Alice checked the pistol's load. She appeared more determined than frightened. Rusty asked her, "You sure you know how to shoot that thing?"

"Mama taught me to shoot before she taught me how to sew. Said every country girl ought to be able to use a gun because there wouldn't always be a man around to do it for her."

The wallow was not deep enough to hide even the wagon, but its shallow bank would provide cover for a person lying on his stomach and sighting a rifle up over the edge. Rusty said, "Andy, your eyes are sharper than mine. Are they wearin' any paint?"

Andy observed them a minute before answering. They had stopped a hundred yards out and seemed to be considering their options. "I don't see any. Probably just out huntin'."

"But they wouldn't pass up three scalps and four horses if they thought they would come easy."

Andy's expression indicated he didn't like what he saw. "I'm afraid that's just what they're thinkin'. They act like they're fixin' to give us a try." He handed Rusty his rifle. "I'm kin, of sorts. I'm goin' out and see if they'll parley."

Rusty thrust the rifle back at him. "You don't look like anybody that's kin to them. They're liable to kill you before you can tell them you're a cousin."

Andy refused the weapon. "If they're bound to kill me they'll do it anyway. Three of us ain't got a chance against them all." He climbed up out of the wallow and paused to add, "Told you about that damned owl."

He moved toward the Indians, his hands in the air to show he was unarmed. Rusty held his breath. An old image flashed into his mind: the sight of Andy's dead mother many years ago, butchered in the cruelest manner. He made up his mind he would not let that happen to Alice. If he saw they were about to be overrun, he would put a bullet through her head.

Some of the Comanches raised their bows. At least three had rifles or shotguns. Andy began making sign talk, and Rusty caught remnants of his words as he spoke. The Indians surrounded Andy. For a few moments he was out of sight. Rusty checked his rifle again. It felt slick against his sweating hands.

Alice said nothing. She held the pistol ready, the hammer cocked back. Her jaw was set like Clemmie Monahan's.

Andy emerged from the circle of Indians. He walked slowly and confidently toward the wallow. The Indians followed at a respectful distance, offering no overt threat. Andy signaled from fifty yards that everything was all right and motioned for Rusty and Alice to lower their guns. Rusty did, but not by much.

Andy stopped at the edge of the wallow. "Told you it was better to talk than to fight. Turned out I know a couple of them. We used to play at stealin' horses together."

"They're past the age for play-actin'. They look like they mean business."

"They're huntin' for buffalo. First thing they wanted to know was if we are, too. They thought maybe the wagon was for haulin' hides. Seems like there's a lot of white hunters workin' the buffalo range north of here. It's got the People pretty mad."

"Tell them those hunters are mostly out of Kansas. We're Texans."

"They don't like Texans, either."

Two of the Comanches ventured up close enough to look down into the wallow.

Rusty warned, "Don't let them see fear, Alice. If they've got mischief on their minds it'll encourage them."

The pair focused their attention on her. She still held the pistol cocked and ready, though she diverted the muzzle a little to one side. She looked cocked and ready, too, if they made any direct move toward her.

Andy said, "It's all right, Alice. It's not often they see a white woman up close."

She said nothing. Rusty suspected she knew her voice would be shaky, and she did not want to reveal that she was frightened.

Andy said, "They asked for tobacco, but I told them we don't have any.

They'd settle for some sugar. You don't find much of that in a Comanche camp."

Geneva had bagged sugar and coffee and salt for use on the trip to the Colorado River. Rusty said, "Give them the sugar, Alice. We can do without it." He liked sugar in his coffee when he could get it, but more often than not he had to drink it straight. He did not consider that a hardship. Through the war years he had gone for long stretches without even coffee.

Some sugar granules clung to the outside of the bag. An Indian wet his finger, ran it through the sugar, then touched the finger to his tongue. He broke into a broad grin.

Andy said, "Alice, you've made a friend for life."

The one holding the bag spoke a couple of words that Rusty assumed were the equivalent of "thank you," then reined his horse around and set off toward the rest of the party in a long trot. His companion followed but did not catch up to him.

Alice finally found voice. "Are they goin' to eat it right out of the sack?"

Andy said, "Sure. Hasn't everybody done that?"

When Andy had first returned from the Comanches he gorged himself on hog lard and raw sugar. The lard evidently made up for some nutritional deficiency. Sugar had been a new and exciting experience. At the time it was still scarce even in the Texas settlements.

Andy went on, "They don't seem as fearsome when you just see one or two up close, do they?"

Alice looked at him askance. "They look scary enough for me."

"You have to get used to them, is all. They're people just like everybody else, except a little different."

Rusty burned to be on his way, but he was hesitant about leaving the dubious shelter of the buffalo wallow until the Indians were out of sight in a direction other than south. He watched them pass the sugar sack around. Apparently there was some dissatisfaction over the fairness of the division, for the last man angrily threw the empty sack at the one who had offered it to him.

Andy said, "See what I told you? They're just like everybody else."

Not until the Indians were out of sight did Rusty motion for Andy to help Alice back onto the wagon. "They may be friends of yours, Andy, but we're travelin' 'til after dark tonight."

Andy said, "I'd worry a lot more about them Bascoms than about my Comanche kinfolks. Them Bascoms ain't civilized."

They paused briefly at the grave of Andy's mother. The marker was down again, buffalo tracks all around it. Even if Andy carried out his vow to build a fence around the site, Rusty knew the buffalo would not respect the fence any more than they respected the marker. They would rub their itchy hides against it until they knocked it down. If the Kansas hunters kept moving south, that problem would be eliminated over time. He would not mention that to Andy, however. It would just raise the young man's hackles.

Alice knew Andy's background, but she had never been here before. Seeing the grave brought the old tragedy to a reality she had not quite grasped earlier. She offered a prayer, spoken so softly that Rusty could not hear most of it. She asked Andy, "Do you remember any of what happened here?"

"A little." He grimaced. "A little too much."

She reached out and touched his arm, then drew her hand away.

Rusty felt impatient. "We can still make some distance before dark." They moved on.

They reached the farm just at sunset. Rusty said, "It's too late to go on to Tom's tonight."

Alice surveyed the place with keen interest. "You've built it up some since we stayed here durin' the war. Broke out some more land and built another cabin."

Rusty said, "The new cabin is Andy's. I thought he ought to have a house of his own when Josie and me . . ." He did not finish. He cleared his throat. "Wonder if Len Tanner is around. Be like him to've gone off on another *pasear*."

Tanner appeared on the dog run of the larger cabin, stretching his long frame as if he had been napping. "Howdy. You-all are just in time for supper. All you've got to do is fix it."

The garden showed signs of fresh work. Evidently Tanner had kept himself at least moderately busy. He had no real obligation to do so because he was not a hired hand. He was not drawing wages. He simply had a home here whenever he wanted it, and in return he contributed a share of the work when he was around. He was free to tie his meager belongings behind his saddle and ride off at any time he felt like it, which was fairly often.

Sight of Tanner momentarily lifted the melancholy that had fallen upon Rusty. "Len, I was afraid you'd be off to hell and gone again."

"I would've been if you hadn't got home when you did."

"Where to this time? Thought you'd seen all you wanted of your kin-folks."

"I have. But now I got other things to do." Tanner looked up in surprise at the girl on the wagon seat. "Alice? Is that you?"

"It's me." She gave him a tentative smile. He had flirted with her and her sisters in the past but had shied away from anything more serious than a stolen kiss, which once had earned him a quick slap in the face.

He said, "You're gettin' to where you look more like your sisters every time I see you. How're they gettin' along?"

Rusty had to look away. Andy said quickly, "Josie's dead. I'll tell you about it later."

Tanner's jolly mood was gone. He stared as if struck by a club. "Damn but I'm sorry." He reached to help Alice down from the wagon.

Andy asked, "You seen any strangers around here?"

Tanner set Alice on the ground. "Gettin' to be a lot of traffic around this place. Sometimes two or three people a day goin' one direction or another. Country's settlin' up to where it don't hardly seem the same anymore."

Andy persisted, "These people would likely have asked about Rusty or Alice."

Tanner shook his head. "Nary a soul."

Rusty said, "The Bascoms couldn't have gotten here ahead of us even if they'd known where we were goin'. For all they know we headed north for Colorado, or east for Arkansas, . . . if they've even found out we're gone."

Andy said stubbornly, "That old woman knows."

Tanner looked from one to another, confused but content to wait until someone saw fit to explain.

Rusty asked, "Know anything about Tom Blessing's wife?"

Tanner said, "She's still poorly. Shanty was here yesterday, helped me plant some tomatoes and okry. He'd been by to see the Blessings a couple of days ago."

Shanty was a former slave. His little place lay between Rusty's farm and the Blessings'.

Rusty said, "I brought Alice to stay with Mrs. Blessing and try to help get her back on her feet."

Tanner nodded his approval. "She's a grand old lady. She'll perk up just from havin' the company."

Rusty knew that Tanner had been smitten by Alice for a long time. He was not sure about Andy. He was aware that Andy had been watching women. For a while he had become somewhat attached to a neighbor girl named Bethel Brackett. That involvement seemed to have faded, probably because of his antipathy for her brother Farley.

Rusty told Alice she could have the bedroom side of the double cabin. As she went inside Tanner said, "I told you to tell her hello for me. I didn't mean you had to bring her all the way here."

Rusty told him as much as he figured Tanner needed to know for the time being. Tanner nodded gravely. "I *am* mighty sorry about Josie. If any of them Bascoms come pokin' around here lookin' for Alice, I'll blow a hole in them you could put a wagon through."

Andy said, "Just a little hole would be enough, long as it's in a place to do the most good."

A hundred times Rusty had imagined himself confronting Corey Bascom. He thought he could probably shoot him in the heart without flinching once. Someday, some way, he intended to do just that.

Tanner said, "Fact is, though, I won't be here. I've just been waitin' 'til you got home. I've joined the rangers."

The word brought Rusty and Andy both to full attention. Rusty said, "The rangers?"

Tanner nodded. "You probably ain't heard. Governor Coke is callin' up a lot of the old hands. The Morris brothers brought the word to me. They've joined up, too."

"Those Morris boys are liable to get you shot."

"I'm too skinny to be hit. I can hide behind a fence post. Anyway, them boys have got their hearts in the right place."

"It's not their hearts that worry me. It's their heads."

Andy spoke up. "How old do you have to be to join?"

Tanner shook his head. "Can't rightly say. If it's the way it used to be, you're old enough now. Got to furnish your own horse and your own gun."

"I have those."

"Don't know what the pay'll be. It doesn't matter much anyhow. I'm used to not findin' anything in my pockets except my hands."

Rusty felt uneasy about Andy's eagerness. "You'd better take a long look before you jump, Andy. It can be a hard life."

"I've never had no featherbed."

Rusty decided upon the wagon to take Alice to the Blessing place. The things she had hastily gathered from home were already in it. That would save having to pack them on a horse. He left Andy with Tanner to clean up the place. Tanner's housekeeping had been of the lick-and-a-promise variety.

They went by Shanty's farm; it was but little out of the way. Shanty had no real last name, though when he had to put his X on legal papers he adopted the surname of his late owner, Isaac York, who had willed him the farm.

Shanty was in his garden, hoeing out shallow trenches and planting seeds, then covering them lightly. His years weighed heavily upon his thin shoulders. He straightened slowly, with obvious back pain. Recognition of his visitors brought him to the garden gate. He removed his hat in deference to Alice, or perhaps to both of them. Old slave habits died hard.

"You-all git down and come in the house," he said.

His house was a cabin built of logs to replace one burned by night riders who had resented the idea of a black man owning a piece of land in their midst. Firm talk by Rusty, Tom Blessing, and other friends had put an end to that kind of devilment. A few neighbors still did not like his being there, but they had been buffaloed into silence.

Rusty said, "We're headed for the Blessing place. You remember Alice?"

Shanty smiled. "I do, but it was a long time ago, and she weren't much more than a thin saplin'. She's growed into a fine-lookin' young lady."

"Alice is goin' to help Mrs. Blessing."

"The Lord will smile on her for that. I been worried about Miz Blessing."

"But one thing, Shanty, . . . if some stranger should come askin' about Alice, you haven't seen her. You don't have any idea where she's at. You don't even know who she is."

Shanty's smile faded into a frown. "Hard to believe somebody'd mean harm to this young lady."

"They do. That's why I've brought her all the way down here." He explained briefly about the Bascoms and Josie's death.

Shanty nodded sadly. "I'll just act like I don't know nothin'. They generally figure that way anyhow." Long years in servitude had taught him how to tell white people what he thought they wanted to hear or to pretend total ignorance, whichever the circumstances called for.

Rusty thought Shanty looked more tired than usual. That concerned him. "You feelin' all right? You haven't been workin' too hard and gettin' yourself too hot?"

"Work and me been friends all my life. And friends know not to crowd one another too much."

Rusty took the remark as a sign that Shanty thought he had been working too hard and not getting enough rest. "We'll be gettin' on to the Blessings'."

"May the Lord walk ahead of you and smooth the road."

CHAPTER

EIGHT

om Blessing's dog announced the wagon's coming and trotted to meet it, tail wagging vigorously. Tom stepped out onto the opening between the two sections of the log cabin and shaded his eyes with his big hand. "Git down," he shouted. "Git down and come in."

Alice looked a little apprehensive. She had gotten to know the Blessings when the Monahan family stayed at Rusty's farm during part of the war years, but she had been only half grown. She had not seen them since. "What if it turns out they've already got somebody to stay with Mrs. Blessing?" she asked.

Rusty suspected that question had been on her mind for some time, but this was the first time she asked it. He remembered the way Tom had answered a question once. He said, "We'll burn that bridge when we get to it."

His comment served only to increase her concern.

Tom raised his strong arms to help her down from the wagon. "Is this Josie?" he asked, smiling. "Lord how you've changed."

"I'm Alice, Mr. Blessing. I've come to stay and help take care of your wife."

"Alice? Then you've *really* changed." He looked expectantly at Rusty. "You left here aimin' to get married. Leave the bride at your place?"

Even after all these days, Rusty still found it difficult to speak about her. "Josie's dead. I'll tell you about it in a little while."

Tom's face fell. His eyes pinched in sympathy. He seemed about to say something to Rusty, but he could not bring it out. He turned back to Alice. "Come on in, girl. Mrs. Blessing will be tickled to see you."

Rusty busied himself unloading Alice's few belongings, placing them in the dog run. He could hear her voice from inside the cabin. It sounded like Josie talking. He leaned against a wagon wheel and stared across Tom's field, but the image was blurred.

Tom came outside in a few minutes. He said, "Alice and the Mrs. are goin' to hit it off real good. It was mighty thoughtful of you to bring her."

"I had a reason. She needs you-all right now as much as you need her. More, maybe." Painfully Rusty explained what had happened to Josie and why he had felt it necessary to bring Alice so far from home.

Tom nodded, his eyes sad. "I reckon this is about as hard a thing as man ever has to take in this life."

"Another hard thing is knowin' that the man who did it is runnin' loose. But he won't stay loose forever. I'm goin' to hunt him down like a hydrophoby dog."

"How you goin' to do that? You've got no idea where to start. He could be ten miles from here or a thousand."

"I'll just give up everything else and hunt 'til I find him."

"That could take years."

"I don't know what else to do."

Tom frowned, deep in thought. "Did Len tell you he's signed up for the rangers?"

"He told me. Andy's itchin' to do the same thing."

"It's not a bad idea. The rangers could be the answer to your problem."

"I don't see how."

"Think about it. You're just one man, lookin' for another man who could be anyplace. If you were a ranger you could put him on the fugitive list. Instead of just one man lookin' for him there'd be a hundred or two, however many rangers there are. And I can send word out to sheriffs around the state to be watchin' for him."

"But I want to be the one who gets him. I want to look him square in the eyes and tell him he's fixin' to die."

Tom frowned. "What's more important, bringin' him to justice or takin' your own personal revenge?"

"The way I feel, I want to do it myself."

"Revenge can poison the soul, Rusty. The man on the receivin' end dies just once, and generally quick. The man out for revenge may die a little every day as long as he lives. Remember after Daddy Mike was killed? You almost let it get the best of you that time."

Rusty remembered. He had been roughly Andy's age. Tom had enlisted him in a frontier ranger company to get him away from home, saving him from killing the wrong man.

Tom said, "Even a justified killin' can eat on a man like slow poison. Say you kill this Corey Bascom but destroy yourself in the doin' of it. Do you think that's what Josie would want?"

"There's no way to ask her."

"Deep down, you know."

"All I know for sure is that I want to see Bascom dead."

"Then at least go about it a right and proper way. Do it through the law."

That, Rusty recalled, was more or less what Preacher Webb had said. It was as though he and Tom had conspired together.

Tom persisted, "You could do a lot of good, bein' a ranger. There's still Indian trouble up north. And what the Yankees called 'reconstruction' spawned enough outlaws to overstock hell. It'll take some strong-minded lawmen to put them down."

"Is that why you let them make you sheriff again?"

"I looked around and didn't see anybody I thought fitted the job. Except maybe you, and you had your hands full with that farm."

"I still do. That's the reason I can't join the rangers."

Tom's frown deepened. "But you'd leave in a minute if you got a lead on Bascom."

"That's different."

The sound of a running horse drew Rusty's attention to the wagon road that led from town. He saw a rider pushing hard, waving his hat. Rusty began to hear his shouting though he could not make out what the man was trying to say.

Tom stiffened. "Nobody's ever come ridin' in that fast to bring me good news." He walked out to meet the horseman. Shiny with sweat, the horse slid to a stop.

The man shouted, though he was close enough that he would not have needed to. "Sheriff Tom, there's been a shootin' in town. And a robbery."

Tom accepted the information with a grave expression. "Slow down, get your breath, then tell me about it."

The rider had the look of a clerk, his shirt white except where sweat had soaked through and attracted dust. His string necktie was hanging askew. He leaned heavily on the horn of his saddle, struggling for air. "Two men. Strangers. Held up the general store. When Mr. Bancroft reached under the counter, they shot him."

"Kill him?"

"I'm afraid so. He was still breathin' when I left, but he looked like a goner." The man pointed. "They rode out headin' west, across country. I followed their tracks part of the way here. They was pretty plain."

Tom grunted. "I ought to be able to cut across and pick them up." He asked for a description, but the one given was vague enough to have fitted Rusty himself, and half the men he knew.

Tom looked back at Rusty. "See what I told you about lawlessness? It's got mighty close to home."

The words popped from Rusty's mouth before he allowed time for consideration. "You want me to help you?"

"I'd be much obliged."

"I'll need to get back home and swap this wagon for my horse. Need to tell Andy and Len, too, or they'll worry about where I'm at."

"I'll swing by your cabin and pick you up after I get a line on them tracks. Want to say adios to Alice?"

Rusty had not had much to say to Alice during the trip. He knew nothing to say to her now. "You do it for me. I'll be gettin' started." He climbed into the wagon and put the team into motion. Looking back once, he saw Alice standing in the dog run, watching him with a big question in her eyes.

Two men. Robbing stores was one of the Bascom brothers' specialties, Alice had said. He knew it was wildly unlikely that they had been the perpetrators here, but the thought was intriguing enough to set his imagination to racing. He pictured himself confronting Corey Bascom. The thought set his skin to burning with impatience. Flipping the reins across the team's rumps, he yelled them into a hard trot.

Approaching the home place, he wondered that he saw no one in field or garden. Long Red and Len's horse were nowhere in sight. Len's in particular was something of a barn lover, usually found within easy reach of feed. Rusty saw his bay grazing alone, near the shed.

He hollered as the wagon rolled past the cabin, but no one answered. He put the vehicle under the shed. Quickly unhooking the team, he pitched the harness into the wagon instead of taking time to hang it up properly. He caught the bay and saddled him, then hurried up to the cabin to fetch his rifle. He had taken only his pistol to Tom's.

He found no fire in the kitchen. On the table he saw a sheet of paper weighted down by a tin cup half full of cold coffee. He held it so that reflected light from the open door made the penciled message readable. He grumbled under his breath as he read it.

Deer Rusty,

    I take pensil in hand to inform you that Me and Andy are gone off to the Rangers. We didnt wait becawz we knowd you would raiz Hell. Dont worry about Andy I will sea that he dont get in no trubbl. With best regards, your verry good frend,

                                         Len Tanner

No trouble. Rusty declared aloud, "Damn that Len." If he was looking out for Andy, who would be looking out for Len? They both needed a guardian, one because he was still young and the other because he would never completely grow up.

Rusty sat down heavily in his chair and weighed the significance of this development. He could go to Andy's ranger captain and argue that Andy was underage. But he had no idea to what company the youngster might be assigned or where it would be stationed. As for age, Andy could pass for his early twenties on the basis of his looks. Rusty could not prove him younger.

This threw a bad kink into his rope.

Tom was not far behind him. He reined up from a hard trot as Rusty walked out to untie the bay. He asked, "Len and Andy goin' with us?"

"They're gone. Went off to join the rangers." As he slid his rifle into the scabbard and swung onto the bay's back he explained about the letter. "I could wring Len Tanner's scrawny neck like a chicken."

"You already told me *he* was goin'. But Andy is a surprise."

Rusty felt too disgruntled to talk about it. "Did you find the tracks?"

Tom nodded. "A couple of miles south of here. They're stayin' off of the roads. Don't want anybody seein' them."

Rusty had a bitter taste in his mouth. "Let's be goin' after them."

He had noted that the young man who brought the message had not stayed with Tom for the long pursuit. Tom explained, "I sent him back to town. The wrong kind of help can get you killed."

Tom led the way, angling southwestward. He cut the tracks in a short time. The fugitives were evidently depending upon fast horses rather than trying to cover their trail.

Tom said, "People noticed them camped outside of town last night but never gave them much thought. There's always folks passin' through.

These were probably watchin' to see where business looked the best. Since we don't have a bank yet, the store must've seemed like the richest pickin's. Old man Bancroft was a gentle feller. He ought not to have reached for a gun."

"Maybe they'd have shot him anyway. There are men like that. Didn't get enough killin' in the war. Or didn't go, and now they're makin' up for it."

Tom's face twisted. "Which means we'd better be careful how we ride up on them. Bancroft's funeral is one too many."

"Another one or two would be all right, long as it's the right men gettin' buried."

Tom gave Rusty a long study. "You've got a hard look in your face. I don't know as I like it."

"Been some hard things happened to me. Andy goin' off like that doesn't make it any easier."

"He's not your son. He's not even your brother. Sure, he's still young, but he's shown that he can think and do for himself. I wouldn't mind havin' him with us right now."

"I'm glad he's not."

The trail presented little challenge. A recent shower had left the ground soft so that the hooves had made deeper than usual cuts in it. Tom stopped to study a place where one of the horses had paused to urinate. He said, "They ain't too far ahead of us. An hour or so, maybe two."

Farther on, Tom pointed to a spot where the ground had been scarred slightly. "Looks like one of the horses stepped in that hole yonder and went down."

Boot tracks showed that one man had walked around a little before remounting. Tom said, "Horse must not have broke its leg, but I'll bet it's limpin' some. That'll slow our boys up."

Presently Rusty saw a single rider ahead of them. At first he could not tell whether the person was coming or going, but soon it became clear that he was moving to meet them. He was on a bareback mule, with wagon harness instead of saddle. He carried the long reins looped like a lariat.

Tom said, "That looks like old man Gillis. What's he doin' ridin' a wagon mule?"

As Gillis approached, it was plain that he had been hurt. Blood had dried on the side of his face. A deep bruise had turned dark from his cheekbone up to the edge of his gray hair. Tom said to him, "You look like you'd been thrown off and drug."

"Two men stopped me. Swapped me a lame horse for my best mule. Taken it right out of the harness. When I tried to argue with them they hit me across the head with a six-shooter."

Rusty rode up close to examine the wound. Gillis said, "If I hadn't had this old wool hat on, it'd have broken my skull like an eggshell."

"Looks bad," Rusty said. "I hope you're not goin' far."

"Headin' for my son's place, over the rise yonder. Him and my daughter-in-law will fix me up. But it makes me madder than hell, losin' that good mule. How do they expect a man to farm without a good pair of mules?"

Tom said, "You're lucky you didn't lose more than a mule. They robbed a store and shot old man Bancroft."

The farmer's jaw dropped. "Old tightwad Bancroft? They must've found out he still had the first dollar he ever made. And most of the ones since." He seemed to regret his words. "I hope he ain't dead."

Tom shook his head. "Don't know. But I expect you'll be gettin' your mule back. I doubt your thief will want to ride him any farther than he has to. He'll be lookin' to steal another horse." He pointed his chin westward. "Who lives yonderway past your place?"

"Young folks named Plumley. Moved in last year and broke out new ground." Gillis's eyes widened as he pondered the possibilities. "I hate to think them young people are in danger. That boy's come and helped me several times. And he's got a mighty sweet little girl for a wife. I'd better come with you."

Tom gripped the farmer's thin shoulder. "No, you'd better go on to your son's place and get took care of. Me and Rusty, we'll see after them young people."

The farmer gave him a better description of the thieves than the town clerk had done. One was tall and lanky with a bushy black beard. The other was of heavier stock and had a brownish mustache with a couple of days' growth of whiskers. An instant before the heavier one had clubbed him, Gillis had seen a long, bluish scar on the back of his hand.

"They both had mean eyes," he warned. "I seen eyes like that in the war. A man with them eyes, there ain't much he won't do."

Tom nodded at Rusty. "Then we'd best not give them time for more than they've already done."

It would have been easy to have missed the Plumley farm had the tracks not led Rusty and Tom to it. The cabin was small, without a dog run, and had been built beneath a hill that hid it from the south. A modest field lay below the cabin. Corn plants stood inches high, for the growing season had barely begun.

Rusty pointed. "The corral yonder. I'd bet you that's Gillis's mule."

No horses were in sight. The thieves were probably gone, but Tom was taking no chances. "That cabin has got no window in the back. We'd better ride up on the blind side."

They dismounted fifty yards away and led their horses, pausing to tie them to a tree. They went the rest of the way with pistols in their hands. They paused to listen a minute before Tom pointed to the front door. Rusty noticed that it was ajar and that it opened to the inside. Oldtimers in the days of frequent Indian trouble usually made sure their doors swung outward so it would be more difficult for anyone to force his way in.

Rusty gave the door a hard shove with his shoulder and stepped quickly inside.

A woman cowered against a back wall. She brought her arms up defensively and screamed. "No more. Please, no more." She covered her face.

Rusty's eyes took a moment to adjust to the room's poor light. The young woman was disheveled, her dress torn from shoulder to waist. As she lowered her arms he saw bruises on her face.

Rusty tried to say something to comfort her, but rage overtook him and left him unable to speak. Tom said gently, "We're here to help you, ma'am. We're not the ones who hurt you." He showed her the badge on his shirt.

She buckled at the knees. Rusty caught her before she went all the way to the floor. He carried her to a wooden chair at the table. Tom said, "There's a pint of whiskey in my saddlebags. You'd better fetch it."

Rusty went out and led the horses up to the house. He fumbled in the saddlebags, found the bottle, and took a long drink before he carried it inside. He lifted a coffee cup from an open shelf and poured whiskey into it. He held it to the woman's bruised lips. "Drink this. It'll do you good."

She choked but got the whiskey down. She began to calm. Tom asked her, "Where's your husband?"

She seemed unable to look him or Rusty in the eyes. Haltingly she explained that her husband had left early in the morning to look for some strayed cattle. He had not yet returned.

In one sense it might have been a good thing he was gone, Rusty thought. He would probably have resisted the thieves, and they would have killed him.

She said, "We just had one other horse. I heard them run it into the pen and shut the gate. When I went out to see what they were up to . . ." She dropped her head even lower.

Rusty walked to the door and stared out, trying to bring his rage under control. Tom comforted her the best he could.

She cried, "My husband . . . what's he goin' to say?"

Tom said, "If he's any kind of a man he'll know you couldn't help what they did. Wasn't none of it your fault. You got any neighbors, somebody we could send to be with you?"

She said she did, a couple of miles southwest. Tom promised, "We'll swing by and let them know. And don't you worry about them men comin' back. We'll stay on their trail 'til we catch them."

Rusty burned inside and knew it was not because of the whiskey. His hands trembled as he untied his horse. "I've seen some bad men in my time. I've known some that would murder a man without battin' an eye and steal anything that wasn't bolted to the floor. But I've never known any that would do a thing like this to a woman."

Tom grunted and climbed into the saddle. "It's a new world. I liked the old one a heap better."

They found the farm Mrs. Plumley had described and told a middle-aged farmer and his wife what had happened. The woman's eyes filled with tears. "That poor girl. Hitch up, Walter. Let's be gettin' over there."

Riding away, Tom said, "With all the new world's deviltry, there's a lot of the old world left. You can still find kindness when you look for it."

Rusty could not reply. He could not shake the image of terror he had seen in the young woman's face. As he reviewed the scene in his mind, her face became Josie Monahan's.

"We've lost time, Tom. Let's be makin' it up."

Dusk came too quickly. Rusty knew they would soon be unable to see the tracks. "They've got to stop sometime. They've got one fresh horse, but the other one has been pushed all day."

"Ours, too. We set off in such a hurry that we forgot about one thing."

"What's that?"

"We haven't got anything to eat."

Rusty patted the blanket roll tied behind the cantle of his saddle. "We're not plumb out of luck. I brought along some jerky left over from our trip down from the Monahans'."

"Jerky." Tom said the word with distaste.

"It's better than nothin'."

"Just barely."

Rusty said, "Indians can get by on it for days. And I ate a heap of it when I was with the rangers."

"Me, too. I always hoped I'd never have to again."

The tracks were hard to see as daylight faded. The fugitives had stopped to water themselves and their horses at a spring some early settler had rocked in but later abandoned. The remains of a picket cabin leaned precariously, threatening to fall over if given a fair push.

Tom asked, "Feel like sleepin' under a roof tonight?" He said it with a touch of humor, but Rusty was in no mood to appreciate it. Hatred simmered for the men they pursued. He said, "That roof would likely cave in on us. Anyway, I'll bet the place is full of snakes."

Reluctantly he conceded that they had no choice but to stop for the night. After watering the bay he staked it on a long rawhide rope so it could graze within a wide circle. Tom did the same, then said, "How about that jerky?"

Rusty unrolled his blanket and took out a bundle wrapped in oilskin. Jerky was strips of meat dried in the sun, usually tasting more of salt and pepper than of beef. Rangers had often carried it with them on long scouts because they had no guarantee of finding fresh game. Though far from sumptuous, it could sustain life until a man found better.

Tom chewed hard. "I've known of men losin' a tooth on this stuff, but I never saw anybody get fat on it."

Rusty realized Tom was trying to jolly him out of his dark mood, but he was not ready to give it up. There was justice to be done. From the description he tried to imagine the fugitives' faces. He could see only one. In his mind they both looked like Corey Bascom.

He said, "I don't understand men like that. What do you suppose gets into them?"

"Hard to say. War soured some of them. Then there's some raised that way by folks that had coyote blood in them. And some are just born with a deep streak of mean. Somethin' missin' out of their brain or their heart. They're hard to cure."

"There's one way. Kill them dead and bury them deep."

Tom frowned and pulled his saddle blanket around him.

Rusty awakened long before daylight. He rolled onto one side, then the other, trying to find a comfortable position. There was none. He felt as if he would willingly trade a good horse for a cup of strong coffee. He dared not light a fire that the fugitives might see. It irritated him to hear Tom snoring peacefully. He itched to be on the move but knew it would be futile to set out before he could see tracks.

At last Tom sat up, throwing back the blanket. Only the faintest hint of light showed in the east. The first thing Tom did was to look around for the horses. That instinct was deeply ingrained into men used to living along the frontier, where a good horse was always a temptation to the light-fingered breed, white or red.

Rusty said, "They're still where we staked them. I've been watchin' them for hours."

"You didn't sleep much?"

"Kept seein' that poor woman, and then I'd think of Josie. I kept thinkin' of her in that woman's place."

"At least that woman is still alive."

"And probably half wishin' she wasn't. There's not much worse a man can do to a woman short of leavin' her dead."

Tom threw his saddle onto his horse's back and tightened the cinch. "Sooner or later you've got to come to grips with what happened to Josie. Otherwise it'll drive you crazy."

"I'll come to grips when I find Corey Bascom. But those two renegades will do for a start."

Rusty chewed on a strip of jerky as he set out impatiently in a stiff trot. It should have been Tom's place to pick up the tracks, but Rusty did not give him time. Once when they lost the trail, Tom was the one who picked it up. Rusty was adequate as a tracker, but he had never considered himself in a class with Tom and other frontiersmen of Tom's generation. Or even with Andy.

As the sun moved upward toward midday and the morning warmed, Rusty became uneasy. He could not put his finger on the cause. It was instinct, a feeling that all was not as it should be. "Tom," he said, "let's wait up a minute."

"You see somethin'?"

"I feel somethin', like cold wind on the back of my neck."

"You sure you haven't been listenin' to Andy too much? He's always got a hunch about somethin'. Hears voices talkin' to him. The Indian upbringin', I suppose."

"I don't hear any voices, and there's nothin' I can see. But I've been around Andy enough to know I'd better pay attention. Do you suppose those renegades could've doubled back? They could be comin' up behind us."

It was an old Indian trick. He had used it himself on the two younger Bascom brothers.

Tom's expression showed he took the possibility seriously. He drew the rifle from beneath his leg. "I should've thought of that. It's been done to me more than once."

Tom jerked in the saddle, dropping the rifle. Almost simultaneously Rusty heard a shot from behind. Whirling the bay around, he saw a puff of smoke behind a small clump of low-growing brush. Without taking time to consider, he drew his pistol and put the horse into a run toward the shooter's position. He fired three quick shots into the brush.

A heavyset man screamed and staggered out into the open. He stared with wide, unbelieving eyes before he buckled. He pressed both hands against his chest, trying to stop the flow of blood seeping between his fingers.

Rusty caught a movement from the corner of his eye. He swung down from the saddle, keeping the horse between him and a bearded man who raised up from behind another bush. Rusty dropped to one knee and knelt low, sighting his pistol under the bay's stomach. His shot and the fugitive's seemed to overlap.

Startled, the bay jerked the reins from Rusty's hands and trotted away, leaving Rusty exposed. He felt a searing along his ribs as he heard the man's second shot. He winced from the burn but leveled his pistol and squeezed the trigger. He caught the man squarely in the chest. The fugitive gasped and went down.

Rusty heard Tom's shout. "Look out."

The first man was up on his knees, both bloody hands gripping his pistol. Rusty shot him before he could fire. The man hunched, the pistol sagging in his weakening grip. His dying eyes were fixed on Rusty. His lips moved as if he tried to speak.

He could say nothing Rusty wanted to hear. Rusty stared into the contorted face, and somehow it became the face of Corey Bascom. Rage overwhelmed him. He had emptied the pistol. In his belt was the one he had taken from little Anse Bascom. He drew it and fired once, twice, three times.

Tom spoke behind him, his voice brittle. "For God's sake, how much deader do you think you can kill him?"

The fury that had swept over Rusty slowly receded. He stared at the dead man lying almost at his feet. "I must've gone crazy for a minute."

"I never saw you like this. You scared me."

"I've scared myself a little, I think."

"Have you sobered up now?"

"Sober enough to remember that you got hit by the first shot. How bad is it?"

Tom gripped his right arm below the shoulder. His sleeve was red, his hand bloodied. "Missed the bone. But I need to get this blood stopped or you'll be carryin' me home like a baby."

Tom squatted while Rusty cut the sleeve off at the shoulder and wrapped it tightly around the wound.

Rusty said, "I'd better get you back to that Plumley place where you can be tended to good and proper."

"And soon. I can feel sickness comin' on. Before long I may not be able to stay in the saddle." Tom jerked his head toward the nearest of the two fugitives. "Somethin' needs to be done about them."

"Let somebody else come bury them, or leave them for the varmints. They're kin to the coyotes anyway."

Rusty gave Tom a boost up onto his horse. The effort brought a sharp pain to his side and reminded him that a slug had grazed his ribs. The bay had trotted off a little way and stepped on the reins. There he had stopped. Rusty fetched him, then looked around for the horses the renegades had ridden. He found them tied to a bush, out of sight from the ambush spot. He checked the saddlebags and found a considerable amount of money. Loot from the store robbery, he assumed. He tied one horse's reins to the other's tail and led the pair back to where Tom waited, slumped in the saddle.

"Feel like you can make it?"

Tom looked pale, but he gritted his teeth. "I've had a wasp bite worse than this."

Setting out, Rusty reached inside his shirt to feel his ribs. The slight blood flow had stopped. The wound was sore to the touch, but he doubted that a rib had been cracked. He would heal.

They had ridden perhaps a quarter of a mile when a horseman appeared. He approached them warily. He was young, a farmer by the look of him. He eased when he saw the badge on Tom's shirt. "I heard shootin'. You-all catch up to those bandits?"

Rusty said, "We caught them."

The young man nodded toward the two led horses. "One of them is mine. They stole him from my place."

Tom asked, "Your name Plumley?"

"Yes sir."

"How's your wife?"

His face darkened. "Fair, considerin' what they done to her. Some neighbors came to help. I thought I'd try to catch up with you-all and be there for the kill. Since you have their horses, I reckon you caught them already."

Rusty said, "If it's any satisfaction to you they're layin' back yonder a little ways. We didn't have time to bury them. The sheriff needs attention."

"I'll help you get him to our place. Later on I'll take a shovel and do the buryin'. It'll pleasure me to throw dirt on them." Riding along, he brooded in silence. Finally he said, "They don't deserve no Christian cere-mony. I'll make sure they won't see Resurrection mornin', either. I'll bury them facedown."

CHAPTER
NINE

Approaching a neat row of canvas tents lined beneath the protective branches of huge pecan trees fronting the San Saba River, Andy Pickard felt apprehensive. "We've come a long ways for me to get turned down. Are you sure the rangers aren't lookin' for somebody with more experience?"

Rusty had always said Len Tanner had the faith of the mustard seed, whatever that meant. Tanner declared, "They'll be tickled to have you. How many fellers your age can brag that they've been as far and seen as much as you have? Time I get through tellin' them about you they'll be rollin' out a red carpet and beggin' you to sign up."

That was one thing worrying Andy. Tanner never knew when enough was enough. He could take a good idea and talk it to a slow and painful death. "I oughtn't to've let you get me into this."

In truth, Tanner hadn't used much persuasion. Andy had toyed with the notion of becoming a ranger from the time he first heard they might be reorganized. But the closer he got, the less confidence he felt.

Tanner said, "Too late to turn back. They've seen us already."

Andy was aware that three men were watching them. He tried to brace up his nerve. "Which do you figure is the headquarters tent?"

"The biggest one, naturally. Officers always get a little the best of it."

The best did not look much better than the others to Andy. Most of the tents were tepee shaped, lined evenly where the heavy foliage would provide partial shade in the afternoon. Beyond the tents and between the trees he could see sun reflected off the clear waters of the San Saba. An officer stood before the larger tent, talking to a couple of men. At least, Andy took him for an officer because his stance indicated authority.

The rangers had no official uniform. They wore what they would wear in civilian life as cowboys or farmers or town merchants. Tanner had told him they did not even have an official badge. Some men made their own out of Mexican silver pesos. Others did not believe they needed one. They expected boldness and a serious demeanor to cow most adversaries. The rest would be dealt with according to the demands of the moment.

Tanner said, "That'd be the captain, I imagine."

The officer turned his attention to the two horsemen. Tanner made a poor excuse of a salute. "Private Tanner reportin' for duty, sir. And I've fetched along a recruit you'll be glad to have in the company."

The officer frowned. "That is a determination I'll make for myself. As for you, Tanner, your enlistment started over a week ago. If you expect to be paid for time absent, . . ."

"Couldn't help it, sir. Things came up. But you don't owe me no more than you figure I got comin'." Money meant little to Tanner except in terms of what he could buy with it, usually as soon as he had the cash in hand.

The officer lowered his voice. "I've been notified of your past service record, so I'll overlook your tardiness. This time." He turned a critical gaze upon Andy. "You say I'll want this young man as a recruit. Tell me why."

Tanner dismounted. "I could talk all day, tellin' you why you want to sign up Andy Pickard."

"I had rather you didn't. Just the pertinent facts will be enough."

"Well sir, in the first place he rides like an Indian. Truth is, it was the Indians taught him. And shoot? He can knock a flea off of a dog's ear at fifty yards and never singe a hair. And he's got more nerve than a mouthful of bad teeth. Why, he once slipped into a Comanche camp and—"

The officer raised his hand. "Let him speak for himself. Tanner, you may put your blankets and gear into that farthest tent yonder, then take your horse out and turn him into the remuda. You'll find it on grass west of camp."

Tanner accepted the order with a nod. "Whatever you say, Captain." He glanced at Andy. "Now, don't you be shy. Tell him everything he ought to know about you. I'll see you after you been sworn in."

The officer watched in silence until Tanner led his horse beyond hearing. "Usually I am suspicious of a big talker, but I am told Tanner was a good ranger in the old days."

"There's a lot more to him than just talk."

"But you are obviously too young to have been in ranger service before. So come into the office and tell me why I should accept you into that service now."

Andy tied Long Red to a rough hitching rack made of live-oak branches. He followed the officer through the open canvas door of the tent the captain called an office. He took off his hat and twisted it in his hands. "First off, sir, Len stretched the facts a little. I can ride, but just about everybody I know can do that."

"How is your shooting eye?"

"Ain't braggin', sir, but I don't generally need two shots. Rusty Shannon taught me not to waste cartridges. They cost too much."

The officer's eyebrows went up. "Rusty Shannon, you say?"

"Yes sir, he's the one raised me, after the Indians. Used to be a ranger along with Len Tanner."

"I've met Shannon. Spotless reputation. I hope he is well."

"Healthy enough, but he lost the woman he was fixin' to marry. It tore him up a right smart."

"Sorry to hear that. But we're supposed to talk about you. What's this about an Indian raising?"

Andy explained that he had been carried off by raiding Comanches when he was small and lived with them until he was around twelve or thirteen. He decided not to go into the circumstances under which he had fallen into Rusty's hands. He doubted the captain would take kindly to the fact that he was trying to emulate his Comanche brothers on a horse-stealing foray. Most people did not like to hear that part of his story.

The captain said, "I'm glad you were rescued. A lot of young people remained prisoners. Grew up Comanche, ruined for life."

Rescued was not exactly the word for it. *Captured* would be a better description, for at first Andy had been an unwilling convert to the white man's road. He had tried to escape back to Comanchería. He judged that this was another aspect of his story best left out. Most white people did not understand how a boy could prefer living in a tepee and following the buffalo with a band of what they considered wild savages most akin to the wolves that also stalked the shaggy herds.

The captain frowned again. "How do you feel about the Comanches now?"

They were still his brothers, most of them, but this was something else the captain would not appreciate. "I've been away from them a long time."

"Part of our job will be to protect settlers from Indian raids. Mainly Comanches to the north, Apaches west and south. If it came to that, would you be able to fight them?" He stared at Andy with an intensity that would not permit evasion.

"I don't know, sir. I guess I could if I had to."

"I need a better answer than that. I can't afford to have men in my command that I could not depend on in an emergency."

"I'll do my duty, whatever that is."

"No matter how difficult it may be for you?"

"If it breaks my back, sir."

The captain chewed his lip in deep thought. "From what I know of Rusty Shannon he would have made you tough enough to do whatever has to be done, however unpleasant it may be."

"He tried awful hard."

"Very well, there are certain requirements to be met. First, you must furnish a horse."

"That's him, the sorrel I tied outside."

"It may be that the state will furnish weapons in the future, but for now you must arm yourself."

"There's a rifle on my saddle. Got a six-shooter and a skinnin' knife on my belt." Tanner had made sure he brought everything he needed.

"Then it would appear you meet the principal specifications. We need to fill out and sign some papers and administer the oath. Have you ever taken an oath?"

"I swore a time or two to tell the truth and nothin' else."

"The ranger oath is a solemn obligation between you and the state of Texas, taken in the sight of God. I don't know what God's punishment is if you break it, but Texas's punishment can be severe."

"If I make you a promise, I won't back away from it."

"Spoken like a good Texan. Now let's see about this enlistment form. I assume you can read."

"Fair to middlin'." Andy's reading ability was about average, he thought, for most Texans aside from teachers, storekeepers, and lawyers. Schooling was sporadic. Many people living in the country and in small towns had no more than a smattering of formal education. Rusty had seen to it that Andy took schooling whenever it was available.

The captain filled out the forms. Andy ran his finger down the pages, lips moving as he slowly read to himself what was written. He signed where the officer pointed.

The captain said, "You understand that you are being accepted on a conditional basis? I have the right to dismiss you at any time you fail to obey orders or live up to expectations."

"Any time I feel like I'm not totin' my load you won't have to fire me. I'll quit."

"That's the proper attitude for a ranger of the Texas frontier batallion."

The captain administered the oath after calling up two rangers to stand witness. He said, "There is room for you in the farthest tent, where I sent your friend Tanner."

The two rangers shook Andy's hand and welcomed him into the company. One introduced himself as Sergeant Bill Holloway. He was a tall, broad-shouldered, flat-bellied man of roughly Rusty's age. His face was burnished brown. His pale blue turkey-tracked eyes had a permanent squint brought on by life in the Texas sun. He said, "I heard you mention Rusty Shannon. I rode with him under old Captain Whitfield 'til the war drawed me into the army. Southern, of course. How come he ain't joined up again?"

"He's had some bad luck lately. Got about all his plate will hold." Andy decided to say no more until he had time to size up the company. He had already told the captain more than he intended. Rusty might not want his personal troubles advertised all over the country.

Holloway said, "A couple more things the captain may not have mentioned. No drinkin' in camp."

"I don't drink."

"And no card playin'."

"Never learned no card games."

The sergeant shook his head as if he could not believe. "I guess you don't cuss, either."

"Yes sir, I do. Sometimes it's the only thing that helps."

The sergeant's squinty eyes laughed, and his mustache lifted at the edges. "That's all right. Just do it judiciously." He turned toward the tent but stopped. "Know any Comanche cusswords?"

"A few."

"I wish you'd teach them to me. Sometimes I use up all I know in English and Spanish and it's still not enough."

Andy untied his blankets and a small war bag of possessions from the saddle. He expected a row of cots inside the tent, but he saw only bedrolls spread on the ground.

Holloway said, "Find you an empty place anywhere. When you're tired enough, the grass will feel like a feather bed."

Andy had slept on the ground during his years with the Comanches and many times since when he was on the move. The Indians had considered it healthy to lie directly upon Mother Earth. A bed put distance between a man and nature, though Andy enjoyed the luxury when he had it.

Holloway said, "A bed just spoils you. Can't take one with you on scout, and the captain sees to it that the nights are short anyway. He'll have you up and goin' before daylight."

Andy said, "I've always heard that beds are dangerous. Lots of people die in them." He dropped his blankets on the ground near the back of the tent, beside the ones he recognized as Tanner's. "How's the food?"

"We have a good cook, blacker than the ace of spades. Old Bo's biscuits would make the angels want to give up their wings and come back to earth."

"Len Tanner will be tickled to know about that."

"I remember Tanner, too. He ever run out of conversation?"

"He hasn't yet."

"He's a man I'd want beside me in a fight, but I wouldn't want to have to listen to him talk about it afterwards."

Andy dropped his saddle on the ground and hopped up on Long Red's bare back. The sergeant pointed. "You'll find the horse herd out that way. One of the drawbacks of ranger service is standin' your day of horse guard every so often."

It stood to reason that the rangers would be careful of their horses. A ranger afoot was essentially useless. Though Indian raids had become less common, they still occurred from time to time. Comanches and Kiowas continued to steal south from the high plains and the reservations to add to their wealth, measured in horses. White horse thieves had increased even as Indian activity had declined. In a state still short of cash money, horses were a leading medium of exchange.

Glancing back once, Andy saw that Holloway still watched him. He decided serving under the sergeant should be pleasant enough, for in some ways he reminded Andy of Rusty. The captain seemed more businesslike and abrupt, but that was probably necessary for an officer. He could not be just one of the boys and still expect them to jump to his command.

Andy met Tanner walking back, carrying his bridle over his thin shoulder. Tanner said, "Looks like the captain taken you in."

"For forty dollars a month."

"Save it and you'll get rich. If you live for a hundred years." Tanner's face took on a worried twist. "You'll find one of your old friends on horse guard out yonder."

"An old friend?"

"Farley Brackett. He's always wanted your horse. He's liable to take him and ride off."

Resentment stung Andy. Of all the people he might run into, Farley Brackett would have been among his last choices. "If he lays a hand on Long Red, I'll . . ." He could not think of anything severe enough to say. "How'd he ever come to be a ranger? The state police rode some good horses to death tryin' to catch him."

"They weren't tryin' near as hard as they made out. They took care not to crowd him too close. The state police are long gone anyway, and good riddance."

"He shot a couple of them that I know of."

"Scallywags and scoundrels. Most folks didn't see it as a crime. Shootin' state police was looked on as a public improvement."

"Well, if he leaves me alone I'll leave him alone."

"I don't suppose the captain said what time they serve supper around here?"

"I didn't ask. Probably couldn't eat anything now." The thought of Farley Brackett being here had already begun to work on Andy's stomach.

He and Brackett saw each other at about the same time. Brackett and another ranger had the horses scattered loosely, giving them room to graze. Brackett rode over to meet him. His attention seemed more on the sorrel than on Andy.

"Howdy, Indian," he said. "You been takin' good care of my horse?"

Andy could think of no suitable answer, so he offered none. Once, under close pursuit by Union soldiers and state police, Brackett left his own tired horse and took one belonging to Rusty. In return, Brackett's father had given Rusty this sorrel, which Rusty turned over to Andy.

Andy demanded, "With your record, why did the rangers ever take you in?"

"They decided that anybody who had killed two carpet-bag state policemen must be all right."

A long scar ran down one side of Brackett's face, result of a wartime saber cut. Deeper internal scars had never healed. Andy had been a reluctant witness when state police cut down Jeremiah Brackett in his own home one dark night, mistaking the father for the son. He could sympathize with Farley's bitterness, but he could not excuse the man's unreasoning violence, or his coveting the sorrel horse.

Brackett's gaze was hard. Andy tried to match it. Brackett said, "I'm surprised the captain accepted you. Did you tell him about your Comanche upbringin'?"

"I did. It's no secret."

"Did you tell him that the first time we get into a scrap with the Comanches you're liable to run off and join them against us?"

"I promised him I'd do my duty. He took me at my word."

"The captain doesn't know you, but I do. If the day comes and you even act like you're fixin' to join your butcherin' brothers, I'll shoot you myself."

"Me and you won't get along. That's plain to see. Maybe one of us needs to ask for a transfer to a different company."

"I was here first. You goin' to turn that horse loose, or not?"

"That's what I came out here for. He'd better still be here in the mornin'." Andy slid from Long Red's back and pulled the bridle down over the ears, then slipped the bits from the horse's mouth. The sorrel hesitated just a moment before turning and joining the other horses. Andy suspected he would not get along with most of them. Long Red tried to dominate whatever company he was in. He would make a friend or two and buffalo the rest of the horses into staying beyond biting and kicking distance.

Andy gave Brackett a final glance but knew nothing more to say. Brackett would be a thorn in his side so long as both of them remained with this company. Andy resolved that he could be a thorn, too.

We'll see which of us hollers *quit* first, he thought.

He walked the three or four hundred yards back to camp. Tanner sat on a crude bench made of branches tied with rawhide strips. He was cleaning his rifle. "I didn't hear no shootin'."

"I didn't do any. But I might if he ever crowds me too hard."

Tanner used a ramrod to push a cloth patch down the rifle barrel. "Maybe it wasn't such a smart idee, me bringin' you along to join the rangers. It's too late to back out, but maybe if I told the captain you lied about your age, . . ."

"I didn't. I told him I don't know just how old I am. So maybe I'm guessin' a little on the high side. That's not the same as lyin'."

"Crowds the hell out of it, though." Tanner shrugged. "Always try to stay where I'll be between you and Farley Brackett. If it looks like trouble is fixin' to break out, I'll have a chance to step in."

Andy disliked the notion that he might not be able to take care of himself. "The man who tries to break up a fight sometimes gets hit from both sides."

"I dodge pretty good."

Andy did not doubt that Tanner would come to his defense no matter the cost. He would not want Tanner hurt on his account. "I'll try to keep my distance from him."

"I ain't the only friend you've got in camp. The Morris boys are in this company. Jim and Johnny are out on a scout."

"Scoutin' for what?"

"Indian sign, horse thieves, robbers, whatever there is. We're west of most settlements here. Good country for them bunch quitters who work in the moonlight so folks don't see what they're up to."

It had taken Andy and Tanner the better part of a week to ride here from the farm, taking their time. They had seen few people the last couple of days. Andy could remember the Comanches bringing their families down from the plains into these limestone, cedar, and live-oak hills to hunt. After white settlement began in earnest they came mainly to raid.

Tanner laid the rifle across his lap and glanced back over his shoulder. "They say there's good fishin' in the San Saba. Catfish so thick they'll crawl out onto the bank to nip at your bait."

Living with the Indians, Andy had spent most of his time in a high, dry country where fish were not plentiful. With Rusty down on the Colorado he had learned to throw a line in the river periodically to vary the menu from venison, pork, and beef. The catching had been all right, but he had not liked the cleaning. It seemed a lot of work for a little bit of eating.

The black cook walked out from the mess tent and struck an iron rod against a dangling piece of wagon tire, signaling time for supper. He gave a wordless holler as if he were calling hogs.

Tanner said, "Let's go see if the boys was lyin' about how good that cook is."

The rangers who lined up were all strangers to Andy, though Tanner knew a few of them by name. No one remained a stranger to Tanner for long. They were a mixed group, mostly young. He saw none who seemed to be nearing middle age. Two or three looked as if they did not have to shave often. That made Andy feel a little less concerned about his youth.

"Fellers," Tanner said, "I want you to meet my compadre, Andy Pickard. Weaned on buffalo milk, brought up by wolves, ripped the hide off of a live grizzly with his bare hands and made himself a bearskin coat. He'd be wearin' it today if the weather wasn't so warm."

Embarrassed, Andy could only stand quietly and look innocent. Sergeant Holloway grinned. "Was that a full-grown grizzly, or was it only half-grown, like that story?"

Andy saw that the rangers were going along with the joke. That eased his self-consciousness. He said, "It wasn't near as tall as Len's yarn. Next time he tells it it'll be two bears."

The grinning sergeant clapped a hand on Andy's shoulder. "Grab you a plate. You never want to miss a chance to eat. There'll be days when you won't get to." He pushed Andy ahead of himself in the line.

Andy decided he need not worry about being accepted. He warmed to the friendliness in the faces around him. He said, "I want to do a good job. Any time you-all see a way I can do better, tell me."

"You can bet on that. This outfit ain't up to strength, so every man has got to pull extra weight to make up the difference." Holloway paused, thinking. "Seems to me I remember some Pickards that used to farm down in the lower country, around Gonzales seems like. Any kin?"

Andy hesitated. "Might be. The only kin I ever met was an uncle. We didn't like each other much."

He did not want to disclose that the uncle had come to see him when he was recuperating from the broken leg that had caused him to fall back into Texan hands. The uncle had rejected him on the grounds that Andy's long exposure to Indian ways had made him unfit for life among white people. Andy had resisted any further attempts to be brought into contact with his blood family. He regarded his real family as a band of Comanches and Rusty Shannon. He also felt an emotional kinship with the Monahans, more than he could ever have with any Pickards who might condescend to accept him.

Holloway said, "You keep an eye on the captain. Watch what he does and learn from it. Sometimes he'll tell you what to do. Other times he'll let you think for yourself."

"Sounds a lot like Rusty Shannon."

"I wish we had Rusty in this outfit. Why didn't you bring him with you?"

"I wish I had." Rusty would be better off in this company than torturing his soul with grief and hatred and hunting for a man who by now might be a thousand miles away. "Right now he's got his own snakes to kill."

After supper Andy heard somebody tuning up a musical instrument. He was a little surprised to find Sergeant Holloway with a fiddle in his hand, adjusting the strings to conform with a banjo held by a young ranger. Holloway had not struck him as a lover of music. Soon the two were playing. Most of the other rangers gathered to listen. Even the captain emerged from his tent and sat on a canvas stool.

Andy found the music pleasant. He tapped his feet to the rhythm.

Farley Brackett ruined his good mood. He said, "I'd've thought a rawhide drum was more to your likin'."

Andy got up and walked to his tent.

CHAPTER

TEN

Rusty had never been to Fort Worth before. About the nearest place he had visited had been Jacksboro during his ranger days. He knew that the town had begun with a military post on the Trinity River before the war. It had grown as farming and ranching spread westward and northward toward the Cross Timbers country and the Red River. In recent times it had become an important stopping point for cattle drives coming up from the southern part of the state on their way to the new railheads in Kansas. It was a resupply center for cattle outfits and freighters, for military units on their way west. There was even talk that a railroad would be coming in soon to lessen the need for trailing herds farther north.

Fort Worth had gained a reputation as a wide-open town where a man could do just about anything he was big enough to get away with. If a little short in stature he could make up the deficit by carrying one of Mr. Colt's inventions on his hip or in his boot top.

This was one of several trips Rusty had made on the basis of tips that Corey Bascom had been seen in one place or another. It was said he had been observed playing poker in Fort Worth's red-light district, beginning to be known as Hell's Half Acre. It was a name common to such districts in many frontier towns. Though previous searches had turned up empty, Rusty started each new one with strong hope. Now hope was about all he had left. The long ride had sapped his energy. Only the image of Corey Bascom kept him in the saddle mile after weary mile.

Each failure diminished his strength but increased his determination. To quit would mean that all his effort had been wasted. He had invested too much of himself in the search to give it up.

He rode through the thinly populated outskirts to a chorus of barking dogs and found a wagon yard a short distance from the courthouse. A young man of about Andy's age met him at the barn's open door. "Put up your horse, mister?"

"I'd be much obliged. And I'll spread my bedroll here tonight, too, if that's all right." He did not want to squander money on a hotel room.

"Sure. May not get a lot of sleep, though. There's two big cow outfits hit town today with herds on the way to the Indian nations. Apt to be a lot of whoopin' and hollerin'."

Rusty shrugged. "I'll just have to put up with it. Town looks a little quiet right now though."

"It's too early in the day. You lookin' for excitement?"

"Mainly lookin' for where the excitement takes place." If Corey was here, he would most likely be found where the action was.

"Wait 'til night. You'll hear it. All you have to do is follow the noise. Or follow a bunch of cowboys. They'll lead you to it."

This would be the drovers' last chance for relaxation and recreation before they hit the Red River and Indian territory. Leaving here they faced a month and more of toil and monotony on the long, dusty trail before they reached the railroad. It stood to reason they would want to let off some pent-up steam and have something to talk about on the tiresome miles ahead of them.

The hostler directed Rusty to a barbershop where he could bathe and have his red hair trimmed. He found a washerwoman to scrub the dirt and sweat out of the clothes he had worn all the way up here. Then he set out walking the dirt streets, locating the saloons and gambling houses where Corey might be. Those he entered appeared to have little business as yet.

A gambler playing solitaire looked up hopefully as Rusty entered. "Interested in a little game, friend?"

"Maybe later. I'm lookin' for a friend of mine. Maybe he's sat in on your game. Name of Corey Bascom?"

The gambler's eyes narrowed. "I know him, but I ain't seen him in a while. You say he's a friend of yours?"

"More like an acquaintance."

"Corey ain't the kind that makes many friends. Nice enough feller, after his fashion, but you got to watch him all the time. He'll cold deck you if you don't."

"That sounds like him. You're sure you haven't seen him lately?"

"No, and I ain't lookin' for him." Suspicion in the man's eyes indicated that he took a dim view of anyone who might be a friend of Corey's. "Even if he's in town he ain't likely to come in this place. He wore out his welcome at my table a long time ago."

Rusty was tempted to ask what Corey had done to earn the gambler's displeasure, but he had not come here to provoke a row, at least with anyone besides Corey.

The gambler said, "On the off chance that he shows up, do you want me to tell him you're lookin' for him?"

"I'd rather you didn't."

The gambler's attitude changed. He smiled thinly. "It's like that, hunh? What's your name, friend?"

"Shannon. Rusty Shannon."

"If I see or hear anything about Corey I'll try to get word to you. Goin' to be in town long?"

"That depends."

"Well, good huntin'."

Rusty returned to the wooden sidewalk and surveyed the street. The buildings were primarily modest one-story frame structures, most of them strangers to paint. A few log houses probably dated back to the town's earliest days. From where he stood he could not see a church anywhere.

A woman in a flimsy gown leaned out of an open window and smiled at him. She said, "Gettin' an early start?"

"Just killin' time."

"Me, too. Goin' to be lots of cowboys in town tonight. I'm apt to get awful busy. But right now I've got lots of time."

He knew an invitation when he heard it. He said, "Thanks, but you'd better get your rest while you can."

Walking away, he heard her call after him, "Later on you'll get to thinkin' about what you missed, and you'll hate yourself."

He passed a uniformed policeman twirling a nightstick. The officer gave him a nod. Then Rusty heard him address the woman by name. He told her, "Them cow outfits'll be in after a while. You better get ready for a busy night."

"I'm always ready. If you find any of them lookin' for a place to light, steer them my way. It'll be worth your while."

"It always is."

Rusty grunted disapprovingly to himself. He had heard that many city policemen shared in the proceeds from illegal activities in return for looking the other way or even, as in this case, participating. It was against all the principles he had learned in his years as a ranger. But that was Fort Worth's misfortune and none of his own.

He walked into a false-fronted building whose sign proclaimed that it offered the finest in spiritous liquors, beer, and hot lunch. It also offered a billiard table. He heard the crack of billiard balls and looked toward the rear of the room where two young men who ought to be at work this time of the day were engaged in a heated game.

A middle-aged man of ample girth and broader smile approached him. "Howdy, friend. If you're lookin' for the best drinks in Fort Worth you've come to the right place."

Something about him struck Rusty as being familiar. The man gave Rusty a moment's intense scrutiny and said, "Seems to me I ought to know you. Sure as hell I do. You're Rusty Shannon. Used to serve under old Captain Burmeister in the rangers."

Rusty remembered. "Right. And so did you." He struggled to remember the name.

"Simon Newfield." The man extended his hand and almost broke Rusty's fingers. "Scouted some with you and old Len Tanner. Reckon he's still alive?"

"Still alive and still talkin'." Rusty grinned, old memories coming back in a rush. He looked around the saloon. It was the fanciest he had seen here, or just about anywhere else he had been. "It's a cinch you didn't buy this place from your ranger savin's."

"No, I came into a windfall." Newfield looked around to see if anyone could hear. "Right at the end of the war I captured me a Yankee army paymaster. Took the money in the name of the Confederacy. But the Confederacy folded, so there wasn't anybody I could legally give it to that needed it worse than I did."

"They're probably still lookin' for it."

"I figured it like a loan. I'll pay it back to them someday when I feel like I've got rich enough. Ain't there yet. What brings you to Fort Worth? I never seen you here before."

Rusty lost his grin. "Lookin' for a man."

"Are you a ranger again? Maybe I oughtn't to've told you about that paymaster."

"No, I'm not a ranger. This is a personal matter. Do you know Corey Bascom?"

Newfield sobered. "Lots of people around here know Corey. Some to their profit and some to their regret. I take it that in your case it's regret."

"He killed the woman I was about to marry."

"That's tough. It doesn't sound much like Corey. Robbery and cheatin' at cards are more his style. But I suppose anything is possible when a man has been listenin' to the owls hoot long enough."

"Seen him lately?"

"He was in here two, maybe three, weeks ago. Never saw him lookin' so sour. Got in a game with a man that was better at cards than he was, and better with a gun, too. Seemed like a stupid thing to do, but Corey tried to egg him into a gunfight. The other feller wasn't lookin' to bloody himself, though. He hit Corey across the head with the barrel of his six-shooter and laid him out cold. Said there wasn't any profit in killin' fools and drunks. Corey left town the next day with a knot so big he couldn't put his hat on. I ain't seen him since."

"Any idea where he went?"

"None at all. Never saw Corey act like that before. It was almost like he was tryin' to get himself killed. Doesn't make any sense."

"It doesn't make sense that he'd come here in the open like that. He's bound to know he's been posted for murder."

"That wouldn't make any difference in the Acre. Jesse James himself could come here and not be bothered. The police keep their hands off of this district. It's a sanctuary, sort of, like church."

"Not like any church I ever saw."

"Poor choice of words. The point is, even if you're not the law any-more, it wouldn't be a good idea to let everybody know you're lookin' for Corey. There's some that would kill you on general principles whether they like Corey or not."

"I'll try not to make a show of it."

"Good. Now let's have that drink. We'll toast old times, and better ones."

While he waited for nightfall Rusty killed time talking with Newfield about long-ago days. Though he did not feel hungry, he partook of the lunch on one end of the bar, boiled eggs, loaf bread, and sliced ham. He washed it down with a beer that would not leave him impaired in the way that whiskey might.

With dusk the crowds began milling. A dozen or so cowboys lined up at the bar. Some moved to the billiard table. Rusty watched them a while, listening to their laughter and loud talk. Most were young, not of an age to be in a place like this. He envied them their youth but wished they were spending it and their money more wisely.

He told Newfield, "I'd better get started if I'm goin' to find Corey."

"Chances are he's not in town. If he was I might've heard. But you won't know 'til you look."

Rusty visited every saloon he could locate, down to a couple of dark dives that made the hair bristle on the back of his neck. Now and then he saw someone who at first glance in dim light looked like Corey but proved not to be. His hopes rose, then fell. Each time they fell they sank lower than before.

He finally returned to Newfield's. The ex-ranger did not have to ask. Rusty knew his face betrayed his disappointment.

Newfield said, "You could hunt every night for two or three months and never find him. You got that much time?"

"No. I ought to be home tendin' the farm. But I've got to look."

"There's no guarantee that he ever will come back here. Gettin' his hair combed with a gun barrel may have turned him away from Fort Worth forever. He could've gone down to San Antonio or maybe over to Fort Smith, even up the trail to Kansas, wherever he might find a card game. If there's paper out on him for murder he might even have sailed to South America like some of them die-hard old Confederates did. You'd just as well try and chase a cloud."

Rusty sighed. "I'll give it another day or two. If I don't find any sign of him, I'll go home."

"I don't like to mess in other people's business, but I'll keep my ear to the ground. If I hear anything I'll let you know."

"I'd be obliged."

"Just don't kill him in here if you can help it, or get killed in here yourself. It's hell to get the blood cleaned up after it's soaked into the wood floor."

Rusty went to the wagon yard and rolled out his blanket on the ground. As the young hostler had said, the place became noisy as cowboys began showing up, full of fun and Fort Worth whiskey. By the time the last of them dropped off to sleep, Rusty had lost the urge. He sat up staring into the darkness and thinking of Josie.

He made up the next day by napping much of the morning after the cowboys departed. At dark he began repeating the rounds he had made the night before. By midnight he had visited every potential place twice. He did not find Corey. He had a strong feeling that Newfield was right. Corey might never come back here.

He decided to give it one more night.

In the late afternoon he returned to Newfield's place. The former ranger came out from behind the bar to meet him, wiping a glass with a white cloth. "Did my boy find you?"

"I haven't seen any boy."

"I sent him out huntin' for you. I got word that somebody named Bascom is in town. Don't know if it's Corey or not."

Rusty's heart jumped. "Where's he at?"

"One of the girls from Fat Beulah's house was in here to buy a case of whiskey. She said a man named Bascom is bedded down with a girl over there. Corey used to take a fancy to the women. He knew every sportin' house in town."

"Thanks, Simon. I'll remember you in my will."

"You better write one before you tangle with Corey. He's tricky."

Rusty was out the door and a couple of houses down the street before he realized he did not know where Fat Beulah's was. He stopped a cowboy and asked. The cowboy pointed. "It's that house yonder. But they got a prettier class of girls over at Miss Flo's place."

Rusty examined his pistol before walking up to the house. The low porch was ornate, with freshly painted gingerbread trim. Three lanterns hung from the edge, but they had not yet been lighted for the evening. He peered through the oval glass in the front door before he entered.

A very large woman sat in an oversized rocking chair, darning a black stocking large enough for two normal legs. Flame in a kerosene lamp gave her light to see her work. She looked up at Rusty but did not stand. "Come in. Come in. It's a little early, but what the hell? Never too early for pleasure or business."

"I'm lookin' for somebody."

"We've got lots of somebodys here. Dark, light, one for any preference. What's yours?"

"It's a man I'm lookin' for, name of Bascom."

Her expression quickly changed from welcome to near hostility. "Don't know no Bascom. Most of our customers go by the name of Smith. Now, as long as you're not interested in my girls I want you to get out of here. If you got troubles, take them someplace else."

"Not 'til I find Bascom."

"All I got to do is blow this whistle and half a dozen policemen will come runnin'." She showed him a whistle on a string, half hidden by the pearls around her thick neck.

He grabbed the whistle and pulled. The string broke, but not before biting into her neck a little. He drew his pistol.

She looked at it fearfully but summoned courage to say, "You wouldn't shoot a lady."

"No, but I'd shoot that lamp on the table beside you. Probably start the damndest fire you ever saw." He thumbed back the hammer.

She slumped deeper into her chair. "All right. The man you're lookin' for is upstairs with Cindy Lou, second door on your right. Only don't kill him here, please. It'll give this place a bad reputation."

Rusty hurried up the stairs, knowing it would not take long for Fat Beulah to work up nerve to fetch the police. The pistol still in his hand, he paused at the door, then kicked it open.

A woman screamed. A man sat up in bed, flinging a blanket aside and reaching for a gunbelt hanging across a high-backed chair. Rusty grabbed it first and flung it out the broken door. "Now, Corey . . ."

His finger tightened on the trigger.

He saw then that this was not Corey Bascom. A strong resemblance was there, but the face was not Corey's. He could not stop his finger from tightening, but he tipped the muzzle up in time. The pistol cracked, and a bullet smashed into the ceiling. The woman screamed again and covered her face with the blanket.

Newley Bascom blanched, his body shaking. "My God, Shannon, don't kill me."

Rusty recognized him as Corey's brother, the one who along with younger brother Anse had tried to ambush him. He found himself trembling a little, too. "I came awful close. I thought you were Corey."

"I'm not. I'm Newley."

"Where is Corey?"

Newley fought to bring his voice under control. "I don't know. I came here lookin' for him. Ain't seen him in weeks."

"I don't know if I ought to believe you or not. I think I ought to just shoot you on general principles."

Newley began to cry.

Rusty felt pity, then disgust. He sensed that Newley was telling him the truth, badly as he wanted not to believe.

But he had to believe. He backed up a step and said, "If you ever do see Corey, tell him he can't go so far that Rusty Shannon won't find him. And when I find him, I'm goin' to kill him." He waved the muzzle at Newley for emphasis. Newley whimpered.

Rusty told the girl, "You ought to give him child's rates. He's not but half a man."

He started out the door. He saw Fat Beulah and a policeman coming up the stairs. He turned back and shouted at Newley and the girl. "Now go on with what you were doin'."

He knew Newley couldn't, not now.

He gave Fat Beulah five dollars for the broken door and the policeman a like amount for his trouble. He did not have the heart to make all the saloons and gambling houses again tonight. He sensed that it would be futile.

Frustration was like acid foaming in his stomach. He just wanted to put Fort Worth behind him. He wondered how far he could ride before dark.

CHAPTER

ELEVEN

The captain gave Andy a little time to settle in and begin to feel at home before he sent him out of camp on any special duties. Unlike military service, the rangers did not require marching and close-order drill, but they did encourage target practice. The state offered a supply of ammunition to help make up for the fact that the men so far had to provide their own weaponry. Targets were marked on scrap bits of board and nailed to the heavy trunk of a pecan tree. A bank of earth behind would stop stray bullets, though any shot that missed hitting the board threw the shooter's marksmanship into question.

Andy watched several rangers take their turns. The first board was soon splintered so badly it had to be replaced. Tanner missed centering the target by only about an inch.

Andy said, "Good shot."

Tanner waved off the compliment. "Sun got in my eyes or I'd've hit it plumb center."

Farley Brackett's turn came before Andy's. He hit the target almost squarely in the middle. Turning away, he ejected the spent cartridge from his rifle. "All right, Indian boy, let's see if you can even hit the board."

Riled, Andy resolved to do better. He took a deep breath, sighted down the barrel, and squeezed the trigger. The bullet cut into the edge of the hole left by Brackett's shot. By a tiny fraction it was nearest to the center. Andy noticed the captain watching him with interest.

Brackett looked surprised. Then he frowned. "A target don't shoot back. The trick is to do the same thing when you're lookin' down the muzzle of somebody's gun."

Andy let malice creep into his voice. "Somebody like the state police?"

"I seldom shot at one but what I hit him."

Andy could not argue with that. Burning with bitterness acquired on the battlefields, Brackett had become a terror to occupation officers who attempted to enforce reconstruction laws.

Tanner edged in between the two. He said, "Andy, you stick your right elbow out too far. Let's go over yonder away from the crowd and practice holdin' that rifle."

Andy knew his stance was all right. It was the one Rusty had taught him. But he realized Tanner was trying to get him away before an argument started. "I'd be much obliged for anything you can show me."

When they had moved apart from the other men Tanner looked back over his shoulder. "Ain't really nothin' wrong with the way you hold your elbow if it feels right to you. It don't matter how you do it as long as you hit what you shoot at."

"I usually do."

"I'm just tryin' to keep you from havin' to aim at Farley Brackett, and him at you. One of you is just as good a shot as the other. You'd probably both go down."

"I don't want any trouble with him. But he keeps pokin' at me every chance he gets."

"A smart fish don't grab at bait that's got a hook in it."

While Andy was taking the measure of the company, the captain had been taking the measure of him. One evening he assigned Andy to night horse guard. "Private Pickard, you will take first watch tonight."

Andy was pleased. He had begun to wonder when or even if he would be given any real responsibility. "Yes, sir. I'll be glad to."

The captain gave him a quizzical look. "You don't have to be glad around here. You just have to do what you're told to, glad or not. And always be ready for the unexpected."

After supper Andy saddled Long Red and checked his rifle.

Brackett leaned against a pecan tree, watching. "Where's your bow and arrow?"

Andy tried not to let Brackett see that his tone stung a little. He pretended he did not hear.

Brackett turned to Jim Morris, just back from a lengthy and uneventful scout. "You know that boy was raised by the Indians? He's a Comanche at heart."

Jim retorted, "I know his heart has got a lot of fight in it. He helped me and Johnny and Len spike a Yankee cannon, with them Yankees shootin' at us the whole time."

That seemed to be news to Brackett. "When was that?"

"Last January, when the carpetbaggers tried to hold onto the state capitol."

"How many of them did he scalp?"

"Not more than five or six. He had to share with the rest of us."

Andy decided Jim could hold his own in a lying contest with Tanner.

Jim said, "They tell me the Comanches called him Badger Boy. He fights like a cornered badger when he's riled."

Brackett appeared impressed, but that did not last long. As Andy started to ride away, Brackett said, "If any of your red brothers come callin', don't you let them get my sorrel horse, Badger Boy." He spoke the name with derision.

Andy said, "Not them, and not you."

Allowed to spread out and graze during the day, the horses had been brought close to camp and pushed into a fairly compact group that could be watched more easily during the night. Though Indians could strike a horse herd at any time, they favored darkness, when they were hard to see and hard to hit.

Andy had come to rely heavily upon his instincts. Sometimes, though by no means always, he had premonitions about future events. He supposed this resulted from hearing about visions that often came to the People like his foster brother, Steals the Ponies. On several occasions he had sought after visions himself, but they never came. Or if they came, they were so vague that he did not recognize them for what they were. Perhaps he had to be a real Comanche, not an adopted one, for visions to work.

He had no premonition tonight. Nevertheless he was determined to remain alert. He listened to night birds settling in the trees. Indians often imitated the sounds of birds and other creatures in signaling to each other.

He did not intend to be fooled. The horses quieted down and began going to sleep, some lying down, others remaining on their feet. Now and then one would snort or stamp the ground or nip at a neighbor that crowded too closely. The one bitten would usually squeal and kick at its tormentor. These were all natural sounds. He catalogued them in his mind so he might recognize any that were not natural.

He had no watch, but Rusty had shown him how to tell time in a general way by the movement of the stars.

The camp routine had kept him busy enough during the days that he had not thought much about the farm. Now, in the long solitude of the night, he thought back on the place where he had spent the years since his return from life with the Comanches. He thought of Rusty and wondered where he was, what he was doing. He wondered if he had made headway in his search for Corey Bascom.

After getting past his initial reticence, Andy had told the captain about Josie Monahan's death. The officer had written down Andy's description of Bascom. "I'll have every man add this to his fugitive list, and I'll send it to the other companies," he said.

Andy had been shown what was called a fugitive book, containing hand-written descriptions of wanted men. The offenses were many and varied: theft of livestock and personal property, burglary, fraud, robbery at gunpoint, assault with intent to do bodily injury, rape, murder. . . . The book was only partially filled, leaving room to add more miscreants to the list. That these pages would eventually be used up was a foregone conclusion. Texas was not a comfortable place for the timid.

No Indians were listed. Few of their names were known. Any found roaming freely within the state's boundaries were automatically considered hostile and in open season, so a listing would have no purpose.

Andy had been instructed to read the book over and over, to memorize the descriptions in as much detail as possible so he might more easily recognize any fugitives he came across. It was considered likely that many were hiding in this thinly settled western country where law was scarce. Local lawmen varied in their diligence, some relentless in pursuit, others tolerant so long as the offenses had been committed elsewhere and were not repeated within their own jurisdiction. In these cases, rangers were the only peace officers likely to bring the offenders to hand.

Andy rode a slow circle around the horses, pausing to listen for any sound he considered alien. He thought the most effective solution would be to build a corral large enough to contain the herd at night. But this campsite was considered temporary. The company might be moved at any time, so nothing of a permanent nature had been constructed.

Even corraled, the horses would have to be watched. Accomplished horse thieves, red or white, could quietly dismantle a section of the enclosure and put the whole bunch on the move before the rangers could muster an adequate defense.

Eventually Andy's relief rode out to take his place.

He called, "Where you at, Badger Boy?"

Andy recognized Farley Brackett's gruff voice. He replied, "Here." Choking down his dislike for the man, he moved over to meet him.

Brackett said, "Anything stirrin' out yonder?"

"I haven't seen or heard a thing."

"You sure you ain't been asleep? Nothin' gets a man fired out of this outfit quicker than bein' caught asleep on guard."

"My eyes are wide open. They have been all night."

"Glad to hear that. Been worried about my horse."

"Long Red is fine. You worry about the rest of the horses."

Andy turned away. He looked forward to a few hours of sleep before daylight.

He heard a movement of horses behind him, then a shouted challenge. The voice was Brackett's. "Who goes yonder?" He heard the jingle of Brackett's spurs as the man put his mount into a run. Andy turned back, trying to see in the dim light of a half moon. Sound more than sight told him the horse herd was moving. A pistol shot echoed through the trees. He assumed it was Brackett's.

He set Long Red into a lope, trying to circle around and head off the running horses. He heard the thieves holler, pushing for more speed. Andy overtook the moving herd and cut in front of it. He shouted, trying to turn the horses back. He fired his pistol into the air. Some of the animals slid to a stop, then ducked aside, frightened by the shot.

For a moment Andy saw the dark outline of a horseman. He brought his pistol up into line but hesitated. What if these were Comanches? What if his foster brother might be among them? Steals the Ponies had been given his name for good reason: he had earned it.

In a moment the question was moot, for the rider was lost in the darkness and the dust.

He saw a blur as another horseman came at him. He thought this was Brackett but he was mistaken. The man rammed his horse into Long Red. The impact knocked the sorrel off its feet and jarred Andy loose from the saddle. He grabbed at the horn but missed. He hit the ground hard on his left shoulder.

The rider loomed over him, his horse almost on top of Andy. Andy felt around desperately for the pistol lost in the fall. He had time for one terrible thought: that a Comanche brother was about to kill him. He saw the rider's hand come down, steadying the pistol.

He heard a shot, but it did not come from the gun that had been leveled at him. The rider pitched forward over the horse's neck. His body fell across Andy's legs.

Brackett's voice shouted, "Get up from there, Badger Boy. We got horse thieves to catch." Brackett turned and disappeared again, his horse in a dead run.

Long Red had regained his feet. Andy pushed the heavy body off his legs. The Comanche side of him regretted the thought of an Indian being shot, though the white side rejoiced that it had not been him instead. Andy remounted and set out in a run after the horses. He heard a few more shots.

He fired at a shadowy figure which crossed his path but knew he had missed. In a way he was relieved.

He found himself in front of the horses again. They were slowing. He shouted until he was hoarse. Gradually they began to mill. Somewhere beyond sight he heard a few more shots, then the night fell quiet except for the nervous stamping of hooves against limestone rocks, the nervous nickering of horses.

He saw a rider coming toward him from the west and brought up his pistol. He lowered it when he recognized Brackett's voice. "Holler out, Badger Boy." The man and his horse were both breathing hard. Brackett struggled for breath. "Got them stopped did you? I hope we didn't lose any."

Andy said, "I never knew Comanches to give up so easy."

"Comanches? Didn't you get a look at any of them?"

"It was too dark, and things moved too fast."

"If they was Comanches, I'm an Apache squaw. They were as white as me and you. Me, anyway."

Several rangers came up, riding hard. They had had mounts staked in or near camp. The captain was among them. "What happened here, men?"

Brackett said, "Just had a little company. They didn't stay long."

"Did we lose any horses?"

"We can't take a good count 'til daylight. Looks like most of them are still here."

"Indians, I suppose?"

"Not this time. I'm sorry to say it, but there's some white men near as bad as Comanches."

The captain accepted the report with a satisfied grunt. "You did good work, Brackett. You too, Pickard."

Andy said, "Captain, one of them went down back yonder. Private Brackett shot him."

"Dead?"

"I didn't wait to see, sir. Seemed more important to catch the horses."

"We'll pick him up as we drive the remuda back."

Andy gritted his teeth. He had rather take a whipping with a wet rope than acknowledge that Brackett had saved his bacon, but he owed it to the man to tell the truth. "My horse got knocked down. That outlaw was fixin' to kill me. Private Brackett shot him first."

The captain was pleased. "I'll put that on your record, Brackett. It might help make you a sergeant one day."

Brackett said, "I'd've done the same thing for the camp cook. Quicker, maybe. He makes good biscuits."

Tanner and the Morris brothers rode ahead of the horses, looking for the raider Brackett had shot. By the time Andy reached them, they had him. Tanner said, "Looky what we found, Captain, tryin' to sneak off into the timber. He's leakin' some, but he's breathin'."

The man was hunched over, holding one arm tightly against his ribs. Andy did not think he had ever seen him before, though a ragged beard covered most of his face except for his frightened eyes.

Tanner said, "We got no jail to put him in."

Johnny Morris said, "We got plenty of trees to hang him from. What do you say, Captain?"

The man cried out, "Somebody help me. Can't you see I'm shot?"

The captain's voice was grave. "You present us with a problem. As Private Morris said, we have no jail to put you in and no doctor to see to your wound. There seems to be but one answer."

Brackett waved a pistol. "It's my fault, Captain. I was movin' fast and in the dark. Couldn't aim straight. I'll make up for it right now if you want me to."

Andy hoped Brackett was just trying to intimidate the prisoner, but he sounded as if he meant it.

The outlaw sank to his knees. "For God's sake, give me a chance."

The captain made a show of struggling with his decision. "My better judgment tells me to put an end to it. But I might consider an alternative if you'd cooperate."

"Anything. Leave me go and I won't stop 'til I get to California. Maybe even further."

"I'll want you to identify your confederates and tell me where we might be most likely to find them."

"I'll tell you all I know. They run off and left me. I don't owe them nothin'."

The captain pointed his chin at the herd. "Pickard, catch him a horse. He can ride to camp bareback."

The outlaw cried, "I can't ride. I been shot. I think my ribs are busted."

"A little hurting will help you repent your wayward life."

Andy doubted that. The only thing this renegade would regret was getting caught. A while earlier he had been willing to murder Andy. Despite his pleas, he was unlikely to reform. He would travel a crooked road until a better-aimed bullet or a strong rope stopped him for good.

The prisoner grunted in pain with almost every step. Andy mustered no sympathy. Leading the horse, he maneuvered it across the roughest ground he could find.

He wouldn't have lost a minute's sleep over killing me, he thought. *What's more, he made me beholden to Farley Brackett.*

That might have been the worst offense of all.

Brackett eased over beside Andy. "I been mullin' this thing over. You thought it was Indians, didn't you?"

Andy wondered what he was driving at. "Thought it might be. I couldn't see much."

"Occurs to me you had a chance to shoot this man before he ran into your horse. Why didn't you?"

"I didn't see him soon enough."

"Or maybe you didn't want to shoot a fellow Comanche."

Andy's face warmed. He was glad the darkness kept Brackett from seeing it. He had told the truth about not having time to fire at this raider, but moments earlier he had seen another. He had a few seconds in which he might have fired, but he had hesitated. Brackett was partially right.

He managed a defiant tone. "Believe what you want to."

"I try to give a man the benefit of the doubt, the first time. And I've damned sure got some doubts about you, Badger Boy."

"I suppose you'll tell the captain about them?"

"I'll keep them to myself for now. But I'll be watchin' you."

The prisoner's horse stumbled on a rock outcrop and almost went down. The man grabbed his side and screeched, "Damn you, can't you watch where you lead this horse?"

Brackett said, "You're lucky we ain't leadin' him out from under a tree limb and leavin' you attached to it."

Andy was grateful that Brackett transfered his malice to the prisoner. He settled into quiet meditation over his own situation. Would he have reacted differently had he known from the first that the horse thieves were white? He was not sure. He feared he might have.

The captain had left a strong guard on the horse herd. At daylight they brought the horses into a clearing at the edge of camp for an accurate count. He and Holloway agreed that they were short only three horses. The thieves might have gotten away with them, or they might simply have strayed away from the main bunch during the excitement. He sent part of the company out on a search for the missing three. Then he watched the cook clean the prisoner's wound.

The renegade protested over the fact that the cook was black. "I ain't never let no dirty nigger touch me."

The captain retorted, "That black won't rub off on you. Keep at it, Bo."

The prisoner squalled as the cook poured alcohol into the wound. Bo grinned and poured more. By the time the bandage had been applied and the ribs tightly wrapped, the prisoner had regained some of his lost courage. When the captain began to question him, he refused to answer. "I changed my mind. I ain't tellin' you a damned thing."

"Regrettable. I hope you realize that if you won't talk, you're of no use to us."

"Never meant to be."

The captain nodded gravely at Holloway. "Sergeant, I have a report to write. Would you take charge of the prisoner? See if you can bring him around to our way of thinking." He retired to his headquarters tent.

Holloway said, "Brackett, bring your rope. We're takin' a little walk down to the river."

The prisoner's eyes widened. "What're you fixin' to do?"

"Like the captain said, you're of no use to us, and we've got no jail." He tied the man's hands behind his back with a rawhide string, then took a firm grip on one arm. Brackett grabbed the other. Though the prisoner dragged his feet, they hustled him along. Andy followed at a short distance, curious.

Holloway pointed at a sturdy pecan limb about ten feet off of the ground. "That one ought to do. Throw your rope over it."

The prisoner blustered. "You're tryin' to bluff me. You wouldn't do this to a man. It's against the law."

Neither Holloway nor Brackett replied. Brackett slipped the loop over the prisoner's head and tightened it around his neck. He pulled the other end of the rope and took up the slack.

The renegade was sweating but tried to show a brave face. "You won't really do this. You ain't allowed."

Holloway nodded, and Brackett pulled the rope. It drew taut. The prisoner choked as his legs straightened. He bent his toes, trying to keep them touching the ground. Brackett pulled until the prisoner's feet were clear by a full six inches. Brackett held him there for a bit, then let him down.

"Got a kink in the rope," he explained. "Need to straighten it out."

The prisoner went to his knees, gasping, his face turning purple. Holloway bent over him. "We forgot to ask if you have any last words for the Lord."

The man coughed but could not speak. Holloway pulled him to his feet. "We'll get it done right this time. Go ahead, Brackett."

As the rope tightened the prisoner found voice. "No! No! For God's sake . . ."

Holloway seemed unmoved. "Tell me why not."

"Get the captain. Ask me anything."

Holloway appeared disappointed, but he turned and winked at Andy. "Don't put your rope away, Brackett. We'll need it if he changes his mind again."

The prisoner was so limp from terror that it took both men's support to get him back to the headquarters tent. A heavy smell indicated he had soiled himself. Holloway said, "Captain, I believe he's come to Jesus."

The captain emerged from the tent, smiling thinly. "He just needed time to consider the error of his ways."

When he quit coughing and regained his breath the culprit became a fountain of information. He said four including himself had been involved. They had planned in the excitement to cut off twelve or fifteen horses and get away with them in the darkness while the rangers chased after the main herd. They had hoped the raid would be blamed on Indians.

He rattled off his accomplices' names without hesitation: Arliss Wilkes, Brewster Pardo, and a boy called Scooter. He didn't know the boy's last name.

Holloway flipped through the pages of his fugitive book. "I find everybody in here except the boy."

The prisoner wailed as the cook rubbed salty bacon grease on his neck, burned red and raw by the rope. The captain told a nearby ranger, "Handcuff him to a chain and lock the chain around a tree. By the time he gets to a real jail he'll think it's the Menger Hotel in San Antonio."

Andy asked Holloway, "Can you do this? Is it legal?"

"Anything is legal if it works, and if you don't let the wrong people see it."

"Somebody is bound to ask about the mark around his neck."

"I'll just say he wears his collars too tight."

The captain chose five men to follow after and attempt to apprehend the thieves. They were Andy, Brackett, Tanner, Johnny Morris, and Sergeant Holloway. "Stay on their trail as long as you feel there's a chance it will be fruitful. Take them alive if it can be done without undue risk to yourselves. Otherwise, shoot to kill. If the rangers are to be respected we must show the outlaw class that we will exact a price for every offense."

Brackett jerked his head at Andy. "Captain, don't you think this boy is a little green?" Andy had not once heard him say *sir*.

"If so, he will ripen with experience."

By the time the five were prepared to leave, the rangers who had sought the three missing horses returned. One reported, "We found them, Captain. Looks like the thieves didn't get anything except experience."

"With a little luck we'll give them more of that."

CHAPTER

TWELVE

It took some circling and searching before Andy found that the three remaining raiders had rejoined one another a couple of miles west from where they had first jumped the remuda. He waved his hat over his head to draw the attention of the other four rangers. Len Tanner had to be sent out to find Johnny Morris, off on a tangent of his own.

Sergeant Holloway said, "Since you found the trail, Andy, we'll let you track for a while. If you run up a stump, somebody else'll take it."

Tanner said, "I'll bet there ain't a better tracker in the company than Andy, unless it's me."

Holloway said, "You may get your chance. We'll see first what Andy can do."

Andy had not expected so much responsibility so soon. He felt a glow of pride, though he knew Holloway was testing him.

Brackett did not allow the glow to last. "Don't you mess up them tracks, Badger Boy. Remember, we ain't trailin' your Indians."

Andy could not think of an adequate retort.

He had left Long Red behind. The sorrel had had a hard run last night and might tire out before this search was finished. The gray he had been lent had a rougher trot than Long Red's, pounding Andy's innards. This was going to be a long, tiresome ride. But at least he was doing something other than following a plow.

The frustrated horse thieves were not experienced at covering their trail. It seemed to Andy that they did not even try. Perhaps it never occurred to them that the rangers would be vengeful enough to follow them inasmuch as they had failed to get away with any horses.

Tanner observed, "They don't seem very smart."

Holloway said, "Most crooks aren't. Very few make much of a livin'. If they'd work as hard at honest labor as they do at mischief they could make somethin' of themselves. They live like coyotes and die like dogs, most of them, dead broke and bleedin' to death in the dirt."

Andy found where the fugitives had camped for the night on a creek. They had built a fire on a flat rock just above the waterline. A couple of dry-ing rabbit skins, covered with flies, remained as evidence of their meager supper.

Tanner said, "Jackrabbit. That's about as far from prosperity as you can get."

Holloway said, "There's misguided kids back East wishin' they could run away and become outlaws. I wish every one of them could see this."

Andy remembered famine times with the People when he had eaten jackrabbit, even rattlesnakes. The thought almost made him feel sorry for the outlaws. But not quite. They had chosen this path. He doubted that anyone had forced them to it at gunpoint. He would reserve his sympathy for people upon whom hard times had fallen without fault of their own.

At midday he approached a small cedar picket cabin, the first dwelling he had seen. Holloway called, "Better hold up, Andy. We'll ride in slow and careful. Tanner, you and Johnny circle way around and come in from the back side."

Andy, Holloway, and Brackett dismounted to present less of a target. They gave the other two time enough to reach their position. Andy said, "Looks like somebody has chopped down an awful lot of cedar." A large area had been cleared around and beyond the cabin. Brush was stacked in piles, probably to be burned when it dried enough.

Holloway said, "I'd figure they're clearin' a field, only this ground has more rocks than soil. I'd hate to try and put a plow in it."

Andy saw a movement and squinted to bring it into focus. "I see a man afoot out yonder. Looks like he's drivin' stakes into the ground. Why would anybody do that in a place like this?"

Holloway shook his head. "Damned if I know. Every time I think I've got people figured out, somebody throws a new puzzle at me."

While the three rode toward the man with the stakes, Andy saw Tanner and Johnny approach the cabin from the rear. Cautiously the pair dismounted and entered, then came back out. Obviously the fugitives were not here. Tracks showed they had passed this way, however.

The man carried a sledgehammer and a long cedar stake, sharpened at one end. Andy saw that he had made a line of stakes stretching to the cabin and beyond.

Holloway raised his hand. "Howdy. We're rangers, on the trail of three riders that came by here. Did you see them?"

The man wiped his sleeve across a gray-stubbled face to clear away a heavy sweat. His manner was jovial, his blue eyes bright though given a wild look by thick, bristly eyebrows. Andy saw that he wore a heavy boot on one foot and a loosely laced shoe on the other. Perhaps that was the only footwear he owned, or perhaps he had not noticed the difference. "They came by early this mornin' and traded me a couple of tired-out horses for two old skates I had. I sure got the best end of that deal."

"Maybe you did and maybe you didn't. Those men are horse thieves. They may have traded you stolen property."

The man's face fell. "You mean you're goin' to take them away from me?"

"We won't, but if the real owners should happen to turn up, you'll lose them."

The eyes brightened again. "By that time maybe I'll be rich enough to buy plenty more horses. I've got me a gold mine here."

"Gold mine?"

"A town. Don't you see it? A town all my own." He waved his hand toward the line of stakes. "I'll be sellin' lots as soon as I finish layin' out the townsite. Pretty soon there'll be houses all over this place. I'll put in a store and later on a bank."

"But a town has to have people. I don't see anybody except you."

"There's thousands of people back East lookin' for a new home. I've got the place for them right here. How about you gentlemen? Any of you want to be the first to settle in Hanleyville?"

"I take it your name is Hanley?"

"Yes sir, Joshua B. Hanley. *Mayor* Hanley."

Andy looked around but saw nothing to attract people to a site like this, certainly not in any numbers. The ground was unsuitable for farming except in narrow little valleys where rains had deposited soil washed down from the rocky hillsides. It might do for grazing cattle or sheep, but cedar was so thick the grass was sparse. He did not see a spring or creek.

Hanley said, "My daddy fought with Sam Houston at San Jacinto. The Republic of Texas gave him this land grant. He never could claim it because the Indians was too thick out here. They're pretty well gone now. I decided it was time to plant a garden in the desert and build a town where there wasn't nothin' but a cedarbrake."

Holloway did a poor job of concealing his misgivings. "Mind if we water our horses before we go on?"

"There's a well up by the cabin. Dug it myself. Take all the water you want."

The town builder resumed stepping off the lots and driving his stakes. Holloway looked back on him with pity. "I've seen many a 'town' like this, somebody's wild dream. Poor devil'll sit out here waitin' by himself 'til he goes crazy. Maybe he already is."

Brackett asked, "What about those horses?"

"They're not ours. Whoever they were stolen from, there's not much chance they'll ever come this far huntin' them. Leave the poor fool somethin'."

Hanley's description of the fugitives, two men and a boy, had matched the one extracted from the prisoner after his early-morning rope dance.

At midafternoon the searchers came across a limping horse, its head down in fatigue. Nearby lay an abandoned saddle, blanket, and bridle.

Holloway said, "The two horses they've got left are probably the ones they traded from Hanley. One of those'll wear down fast, too, carryin' double. We'll have them pretty soon."

Shortly before sundown Andy caught a whiff of woodsmoke on a warm breeze from the west. He had not seen sign of a human since after they had left Hanley's townsite. It stood to reason that the fugitives had found what they considered a good place to camp. He waited for the others to come up even with him.

Holloway sniffed. "I smell it, too. They can't be far."

Andy flinched at a shot, followed quickly by another. By instinct he was half out of the saddle before he realized the sound came from far away. The shots had not been aimed at the rangers.

Holloway said, "Probably tryin' to get a deer or somethin' for supper. They need it, judgin' by the jackrabbits they ate last night."

The rangers moved into the edge of a cedarbrake and waited, listening. Andy heard nothing else. Either they hit their game with the first shots or it got away and they hadn't found anything else.

Brackett said, "I could stand a chunk of venison myself. Bo's cold biscuits are startin' to taste like horse sweat."

Holloway said, "They'll have to do for now. We'll wait here 'til dark, then close in on them. Maybe they'll have their bellies full and drop off to sleep." He glanced at Andy. "Nervous?"

"Am I supposed to be?"

"Most people are the first time they come up on a situation like this."

"This isn't my first time."

Tanner said, "Andy could tell you lots of stories."

Holloway said, "Another time. I'm fixin' to catch a little nap while I can."

Andy wondered aloud how the sergeant could drop off so quickly and easily.

Brackett said, "I was with him several times in the war. He could go to sleep twenty minutes before a battle or after one. Ain't much that scares him, aside from gettin' old. Bein' a ranger, he may not ever *get* old."

Andy realized that Brackett respected the sergeant. That surprised him. He had not seen Brackett show much respect for anybody.

What'll it take for him to respect me? he wondered.

Holloway awakened at good dark, as if he had planned it that way. He dug one of the cook's leftover biscuits from a canvas bag tied with his blanket roll. He watched Brackett while he ate it. "Horse sweat don't taste too bad," he said. "You just hold your breath and swallow, like it was gyppy water."

He checked his weapons, a silent indication that the others should do the same. He said, "We'll take them alive if we can. If we can't, it's their hard luck. Johnny, you and Tanner circle around. We'll come in on them from this side. Just be careful you don't shoot one another in the dark. I don't want to bury anybody but those horse thieves, and not even them if we don't have to."

The three thieves were either supremely overconfident or not very good at their calling. The rangers took them by complete surprise. They looked at their captors with disbelief for the few seconds the rangers required to take charge of their weapons. One made a grab for a rifle just as Brackett picked it up. Brackett swung it and struck him across the head. The outlaw went down like a sack of potatoes.

Holloway said, "You-all just sit right still and don't twitch an eyebrow. Brackett, you and Johnny put the handcuffs on them."

Two of the thieves were grown men. One snarled at the other, "You said they wouldn't come after us because we didn't get none of their horses. I told you we oughtn't to've built a fire like that."

The other was the one Brackett had struck. Blood trickled down his forehead. "It was you that kept hollerin' about bein' hungry and wantin' to stop and eat."

The third sat quietly and looked frightened. He was a boy of perhaps fourteen or fifteen years. His wrists were so thin that Brackett could not make the cuffs fit tightly.

Holloway asked, "What's your name, son?"

The lad would not look at him, nor would he answer. Holloway tried again without result. He asked, "Son, is one of these men your daddy?"

That seemed to irritate the boy. He exploded, "Hell no they ain't." Then, in a subdued voice, he added, "They're friends of mine."

Holloway asked the men their names, though he already knew from their confederate's confession back at the ranger camp. One said he was John Smith. The other was John Jones. Holloway made a wry smile. "Smith and Jones. I've arrested a lot of your kinfolks in my time."

"We're from big families," the oldest man retorted.

"Of all the victims you could've picked, what made you think you could get away with a raid on ranger horses?"

"We don't know nothin' about no ranger horses. We're just honest settlers mindin' our own business, lookin' for a place to make our homes."

"I don't think you'll need to worry about a home for the next few years. The state of Texas is fixin' to give you one. Maybe I can help get your terms shortened if you'll talk to me straight."

"Straight about what?"

"Whatever I decide to ask you." Holloway turned to the boy, who by now seemed to have lost most of his fear. "I'm askin' you again, son, what is your name?"

The answer was curt. "Brown. Bobby Brown."

"Jones, Smith, and Brown. You got yourself tied in with some real gallows bait, son. They'll get you nothin' except a hard life and an early death."

"I already had the hard life. Maybe death ain't so bad."

"Don't you believe in hell?"

"Hell can't be no worse than what I've already had. And the devil can't be no meaner than some people I know."

Andy felt a swelling of pity. It was clear that this boy had been badly treated for a long time.

The outlaw who called himself Smith quickly put in, "It wasn't us. We been good to him. Treated him like a kid brother almost."

Holloway's voice had acid in it. "Teachin' him to be like you?"

"Teachin' him how to get along in a hard world. Every boy needs to learn a trade."

"Some trade, stealin' horses."

"We ain't stole no horses. You see any of your horses in this camp?"

"It's not because you didn't try." Holloway studied the boy a minute. "We ought to hang the two of you right here for leadin' this kid astray."

The boy came to their defense. "Wasn't nobody around to take care of me after my mama died. My daddy's in jail. Goin' to be there for a long time. Arliss and Brewster, they picked me up and let me come along with them. Didn't nobody else care if I lived or died."

Holloway almost smiled. "Arliss and Brewster. Not John." He had known that all along.

Smith growled, "Them's our middle names."

Part of a deer carcass was hanging from a cedar limb, a butcher knife stuck in it. Holloway said, "Well, Arliss and Brewster, I'm grateful to you-all for providin' that venison. We've made do on cold biscuits and air all day." He jerked his head toward the deer. Tanner moved quickly to the task.

After eating his fill, Holloway fetched the fugitive book from his saddlebag. "Arliss Wilkes and Brewster Pardo. Both of your names are on the list. You're wanted for several things besides horse stealin'."

Arliss said, "We get blamed for things we didn't do."

"Accordin' to our information the boy's name is Scooter. But Scooter's not a Christian name." He looked at the youngster. The boy said nothing.

Arliss was the one who had called himself John Smith. He said, "Ain't heard no other given name but Scooter. His last name's Tennyson."

Holloway smiled. "That's more like it. See, it's not hard to talk to the rangers."

"We don't have much choice when you got guns on us."

Brackett growled, "At least we know what names to put on your headboards if you-all give us any trouble. Every man ought to have his right name on his headboard."

Later, chewing on a half-broiled strip of meat, Andy studied Scooter Tennyson. He looked as if he had been brought up in a brush thicket. His hair was a-tangle. Someone had made a bad effort at cutting it, leaving a ragged job that looked more like the work of a butcher knife than of scissors. His shirt was too large for his thin frame. It hung on him like a partially collapsed tent. His trousers, also too big, had patches on both knees and holes in both patches.

Andy let his imagination run free. He could have been in the same situation at almost the same age had it not been for Rusty Shannon. Fate had been kind to him. It appeared that nobody had been kind to this boy.

In a quiet voice he asked Holloway, "What'll happen to the kid when we take him in?"

"The state has got a home for boys like this."

"It's like a junior penitentiary, isn't it?"

"Pretty much, I guess. I've never seen it."

"Doesn't seem right. He's never had much of a chance."

"He's old enough to know right from wrong. Some people set out on a crooked trail earlier than others. He said his daddy's in jail. It's probably in the blood."

"I don't believe that. I'll bet if he was among decent folks a while he'd straighten out."

Holloway's face showed his doubt. "Maybe. You want the job?"

"I don't know that I'm the one to do it. I'm not but a few years older than him. And I've got a job as a ranger."

"I'll talk to the captain when we get back to camp. Maybe he'll see his way clear to do somethin' for the boy. What's your interest in him?"

"Maybe it's because when I look at him I see what could've become of me."

Talking to Scooter was like talking to a post. The boy turned away and made a show of ignoring Andy. His patience strained, Andy said, "I'm just tryin' to help you, kid."

"Don't need your help. Don't need nothin' but a good leavin' alone."

"You won't get much leavin' alone if they put you behind the bars."

"Maybe that's what I was born for."

"Nobody's born for a life like that. They choose it or get pushed into it. Looks to me like you've been pushed. I'd like to see you get a decent chance."

"You a preacher or somethin'?"

"No, I'm just a ranger, and a new one at that. Mostly I guess you'd say I've been a farmer."

"Then go back to your plow and leave me alone."

Andy caught a look from Holloway that said for him to ease off. The boy pulled away from Andy and closer to his outlaw friends. Holloway beckoned Andy away from the campfire, out into the darkness.

He said, "You're wastin' your breath."

"Maybe he hasn't had time to understand the trouble he's in. Once he does, he might be easier to talk to. It took me a while when I was where he's at."

"I tried once to raise an orphaned coyote pup. Thought since I'd caught him young he'd train like a dog, but he never did. He never was anything but a wild chicken-killin' coyote. I finally caught him killin' a baby calf. Bad as I hated to, I had to shoot him."

"There were folks who thought the same thing of me, comin' out of a Comanche camp."

"From what Tanner has told me, some good folks took an interest and set you right."

"Maybe that's all Scooter needs."

"I think you're puttin' yourself in for disappointment, but I'll talk to the captain."

Andy went back and sat down near Scooter, trying to think of an approach that might work. It was Scooter who made the approach. The boy said, "I heard some of what you were sayin' out there. What's this about you and the Comanches?"

Andy took the boy's interest as a hopeful sign. "They killed my folks and carried me off when I was little. Raised me for several years. I was luckier than you. Some good people cared enough to take me in and give me a home."

"I never found no good people except Arliss and Brewster. Arliss was in jail a while with my daddy. He got a notion Daddy had buried money someplace and I might know where it was. But my daddy never had enough money that he could afford to bury any."

"Arliss and Brewster aren't the kind you ought to be travelin' with."

"They're all I got." The boy went pensive. "We come across another feller a few days ago. He was nice to me. Him and Arliss and Brewster robbed a little bank over at a burg called Brownwood. But he didn't cotton to the notion of stealin' ranger horses, nor of goin' farther west. Said there wasn't no banks out there, so he left us. I kind of wished he'd stayed. Seemed smarter than Arliss and Brewster. Maybe we wouldn't have got ourselves caught."

"You were bound to get caught sooner or later."

"I felt kind of sorry for him. Said his wife got shot a while back. He was still takin' it hard."

Andy felt a tingling along his spine. "Who was he? Did he give a name?"

The boy thought for a moment. "Bascom, it was. Yeah, Bascom. At least that's what he told us."

"Corey Bascom?"

"I believe so."

Andy's excitement built. "Did he say where he was goin'?"

The boy looked at him as if he did not believe the question. "I don't never ask a thing like that. Anybody wants you to know, they'll tell you."

So Bascom had been with these two-bit badmen as recently as the last day or two. It was a starting place, at least. Andy could hardly wait to write Rusty a letter. He would do it as soon as he got back to camp.

Sometime during the night he awakened to the sound of a running horse. Brackett shouted, "That damned kid has gotten away."

Andy flung his blanket aside and pulled on the boots he had put beneath it to protect them from dew. He saw Brackett pick up a pair of handcuffs.

Brackett said, "Those cuffs were too loose on him. He slipped them off."

Holloway declared, "Andy, you're so interested in givin' the boy a chance, go see if you can catch him and bring him back. Brackett, you'd better follow along."

Wilkes and Pardo were handcuffed to the trunks of young trees. Scooter had been, too. Wilkes said, "Good for the boy. I hope he gets plumb to Mexico."

Holloway took a quick inventory of the horses. "At least the kid has an eye for horseflesh. He took mine. You'll have to ride hard to catch him."

Andy could not see far in the darkness, but the hoofbeats had told him the boy was headed west. He wished he had Long Red with him. The sorrel had outrun almost everything Andy had ever pitted him against. He had not tested the gray for speed, but he gave it the spurs. He felt the rush of wind in his eyes and ears. Limbs whipped him across the face and shoulders.

Brackett shouted, "You'd better slow down. That horse is liable to fall and bust his leg."

The horse had better night vision than Andy, for it leaped over fallen limbs and cut around trees Andy had not seen. He leaned low in the saddle and gave the animal its head.

He saw the dark shape of the fugitive ahead of him, making a crooked trail through the cedar brush and live oaks. "Scooter," he shouted. "Stop."

Scooter shouted a reply. Andy could not discern the words, but the tone left no doubt about their meaning. The boy was outlining Andy's ancestry in scathing detail.

The chase came to a sudden stop as a low limb caught Scooter across the chest and held him while the sergeant's horse ran on without him. By the time Andy reached him the boy lay curled up on the ground like a wounded caterpillar, gasping for lost breath. Andy demanded, "What the hell were you tryin' to do? You've just added another horse-stealin' charge to your record."

Scooter tried a sharp answer, but he could only wheeze. Brackett went after the runaway horse. It stopped when it realized it had lost its rider.

Andy gave way to anger. "There I was, beggin' the sergeant to give you a chance. Then you pull a stunt like this."

The boy was not as helpless as he had appeared. He jumped to his feet, pushed Andy aside and made a grab for the gray horse. Andy caught his shirt and pulled him away just as the boy's left foot hit the stirrup. He gave Scooter a hard shove that put the boy on the ground again.

Brackett came back, leading the sergeant's horse. He seemed to be enjoying himself. "Looks like that kid's got some badger in him, too, Badger Boy."

Andy's anger subsided. He remembered that he had tried to fight back when he was first recaptured from the Comanches. The difference was that a broken leg gave him no chance of winning. He had tried once to run away, but the weak leg had betrayed him.

"I guess we can't blame him too much for tryin'." He nodded at Scooter. "Get back on the sergeant's horse." He cut a long leather string from his saddle and tied Scooter's hands to the pommel. "I'll bet you don't slip out of that."

The boy tugged at the bonds, then began crying softly.

The last of his anger drained, Andy wanted to comfort him. "Maybe the worst thing you've done is fall in with bad company. They can't do much to you for that."

Brackett said, "He's a horse thief."

"He's just a little reckless about his borrowin'. Seems I remember you takin' one of Rusty Shannon's horses once."

"But I left another one in his place."

"One you'd 'borrowed' from the U.S. Army. Got Rusty into a lot of trouble."

"That was a whole other time. Things are different now. And this boy ain't you. He's somethin' else entirely. Pretty soon you'll be wishin' you'd never seen him."

Andy already wished that. But he *had* seen him, and he could not give up on him, any more than Rusty Shannon had given up on a half-wild kid named Badger Boy.

CHAPTER
THIRTEEN

Rusty Shannon leaned on the hoe and looked across the field at the weeds still to be chopped out of his growing corn. It was a job without an end, for before he could get the last row finished, the first would need hoeing again. He missed Andy and Tanner. Andy had always been a diligent worker. Tanner could be, too, when the mood was upon him and he wasn't fidgeting to go somewhere.

Old Shanty had ridden over here yesterday on his mule and offered to help, but Rusty had politely declined. Shanty had work enough of his own. A man of his age and frail constitution needed a lot of rocking-chair time.

"Your eyes show the miseries," Shanty had said. "This old place just keeps you studyin' about the girl you was fixin' to bring here."

"I stay busy, but it doesn't help much."

"Swingin' a hoe don't tie up your mind. Leaves you free to think too much. You need to get away a while."

"I'd be thinkin' about her no matter where I went."

He had left here twice following false rumors that he had hoped would lead him to Corey Bascom. He had ridden for days, only to be left frustrated and sick at heart. So far as he knew he had never been anywhere close to Corey.

Shanty had suggested, "Everybody says you was a good ranger once.

The man you been lookin' for could be way down in Mexico by now or plumb out to the California ocean. But there's a-plenty other sinners runnin' loose. They need catchin'. Maybe you'd ought to be a ranger again."

"It wouldn't be the same."

"Sometimes the Lord don't hand us a full bucket. We give Him thanks for what we do get, even if it's just half a bucket."

Rusty recognized Sheriff Tom Blessing's big horse coming in on the trail from town. He gratefully carried the hoe to the turn row and laid it down. Tom usually opened his conversations with either the weather or the state of the crops. He hollered, "Your corn's lookin' good."

"Not as good as the weeds."

Tom dismounted, and Rusty shook hands with him. Tom took another look across the field. "You need to go to town and hire a boy or two to help you."

"I wouldn't want to take anybody away from school."

"School's out. And workin' in the fields will teach them more practical stuff than studyin' about the history of England and all them other places a long ways off from here."

"I'll think about it. How's Mrs. Blessing?"

"Better every day, thanks to Alice." Tom frowned, waiting. "Ain't you goin' to ask me about Alice?"

Rusty thought he probably should. "How's Alice?"

"She's a good-hearted girl. Homesick, of course. And she's still afraid you resent her because she's alive and her sister's not."

At a conscious level Rusty had tried to put such feelings aside, but they still rose to the surface at unexpected times when he was not prepared to confront them. "I know it wasn't her fault. Except for her bad judgment in marryin' Corey Bascom."

"Speakin' of Corey Bascom, . . ." Tom reached into his shirt pocket. "While I was at the post office gettin' my mail I found you had a letter, too. It's from Andy. He thinks he's got a line on your man."

The envelope had been opened. Tom had read the letter. Rusty did not mind. He had far too much privacy out here anyway, living by himself. He hurried to unfold the letter, running his finger along the lines as he read.

Tom said, "They sent Andy and Len to a frontier ranger company camped way out on the San Saba River. That's where he heard about Corey Bascom."

Rusty hurried ahead to the part of the letter that told about a kid who

had ridden a short time with Bascom. His hands shook so that it was difficult to read the lines. "Reckon how many days it'll take me to get to that
camp?"

"A bunch. It's liable to be a cold trail anyway."

"No colder than others I've tried. At least we know Bascom has been
there, or close by." He turned his eyes to the west. "I've never been that far
out yonderway." He started walking toward the barn.

Tom rode along beside him. "Me and my boys will keep an eye on the
place while you're gone. Can't guarantee to cut all the weeds down, though.
If a man could get his crops to grow as good as his weeds . . ."

"To hell with the weeds."

"What about that hoe you left layin' out there?"

"To hell with the hoe, too. I've got some country to cover."

Together he and Tom sketched out a rough map. Tom said, "You've
been to Austin, so you know the road that far. From there you'll head west
into the hills. I'm a little hazy about the towns, but you'll pass through
some German settlements like Friederichsburg. From what Andy says in
the letter the camp is west of Fort Mason, close to a settlement called
Menardville. Feller told me he saw ruins of an old Spanish mission there.
Jim Bowie's name was carved over the gate."

"I'll ask directions as I go along," Rusty said.

"I wouldn't be tellin' everybody my business was I you. There's some
wild old boys out yonder. They may get hostile if they find out you're after
one of their own kind."

"I take pretty good care of myself."

"You haven't always. I've seen a couple of your scars." Tom thrust his
hand forward. "Don't worry about your farm. And don't worry about Alice.
Me and the missus never had a daughter before. It's nice havin' one for a
while."

Rusty packed a smokehouse ham and a slab of bacon as well as flour
and salt and coffee. There had been a time he could usually sustain himself
on wild game for days on end. But wherever settlers moved in, the game
tended to thin out. He saddled the bay horse and tied his pack onto a fancy-
stepping Spanish mule he had acquired at a trade day in town.

Tom warned, "I never trusted them little mules. They can kick so fast
you can't see it comin'. They'll break your leg before you can spit."

"I'll be careful."

Tom watched as Rusty rode away. He hollered, "Anything you want me
to tell Alice?"

"Just don't let any strangers see her."

In his eagerness he rode far into the first night and had to search in the darkness for a grassy spot to stake the horse and mule and for wood to build a fire. He resolved not to do that again. The road was familiar as far as Austin. He wasted no time there reminiscing about last January's confrontation over possession of the state capitol. He sought directions and nothing else.

He found the topography changed abruptly west of Austin. The road led into rocky cedar-covered hills and scattered live-oak mottes. The land was drier. He wondered at the feasibility of cultivating it. Settlers so far had restricted the plow to valley flats. A scattering of cattle, sheep, and Mexican goats made use of the hillsides, grazing the short grass, browsing whatever parts of the brushy plants were edible.

Looks like a hard place to make a living, he thought.

Yet the first settlement he encountered had a more prosperous look than he would have expected, given the land's meager prospects. The buildings were mostly of native stone, the individual pieces carefully chiseled to fit closely together. The roofs were shingled with cypress, which some artisan had trimmed to just the proper dimensions.

His second night out of Austin he reached the German town Tom had told him about, Friederichsburg. The streets were wide and generous. Most of the signs were in words he did not know, though he could figure out some that bore a passing resemblance to English, such as "Bäckerei" and "Drogerie." He found a tall wooden building with an odd steamboat-looking front. The sign proclaimed it the Nimitz Hotel.

He would not spend money on a hotel room, but he decided to treat himself to the luxury of a dining-room meal. The staff spoke English with an accent that reminded him of the way old Captain—now Judge—August Burmeister talked. After a pleasant supper of venison, gravy, and hot bread, he rode up the Hauptstrasse to look at the rest of the town. Evidently these people had wrung a living from the land despite its less than impressive appearance.

He tipped his hat to a middle-aged woman of generous proportions who was watering a flower bed from a metal bucket that had holes punched in its bottom. Her husband pulled weeds by hand from a vegetable garden beside the stone house. A young girl carried a bucket of milk up from a cow pen in back.

Rusty could see how they prospered against the odds. Everybody worked.

He received directions to the Fort Mason road and left at daylight. The little mule seemed to like Friederichsburg and resisted leaving it until Rusty applied the quirt across its hindquarters. It kicked at him and missed, then gave him a resentful look that said it would exact revenge sometime when he was not looking.

A friendly storekeeper had told him Fort Mason was forty miles away. He also hinted that trouble was brewing between some of the German settlers and a segment of the English-speaking citizens for no good reason that met the eye except that they came out of two different cultures. "Might be a good idea if you take roundance on that town," he said.

Rusty had traveled forty miles and more in a single day when the occasion demanded it, but it was hard on the animals. He decided not to push them. Chances were that Bascom's trail would be cold, as Tom had said. But if it wasn't he would not want to take it up with a worn-out horse and mule.

He camped on the bank of the James River. A German family came along in a wagon, heading in the opposite direction. They said they had found the atmosphere uncomfortable in Mason. "It is for the children that we go," the father explained, his words labored. "It is not good that they see men fight."

Rusty was aware that during the Civil War many German settlers in the hill country had remained loyal to the Union. They had suffered severely for it. Whatever the current trouble was, he suspected it had its roots in the war years and the distrust created between neighbors, even within families.

These people were short of provisions. Rusty gave them most of his flour and coffee, knowing he could replenish his supply in Mason.

He reached the town toward mid-morning. Riding in, he noticed that people watched him with suspicion. It was much like the reception he had received in Austin some months ago when that place was threatened with violence over possession of the governor's office.

The proprietor of the store where he chose to stop spoke with a German accent. He offered no pleasantries but simply sacked up some flour and coffee beans and laid them on the counter. His mistrust was palpable though his manner was civil. Rusty asked, "Where do I find the road to Menardville?"

The storekeeper seemed a little friendlier. "You do not stay here?"

"Just passin' through. Got business at a ranger camp over there."

"You are not here for the trouble?"

"Whatever your troubles may be, they're none of mine."

Leaving the store, Rusty found three men standing in the dirt street, watching him. Their grim faces indicated that their intentions were not benign. Rusty tied his provisions on the little Spanish pack mule, then turned to face the men. "You-all got business with me?"

One appointed himself spokesman. He took a step forward. "We got business with any stranger that drifts into town. How come you to stop at that Dutchman's store?"

"It was the first one I saw."

"Around here these days a man has got to know which side of the fence he stands on. There's them, and there's us. Which are you?"

"Neither. I'm a passin' stranger, and I'm fixin' to pass." He swung into the saddle, feeling angry.

Damn it, he thought, I didn't come all this way to get tangled up in somebody else's fight.

Looking back, he saw that they had caught up horses and trailed behind him. He suspected they would follow him out of town, then challenge him or perhaps even waylay him. He decided to meet their challenge here and now. Reaching down, he brought up his rifle. He turned abruptly and faced them. "I can find my own way. I'm not lookin' for any escort."

The spokesman said, "Just because you talk good English don't mean you're all right. There's some Americans around here sidin' with the Dutchmen. I'm goin' to see what you got on that pack mule and make sure you ain't smugglin' guns."

Dismounting, the man walked up to the pack mule and reached for the rope that held the pack in place. The little mule whirled half around and kicked him on the leg. The impact sounded like a small-caliber gunshot. Grabbing his knee, the man gave a cry of pain and crumpled. The other two got down to see about him while he howled that his leg was broken.

Rusty spurred the bay into a fast trot toward the Menardville road. The little mule had to trot extra fast to keep up.

He could not remember exactly what he had paid for the animal, but he decided it had been cheap at the price.

He met a horseman wearing a badge and found him to be a deputy sheriff. The lawman asked, "What was the argument down yonder?"

"No argument. Some feller got a little too close to a mule."

He could tell that he had not fooled the deputy. The man said, "Stranger, ain't you?"

"First time I was ever here. Nice lookin' town, but it's got some testy citizens."

"Was I you, I wouldn't linger. Them boys yonder belong to one side. They probably suspicion that you've come to throw in with the other." He narrowed his eyes. "Or maybe that's why you're here."

"I'm just tryin' to find my way to a ranger camp over on the San Saba."

"You a ranger?"

"Used to be."

"You're in luck. Been some rangers in town tryin' to stop trouble. A couple of them are fixin' to report back to camp. If you was to ride along with them, nobody'd bother you none."

"Just point me to where they're at."

"This used to be a pretty good town. Will be again when we get rid of a few rotten apples."

Rusty was pleased to find Jim and Johnny Morris preparing to leave Mason. He had a feeling the deputy did not fully trust him until he saw the welcome the brothers gave him, pumping his hand, slapping him about the shoulders.

The three men who had accosted him made no attempt to follow. He mentioned that to the Morris brothers.

Jim said, "You're in West Texas. A lot of frisky old boys come here when they've wore out their welcome everywhere else. Mason's not the only place that's got a two-bit local feud goin' on."

Johnny put in, "If you think there's some hard *hombres* here, you ought to see Junction City."

"Right now I'm just lookin' for Andy."

Jim said, "I hope you ain't come to take him home. Andy's took to rangerin' like a duck takes to water."

"No, I felt that way myself once. I won't try to get him to quit."

Johnny asked, "Why don't you join up with us? Captain's still got some openin's left, and you can see how bad the rangers are needed out here."

"I have my farm to worry about. And other things."

"We know about the other things. Len Tanner told us."

That was no surprise. Len had never recognized a secret in his life. Rusty explained about Andy's letter.

Jim said, "Yeah, that boy Scooter's still in camp. Rougher than a corn-cob. Andy's tryin' to work the rough edges off of him, but the kid has got a coyote eye. I wouldn't want him sneakin' up behind me."

Rusty could understand Andy's sympathy for a boy like that. Andy had been in much the same position a few years earlier. "He thinks the boy might give me a lead on Corey Bascom, the man I've been lookin' for."

"The captain's already made inquiries about that bank robbery. Andy talked to them three horse thieves 'til he was blue in the face, but he didn't find out much about Bascom. It's been so long now that I'm afraid you won't be able to pick up the trail."

"I'd like to talk to the boy, anyhow."

"Gettin' him to talk to *you* will be the hard part. He can cuss like a muleskinner, but he don't put out much information."

Sight of the ranger encampment brought back memories, most pleasant, a few painful. It looked much like the wartime camp he remembered far to the north near Fort Belknap. This one appeared better equipped, for the state's Confederate government had always teetered on the edge of bankruptcy. Necessities had been scarce, luxuries not even considered. Postwar Texas was hardly wealthy, but it was better off than ten years ago.

Jim said, "I'll introduce you to the captain."

"I'm much obliged."

Rusty remembered meeting the captain a long time back. The officer said, "Welcome to camp, Mr. Shannon. I hope you have come to enlist."

"No sir, I have other business here."

Sergeant Holloway walked into the headquarters tent. Recognition was immediate, and he grasped Rusty's hand. He said, "Captain, me and Rusty rode together up at Fort Belknap. Chased outlaws and Indians. Even caught a few now and then."

The captain said, "If you have not come to join us, what brings you so far west?"

Rusty explained about his mission and showed Andy's letter. The captain nodded grimly. "I'm afraid you've come a long way for nothing. We interrogated the three prisoners at considerable length before we sent them away to jail. All we got out of them was that a man named Bascom was with them in the bank robbery. He left them before they made a try at our horses. I sent men out to try to pick up a trail, but evidently your man traveled a public road long enough to mix his tracks with a hundred others."

"What about the boy?"

"He is still here in camp, to everybody's regret. Private Pickard thinks he can redeem him. I had about as leave try to redeem a wildcat cub."

"Andy's got a good heart."

"One that outweighs his judgment, I am sad to say. I'd have already sent that young heathen back east to the dubious mercy of the court if

Pickard hadn't put up such an argument for him. But the boy has pushed me almost to the end of my tether." The captain glanced at Holloway. "Where *is* Pickard?"

"Out on horse guard."

"Send someone to replace him and tell him he has company." The captain gave Rusty a quiet and calculating study. "This company could use a man of your experience. Are you sure you would not like to enlist?"

"It wouldn't be fair to you. The first time I heard something new about Corey Bascom I'd be up and gone."

Andy arrived at the headquarters tent, riding his sorrel. Rusty imagined he looked older and more mature, but only a few weeks had passed since they had last seen one another. After the howdies Rusty said, "I got your letter."

Andy appeared troubled. "I didn't realize how long it would take you to get it and how long it'd take you to reach here. I'm afraid you've wasted the trip."

"I'd still like to talk to that boy."

"Don't judge Scooter too quick. He looks rough and talks rough, but he's never had much chance to be otherwise. I'd like him to get that chance."

Andy's eyes looked so earnest that Rusty could only go along with him. "All I want to do is talk. Maybe there's somethin' he's forgotten to tell."

Andy led Rusty toward the cook tent. He said, "I hope you weren't mad at me, leavin' sudden like I did. Len was goin' to report to the rangers, and it seemed like a good idea to ride along with him."

"You're old enough to know your own mind. I wasn't any older the first time I joined."

Andy showed him a boy he took to be twelve or thirteen, peeling potatoes for the black cook. A dark scowl showed his opinion of the job.

"Boy," the cook said, "there's too much tater goin' out with them peels."

The youngster flourished the knife as if threatening to use it for a weapon. "There'll be an old darkey throwed out with them if you don't leave me the hell alone."

"Captain says you've got to work if you're goin' to eat. Otherwise he's fixin' to send you where he sent them friends of yours. Be a long time before they see freedom."

"I'd be in better company than what I got here."

"I swear, youngun, I don't know what to do with you."

"You don't have to do nothin', just let me be."

Rusty gave Andy a quizzical look. "You really think you can reform that?"

"You reformed me."

"I don't remember you ever sassed me that bad."

"I'd about forgotten how to talk English. By the time I learned it again I'd smartened up." Andy moved into the cook tent. "Bo, can I borrow your helper a little while?"

"Borry him? You can *keep* him. He ain't much help to me."

Andy introduced Rusty. "Scooter, this is the man who raised me after I came back from the Indians."

Scooter gave no sign that he was impressed. To Rusty he was a freckle-faced ragamuffin in donated ranger clothes so large they swallowed him up. His hair was badly in need of barbering. His eyes were his only outstanding feature. Brown and dark as coffee beans, they seemed to be searching for a fight.

Rusty said, "I want to ask you about Corey Bascom."

Scooter's voice was full of resentment. "I already told them all I know. They've asked me twenty times."

"Didn't he give you any idea where he was goin' when he left you?"

"Didn't even say he was leavin'. Just pulled out. Told Arliss and them it was a fool idea tryin' to steal horses from the rangers. He wasn't havin' no part of it."

"What direction did he go?"

"I didn't watch." The boy stuck out his chin in a challenging gesture. "For all I know, he went straight up."

Andy gave Rusty a quiet look that said it was no use. Corey Bascom was too cagey to tell his plans to a kid he had just met. Even if the boy knew more, which was unlikely, he had no intention of sharing it.

Rusty sent him back to his potato peeling. In a show of rebellion, Scooter cut the first skin even thicker than before and flipped it at the cook.

Bo said, "Youngun, I'd like to get a preacher ahold of you. A fire-and-brimstone Baptist."

Rusty and Andy looked at one another. Andy said, "Preacher Webb."

After reflection, Rusty rejected the idea. "Preacher's gettin' too old to take on a wildcat like this."

Andy said, "But you're not."

"Don't try to push that job off onto me. I've already been down that road once, with you."

"I turned out pretty good, didn't I?"

"This boy isn't you. Like as not he'd run off the first chance he got. And if he didn't, he'd make me wish he had."

"Think about it at least. Don't be quick to say no."

"I've already said it."

Andy accepted defeat, if only for the time being. He said, "I'd better go out and finish my turn on horse guard. See you about supper." He untied the sorrel horse.

Rusty said, "I see that Farley Brackett hasn't talked you out of Long Red."

Andy leaned forward and patted the sorrel on the shoulder. "He knows he'd be wastin' his breath."

Rusty watched Andy ride out to where the rangers' extra horses were loose-herded on grass.

The captain said, "I understand you raised Private Pickard."

"Mostly he raised himself, after the Comanches. I just tried to point him in the right direction from time to time and keep him from gettin' killed."

"Now he has a notion he can do the same for that vagabond kid. I'm afraid he is letting himself in for a terrible disappointment. A tree grows as the sapling is bent. This boy has been bent the wrong way too long."

"I guess Andy feels that he owes me, and the way to pay the debt is to do for somebody else what I did for him."

"That speaks well for his intentions, if not his judgment. You'll stay the night with us, won't you, Shannon?"

"So you can keep tryin' to recruit me?"

"You've already said no. I'll not make a nuisance of myself."

"Then I'll be glad to stay. Reminds me of old times."

The cook rang the supper bell. The rangers gathered around, filling their plates from pots and Dutch ovens. The captain glanced about, then asked, "Bo, where's your young helper?"

"He ain't no helper of mine. Sneaks off every chance he gets. Didn't finish half the spuds I gave him to peel. You ever looked at his neck?"

The captain seemed puzzled. "Can't say that I have."

"He's got a ring around it. Born for a hangman's noose, if you ask me."

"That's just dirt."

After supper Len Tanner and two other rangers rode out to bring the horses up close to camp and relieve Andy of guard duty. The horses came in, and the rangers, but Rusty saw nothing of Andy. He walked up to Tanner.

"Where's Andy?"

"Didn't see him. The horses was scattered more than they ought to've been. It ain't like Andy to've rode off and left them."

Rusty felt stirrings of concern. "No, it's not. Wait 'til I get my horse. We'll go out and look for him."

Jim and Johnny Morris joined them without having to be asked. When they reached the area where the horses had grazed, Jim said, "Me and Johnny will split off and go around this way."

Rusty jerked his head at Tanner. "We'll take the other side."

He had ridden about two hundred yards when he saw Andy rise up out of the grass and stagger to his feet. Rusty whistled to Tanner, who had ridden a wider outside circle. Tanner came in a run.

Rusty saw a bloody streak down Andy's forehead, all the way to his jaw. Andy swayed as if about to fall. Rusty stepped down quickly from the saddle and caught him.

"Did Long Red fall with you?" he asked. So far as he had ever seen, the horse was surefooted.

Andy turned and caught hold of Rusty's saddle to steady himself. "Wasn't Long Red. It was Scooter."

"That kid?"

Tanner and the Morris brothers rode up. Tanner dismounted and took a critical look at Andy's head. "Looks like somebody gave him a six-shooter shampoo."

Andy started to nod but raised his hand to his head and grimaced. "Twice. You wouldn't think a boy that small could hit so hard."

Jim Morris said, "I been warnin' you about him. A little rattlesnake can bite you as bad as a big one."

Rusty said, "Let's get him back to camp. He can tell us about it there."

Jim pointed northward. "We found tracks of a horse headed off yonderway."

Andy said, "He took Long Red."

Tanner spat. "Thievin' little coyote." He mounted his horse, then freed his left foot from the stirrup. "You-all boost Andy up here."

Riding toward camp, Andy explained that Scooter had walked out around the horse herd. "Said the captain wanted to see me right away. He had stolen a pistol somewhere. Soon as I let him swing up behind me, he hit me over the head with it and shoved me out of the saddle. Then he hit me again for good measure. Next thing I remember was Rusty ridin' toward me."

"Ungrateful little whelp," Jim said. "He'd already be in jail if it wasn't for you."

Rusty said, "Not much chance of catchin' him now. It'll be dark pretty quick. By mornin' there's no tellin' how far he'll be gone."

"And on my horse," Andy lamented.

CHAPTER

FOURTEEN

A ndy's head throbbed so painfully that there were moments when he thought he might die. There were other moments when he feared he might not. He expected the captain to lecture him on his misspent sympathy for a wayward boy, but evidently the officer decided the experience was lesson enough in itself. At daylight the captain detailed the Morris brothers and another ranger to find Long Red's tracks and determine if they could be followed. By late afternoon the men were back. They had lost the trail.

Andy had expected Rusty to start home, but instead he remained in camp. For the time being, at least, he was more concerned about Andy than about trying to find Corey Bascom.

Andy was sick at heart, partly from loss of the sorrel horse but more from the realization that his good intentions toward Scooter had gone for nothing. He felt betrayed. He kept wondering if he might have done more, or done better. In a way he could not analyze, he even felt that he had let Rusty down. Rusty had taken a chance on Andy against long odds a long time ago. What Andy had tried to do for Scooter had been meant as an oblique thank-you to Rusty.

Rusty seated himself on the ground near the spread-out blankets on which Andy lay, a wet cloth across his forehead. He said, "If it's any consolation to you, Farley Brackett is mad as hell. He says if anybody deserved to steal that sorrel horse, it was him."

Andy was too miserable to appreciate Rusty's dark humor. He said, "Everybody kept tellin' me. I thought I could change Scooter the way you changed me."

"Maybe it was in his blood. More likely it's because he's been mistreated all his life. Beat a young horse every day and he'll outlaw on you. He'll reach a point where there's nothin' much you can do except shoot him. Else he's liable to kill you. That boy was ruined before you ever saw him."

"I guess. I just hoped for better."

"Look at the fugitive list the captain has. Most of the men on it had mothers and daddies who did the best they could to make somethin' out of them. Somewhere, every one of them came to a fork in the road and took the wrong direction. Most of them will never turn around. They'll stay on the devil's road 'til it leads them to the cemetery."

"You figure that's the case with Scooter?"

"He'll end up on the fugitive list, if he lives that long."

After two days Andy felt much better. He expected Rusty to start home, but Rusty showed no inclination to leave. He said he was hanging on a few days longer, hoping some word might come about Corey Bascom. Andy suspected one strong reason was that he enjoyed the rangers' company and the camp life that reminded him of other times.

Whatever the cause, Andy was comforted by Rusty's presence.

The third day after Scooter ran away, Andy saw a horse gallop into the edge of camp, lathered with sweat. The rider pulled up in front of the headquarters tent and dismounted, so exhausted he almost went to his knees. In a weak voice he called for the captain.

The officer came out before the rider could yell a second time.

The man struggled for breath. "Indians, Captain. We got Indian trouble."

Andy turned toward Rusty. He felt a cold dread. "I hoped I'd never have to face this."

Rusty said, "You had to know it was bound to come."

The captain called the company together. He asked Sergeant Holloway, "How many men could be ready to go right away?"

"We have four out on detail. Leaving a few to guard the camp, we have a dozen available men at best, sir, including ourselves."

"Very well, send a detail to bring up the horses."

Farley Brackett had not spoken directly to Andy since Scooter had absconded with the sorrel horse. Andy was conscious now of Farley watching him. He imagined the thought behind the critical eyes: that in a show-down Andy would not be able to go against his Comanche friends.

Rusty gave Andy a gentle nudge. "Somebody's got to help guard the camp. If you don't feel right about this, why don't you stay? Tell the captain you're still not up to a hard ride."

Andy wished he could. "I took an oath. Whatever the captain gives me to do, I'll do it."

"Would you feel better if I went along?"

Andy was not certain what his reaction should be. Rusty's presence always gave him a feeling of security. But in this case it might indicate doubt about Andy. "You're not a ranger anymore. It ain't your fight."

"If there's people bein' killed, it's everybody's fight."

Grim faced, the captain approached Rusty. "Shannon, we are short-handed, as you can see. You have no obligation to us, and I would not be so bold as to ask you. But if you should decide to ride with us of your own free will, I would happily accept your company. I cannot promise that the state will pay you for your services."

"Half the time I *was* a ranger I didn't get paid for it. I'm not askin' for anything now."

"Spoken like a true Texan." The captain looked at Andy. "Perhaps you should remain here."

Andy said, "I heal fast. I'll go."

He knew the chances of Indians hitting this camp were remote. The report had them many miles to the north, where they had hit a group of cowboys on roundup and had driven off a substantial number of cattle as well as horses.

Farley said, "I can't figure what the Comanches would want with cattle. Their preference runs to buffalo."

Andy replied, "The cattle are for tradin', not eatin'. They drive them north to the canyon country and swap them to Comanchero traders for white-man goods. They don't know much about money, but they know how to trade. They've been doin' it a long time."

Farley grunted, malice in his eyes. "You'd be the one to know."

Andy clenched a fist. One of these days, he thought, me and you are going to knock heads. I'm betting that mine is harder.

The rangers pushed their horses as much as they dared, stopping to camp at dusk. Andy was tired, his head aching. Rusty, on the other hand, seemed rejuvenated. He said, "I feel like I never left the rangers. It's like I've stepped back into old days at Fort Belknap."

Andy said, "The captain would be tickled to have you sign on permanent."

"I might if it wasn't for Corey Bascom. And the farm."

"People like Bascom generally come to a bad end. Sooner or later he'll try to rob the wrong outfit and somebody'll blow his light out. It doesn't have to be you." He realized that what he said about Bascom sounded more than a little like Rusty's comment about Scooter.

Rusty frowned. "If it happens that way, well and good. But if it fell to me to be the one, well, . . . I owe him for Josie."

"Do you think you have to kill him before she can be at rest?"

"No. Before *I* can be at rest."

The ranch was little more than a rough cow camp, its few structures having picket walls and dirt-covered roofs. Its owners clearly intended it to be temporary. None of the cowboys had been killed, but the outfit had been shot up and had lost most of its horses, including several with saddles on.

The wagon boss walked out to meet the rangers. His left arm rested in a sling made of tarpaulin torn from a wagon sheet. His face reddened as he described the incident. "Caught us flat-footed, the boys all scattered around the herd. Took cattle, horses . . . even the camp dog followed and never came back."

The captain said, "I'm sorry we don't have a doctor."

"We taken care of ourselves." The boss raised his wounded arm a little and winced. "This don't hurt near as much as losin' the outfit. I am madder than hell. At them, at us. I'm even a little mad at you for not bein' here when it happened."

The captain nodded. "I suppose you're entitled. Would any of you like to ride with us?"

"We ain't got but two men still on horseback, but they're rarin' to go. It's been all I could do to keep them from chasin' off after the Indians alone." He cursed. "A cowboy with no horse is a sorry sight to behold."

The rangers tarried only long enough to water their mounts and for the two hands to saddle up and join them.

The wagon boss shouted as the riders moved away, "Give them hell, rangers."

The cowboys led the way to where the attack had taken place. "Lucky none of us got killed," one said. "They seemed more interested in gettin' away with the horses and cattle than in takin' scalps."

Holloway told the captain, "If they'd just taken horses they'd be hard to catch up with. But the cattle will slow them down a right smart."

The captain said, "That is our main hope. Otherwise they would probably be out of our reach already."

Andy knew from experience that the raiders would abandon stolen horses only under heavy pressure, for these quickly became regarded as personal property. They would more readily abandon the cattle if they discovered close pursuit. Those, after all, had value to them only for trading.

He hoped they would give up the cattle and push on at a fast enough pace that the rangers would not catch them. Long ago he had been forced to a reluctant choice between white people and red. But his stomach churned with a dread that he might have to fire upon those he had for years regarded as his own.

He felt Rusty's speculative gaze. Rusty, more than anyone here, should understand Andy's conflicting emotions. Farley Brackett studied him with open distrust.

Andy might stretch the facts about his age, but he had given a man's word. He would not back down from it.

A trail left by stolen horses could sometimes be difficult to follow, but to hide the tracks of a cattle herd was impossible. Andy could have followed it with one eye shut. The Indians must have been confident that the cowboys would not be able to follow and chastise them. It was possible they were unaware so far of the rangers' reinstatement. In the past they had feared rangers more than the army or civilian volunteers. They had regarded rangers as a warrior society of unyielding determination and fearsome power.

The trail became fresher, the tracks cleanly cut, the droppings soft and still warm enough that Andy could smell them. For a while now the rangers had been coming across young calves the Indians had left behind because they could not keep up the pace. Andy heard cows bawling. His nerves tightened. He saw Rusty quietly slip the rifle from beneath his leg and bring it up to the pommel of his saddle.

The captain gave an order for the men to stop and tighten their cinches. A slipping saddle could be fatal in a running fight. He said, "If anybody feels like communing with his maker, this would be the proper time."

Andy had a dark feeling it was too late to pray for what he had hoped most, that the Indians would slip away without confrontation.

Holloway asked, "Any orders, Captain?"

"Just one, Sergeant. When we see that they've spotted us, charge. Don't give them time to take count."

Rusty said, "Sounds like old Captain Whitfield. Bible in one saddlebag, whiskey in the other. He was hell on horseback."

The Comanches had three men trailing the herd as a rear guard. They appeared surprised by sight of the rangers riding up over a stretch of rising ground. They hesitated for a moment, seemingly undecided whether to stand and give fight or to run and give warning. One carried a rifle. He threw a quick shot in the rangers' direction and wheeled about, riding away at a high lope. His partners struggled not to be left behind.

The captain said, "We've caught them asleep. Let's wake them up." He motioned with his hand and spurred his horse into a run.

The rangers split around the herd. The cattle spooked at first, splitting off in various directions. Andy thought there might be a hundred or more. The animals stopped their forward movement once the rangers pulled back together beyond the herd.

Ahead, Andy saw dust kicked up by the remuda. The Indians were whipping them into a run. The two cowboys, eagerly responding to sight of their quarry, pulled ahead of the rangers. The captain tried to call them back, but they did not hear. Or perhaps they chose not to.

Rusty spurred his bay horse. He shouted at Andy, "Let's try and catch up to those cowboys. They're liable to get themselves into a fix."

Farley Brackett pushed his horse into a run that put him a little ahead of Andy and Rusty.

The Indians stopped running. Having stampeded the stolen horses, they pulled together into a defensive line. Rough-counting by twos, Andy guessed they numbered twenty or so. They looked like a solid wall.

The captain shouted, "Don't hit them head-on. Cut around the end."

The flanking maneuver momentarily confused the Comanches, but the surprise did not last long. They broke out of the line and made for a stand of timber. Several hung back, fighting a rear-guard action. Rifles and pistols cracked, raising clouds of white smoke. Arrows whispered like wind in a stovepipe. Andy saw a couple of warriors on the ground. He heard a ranger cry out as he was hit. The vanguard of the Indians reached the timber and turned to mount a defense.

The captain shouted, "Smite them hip and thigh."

The rangers lost any semblance of a line. They plunged into the timber by ones and twos. The combat was almost hand-to-hand. Gunfire racketed in Andy's ears. He saw several Comanches who offered good targets, but he could not bring his pistol to bear on them.

He became aware that Farley had gotten himself isolated out to one side and had the full attention of three warriors. His horse was down. The ranger dodged among the trees, afoot. Andy wanted to laugh over his antagonist's precarious situation, but he sobered quickly. Farley stood a strong chance of being killed. He forced down his resentment and spurred in that direction.

Andy wanted to give the Indians a chance to escape. In Comanche he shouted, "Get away! Run!"

One paused long enough to snap a shot at him with an old muzzle-loading rifle much too cumbersome to be effective from horseback. Two warriors disappeared into the heavier growth.

The third appeared determined to bring Farley down. Farley tripped over a deadfall limb. The Indian rushed his horse toward him, drawing back an arrow in his bow. Farley turned over onto his back, eyes desperate. His hands searched for a pistol that had fallen out of his reach.

Again Andy shouted in Comanche, "Get away!"

The Indian turned, swinging the point of the arrow toward Andy. Andy saw the face and recognized it. Holding his breath, his skin afire, he aimed his pistol, then let it drift to the warrior's left. His shot missed. So did the arrow. The Indian turned his horse away and followed the others into the trees.

Andy trembled. His pounding heart seemed about to burst. The man he had almost killed was a friend to Steals the Ponies.

Ashen faced, Farley struggled to his feet. He picked up the weapon he had dropped and quickly glanced around. "Let's get out of here before they decide to come back."

Andy extended his arm. Farley grabbed it and swung up behind the saddle. He almost jerked Andy from the horse. Andy felt as if his arm had been wrenched from the shoulder.

Farley's voice trembled in the aftermath of fear. "Where's the rest of the rangers?"

Andy found it difficult to speak. "I lost sight of them in the trees. Whichever way we go, we're liable to run into Indians."

"Let's go someplace, even if it's wrong. I don't like it here atall."

Andy could understand that. "Which way?"

"Back out of this timber to where we can see somethin'."

Andy pointed his horse south, where open country showed through the trees.

Farley said, "I felt the devil's breath on my neck. It had the smell of brimstone."

Andy waited for Farley to thank him but soon concluded it was going to be a long wait. Instead Farley said, "You've got a reputation as a good shot. Wasn't no reason for you to've missed that Indian."

Andy would not admit that he had done so on purpose. He wondered if the Comanche might have missed for the same reason. "It's hard to hit a target when you're whippin' through the timber."

"Especially when it's a Comanche. Friend of yours?"

Andy did not reply. He reined up at the edge of the trees, hoping to see the other rangers. He heard continued firing at some distance and wondered how Rusty was doing. He wished they had not become separated in the excitement of the skirmish.

He heard a running horse and whirled around. A Comanche warrior was almost upon him, arrow drawn back. His mouth was open, making a war cry meant to chill the blood of an enemy. By instinct more than calculation, Andy fired. The arrow drove into his shoulder, knocking him back against Farley. He would have fallen had Farley not held him. Shock was instant. Andy's head reeled. His stomach turned over.

He was aware that the Indian had fallen from his horse and lay in a twisted heap. His face was turned upward, his dying eyes open. Andy recognized him. He was from Steals the Ponies' band.

Andy's meager breakfast came up. He felt himself slipping from the saddle. Farley pulled him back. "Don't you fall, boy. You're liable to drive that arrow plumb through. I don't want two dead Indians on my hands."

Through a red haze Andy saw several rangers ride out of the timber, driving some of the reclaimed horses. Half a dozen Indians came out in an effort to head them off. They quickly spotted Andy and Farley and moved toward them. More Indians appeared behind, blocking escape.

Farley reloaded his pistol. "Hang on. We're fixin' to ride like hell." He put the horse into a hard run straight toward the half dozen warriors. He fired one shot after another, as rapidly as he could pull the trigger. He shouted at the top of his lungs.

"Out of the way, you dog-eatin' sons of bitches!"

Andy felt consciousness slipping away, yet he found enough resentment to murmur, "Comanches don't eat dog."

He was aware that the Indians were surprised by Farley's audacity. They pulled apart, letting him pass between them, then shooting at him in vain. Incongruously Farley laughed aloud. He fired once more and brought a man down.

Farley pulled up. The rangers circled protectively around him and Andy. Andy heard Rusty's worried voice. "Lift him down. We've got to get that arrow out."

Someone said, "The horses are gettin' away."

"To hell with the horses."

Several hands eased Andy from the saddle and lowered him onto his back in the grass. Andy could see swirling images of the men through a reddish haze. He felt his shirt being ripped open.

Rusty said, "A couple of you hold him down. I sure hope that arrowhead ain't barbed."

Andy felt a sharp pain as Rusty tested the shaft, trying to determine how deeply the arrow had penetrated. Rusty said, "Grit your teeth, Andy. This won't be any fun."

Andy started to say, "I'm grittin'," but the words never quite made their way out. Instead he gave a sharp cry as Rusty gripped the shaft and jerked it free. Andy felt as if he were spinning backward, sinking into a bottomless well that blazed with flame, then went dark. The hurting diminished, and he was briefly at peace.

Rusty examined the arrow. He said, "The point is broken off. I'm afraid it may still be in there, too deep to dig for."

Andy's sense of peace was shattered by searing pain as Rusty cauterized the wound with a red-hot knife blade. Andy was aware of a sharp smell of burning flesh. He knew it was his own.

Rusty said, "Sorry. I had it done to me once, and I know it hurts like hell. But out in the field there's no other choice."

Consciousness slipped away again. Andy could hear, but he was not sure what he heard was real. It might be a dream. He thought he heard someone say, "Maybe we can fix up some sort of drag, like the Indians do."

Rusty said, "Too bumpy a ride. Liable to kill him. Let's cut down a couple of those small trees. We'll make a stretcher."

Andy had a sense of floating on air. It took some time for him to realize that the rangers had rigged a makeshift stretcher with blankets and poles.

He was being carried between two horses. The ends of the poles were tied into stirrups on each side.

He hoped the horses were gentle enough not to spill him. He had a feeling he would break like an eggshell. The wound in his shoulder felt as if a fire were burning in it. His mouth was so dry that when he ran his tongue over his lips he felt no moistening.

Rusty rode alongside him. Seeing that Andy had awakened he said, "Lay still. Else you're liable to get the blood started again. We like to've not got it stopped in the first place."

Andy had no intention of moving. It hurt too much. He was being jostled enough by the horses that carried him.

Andy found voice, though it was weak. He felt choked. "I killed a Comanche."

"You didn't have a choice. He was set on killin' you."

"But I knew him. He was one of my people."

"Maybe he knew you, too. That didn't stop him from comin' after you. Farley said—"

"Farley." Speaking the name came hard. "If I hadn't gone to pull him out of a tight spot I wouldn't have had to kill anybody."

"That's one way of lookin' at it. Another way is to realize that Farley saved your life, too. He held onto you and got you out of there."

"Where *is* Farley?"

"Helpin' drive the cattle. We got them back. Some of the horses, too."

"Anybody killed?"

"Not on our side. Couple of boys were wounded a little but not as bad as you. Can't say about the Indians."

Andy closed his eyes. He kept seeing the man he had killed. It was a face he knew. He did not want to remember the name, but it came nevertheless. The warrior had been known as Bugling Elk. He had had a piercing voice that could reach far across the prairie. Andy recalled hearing his war cry just before the warrior loosed the arrow. That cry would echo in his mind again and again, perhaps for the rest of his life.

He turned his head to one side.

Rusty said, "Hang on. I know it hurts."

It was not the wound that hurt most.

After long hesitation Rusty said, "There's somethin' else. It's good news in a way. It's also bad."

"How can it be both?"

"We found a sorrel horse amongst those we got back from the Indians. He's your Long Red."

It took a moment for Andy to grasp the ramifications. "What about Scooter?"

"We'd have to figure that the Indians got him."

Andy wanted to cry, but he was too old for it.

CHAPTER
FIFTEEN

Corey Bascom studied the cards he had dealt himself, then looked across the table into his adversary's eyes. He searched for a flicker of emotion that might betray the quality of the cowboy's poker hand. He saw a fleeting disappointment, quickly covered. He bet and the cowboy folded, as had two other players before him.

Corey had smiled little since learning of Alice's death. He did not smile now, smothering a momentary elation over winning. The penny-ante bank out at Brownwood had not been as flush as expected, and a four-way split had left him only a few days' traveling money. Since coming to Fort Worth he had more than doubled his stake, however. The lamp-lighted poker tables in Hell's Half Acre had been good to him. They usually were.

In recent years Fort Worth had become his favorite place to go for liquor, women, and some rewarding poker. Here trail outfits on their way to Kansas resupplied for the long trip that still faced them. Their cowboys grabbed a last chance to see the elephant and buck the tiger before beginning the last long leg of their trip north. They often stopped again on their way home.

For a man better than average at manipulating the pasteboards, it was a good place to pad out his roll so long as he did not pit himself against the real professionals from places like Chicago and Kansas City. The district's rowdy action had long offered temporary relief from his family's stifling influence. Though Bessie Bascom was his mother, and he had the affection for her a dutiful son should, she often rubbed him raw like burrs in his underwear. An occasional visit to Hell's Half Acre was akin to a safety valve on a steam boiler.

It had been several weeks since he had left the family, bitter that Lacey had shot Alice on his mother's orders. He had to leave, for had he stayed he might have killed Lacey. The temptation had been strong. His bitterness had only deepened since. For a time he had lost his grip to a point of feeling suicidal. He had provoked a fight with a gambler whose skill with a gun he knew was superior to his own. The son of a bitch had clubbed him to the floor with the heavy barrel of a Colt Navy revolver but had left him alive. Perhaps he had recognized Corey's brief madness for what it was and chose not to take advantage of it.

The close encounter with death had been shock enough to revive Corey's desire for life. He had wandered without purpose, always aware that local law enforcement might be on the lookout for him because of past offenses. Here in this raucous section of Fort Worth he felt relatively secure. Its peace officers were not inclined to be foolhardy. Some had a financial stake in the prosperity of Hell's Half Acre, exacting a percentage of the take as protection money. Several were known to own a substantial interest in some of the district's illicit enterprises. They were selective in their diligence as keepers of the law. Others who had no financial ax to grind were nevertheless aware of their own mortality and did not arbitrarily poke at hornets' nests.

Before he met Alice, Corey had invested enough in commercial female companionship to have bought a small ranch. Since her death the notion had repelled him. Odd, he thought. He had never expected one woman to take such a hold on him that he lost interest in all others. He had tried a couple of nights ago to break Alice's spell by going upstairs with a dark-eyed raven-haired beauty who affected a French accent and claimed to be from New Orleans. To his dismay he had not been able to get past her doorway.

He had never thought about ghosts enough to believe or disbelieve. Now he wondered if Alice's ghost might be riding on his shoulders.

Well, that New Orleans queen was probably just from Arkansas, anyway. Fort Smith, more than likely.

A rough voice demanded, "You goin' to play or just daydream about it?" The other players had shoved back from the table, but the cowboy evidently had not yet lost all of his money. Corey felt honor-bound to oblige him and see that he did not leave here overburdened. He ordered the cowboy a fresh drink and resumed the game.

As his pile grew and the cowboy's shrank, Corey became aware that a couple of men were watching him with more than casual interest. Their clothes were threadbare and dirty, as if they had been sleeping beneath a porch or in a haystack. He knew the breed on sight: two-bit footpads and pickpockets, feeding on the fringes of the real action like dogs prowling under a table in search of scraps fallen to the floor.

He sensed also that they had picked him as a target. Unless he stayed and played until dawn, he eventually had to leave the lamplight and venture out into the darkness. There they would pounce on him like coyotes on a rabbit.

Well, boys, he thought, you may be coyotes, but I ain't no rabbit.

The cowboy threw in his final hand with a gesture of disgust. "You just cleaned my plow."

Corey gave him back five dollars. "Never like to see a man leave the table dead broke." The cowboy hesitated. Pride told him to refuse. Practicality told him to take it. He took it.

Corey cast a quick glance at the two thugs. They were still watching him. He said, "Cowboy, step over to the bar and I'll buy you a drink."

Once there he said in little more than a whisper, "How would you like to earn some of your money back?"

"How? There ain't much I know to do except on horseback. I just proved I ain't no poker player."

"This won't take any skill. All you have to do is go out that door and start walkin'."

Suspicious, the cowboy said, "I was fixin' to do that, anyway. What's the catch?"

"Don't look behind you. Look in the mirror back of the bar. See those two ginks yonder in the corner? One's got a black wool hat. The other one's wearin' a cap he probably stole off of a railroad conductor."

"I see them."

"I think they've got it in mind to lift my roll. I'd like to see them disappointed."

"Then you'd ought to get you a policeman. I'm a trail hand, is all."

"Any policeman I'd find around here may be a friend of theirs. I want you to walk out ahead of me, then wait for me just out of the lamplight."

"You fixin' to use me for a decoy?"

"They won't hurt you. I won't give them the chance."

The cowboy thought it over for a minute. "I wouldn't do this if it wasn't for the money. If you let them kill me I'll be mad as hell."

"Don't worry. I'll be right behind you."

"So will they." The cowboy finished his drink. "Oh well, I'll probably get drowned anyway when we reach the Red River."

Corey watched the drover walk to the door, then pause to look back at the would-be robbers. He feared that might arouse their suspicion, but the thugs were paying no attention to the cowboy. Their gaze was fixed on Corey. He nodded a silent good night to the bartender, then strode at a leisurely pace across the room and out onto the wooden sidewalk.

The cowboy awaited him, just beyond the lamplight that fell upon the dirt street. Corey said, "Here, swap hats with me. Now start walkin' yonderway. Walk slow and stay out of the light."

He ducked into a dark passageway between the saloon and a mercantile store. In a moment he heard footsteps on the boards. A man's low voice said, "There he goes. Let's catch him before he gets to that next streetlamp."

The two footpads passed Corey's hiding place but did not glance in his direction. He stepped out behind them. Without a word he swung his pistol and slammed it against the woolen hat. The thug went to his knees. His hat rolled across the boards and out into the dirt. Corey clubbed him again for good measure.

The second robber spun around, a small derringer in his hand. Corey struck the pistol barrel down across the man's hairy knuckles, causing him to drop the tiny weapon. He jammed the muzzle of his six-shooter into the man's wide-open mouth.

"If you don't want me to blow all your teeth out, you'll raise those hands," he declared.

The thug's hands shot into the air.

Corey called, "Cowboy, you can come back now."

The cowboy stopped but took a moment to size up the situation before he risked returning. He looked down at the robber crumpled on the sidewalk. "You must've scared him to death. I didn't hear you shoot."

"Just gave him a Sam Colt massage. He'll come around directly. Search this one. Be sure he doesn't have another gun on him."

The cowboy found no weapon. Corey poked the muzzle into the thug's stomach. "Are you a fast runner?"

The robber tried to answer but could not summon voice.

Corey said, "Let's find out. I'll let you start runnin'. I'll count to five, then shoot. Now go."

The cap fell off halfway across the street, but the thug did not stop to retrieve it. Corey counted to five, then put a bullet into a wall just behind the running man. It seemed to encourage him in his speed.

He knelt and went through the fallen robber's pockets. He found a watch and some folding money. He said, "I'll bet you don't even have a pocket watch, cowboy. Here, take this one." He picked up the derringer. It was an over-and-under model that allowed two shots. "How would you like an extra gun?"

"I wouldn't even shoot a rabbit with that little thing. It'd probably make him mad enough to come after me with his teeth bared."

"Well, I'll keep it. Never know when somethin' like this might come in handy." It was small enough that a lawman might overlook it. He stuck it in his pocket. Corey also kept the money. That seemed just inasmuch as the thug had intended to take *his*.

He was a little surprised that the shot did not attract curious onlookers. It took more than a single shot to excite the citizens of Hell's Half Acre. He counted off roughly half the money he had won from the drover. "Much obliged for the help, cowboy. Like a little advice?"

"As long as it don't cost me nothin'."

"Maybe it'll save you somethin'. Stick to playin' mumblety-peg. Poker ain't your game."

He was staying in a little ten-by-twelve room above a whiskey mill. He had used it several times during his visits here and knew he did not have to worry about the management giving him away to any policeman who had more curiosity than judgment. The room key had long since been lost, but a door key would only lead to overconfidence. Any burglar worth his salt could pick a lock as easily as he could pick his teeth. A pistol beneath the pillow was much more reliable for protection.

He climbed the outside stairs and started down the short hall toward his door. Instinct told him to pause. He had left the door closed, but now it was slightly ajar. A thin streak of lamplight showed around its edges. Holding his breath, he drew his pistol. He hit the door hard and rushed into the room, then jumped to one side in case someone was waiting for him with a gun.

He almost shot his brother Newley.

The surprise left him speechless, his heart pounding hard. "I like to've killed you," he said when his breath came back. "What the hell are you doin' here?"

Newley was his next to youngest brother and his favorite of the three. Lacey had always been an irritant to him, cruel and a little dangerous when left to his own devices. Little Anse had always been headstrong and impervious to advice from anyone except Ma and Lacey. Newley was his mother's obedient lackey to the best of his limited abilities, but he showed occasional signs of thinking for himself when he was not under her shadow.

Newley was in deeper shock than Corey had been. He was still looking down the muzzle of Corey's pistol. Shakily he said, "For God's sake put that six-shooter away."

Corey did. Newley swallowed hard. The color began coming back into his face. He said, "That's the second time lately I've come near gettin' shot on your account."

"You oughtn't to surprise me like this."

"I've been huntin' you from Fort Griffin to kingdom come. This is the third time I've been to Fort Worth. I figured you'd show up here sooner or later."

"What do you want with me? I told Ma when I left that I wasn't comin' back, after she had Lacey kill Alice."

"That's one thing I came to tell you. Alice ain't dead."

Corey went stiff, his body tingling. He stared at his brother, not sure he had heard correctly. "Not dead?"

"Lacey got the shakes and picked the wrong target. It was Alice's sister he shot, not Alice."

"Her sister?" Corey's head seemed to spin.

"The one called Josie. It was a natural mistake. Ma was awful put out about it, though. She's still bound and determined to get Alice."

A chill passed through Corey. "Not if I can stop her, and I'll stop her if I have to kill her." He sat down heavily on the edge of the bed. Hell of a thing to say about one's own mother, he thought, but there weren't many mothers like Ma Bascom. "I'm glad you found me. That's good news about Alice."

"It ain't all good. You know Josie was fixin' to marry a farmer named Shannon."

"I remember some talk."

"Shannon thinks you're the one that shot Josie. He's huntin' for you with

blood in his eyes. He mistook me for you. Came within an inch of killin' me."
He explained about Shannon breaking into the room at Fat Beulah's.

Corey demanded, "Didn't you tell him it wasn't me that shot Josie?"

"I never got the chance."

"You were probably too scared to think about it."

This was a new experience for Corey, being sought for something he
didn't do. Up to now he had always been guilty as charged. "If he finds me
he'll wish he hadn't. There ain't no clodhopper goin' to get the best of me."

"This one might. He used to be a ranger. And he killed little Anse."

Corey was jarred again. "Little Anse?"

"You know he always thought he could do anything but walk on water.
He thought he could draw and shoot faster than Shannon. But he couldn't."
Newley explained that Ma had sent him and little Anse out to search for
Shannon, to try to kill him before he could find Corey. Shannon had out-
smarted them.

Corey's sense of loss over his youngest brother was tempered by his
learning that Alice was still alive. He said, "I saw Shannon once at the
Monahan place, so I'll know him on sight. But first I've got to think about
Alice. If Ma has her mind set on seein' her dead, . . ."

"You know Ma. She says it has to be done. If Alice ever testified in
court she could send us all to the penitentiary. Maybe worse."

"I'll worry about Shannon later. First thing I'll do is go to the Monahan
place and steal Alice away. I'll take her so far that Ma and Lacey will never
find her."

Newley seemed to approve. Like Corey, he had sometimes questioned
Ma's opinions, though seldom to her face. That took more courage than he
could usually muster. "I'll help you any way I can."

Corey was aware that Newley had had feelings for Alice. During the
time she had been with the Bascom family he had seen Newley watching
her with sad hound-dog eyes, wishing. Corey had no intention of sharing
her, but he knew Newley would help him get her away. Once Corey and
Alice were safe from Ma and Lacey he would cut Newley loose on his own.
The boy was weak, but maybe he could find some backbone if he were free
from Ma's poisonous influence.

"We'll leave come daylight," Corey said.

Ma always kept a dog or two. They were essentially worthless except that
they alerted anybody within hearing when someone approached the cabin.

Corey had heard her say she never expected much of a dog, so no dog had ever disappointed her. She had often been disappointed in her sons.

Corey remembered a number of occasions when she had also been disappointed in her husband, the late Ansel Bascom. She would chase him away with orders never to come back. He would return, however, and she would grudgingly accept him. After all, he usually brought money with him. She had carried on at the top of her lungs when the state police killed him, but Corey had suspected a lot of it was for show. At least she would never have to wonder anymore where he was.

Right now Ma was down to one dog. It barked long and loud until Corey dismounted and chunked a rock at it. It retreated behind the saddle shed and resumed the alarm. Ma stepped out of the picket house, a shotgun in her hands. She lowered it when she recognized the arrivals, but her stern face offered no warm greeting for the prodigal son.

She said, "I'd about decided you never was comin' back."

"I hadn't figured on it 'til Newley told me Alice is still alive."

Her face took on an ugly twist. "Only because Lacey ain't been able to get close enough to the Monahan house for a clean shot. She don't let herself be seen. I don't reckon you've worked up spine enough to do the job yourself?" She studied him a moment. "No, I didn't figure you would."

"I came here hopin' I might talk you into leavin' Alice alone. I'll take her far away, to where the law never heard of us."

"Sooner or later she'd get dissatisfied and want to come home. She's like a dagger hangin' over this family."

"Not if I take her plumb out of the country."

"You'll have to kill a bunch of Monahans to get her, and she wouldn't have anything to do with you after that. If she wanted you she'd have come back here already."

"Knowin' you intended to kill her? She's not a fool."

"Maybe not, but you are. If she ever got on a witness stand she'd talk like a revival preacher. Whatever me and Lacey done, we done to protect this family."

"Shootin' the wrong woman and settin' a ranger on my trail? The best protection I can think of is distance. Once I get Alice, you won't see any more of me or her."

"You ain't got her yet. We don't even know for sure if she's still at the Monahans'. Lacey thinks they might've spirited her away someplace."

"If so, they can't take her so far that I can't find her."

"Then you'd better be sure you find her before me and Lacey do. Otherwise . . ." She shook her head sadly. "I thought I'd raised you better than to let a pretty face turn you against your own. Your poor old pa would be mightily ashamed."

"My poor old pa never felt ashamed for anything in his life except gettin' caught. Where *is* Lacey, anyway?"

Ma jerked her head toward the cabin. "Catchin' him some rest. He's laid up many a night watchin' the Monahan place, hopin' for another chance at Alice."

"You tell him that if he tries again I'll kill him."

"You'd kill your own brother?"

"Dead as a gut-shot mule." Corey could not remember a completely happy day he and Lacey had ever spent together. He glanced at Newley. "You comin' or stayin' here?"

Newley shrugged as if neither choice offered any pleasure. "I reckon I'll go along with you."

Newley showed him where they had buried little Anse beneath a tree a couple of hundred yards from the house. The marker was a cross made from two pieces of pine lumber. Painted on it in crude letters was *Ansl Bascom*.

Couldn't even spell his name right, Corey thought. It didn't matter much. Nobody was likely to see it except family. The paint would weather away, the cross would fall over and rot, and the grave would be forgotten. It would be as if little Anse had never lived. Other than immediate family and the Bascoms' victims, no one had ever cared.

Poor kid never had much chance. He let Ma run his life, and obeying her had caused his death. Corey felt more resentment toward his mother than toward the man who had shot little Anse.

He asked Newley, "Are you' set for a few more days' ride? I figure on goin' to the Monahan farm."

"Why not? All I've done lately is travel."

Corey and Newley sat on their horses in the edge of the timber and studied the Monahan farm three hundred yards away. It looked no different than the last time Corey had seen it. He knew things had changed drastically within the family, however. He could only imagine what a shock Josie's death must have been, coming on top of Clemmie's illness. He had developed a grudging liking for the Monahan family, though he knew his elopement with Alice had created a hostility he would never be able to over-come. It would be useless to ride in boldly and assert his claim to his wife, even if he argued that it was the only way to save her. James Monahan would probably shoot him on sight. If he didn't, and Clemmie had recovered enough to hold a gun, she would probably do it.

No, the only way would be to slip in there in the dark hours of early morning and rush her away before the family could react. That would be no easy matter. If it were, Lacey would already have sneaked in and killed her. Lacey had a streak of cowardice that limited the risk he was willing to take. Corey told himself he had no such shortcoming. Being brave did not have to include being foolish, however. He would study the situation and plan his move carefully.

The time he had worked for the Monahans had made Corey familiar with the layout of the farm, where its buildings stood in relation to one another, where he could hide horses as near as possible and the route he could take to get into the main house. He remembered the configuration of the rooms and where Alice would be sleeping. This was knowledge Lacey did not have.

It was almost certain that someone would stand watch at night. Corey was confident he could find and take care of the guard. He felt he could get into the house and into Alice's room. The real trick would be getting her out and to the horses, especially if she resisted and put up a holler. The quickest way would be out the window. The Monahans probably would not risk shooting at him for fear of hitting her in the dark.

Newley asked, "What if she ain't there? What if they've snuck her away like Ma said? You might get in the house, but you're liable to have hell gettin' out."

That question had nagged Corey, too. "I wish there was some way to be sure she's there before I go dancin' around a bear trap."

"It's a cinch you can't just ride in there and ask them."

A horse left the barn and moved in their general direction. A small boy sat on its back.

Corey motioned for Newley to pull a little farther into the trees. "Yonder may be the answer. That's Clemmie's grandson Billy. I used to saddle his pony for him so he could ride. Him and me got along real good."

"Things may be different with him now. He's old enough to know that they don't speak your name anymore without addin' a cussword to it. And if he tells his folks he saw you, they'll figure out what you've got in mind."

"We'll keep him with us a while. When he doesn't come in for supper the menfolks'll start out huntin' for him. That'll make it easier for me to grab Alice and go."

Newley shrugged. "We've been charged with everything else. Kidnappin' a kid will be somethin' new."

"Not kidnappin'. Just borrowin' for a little while."

He waited until the boy had skirted around the edge of the timber and was out of sight should anybody be looking in his direction from the houses or barn. "You stay back," he told Newley. "He doesn't know you. You might scare him."

Corey rode out to intercept the youngster. Billy reined up, surprised.

"Howdy, Billy. How's my boy?"

Billy said nothing. He lifted the reins as if he were about to turn and run away.

Corey said, "Don't be scared. I'm not fixin' to hurt you. Just want to talk. What're you doin' out here by yourself?"

Billy swallowed hard. "Lookin' for a milk cow. She ain't come in for a couple of days. Daddy says she's probably had her calf and she's hidin' it out."

"Cows do that."

"Everybody's mad at you. They wouldn't want me talkin' to you."

"I know. They think I killed your Aunt Josie, but I didn't. I wasn't even here."

Billy seemed to want to believe. "You wasn't?"

"No. If I'd known it was goin' to happen I'd have stopped it. How's your Aunt Alice?"

"I don't know."

"But she's livin' right there in your grandmother's house. How come you don't know?"

"Because she's not there. Rusty Shannon took her away, him and Andy."

Somehow Corey was not especially surprised. They had smuggled Alice out under his brother Lacey's nose. He even began to see a little humor in it. "Where did they take her, Billy?"

"Down to Rusty's farm, I guess."

"Where is his farm?"

"I've never been there. They say it's a long ways. I've heard them talk about the Colorado River."

That did not tell him much. The Colorado River cut across most of

Texas, starting somewhere up in Comanche country and flowing generally southeastward all the way down to the Gulf of Mexico. During the time Corey had worked for the Monahans he had heard them mention Shannon's farm a few times. He reasoned that it must be somewhere downriver, probably around Austin or farther east, where the settlements were no longer new.

He asked, "Are you sure they haven't mentioned the name of a town?"

Billy thought a moment. "Alice has written Granny a couple of letters. Postmark had the name of a place called Columbus."

Corey knew in a general way where Columbus was. He also knew that the letter had probably been posted miles from where Alice was staying. That was a logical precaution in case the wrong people saw it.

But Columbus was a starting place. It narrowed the search.

"Billy, it might be a good idea if you don't tell your folks you talked to me. I wouldn't want you to get a spankin' on my account."

"I wouldn't want one, either."

"And believe me, I didn't kill your aunt." He had developed a soft spot for the boy while he had lived here. Billy's approval meant something to him.

Billy said, "You were always nice to me. I never wanted to think you done what they said."

"You're a good boy. You'll be a good man someday. Now, you go find your cow. And remember, don't tell anybody about me."

The boy went on. Corey watched him a while, glad there was no reason to hold him, after all.

Newley rode closer. "You just lettin' him ride off?"

"There's no point in keepin' him. Alice is gone."

"I heard some of what he said. Where is this Columbus town?"

"Down on the Colorado River."

"What'll I tell Ma?"

"Don't tell her a damned thing. I'm goin' down there and hunt 'til I find Alice."

"And then what?"

"I'll cross that river when I get there."

CHAPTER
SIXTEEN

essie Bascom was churning butter when she heard the dog start to bark. She muttered under her breath, for she hated to be interrupted in her work. She picked up her shotgun and checked to be sure shells were in the chambers, then she stepped outside. She could not remember the last time a stranger had brought good tidings to her door. Her tensed-up shoulders relaxed when she saw that the incoming rider was her son Newley. He was alone.

"Where's your brother Corey?" she demanded as soon as Newley came within hearing distance.

"Gone."

Drawing a reluctant answer out of her sons could be almost as difficult as pulling their teeth. It always irritated her. When the boys became evasive it was a sign things were not going just right. In trying to avoid touching off her volatile temper they often carried her to the brink of violence and sometimes pushed her over. Every one of them bore marks left by her quirt, testimony to past outbursts.

"I ain't blind," she replied, "but where did he go?"

"Off huntin' for Alice. She's not at the Monahan place."

She had suspected that. "Has he got any notion where she's gone to?"

Her son's hangdog manner told her he was holding back. Dismounting, he did not look directly into her eyes. "Didn't tell me nothin'. Just rode off."

"Whichaway?"

"South."

"He must've had some notion, then. You sure you're tellin' me all of it?"

"As much as I can."

Now she was certain he knew more than he was admitting. She heard footsteps and saw her son Lacey walking up from the barn. She said, "Lacey, you've always had a knack for keepin' your younger brothers in line." He was half a head taller and thirty pounds heavier than Newley. "Corey has gone off after that Monahan wench. I think Newley knows where, but he ain't tellin'. See if you can persuade him."

Newley backed away. "I've done told you all that Corey told me. Ain't no use in us fightin'."

There was not much fight to it. Lacey got an arm under Newley's and around the back of his neck. He applied pressure until Newley cried out, "Enough."

Ma asked, "How's your memory now?"

She thought for a moment Newley was going to cry. Damned poor conduct for a grown man, in her opinion. He took after his old pa in some ways she could not abide. Ansel Bascom had always had more mouth than guts despite the glowing image of him she held up to her sons. She had wanted to make them better than their father had been, but she was often disappointed.

Newley regained his composure, to a degree. "He's just tryin' to save Alice. He knows you and Lacey want to kill her."

"Damned right we do. She's bad medicine for all of us, you included, if you had the sense to see it. Now, where's he gone?"

"He didn't tell me hisself, but I heard that little boy of the Monahans's say somethin' about a town called Columbus. It's way down on the Colorado River, the other side of Austin. Seems like that ranger Shannon has got a farm down there someplace."

"The one that killed little Anse?"

"That's him."

"So Corey figures if he can find Shannon he can find Alice."

Newley's voice took on a pleading tone. "He still loves her, Ma. Says if he finds her he'll take her a long ways off. She won't be talkin' to no court, nor testifyin' to nothin'."

"She sure won't if we can find her. And if Corey can, we can, too. You boys catch us some fresh horses to ride. And a pack horse. I'll go rustle up grub for the trip."

Newley protested, "I don't want no part of this."

"You'll go if I have to whip you like a chicken-stealin' hound. I swear I don't know what it'll take to put some manhood into you."

Lacey grabbed Newley by the collar and pushed him toward his horse. "Get goin'. I expect Corey has got a good start on us. We have a lot of country to cover."

Rusty and Tanner lifted Andy from the improvised stretcher and placed him upon a blanket on the ground. Fully conscious, Andy was aware that they had reached the cow camp. His shoulder burned all the way through. He imagined he could still feel the searing of the cauterizing blade.

Rusty asked, "You feelin' all right?"

Damn fool question, Andy thought, but he chose not to be sarcastic. He lied, "I'm makin' it fine."

The wagon boss was exuberant over recovery of the cattle. He counted the horses and accepted the losses with good grace. "You got back more than half of them," he said. "I'd already said good-bye to the whole bunch."

Though Andy knew the feeling was disloyal, he was glad the Comanches had held onto some of the horses. They had paid a considerable price. At least they would not have to return to their encampment empty-handed.

He was gratified to have Long Red again, but he grieved over the cost. He could only guess what had happened. He did not want to think about it, but the image refused to leave him. The kid probably had but one thought, to get away, and had ridden blindly into the Indian raiding party. Had he been only five or six years old they might have kept him as they had once kept Andy. But he was old enough that they would regard him as a man, a potential warrior against them. They would have made short and bloody work of him.

Perhaps everybody had been right, that Scooter was fated to a violent end, if not this way, some other. But Andy thought he had deserved at least one more chance to compensate for suffering through a life of abuse and deprivation.

Rusty had tried to ease Andy's distress. "Been many a boy even younger killed for no fault of his own. He brought this on himself."

The wagon boss gave Andy a minute's brief sympathy for his wound before turning to other matters. He told the captain, "The least I can do is make you the loan of a wagon so you can carry your wounded back to camp. And we'll whup you-all up some dinner so nobody goes away from here hungry. I hope you like beans."

The captain said, "When men are hungry, a pot of red beans is like ambrosia."

The thought of food made Andy nauseous. He knew he was running some fever.

Farley had given Andy little attention since the skirmish. Now he walked up to the blanket where Andy lay and stared down at him with accusing eyes. He said, "We're even now. You ran off the Comanche that wanted my scalp. I toted you out of there before some other heathen could snuff you out. We don't owe one another nothin', do we?"

His tone of voice rubbed Andy like coarse sand. He muttered, "Not a damned thing."

"Good, because the captain needs to know what happened out there."

Rusty butted in. "And what *did* happen?"

"This boy had a clean shot at that first Comanche. Wasn't no way he could've missed unless he wanted to. I'm thinkin' he wanted to. If that Indian hadn't got scared off he'd have killed me deader than hell."

"But he shot the next one."

"It was *his* life on the line that time. If he hadn't fired, that arrow might've gone into his heart."

"You're makin' a serious charge. You'd better think about it twice before you talk to the captain."

"I'm tellin' it the way I saw it."

"You saw it the way you wanted to see it. You've carried a grudge against Andy for a long time. Now, if you're lookin' for a fight, . . ."

Andy raised his good hand. "Rusty, don't. There's no use you and him bloodyin' one another. The truth is, he's right."

Rusty did not show as much surprise as Andy would have expected. He had probably sensed it all along but was willing to fight for Andy's sake.

Andy said, "I recognized the one that was after Farley. He used to teach me how to track game. I hoped I could scare him off without killin' him."

Farley said, "So you left him alive to raid again."

Rusty retorted, "Killin' or not killin' one Indian ain't goin' to make much difference. There's still aplenty more."

Farley said, "The point is that when it came to makin' a choice, he chose the Comanches over his friends."

Rusty argued, "You never was his friend. A friend wouldn't carry a story like this to the captain."

Their voices were becoming strident. Andy tried to shout to get their attention, but he could not muster the strength. He waved his hand. "You-all back off. I'll tell the captain myself."

Farley continued to glare at Rusty. "All right, but I want to be there to see that you tell it straight."

Rusty said, "Andy doesn't lie."

The captain came around when one of the cowboys brought up a wagon. "Pickard, you and Private Mitchell will ride in this the rest of the way back to camp. It should be more comfortable than that makeshift stretcher."

Andy said, "Captain, you may want to leave me behind after you hear what I have to say."

"That you hesitated about shooting an Indian?"

Andy had not anticipated that the captain might already know. "Somebody told you?"

"No, I guessed. I halfway expected it, under the circumstances."

"And you still let me come along?"

"I doubted it would make a life-or-death difference."

"It almost did. Maybe I'd have made the second shot good if Farley's life had depended on it. Maybe not. I can't be sure."

The captain frowned. "You're hurting, and you look feverish. This discussion can wait until we get back to camp and you are better fixed to know your mind." He motioned for a couple of rangers to lift Andy into the waiting wagon. They stretched him out on a folded blanket.

Rusty leaned worriedly over the sideboard. "If the ride gets too rough, be sure to holler. The point of that arrowhead may start workin' around in your shoulder."

Andy felt it would be fitting if a little of the arrow *was* still imbedded. It would afford a punishment of sorts for his having killed one of those he had considered his own people. It would be his penance.

Andy caught the welcome smell of wood smoke and knew the trip was almost over. By any standard the ranger camp was Spartan, but the line of tents looked like home. Reaching it meant an end to the wagon's jolting and jerking. The black cook came out to meet the arriving rangers. Andy saw him pointing with his forefinger, silently counting them one by one, smiling when he saw that none were missing. He turned his attention to Andy and Private Mitchell, the only two other than the wagon driver who did not come in on horseback. Mitchell had taken a bullet in his thigh, but it had passed through without striking a bone.

Bo clucked in sympathy. "Looks like you-all found the Indians you was lookin' for."

Tanner rode up and said, "We whupped up on them pretty good." He described the fight in more detail than the cook probably wanted to hear. Andy cringed, especially at the account of his killing an Indian.

Rusty noticed his discomfort. He said, "Len, I think I heard the captain call your name."

Tanner left. He was back in a while. "All that shootin' must've done somethin' to your hearin', Rusty. Captain wasn't lookin' for me, after all."

By then the cook was busy in the mess tent, preparing supper. Tanner went in to finish his story, but Andy did not have to listen to it.

The captain came around to check on his wounded.

Andy said, "Captain . . ."

The captain waved him off. "Get some rest, Pickard. We'll talk about it tomorrow. Or maybe the next day."

Rusty waited until the captain was out of earshot. He said, "Leave well enough alone. The captain isn't blamin' you for anything, and you shouldn't be blamin' yourself."

"I can't help it. I didn't do right by the rangers when I pulled my aim off of that first warrior. And I didn't do right by the People when I shot the other one."

"You did right by yourself. If you hadn't you'd be dead and I wouldn't be standin' here tryin' to pound some sense into you."

"When do you figure on goin' home, Rusty?"

"I haven't decided. I was kind of enjoyin' the camp. Took me back to the old days. For a little while it even made me think maybe I'd like to join up. But that skirmish took me back to a part I never did like. The farm gets to lookin' pretty good."

"Will you take me with you when you go?"

"Thought you was tired of the farm."

"Like you said, that fight has made the farm look pretty good."

"You ain't been a ranger long enough to draw your first pay, hardly."

"It'd be blood money if I did."

"That's the fever talkin'. Wait a couple of days before you jump off into a ditch you might not be able to climb out of."

The next day Andy felt like leaving the blanket and walking around the camp a little. The cook waylaid him at the mess tent. "What you need for healin' is lots of meat, wild meat. Ain't nothin' better for you than venison. Come, let me fry you up a piece of backstrap."

"You gave me more at breakfast than I could eat."

"That was a while ago. This'll put strength in your legs, let you run like a deer."

"I don't care about runnin'. I just want to get to where I can ride so I can go home."

"What's this about goin' home? Mr. Tanner been tellin' me what you done out there. You're too good a ranger to be quittin' on us now."

"Don't take what Len tells you as gospel. If hell has a place for liars, he's due a good scorchin'.'"

"Just don't be in no hurry. My old master was bad to make fast judgments. Most generally they was wrong, like the time he seen somethin' in the brush, movin' toward his hog pen. Figured it was a mongrel dog. He went chargin' in there throwin' rocks. Turned out it was a bear. You never seen a fat old man run so fast."

The next day Andy asked Rusty to saddle Long Red for him. He rode him around the outside of the camp. His shoulder ached a bit but not as much as he expected. Rusty waited for him at the corral, silently asking with his eyes.

Andy said, "It's not so bad."

"You just made a little circle. It's several days' ride back to the farm."

"Give me a couple more days. I can do it."

"That Indian still weighs heavy on your mind. Do you think a couple hundred miles will make him go away?"

"It'll put me where I'll never have to do that again."

By the third day Andy was convinced he was ready. Rusty followed him to the captain's tent but remained outside. Andy asked, "You got time to talk to me, Captain?"

The captain studied him, then shrugged in resignation. "Your face betrays your decision. You are not a good poker player."

"I've decided to resign. I'm goin' home with Rusty."

"I believe you have it in you to become an exceptional ranger. Perhaps even an officer someday. May I suggest an alternative course?"

"Won't hurt to listen to it."

"In view of your wound and the healing time it will require, you are due a leave of absence. Without pay, of course. At the end of that time, if you are still of the same mind, I will accept your resignation with regret."

Andy considered. This was a way of leaving the door ajar without firmly committing himself. "Sounds fair to me, sir. I'll write you if I decide not to come back."

The captain extended his hand. "Don't push yourself too hard. You may be hurt more than you realize."

More than *you* realize, Andy thought. The pain was not all physical.

Andy hesitated at the front opening. He turned back. "If you ever find out just what happened to Scooter, . . ." Someone, sometime, might come across the boy's body.

"It's not likely we'll ever know."

Rusty frowned. "Looks to me like you're carryin' a double load, that boy and that Indian. You couldn't help either one of them."

Like you couldn't help Josie, Andy thought. Me and you are both saddled with ghosts.

They prepared to leave the ranger camp after breakfast. Rusty made one last attempt to postpone the trip. "A couple more days would make you stronger."

"In a couple of days we'll be closer to home."

Rusty took the pack mule's lead rope. After a mile or so he could turn the mule loose and trust it to follow the horses. "If that shoulder really gets to hurtin', let me know. We'll stop and rest."

"I'll holler." Andy had no thought of doing so unless the hurting became more than he could handle. He had made strong talk and intended to back it up. By mid-afternoon he was gritting his teeth in an effort not to give in to the pain. Rusty must have sensed it. He dismounted beside a narrow creek.

"We've come twenty-five miles or so. My bay is commencin' to slow down."

Andy was grateful but felt obliged to put up a good front. "Me and Long Red are doin' fine."

"We've got to consider the stock." Rusty unsaddled and caught the mule. He lifted the pack of provisions from its back. "Bo gave us enough vittles to get us to Friedrichsburg or maybe Austin. We can swing around and miss the troubles in Mason town."

"You know about them?"

"I didn't get a very warm welcome there. It's a local feud. No point in us gettin' mixed up in it."

"The rangers *are* mixed up in it, a little. The captain's been sendin' men over to try and hold the lid down."

"It's a good thing Texas has rangers again."

"It is. But there's no law says I have to be one of them."

They reached Friedrichsburg on the third day of a slow trip. Rusty said, "Bo was right good for a camp cook, but you're fixin' to get one of the best meals this side of Clemmie Monahan's table." He took Andy into the Nimitz Hotel for supper. Andy felt out of place with the white tablecloths and fine tableware.

Rusty said, "I could get spoiled in a hurry with fixin's like this."

Andy realized Rusty was trying to lift his spirits, to relieve for even a while the darkness that had come over him since the fight. He made up his mind to smile and enjoy it whether he wanted to or not.

At the easy pace Rusty set, they were more than a week in getting back to the farm. At a glance Andy knew someone had been taking care of the place in Rusty's absence. Tom Blessing and his sons, he guessed, and perhaps old Shanty. The corn was near shoulder-high. In the garden, cut and shriveled weeds showed the mark of a hoe.

Rusty said, "Maybe your shoulder will be a lot better by the time the garden needs much work again."

"It feels better this mornin' just by us gettin' here. I don't aim to lay around doin' nothin'."

"I don't want you takin' on very much for a while. You might ruin that shoulder. I'd have a cripple on my hands from now on."

"The place won't be the same without Len Tanner comin' around every so often."

"Ranger or not, he'll find a way. You go in and get a fire started so we can fix dinner. I'll unsaddle the horses and unpack the mule."

Tom Blessing came by in the early afternoon. He shouted, "Hello the house" before riding all the way in. Rusty and Andy walked out on the dog run to meet him. Tom dismounted and led his horse up to the hitching post.

"Saw smoke from your chimney, but I couldn't be sure if it was you or some passin' stranger stopped to fix him a meal. Glad to see you home." He looked at Andy. "Thought you joined the rangers." He noticed Andy's bandaged shoulder. "What did you get in the way of?"

Rusty answered for Andy. "A Comanche arrow. Andy hasn't made up his mind if he wants to be a ranger anymore. How's Mrs. Blessing?"

"That Alice girl has been like a tonic to her. She's startin' to act like she's thirty again. Forty, anyway." Tom's smile gave way to an expression of concern. "I'm glad you've made it home. We've got to do somethin' about Alice."

Rusty turned apprehensive. "Somethin' happened to her?"

"Not yet, but she's awful homesick. Wants to go see her mother. Every time I leave the house, I worry that she may not be there when I get back."

"You think she'd go all by herself?"

Tom nodded. "I wouldn't be surprised. She's got nerve."

"Nerve runs in the Monahan family. But she can't take care of herself against the likes of Corey Bascom. He already tried once to kill her. He might get it done the next time."

"I wish you'd go talk to her. My wife tends to take Alice's side. Neither one of them seems to realize the danger she'd put herself in, strikin' out alone."

Rusty did not study long. He said, "I'll ride over there with you."

"You'll have to go by yourself. I'm on my way to town. Got to be in court for a couple of days."

"I'll try to talk her into stayin' a while longer."

"Stayin' may not be a good idea, either. I heard a feller was in town askin' how to find your farm."

"Corey Bascom?"

"Might be. The description fits what you've told me."

Rusty smiled coldly. "Maybe I won't have to hunt him anymore. Maybe he'll come huntin' me."

Tom said, "The only reason he'd be lookin' for you would be to locate Alice. If he can find out where you are, it's only a matter of time 'til he learns where Alice is. We need to move that girl to a safer place."

"I could bring her here. And when he comes for her, I'll have him."

Tom gave him a look of disbelief. "Use that girl for bait? It's not like you, Rusty. What if somethin' went wrong?"

Rusty reconsidered. "You're right. It was a fool notion that just popped into my head."

"The reason you brought her to my place was so her husband couldn't find her. Now I'm afraid he's fixin' to. She's been wantin' to go home, and I'd say that's the best place for her, amongst her own folks. They can protect her better than I can."

Andy had listened without saying anything. Now he told Rusty, "You snuck her away from home in the dead of night. You could do the same thing again."

Rusty nodded. "Looks like that's what I've got to do. Think you can take care of yourself 'til I get back?"

"You're talkin' to a ranger. Used-to-be ranger, anyway. Go and do what has to be done."

CHAPTER

SEVENTEEN

Rusty had just finished unpacking the mule. Now he packed again with provisions for the several days' ride to the Monahan farm. Andy helped where he could, though he had but one hand to work with. He said, "There's liable to be gossip, you and Alice goin' all the way up there by yourselves. It'll take several days . . . and nights."

"I've got no interest in Alice, not in that way. I'm just tryin' to save her life."

"And maybe playin' hell with her reputation."

"Reputation doesn't plow a field or put money in the bank, and gossip doesn't draw blood. Everybody knows it was Josie I wanted. Alice is too young for me."

"Not that much younger than Josie was. Looks a lot like her, too. All three of them Monahan girls favored one another."

Rusty felt a rising irritation. In an oblique way Andy was reminding him that he had lost Geneva, then had first been attracted to Josie because she resembled her older sister. True, Alice looked a bit like Josie, but that was different. Besides, she was married, or would be until justice overtook Corey Bascom. It wasn't in Rusty to trifle with a married woman even if she did remind him a little of Josie and Geneva.

Riding toward Tom's place, he considered the long trip ahead. He did not expect pursuit if they got away in the dark of the moon. They would strike out across country instead of following the usual trails, so interception would be unlikely even if Corey outguessed them.

He had an uneasy feeling that he was being followed. Looking back, he saw no one.

Getting Indian notions like Andy, he thought.

After a time he came to a dry creekbed and took advantage of its cover to double back on his trail. Still he saw no one. He decided Tom's report had cut the reins on his imagination.

Alice stood on the dog run, watching his approach. For a moment the sight of her was unnerving. He could easily have mistaken her for Josie. Andy's words came back to him. By the time Rusty reached the double cabin, Mrs. Blessing stood at Alice's side. She looked stronger than he had seen her in the past year.

Rusty took off his hat and spoke first to Mrs. Blessing because she was the oldest and due the deference. Then he told Alice, "I was talkin' to Tom. He said you're itchin' to go home."

"Don't try to talk me out of it. I've been away too long."

"Hear anything from your mother?"

"Her letters say she's a lot better. Walkin' on her own, doin' most of the things she wants to. But she still needs my help."

She sounds like Josie, too, he thought.

Mrs. Blessing said, "I hate to lose Alice, but she's right. It's time you took her home. She'll be a godsend to her mother like she's been to me."

Rusty had argued with himself on the way over here. Should he tell Alice that Corey might be about to track her down? He had decided she was entitled to know about the danger she faced. He said, "Somebody's been askin' questions about my farm. Tom thinks it was probably Corey. Once he finds me it won't take him long to find you."

The news did not disturb her as much as he had thought it might. "All the more reason I ought to go home."

"That's what I brought the pack mule for. Soon as it's good and dark we'll leave. You'd best pack whatever you want to take."

Alice smiled the way Josie used to smile, and Geneva. "*Home.* The prettiest word I know."

Mrs. Blessing said, "I'll miss you, but it's for the best if you're in danger here."

Rusty led the bay horse and the mule down to the barn. He took off the saddle and pack and poured some dry oats into a wooden trough. "Eat good, boys. You've come a long ways, and you've hardly got started yet."

The two women cooked supper, the best meal Rusty had eaten since the hotel in Friedrichsburg. Afterward he stood on the dog run or walked around the outside of the cabin, looking for anyone who might be out there watching. Dusk seemed to last for hours. He tingled with anxiety to be on his way.

At last, when he thought it was dark enough, he went out to the barn and packed the mule, then saddled the two horses. He was about to lead them from the corral when the mule snorted and poked its long ears forward. Rusty turned quickly, but not quickly enough. He caught a glimpse of a dark figure just before a gun barrel came down on his head. It knocked him to his knees and elbows.

A rough voice said, "I always found that the best way to win a fight is to get in the first lick. That one was for little Anse. Try to get up and I'll hit you again. That one will be for me."

Rusty felt paralyzed, unable to move. He knew this was Corey Bascom. He wanted to shout to Alice to stay away, but he could not summon voice.

He sensed that she was on her way to the barn. He could hear her footsteps. She opened the gate and said, "I'm ready, Rusty."

Corey said, "Rusty ain't ready, but I am."

She made a sharp, involuntary cry before he grabbed her and clapped a hand over her mouth. "Don't holler. I wouldn't want somebody else to come out here and get hurt."

He removed the hand from her face. She gasped. "Corey! What're you fixin' to do?"

"Same as he was, gettin' you away from here before Ma and Lacey find you. I know they're lookin' because I've felt their breath on the back of my neck."

"What makes you think I'd go with you?"

"Because I ain't givin' you any choice. Listen, woman, I'm tryin' to keep you from bein' killed."

"Like you killed Josie?"

"I didn't kill Josie. That's the God's truth. Lacey done it. He thought she was you. Next time he may not miss."

She took a moment to consider that. "I'm inclined to believe you. But Rusty was fixin' to take me back to my people."

"That's too close to *my* people. I'm takin' you someplace where they'll never find you."

Rusty reached for the corral fence, trying to pull himself up. Corey raised the pistol. Alice caught his arm. "Don't, Corey, please. He was just tryin' to help me."

"From now on that's my job. You're still my wife. What's this man to you, anyway?"

"A family friend, that's all. Josie and him was plannin' on gettin' married."

"There ain't nothin' goin' on between the two of you?"

"Of course not. But please don't hurt him any more. He's already been hurt a way too much."

"I won't hurt him if you'll get on that horse and behave yourself. We're leavin' here." He threw Rusty's pistol over the fence. He unsaddled Rusty's horse and ran it out of the corral. He remounted his own and grabbed the reins of Alice's horse. He said, "I don't know what all is packed on that mule, but it'll come in handy on the trip. Let's go."

As the two rode by the cabin, Mrs. Blessing stood on the dog run, a silhouette against lamplight from the kitchen. She shouted, "Alice, I thought you-all were headed north."

Corey said, "Don't answer her."

Alice shouted back anyway. "Rusty's hurt. Out at the barn. Go help him."

"Then who's that you're with?"

Alice tried to answer, but Corey gave her horse's reins a rough jerk. She swallowed the words.

Though the rising moon was little more than a sliver and yielded faint light, she knew they were traveling south. She kept looking back in the darkness, half hoping Rusty was coming, yet afraid of what might happen if he was. She believed what Corey had said about Lacey having killed Josie. Though Corey was capable of violence, she had found it difficult to believe he could have shot her sister. Lacey, on the other hand, . . .

They rode in frosty silence a long time. Finally he demanded, "Ain't you goin' to say somethin'?"

"There's nothin' to say. You've said it all."

"You might cry a little then, so I'll know you're still breathin'."

"I got over cryin' a long time ago, after Josie died."

"I told you I had nothin' to do with that. I came near killin' Lacey for what he done. I never intended for you to be hurt, nor none of your family. Damn it, Alice, I love you."

"Is this the way you show it, by kidnappin' me?"

"I'm not kidnappin' you. You're my wife. I'm takin' you where you'll be safe."

"And where is that?"

"Mexico. I figure we can lose ourselves down there. Nobody'll find us."

"What can we do in Mexico? I'd never feel at home there. I don't even speak any Spanish. Do you?"

"A few cusswords is all."

"I don't want to go to Mexico. I want to go home. I want to see my mother walkin' again. I want to see her movin' and talkin' natural."

Corey rode a while before he spoke again. "What happened to Josie was awful. I don't want it happenin' to you."

"It won't. My family would see to that."

"What about me? Chances are your brother James would kill me, or try to. Maybe you'd like to see me dead."

"No, I wouldn't. But I believe I could handle James."

"Think you could handle your mother, too? Clemmie's cut from pure rawhide."

"I'd tell them you're still my husband, that I still love you."

"Do you, or are you just sayin' that to get what you want?"

Alice fumbled for an answer that wouldn't come. "I did love you once. Lord knows I don't want to, but maybe I still do, a little. I don't know."

"There's a way to find out." He reined his horse in beside hers. He drew her up against him and kissed her. She pulled back in surprise, unsure how to react. He kissed her again, longer and harder. She felt an unexpected flush of warmth. She found herself responding with an eagerness for which she had not been prepared.

"See?" he said. "It's still there."

She tingled, not yet quite accepting what had happened to her. "Maybe a little bit."

"I never got over you, Alice. Seems like you never got over me, either, even if you thought so. We'll make us a good life together. You'll see."

"But I still want to go home, at least long enough to see for myself that Mama is all right. Take me there, and then I'll go with you wherever you want. Colorado, California. Any place."

"Is that a promise? You're not just sayin' it to stall for time 'til you can get away from me?"

"Us Monahans were taught never to lie."

He reined up. "All right. You know the risk. But if you're willin' to take it, so am I."

"I don't understand why your mother is so bent on seein' me dead. If I intended to tell what I know about the Bascoms I'd have done it a long time ago."

"That's what she was fearful of at first. I have a feelin' it's gone way past that now. Us three sons are all she's got left in the world. She sees you takin' me away from her. She's jealous, and she's afraid."

"And maybe a little bit crazy."

"Maybe. Anyway, Oregon is way out of her reach, and they tell me it's a pretty country."

"Just one more thing. I don't want to spend the rest of my life dodgin' the law with you. Are you through with robbin' stores and banks and such?"

"Never was very good at it in the first place. There's other things I can do. I'm a pretty good carpenter and a damned good blacksmith. I could even farm if I had to. I'll make us a livin' and do it honest. I swear."

She turned her horse around and pointed toward the north star. "Home is that way."

Reluctantly he reined up beside her, pulling the pack mule after him. "You know what we might run into." He reached into his pocket and withdrew a small derringer. "Picked this up in Fort Worth a while back. Worst come to worst, you might need it."

She had been taught the use of guns ever since she was old enough to hold one. She had never handled one this small. "Looks like a toy."

"It's not. It can kill if you put the bullet in the right place."

She had never been far south of Rusty's farm. The darkness offered no landmarks, anyway. She trusted that if they rode north long enough they would come upon familiar ground. As she rode she puzzled over her contradictory emotions. She had believed any affection she once felt for Corey was gone, killed by his mother's cruelty and his own rough nature. But at least a remnant of it had survived, rekindled now by his presence. She found herself wanting him to take her in his arms and kiss her again. The thought made her ashamed, yet she took a guilty pleasure in it.

How could she hope to understand people like Corey and the whole haywire Bascom family if she did not even understand herself?

A glow in the east told her it would soon be daylight. Maybe now she could see a farmhouse and get some idea of where she was. She watched for chimney smoke. It was time for farmers and their families to be up and making breakfast. But she saw no smoke.

As the sun broke over the horizon and spilled early light across the land, she saw two horsemen.

Corey saw them, too. He said, "Damn. I hope that ain't Ma and Lacey." He drew his pistol. "Keep behind me."

The riders' faces were in shadow so that she did not recognize Rusty and Andy until they were within fifty yards. Rusty was hatless, a white bandage around his head.

She moved a little past Corey, trying to block him. "Don't shoot. They're friends."

"Not of mine." Corey brought the weapon up and drew back the hammer.

Rusty was quick to recognize Alice and Corey. He drew his pistol before he reached them.

Andy warned, "Careful. He's packin' as much artillery as you are."

Anger boiled up and strained Rusty's voice. "Move aside, Alice." He motioned with the weapon. "It's time for Corey to pay the preacher."

Her eyes pleaded as strongly as her voice. "You're wrong about him. He didn't kill Josie."

Rusty barely heard her. His hands shook with pent-up fury. "You don't owe him nothin'. I said move aside."

Andy had watched and listened, his mouth wide open. Now he pulled in front of Rusty and grabbed the hand that held the pistol.

"Hold on, Rusty. Hear her out."

"What's there to hear? He's lied to her and got her to believe it."

Alice said, "It wasn't Corey. He wasn't even there. It was his brother Lacey. He thought Josie was me."

Rusty did not want to believe. He had carried his hatred for Corey too long to turn loose of it easily. He jerked his hand free of Andy's grip and fired past Alice. Corey dropped his pistol and grabbed his right arm. He made a cry of surprise and pain.

Rusty saw that in his haste he had hardly more than scratched Corey. He leveled the pistol again. Andy grabbed Rusty's hand and gave it a twist. The muzzle pointed downward. Andy shouted, "Pull that trigger and you'll kill your horse."

"Turn me loose. Corey's got it comin'."

"By law I'm still a ranger, Rusty. I didn't resign. I just took a leave. I'm arrestin' Corey, and if you don't cool down I'll have to arrest you, too."

Rusty glared at him but found that Andy stared back with eyes that reminded him of a Comanche about to kill. Andy said firmly, "Corey's my prisoner. He's got my protection."

Slowly Rusty relaxed his grip on the pistol. Andy wrested it from his fingers and stuck it in his waistband. He said, "Maybe she's right, Rusty. Maybe Corey didn't kill Josie. And again, maybe he did, but it's up to the law to sort it all out. You were a ranger long enough to know that."

Rusty was confused, a hot streak of anger still burning. "First time you ever laid a hand on me, Andy."

"I oughtn't to've had to. You just lost your head for a minute. Once you've cooled off you'll see that I'm right."

Alice broke in, "Corey's bleedin'."

Rusty's bullet had cut a gash along Corey's forearm.

Andy said, "See what you can do for him." He stepped down to retrieve Corey's fallen pistol. He stuck it into his waistband along with Rusty's.

Alice ripped off Corey's sleeve, already torn by the bullet. She wrapped it around the wound. "That'll hold 'til we get to Rusty's cabin. Then we can fix it proper."

Rusty wrestled with his emotions. He looked in Alice's anxious face and saw Josie. He had faced the man he had searched for, then he had missed a chance to kill him. He felt uncertain and deeply frustrated. "I've ridden a thousand miles tryin' to find him. Now you're tellin' me I ought to've been huntin' for somebody else all the time." His hands trembled.

"I'm sorry, Rusty. We were all wrong about Corey. He's been tryin' to help me in his own left-handed way."

Rusty turned aside. He did not want her to see the turmoil he was going through.

Andy broke his silence. "Alice, how come you-all to be headin' back this way? Rusty came by and asked me to help him cut your trail. He figured Corey was takin' you to Mexico."

"That was his intention. I talked him out of it. I told him if he'd take me home first I'd go with him anywhere he wanted."

Rusty regained some of his composure. "You'd go with him willingly? Surely you don't still love him?"

"I didn't think so. I thought I was over him. I guess I didn't know my own feelin's."

"They're wasted on him. Even if he didn't kill Josie, they could put him away for life for what he *has* done. He's wanted for robbin' a bank over at Brownwood. Lord knows what else."

Corey complained, "I'm leakin' my life's blood. If you-all stay here talkin' all day I won't live long enough to see the jailhouse."

Rusty said, "It'd serve him right to just leave him afoot and let him die in his own slow time."

Andy said, "You know we can't do that. Even an outlaw has got certain rights."

Rusty shrugged, still conflicted. "Just so he doesn't get away. If he does, I'll kill him for sure the next time."

CHAPTER
EIGHTEEN

Rusty rode in silence, nursing his doubts, fighting confusion. His stomach was uneasy. His head still ached from the blow Corey had struck last night. He only half listened to Andy throwing questions at Alice.

"What you goin' to do about bein' married to Corey? The preachers say 'for better or worse, richer or poorer,' but they don't say what you do if your man goes to jail."

"I guess that's part of the 'worse.'"

"A lawyer could get you a divorce."

"I don't think a Monahan has ever been divorced, not as far back as anybody knows. It'd raise a scandal from here to Georgia."

Rusty saw his farm looming up ahead. He glanced at Corey, who had both hands clasped around the horn. He had paled from shock and loss of blood.

Alice said, "We're almost there, Corey."

Rusty said, "*He* wouldn't be if I was a better shot."

They stopped in front of the cabin. Andy dismounted and moved to help Alice down from her saddle, then Corey. Rusty took his time. He did not offer assistance.

Andy said, "We'll find some clean cloth and bandage him right."

Rusty grunted. "Do what you want to. He's your prisoner." He had rather have left Corey out there alone and let nature take its course.

Alice took Corey's left arm. "I'll help you with him, Andy." She started to move, then halted abruptly. Rusty saw shock in her face.

Two men and a woman stepped out of the kitchen and blocked the way onto the dog run. Bessie Bascom held her double-barreled shotgun. Lacey and Newley stood on either side of her. The old woman said, "Well, look who showed up. You people are the devil to find. Now you-all drop your guns on the ground."

Rusty had no weapon to drop. Facing the business end of those two barrels, Andy reluctantly placed his own pistol on the ground along with those belonging to Rusty and Corey.

Bessie's malevolent gaze fastened on Alice, then shifted to Corey's crudely bandaged arm. "What's the matter with my boy?"

Alice said, "He's been shot."

Bessie shifted the shotgun's muzzle toward Rusty. "Who done it? Him?"

Rusty swallowed, expecting her to shoot him.

The old woman stepped toward her son and reached out to touch the bandage. Most of the blood had dried, but a little was fresh enough to shine in the early morning sun. It stuck to her palm and fingers. She looked at her hand with revulsion and shifted her gaze back to Alice. "That comes from havin' truck with such as you. I told him you were a Jonah from the start." She swung the shotgun up into Alice's face. "You ain't puttin' a spell on any more sons of mine."

Corey stepped in front of Alice. He swayed a little but remained on his feet. "No, Ma, I ain't lettin' you."

"Get out of the way, boy."

"Before you can kill her you'll have to kill me."

The woman's eyes bulged with rage. "I'd kill anybody to protect what's left of this family."

"Not your own son."

"You've betrayed the family, just like your pa done. I killed him. I can kill you."

"It was the state police that killed Pa."

"They shot him, but I was the one told them where he'd be."

"You? Why?"

"I always kept this from you boys. He was fixin' to desert the family and run off with a saloon trollop. Now you're tryin' to run off with this piece of baggage."

Corey seemed shaken by the revelation. "She's my wife, and I love her. Killin' Alice will just make bad things worse. There's witnesses here, and one of them is a ranger."

"There won't be no witnesses when we leave." She laid the shotgun barrel against Corey's good arm and attempted to shove him aside with it. "Damn you, boy, I said move out of the way."

Corey tried to wrest the weapon from her but lacked the strength. He gave it a hard push instead, striking her chin with the barrel. She staggered. In attempting to regain her balance she let the shotgun tip down. One barrel fired.

Corey took the load in his chest and hurtled backward.

The old woman screamed. "Corey!"

She froze for a moment, choking down a rush of grief. Then she turned her fury back upon Alice. "You miserable Jezebel!" She brought the shotgun up again.

The tiny derringer flashed in Alice's hand. The shotgun tilted toward the ground and discharged its second barrel. It raised a small eruption of dust. Bessie shivered, her confused eyes fixed on Alice. She protested, "I kept tellin' him . . ."

Blood trickled from the corner of her mouth. She leaned forward, then struck the ground like a felled oak.

Rusty grabbed up his pistol from the ground. Lacey shouted, "Ma!" He reached for the weapon at his hip. It had just cleared the holster when Rusty's bullet struck him. He teetered, trying to level his pistol. Rusty fired again, twice. Lacey crumpled.

Rusty muttered, "That's for Josie."

Newley went to his knees, sobbing as Rusty and Andy swung smoking pistols in his direction. "Don't kill me. Please don't."

Alice found her voice. "Don't shoot him. He's harmless."

Rusty felt his finger tightening again on the trigger. He had to stop himself from following through as Andy moved in front of him.

Andy said, "Maybe you know him, Alice, but we don't." He took Newley's pistol. "I hope you ain't goin' to give us any trouble, Bascom. Been killin' enough already."

Newley shook. He tried to speak but brought forth only a little jibberish.

Andy surveyed the carnage. "Lord, what a mess."

Wearily Rusty seated himself on the ground. He extended his arms across his knees and rested his aching head on them. He felt his stomach churning. He had hoped avenging Josie would give him satisfaction. It had not. "I thought I'd shoot Corey and that'd be the end of it. I didn't figure it would come to all this."

Alice knelt beside Corey. She could do nothing for him. She lowered her head and wept.

Andy said, "Looks like he did love you, after all."

She was slow to answer, her voice subdued. "In his way . . . I guess he did."

Andy turned to Rusty. "At least it was the old lady that killed him, not you. You don't have to carry Corey on your conscience."

Rusty looked at the still form of Bessie Bascom. He felt he should have some regret about the old woman, but he did not. His only sympathy went to Alice. "You don't have to report that Alice shot her. Tell them I did it. It'll save her some trouble and grief."

Andy nodded. "Trouble maybe, but not grief."

Alice held Corey's limp hand. A tear rolled down her cheek. In a thin voice she said, "I never saw anybody so poisoned with hate as she was. She always talked about protectin' her family, but she destroyed it herself."

"All but one." Andy nodded toward Newley, who was still on his knees, trembling.

She said, "He never was quite like the others. They always drug him along against his will."

Andy asked Rusty, "What do you think we ought to do with him?"

Rusty felt empty. At this point he did not care. "You're the law. You call it."

"I don't have a fugitive list with me. If he's wanted for anything I don't know about it." He approached Newley. "Stand up."

Newley arose on wobbly legs.

Andy said, "Get on your horse and see how far you can go before dark. Don't let your shadow fall on this side of the Colorado River ever again."

After a silent final look at his mother and brothers, Newley hurried to the barn where the Bascoms had hidden their horses. Shortly he rode out of the corral and put his mount into a lope, heading northward.

Andy returned to Alice. "Does that suit you?"

She nodded. "He's got the Bascom taint in his blood. It'll probably get him killed, but it won't be our doin'."

Andy said, "I'll have to go tell Tom Blessing about this. I'm still a ranger, but he's the local law."

Rusty raised his head and gave Andy a long study. He did not look like a boy anymore. He said, "You did good today. It's a pity you've decided to resign."

"I never said that. I said I was comin' home to heal up and to think about it. I'm still thinkin' about it."

Rusty arose, his legs weak. He walked into the cabin's kitchen and slumped into a chair. He felt wrung out, exhausted.

Alice followed him worriedly. "Are you all right?"

Rusty shook his head. "No. Maybe next week I'll be all right again, or next month. Right now I just feel used up."

Alice looked at him with sad eyes. It struck him again how much she resembled her older sisters. But she was not them, not Geneva and not Josie. She was Alice, just as Josie had been Josie and not Geneva.

Well, at least Josie could rest easy now, he thought. He wondered when *he* would.

Several days' ride brought a nagging ache back into Andy's shoulder, but he had no intention of telling anybody about it. He followed the San Saba River, hoping the cook had been out there with his pole and line. A mess of fresh-fried catfish would make for a tasty supper after all the fat bacon he had eaten on the trail.

He saw the tents ahead and was pleased that the ranger camp had not been moved in his absence. If he ever decided to get a place of his own and settle down he might very well choose such a pleasant spot on this river where tall pecan trees spread their heavy shade along the banks and the water ran clear and cool. It carried him back in memory to some of the better times he had spent with the Comanches.

The Comanches. Reports lately from the high plains had left him with mixed feelings. It was said the army had defeated them after an almost bloodless encounter in a faraway canyon and had run off their horses. They had no choice but to give up and start a long, sad walk to the reservation. That meant he would probably never be called upon to fight them again. The rangers could shift their main attention to lawless white men instead of Indians. Yet his sympathy went to the People, like his foster brother Steals the Ponies, afoot, confined, forced to accept the dubious charity of the federal government. It was too much for a proud race to have to bear. He grieved for them.

Len Tanner was on horse guard. He hollered and put his mount into a long trot to overtake Andy. "Hey, button, how's the shoulder?"

"What shoulder?"

"You back to stay?"

"If the captain will have me."

"He's been hopin' you'd show up. Where'd you leave Rusty?"

"At home. He's decided bein' a farmer is more restful than bein' a ranger."

"Rusty ain't gettin' no younger. The ranger life is for young men like me and you."

Tanner had some gray streaks in his hair, but Andy knew that to mention it would set him off into a longer speech than Andy wanted to hear. "Where are the Morris brothers?"

"On patrol. We been havin' a lot of fun chasin' after outlaws over in Kimble County. You'll enjoy it." He turned serious. "Did Rusty ever find that feller he was huntin' for?"

"Corey Bascom? Yes, that's over and done with."

"And Alice?"

"Rusty took her back to her folks. She's safe now."

"I sort of hoped her and Rusty . . . well, it would kind of make up to him for losin' Josie like he did."

"Who knows? Rusty took a mighty deep wound, a lot worse than what I got in my shoulder. Such things take a long time to heal." Andy looked toward the row of tents. "I'd better report to the captain. Let him know I'm ready for whatever he wants me to do."

A broad grin creased Tanner's freckled face. "He'll be tickled to see you."

The captain stood in front of the headquarters tent, watching Andy approach. Andy dismounted and gave him what passed for a salute in ranger circles.

The captain returned the salute in a manner even less military than Andy's. "I've been wondering about you, Pickard. Have you healed up?"

"Enough, sir. Reportin' for duty."

"Glad to have you. I'll put you back on the pay roster. And Mr. Shannon?"

Andy shook his head. "He won't be comin'."

"A pity. But we must all make choices in this life. If you're hungry, go ask Bo to fix something for you."

Andy saw a boy sitting at the mess tent, peeling potatoes while the black cook watched. He asked, "Is that . . . ?"

The captain nodded. "It's Scooter."

"I thought the Indians got him."

"So did we all. But when the boy saw they were about to overtake him he ran into a cedarbrake and hid. The Comanches hunted for him. They came so close that he said he could hear them breathing. He laid in the cedar all night, scared to death. But at daylight they were gone. He wandered around afoot for several days, hungry, dodging rattlesnakes. Finally some cowboys found him, fed him, and brought him to us."

"Maybe he learned somethin'."

"That he did. This experience took him to the edge of hell and showed him what death looked like, face-to-face. It turned him completely around. He even says 'sir' now."

"I guess I ought to go speak to him, tell him I've still got my horse."

"Good idea." The captain smiled. "Welcome back, ranger."

TEXAS
Vendetta

To Felton Cochran,
bookseller extraordinaire

CHAPTER
ONE

For the last twelve or fifteen miles Andy Pickard and Farley Brackett had ridden in almost total silence. One ignored his partner, and the other tried to. They talked no more than the surefooted little Mexican pack mule that followed them across the Texas hill country's rocky ground. That suited Andy fine, for Farley was unlikely to say anything he wanted to listen to.

Andy speculated that the Ranger captain might have been sore at him for some reason, detailing him with dour Farley Brackett on this locate-and-arrest mission. The captain had said, "Brackett's a man I'd like to have beside me in a fight, but be damned if I'd want him for company before and after."

Farley usually looked as if he had just come back from a funeral. The captain had probably been glad to get him out of camp for two or three days and let the sunshine in.

Andy had to squint, riding directly into the setting sun. "Fixin' to be sundown pretty quick."

Farley grunted as if to say he could see that for himself and he resented the break in silence.

Night was going to catch them before they reached the Leach place. That was all right with Andy. He liked a little low-level excitement, but he had no interest in getting killed. He said, "We'd make too good a target ridin' up in broad daylight anyway. Captain told us those folks are apt to put up a fight if we don't catch them off guard."

Farley's eyes were as grim as the muzzle of a shotgun. "Anybody is liable to put up a fight when they're lookin' at a stretch in the penitentiary. These people ain't bright, but even a fool can sight down a gun barrel and kill you."

Andy and Farley carried a warrant for the arrest of one Joseph Bransford on a charge of robbery and attempted murder. He had ambushed a stock farmer back in Colorado County, leaving him for dead after taking money the farmer had collected for selling a team of mules. The captain had received a tip that Bransford was hiding out north of the Llano River on a hardscrabble homestead operated by his sister and her husband, Abner Leach. Leach claimed to be a farmer, but he was suspected of operating a way station for stolen livestock. No one had been able to prove it to the satisfaction of a jury.

So far as the captain could determine, Leach was not currently wanted by the law despite his shady reputation. However, it was probably only a matter of time before he was caught knee-deep in some ill-conceived activity that would put his name on the Rangers' fugitive list.

Farley said, "If we was to shoot them both, the taxpayers wouldn't have to foot the cost of a trial."

Coming from some people, that would be considered idle talk. In Farley's case, Andy doubted it was idle. "There's no charges out against Leach."

"There will be sooner or later. Shoot him now and we'll save some squatter from gettin' his livestock stolen."

Andy could see a certain twisted logic in Farley's view of summary justice, but it went against many stern lectures peace officers like Rusty Shannon had preached to him about the importance of law, about the presumption of innocence until guilt was proven. He wished he had Rusty with him now instead of Farley. "Rangers don't go around shootin' prisoners."

"Wake up and look around you, boy. Sometimes justice gets served out in the brush, where there's no witnesses. No petty-foggin' lawyers, no bought-off jury. Time you get a few more years on you, you'll know what I mean."

Farley had touched a sore spot. Andy was evidently the youngest man in the company, though nobody knew his age. The best guess was twenty years or a little more. Indians had killed his father and mother when he was small and had carried him off to raise as their own. Circumstances had thrust him back into Texan hands about the time his voice began to change. He had had to learn English all over again and stumble along on the white man's road, learning the hard way by trial and error—lots of error. Even with Rusty Shannon's guidance, it had been a rough road to follow after knowing only the ways of the Comanche.

He was keenly aware that he still looked young to be riding with the Rangers. He had recently tried growing a mustache in an effort to appear older. He had shaved it off after three weeks because it looked pathetically thin and weak.

Farley had remarked, "Old men try to look young, and young men try to look like their daddies. They're all lyin' to theirselves."

Andy was aware that an element of truth existed behind Farley's talk about shooting prisoners. He had heard whispered stories about outlaws shot "trying to escape." If a man was considered dangerous, it was safer to carry him in dead. And a quick burial was cheaper on the county. No criminal ever climbed out of the grave to file an appeal.

Many people were afraid of Farley Brackett, with cause. He had come home from the Yankee war with a long scar on his face and a deeper one etched into his soul. During Reconstruction years he had become a scourge to the federally backed authorities. The unionist state police had chased him often but had learned from bitter experience not to get close enough to catch him.

Once the old-time Texans regained political control of their state, transgressions against the former government had been forgiven, even applauded. The reorganized Rangers had been glad to have Farley join their ranks. He knew how men on the dodge thought and acted because he had been one. Andy thought he still had the shifty wolf eyes of a fugitive.

In the fading light of dusk Andy could make out a dim wagon trail. "You sure these tracks lead to the Leach place?"

Farley grumped, "Of course I'm sure. I'm always sure. I came this way before, huntin' a pal of Leach's that stuck up a Dutchman over in Friedrichsburg. Leach tried to point me onto the wrong trail. I ought to've shot him when I had the chance. We wouldn't have anybody to worry about now but Bransford."

They followed the wagon tracks until Andy saw lamplight ahead. "Looks like we've found the cabin."

"It never was lost. I knew where it was at."

"I guess we'll wait till they're asleep, then bust in?"

Farley assumed command by right of seniority and age. He looked at Andy as if the suggestion were the dumbest thing he had ever heard. "No, we'll make a dry camp and wait for mornin'. Bust in now and we'd have Bransford and Leach both to fight. That ain't countin' the woman, but I expect she'll just scream, faint, and fall down."

Andy argued, "In the mornin' they'll all be awake."

"We'll wait till the men are separated so we can handle them one at a time. Last time I was here, Leach came out about daylight to milk. We'll surprise him at the cow lot."

"And Bransford?"

"He'll give up when he sees we're fixin' to burn the cabin down around him."

"Or he'll come out shootin'."

"Good. We can finish him off legal and proper."

Andy protested, "We can't burn a cabin with a woman in it."

"She'll come out soon as her skirts start smokin'. With people like them, you don't ask permission or beg their pardon."

"I doubt the adjutant general would approve of it."

"The adjutant general!" Farley snorted. "Sittin' comfortable at a desk in Austin, writin' rules like he was dealin' with law-abidin' citizens. Out here the owl hoots in the daytime same as at night, and things look a lot different."

They moved back to the far side of a cedar-crowned hill where they could build a small fire without its being seen from the cabin. Farley commanded, "Cook us somethin' fit to eat."

Andy started to say, *You're a private same as me*, but changed his mind. The day might come when he had a showdown with Farley, but it would have to be over something more important than this. He took a pack from the back of the mule while Farley coaxed a small pile of dead wood into a blaze. Andy wished he had some of the dried buffalo meat that Comanches carried on long rides or the pemmican they made by pounding dried meat, berries, and nuts together. He preferred it over fatback broiled on the end of a stick. But he would settle for fatback because that was what he and Farley had brought, that and cold biscuits dried hard enough to drive a nail.

He knew no fat Rangers.

Water from their canteens yielded a cup of coffee apiece. Farley sat back, stretching his long legs, and slowly sipped his coffee as he might nurse a shot of whiskey. He seemed to withdraw into some private part of his mind, as distant as if he were back in the company headquarters camp on the San Saba River.

Andy broke a long silence. "I wish Rusty was with us." Rusty Shannon had taken charge of Andy when he was separated from the Comanches. He had become like an older brother.

"What's the matter, Badger Boy? You need a nursemaid?"

Farley took perverse pleasure in using the English version of the name by which the Comanches had known Andy. He was like some malevolent shaman who could summon up a dark and rumbling cloud from a bright and sunny sky.

Andy said, "Rusty always knows what to do."

"He's not a Ranger anymore, and it's probably a good thing. He always allowed the other feller too much of an edge. Sooner or later he'd get himself killed takin' pity on people that have got no pity comin' to them."

That was one thing Farley could never be accused of, Andy thought. "Rusty had pity on *me* when I needed help. And God knows I caused him trouble enough for a while."

Rusty had taken Andy into his log-cabin home on the Colorado River. He had managed to maintain his patience while Andy made the slow and painful transition from Comanche life. Andy had run away more than once, trying to return to his adoptive Indian family. He had fistfought boys for miles around when they ridiculed him for the Indian braids he refused to cut and the moccasins he wore instead of shoes.

The braids were gone now, and so were the moccasins. He wanted to fit in, to be the kind of Ranger Rusty had been. But he retained a remnant of Indian upbringing. It would probably always be there.

Drinking his bitter coffee, he lapsed into silence, pondering tomorrow and wishing he were as sure of himself as Farley seemed to be.

Morning was a long time in coming. Andy lay awake most of the night, visualizing the expected confrontation, imagining the worst that might happen. He pictured Leach's woman lying dead after the smoke cleared, much as he had seen his white mother dead years ago. It was one of his earliest memories, long suppressed because it was so terrible. The image still returned from time to time like a nightmare that would not wait for the night.

Farley seemed to harbor no misgivings. Andy listened to him snoring peacefully.

The stars still glittered when Farley came out from beneath his blanket. He looked up at them to get a rough notion of time. "We'd better be gettin' ourselves in position before daylight. Leach wakes up the rooster."

Andy was hungry. "Hadn't we ought to fix some breakfast first?"

"When we're done we'll make Leach's woman cook us a proper meal."

"Thought you were goin' to burn her cabin down."

"They raise pigs. We'll catch us a juicy shoat and have her roast it over the coals."

Andy started to pack the mule. Farley stopped him. "Don't you know a stupid mule is liable to smell feed and go in there brayin' his head off? We'll leave him here and pick him up when the job is done."

Chastened, Andy tied the mule.

The cabin was still dark as the two Rangers circled around to come in behind the milk shed. They left their horses in a clump of trees. The cow stood outside the gate, waiting in bovine patience for the grain that awaited her in the stanchion. She turned her head to watch the men approach on foot. She seemed to know they were strangers and drew away. She did not go far because she had not yet nursed her calf or had her morning feed. Hogs in a nearby pen grunted but quickly settled back down. Andy's nose pinched. He never had gotten used to the smell of pigs. Horses disliked them, and so did Comanches.

Presently he saw lamplight in the cabin window. A man came out carrying a bucket.

Farley said, "That's Leach. He's meaner than a boar hog with the hives. Be ready for real trouble."

"You don't figure on shootin' him, do you?"

"Not without he gives me cause. But if he gives me cause I sure won't take a chance with him."

Andy's hands were tense on his rifle. He could handle a pistol, but a rifle felt steadier and seemed to carry more authority. He could not see if Leach was armed. The man's face was featureless in the dim light of early dawn, but Andy could see that his body was broad and muscular. He looked as if he would be hard to handle in a fight.

Farley whispered, "He's got a six-shooter in his boot. Get set. It's liable to be a hell of a scrap."

Farley waited until Leach opened the gate for the cow to enter the lot. He stepped out into the open and said, "Hands up. We're Rangers." He shoved a pistol forward, almost in Leach's face.

Leach wilted and raised trembling hands. "Don't shoot. For God's sake, Ranger, don't shoot."

Farley seemed let down by the lack of resistance. "You're harborin' a fugitive. We got a warrant for Joseph Bransford's arrest."

"Go help yourself," Leach said in a quavering voice. "He's in the cabin. Only please don't shoot. I'm a married man. My wife depends on me."

Disgusted, Farley told Andy, "Cuff this cowardly son of a bitch to the fence post." He turned back to Leach, waving the pistol in his face. "If you holler I'll blow a hole in your brisket."

Fear gave Leach's voice a high pitch. "I won't make a peep."

Andy said, "That was easy."

Farley did not hide his disappointment. "Bransford is apt to come at us like a mad bull. Be ready to shoot him."

"What about the woman?"

"Don't worry none about her. She'll wilt like bluebonnets in June."

A wagon stood in front of the cabin. Farley placed himself behind it. He motioned for Andy to take cover behind a dug well ringed by a circular rock structure about three feet high, with windlass and wooden bucket on top.

Andy thought it would be more effective to burst into the cabin and take Bransford by surprise, giving him no time to put up resistance. But Farley preferred confrontation in broad daylight, where he could see his target and have plenty of room to move around.

Farley shouted, "Joseph Bransford, listen to me. We're the Rangers. There's ten of us, and we've got this cabin surrounded. Come out with your hands up or we'll burn the place and roast you like a pig."

Andy heard a woman's angry shout from inside.

For emphasis Farley fired a shot that showered splinters from the upper part of the door. He called, "Let the woman come out first. We got no paper on her."

The woman came out waving a heavy chunk of firewood. She made straight for Farley, cursing him for twelve kinds of egg-sucking dog. She was tall and broad and looked as if she could wrestle a mule to its knees. As Farley raised his arms for defense, she struck him twice. Startled, then stunned, Farley almost went to his knees. He raised his arms, trying to fend off her blows.

"Damn you, Badger Boy, do somethin'."

Farley's hat rolled on the ground. His head was bleeding.

Andy twisted the firewood from her hand and cast it away, but she closed in enough to leave deep tracks of her fingernails upon Farley's whiskered cheek.

"Get this civit cat off of me."

Andy got an arm around the woman's wide waist and dragged her away from Farley, only to have her turn on him instead. He managed to grab her strong hands and pull them behind her back. He handcuffed her to one of the posts that supported the windlass. She cursed until her voice went hoarse.

Both men struggled for breath. Farley raised a hand to his head and then looked at it. He saw blood. "Damn you, boy, how come it took you so long?"

"I thought you said she was goin' to scream, faint, and fall down."

Farley gave him a look that would wither weeds. He dragged a sleeve across his sweating face and fired a shot through the open door. "You comin' out, Bransford, or do you want to fry like a slab of bacon?"

A shaken man appeared in the doorway, hands above his head. "I give up. You don't need to shoot no more."

The woman turned her fury on him. "You ain't no brother of mine, you snivelin' coward. There ain't but two of them. You could've got them both." She looked around with wide eyes. "Where's my husband? What you done with my man?"

Farley was too choked with anger and embarrassment to answer. Andy said, "He's down at the shed, holdin' on to a fence post. Ain't done his milkin' yet."

The Rangers had just one set of handcuffs apiece, and those were both in use. Andy tied Bransford's hands with a leather string cut from his saddle. He drew the binding down tightly enough that Bransford complained about the circulation being cut off.

Farley said, "Ain't near as tight as a noose around your neck. You're lucky that farmer didn't die. Now, where's the money you took off of him?"

The woman said, "Don't you tell them nothin', Joseph. That money's ours if you'll just keep your damn-fool mouth shut."

Farley tapped the muzzle of his pistol smartly against Bransford's upper teeth. "Bad advice can get a man killed. Tell me where that money's at or I'll scatter your brains for the chickens to peck on."

Andy hoped the prisoner would see that Farley was not bluffing.

Bransford was eager to tell. "It's in there," he said, pointing to the cabin. "Come and I'll show you." Andy followed him while Farley remained outside, wiping blood from his forehead. Bransford pointed his chin toward a wooden box beside the iron stove. "It's at the bottom."

Andy said, "Stand back yonder and keep your hands high in the air." He dug the stove wood out of the box until he found a canvas sack. He could tell by the feel that it was full of paper. Coins clinked together in the bottom when he shook it.

He demanded, "Is it all there?"

Bransford was trying not to cry. All that effort and nothing left to show for it. "Just spent a little on whiskey. And I left a few dollars with a woman over to Fort McKavett." He was trembling with fright. "What you Rangers goin' to do with me?"

Andy said, "Farley is plumb sore that you didn't put up a fight. But if I can keep him from killin' you, we'll take you to camp. Then I expect they'll send you to Colorado County to stand trial."

"What you reckon they'll give me?"

"Ten to twenty years, the captain said."

Bransford mumbled, "Ten to twenty years. Seems like an awful long time for no more money than I got."

"You shot the man you took it off of."

"I wouldn't have if he'd given it to me right off like I told him to."

Andy motioned for Bransford to walk outside ahead of him. The prisoner avoided his sister's smoldering eyes. He stared at the sack, his expression solemn. "Looks like by rights that money ought to be mine, seein' as I'm goin' to give up ten to twenty years payin' for it."

Farley shook his bleeding head in disbelief. "We sure got a sorry class of criminals these days. At least the Indians gave us an honest fight."

Andy said, "I'm takin' that as a compliment."

It was as much of one as he expected to receive from Farley.

A couple of horses grazed a few hundred yards away. Andy rode out and brought back the better of the two, a grulla gelding, for Bransford to ride. The woman fought the cuffs that held her against the well. "That's my husband's horse." She resumed cursing as the three men went down to the shed.

Bransford pointed out his saddle, and Andy put it on the horse for him. "Mount up." When Bransford was in the saddle, Andy fetched up his own and Farley's horses. He unlocked Leach's cuffs and transferred them to Bransford.

Leach rubbed his raw wrists, his face twisting. "You damned Rangers think you run the world."

Farley said, "We do, and we'll be back to get you the first time you let your foot slip."

"That's my horse you put Joseph on. His is that jug-headed bay out yonder."

Farley had no sympathy. "You just traded. They're probably all stolen anyway." He mounted his horse and poked the muzzle of the pistol in Leach's direction. "Come on back up to the cabin. We ain't plumb finished with you."

When they reached the dwelling Andy leaned down from the saddle and handed Leach the key to the handcuffs that restrained his wife. "Turn her a-loose, then give me the cuffs and the key."

Farley argued, "We ought to just leave her thataway. While her man filed those cuffs off of her, she'd have time to study on a woman's proper place."

"You want to pay the captain for the cuffs?"

"I reckon not. But watch her close when you turn her loose."

Fortunately the woman seemed to have used up most of her fight as well as all the profanity she knew. She stood in fuming silence, trying to kill Andy and Farley with the hatred in her eyes. Leach handed Andy the cuffs and key.

As the three rode away the woman shouted, "Our old daddy's turnin' over in his grave, Joseph, you givin' up so easy. You better ride way around this place when you come back."

Farley turned in the saddle. "Lady, he ain't comin' back."

Andy said, "Some lady."

Farley took a final glance at the cabin. "That place would look a hell of a lot better if we'd left it in ashes."

Bransford said, "You'd really burn it down with me in it?"

"I had the matches in my hand."

Andy remarked, "Thought we were goin' to have her fix us some breakfast."

Farley shook his head. "She'd poison us."

They fixed their own when they got back to where they had left the pack mule tied.

Andy asked Farley, "How's your head?"

"If she didn't break my skull, she bent the hell out of it. And you just stood there watchin'."

"I jumped in as fast as I could." Andy saw that Farley had no interest in his side of the story. "First water we come to, we'd better wash the blood off of your face. I've seen butchered hogs that bled less."

Farley gingerly felt of his head. "Look, it's enough that we bring the prisoner in like the captain told us to. There's no reason we've got to tell him about that woman."

CHAPTER

TWO

Nearing camp, the three riders came upon the company horses scattered to graze on an open flat. They were watched over by two Rangers taking refuge from the sun's heat by shading up under a live-oak tree. The end of the long ride lifted Andy's spirits. Fatigue seemed to slip from his shoulders. The prisoner had been sullen and quiet, slouching in the saddle. Andy could understand, given the likelihood that he faced a long prison sentence. Farley had spoken little. He carried his hat on his saddlehorn, for it had been painful to wear over the knot swollen on his head.

The sound of gunshots made Bransford sit up in alarm.

Andy tried to calm him. "Just some of the boys at target practice." The captain provided an ample supply of cartridges, encouraging his men to sharpen their marksmanship. Cartridges were one of the few things besides food that the Rangers were not obliged to furnish for themselves. Even food was supplemented by whatever game they could shoot or fish they could catch.

The company camp had been established on the bank of the wide, clear San Saba River. Tall pecan trees sent roots deep into the mud and cast a cool shade over a row of canvas tents. To this company of Rangers it was home. It was an easily movable home, its location subject to the region's changeable law enforcement needs.

Earlier, the frontier batallion had busied itself primarily with keeping hostile Indians out of the settlements or chasing those who managed to get in despite the long picket line of Ranger outposts. Now that task had been largely eliminated by a relentless army push against the warring Plains tribes. A concentrated military offensive, moving in from three directions, had forced most of the Indians to give up the fight and repair to the questionable mercies of the reservation. Except for occasional limited outbreaks, the Comanches, Kiowas, and Cheyennes had been put out of action.

Apaches still roamed the far western part of the state and prowled rough hills down along the Rio Frio and upper Nueces, but the most destructive of the Indian raids were over. Of late the Rangers had turned their attention to the criminals who infested the state, especially its less settled portions, where escape was often fast and easy. Nowhere were they worse than in the limestone hills west of San Antonio, where dense cedar brakes and deep, rugged canyons offered sanctuary, where water and game were plentiful and a man could live off the land if the climate elsewhere became too hot.

Thus the principal Ranger mission had shifted from Indian fighting to domestic law enforcement, to chasing murderers and thieves and border-jumping bandits, to breaking up feuds that broke out occasionally among a prideful, independent people hardened to violence and easily stirred to deadly force.

Protocol demanded that Andy and Farley deliver their report and their prisoner to the captain before they did anything else. Bransford cast anxious eyes at the camp as if he expected someone to step out of a tent and gun him down. He sweated more than the summer heat called for.

Several Rangers emerged from the tents or from under the shady trees to observe the three men coming in. Bransford's expression became even bleaker.

Andy said, "They won't shoot you in the middle of camp, not without you give them reason to."

Farley had transferred to Bransford most of the blame for his injury. "Even if they did, who's to tell? One Ranger ain't goin' to call down the law on another. We're decent people."

Bransford cast a fearful glance at him. He had probably expected a bullet in the back all the way from the Leach farm. Andy had said nothing to disabuse him of the notion, hoping fear would have a positive effect on his behavior.

Len Tanner's clothes were always too large for him except for the trouser legs. They were a little short. The lanky Ranger walked up and stared at the prisoner. "This the gink that goes around robbin' farmers?"

Andy said, "That's the charge, but he ain't been tried yet."

Farley studied Bransford like a hungry wolf eyeing an orphaned calf. "He's guilty, all right. You can tell by lookin' at him."

Andy said, "If that was the case, we wouldn't need judges and juries."

"Far as I'm concerned, we don't. If we shot them where we find them we'd save a lot of bother."

Sergeant Bill Holloway ducked to step out of the headquarters tent, then straightened his tall frame. He squinted against the sun. Deep turkey tracks pinched around bleached blue eyes. "I see you got your man."

Farley took offense. "We wasn't sent out there to *not* get him. We've come to turn him over to the captain."

"I'll take charge of him. Captain's busy right now."

Andy could hear the captain's angry voice through the canvas. Holloway jerked his head as a signal for the men to move away from the headquarters tent. He followed them far enough that they could no longer hear the voice.

He said, "Captain doesn't like to be disturbed when he's bawlin' a man out. Dick Landon put away too much bad whiskey last night over at Fort McKavett. Got into a cuss fight and tried to bend the barrel of his six-shooter over a citizen's skull. Lucky it was one of them hardheaded Dutchmen."

It was a seldom-discussed fact of Ranger life that isolation, boredom, and frustration led some men to drink heavily when off duty, and occasionally even on duty. This could result in unjustified confrontations with civilians unlucky enough to get crossways with them. Those men who became a frequent problem to their commanders were likely to be discharged quietly and encouraged to move on lest they taint the reputation of the service.

Landon had caused disturbances before. The captain had kept him on because he was a good Ranger when sober, bold when the occasion called for it, a crack shot with pistol or rifle. Drunk, he tended to create trouble where there had been none. It was said he came from a fighting family.

Farley grumbled, "Dick ought to never drink. Whiskey makes him mean."

Andy said, "Some people don't need whiskey for that."

Farley gave him a cold stare. "If you mean me, I don't go huntin' trouble. But if it comes, I don't run."

Farley had gone out of his way during Reconstruction times to antago-
nize the state police, who were easily aroused. But Andy saw no point in
pressing the issue. Farley would never concede defeat.

Farley said, "I never shot a man that didn't need killin'. The only
regrets I've got are over some I ought've shot but didn't."

Holloway said, "I reckon Dick had reason enough to get drunk. He
helped bring his own brother in yesterday on a murder charge."

Puzzled, Andy asked, "How could he do that?"

"He's a Ranger. Dick joined to get away from a feud back in his home
county. Seems like his brother Jayce killed a man on the other side and
came out hopin' for Dick to give him protection."

"Instead, he brought him in?"

"Rangers do their duty or they quit."

"I don't know if I could do what Dick did."

"I think you would if the chips were down." Holloway led them around
the cook tent and pointed. "We'll take your man down there."

The camp had no jail. For temporary confinement, prisoners were
handcuffed to a chain locked around the thick trunk of a pecan tree a few
steps up from the river. Most were removed to a regular jail as soon as possible.

Holloway said, "We'll throw your man in with Jayce Landon."

Landon sat on the ground, one arm locked to a sturdy chain. A big man,
he stared resentfully at the officers and did not attempt to stand up. Andy
untied a leather thong that had secured Bransford's handcuffs to the horn of
his saddle. "Get down."

Bransford's legs were wobbly. Andy unlocked one side of the cuffs. He
was aware that Farley watched closely, a hand on the butt of his pistol in
case Bransford decided to make a break. Andy relocked the open cuff
around the chain. This allowed movement up and down the chain but not
away from it. Bransford tugged at the chain and found it heavy. "I've seen
dogs treated better than this."

Farley said, "Dogs don't go around shootin' the taxpayers."

Holloway intervened. "There's no need to taunt the prisoner. Farley,
you and Private Pickard go get yourselves some grub. I can hear your bellies growlin' all the way over here."

Bransford asked, "What about me? I'm starved half to death."

Holloway had no patience for complaining prisoners. "You'll eat when
we're good and ready to feed you. Till then an empty belly will help you
contemplate your sins." He walked off with Farley toward the mess tent.

Andy remained a minute, studying Jayce Landon. His face bore a striking resemblance to that of his Ranger brother. At a little distance he might mistake Jayce for Dick.

Andy had been trying to discern if there was any way to recognize a criminal on sight. So far he had not come upon any common denominator. Bransford looked the part, at least as Andy visualized the outlaw type. He would have taken Landon for a preacher. Or perhaps a Ranger.

Bransford looked up at the open sky. "What if it comes a rain? We'll drown out here."

Andy had not observed a decent cloud in two weeks. "You can climb the tree and drag the chain with you."

Bransford groused until his fellow prisoner turned on him irritably. "Don't go rilin' them up or we won't get any supper. Some of these Rangers would throw their own brother in jail and lose the key."

Bransford shivered involuntarily. "That Farley Brackett kept starin' at me like I had a target painted on my back."

Landon showed no sympathy. "You're lucky if jail is all you're facin'. I'm lookin' at a rope. Gettin' shot might be the better way out." The prisoner rubbed his raw knuckles. Evidently his capture had not been without incident.

The black cook grinned at the Rangers as they approached. Andy grinned back in anticipation. He had rather eat Bo's high-rising sourdough biscuits than cobbler pie. Bo could make sowbelly seem like beefsteak. Somebody had been out hunting, so Bo was able to fry up some venison backstrap to go with Andy's and Farley's red beans. Andy believed in the Comanche adage that one should eat all he could hold when he could get it because it might be a while before he had it again.

Farley, for all his complaining nature, was normally a hearty eater. Today he nibbled tentatively at what Bo offered. By that, Andy knew he still had a considerable headache.

Bransford *was* lucky he had not been shot.

A towheaded boy brought a blackened coffeepot. He gave a glad shout at the sight of Andy sitting there. "Hey, Andy, did you get your man?"

"We always get our man." That was a shameful stretch of the truth, but the boy had begun taking pride in his loose association with the Ranger company. Andy wanted to encourage that feeling, for Scooter Tennyson had been headed down the slippery road to an outlaw life when the Rangers took him in.

Andy held out his empty tin cup. "You been stayin' out of trouble?"

The boy glanced at the black cook. "I ain't been allowed time enough to get in trouble. Give a darky a chance to give orders to a white man and he'll work him to death." He smiled at the cook to indicate he did not really mean it.

The cook smiled back, but his dark eyes showed he knew Scooter *did* mean it. "You finish washin' them dishes, boy, then fetch me up some firewood. After that you can go fishin' if you're of a mind to."

Scooter's mother was dead. His father was in the penitentiary. The boy had been riding with some of his father's outlaw friends until the Rangers captured him. Finding no relatives, they had more or less adopted him to steer him away from a pathway already blazed for him by his father. Andy had taken a special interest because of parallels with his own boyhood experience.

Scooter had been skinny and hungry-eyed when the Rangers first found him. He was filling out now, putting on weight. Andy said, "Looks like Bo's cookin' is good for you."

"I just wisht he didn't make me work so hard for it."

The boy was earning his keep by doing light chores around the kitchen tent and fetching wood, nothing that would cause him undue strain.

In a severe voice Farley said, "Work'll make a better man of you. Maybe you won't follow your daddy into the pen."

Stung, the boy took the coffeepot back to the fire.

Andy frowned. "You didn't have to say that."

"It's the truth. That kid was far gone before you got ahold of him. It'll be a wonder on earth if he doesn't wind up lookin' out through the bars just like his daddy."

"It doesn't have to happen that way if we give him a chance."

"*You* give him a chance. I ain't got the time or the patience."

The captain came along soon after Andy and Farley finished eating. Andy wanted to ask if he had discharged Dick Landon, but he knew it was not his business. He would know in due time.

The captain had regained his composure after dressing down the wayward Ranger. He said, "You-all did a good job."

Farley shrugged, then paid for it as pain stabbed him. "It's what we get paid so high for."

"Did you have much trouble?"

Farley did not answer, so Andy put in, "Not with the prisoner." He was tempted to tell about Leach's woman but chose not to rub salt into Farley's wound.

The captain bent to look at Farley's face. "You look like you tangled with a wildcat."

Farley looked into Andy's eyes with a silent warning. "Horse fell with me."

The captain studied him thoughtfully. "At least it didn't cripple you. I have another job for you and Private Pickard."

Farley went defensive. "To do what?"

"You two will deliver the prisoners back east to where they're wanted."

Farley was not pleased. "Handlin' two prisoners is a big responsibility. I'd rather take somebody older. This young'un is green as grass."

"Pickard is young, but he's not inexperienced. You were with him when he took an arrow wound."

"Delivered by one of his redskinned cousins. Gettin' wounded ain't no accomplishment. Anybody can do it."

"You two are the only men I can spare. If you don't feel that you can go, I will regretfully accept your resignation."

Farley glared at Andy. "I can put up with him if I have to."

Andy asked, "Where are we takin' the prisoners?"

"Southeast Texas. You'll deliver Bransford to the sheriff of Colorado County. Jayce Landon is wanted over the other side of Columbus. It seems an old feud has fired up again." The captain looked back to see if anyone could hear. "Dick helped bring his brother in, then went off on a drinking binge."

Andy said, "I can see why he would."

"Discipline has to be maintained or everything comes apart."

Andy studied the chained prisoners. "It's hard to figure people. Bransford looks like a hard case, but Landon looks like he ought to be preachin' Sunday services."

The captain shook his head. "You can't judge by appearances. Sometimes the men who seem the meekest and mildest have the bloodiest hands. And I've seen some ugly-looking preachers."

Andy saw a bright spot in the assignment. "If we take Bransford to Colorado County, I'll have a chance to stop by Rusty Shannon's farm." He looked at Farley. "And you could visit your mother and sister."

Farley grunted. "They don't want to see me. I brought too much grief down on them."

Andy was strongly conscious of family ties, having none of his own. He could not understand anyone rejecting family or being rejected by them. "That was a long time ago."

"Not long enough." Farley turned away. "If you're done with us, Captain, I'll go see after my horse."

"You're dismissed." Watching Farley retreat, the captain said, "He ought to be a sergeant by now, but he has a dark streak in him that confounds me. What's this about his mother and sister not wanting to see him?"

The memory still made anger rise in Andy. "It was back in the time of the state police. They mistook his daddy for Farley and killed him. Wounded his mother so bad she almost died. Farley figures his family blames him for all the trouble they had."

"Do they?"

"I doubt they do anymore. They know the war twisted him up inside."

"He's unpredictable, even a little dangerous. In some ways that makes him an effective Ranger. It also makes him risky to be around."

"He's like a bear I saw on a chain. Even when he acts quiet, he's liable to turn on you and bite your arm off."

"It's obvious I can't send Dick Landon on this mission. It would put him in an impossible situation. So it's up to you and Farley."

Andy shrugged. "At least I'll have a chance to see Rusty."

The captain nodded. "Tell Shannon that anytime he wants to be a Ranger again, he just needs to let me know. He's welcome in this company."

"I'll tell him, but he's had more than his share of trouble. I think now he just wants to be a farmer."

Scooter was carrying wood and dropping it into a pile near the cook's fire pit. Andy pitched in to help him. Scooter did not thank him verbally, but his eyes showed he was pleased. He said, "Soon as I get done fetchin' wood, I'm goin' fishin'. I never got to do no fishin' till I come to this camp."

"You like fishin', do you?"

"It's about the most fun thing I ever done." The boy had never been given much chance for fun, riding with a criminal father and his father's lawless companions. When he tried to read he followed the lines with his finger, mouthed the words slowly, and often gave up in frustration. What little writing he could do was in block letters, the words so badly misspelled that it was a struggle to decipher their meaning.

Andy said, "I never did any fishin' either before I went to live with Rusty Shannon. The Comanches leaned to buffalo meat."

"Somethin' else I'd like to do someday is hunt buffalo. I'll bet that'd be fun."

"I was too young to ride with the hunters. They made me stay with the women and children. We skinned out the meat after the hunters got through. That was the work part, not the fun part."

"I ever get the chance, I'm goin' to kill me a buffalo."

Andy shook his head. "You may never get the chance. They say hunters have scattered all over the Plains, killin' for nothin' but the hides. Pretty soon there won't be any buffalo left."

"How come the Indians don't stop them?"

"They've tried, but there's too many hunters. The army has driven most of the Indians to reservations. Tryin' to teach them to farm and eat beef." Sadness fell over him. "The ones I knew are too proud to take to the plow. I don't know what'll become of them."

"You ever think about goin' up yonder to see them?"

Andy dropped an armful of wood and looked northward past the river. "Sometimes. I've got lots of friends there. But I've got a few enemies, too."

"Take me with you. I'll help you fight your enemies."

"Maybe someday." Andy dusted himself off. "I'd best go see after my horse."

Scooter grinned. "I'll catch a fish for your supper."

Andy tousled the boy's unkempt hair. "Just what I've been hopin' for."

Farley was brushing his horse's back. He frowned as Andy approached. "You're wastin' your time tryin' to reform that dogie kid. He's got a taint in his blood. It's waitin' for a chance to bust out like a boil on the butt."

"It doesn't have to. If we treat him right . . ."

"I knew some folks who tried to make a pet out of a coyote pup. The wild blood always showed through. They finally had to shoot it."

"People told Rusty the same thing about me."

Escorting prisoners carried a degree of risk. The more severe the crime and the probable punishment, the more the risk. Andy had little concern over Bransford, who had shown his fearsome reputation to be all smoke and no fire. However, he had misgivings about Landon. The captain's information was that Landon and his kin were carrying on a blood feud with a family named Hopper. Family feuds in Texas could be long-lasting, and deadly as a den of snakes. Landon had waited for and shot one Ned Hopper on a lonely country road. Cornered by the Hopper-controlled law, he had wounded a deputy sheriff and made his escape, traveling west to seek help from his brother Dick. He had not considered that the telegraph was faster than the horse.

"You-all watch him," the captain warned as they prepared to leave early the next morning. "Don't give him any slack just because he's Dick Landon's brother."

Farley showed no concern. "If he makes a false move, it'll be his last one."

"Don't shoot him unless you absolutely have to. They want him alive back there."

Farley checked to be sure the two prisoners' hands were securely cuffed and the cuffs tied to their saddles. "Either of you makes a break, you're dead," he warned.

Ranger Dick Landon had watched from the front of the tent in which he slept. He came forward, his eyes full of pain. His face and his halting walk showed the lingering effects of his drinking spree. He said, "Jayce, I'd give all I've got if I could've kept it from comin' to this. I came out here to get away from the feud. I wish to hell you'd brought Flora and done the same."

Jayce Landon turned his head away, not looking at his brother. He stared into the distance. His voice stung. "You went off and left the family. I done what needed doin'."

"When's it goin' to stop?"

"When we've filled up the graveyard with Hoppers."

Ranger Landon turned toward Andy and Farley. "I know he's wanted for murder, but he's still my brother. Don't mistreat him."

Farley said, "If anything happens to him it'll be of his own doin'." He jerked his head as a signal to start. Bransford led off. Farley followed closely behind the prisoners. Andy brought up the rear, leading a little pack mule.

Looking back, he saw Ranger Landon hunched in an attitude of misery. Andy told Farley, "I feel real bad about Dick."

"I've got my own worries. I ain't takin' on none of his. Dick had best watch out for himself and let the rest of his family go to hell."

"That's a cold way of lookin' at it."

Farley turned on him. "Don't be botherin' me with other people's troubles. Or yours either. Else I'm liable to leave you afoot and take the prisoners by myself."

Anger warmed Andy's face. "Looks like we understand one another."

"The important thing is that you understand *me*."

People who had known Farley as a boy said he had been a kindly youngster who enjoyed hunting and fishing and had sung in church. The war and the angry years that followed seemed to have burned all kindness out of him.

Once clear of camp, Andy turned the mule loose. It followed without having to be led. The morning sun was in their faces. The captain had suggested that they push hard to reach Friedrichsburg before dark so they could lodge the prisoners in a secure jail. That way both Rangers could get a good night's sleep without having to stand guard.

The day passed without notable incident, though Andy sensed that Landon was on edge, watching, wishing for a chance to escape. No such chance presented itself. Farley was always close by, a dark and brooding presence. They occasionally met travelers on the trail. Farley scrutinized them suspiciously and kept his hand on the butt of his pistol while they were within range.

"Landon was mixed up in a feud," he told Andy, "so we've got to watch out for both sides. His own people will look for a chance to free him and the other bunch will be lookin' to kill him. Both sides see me and you as enemies. Us bein' Rangers won't make a particle of difference."

Andy began to fear that night would catch them before they reached Friedrichsburg. Darkness would increase the danger in traveling with prisoners. He was relieved when they came into a wide valley and saw the German settlement. Though the town was relatively young, as were most along the western fringes of the state, its broad dirt streets were already lined with sturdy stone and brick structures built in a style brought from the Old World. They were a sign that its citizens were not transient. They had established deep roots and intended to stay.

A deputy received the Rangers at the jail. His English was heavily accented, his manner efficiently professional. He locked the prisoners in separate cells and suggested that the Rangers would be comfortable in the Nimitz Hotel.

Farley demurred. "I'm never comfortable spendin' my money foolishly. I'll sleep in the wagon yard."

Andy suspected the captain would have chosen the hotel, but the captain was better paid. Privates rode for thirty dollars a month. At least nowadays they actually received it. Rusty had told him that in earlier times they often went unpaid for long stretches while the state struggled with a thin and leaky treasury.

Andy followed Farley from the jail to the wagon yard, each carrying his rolled blankets. Farley turned on him and pointed up the street. "You don't have to copy after me. Go to the hotel if you're of a mind to."

"They don't pay me any more than they pay you." He knew it would look awkward if he, the junior of the two, took better accommodations. Farley was sure to let the other Rangers know. Some would take it as a sign that Andy was being uppity. Among proud Texans, that was a cardinal sin.

Andy let Farley stay a few steps ahead, befitting Farley's seniority. Anyway, he could do without Farley's company.

He thought about how pleasant it would be to order supper in the hotel, where they served meals on a white tablecloth. Maybe someday, when he had more money in his pocket. A working cowboy earned as much as a Ranger and seldom if ever had to face somebody with a gun and criminal intentions.

He bought a loaf of freshly baked bread and a spicy sausage to share with Farley. Farley bought a bottle but did not offer to share it. Nor did he bother to thank Andy for the supper. The man and his contradictions intrigued Andy as much as they offended him.

The darkness was compromised only slightly by a lighted lantern at the open front doors of the stable. Andy sat on a wooden bench, watching Farley tip the bottle. He broke a long silence. "I heard you say some people oughtn't to ever drink."

"I don't drink enough to let it get in my way."

Andy watched a match flare after Farley rolled a cigarette. He said, "Not that I give a damn, but I wonder what makes you itch so bad. You've never liked me from the time we first met."

The observation caught Farley off guard. "I never thought much about it. Didn't seem important. But now that you mention it, I *don't* like you. You stole a horse from me once."

"He never was yours in the first place." On the run from the state police, Farley had abandoned a worn-out horse and had taken one from Rusty. Farley's father gave Rusty a sorrel in return. Rusty turned the animal over to Andy, who named him Long Red.

Farley said, "I'd told my daddy I wanted that horse. Figured I'd earned him for all the work I did for nothin' on that man-killin' old farm."

"Guess he didn't see it like you did."

"Lots of things he didn't see like I did. Got to where I couldn't stay around him anymore. But those damned state police had no call to kill him." Farley's voice was bitter.

"You gave the carpetbaggers a lot of trouble. Don't you think you came out about even?"

"I tried to give them back as good as what they gave me."

"Why, then, did you wind up joinin' the Rangers?"

"The state police was mostly scallywags. The Rangers are *us*, the old-timey Texans. You think after all I went through in the war and with the carpetbaggers that I could ever settle down on the farm again? You think *you* could, after livin' with the Comanches?"

"If I set my mind to it. I just got a little restless, so I joined the Rangers. Wanted to see if I could ever be as good as Rusty Shannon."

On that question he was still undecided. He knew he was not yet. He wondered if he ever would be.

Farley asked, "What do you think of the service, now that you've been in it awhile?"

"I didn't look for it to be fun. Mostly it's been long days in camp standin' horse guard or out followin' long trails that fade away before we find anybody. I can see why men like Dick Landon slip off and get drunk."

"Excitement is considerable overrated. Now you'd better go to sleep. We'll try and make Austin by tomorrow night if the horses hold up."

Farley had put his finger on one problem Andy saw with the Rangers. Not much consideration was given to how well the men held up. They were expected to perform regardless of circumstances. But allowances had to be made for the horses. A horse couldn't tell an outlaw from a Baptist preacher.

On reflection, Andy realized that he couldn't either.

They got an early start on what was going to be a long day's ride. Bransford griped about being rousted out before sunup. Landon said nothing, but his eyes were constantly at work, searching for a chance to get away. The same deputy who had checked the prisoners in checked them out and had Farley sign a release absolving Gillespie County of any blame should either prisoner make a break after leaving the jail.

"You watch that man," he warned, pointing at Landon. "All night his eyes are open. Look away from him this long"—he snapped his fingers—"and he will be gone from you."

As a precaution the deputy had put a set of leg irons on Landon. Fumbling with the key, Andy bent to unlock them so Landon could mount his horse. Landon brought his handcuffs and his fists down on the back of Andy's head, knocking him to his knees. Landon grabbed at the pistol on

Andy's hip. Andy twisted away, falling on his side so Landon could not reach the weapon.

Farley shouted a curse and slammed the butt of his rifle against Landon's head. Landon staggered. Farley grabbed the back of the prisoner's collar and shoved him up against his fidgeting horse. "I've made allowances for you because you're a Ranger's brother. Next time I'll bust your head like a watermelon."

Andy pushed to his feet, his head aching.

Farley said, "See what comes of bein' reckless? Didn't the Comanches teach you to watch out for yourself?"

"My hat took the worst of it."

The deputy had observed the incident but had not been close enough to help. He told Farley, "Like I said, better you watch that man. The devil looks from his eyes out."

"I've got three men to watch after, and one of them is a careless kid who's supposed to be helpin' me. You want a Ranger job?"

The man smiled thinly. "I am better paid being a deputy only."

They rode out of town, the prisoners securely handcuffed to their saddles. Bransford glared at Farley. "You could've broke that man's head like an egg."

"He had it comin', and so will you if you keep exercisin' that jaw."

Andy's head drummed with pain. That was Landon's fault, but he could not condemn the prisoner for it. In Landon's position, standing in the shadow of the gallows, he thought he too would probably grab at any straw, no matter how flimsy.

By pushing hard they reached Austin at sundown. Andy worried about the horses' ability to stand the pace. Farley assured him, "They'll make it. The tireder we keep the prisoners, the less trouble they're apt to give us."

Once Bransford and Landon were secured in jail, Farley and Andy reported to Ranger headquarters at the state capitol. It was a matter of form. Farley said he hoped local Rangers would be assigned to finish delivering the prisoners, but the officer in charge simply wished him an uneventful trip.

Andy was pleased, for he had counted on a visit to Rusty's farm. "Like it or not, Farley, you ought to see your mother and sister. They'll be disappointed if they find out you got so close and didn't stop."

"Mind your own business."

They left town on borrowed horses, for two hard days' travel had exhausted their own. Toward the end of the second day out of Austin they turned Bransford over to Sheriff Tom Blessing as ordered. Blessing, a large, blocky man built like a blacksmith, had known Andy since he had returned from his life with the Comanches. Andy asked him about Rusty and black Shanty York and others he knew around the county.

"Rusty's got thin enough to hide behind a fence post. He don't sleep enough and don't eat right. Still grievin' over that girl he lost. He's got a good crop in the field, though. As for Shanty, you know how it is with them darkies: you can't tell their age by lookin'. That black skin hides the lines."

Andy said, "I'll be goin' by to see Rusty once we've delivered this other prisoner."

Blessing frowned. "The word's already out that you're on the way with Jayce Landon. There's liable to be people waitin' for you. If I was you I'd deliver him in the dark of the night."

Farley had been listening to the conversation. "And act like we're afraid of his friends?"

"He's got more enemies than friends. If I was you, I'd be afraid of them all."

CHAPTER

THREE

Rusty Shannon leaned on his hoe and looked beyond the waving green corn toward a dark cloud boiling on the horizon. One more soaking rain should finish bringing the corn and his other crops to maturity.

I wish Josie could have been here to see this, he thought. But the prospect of rain brought no real pleasure. Very little did anymore, not since Josie had died.

A rider approached him, mounted on a mule. Rusty recognized Old Shanty's slight, bent form and walked out to the edge of the field to meet him. He removed his hat to wipe sweat from his brow and the reddish hair that had given him his nickname. Sprinkled with gray, it was uncut and shaggy because he'd lost interest in his appearance. He had not shaved in a week.

He lifted his hand in what he meant to be a welcoming wave, though it fell short. "Get down, neighbor, and give that old mule a rest."

Many white men would not shake hands with a black. Rusty did so without thought. Shanty had been a friend too long for racial proprieties to stand in the way.

"How do, Mr. Rusty. Kind of hot. Buildin' up to a summertime shower, looks like."

Shanty always addressed him as *Mister*. He had spent a major part of his seventy or so years as a slave, and old habits died hard, if at all. He had inherited a small farm from his former owner. For a time he had had to struggle to hold it in the face of opposition from some in the community who resented his being an owner of property. That battle had been fought to a standstill with help from Rusty, Andy, and others like Sheriff Tom Blessing who had kindly feelings toward him.

Since losing Josie, Rusty had found it difficult to arouse much interest in his own farm. He frequently rode over to Shanty's place to help him with heavy work that had become too much for the old man to handle alone. In return Shanty felt obliged to repay in kind, whether Rusty needed his help or not. He had spent more time in Rusty's garden than Rusty had.

Rusty said, "I judge by the direction that you're not comin' from your own place."

"I been over to Mr. Fowler Gaskin's, helpin' him work his vegetable patch. Hoed his weeds. Picked him some squash and beans and tomatoes so he's got somethin' to eat. He's a sick man, Mr. Gaskin is."

Rusty snorted. "Sick of work, mostly. That old reprobate has enjoyed bad health ever since I can remember."

Gaskin was notorious for sloth, feigning illness and using his age as a crutch. He had made an art of chiseling others into doing for him the work he did not want to do for himself. His neighbors had long since learned to watch their property when he came around because he was likely to leave with some of it.

Rusty said, "You've done a lot of work for him, and I'll bet he hasn't paid you a dollar."

Shanty shrugged. "Mr. Gaskin's a poor man. Besides, the Book says I am my neighbor's keeper."

"He never was *your* keeper. He did his damndest to run you out of this country. He was one of them that burned your cabin down."

"We never did know that for certain sure. We just supposed. Anyway, I can't be grudgin' agin a sick old man. He says it won't be long till he's knockin' on them Pearly Gates."

Rusty could think of few things that would improve the community more than a funeral service for Fowler Gaskin. People would come from miles around to attend, just to be sure he was gone. No hog pen or chicken house was safe so long as he drew breath.

Shanty said, "He's been speakin' remorseful about all the wrong things he's done. Cries when he talks about his two boys that was killed in the war."

For years Gaskin had been using his sons' death in an effort to arouse sympathy. Most people around here had learned the truth long ago, that his sons had not died in battle. They had been killed in a New Orleans bawdy-house brawl.

"That's just to get you to do his work for him, and do it for nothin'. He still hates you, but that doesn't mean he won't use you."

Shanty shrugged. "I'm just tryin' to serve the Lord any which way I can. Someday I may be old and sick myself. Maybe Mr. Gaskin will come and help *me*."

Perhaps, when cows fly over the moon, Rusty thought. It was pointless to continue the argument. Shanty was of a trusting nature. Freedom had not come to him until well into his middle age. Up to then it would have been considered presumptuous of him, even dangerous, to pass judgment on anyone white. Now he did not know how.

Rusty made up his mind to ride over to Fowler Gaskin's soon and read the gospel to him.

Shanty gave Rusty a quiet appraisal. "You're lookin' kind of lank, Mr. Rusty. Ain't you been eatin'?"

"It's been too hot to eat."

"It don't ever get *that* hot. That girl's still heavy on your mind, ain't she?"

"Some things ain't easy forgot."

"You don't have to forget. Just take the things that trouble you and set them on a high shelf where you won't be lookin' at them all the time."

"I've tried, but life has sort of lost its flavor around here."

"Maybe supper would taste better to you if somebody else cooked it. I could stay and fix you somethin'."

"Thanks, but by the looks of that cloud, you'd better be goin' home before you get soaked. I'll fix for myself if I get hungry."

Shanty soon left. Rusty knew it was too late to visit Gaskin. Tomorrow would be soon enough, or the next day. The extra time would allow him to think of more shortcomings to call to Gaskin's attention.

He was about ready to quit the field and do the evening milking when another visitor appeared. Rusty had counted Tom Blessing as a friend as far back as he could remember. Tom was a contemporary of Daddy Mike Shannon, who had been a foster father to Rusty. As a small boy more than thirty years ago, Rusty had been carried away by Indians after they killed his parents. Unlike Andy Pickard, he had been rescued a few days later. Because of Daddy Mike and Tom Blessing and several others, he had not spent years among the Comanches as Andy had.

After howdying and shaking, Rusty said, "Follow me up to the cabin, Tom. I'll fix us some coffee and warm up the beans."

"Beans." Tom gave Rusty the same critical study that Shanty had. "You don't look like you've been eatin' regular, not beans or anything else."

"It don't taste all that good when you're by yourself."

"You oughtn't to be by yourself."

Tom had been arguing that Rusty needed a wife. He even had one picked for him. But the suggestion stirred up painful memories Rusty was still struggling to cope with. He side-stepped the subject. "I could fry up some bacon."

"Sorry, but I ain't got time. Need to get home and do the chores before it rains." Tom pointed with his chin. "I happened into Shanty on the road. Said he'd been by here."

"He was over at Gaskin's, doin' work Fowler ought to do for himself. Fowler needs a load of fire and brimstone dropped on him."

Blessing smiled. "If you do it, just don't kill him. The court docket's already full enough." He looked toward the building cloud. "I'd best get into a high lope."

The cloud had grown considerably since Rusty had last paid attention to it. "And I'd better get the cow milked. Need to carry some dry wood into the house too."

The cow was waiting at the milk-pen gate. Her calf was penned inside so that the two were separated all day. Rusty allowed the calf to nurse long enough that the cow let down her milk, then penned the cow and took the milk he needed for his own use. Done, he let the calf in again to finish what remained.

The cloud was coming up rapidly. Rusty hurried to the cabin with the bucket of milk, set it on the kitchen table, and went outside to fetch in a couple of days' supply of dry wood for the fireplace. He had barely finished when the rain started. The drops were large and in the first moments struck the ground with force enough that they raised dust.

He became aware of a roaring noise, rapidly growing louder. He knew immediately that it was hail.

"Oh damn," he said under his breath.

The air, so warm earlier, quickly chilled. The initial stones were no larger than the first joint of his little finger. Quickly, however, they became much larger, hammering the ground. Though he stood in the shelter of the open dog run, some of the hailstones bounced up and rolled against his feet. He stepped back into the kitchen door. The impact of ice pellets against the roof was loud as thunder. Soon the ground was white as if a heavy snow had fallen.

He shivered, but some of the cold came from within. An hour ago he had every prospect of a good crop. Now he wondered if a stalk remained standing.

As quickly as it had come, the hailstorm was gone. A slow, steady rain followed, the kind of rain he had needed in the first place. Water dripped down into the cabin from holes in the roof. He would have to replace a lot of shingles, perhaps all of them.

He pulled a slicker over his shoulders and stepped out to survey the damage. He did not have to walk all the way to the field. He could see it through the rain. Everything in it was beaten to the ground.

He had known people who worked off their frustrations with a burst of profanity. He stood in stony silence, shivering from the cold wind that had come with the hail. Rain rolled off the brim of his hat and spilled down his shoulders.

He saw a couple of dead chickens on their backs, their legs in the air. They had not made it to the shelter of the crude henhouse. Hailstones floated in the spreading puddles of rainwater.

Feeling as if a horse had kicked him in the belly, he trudged back to the cabin, mud clinging to his boots. He had to move the bucket of milk because water was dripping into it. He brewed a pot of coffee and slumped into a chair, holding a framed photograph from the mantel over the fireplace. His throat tightened as he studied the face that smiled at him from the picture.

His shoulders were strong. They could bear this new burden; they had to. But they would bear it better if Josie could have been here.

He imagined what old Preacher Webb would say: *The Lord giveth, and the Lord taketh away.*

Rusty bowed his head. He sure as hell took it all, he thought.

The light of day brought no comfort. The rain was gone, and the morning sun was bright through breaking clouds. He walked first to the garden, where his tomato and okra vines looked as if a herd of cattle had trampled them. He had not removed the two dead hens. The other chickens pecked around them, oblivious to their sisters' fate. Some were half-naked, feathers stripped away.

His field was a muddy ruin. The only salvage he could see was to turn cattle in on it when the ground dried enough. They might find a few days' forage. But he would have nothing to put in his corncrib, much less to haul to town and sell.

He was well aware that a farmer's life was a constant gamble. Each year he bet his land, labor, and personal welfare against the threats of drought, excessive rainfall, heat, and untimely cold as well as insects and various orders of blight. Every so often the farmer would lose his bet, and the best he could hope for was a better next year.

Next year seemed a long way off, for this was still summer.

Rusty returned to the cabin and fixed breakfast, though he could bring himself to eat but little.

Tom Blessing rode up and hollered. His eyes were sympathetic as Rusty walked out to meet him. "Just ridin' around checkin' on my neighbors," Tom said. "Looks like that hail knocked the whey out of you."

Rusty could only shrug. "What about your place?"

"Not enough to break an egg, hardly. Looks like there was just one strip of heavy stuff, and it hit you the hardest of anybody. Missed Shanty's place altogether."

Rusty was gratified to hear that. "I may have to move in with Shanty this winter. What about Fowler Gaskin?"

Blessing shook his head. "I haven't been over there yet, but it doesn't look like the hail went that far."

Rusty felt regret. If Providence was even half-fair, Fowler's place should have been beaten into nothing but a puddle of mud.

Blessing said, "Preacher Webb always claimed everything happens for a reason. Said no matter how cold and cloudy the day, the sun is still shinin' someplace. Maybe you can replant."

"Garden stuff, maybe, but it's too late for corn. I won't be puttin' away any fresh money for a while."

Blessing faced the cabin. "Looks like your roofs got beat real bad. Want me to have a load of shingles sent out from town?"

"Can't afford to buy what I can make for myself. I've got plenty of timber down on the river. Tell you what you *can* do, though: see if you can find me a job."

"I'll try, but I'm afraid there's not much to choose from around here. Times are slow."

Rusty had not inventoried his toolshed in a while. He found his saw was missing. So were the froe and mallet he used to split shingles the time he had helped rebuild Shanty's burned cabin. He was certain he had brought them home after that job was done.

He knew where he was most likely to find them, at Fowler Gaskin's. That scoundrel had a habit of borrowing without asking. Stealing, most people would call it, for he brought nothing back except under duress. Rusty had never liked going to Gaskin's place, but he had already decided to raise Cain with the old heathen over his abuse of Shanty. He hitched his team to the wagon. The tools would be unhandy to carry home on horseback. He had no way of knowing what-all of his property he might find, things he had not yet missed.

For years Gaskin's cabin had leaned to one side, away from the prevailing winds. Logs had been propped at an angle against it to keep it from falling over. Trash and debris littered the premises around it. Gaskin sat on a bench in the shade at the front of the cabin, a jug within easy reach on the ground. He was rail-thin, his skin sallow. His ragged beard was mostly gray, laced with rusty streaks left by tobacco juice dribbling down his chin. He squinted bleary eyes in an effort to bring Rusty into focus.

"What the hell you doin' here?" he demanded. "I ran you off of this place, didn't I?"

Rusty climbed down from the wagon. "You've never run me anyplace that I didn't want to go. I believe you've got some tools that belong to me."

"No such of a thing. Ain't nothin' of yours here." Gaskin arose on wobbly legs, then dropped back onto the bench. "You've got no cause to come accusin' me. I'll sic my dogs on you."

Gaskin's two dogs had barked once, then had slunk away at the wagon's approach. They had much in common with their master.

Rusty did not wait to hear any more of Gaskin's protests. He walked out to a half-collapsed shed and began to dig through tools and implements piled there in a heap. He found his froe and mallet. They bore the initials *RS*, which he had burned onto the wooden handles with a steel rod heated to a red glow. He also found his timber saw and a sledgehammer that belonged to him. He carried them back and placed them in the bed of the wagon.

Gaskin protested, "You got no right to carry a man's tools away. I'm liable to need them."

"Not unless you can get somebody else to use them for you. It's too bad you don't have four hands, Fowler. You could steal twice as much."

Gaskin stood up again, bracing one hand against his cabin. Rusty thought it was a toss-up as to which might fall first. Gaskin said, "You come on my land, you steal my tools, then you insult me to my face. If I wasn't old and sick I'd whup you good and proper."

"Speakin' of bein' old, you've been playin' on Shanty's sympathy when the truth is that you're younger and stronger than he is. I'm tellin' you to stop it or else."

"Or else what? You goin' to hit a poor old man?"

Rusty clenched his fists. "I might. I sure as hell might."

He climbed into the wagon and clucked the team into motion. Gaskin followed in short, shaky steps, shouting his opinion of Rusty and all his ancestors. The dogs came out from hiding and barked from a safe distance.

Gaskin had only a small field, for planting required work. But his corn stood tall, the stalks rustling in the wind. The hail did not seem to have touched him.

Rusty looked up and said, "Lord, next time You send us a storm, I hope You have a better sense of direction."

Reaching home, he carried the tools down to the river. With an ax he cut a deep notch in a tree in the direction he wanted it to fall, then used the saw. When the tree was down, he sawed it into shingle lengths. He dropped several trees before he thought he had enough. Then he began splitting off shingles.

In a couple of days he had a supply of them piled behind the cabin. He was on the roof, removing damaged ones when he saw a wagon and several riders approaching on horseback. He recognized Shanty on his mule. Tom Blessing loped ahead, one of his brothers spurring along behind.

Blessing shouted, "Got a bunch of your neighbors here. We can't do anything about the crop you lost, but we've come to help you put your roofs back on."

Rusty's dark mood lifted. It was a custom in rural Texas communities that neighbors work together. If a man was sick or hurt, his friends came to do whatever work was necessary. If hard luck befell him, the neighbors pitched in to set things as nearly right as possible. No one could guess when his own time might come.

Rusty climbed down the ladder and walked out to greet the visitors, shaking hands with each in his turn.

Blessing smiled broadly. "You need some good news after all that's hap-pened to you. I saw Andy. He'll be by to visit you in a few days."

Rusty grinned. That *was* good news. "His arm wasn't broke, was it?

He's written me just one letter since he's been in the Rangers, and it took up only half a page."

"He looked healthy to me. Him and Farley Brackett delivered a prisoner to me and had another they were fixin' to take a little farther. Said he'd see you before he heads back to the Ranger camp."

Rusty's grin faded. "He was with Farley Brackett?"

"I know him and Farley don't gee-haw too good, but I suppose he had no choice. A young man needs to learn how to take orders so he'll know how to give them when his time comes."

Rusty said, "Farley wakes up every mornin' with a dark cloud over his head. And he's got a wild hair in him that pops out every now and then."

"Andy can think for himself. It's good for him to learn how to get along with all kinds of people. Even somebody like Farley."

Two women rode on the wagon seat, the younger one driving. The older of the pair was Tom Blessing's wife. Rusty had to look a second time before he realized the other was Bethel Brackett, Farley Brackett's sister.

Mrs. Blessing said, "Bethel and me are goin' to fix dinner for the workin' crew. Mind helpin' us carry some vittles into your kitchen? Looks to me like you need a good square meal."

"Been livin' on my own cookin', such as it is."

"What you need here is a woman." Mrs. Blessing quickly had second thoughts about what she had said. "I'm sorry. I wasn't thinkin'."

Rusty's momentary cheer left him. He forced a thin smile, though he did not feel it. "Been a while since I lost Josie. I think I've pretty well got over it."

He had not. He did not know if he ever would.

He turned toward Bethel. He remembered that Andy had shown a considerable interest in her once. Rusty had long wondered how a girl so pleasant-looking could have a brother like Farley. If he did not know her mother to be a woman of stern moral standards, he might wonder if the two had the same father.

He said, "Welcome, Bethel. Been a long time since that day you came here with your daddy, bringin' me a sorrel horse."

"The horse you gave to Andy." She smiled. "Have you heard anything from Andy lately?"

"Andy's not much for writin' letters."

"So I've noticed."

He suspected the sheriff had not told her Andy was due soon for a short visit. That meant she probably did not know Farley was with him. Perhaps Blessing had a good reason for not telling her. It might be that Farley had said he did not plan to visit his mother and sister. In that case it was just as well they did not know. Farley had caused them pain enough over the years.

Mrs. Blessing followed Rusty into the kitchen with a sack of flour. She looked back to be sure the girl was not within hearing. "Bethel has turned into a right pretty young lady, don't you think?"

Rusty sensed where she was heading. "But too young for me, and I'm sure I'm too old to interest her. She's more Andy's age."

"But Andy's not here. You are."

"I'm just not ready to be thinkin' in that direction."

"If not Bethel, then how about Alice Monahan? Alice is a sweet girl. She was a godsend to me when I was sick for so long. And she *is* a sister to Josie, or was."

Rusty had been in love with two of the Monahan sisters, Geneva and Josie. He had lost them both. He would not allow himself to consider another. "Looks like the Lord intends for me to be an old bachelor."

"It's not for us to say what the Lord intends, but I can't believe He wants you to spend your life alone."

Rusty was grateful for an interruption by Tom Blessing. "Rusty, let's get started on that roof."

Tearing out old shingles, placing new ones where they had been, Rusty told Blessing, "Thanks. You came in at just the right time."

"I know. When my wife takes a notion about somethin', she's like a cold-jawed horse. There's no turnin' her back. I just let her play it out to the end of the string." He frowned. "But you know, she's right. That hail didn't leave you much reason to stay around here till plantin' time comes again. If I was you I'd take a ride up to the Monahan farm. Alice might surprise you."

"I'm not lookin' for surprises. Unless you can surprise me with a good job."

"I've asked around. Haven't found anything."

Rusty felt the bleak mood settling over him again. "It's liable to be a long fall and winter."

CHAPTER

FOUR

The trip had not made Jayce Landon any less of a puzzle to Andy. In comparison to Bransford, who had been left in Tom Blessing's custody, Landon still looked as if he might be a preacher, or at least a law-abiding storekeeper. But Andy had a sore place on the back of his head from Landon's attack. And Landon had laid in wait to shoot a man. Bransford had never done that so far as Andy knew.

Farley Brackett said, "Don't waste sympathy on him. He's got blood on his hands."

"How about the state policemen *you* killed?"

Farley said, "They was lookin' at me. They could've shot me as easy as I shot them."

"Do they ever keep you awake at night?"

"Dead is dead. They don't come back."

Andy did not like the look of five horsemen riding to meet them from the direction of Hopper's Crossing. He tensed, and again he wished Rusty Shannon were there. "What do you think, Farley?"

"I think *damn it*. I hoped this wouldn't happen." Farley reached across to recheck Landon's handcuffs and the rawhide strip that bound them to the saddlehorn. "Take a good look at them, Jayce. Are they friends of yours, or enemies?"

For the first time since the trip began, a smile creased Landon's face. "Some of my kin and a couple of my neighbors. They won't like it, seein' me shackled like a runaway slave."

"They'll like it even less if they try and turn you loose because I'll shoot you dead. Badger Boy, you better draw your weapon."

Andy already had. He was not surprised about being met on the road. Tom Blessing had warned that the word had gone out ahead and that it was wise to be prepared for anything.

Thirty feet from the approaching horsemen, Farley stopped. He placed the muzzle of his pistol behind Landon's ear. "You men had better put aside any foolish notions. The only way you'll get this prisoner away from us is if he's dead. And some of you will ride to perdition with him."

Andy's mouth went dry as he tried to read the men's intentions.

One rider pushed his horse a little past the others. His facial features resembled Jayce's so much that Andy guessed they might be brothers. Dick Landon must have come from a large family. "Now, Ranger, we just come to make sure he gets to town alive. The Hoppers would like to see that he don't."

Farley said, "And they'll have their way if you make a move to help him. I want all of you to turn around and ride out ahead of us. Way ahead of us."

The men argued among themselves. Farley brought the conversation to a close by cocking back the hammer. Jayce gasped. Andy held his breath.

Jayce said, "You-all better do what he says, Walter. This Ranger is one mean son of a bitch."

The man called Walter jerked his head as a signal for the rest to comply. He said, "Don't you let your finger get nervous, Ranger. If somethin' happens to Jayce, you'll be dead two seconds after he is."

Andy sensed that whatever intentions the five might have had, had been thwarted by Farley's unyielding stand. They were not likely to try anything unless circumstances changed drastically in their favor.

Farley said, "Take a lesson from this, Badger Boy. Never give an inch or they'll run over you."

"You'd really have shot him, wouldn't you?"

"If it was the last thing I ever did."

Sweat rolled down Jayce's face. He trembled in fear's aftermath. "God, Ranger, but you're cold-blooded."

"I am, and don't you forget it."

"You don't know what kind of a man I shot."

"Makes no difference. Me and Badger Boy are paid to deliver you to the local sheriff. The rest is up to the jury that tries you."

"The judge is old Judd Hopper. He's a direct grandson of the devil himself. Him and the rest of them Hoppers'll do all they can to see me hung."

"You've got a brother who's a Ranger. Have you got one who's a lawyer?"

Landon looked behind him as if expecting pursuit. "This fight goes way back. Why can't the law stand aside and let the families work it out for theirselves?"

"I know how crazy-mean these feuds can get. You kill an enemy, then one of his family has got to kill one of you. It goes on and on till just about everybody is dead. Better for the law to hang you instead of one of your enemies shootin' you. Maybe that'd put an end to it."

"It won't end till that Hopper bunch is all dead and gone."

Andy shook his head. "I'll bet you don't even remember what started it."

"It commenced over an election for the county seat, but that don't matter anymore. It's a blood thing now."

Farley looked at Andy and shrugged. "No use arguin' with him. You can't talk sense to people like that."

Andy said, "It's a good thing for Dick Landon that he joined the Rangers and got away from the trouble."

Farley grunted. "Even Dick'll bear watchin'. He's got bad blood in him."

Andy could count on one hand the times he had heard Farley speak well of somebody, and he could give back a couple of fingers.

Jayce said, "If you think the Landon blood is bad, wait till you meet the Hoppers."

Hearing hoofbeats behind him, Andy turned in the saddle. He counted six riders. Farley demanded, "Who are they, Jayce?"

Jayce looked back in dismay. "They're Hoppers . . . Hoppers and their kin."

Andy said, "Five Landons in front, six Hoppers behind, and us in the middle."

Farley growled, "Best thing would be for us to pull out of the way and let them settle their stupid feud for good."

Andy considered the situation, then moved his horse toward the six men.

Farley shouted, "What do you think you're doin'?"

Andy did not answer. He drew his rifle from its scabbard, laid it across his lap, and rode almost within touching distance of the horsemen. "Which one of you is in charge of this bunch?"

A big bear of a man with a short, curly beard said, "Ain't nobody in charge. We're workin' together to see justice done."

"And your name?"

"I'm James Hopper. Big'un, they call me." He looked strong enough to wrestle a bull to the ground from a standing start. He was half a head taller and fifty pounds heavier than any of the men who rode with him.

Andy swung the rifle muzzle around to point at the man's belly. He jerked his head. "Come on, Big'un. You're ridin' up there with us. The rest of you stay back. If one of you makes a move against us and our prisoner, I'll blow this gentleman's lights out."

The bearded man protested, "I'll have you know that I'm a deputy sheriff. Appointed by the county judge hisself. What gives you the right to tell me what to do?"

"This rifle does. Are you comin' or do I shoot you right here?"

Hopper did not consider long. "I'm comin'. The rest of you better do like he says."

One of the riders was a smaller man but had the same facial features as Big'un. He said, "He's bluffin'. Say the word and we'll take him."

Big'un declared, "Shut up, Harp. We don't need no blood spilled here. Not mine anyway."

Andy started Big'un moving toward Farley and Jayce. Big'un said, "You look kind of young to pack so much authority."

"A gun makes everybody the same size."

Farley looked the deputy over, then turned critical eyes on Andy. "What did you bring him for?"

"For insurance."

"You think you could really kill him if you had to?"

"You said to never give them an inch."

Farley almost nodded in approval but caught himself. "Lookin' at you right now I'd swear you're a Comanche after all."

Andy took that as a left-handed compliment, the only kind Farley Brackett gave.

Jayce's face hardened, displaying his hatred of the bearded man. "Well, Big'un, looks like they've got you the same as they've got me."

Hopper's eyes burned with malice. "Not quite the same. They'll turn me loose when we get to town. They're already stackin' lumber over by the jailhouse to build your scaffold."

Farley broke in. "I've got half a mind to cut you two coyotes loose and let you go at one another, but there's probably some fool law against it. So both of you shut the hell up."

A mile from town they were met by the county sheriff. Jayce's supporters pulled to one side but did not leave. The Hoppers started to move up, but Andy made a show of pressing the rifle's muzzle against Big'un's midsection. That stopped them.

Big'un complained, "Damn it, Ranger, you got to bruise my ribs?"

A middle-aged man with gray hair and a slight paunch, the sheriff reacted sharply at the sight of Big'un being held at gunpoint. "What do you think you're doin' with my deputy?"

Andy said, "He was fixin' to get himself in trouble. We're protectin' him."

The sheriff turned his anger on Big'un. "Damn it, I told you to stay home, and keep all the Hoppers there too."

Big'un bristled. "We just come to make sure none of Jayce's kinfolks let him loose."

"That's my job." The lawman turned back to the Rangers, making no secret of his antagonism toward Jayce Landon. "Thank you, Rangers, for deliverin' this murderer. I'll take over from here."

Farley gave Andy a severe look that warned him to be alert. "Our orders are to deliver him safe to your jailhouse. Till then, he's still ours."

Andy watched the Ranger and the sheriff glare at each other. He knew Farley would stand his ground if it took all afternoon. The sheriff evidently came to the same conclusion. He said reluctantly, "All right. Another mile won't make much difference."

Big'un looked back for support. "A trial is goin' to cost us taxpayers money. There's a good, stout tree yonder. I say we drag Jayce over there and hoist him like a fresh beef."

The sheriff's voice crackled, "Shut up, Big'un. The judge crowded me into takin' you and Harp as deputies, but I don't have to listen to you talk like a damn fool." He pointed his thumb toward town. "All right, Rangers, Jayce is still yours till we get him to jail. Let's go before some idiot takes a notion to show how stupid he is." He looked at Big'un again.

A crowd had gathered to watch Jayce being brought to town. Andy had never seen so many angry people. Some supported Jayce, but it appeared that the majority were hostile to him. A couple of fistfights broke out as the horsemen approached the jailhouse door.

Farley muttered, "Keep a close watch. There's no tellin' what some hothead might do." He cut the leather thong that bound Jayce's hands to the saddlehorn, but the cuffs remained on the prisoner's wrists.

Andy stayed in the saddle, holding the rifle in a firm grip. Big'un slipped away from him and rejoined the five who had ridden behind. The sheriff opened the front door of the jailhouse but stood in the middle, blocking it for what seemed to be several minutes.

Giving somebody a good chance to shoot Jayce, Andy thought. He studied the people with anxious eyes.

The long road to justice had many a shortcut.

Farley took a firm grip on Jayce's arm and led him through the doorway, past the sheriff. This time Jayce showed no resistance. Instead, he seemed in a hurry to get inside away from the crowd. Andy dismounted and followed, walking backward, the rifle ready.

Farley said, "Badger Boy, would you mind fetchin' my saddlebags?"

Andy could not remember that Farley had ever asked him to do anything. He had always just told him.

A woman burst through the door and ran to the prisoner, her arms outstretched. "Jayce," she shouted. "Jayce!"

The sheriff tried to restrain her, but she was strong enough to break free. She embraced Jayce, sobbing loudly. Too loudly, Andy thought. He sensed that she was making a show of it. After letting her cry for a bit, Jayce's brother Walter pulled her away. "Come on, Flora, you oughtn't to act like that in front of these Hoppers. They've had too much satisfaction already, just seein' him brought in."

She launched a tearful tirade at the sheriff. "My Jayce is a better man than you, Oscar Truscott." She turned on the crowd. "He's better than the lot of you. All he done was kill a man that needed killin'. There's a whole bunch of you Hoppers needs killin'." She seemed to concentrate particularly on Big'un.

Andy thought he saw a look of satisfaction in her eyes as Walter Landon led her outside. He wondered about it.

Farley withdrew some papers from the saddlebags Andy had brought. He handed them to Sheriff Truscott. "Me and Pickard have done what the captain ordered. Jayce belongs to you, but you'll need to sign this release."

Truscott signed with a flourish, smudging a little ink. "It'll be like havin' a box of dynamite in here, but I'm glad to have him. I hope the trial don't take long."

Big'un grinned. "It won't, not with Uncle Judd on the bench."

The wooden floor trembled as an iron door slammed heavily. The sound made Andy feel cold even though he was not the one being locked away.

Farley told the sheriff, "There's lots of people out yonder that would like to do the prisoner harm."

"You don't have to tell me my business. You Rangers have done your job. I expect you'll want to head west and put some miles behind you before dark." His voice was hopeful.

"Our horses need a rest. We'll bed down at the wagon yard and make a fresh start in the mornin'."

The sheriff shrugged. "Suit yourselves. There's a fair-to-middlin' eatin' joint down the street yonder, run by one of my wife's nephews. Nothin' fancy, but it's cheap."

"Sounds fine to me." Farley beckoned to Andy. "Let's go see to our horses."

Walking outside, Andy sensed the tension. His scalp tingled as if an electrical storm were building. It would take but little to set off a riot. The fight would be one-sided, for the Hopper crowd appeared to outnumber the Landons by a considerable margin.

Farley growled, "Don't look to the left nor the right. Just walk straight ahead. This don't concern us anymore."

"Jayce won't get a fair trial in this town."

"Don't matter. Even a fair trial would end up hangin' him. He's as guilty as sin."

Andy rubbed his throat. The thought of a rope around it gave him a chill.

Farley said, "It would've been better for him if he'd made a break along the way. We would've shot him, and it would already be over with. Now he'll sit in that jail cell broodin' about it. He'll die a thousand times before he ever feels the rope."

They ate a mediocre supper. A good one would have had no more appeal to Andy under the circumstances. He asked, "Doesn't it bother you that we brought Dick Landon's brother here to die?"

"Jayce put the rope around his own neck when he took aim on Ned Hopper. He tripped the trapdoor when he walked up and shot him a second time. It wasn't none of my doin', nor yours."

The stable keeper was a small man with a flushed face that indicated he was a favored customer at some bar up the street. He seemed to fancy the sound of his own voice. "You-all are the Rangers that brought Jayce in, ain't you? Bet you didn't know what a hornet's nest you was fixin' to stir up. Soon as it gets dark and some of the Hoppers get enough liquor in them, you'll see the biggest fireworks we've had around here since the Yankee war."

Farley said, "It's nothin' to us. We just want to get some sleep and head out in the mornin'."

"May not be much sleepin' done in this town tonight. Me, I ain't takin' sides. Their money all looks the same to me. I'll still be here when it's over."

Farley scowled. "It's a smart man who knows how to mind his own business."

"But ain't you Rangers supposed to keep the peace? Looks to me like you'd be out there amongst them, holdin' the lid down."

"Our orders were to deliver Jayce to the sheriff. From now on it's up to him and the court."

"The sheriff's married to a Hopper. He's got some inlaws he ain't real fond of, like Big'un and the judge, but they come with the deal."

Andy said, "It's a cinch there won't be anything fair about Jayce's trial."

The stableman looked around to see if anyone else could hear. "Ain't goin' to be no trial. Talk is that they're goin' to stage a fight and draw the sheriff away after dark. The jailer is a Hopper cousin. When his kinfolks come callin' they won't have to tell him twice to raise his hands."

Andy's jaw dropped. "They're goin' to take Jayce out and hang him?"

"No, they'll shoot him right there in his cell and scatter before the sheriff or the Landons have time to do anything about it."

Farley frowned. "Are you sure about this?"

"I got it from one of the Hopper boys. He was already tanked up on Kentucky courage."

Andy told Farley, "We've got to do somethin'."

Farley shook his head. "What's the use? They'll just keep tryin' till they get him. Feuds are nasty business."

He forked dry hay onto the ground and spread it evenly, then unrolled his blankets on it. "Best thing is to let the damn fools fight it out. Then we can hang the winners or send them to the penitentiary."

"I'll bet that's not in the captain's rule book."

"The book has got blank pages in it so we can write our own rules when we have to."

Andy did not consider long. "I didn't make this ride just to stand back and watch them lynch our prisoner." He drew his rifle from its scabbard on his saddle and dug into his saddlebag for extra cartridges.

Farley arose from his blankets. He gripped Andy's shoulder tightly enough to hurt. "They'll cut you to ribbons, and for what? Jayce is goin' to die anyway. If he doesn't do it tonight, he'll do it when the trial is over. Leave it alone."

"I can't."

"Listen to me, Badger Boy. Even if you *are* half Indian, you're worth more than Jayce Landon."

Andy thought that was an amazing admission for Farley. He could not think of an adequate response. "Like the man said, we're supposed to keep the peace."

"Ain't goin' to be peace in this town till they've killed enough of one another that they gag on the blood. You'd best look out for your own skin."

"What'll the captain say if we tell him we delivered Jayce and then stood by while a mob shot him to pieces?" Andy cradled the rifle across his left arm and walked out of the stable into the darkness.

The jail was a little more than a block away. He had a strong feeling of being watched, but he could see no one. He heard a horse somewhere behind the buildings, moving into a slow lope.

He pondered whether he should go inside the jail or wait for the Hoppers in front of it. He had heard of mobs burning a jail to get a prisoner. In such an event he could do little from inside. Besides, the jailer was in on the deal. He would probably do whatever he could to put Andy out of the way. He decided to take a stand outside, blocking the door.

The street remained quiet for a while. Andy began to wonder if the hostler's information was overblown. People sometimes made bold talk but did not have the stomach to follow through. Then he saw several men moving up the street toward him. He tightened his grip on the rifle. Though he could not distinguish the faces, he sensed that these were of the Hopper clan.

Sternly he said, "That's close enough."

A gruff voice shouted, "Step out of the way, Ranger."

Andy thought the voice sounded like Big'un's. He said, "I'm tellin' you to disperse."

The men moved closer but stopped when Andy leveled his rifle on them. Big'un declared, "You've got no jurisdiction here. You finished your job when you brought Jayce in."

Andy's throat was too tight for a reply. He hoped silence was more threatening than anything he might say. The men huddled, murmuring among themselves. Several more came up the street, joining them. By Andy's rough count there were fifteen, perhaps more.

One man edged beyond Big'un and the others. He said, "You're just a shirttail kid. You won't really shoot us." He paused a moment, gauging Andy's reaction, then moved forward again with confidence in his step.

Andy aimed the rifle, but he could not bring himself to squeeze the trigger. The blood rose warm in his face.

He sensed a movement on the street. A pistol blazed, and the man went down. He gripped his leg and squalled in pain.

Farley's voice was deadly. "Next shot goes in somebody's gullet." He fired again, kicking up dust in front of the mob.

Andy expelled a pent-up breath. Farley walked up and joined him in front of the door. His stern gaze never left the Hoppers as he muttered, "The graveyards are full of people who wouldn't pull the trigger."

"I tried. I just couldn't."

The wounded man lay on his back, gripping his bleeding leg. He kept hollering.

Farley said with contempt, "Listen to that brave son of a bitch, squealin' like a pig stuck under a gate."

Members of the mob conferred among themselves. Big'un shouted, "You're protectin' a murderer."

Farley said, "He ain't been tried yet."

"We come here to give him all the trial he needs."

Farley muttered, "If they rush us, shoot the foremost. That'd be the one called Big'un. If that doesn't stop them, shoot another."

"You'd do that for Jayce Landon?"

"No, for us. Right this minute we're in worse danger than he is."

Big'un shouted, "You Rangers can't stay here forever. We can wait."

Farley pointed the pistol at him. "You'll have to. Now you-all had better scatter because in one minute I'm goin' to shoot every man I can see." He held up his watch so he could read it in the moonlight.

The men lingered a little, then began to peel away. Some, like Big'un, shouted threats back over their shoulders, but soon all had retreated beyond sight, carrying their wounded man with them.

Farley said, "You have to talk to people in a way they understand, then be ready to back up what you tell them. Remember that and you'll live longer."

Andy shuddered. "You were really set to kill somebody."

"I would, if there'd been a brave man amongst them. But after one shot everybody started thinkin' about home and mother. That's generally the way."

"You told me at the stable that you wasn't comin'."

"I didn't intend to. I don't give a damn about Jayce Landon, but I didn't want to have to tell the captain I stood back and let a mob kill a Ranger. Even an ignorant Comanche Indian."

A stubborn streak would not allow Andy to show his pleasure. He had taken too much abuse from Farley to grant him the satisfaction. He looked down the dark, empty street. "I don't understand why none of the Landon bunch was here. Looks like they'd have turned out to protect Jayce."

"That does strike me a little peculiar. It goes to show that both sides are crazy."

After they had watched for ten or fifteen minutes Farley said, "I don't think they'll be comin' back for a while. I want to do some Dutch talkin' to that jailer."

Andy was not surprised to find that the front door had been left unlocked. He said, "I guess the jailer wanted to make it easy for them. All they had to do was walk in."

Inside, he locked and barred the door in case some of the Hopper people drank enough courage to come back. He did not see the jailer. Farley walked through the door that led back to the cells. He called, "Come here, Badger Boy. This is a sight to tell your children about if you live long enough to have any."

The jailer was handcuffed to the bars of a cell. The cell door was open. Jayce was gone.

Farley snickered at the jailer. "Now ain't you a pretty sight? How did you get yourself into this fix?"

The man's eyes were downcast. "Jayce has escaped."

"I figured that out for myself. What did you do, go to sleep on the job?"

"No such of a thing. The sheriff went to see about a fight. Soon as he was gone, Jayce pulled a gun on me. Just a little derringer, but it could kill a man."

Farley gave Andy a speculative glance. Jayce hadn't had a gun on him when the Rangers brought him into town.

Andy did not have to think about it long. He remembered how Jayce's wife rushed up and hugged him. He would wager a month's pay that she stuck it inside his shirt during the moment of confusion.

He chose not to mention it. The woman had misfortune enough just by being Jayce's wife.

The jailer wailed, "Are you-all goin' to get me out of this mess?"

Farley came dangerously near smiling. "We ain't got the key."

"Look in the top desk drawer out yonder."

Andy rummaged around and found it. Freed, the jailer rubbed his wrist, raw from straining against the handcuff. "I think Jayce went out the back door. I heard a horse lope away. Some of his kin must've been waitin' out there."

Farley grunted. "So now he's took to the tulies."

The jailer wailed, "If the sheriff doesn't murder me, my kinfolks will."

"I've got half a mind to do it myself. On account of you, me and Pickard made a long ride for nothin'. And that mob out yonder could've killed us."

"You got to tell them it wasn't my fault."

Andy suggested, "Might be a good idea if we left town. They're liable to think we had a hand in this."

"Run away?" Farley took offense at the suggestion. "Last time I ran from anybody it was the state police. I swore I'd never run again. No, we'll stay and tell them how it was. Next time maybe they'll hire better help."

Someone began beating against the front door and shouting for the jailer to open it. The jailer appeared about to wilt. "Oh God, that's the judge."

Andy assumed that thwarted mob members had carried their frustration to the Hopper family leader.

Farley said, "Just as well let him in. But nobody else. This place could get crowded in a hurry."

Reluctantly Andy slid back the bar and opened the door just enough for Judge Hopper to enter. Several men were with him, but Andy pushed the door shut and barred it before any of them could bully their way in. Big'un shouted threats from outside.

Judd Hopper was a tall, angular man with gray chin whiskers and angry eyes that cut to the quick. "What are you Rangers doing here? Protecting the prisoner is the sheriff's responsibility."

Farley did not waver under the tirade. "I'm glad you said that. I think your jailkeeper has got a little news for you."

The jailer hung his head. His voice was little more than a thin squeak. "Jayce is gone."

"Gone?" The judge took long strides into the back room. His face reddened as he saw the open cell door and absorbed the full import of Landon's escape. He whirled around, jabbing an arthritic finger at Andy and Farley. "You-all turned him loose. I'll send you both to the pen."

Farley gripped the jailer's wrist so hard that the man cried out. "Tell him the rest before I twist your arm off and beat you to death with it."

Defensively the jailer explained that Landon had produced a pistol and forced him to unlock the cell. "Next thing I knowed he had me handcuffed to the bars. I hollered, but nobody heard me. Wasn't nothin' I could do."

The judge fumed. "I wish he'd killed you. I guess you know you're fired. You'll be lucky if some of my nephews don't flay the hide off of you. How did he get ahold of a pistol?"

Andy and Farley stood silent. The jailer spoke in a subdued voice. "We didn't make him take his boots off. Maybe he had it in one of them."

The judge slammed the cell door shut and then shook it in rage, gripping the bars tightly enough to turn his knuckles white. "I'll make somebody wish he was in the fires of hell instead of in Hopper's Crossing."

Farley beckoned to Andy. "I don't see nothin' more for us to do here."

Hopper demanded, "You're goin' to help us hunt him down, aren't you?"

Farley showed his disdain. "Ain't our fault you-all couldn't hold him. Our assignment was to deliver him to the sheriff. We done that, so now we're leavin'."

Andy slid back the bar and opened the door. As he and Farley left, a dozen Hopper partisans rushed in, bumping one another against the door in their haste.

Andy said, "The judge is liable to tell them it was our fault. Anything to shift the blame. We better get away from here."

"We ain't runnin'. We're walkin'. We'll show this bunch we ain't afraid of nobody."

"Maybe you're not, but I am."

Farley set a slow and deliberate pace toward the wagon yard. They had not gone far before Andy heard someone shout a curse. The voice sounded like Big'un's. A shot was fired. Farley spun half-around, grabbing his right side.

A man stood in lamplight that spilled through the open jailhouse door. He held a pistol. Andy raised his rifle and made a quick shot. The man went down, twisting in the dirt.

Farley swore under his breath. Andy asked, "How bad are you hit?"

"I don't know. It hurts like almighty hell."

"We'd better keep movin'. They didn't get to kill Jayce Landon, and they're fired up to kill *somebody*."

Andy took Farley's left arm to give him support. At the wagon yard he found the stableman standing in the open front doors, staring into the dark street. "Heard some shootin'. What . . ." He seemed to lose his voice when Andy and Farley came into the lantern's light and he saw Farley's bloody shirt.

Andy said, "Saddle our horses for us and throw our pack on that mule. Be quick." He helped Farley to a straight wooden chair and brought the lantern up for a close look. The bullet had struck high up and from behind. "Can you move your arm?"

Farley raised it a little.

Andy said, "Could've busted some of your ribs. You're bleedin' like a stuck hog."

Andy took out his handkerchief and pressed it against the wound. "Feel like you can sit in the saddle?"

"I don't see I've got much choice. Them crazy Hoppers'll be lookin' to finish the job."

The stableman brought their horses and the mule. "If I was you-all—"

Andy interrupted. "Is there a doctor in this town?"

"There is, but you'll be needin' an undertaker instead if you've got yourselves in Dutch with them Hoppers."

The stableman reluctantly gave directions, then helped Andy boost Farley into the saddle. Andy found the doctor's house, but he saw that several of the Hopper people were already there. The doctor would be treating the man Farley had shot. The one Andy had shot would probably be brought along shortly.

He said, "We'd better not stop here."

Farley nodded in painful agreement. "Doctor may be one of them Hoppers anyway. Whole town seems to be infested with them."

"I'm afraid you'll have to tough it out for a while."

Farley grumbled under his breath, "Badger Boy, you're a damned Jonah. You'll get me killed yet."

CHAPTER

FIVE

Andy feared he might have to hold Farley in the saddle, but Farley hunched over the horn and stubbornly refused help. The horse's every step hurt him.

They rode back down the road they had come on for what Andy thought must have been two or three miles. He saw lamplight in a window. "Farmhouse," he said. "Maybe they'll help us."

Farley's voice choked with pain. "If they ain't Hoppers."

"Even if they are, maybe they don't know what happened in town. No need in us tellin' them."

Andy strode up onto a wooden porch and knocked on the door. He heard a floor squeak as someone walked across it. The door opened, and a woman stood there, a shotgun in her hand. A cold feeling came to Andy's stomach. He recognized Jayce Landon's wife.

Her voice was like ice. "You're one of them Rangers. What do you want here?"

"I've got a hurt man outside. He needs help."

She looked at Farley but offered no sympathy. "You-all brought my husband back and turned him over to them Hoppers. Now you've got the nerve to ask for my help?"

An old man's voice came from a back room. "Who is it, Flora?" He came out carrying a pistol and squinted at Andy in the dim lamplight.

She said, "It's them Rangers, Papa. By rights we ought to shoot the both of them."

The bewhiskered old man poked the muzzle of his pistol toward Andy. "What you got to say for yourself?"

"I need help for my partner. He's been shot."

"By who?"

"By one of the Hoppers."

The pair's hostility began to fade. The old man said, "Thought you was in league with them, fetchin' Jayce in like you done."

"That was our job. But afterwards we stood guard on the jail to keep a mob from bustin' in. We didn't know Jayce had already broke out." He allowed a hint of accusation into his voice. "But I'll bet *you* knew it."

A satisfied look passed between the pair. The woman spoke first. "We ain't ownin' up to nothin'. But if you're lookin' to catch Jayce, you'd better have some damned fast horses. He left town on the best runner in the county."

"Right now I'm just interested in gettin' help for Farley Brackett."

The old man's attitude quickly mellowed. "Brackett, you say? Is he the one that gave them state police so much hell durin' the Yankee occupation?"

"He's the one."

"Lord amighty. Bring him on in here, boy. We'll see what we can do for him."

The woman still seemed reluctant, but she deferred to her father's judgment. Andy helped Farley out of the saddle and up the step.

The old man said, "Any enemy of the Hoppers is a friend of ours."

Farley growled, "I ain't their enemy, and I ain't your friend."

The old man appeared to take no offense. "He's probably half out of his head. Set him in that chair. Let's see how bad he's hurt."

They took off Farley's blood-soaked shirt, then peeled his long underwear down to his waist. Flora Landon held a lamp close and examined the wound, probing with her fingers while Farley ground his teeth. Andy got his first good look at her face. He thought her handsome, at least for a middle-aged woman. He figured her to be about thirty.

She said, "Looks to me like the bullet glanced off of the ribs. Gouged a pretty good hole comin' and goin', but it's a long ways from the heart. If he's got one."

Farley winced against the pain. His face was pale. "Ain't the first hole I ever had shot in me."

She frowned. "If you get blood poisonin' it may be your last. Grit your teeth, because this is fixin' to burn like the hinges of hell's front door." She washed the wound with whiskey. Andy thought for a moment that Farley might faint. She said, "We'll bind them ribs good and tight."

The old man said, "A broken rib is liable to punch a hole in his lung and kill him deader than a skint mule. Be better if he didn't ride horseback for a while."

The woman studied Farley with her first hint of sympathy. "I don't see where he's got a choice. Right now them Hoppers are probably searchin' all over Jayce's and my farm. When they get through there they'll be comin' here. I don't think you Rangers'll want to be around."

Andy said, "I was wonderin' if you folks have got a wagon I could borrow."

Flora looked questioningly at her father. He said, "This man faced up to the Hoppers and led them scallywag state police on a merry chase. You bet he can have my wagon." He jerked his head at Andy. "Come on, boy. Help me catch up my team."

He walked out onto the porch and stopped abruptly. "Daughter, you'd better come and look."

Andy saw flames in the distance. He could not guess how far away they were.

Flora gasped. "They're burnin' down our house, mine and Jayce's."

The old man nodded. "This place'll be next."

Andy heard horses coming. "Sounds like they're already here."

Flora declared, "Be damned if they're goin' to burn my papa's house." She reached inside the door and grabbed her shotgun.

The old man's bony hand pushed the shotgun muzzle down. "This house ain't nothin' but lumber and nails. I can build a new one. But the Lord Hisself can't build a new me or you."

Andy said, "It's too late to run. You-all get back inside and blow out the lamp. I'll talk to them."

Flora said, "I doubt as they're in a listenin' frame of mind."

"They'll listen to me or they'll answer to the state of Texas." He made his voice sound more confident than he felt. He stepped out to where he had tied his and Farley's horses. He lifted his rifle from its scabbard and got Farley's as an afterthought. He stood in the moonlight on the edge of the porch, his own rifle in his hand and Farley's leaning where he could reach it without much of a stretch.

He counted seven horsemen. An eighth followed behind. The deputy

Big'un was in front as the riders came to a stop. He recognized Andy. "You Rangers again. Seems like you're everywhere."

"We try to be where we're needed."

"You know who we're after."

"Jayce Landon isn't here. I can vouch for that." He really couldn't. He had not seen anything here except the front room of the house. But the imperious lawman did not need to know that.

Big'un declared, "You Rangers have stepped way over the line. You helped a fugitive get away."

"He didn't escape from *us*. We delivered him like we were ordered to. He was the sheriff's prisoner. It was the sheriff's responsibility to see that he didn't bust out."

"I expect that woman of his knows where he's at. This is her daddy's house, and I'm bettin' she's in there."

Flora came out onto the porch, shotgun in hand. Andy started to tell her to go back inside, but he knew she would not heed him. She looked like a woman who would charge a bear with a willow switch.

She said, "I'm here, Big'un Hopper, and here I'm stayin'. It don't take much of a man to burn my house down, but it'll take a better man than you to run me out of this country. You or any of your other line-bred Tennessee ridge-runner kin."

The deputy moved his horse up closer to the porch. "If we ever find out you helped Jayce get away, you wouldn't be the first woman ever hung in Texas."

Andy shifted his rifle to point at Big'un. "There'll be no more talk about hangin', especially of a woman. You'd better back away if you don't want the whole Ranger force swarmin' this county like a nest of hornets."

"It ain't the Rangers' business to take sides in a local affair."

"It is when it comes to killin'."

Hopper seemed not to hear. "Flora Landon, I'm placin' you under arrest for aidin' and abettin'. You come down here."

She did not move. "You come up here and get me if you don't mind a load of buckshot in your belly."

For a minute Andy was not sure which way the pendulum would swing. Big'un seemed to weigh his chances, and anger appeared stronger than caution.

Farley Brackett walked out to join Andy and the woman on the porch. He held his arm tightly against his ribs, but in his hand was a pistol. He said nothing. He let his eyes deliver his threat.

Looking at Farley, the deputy took fresh stock of his situation. "Somethin' about you seems familiar to me. But I don't recollect that I heard your name."

"I'm Farley Brackett."

The name jarred Big'un. "From down in Colorado County? Somebody told me you was dead."

"I ain't heard about it."

Andy said, "And I am Andy Pickard." That name carried no weight with the deputy, but Farley's had drawn his full attention. Andy thought it was time to try to close the conversation. "You've got no grounds to arrest Mrs. Landon. You're trespassin' here on her daddy's place. You'd best be movin' on, or you're biddin' fair to see inside one of your own cells."

Big'un reluctantly began to cave. "You Rangers won't be stayin'. We can wait till you're gone." He pulled his horse around and started back in the direction of town. The other men followed, some grumbling about not finishing their job.

Flora looked at Farley. "Big'un almost lost his breath when he heard your name. You must've left some deep tracks."

Farley started a shrug but pain stopped it. His face pinched. "Would you have shot him in the belly?"

She replied, "I don't say anything I don't mean."

She went back into the house. Farley was ordinarily sparing with admiration, but he said, "There, Badger Boy, is what I call a woman!"

In the house, Andy said, "That was brave talk outside, but the Hopper bunch has got killin' on their minds. It would be smart if you folks left here for a while."

The old man told his daughter, "Get your stuff together and we'll go with these Rangers."

She resisted until her father said, "There ain't no shame in runnin' when it's the only way out. Jayce has done it. At least we'll live to hit them Hoppers another day."

Andy asked, "Where's Jayce runnin' *to*?"

The old man shook his head. "If I was to tell you that, you'd go after him."

"We would if it was our orders."

"Jayce ain't an easy man to warm up to, but he's the only son-in-law I've got. That's why I ain't tellin' you. Let's get that team hitched up. I don't fancy bein' around to entertain that bunch when they swaller a little more panther juice and come back."

———

Andy did not ask at first where Flora Landon and her father wanted to go. He simply turned the team away from the direction of town and the fire still burning in the distance. He and Flora sat on the wagonseat. Farley lay on blankets in the bed of the wagon. Flora's father rode Andy's horse. Farley's was tied on behind, trailed by the little pack mule. They traveled a couple of miles in silence, though Andy stopped the wagon several times to listen for sounds of pursuit.

He saw a new fire and knew the house they had left was burning. The old man cursed under his breath. "I'll build it back, and I'll bury a couple of Hoppers in the backyard for good luck."

Flora said, "I'll help you dig the hole."

Andy asked, "You-all got kinfolks you'd like to go to?"

Flora said, "Not till things die down some. We'd bring more trouble on them, and they've got trouble enough just bein' Landons and kin. Where are you headin'?"

"To Colorado County, to some folks that will take care of Farley."

"Mind takin' us with you? Papa and me need to be scarce for a while."

"What about your husband? He won't know where you're at."

"We'll come back when the Hoppers ain't lookin'. They'll find out that their houses can burn just as easy as ours did."

The bitterness in her voice reminded Andy of what Farley had said about feuds. Often starting over some trivial incident, they tended to grow out of all proportion into a senseless succession of brutal killings. Andy had heard of one bloody vendetta that began over nothing more than mistaken accusations about a few missing hogs.

He doubted that Flora knew the origin of the Landon-Hopper feud, but he asked anyway. That started a mild argument between her and her father.

She said, "It was when Old Man Hopper shot at Jayce's daddy and took a chunk out of his shoulder."

"No," the old man countered, "that come later, after one of them Hopper boys and his cousin tried to beat up on Jayce's granddaddy. That old man whipped the britches off of them all by hisself, then whittled a swallow fork in the Hopper boy's ear."

The talk left Andy with a feeling of futility. Families killed one another though they could not agree on what had started the fight. It was a process with no foreseeable end.

Farley became feverish, drifting in and out of reality. From time to time he mumbled incoherently. At other times he was lucid enough to ask, "Where we goin'?"

Andy would tell him, "You'll see." He feared that a better answer would touch off an argument.

Flora occasionally checked the bandage while Andy stopped the wagon. She asked, "How'd he get that scar on his face?"

Andy told her he had brought that home from the war.

She said, "I have a feelin' he's got other scars on him that don't show. He must be a hell-bender in a fight."

Andy admitted, "He takes care of himself."

"Didn't do so good this time, did he?"

"Somebody shot him from out of the dark. He didn't have a chance."

Seeing the Brackett farm took Andy back to a terrible night when Reconstruction state police had shot up the house in the mistaken belief that Farley was there. They killed Farley's father, Jeremiah, and wounded his mother. Ironically, Farley was miles away at the time.

Lying in the wagon, Farley was unaware of Andy's destination until they were within a hundred yards of the house. He pulled himself up to look over the sideboards. Sight of the place jarred him out of his dreamy state. "Damn you, Badger Boy, I didn't want to come here."

"You need lookin' after. Who'll do it better than your mother and your sister?"

"They won't want to see me." Farley made a feeble try at getting up, but he hurt too much to do it on his own. He managed to say, "I'll whup you, boy, soon as I get my strength back."

"You can try. Right now you couldn't whip a sick kitten."

Andy shouted as soon as he thought he was within earshot. "Hello, the house."

A young woman stepped out onto the porch, shading her eyes with her hand. "Andy?"

"I've got Farley here, Bethel. He's hurt."

She hurried toward the wagon. Her flaring skirts startled the team, and Andy had to draw hard on the reins. Bethel gave Flora and the old man only a glance. She looked anxiously over the wagon's sideboards. "What happened to him?"

Andy said, "He's been shot."

Flora said, "He lost a right smart of blood."

Elnora Brackett and a black woman came onto the porch. Farley's mother watched anxiously as Andy and Flora helped Farley climb the steps. Color drained from her face. She said, "Bring him in. We'll put him in his own bed."

This was a large house in comparison to most Andy knew. Jeremiah Brackett had been a prosperous farmer before the war and before confiscatory Reconstruction taxes had stolen much of his property.

The black woman led the way down the hall and into a spartan room devoid of furniture except for a bed and a chair. Farley had not spent much time in this house after going off to war and later coming home to the desperate life of a fugitive, defying the occupation authorities.

His mother said, "That bandage is soaked. It needs changing." She held her son's hand as Andy cut through the bloodied cloth. "Is Farley in trouble again?"

She had reason to ask, for her son had led a reckless life after returning from the war. Andy told her, "No, he got this in the line of duty." He explained about delivering Jayce Landon, about standing off a mob, and about shots fired on a dark street. He said, "I brought Farley here because I thought his family would take better care of him than anybody."

Bethel touched Andy's arm. "You did the right thing."

"He didn't want to come. He thinks you-all still hold it against him for his daddy gettin' killed."

Bethel seemed surprised. "We got over that a long time ago."

Mrs. Brackett had lost two sons in the war and her husband in its aftermath. She said, "He's the only son I have left. He should know we'd stand by him."

"That's what I told him. Maybe he'll believe it, comin' from you." Andy doubted Farley was in any condition to follow the conversation. His eyes were vacant, staring at nothing.

The wound looked angry around the edges. Elnora fretted about the possibility of blood poisoning. She cleansed the opening and replaced the bandage with help from Bethel and the black woman.

Only then was there time for Andy to introduce Flora and her father and explain why they were with him.

Bethel said, "Thank you-all for your help. You're welcome to stay here as long as you want to."

Flora said, "It won't be long. Soon as I think them Hoppers are lookin' the other way . . ."

Andy said, "I'll go over to town and fetch the doctor. We don't want to take any chances with Farley."

Bethel asked, "Have you had anything to eat?"

"I guess I did, but I don't remember when it was."

"I'll fix you something before you go. Maybe we can get Farley to take some broth."

In the interest of time Andy settled for warming up some beans and smearing a heavy load of butter on cold biscuits. He was aware of Bethel's eyes. She stared at him while he ate.

She said, "You quit coming around to see me."

"I've been tied up with the Rangers."

"Before that, though. I hope I didn't say or do anything . . ."

"You didn't. I just got real busy. Anyway, it seemed to me like you were havin' company enough without me. And I had a notion that I reminded you of the night the state police came."

The memory darkened her expression. "I would remember that anyway, with or without you. I kept hoping you'd come around. You will come back, won't you, with the doctor?"

"Yes, I'll want to see what he thinks about Farley and how long he'll be laid up. Then I'll visit with Rusty before I report back to the captain."

She touched his hand. "If what happened to my brother is any measure of life with the Rangers, I don't want to see either one of you go back."

He did not pull his hand away. In the past he had wondered how a girl like her could have a brother like Farley. He stared at her, trying to find any facial resemblance. He said, "It's a pretty good life most of the time. There's more boredom than excitement. The food's good when we're not out on patrol."

"The pay isn't much, is it?"

"I don't need much. They feed me. Rusty Shannon never let me pick up any wasteful habits."

"Maybe you could use some. Maybe you could come and see a girl once in a while."

"You mean that?"

"If I say it, I mean it."

He had heard that statement from Farley several times. Farley and his sister might not look alike, but they thought alike in some ways.

Bethel came outside to watch Andy get on his horse. He said, "Looks like you-all have had a good rain." The ground was muddy, and water stood in the fields.

"A storm passed through here a few days ago. All we got was rain, but your friend Rusty caught a terrible hail. It just about wiped him out."

"Sorry to hear that." Andy paused a moment, feeling a rush of sympathy for Rusty. "I'll be back with the doctor soon as I can."

CHAPTER
SIX

Andy was not prepared for the ruin that had been Rusty's field. A maturing crop of corn had been battered into nothing more than stalks, standing bare and broken. Leaves and half-developed ears were pounded into the muddy ground. The devastation was complete.

Approaching the cabin, he saw that its roof was newly shingled, as was the roof of a smaller cabin Rusty had built for Andy when he had expected to bring Josie Monahan home as a bride. Several chickens pecked about the yard. Some had lost many of their feathers. Patches of bare skin showed through.

Andy called out. He heard an answer and reined his horse toward the shed where Rusty kept his farming implements and tools. Rusty stepped out into the open, leather harness in his hand. Recognizing Andy, he forced a smile, though Andy knew smiling must come hard to him these days.

"Hey, Andy, I'll put this stuff away, then we'll go up to the house." Rusty went into the shed, emerging without the harness. The smile was gone. He looked haggard. "Tom Blessing told me you'd be comin'. I suppose you got your prisoner delivered."

Andy dismounted to shake Rusty's hand. "For what it was worth." Andy would tell him about it later. Right now he was having difficulty absorbing the damage he saw around him. "Looks like you had a buffalo stampede."

Rusty had always stood tall and straight. Now his shoulders sagged. His voice was weary. "You can put up a fight against most things that come at you. You can whip down a fire or dam up against a flood. But a storm like this, all you can do is hunker down and watch it happen."

"I see you got new roofs."

"Neighbors." Rusty led Andy into the kitchen. "Had anything to eat?"

"Ate dinner with the Bracketts."

For a moment Rusty's eyes seemed to light up. "I'm glad you went by to see that Bethel girl. She's been askin' about you."

"It wasn't on account of her." Andy explained about the Jayce Landon affair and Farley's being wounded.

Rusty frowned. "Farley always did draw lightnin'." He and Farley had had their differences. "Lots of young men around here think Bethel Brackett is the best-lookin' thing in a hundred miles."

"She looks all right."

"Just all right?"

Andy was aware that Rusty had been trying a long time to promote a romance between Andy and Bethel. "Why don't you pay court to her yourself?"

Pain came into Rusty's eyes. "You know the luck I've had when it comes to women."

Andy wished he could take back what he had said. It had slipped out. "I'm sorry."

"No matter. I've halfway come to accept things like they are. I didn't need that hailstorm, though."

Rusty turned away, but not before Andy saw grief rekindled in his eyes. On the mantel stood a tintype of Josie Monahan. Andy could only imagine how many times a day Rusty must look at that picture.

He asked, "Ever hear anything from Alice?" Alice was Josie's younger sister.

"Not directly. Got a letter from her mother. Clemmie said the boy Billy keeps askin' about you."

"Nothin' from Alice herself?"

"I've got no reason to expect anything. There's nothin' between us. Never was."

Andy had hoped there might be.

Rusty poked at coals banked in the fireplace until they glowed red. "I'll boil us some coffee. It'll tide us over till suppertime."

Andy placed small sticks of dry wood atop the coals. "What're you goin' to do, Rusty? You've lost the year's work. It's too late in the summer to replant your field."

"I've got meat in the smokehouse and hogs runnin' loose on the river. I won't starve."

"You're not one for sittin' around idle."

"There's always work to do if I feel like lookin' for it. But lately I've been askin' myself what's the use?"

Rusty's dark mood made Andy uneasy. He said, "How about gettin' away from this place for a while? Come back to camp with me. You could sign up with the Rangers for three months or six months, however long you want to. The captain said he'd be tickled to have you."

Rusty toyed with the idea but resisted at first. "Rangerin' is for young men like you."

"There's older men than you in the force. Len Tanner is about your age. The Morris boys ain't far behind."

"I'll admit it'd be good to ride with them again." Rusty walked to the door. He looked out past the dog run to his ruined field. "The thing is, I'm gettin' to where when night comes I want a real bed, not a blanket on the hard ground."

Rusty was thin and drawn. Andy wondered how many meals he had cooked, then not eaten. "I always thought you enjoyed your time with the Rangers."

Rusty nodded. "I did, even with the long trips and the days I didn't eat. There's a lot of satisfaction in ridin' with a bunch of men you like and respect."

"Then come along with me. I guarantee that the captain will be pleased to see you."

"I'll admit I'm a little tempted."

"It might do you good to see some fresh country. This farm could pretty well take care of itself from now till spring plantin'."

Rusty gradually warmed to the idea. "I could turn the milk cow and her calf out together. I could take the chickens over to Shanty so the coyotes don't get them."

Perhaps later, when more healing time had passed, Andy could talk Rusty into traveling up north to visit the Monahans. If he spent time close to Alice, he might finally see what everybody around him already knew.

Bethel Brackett stood on the porch watching as Andy and Rusty dismounted in front of her house. She spoke first to Rusty, then to Andy. "Going back to camp already? I hoped you might stay awhile longer."

Andy said, "It's time I reported for duty. Just came to see about Farley so I'll know what to tell the captain."

He caught a moment's disappointed look before she hid it. She said, "Farley's stubborn and hard to get along with, but he always was. He's raisin' a ruckus about wantin' to go back to camp."

"He can't be ready yet."

"No, but he thinks he is. Nothing counts with him except what he thinks."

"What about Flora Landon and her daddy?"

"They're still here. Farley actually smiles when Flora comes into his room. I think he's a little taken with her."

Guess he's got some human feelings after all, Andy thought. "Reckon they know where Jayce is at?"

"I make it a point not to ask questions. If anybody comes around hunting for information, I won't have to lie to them." She managed a weak smile. "You-all are not in too much of a hurry to stay and eat dinner with us, are you?"

Rusty took the decision out of Andy's hands. "We'd be much obliged."

That was how it had always been, Andy thought. He never got to make a decision of his own unless he was by himself. He was always in Rusty's shadow, or someone else's.

He remembered how to reach Farley's room, but he chose to follow Bethel anyway. He enjoyed looking at her, though he would not tell her so, or Rusty.

Farley lay on his bed, atop the covers. Pale, unshaven, he was fully dressed, even to his boots. His shirt was only partially buttoned because of a bulky bandage wrapped around his ribs. He grunted at the visitors, either a halfhearted greeting or a dismissal. He had always lacked confidence in Andy, and he had only a strained tolerance for Rusty. Both had gotten in his way more than once.

Farley said, "I hope you're ready to ride, because I sure am. I may just beat you back to camp."

Andy saw worry in Bethel's eyes. She said, "You wouldn't get ten miles from home before you fell off of your horse. You'd lie there and bleed to death."

Farley said, "I got hurt worse than this in a skirmish with the Yankees and still rode thirty miles before dark."

Bethel shrugged. "How can you talk sense to a man like that?"

Andy saw no reason to tell her it was useless to try. She knew it better than he did. But he sensed that Farley understood the truth. Despite his blustering, he was not ready to ride, nor would he be for a while.

Rusty said, "Farley, I hear you and Andy turned back a mob."

Farley grunted. "It was a damn-fool thing to do, seein' as the man they was after had already lit out."

"You didn't know that at the time."

"This Badger Boy of yours was all set to try it by himself. When he takes it in his head to do somethin', you couldn't beat it out of him with a club."

Rusty nodded. "I've got no quarrel with that."

"Fool kid could've got us both killed." Farley glowered at Andy. "Look what happened to me. I deserve it for takin' pity on him."

Rusty said, "You got it for doin' the right thing."

"That Jayce Landon is a knot-headed idiot. The only reason I'd give a damn what happens to him is that he's got a wife who ought to've done better for herself. And a goodhearted daddy-in-law. Do you know he's out in the field right now, workin' like a hired hand? And her with him."

Andy took that for a sign Farley might be mellowing. The Bracketts still had the help of a black woman who once had been their slave. She now worked for her keep and received a modest wage when Elnora and Bethel had any money to pay her. When they did not, she stayed anyway. She had nowhere else to go. Andy could hear her clanging pots and pans in the kitchen. It reminded him he was hungry.

Farley tried to get out of bed but gave up. "I'm damned tired of takin' my meals in bed like a baby."

The black woman brought him his meal, but he ate only a little of it. He stared at the window and offered no more conversation.

Flora Landon and her father came in for dinner. Andy noticed that the first thing she did was go to Farley's room to see about him. She came back shortly, grinning. She said, "I thought Jayce knew every cuss word in the language, but I believe Farley could teach him some. When he finally gets up he's liable to drag that bed outside and burn it."

Her father asked Andy, "Seen any more of Sheriff Truscott or Big'un?"

"No, but I ain't been lookin' for them."

"Watch out. They're liable to come lookin' for *you*."

The meal finished, Andy felt reluctant to leave. For one thing, visiting with Bethel and her mother seemed to have brought some life back into Rusty's eyes. But duty's call was loud. Andy jerked his head at Rusty. "It's a long way to the San Saba."

Farley shouted from his bedroom, "Saddle my horse for me. I'm goin' too."

Bethel cast a sad glance at Andy.

Rusty said, "Farley knows he can't. It just gets under his skin to have to depend on other people."

Andy and Rusty said their good-byes to Elnora and the Landons. Bethel followed them out onto the porch. She told Andy, "Write me a letter once in a while. Let a body know you're still among the living."

"I'm not much of a hand with pencil and paper. But I'll try."

Rusty said, "I'll see that he does."

Riding away, Andy looked back. Bethel remained on the porch, watching them.

Rusty said, "One word from you and she would follow you anywhere."

"To a Ranger camp? What could she do there?"

"You won't stay with the Rangers all your life. Nobody does."

They rode awhile before Andy said, "I'm tempted to go back up the river and see if there's any news about Jayce. Dick Landon would want to know about his brother."

Rusty threw cold water on the idea. "I've heard stories about the Hoppers and the Landons. Especially the Hoppers. I'd as soon see you stick your head into a rattlesnake den."

"I wish there was somethin' we could do about that double-dealin' Big'un."

"Time has a way of payin' off his kind of people. Chances are that some Landon will clean his plow or he'll get caught dippin' his hands into the county treasury."

"I hate to ride away and leave things hangin'."

"If trouble is lookin' for you it'll find you without you huntin' it. Let the Landons and the Hoppers fight it out amongst theirselves."

The next morning they rode for several miles in brooding silence. Andy was thinking about the unfinished business with Big'un Hopper and his kin. He suspected Rusty was thinking about his farm and Josie Monahan.

At length Andy said, "Folks holler about savage Indians, but I don't see that they're any more savage than people that go feudin' and killin' one another. Most of them don't even know anymore what the fightin' is about."

Rusty pointed out, "Comanches kill Apaches any time they can. And Apaches kill Comanches the same way."

"That's different. They're blood enemies."

"Why? What started it?"

Andy tried in vain to remember if anybody had ever told him. "I'd guess it might've commenced over horses a long time ago. Somebody stole them and somebody else wanted them back. Or maybe somebody insulted somebody. With Apaches, who cares?"

"See, you ain't got past all of your Comanche raisin'. You hate Apaches without knowin' why. Comanche or Apache, they're all Indians. It's a family feud just like with the Landons and the Hoppers. And it doesn't make a lick of sense."

That stung, although Andy could not quite reconcile himself to Rusty's viewpoint. Every Comanche knew that Apaches were like rattlesnakes, to be killed wherever they were found. Children were taught that lesson as soon as they were able to learn. "It's the People's way," he said.

"Killin' one another is the Hoppers' and the Landons' way. The Lord never made any perfect humans, Indian or white."

West of Austin the rugged topography always lifted Andy's spirit. It seemed to lift Rusty's too, for his eyes brightened as he surveyed the rough terrain, the live-oak flats, the limestone layers that were like broken stair steps up the sides of the hills. He said, "I never spent much time out in this part of the country. I wish I had. It's pretty."

"Pretty wild."

"If I was just startin' out and didn't already have my farm, I think I'd find me a place out here. I'd set my roots deep and never leave it the rest of my life."

Andy was gratified to see Rusty beginning to come out of the darkness. "I've studied on it some myself."

He remembered older Comanches' accounts of long hunting trips down into this land rich in water and grass and game. By the time he was with them they never ventured this far south anymore except to raid. The Texans had made it too dangerous for them to stay. In Andy's view the hill country had not yet been spoiled by civilization. Most of it was too rough to be violated by the plow except for narrow valleys where soil had washed down from the steep hillsides to accumulate deep and rich. In springtime it was like a boundless garden exploding in color with bluebonnets and other wildflowers. Now in summer the season of blooming was gone and the maturing grass was more brown than green. Spring was short, but the memory was long.

It was a perfect haven for grazers and browsers, wild and domestic. Now and then Andy glimpsed white-tailed deer. Alert to danger, they bounded into the cedar thickets and live-oak mottes long before the horsemen reached them. A hunter needed stealth and steady nerves to stalk them with a rifle. How much harder it would be, he thought, to stalk them with a bow and arrow as the Indians traditionally did.

He saw wild turkeys too. He brought one down with a well-aimed shot to the head.

"What did you do that for?" Rusty asked. "It's hard to strip off the feathers without boilin' water to scald the bird."

"I'll skin him like a squirrel. He'll make a nice supper." Andy was proud of his shot. Bringing down a turkey with a rifle was a test of marksmanship. Rusty had taught him so well in the use of the rifle that Andy was now the better shot. In fact, when he gave it any thought he realized that Rusty had taught him most of what he knew about living in the white man's world.

Having finished all he wanted of the turkey, he sat on the ground a little way from the dwindling campfire. The night was warm enough that he did not need the heat. He said, "You're studyin' me awful hard."

Rusty said, "I was wonderin' with your Indian raisin' why you ever decided to be a Ranger. Rangers and Comanches have fought one another ever since Stephen F. Austin's time."

"It's more like the life I had with the Comanches than the life I had on your farm."

"But it's not a job you'd want to spend the rest of your years at. Even if you could depend on it, which you can't. The state is always runnin' out of money. You never know from one month to the next if you'll get paid."

"Money's not the main thing."

"It's easy to say money's not important when you've got a little in your pocket. It looks different when you don't have any. First time the state's money gets tight they'll cut the Rangers again. Folks back in East Texas will say the Indian fightin' is done so there's no use spendin' that tax money. But let a bank get robbed or somebody get killed and they'll holler, 'Where's the Rangers?' "

An owl hooted. Andy felt a chill. "Hear that?"

"It's just an owl in the tree yonder. He's probably lonesome for company."

"I don't like owls. They bring nothin' but bad luck."

"That's just an old Comanche notion."

"Some Comanche notions are real. Owls are bad medicine."

Andy lost himself awhile in memories of his Comanche life. He was shaken back to reality by the sound of a horse's hoofs striking against the limestone rocks. He reached for his rifle.

A voice called from the darkness, "Hello, the camp. All right if I come in?"

Rusty shouted, "Come ahead." He was watchful but did not seem worried. Andy's instincts told him to keep his hand on a gun.

The rider dismounted at the edge of the firelight and tied his horse where it would not kick dust into the cook fire. He appeared to be of middle age. He had several days' growth of whiskers, though his hair was cut short. If he carried a weapon it was hidden. "Glad I seen your fire. I was about to make a cold camp, and a hungry one."

Rusty said, "You're welcome to what's left of a skinny turkey. You've traveled a ways by the looks of you."

"Several days, but I think I'm gettin' close to what I'm lookin' for. You-all know anything about a Ranger camp out thisaway?"

Rusty said, "Reckon we do. You thinkin' about joinin' up?"

"Me join the Rangers? Not hardly." The visitor seemed to find dark humor in the thought. "But I've got business with them."

Andy was still tense, trying to gauge the stranger's tone of voice. "You got a quarrel with the Rangers?"

"No, I stay away from the law and hope it stays away from me. Took me a long time to learn that, and I've got the gray hair to show for it. You say you know where the camp is at?"

Rusty said, "We're headed that way ourselves."

The stranger stiffened. "You're Rangers?"

Andy did not like the reaction. "I am. Rusty's fixin' to be. Is there somethin' we can do for you?"

"The Rangers been keepin' somethin' of mine."

Andy burned to ask for more details, but he considered it ill manners to be inquisitive without a clear reason. The visitor attacked the remnant of turkey as if he had not eaten in two days. Andy boiled a can of fresh coffee. The stranger blew steam from a cupful and drank it without waiting for it to cool.

Rusty said, "It ain't much, but it's the best we can do travelin' across country."

The stranger made a gesture of approval. "It's mighty fine. Where I been they don't know nothin' about makin' coffee, or much of anything else."

Andy itched to ask him where that was, but if it was important he would know in time. If it wasn't, it made no difference.

The stranger rubbed his stomach with satisfaction. "Couldn't be no better if you'd served it on golden plates. I'm obliged." He poured the last of the coffee. "Be all right with you fellers if I spread my roll here tonight and ride along with you tomorrow?"

Andy had doubts. But Rusty said, "I don't see any reason not to."

"I ought to let you know right off. I just come from a stretch in the penitentiary. You might not be comfortable with the likes of me around."

Andy's suspicions were confirmed. "If you escaped, we'll be honor-bound to take you in."

"No, I served my time and got out legal. They gave me a few dollars and a suit of clothes. Said they didn't want to see my ugly face no more, and I promised them they wouldn't."

Rusty said, "As long as you've paid up fair and square, I don't see where we've got any kick comin'. I'm Rusty Shannon. This is Andy Pickard."

The stranger nodded but did not offer to shake hands. "My name's Tennyson. Lige Tennyson."

Tennyson. Andy's pulse quickened. "Have you got a boy that goes by the name of Scooter?"

The stranger spilled some of his coffee. "You know him?"

Andy stared into the fire, his stomach uneasy. "I know him."

He was sure now why Lige Tennyson had come looking for the Rangers.

CHAPTER
SEVEN

ennyson walked off into the darkness to take care of necessities. Andy said, "We can't let him take Scooter away."

"He's the boy's daddy."

"But he's an outlaw. He's been in the pen."

"He's served his time."

"What if he goes back to his old ways and drags Scooter along with him? We can't let that happen."

Rusty was sympathetic but offered little comfort. "If his mind is set, the only thing apt to stop him would be the court. You know a good judge?"

"I don't even know a bad judge. Well, Judd Hopper. I just know that kid was on the road to hell before me and some of the others took him by the scruff of the neck. We may not be able to rescue him the next time."

"Maybe Tennyson has decided to walk a straight line. I've known men that slipped once but never did it again."

"An old horse doesn't change his color. I've got a bad feelin' way down in my gut."

Though he knew it was unlikely, Andy could not shake a suspicion that Tennyson might steal their horses and make off with them in the dark. He dozed fitfully, never falling into deep sleep.

Tennyson snored all night.

Frying bacon for breakfast, Rusty noticed the droop of Andy's shoulders. "It won't help for you to lay awake frettin'. If the boy's daddy wants him there's not much you can do."

"Maybe the captain can."

Andy studied Scooter's father as they rode. It had long seemed to him that there should be something in a criminal face that marked it as different. He could find nothing unusual in Tennyson's unless it was the restless eyes, constantly searching. He had seen the same characteristic in frontiersmen used to being in Indian country, ever on the lookout for danger. Watchfulness was not necessarily a sign of a criminal mind.

Tennyson asked many questions about his son. "I'll bet he's growed up to be a man, almost. It's hard to picture him that way. Last time I seen him he stood about waist-high to a tumbleweed."

Andy looked for any sign of hope. "You may not know him, and he may not know you. You might've grown too far apart to fit back together again."

"Give us a little time. Blood will always tell."

Blood. That was what Andy worried about. Lige Tennyson's blood ran in Scooter's veins. It was an outlaw strain.

Andy said, "Scooter's come a long way. Sergeant Holloway's been schoolin' him in readin' and writin' and figures. It'd be a shame to take him away from that."

"I studied a few books while I was boardin' with the state, and I was always pretty good at figurin' up sums. I'll teach him all I know."

That was the problem, Andy thought. Lige knew too many of the wrong things.

They rode into camp at midafternoon and reined up in front of the headquarters tent. Sergeant Holloway stepped out, his turkey-tracked eyes pinched against the sunshine. Holloway gave Tennyson a glance, then turned to Andy and Rusty. "Rusty Shannon! It's good to see you back. You figurin' to stay awhile?"

"If you-all will have me."

Holloway asked Andy, "Where's Farley? Don't tell me he decided to resign." He looked a bit hopeful.

"Farley got shot up a little. I left him with his family till he heals up enough to ride."

Andy was about to give Holloway the details when the captain emerged from his tent. He acknowledged Rusty and told him he would be glad to have him sign up for whatever period Rusty might choose. Then he diverted his attention to Andy. "I received a wire saying you and Brackett delivered your prisoners all right."

"Delivered and signed for. But Jayce Landon didn't stay a prisoner for long."

"So I understand."

Andy explained about Jayce's escape from jail. He omitted his belief that Jayce's wife had slipped him the derringer, for she was in enough trouble with the local law. She didn't need the Rangers hounding her as well.

Dick Landon came up in time to hear most of it. He smiled broadly as he listened to the account of his brother's flight. "I figured he'd get away if he had even a ghost of a chance."

"Got away slicker than wagon grease. My guess is that he put the county line behind him as fast as his horse could run. He left a bunch of disappointed Hoppers, not to mention the county judge."

"Judd Hopper!" Dick spat the name as if it were a wad of bitter tobacco. "The old son of a bitch has stolen half of the county."

Andy said, "Sheriff Truscott seemed like a decent sort, considerin' what-all he's got to deal with."

"But he's got Judd Hopper's leash around his neck."

Tennyson listened intently, saying nothing as his eyes cut from Andy to Dick to the captain.

The captain impatiently changed the subject. "Tell me again how Brackett got wounded. The wire was much too sketchy."

Andy repeated the account. The captain asked, "And you're sure you shot whoever did it?"

"I saw him fall and grab his leg."

The thought seemed to please the captain. "There's nothing so stupid as a feud, and Texas seems to be suffering an epidemic of them. The trouble isn't over just because you-all managed to ride away. It may follow you out here."

That thought was not new to Andy. "Any shots we fired were in self-defense, plain and simple."

The captain said, "From what I know of that county, the court belongs to the Hoppers. If they take a notion you've thrown in with the Landons, your testimony in court wouldn't be worth a Continental." His face indicated concern. "I'll need you to write a full report at your first convenience. Perhaps I can get it to Austin ahead of any protests from the judge or the sheriff."

The captain turned his attention to the visitor. "You say your name is Lige Tennyson? Somehow that has a familiar ring."

Tennyson shrugged apologetically. "I'm sorry to say that too many people used to know my name. Five years down at the state hotel has taught me that the outlaw road is all uphill, through flint rocks and cactus. But I've wrestled with the devil, and I've finally pinned him to the floor."

"Well and good, but what brings you to this camp?"

"I've come to claim my son. He's the boy called Scooter."

The captain's brow wrinkled. He gave Tennyson a more intense scrutiny. "I believe I see a family resemblance."

"The Tennyson blood has always showed out strong. Ain't goin' to be no trouble about me takin' my boy, is there?"

"I'll have to satisfy myself that it's the right thing to do. I'll want to see what the boy says."

"He's his daddy's son. He'll want to go."

"That I shall determine for myself. Follow me, Mr. Tennyson." The captain strode toward the cook tent. Tennyson took long steps to catch up with him. Andy trailed along. Rusty stayed behind, talking to Holloway.

The black cook looked up from his Dutch ovens, puzzled by the crowd converging on him. "Howdy, Captain. A little early for supper. Got coffee ready, though."

"We're looking for Scooter."

"He's out draggin' up firewood. Ought to be back right soon." Bo's forehead creased with worry. "He ain't got in no trouble, has he?"

"No trouble. His father has come to see him."

Bo seemed at a loss for words. He started to extend his hand but reconsidered and drew it back. He would not expect a white stranger to shake with him. "You're Scooter's daddy?" His voice hinted at the same misgivings Andy felt. "You and him been away from one another a long time."

"Too long, but I'm fixin' to make it up."

Bo looked at the captain and at Andy, a silent pleading in his eyes. "I hope you ain't fixin' to take him away. That boy's been a right smart of help to me."

Instead of replying to Bo, Tennyson turned to the captain. "You got him takin' orders from a nigger?"

The captain stiffened. "He listens to all of us. That's how a boy learns."

"Not a boy of mine. I want him growin' up proud and strong. He's got no business playin' servant to anybody, least of all a nigger."

The captain's face flushed as he struggled for an answer. Andy knotted his fists.

They were distracted by a scraping sound. Scooter approached on horseback, dragging several long, dead tree branches at the end of a rawhide rope. He brought them up even with a remnant of woodpile and jumped to the ground. He retrieved the rope and coiled it. "That ought to last a couple of days, Bo. You want me to chop it up?"

Bo's eyes were troubled. He did not answer.

Tennyson said, "You're through doin' chores around here, son."

Scooter noticed the visitor for the first time. He blinked in confusion.

Tennyson bent down. "Don't you recognize your old daddy?"

Scooter appeared at first to disbelieve what his eyes told him. "Pa?"

"Son, I've come to fetch you away from this place. It's time me and you was partners again." He opened his arms.

Scooter hesitated another moment, then accepted his father's hug. "Pa, I didn't know who you was."

"Five years make a lot of changes in a man. But not as many as in a boy." He pushed his son off to arm's length and gave him a long study. "You've growed a sight bigger than I expected. You're might near a man."

"Might near."

"Have you missed me?"

"I didn't think I'd ever see you again."

"There was times I wondered too, but you'll see a lot of me from now on. We've got places to go and things to do."

"Where we goin'?"

"We'll talk about that. How long before you're ready?"

Scooter looked to the officer for an answer. "Is it all right with you, Captain?"

The captain was slow to answer. "Son, you're free to do whatever you want to. Just be sure you know your mind."

"This is my daddy." Scooter looked at Bo. "You're always talkin' about Scripture. Don't it say in the Book that I'm supposed to obey my daddy?"

The cook's words came reluctantly. "It ain't for me to tell you what you should do. All I know is that you've been a changed young'un since you've been with us."

Scooter turned back to his father. "These Rangers have treated me real good."

Tennyson said, "But they ain't your kin. Blood is what matters most in this world."

Scooter pondered his dilemma, his freckled face twisting. "I guess I belong with my daddy."

The captain nodded gravely. "If that's your choice."

Andy protested, "Scooter, you were ridin' with outlaws when we found you. You don't want to be doin' that again."

"I'll be ridin' with my daddy."

Andy wanted to grab the boy and shake him until he changed his mind, but he could not bring himself to lay a hand on Scooter. He said, "You're makin' a mistake."

The captain said, "Leave him alone, Pickard. I told him the choice was his."

"But he's makin' the wrong one."

Tennyson said, "Keepin' a boy away from his kin is like cuttin' off the roots to a tree. It ain't right. He needs to know who he is and who his people are."

Scooter asked, "We don't have to leave today, do we?"

Bo put in, "Stay a little longer and I'll fix this boy a supper like he ain't never had before."

Tennyson considered. "Supper? Sounds all right to me. My horse is about give out anyway."

Andy had found that tired horses were always a logical excuse for inaction.

Rusty had come up by then. Taking him aside Andy told him, "Maybe this'll give me time to talk Scooter out of the notion."

Rusty frowned. "Careful. If you push him into a decision he comes to regret, he'll resent you the rest of his life."

"If he makes the wrong decision, he'll resent me for not advisin' him better."

Rusty shrugged. "Looks like you're rimfired either way you go."

Bo joined them. He seemed unable to conceive of the boy going away. He said, "When he first come here I felt like skinnin' him alive. But us all workin' together, we've made a pretty good kid out of him. Maybe he'll still decide not to go with his daddy."

Andy said glumly, "Maybe. But if *my* real daddy was to show up, I guess I'd want to go with him. Kin is kin."

"There's a difference. Your real daddy was a peaceful farmer, so they say. He wasn't no outlaw."

Andy noticed that Tennyson sought out Dick Landon and talked with him at length. Later, when he had a chance, Andy asked Dick what Tennyson had been so interested in.

Dick said, "He asked a lot of questions. Told me he heard talk in the pen about the fight between the Landons and the Hoppers. I told him I've been tryin' to stay out of it, but it's hard when so many people are tryin' to hunt down my brother."

"Maybe Jayce has got to Mexico by now."

"I doubt he'd go there without Flora. No, he'll stay close enough to keep in touch with her and the rest of the family."

"Then he's always in danger of bein' found."

Dick's face darkened. "Them that find him, they'll wish they hadn't."

Andy had expected trouble to come sooner or later from Sheriff Oscar Truscott or at least his deputy, Big'un Hopper. He had not expected the county judge to show up at the Ranger camp in a buggy, sided by Big'un and another Hopper on horseback. Andy remembered Big'un calling this one Harp. The family resemblance was strong.

Judge Hopper looked to be in the final stages of dyspepsia. He stopped at the headquarters tent first, conferring awhile with the captain. The captain in turn sent for Andy.

The captain's face was sober, but Andy could sense anger simmering beneath the surface. "Private Pickard, Judge Hopper has made grave charges against you and Private Brackett."

Andy stood straight and defiant. "We expected somebody would." He wondered why Sheriff Truscott had not come instead of the judge. He had sensed almost from the first that friction existed between the sheriff and his in-laws.

Big'un poked a thick finger toward Andy's face. "This man and his partner contrived for a prisoner to escape."

The captain maintained a stern attitude. "And how did they do that? Private Pickard brought me a signed release certifying that the prisoner had been delivered into the sheriff's hands. All further responsibility was the sheriff's."

Big'un said, "They claimed they'd searched him, but he had a gun on him. He forced the jailer to turn him aloose."

Andy said, "Didn't you or the sheriff search him too before he went into the jail?"

"We took you-all's word."

"I distinctly remember seein' you feel of Jayce's pockets."

"He must've had it someplace else. In his boot, maybe. We trusted you

Rangers to be sure he didn't carry any weapon when you turned him over to us."

"He didn't." Andy was gratified that the Hoppers evidently had not figured out something that seemed obvious to him: Flora Landon had slipped her husband the derringer. He did not want to make their job easier or the woman's life harder than it already was.

Big'un declared, "One of them Rangers wounded a cousin of mine. Took a chunk out of his leg. He'll never walk straight again."

Andy retorted, "The way most of them were liquored up that night, he wasn't walkin' very straight before."

The captain frowned at Andy, a quiet signal for him to tread lightly.

The judge looked up the row of tents. "Where is that other Ranger, the one named Brackett? Why is he not out here?"

Andy did not answer. He decided that was for the captain to do if he so chose.

The captain said, "He is recuperating from a wound some of your people inflicted upon him."

"I asked you where he is."

"And I have chosen not to say. Any business you have with him, you can take up with me." The captain's firm stance made it plain that he did not intend to tell more than he already had.

Big'un broke in, "We understand you've got a man here by the name of Landon."

The captain said, "Yes. Private Dick Landon."

"Do you know he's a brother to the fugitive?"

"I do, but I've kept Private Landon here in camp or on assignment nearby. You cannot implicate him in this fiasco."

"He didn't have to be there. I'm bettin' that him and Pickard and Brackett were in cahoots. And I'm bettin' he knows where his brother is at. He may even be hidin' him somewhere close to this camp." Big'un's voice rose as he spoke.

The judge said, "I have sworn out a warrant for the arrest of Pickard and Brackett and your Ranger Landon. I intend to bring them before the grand jury." He removed some papers from his vest pocket.

The captain planted his feet a little farther apart. "You are out of your jurisdiction." Nevertheless, he gave the documents a cursory inspection. His voice edged toward the sarcastic. "Signed by Judge Judd Hopper. I wonder why the Hopper name does not surprise me."

"I was duly elected by the voters of the county. Those papers are as legal as if they were signed by Sam Houston himself."

The captain handed back the documents. "I cannot accept these. I do not know if the signature is genuine."

"I just told you."

"I do not know if *you* are genuine. You have shown me no documentation to prove you are who you say you are."

Big'un said, "You can see my badge."

"Any half-sober silversmith can counterfeit a badge. The men you seek are Rangers under my command, duly sworn. You will not have them unless I receive direct orders from the adjutant general."

Big'un said, "He's way to hell over in Austin."

"Probably, if he is not away on an inspection tour somewhere across the state. I suggest you go to Austin and wait for him."

Big'un started to turn his horse away but paused to curse the captain. "We ain't done yet. You'll be wishin' you'd never heard of us Hoppers."

The captain said, "I already do. Leave this camp, or I shall place you under arrest for disturbing the peace. I may come up with another charge or two if I set my mind to it."

Andy watched the judge's face flush a deep red. He thought Hopper might be in some danger of bursting a blood vessel. Big'un gave the judge a cautionary look. "Better ease off, Uncle. You know what the doctor told you about them conniption fits." He turned his eyes to the captain. "Looks to me like he needs a drink."

"We don't keep liquor in camp."

"Some water, then."

The captain offered no sympathy. "There's a whole riverful of it down yonder."

Big'un and the judge rode down toward the river. Harp followed a length behind. He had never spoken. Andy surmised that he simply rode in his kinsmen's shadow.

Sweating heavily, Andy said, "Thanks, Captain. I was afraid you might give them what they asked for."

"The Rangers stand by their own."

"Those Hoppers are a hard bunch. From what I heard, so are the Landons. Dick is an exception."

"Perhaps. Given sufficient provocation, there is no telling what any man might do, including yourself. I gather you have had no experience with a real Texas family feud."

"Not like this one."

"They can be vicious. They can draw in an entire community, including people who are no blood kin. Back in the time of the republic, two groups known as the Regulators and the Moderators went to war against one another. It took Sam Houston and the Texas army to stop the bloodshed."

"I've heard about that one."

"Sometimes it's hard to stay neutral, but we have to. It's our job to keep the peace, even if we have to kill some people to do it."

"Big'un Hopper is a determined man, and so is the judge. Do you think they'll just turn around and go back?"

"I'll see that they do. I'll send Len Tanner as an escort to see the three of them safe from Indian attack the first forty or fifty miles."

"There hasn't been an Indian attack around here in years."

The captain smiled thinly. "And we want to keep it that way."

Andy thought by the time the Hoppers listened to a one-sided conversation from Len for fifty miles, they would not want to come back. He could talk the ears off a dead mule.

CHAPTER

EIGHT

The Ranger company had given Scooter an unclaimed fourteen-year-old horse recovered from a thief, along with an old saddle and a bridle acquired the same way. He had been as proud as if the rig were brand-new and the horse a three-year-old. He rode beside his father, who had not told him their destination but had set out after breakfast in an eastward direction.

A squirrel chattered at them from the limb of a pecan tree. Lige said, "There's supper." He drew his pistol and fired. The squirrel toppled, its head gone.

Scooter whistled. "Man! I never even seen a Ranger shoot like that."

"It ain't nothin' you can't learn to do. Just got to set your mind to it. I'll learn you."

Lige motioned, and Scooter dismounted to retrieve the squirrel. Lige said, "Keep watchin' for another. We can have us a regular feast as good as what that darky's been fixin'."

"Ain't many can cook like Bo."

Lige frowned. "Them Rangers had no business lettin' you do chores for the likes of him. You're white, and don't you ever forget it."

"Bein' black ain't Bo's fault. He's good people."

"As long as he knows his place."

At dusk they sat before a campfire, watching two squirrels broiling on the ends of long sticks. Scooter said, "Been a long time since we camped together. So long I can barely remember it."

"We'll do it a lot more. We're partners, me and you." Lige leaned forward for a look at the squirrels. "I done a lot of campin' when I was younger. Bet you didn't know I lived for a few years up in the Cherokee nation."

"With the Indians?"

"They was good Indians."

"I didn't know there *was* any good ones. Comanches come awful close to killin' me once. I hid out to where they couldn't find me, but they sure tried. They come so close I swear I could smell their breath."

"The Cherokees are a different breed. I had me some good friends amongst them, and we cut some real shines together. Of course I was a sight younger then." Lige mused for a while, staring into the fire. "I got it in mind to go back up to the nation and find me a Cherokee wife. They each got a head right to some land. Me and you could get us a good little farm that way."

"You'd marry an Indian just to get some land?"

"It ain't easy for a poor man to get ahold of good land these days. Besides, there's other advantages to bein' married. Me and your mama had a pretty good life together. I miss her."

"I don't know how I'd take to havin' an Indian mother. I'd keep thinkin' about them Comanches wantin' to scalp me. I'd wonder if she had the same notion."

"Them Cherokees live like white people. Got their own government. Even got their own newspaper."

"Still, I don't know as I'd like it. I might not go with you up there."

"You'll go where I say." Tennyson's face clouded with anger that came quickly and faded the same way. "The Good Book says to honor your father."

"You've read the Good Book?"

"Parts of it."

"You believe everything it says?"

"The parts I agree with. I heard a lot of preachin' while I was back yonder workin' for the governor. So we'll follow the Book, and you'll go where I go."

Scooter had forgotten how mercurial his father's moods could be. He remembered how hard his father could slap him with an open hand, then hug him tenderly. He decided to step with caution. "And where'll that be?"

"Back where that feud is goin' on. I talked to Dick Landon, and I watched that judge and the deputies. I figure a man good with a gun ought to be able to hire out to one side or the other for high dollars. That'd set us up fine for goin' to the Cherokee nation. But first we need us a little road stake."

"Road stake?"

"Travelin' money. There's a nice little bank over in Kerrville. I think I could talk them into makin' us a loan."

Scooter did not hide his misgivings. "When you say loan, you're really thinkin' robbery."

"Robbery is an ugly word. *Borrowin'* touches softer on the ear."

"I doubt as the Rangers would see the difference."

"You're not with the Rangers anymore. It's time you quit worryin' about what they think."

"I was with Arliss and Brewster and another feller when they held up the bank in Brownwood. Scared me near as bad as them Comanches did."

"There's nothin' to be scared of when you know what you're doin'. Watch me and learn. Every boy needs to master more than one trade."

The Rangers had told Scooter that Kerrville and several other towns in the hill country had a strong German influence. They explained that in the years before the war, many groups of Europeans—German, Polish, Alsatian, Irish—had immigrated into Texas, usually settling into enclaves among their own kind, where they felt comfortable.

All he knew about Germans was that they talked differently from most people though they looked like just about everybody else. He wondered if the men in the bank would understand Lige's words. But of course they would understand his meaning. Everybody knew what a gun meant when they looked at it from the front end.

He was sure Andy and Bo and everybody else back in camp would be furious at him and Lige both. But he knew he could not talk his father out of the notion. Lige was better at talking than at listening.

Lige gave the bank several minutes' scrutiny. "I was in there six or seven years ago. Doubt it's changed much."

"You've robbed it before?"

"I looked at it as a loan. Never intended to keep the money permanent. I always figured on payin' it back someday when I could. Just ain't been able to. Besides, it ain't right, some people havin' so much money and some not havin' none. What the government ought to do is take up all the money in the country and divide it equal. When you look at it that way, all I'm doin' is seein' that we get our share. That's what democracy is all about."

Scooter saw three horses tied in front of the bank. He wondered if their riders would stand idle while Lige single-handedly robbed the place. "Hadn't you better go in and look things over first, Pa?"

"They might recognize me from last time. Best thing is to get straight to business. Now you stay in the saddle and hold my horse. I'm liable to be in kind of a hurry when I come out."

Hands shaking, Scooter took the reins his father handed him. "What if things go wrong and you don't come out?"

"Then run like hell. The penitentiary ain't no place for a growin' boy." Lige turned away, carrying his saddlebags over one arm.

Scooter's stomach churned. He tried to ease the tension by pretending that his father was only teasing him, that he actually intended to negotiate a legitimate loan. The fantasy faded like a wisp of smoke. The truth was as solid and forbidding as that stone bank building.

A friendly voice called, causing him to freeze. "Howdy, Scooter. What you doin' so far from camp?"

He turned, trembling. Ranger Johnny Morris walked toward him. Scooter stammered, trying for some kind of answer. He remembered that the captain had sent Johnny on a mission of some kind a few days ago.

"I'm with my pa," Scooter managed. "He came and got me."

"Your pa? I thought he was in . . ." Johnny broke off. "Where's your pa now?"

"He went in the bank."

"The bank!" Johnny turned on his heel, drawing his pistol as he ran. He barely had time to enter the front door before Scooter heard a shot from inside.

Lige rushed out, a smoking pistol in one hand, the saddlebags slung over the other arm. He tossed the bags to Scooter and grabbed the reins from Scooter's hand. "Hang on to them bags. Hold them tight."

He swung into the saddle and fired a shot through the open bank door. Someone stepped quickly back out of sight.

Lige shouted, "Let's go. This town ain't got no friendlier."

Scooter was too frightened to talk until they had cleared the outskirts of town. They galloped eastward alongside the rock-strewn Guadalupe

River and its tall cypress trees. Looking back, he could see no one in pursuit, but he reasoned that they would soon be coming. "I hope you didn't kill somebody."

Lige cursed. "Everything was goin' just dandy till some feller come stormin' in with a six-shooter. Wasn't nothin' I could do but shoot him before he could shoot me."

"That was a Ranger. He was a friend of mine."

"When it comes to the law, us Tennysons ain't got no friends."

Scooter wanted to cry but couldn't. "Did you kill him?"

"Things went too fast. I just know I hit him. He ought to've minded his own business. I was mindin' mine."

Scooter felt a measure of relief, but not enough. "That *is* his business, chasin' robbers."

"Don't call me a robber again or I'll take my belt to you. I swear, young'uns these days have got no respect."

Scooter's anger flared, the aftermath to his earlier fear. "If you ain't a robber, what are you?"

"A rebel. They got too many laws in this country, and I've fought against damn near all of them. I was born free. I intend to stay that way."

Scooter thought that might not be easy. "The Rangers will all be after us now, and they don't stop at no county lines."

The news from Kerrville brought all the off-duty Rangers to the headquarters tent. The report was that a bank robber had badly wounded Johnny Morris. A boy had been with him. The message did not offer any names, but Andy was sure Lige Tennyson was the culprit. Scooter was a witness at the least, perhaps even an unwilling accomplice.

Andy told the captain, "I had a bad feelin' about Tennyson from the start. I want to go over there."

"I don't think I should let you. You're too close a friend to the boy."

"Everybody in camp was friends with Scooter. He's liable to end up killed if we don't get him away from that outlaw daddy."

The captain's face indicated that he was going to turn Andy down, but he said, "All right. I'm sending Sergeant Holloway and Rusty Shannon. You can accompany them. Saddle up. You'll leave in twenty minutes."

Rusty and Andy were sitting on their horses in front of the headquarters tent when Sergeant Holloway came out carrying his rifle. They had blanket rolls tied to their saddles, grub from Bo's kitchen hanging in cloth sacks. The sergeant walked to where a Ranger had Holloway's horse sad-dled and waiting. He said nothing. Conversation tended to be sparse on a serious Ranger mission.

The three Rangers rode far into the night, following a wagon road that wound through the valleys and between the hills. Andy judged that it was past midnight when they rode up to the jail in Kerrville. For the last couple of hours he had felt the horse gradually tiring beneath him. He doubted the animal had another hour of travel left.

The sergeant knocked on the door several times before a sleepy-headed deputy sheriff answered, holding a lamp so he could see the faces before he opened the door all the way. He recognized Holloway on sight. "I was sort of expectin' you Rangers, but not at this hour of the night."

Holloway said, "Rangers don't get much sleep when outlaws are on the prowl. How's Johnny Morris?"

"He'll live, but he was hard hit. Goin' to be a long time before he does any Rangerin' again."

Rusty asked, "Where's he at?" He and the two Morris brothers had been friends for years.

"Over at the doctor's house. I wouldn't go beatin' on the door now, though. Him and the doctor both need sleep. You can bunk down here till daylight. I got some empty cells."

Holloway thanked him for his thoughtfulness. "We'll need to put our horses away first. I'll want to talk to witnesses as soon as we can. We're pretty sure we know who the culprit is."

The deputy nodded. "Your Ranger told us the boy's name is Scooter Tennyson. The robber was the boy's daddy."

Andy asked, "Did Scooter help with the robbery?"

"The Ranger said it looked to him like the kid was holdin' the horses. Said he hoped the young'un didn't realize what was goin' on."

The sergeant frowned at Andy. "For the time bein' we'll give Scooter the benefit of the doubt. But if he knew what his daddy was doin', and he helped, we'll have to consider him an accessory."

"He's just a kid."

"A kid can pull a trigger."

Andy found a jail cell a poor place to sleep. The bunk was rock-hard. He had never given much consideration to the comfort of people he helped to arrest. He thought perhaps in the future he might be more conscious of prisoners' rights.

Holloway had little use for a bed after sunup nor was he sympathetic with others who would rather sleep than meet the new day. He hollered, "Daylight!" at the top of his voice. He was not accustomed to saying it twice. Andy had slept in his clothes, all but boots and hat. He donned the hat first, then pulled on his boots.

The deputy soon emerged from his living quarters. "Got water and a wash pan out by the back door. I'll see if I can scramble up some breakfast."

Andy appreciated the fresh eggs, though the deputy cooked them too long and gave them a scorched flavor. The biscuits were soft and warm. He smeared them liberally with fresh butter and dipped them in blackstrap molasses. Good biscuits could make up for a lot.

His thoughts ran to Scooter. He wondered where the boy was now. Camped out along a trail somewhere, more than likely, possibly hungry and frightened. He thought of Johnny Morris lying in the doctor's house, in pain from a bullet wound that could easily have killed him.

Damn Lige Tennyson. Andy wished there were a dozen of Tennyson, and every one of them was locked up in the Kerrville jail. Or better, buried at the back side of the Kerrville cemetery.

Andy kept glancing at the sergeant, wanting him to hurry his meal. Holloway took note of his impatience. "In due time. Johnny may still be sleeping."

The deputy said, "The robbers headed east along the river road. We trailed them a ways, but we lost their tracks because they was mixed with so many others. There's no tellin' which way they went once they got plumb clear of the town."

Johnny Morris was awake and propped up in bed. His face was pale, his cheeks drawn in, but his eyes lit up when he saw his fellow Rangers. He said in a thin voice, "I thought for a while I was fixin' to go absent without leave."

The sergeant smiled. "That'd be desertion. You're too good a Ranger for that." He quickly got down to business. "We figure the robber was Lige Tennyson. Are you sure it was Scooter you saw?"

Johnny said, "It was him, all right. I was surprised to see him sittin' there holdin' a second horse. When I asked what he was doin', he said he was waitin' for his daddy. I remembered that his daddy was supposed to be in the pen, so I figured he didn't go in the bank to make a deposit."

"And you set out to stop him?"

"The bank was dark. Comin' in from the daylight, I couldn't see much. The robber shot me before I got a good look at him."

Andy said, "Reckon Scooter knew what his daddy was up to?"

"Maybe there wasn't nothin' he could do about it."

The sergeant said, "He could have ridden away and left his father."

Andy argued, "You couldn't expect him to do that. He hadn't seen his daddy in five years. He wouldn't leave him so soon."

"In the eyes of the law he's old enough to make choices, even the hard ones."

A visit to the bank filled in some extra details but did not change the cardinal fact that the holdup man was almost certainly Lige Tennyson. A quick-thinking teller had filled the saddlebags with low-denomination bills and a stack of blank counter checks so that the bank's loss was minimal. Tennyson must have been sorely disappointed when he stopped to count the fruits of his labor.

Holloway said, "Comin' up short, he'll likely pull another robbery before long. I'll wire Austin a description, and the adjutant general's office will send it across the state. I doubt that Tennyson has any idea how the telegraph lines have spread durin' the time he was in the pen."

Impatience stung Andy like a case of hives. "Every time he does it he puts Scooter in danger. Sooner or later they'll run into somebody who's a good shot."

"We'll try to pick up his trail. Maybe we'll have better luck than the townfolks did."

Andy burned inside. He wished he had Lige Tennyson in front of him right now. He would gladly shoot him, even if Scooter hated him for it afterward.

Lige Tennyson had been in a dark mood since he had stopped to open the saddlebags and find out how rich he was. Scooter watched him uneasily, fearful that he might become the whipping boy for his father's frustrations. So far he had not, but Scooter remembered harsh punishment inflicted long ago for minor infractions.

Lige had turned the air blue. "Damned teller with his clean white shirt and necktie. A dirty crook is what he is, cheatin' me thisaway. I wouldn't put it past him to've stuck the real money in his pockets and then claim I got it all."

Scooter considered the implications. "That'd be double robbery, wouldn't it, robbin' you and the bank both? He could go to jail twice."

Lige rumbled on, "I'd go back and blow his lamp out, but the town'll be swarmin' with Rangers by now. We got to keep movin'."

Scooter figured his father was probably right about the Rangers. He wondered if Andy and the others were on the trail right now. Lige had been careful to stay on the river road at first so their tracks would be difficult to separate from the others. They had turned off at a place where the road crossed a field of gravel deposited by some long-ago flood. They had not left a track that he could see.

He was torn between a wish that the Rangers would catch up with them and a fear that if they did, they might shoot first and discuss consequences later. He had heard enough talk in camp to know that at times it was considered good judgment to bring a prisoner in dead rather than alive. Under stressful circumstances the Rangers were prone to be both judge and jury.

Lige muttered, "We ain't got near as much money as I figured. We're goin' to have to find us another loan."

Scooter said, "We don't have to *borrow* money that way. We could find work and earn it fair and square."

"Doin' what? I never was no good at a town job. Tried clerkin' in a store once. Pretty soon I was talkin' to myself. I done a little work as a ranch hand, but I never saw an outfit that didn't have a bunch of rank horses they expected you to ride. I'm gettin' too old for that. Banks, now, that's somethin' I know a right smart about. You just walk in, get their attention in the right way, and they'll generally loan you anything you ask for."

"Sometimes they've got guards with guns."

"If you want money, you've got to go where the money is at."

They came in sight of a modest frame farmhouse. Lige signaled for Scooter to stop. He studied the place awhile, then observed, "Crops ain't well tended. Weeds look to be doin' better than the corn."

Scooter smelled wood smoke and saw that it was coming from the backyard. A skinny middle-aged woman carried water from a steaming wash pot to a wooden tub, her thin back bending under the strain. She began scrubbing clothes.

Lige speculated, "Widder woman maybe. If she had a man the weeds wouldn't be takin' the field that way."

Scooter worried, "We ain't fixin' to rob her, are we?"

Lige seemed scandalized that his son would think such a thing. "There's no gain in holdin' up poor folks. They've got nothin' to give you anyway. But maybe we can get us a woman-cooked meal. You're lookin' a little drawed."

Scooter had not had much to eat except for squirrel and somebody's young shoat they had caught rooting for acorns. "Whatever you say, Pa."

The woman raised up from her scrub board as they approached the rear of her house. She seemed unconcerned. Scooter supposed she reasoned that a man traveling with a boy at his side presented no threat.

Lige touched fingers to the brim of his misshapen hat. "How do, ma'am. Me and my son are just passin' through. We noticed that your garden stands in need of weedin'. We wondered if we might trade a little service for a good meal. The boy ain't et proper in a while."

Scooter thought the woman looked a little like his mother when she gave them a weary but grateful smile. She said, "That'd be a mighty welcome trade. My husband's laid up with a broke leg, and things around here have got away from me some. Soon as I get these clothes on the line I'll see what I can cook up for you."

Lige nodded. "If you'll kindly direct us to where your husband keeps his workin' tools, me and the boy'll get busy."

She accompanied them to a small frame barn where a hoe, a rake, and smaller tools were neatly arrayed. She said, "You wouldn't see things in this shape if my husband was able to work. Neighbors come now and again to help, but they got needs of their own to see after."

Lige said, "We'll do the best we can."

There was only one hoe. Lige told Scooter, "I'll pull up the big ones by hand. You foller along and cut down the littler ones."

Lige worked faster with his bare hands than Scooter could with the hoe. "Pa, you act like you've done this before."

"I got lots of practice while I was studyin' at the state school. They expect you to earn your keep. When we get that farm of our own up in the territory, we'll be doin' a lot of this. Watch out you don't cut them tater vines instead of the weeds."

Scooter soon worked up a sweat. He was not sure he looked forward to that farm of their own, but maybe it would keep Pa happy enough to give up his forays into the banking business.

Between them they finished most of the garden before the woman called them to supper. The food made up in quantity what it lacked in variety. She said apologetically, "It ain't fancy, but there's nourishment in it for a growin' boy. Lucky we still got ham and fatback and such in the smokehouse from last winter."

Lige said, "It's mighty fine."

The woman's husband had limped to the table, aided by crutches. One leg was immobilized by splints bound securely with strips of cotton cloth. He said, "I'm much obliged to you fellers. As you can see, I been about as much use around here lately as teats on a boar hog."

It was obvious to Scooter that the place had been a long way from prosperity even when the farmer had full use of both legs. The little furniture he saw looked as if its best service would be as kindling to start a blaze in the fireplace. Newspapers had been pasted to the wall in lieu of wallpaper. They might block the wind that pushed between the siding's raw pine boards, but they would do little to shut out summer heat or winter cold.

The woman noticed Scooter's silent appraisal of the room. She said, "It ain't much, but it's ours. We done it all ourselves. Grubbed it out of the ground, me and my husband, with the Lord's help."

Lige said, "Glory be to the Lord."

That startled Scooter. He doubted that his father had given the Lord much thought when he robbed the bank in Kerrville.

The farmer said, "If you-all ain't in too much of a hurry, you're welcome to stay all night. Eat breakfast before you go on your way in the mornin'."

Lige said, "That's kind of you. We couldn't go much farther before dark."

Scooter observed that his father enjoyed other people's cooking far more than his own. That was probably one reason he was eager to find himself a Cherokee woman, beyond the possibility of profiting from her head right to land in the territory. Scooter worried that somebody might have picked up their trail and be following it even as they idled at this farmer's table, but Lige seemed not to share his concern. With a warm and solid meal in his belly, he appeared content to accept the world on its own terms.

There being no sign of rain, Lige elected to spread a little hay on the ground and unroll his blanket on top of it. "Ain't nothin' healthier than the clean outdoors with the stars for your ceilin'," he said. "For five years the only stars I seen was through a high window with bars in it."

"Pa, are you sure a farm is what you want? These folks have got one, and they're as poor as church mice."

"Because they ain't got enough land. Me and you, we ain't goin' to settle for nothin' small like this. We're goin' to have a big farm with a big house and lots of stock. We'll have cornfields stretchin' as far as the eye can see. I've had lots of time to plan it all out. I know just where everything is goin' to be—the house, the barns, the fields."

"All that is goin' to take lots of money."

"The reason most people don't have enough money is that they don't have the guts to go where it's at and get their fair share."

As they finished breakfast Scooter saw his father stick a roll of bills into the sugar bowl when the farmer and his wife were looking away. He said nothing about it until they had put the little farm behind them.

"You said we ain't got much money, but I seen you leave a wad of it for them folks."

"Do good where you see the need and the Lord will reward you. Next time maybe He'll lead us to a bank where the teller ain't a crook like that last one was."

CHAPTER
NINE

Sergeant Holloway held out little hope of finding Lige's and Scooter's tracks. Too many others had been made along the river road that led eastward from Kerrville, including those of the earlier posse. The sergeant was about ready to give up.

He said, "Anywhere there's a telegraph, the local authorities will be on the lookout for Tennyson and the boy. These modern communications are the wonder of the world. Did you know a man can board a train in New York and get to San Francisco in less time than it takes to ride horseback from Fort Worth to San Antonio?"

Andy argued, "But we're not goin' to San Francisco, and most of Texas doesn't have a railroad yet. Lots of places ain't even got a telegraph."

He chafed with impatience, but he was just a private. It was the sergeant's place to make decisions.

Rusty recognized Andy's anxiety. "We've come this far, Bill. Won't hurt us to try a little longer."

Holloway reconsidered, respecting Rusty's long experience. "Wouldn't want the captain sayin' we quit too quick. Andy, how's your trackin' eye?"

Andy feared his reputation was better than his ability, for most people assumed his Indian background gave him an advantage in following trails. But a show of confidence might keep Holloway from abandoning the search. "Nothin' wrong with my eyes."

He had found long ago that he had better hunches than most people. He wondered if it might come from his association with the Comanches, who put a lot of faith in intuition, visions, and dreams. When the three riders reached a place where a flood had deposited a large bed of gravel at a bend in the river, he had one of those hunches. He said, "If I was wantin' to cover my trail, right here is where I'd quit the road. A buffalo herd wouldn't leave tracks in that gravel."

Holloway said, "It's your hand. Play it."

Andy moved forward while Rusty and the sergeant waited so they would not add their horses' tracks to any already there. He rode along the leading edge of the gravel deposit until he found the trail of two horses. A light shower had created a thin skim of mud. The tracks had dried hard enough to preserve them from the wind's destructive touch. His hunch told him these marked the passage of Lige and the boy. He waved his arm.

"We're on the money," he shouted.

Rusty dismounted and studied the tracks. "One horse's forefoot turns out a little, like he might've been crippled at some time."

Andy said, "That'd be Scooter's. I remember the old brown they gave him had a funny way of walkin'. Kind of paddle-footed." He felt a rising excitement. "What about it, Sergeant?"

Holloway pointed his chin eastward. "We came to catch a bank robber. We're not doin' it sittin' here."

It occurred to Andy after a while that Lige had evidently not put much effort into hiding his trail. He probably thought he had followed the well-traveled road far enough to throw off a posse. Now and then the trail would disappear on hard ground or in thick grass, but Andy would manage to pick it up again a little farther on. Lige's direction seemed well set.

Holloway said, "Looks like he's headed almost due east. We can afford to lope up some. Even if we lose the trail awhile, we ought to be able to cut it again. Maybe we can gain on him."

The second day they had not seen the trail in a while but were traveling on faith and hope. Spotting a small frame house, they stopped to water their horses. A gaunt, hard-used farm woman came out to greet them. The sergeant introduced himself. "We're obliged for the water. We'd be glad to pay for it."

She demurred. "I don't see how I can charge you for water. It's a gift from the Lord."

The sergeant smiled. "The Lord didn't dig that well for you, did He?"

"No, sir, me and my husband done that. But the Lord was lookin' on and made sure we found water."

Holloway handed her a silver dollar. "I'll pay the Lord His share next time I get to church. Been any strangers pass this way the last day or two?"

"The only people been by here lately was a man and a boy. Fine folks. They taken time to hoe the garden for me. My husband is laid up and can't work."

Andy stiffened. "Did you hear any names?"

"I don't recall that he ever introduced himself, exactly. And the boy just called him Pa." She frowned, trying to remember. "Seems to me I heard him call the boy by name, but I can't remember what it was."

"Could it have been Scooter?"

Her face brightened. "I believe it was. You know them?"

Holloway said, "We do. Were they still travelin' east when they left here?"

"They was. But I can't imagine what interest you Rangers would have in God-lovin' folks like them. Even after workin' for their keep, they left some money for us."

Kerrville bank money, Andy guessed. Tennyson could afford to be generous with it. It wasn't his.

The sergeant said, "May I be so bold as to ask how much?"

"Close to fifty dollars. I wanted to give it back, but they was gone by the time I found it."

Andy said, "It doesn't make sense, him *givin'* somebody money."

The sergeant said, "It's a waste of time to try and figure out people like Tennyson. They serve the Lord one minute and the devil the next. Tryin' to stay in good with both sides, I guess."

Riding away, Holloway seemed cheered. "He gave those folks most of the little bit he got in Kerrville. He'll be needin' more. We already wired Austin to send a warnin' to all the banks. Next time Tennyson tries to make a withdrawal, he may find himself lookin' down a dozen gun barrels."

Andy felt a dark foreboding. "What about Scooter?"

"Let's hope his daddy thinks enough of him to leave him out of harm's way."

Rusty brooded. "I can't figure Lige. If it was me and I was on the dodge, I'd go west to where law is scarce. I wouldn't go back where there's a badge on every section corner."

Holloway said, "Where law is scarce, there aren't many banks either. A workin' man goes where the work is. Or in Tennyson's case, where the money is."

Rusty said, "If I didn't know better I'd say he's headed almost directly toward my farm."

Andy said, "He'd have no reason to be goin' there."

Holloway said, "You can bet Tennyson knows what he's doin', or thinks he does. He wouldn't be travelin' this direction without he had cause. I'd give a month's pay to know what it is."

The third day Andy lost the trail and could not find it although he criss-crossed several times, returning always to a generally eastward direction. Toward dark the three Rangers came upon a family of movers camping with a tarp-covered wagon and a trail wagon hitched behind. The wagon tongue was pointed west. A young boy herded half a dozen cows and a bull. Andy could only guess at the disappointments that had put these people on the road to new country and a fresh start.

Holloway hailed them in an easy, smiling manner. "How far you-all headed?"

The man was straightening harness. "Pecos River or bust. We hear there's cheap land out there."

Cheap for a good reason, Andy thought. Charles Goodnight had called the Pecos River "the grave of a cowman's hopes." But settlers were starting to drift out that way regardless. So long as there was new land, there was always a chance, or at least the illusion of one, even where it didn't rain enough to grow much more than greasewood and prickly pear.

The Indians were not alone in following dreams.

As he had with everyone else they met, Holloway asked if they had seen a man and a boy traveling east.

The mover said, "We did. They rode into camp just as we was fixin' to have supper last night. Ate with us and rode on. Nice-actin' folks, they was."

The woman said, "Shy kind of a boy, though. Acted like he was scared to talk. I reckon he hasn't been out among strangers much."

Rusty asked, "Did they give any names?"

The man thought about it. "Not that I remember, and we didn't ask. I always figure if a man wants you to know what his name is, he'll tell you. If he doesn't want to, he's probably got a good reason."

Holloway politely turned down an invitation to stay for supper, explaining afterward that the people didn't look as if they had enough that they could afford to share. He said, "At least we're travelin' in the right direction. If we can find where those folks camped last night, maybe we can pick up Lige's tracks again."

The effort proved fruitless. They came across evidence of several campsites where fire pits had been dug and wood burned for cooking. Some were fresh enough to have been used within the last night or two. But Andy found no tracks he could identify as the paddle-footed brown's.

Holloway looked discouraged. Andy feared he might decide to quit. He had another hunch, that they were closer than they had been since they started, even if he could find no trail. But hunches would not carry a lot of weight with the sergeant. He was inclined to believe only what he could see, hear, or feel.

The land became increasingly familiar. Andy realized he had ridden over it with Rusty, looking for strayed cattle. Rusty acknowledged that they were not far from his farm.

Holloway asked, "Do you want to go by and see if everything is all right?"

Rusty said, "I haven't been gone long enough for much to've gone wrong. Unless Fowler Gaskin has come over and carried everything away." He had to explain about Gaskin.

Holloway understood. "I used to have a neighbor like that. He finally threw a conniption fit and died. You never saw so many people smilin' at a funeral."

"I doubt the Lord is anxious for Fowler to show up. He'll probably out-live us all."

Rusty's horse stumbled over a rough spot on the trail. "He's tirin' out. I expect they all are. How about we ride over to Sheriff Tom Blessing's and see if he can get us a change of horses?"

Holloway frowned. "We've already stretched pretty far past our district."

The Rangers did not have to stop at county lines. They were free to operate anywhere in the state. However, efficiency required that they remain within their own appointed areas of responsibility unless in pursuit or on a specific assignment.

They stopped at Rusty's farm. Nobody was there, a relief to Rusty. "I was half-afraid we'd find Fowler takin' up residence while I was gone. He did it once before when I was off chasin' after Indians."

The fields were as desolate as when Andy had last seen them in the wake of the hailstorm. Some plants were making a feeble try at regrowth, nature's eternal effort at survival, but they were stunted and doomed to be killed by frost before they could mature. In contrast to the fields, the garden showed signs of fresh work, freshly risen greenery.

Rusty said, "Shanty's been over here."

They went into the cabin and cooked a meager dinner. Andy noticed that Josie's photograph was missing from the mantel. Rusty must have carried it with him, though Andy had not seen him looking at it. He probably did that in private. Grief was taking a long time to heal.

Done with the meal, Rusty said, "Let's get on to town. Stoppin' here is like visitin' a graveyard."

They came upon Shanty's cabin. At Rusty's call, Shanty came out grinning. "Mr. Rusty, Andy. You-all ain't already quit bein' Rangers, have you?"

Rusty introduced him to Sergeant Holloway. "We've been trailin' a bank robber. He's got a boy travelin' with him. Anybody like that passed this way the last day or two?"

"Not as I noticed. I see most folks that come along this road. Anyway, what would a bank robber want with me? I don't have nothin' anybody'd want to steal."

"This one might've *given* you money."

"Then he sure ain't been by, because there ain't nobody given me nothin'."

Holloway grimaced. "I'm afraid we've played out our string. Tennyson may not stop till he gets halfway across Louisiana."

Andy clenched a fist in frustration. "You mean we're turnin' back?"

"I'll wire the captain and ask him what he wants us to do."

Andy said, "As long as we're this close, don't you think we ought to go by the Brackett place and see about Farley? He may be healed up enough to go back to camp."

"You and Rusty can do that while I stay in town and wait for the captain's answer."

Andy had a bitter taste in his mouth. He had far rather be taking Scooter back to camp, but he might have to settle for Farley Brackett.

At least he would see Bethel for a little while.

Scooter sat nervously on his horse half a length behind his father's while Lige quietly studied the town that lay before them. He had seen Lige count his money last night and frown.

Lige said, "Can't tell from here if this place is big enough to have a bank. Only way to know is to ride in and see."

Scooter asked, "How many times we got to do this, Pa?"

Lige turned to study him. "You're shakin', boy. Ain't nothin' to be scared of. Your old daddy knows what he's doin'."

"So do the Rangers. How do you know there ain't a bunch of them waitin' for us?"

Lige's eyes narrowed. "I can tell you ain't cut out for this business. That's why we need to travel on up to the territory and get us that farm as soon as we can. But we got to have money first, don't you see?"

"Most people don't get it this way."

"Everybody has got to find out what he's good at. I'm good at the bankin' business. Now come on, let's see what this place has to offer." His spurs jingled against his horse's sides. Scooter hesitated, then followed, his eyes searching for something to be afraid of. There was plenty, most of it imaginary.

They rode down the length of the short street. Lige slumped in disappointment. "This burg ain't big enough to support a bank. I'd settle for a good general store, but the only one I see don't look very prosperous. I wonder when the hard times are goin' to be over with."

"Seems like it's been hard times ever since I can remember."

"That's on account of the war. It's been more than ten years, but Texas ain't got over it. Times was flush before the Yankees started all that trouble. There was money enough for anybody who had the nerve to go and get what was due him. I can remember when I had so much gold that I had to have a packhorse to carry it."

"What went with it, Pa?"

"Money's like water. It dribbles out between your fingers no matter how hard you try to hold on to it. And who knew those good times were fixin' to end? We thought they'd go on and on."

They turned and rode back up the street the way they had come. Lige's attention was fixed on the general store. It was a square-fronted frame building innocent of paint. Farming tools and wooden barrels were displayed on the plank sidewalk, against the wall. A sign in the window advertised chewing tobacco and prickly bitters. Lige said, "I wonder what day it is. Used to be that Saturday was when all the farmers came to town. A good general store would have a lot of cash on hand."

"I think it's Wednesday, Pa. Or Tuesday."

"We can't wait around for Saturday. When you can't have all you want, you settle for what you can get." He dismounted in front of the store, stretching his arms and back. Scooter had heard him complain about rheumatism.

Lige handed over his reins. "Hold them. I'll go see to business. Stay awake, because when I come out I'll be lookin' to travel."

Scooter accepted reluctantly. "I'll be right here."

Lige patted him on the leg. "You're a good boy. You've got the makin's of a good man."

If you don't get me killed, Scooter thought.

A large man with a black mustache and a dark expression blocked Lige's entry into the store. He held up a hand that looked as big as a hindquarter of beef. The other hand rested upon the butt of a pistol high on his hip. "Just a minute, stranger. I need to know your name."

Scooter saw a small silver badge on the man's vest. A chill went all the way to his toes.

"My name?" Lige seemed momentarily taken aback. "What for?"

"I'm a deputy sheriff. We got a wire tellin' us to look out for a man and a boy that robbed a bank out west someplace. You've got a boy with you."

"My son," Lige said. "What do you mean, you got a wire?"

"Ain't you heard about the telegraph?"

"I've heard tell, but I never knew it'd come to a little place like this."

"They're gettin' it just about everywhere. There ain't a horse alive that can outrun it. Now what's your name and what you doin' here?"

Scooter searched Lige's face for a clue about what his father might do. He wondered if he might shoot this deputy the way he had shot Johnny Morris at the bank in Kerrville. He froze in dread.

Lige tried running a bluff. "My name's Simon Good. That's my boy Willy. We're just poor farmers passin' through on our way to help my baby sister over in Colorado County. Her husband is laid up with a broken leg and can't work his field."

Scooter realized his father was drawing on the experience of the farm couple with whom they had spent a night.

The deputy demanded, "You got any papers to prove you're who you say you are?"

"What would I carry papers for? Ain't got but little money, either. If we'd robbed a bank, don't you think we'd be carryin' a lot of money? You can search us. If you find more than twenty dollars you can keep it."

The deputy had developed a deep and doubting frown. He approached Scooter. "Is that right, kid? Is your name Willy Good?"

Scooter could not bring himself to speak. He could only nod.

The deputy asked, "Is the boy slow-minded that he can't talk?"

Lige said, "He's hardly ever got off of the farm. Ain't used to town. It's natural that he'd get a little scared when a sheriff starts askin' him questions. It never happened to him before."

The deputy softened. "Didn't mean to upset you, son. Just doin' my duty, is all. You and your daddy have got honest faces. It's plain to see that you ain't the bank robbers they're lookin' for. Besides, their name is Tennyson, not Good."

Lige blinked at the sound of his name, then shook his head. "What would bank robbers come into a little town like this for?"

"Right enough. We ain't even got a bank."

"This town'd probably starve a banker to death. All right if we go on about our business?"

"As long as it ain't bank robbery." The deputy laughed at his own joke. No one else did.

The lawman walked on, ambling toward an ugly stone courthouse that stood two stories tall at the end of the street. It had a cupola with a clock that either was not running or was off by several hours. It was a poor town, Scooter thought, that couldn't afford to fix a clock.

Lige watched the deputy. "Damn. They already know my name. Makes me want to cut down every telegraph line I come across."

"Maybe we ought to forget that road stake and go straight to the Cherokee nation."

"We can't go there broke." Lige considered for a minute before going into the store. To Scooter's surprise he was not in a hurry when he came out. Lige bit a chaw from a plug of tobacco he had just bought.

Scooter said, "You didn't do any business?"

"One look and I could tell there wouldn't be enough money in the till to make it worth the risk. We'd have that deputy on our tail before we could clear town. Probably the sheriff too, and no tellin' how many townfolk. We'll have to give up the luxuries and get by on what we've got till we get to where they're havin' that feud. Our luck will change there, you just wait."

Scooter tried to recall what luxuries they had had. Off-hand, he could not remember any.

When they reached the edge of town he said, "I'm a Jonah to you, Pa."

"How do you figure that?"

"You heard him. They're lookin' for a man and a boy travelin' together.

If you was by yourself, they wouldn't look at you twice. The next place we come to, they might not be as easy to fool as that deputy was."

"We ain't splittin' up, if that's what you're gettin' at. We already been apart way too long. Anyhow, where would you go?"

"Back to the Ranger camp. They're good to me there."

"They wouldn't be good to you no more. They know you was with me in Kerrville. Like as not they'd send you to one of them reformatories and keep you there till you're old enough to shave. I've heard stories. They'd feed you bread and water and put the whip to you every day."

Scooter shuddered.

Lige said, "We'll take roundance on the towns from now on till we get to where we're goin'. Me and you are stickin' together. Father and son, like it was before I went off to work for the governor."

CHAPTER
TEN

One of the Bracketts' black field hands sighted the two Rangers' approach and went running to the main house ahead of them. His frantic manner said he was on his way to give warning.

Rusty took that as a sign of trouble. "He acts like he's afraid of somethin'."

"Probably didn't recognize us."

The sight of strangers would not ordinarily arouse fear on the Brackett farm, though memories lingered of times during Reconstruction when Farley was having difficulties with carpetbag authorities. Seeing the visitors before the visitors saw him had been the difference between life and death.

"Got any hunches, Andy?" Though Rusty on occasion had played down Andy's hunches, he was aware that they proved correct often enough to be disturbing. It was as if Andy had some supernatural power, though Rusty had not brought himself to accept that premise.

Andy said, "Maybe Farley has threatened to peel the hide off of him if he lets somebody come without lettin' him know."

"That sounds like Farley."

Bethel stood on the porch, arms folded in an attitude of defiance until she recognized Andy and Rusty. She hurried down to meet them, her eyes anxious. "Lord, I've prayed for you-all to come."

Andy's pulse quickened. "Trouble?"

"Two days ago. A deputy sheriff showed up looking for Flora Landon."

"Did he find her?"

"Yes. He dragged her away, him and five others. He took Farley too. Wouldn't listen to us trying to tell him he was still too hurt to ride."

A large bruise darkened her cheekbone. Andy demanded, "Who did that to you?"

"The deputy, when I tried to hold on to Farley. He was a big fellow. Pushed Mother off of the porch too. She's stove up so badly she can barely walk."

Andy's face heated. "That'd be Big'un Hopper. What about the old man, Flora's daddy?"

"He was out in the field. They missed him. He slipped away as soon as the posse was gone. Probably went to tell Jayce Landon."

Andy dismounted for a closer look at Bethel. He touched her cheek. "Are you sure you're all right? Nothin' worse than that bruise?"

She reached up and pressed her hand against his. "Nothing that won't heal. Except I'm still mad enough to chop that big deputy into little chunks and feed him to the hogs. I'm worried about what they might be doing to my brother. They accused him of helping with the jailbreak."

"Big'un has accused me too, but he's a liar. He knows me and Farley had nothin' to do with that."

"Just the same, I'm afraid. They treated Farley rough. They knew he was wounded, but they didn't care. That deputy seemed to take pleasure in hurtin' him."

Andy's antipathy for Farley Brackett mattered little now. Farley was a fellow Ranger. "What're we goin' to do about it, Rusty?"

"By rights that's a decision the captain ought to make, or at least the sergeant."

"They're not here. So what would you do if you had to make the decision?"

Rusty said, "The Rangers have always taken care of their own."

"The longer we wait, the more time they've got to torment Farley. And Flora Landon."

Rusty had one reservation. "Don't forget that the law over there would like to jail you too."

"Just let Big'un try. He'll see hell from the bottom side."

Bethel agreed to send a field hand to town to find the sergeant and advise him that Andy and Rusty had proceeded on their own volition. She asked, "Do you know how you're going to handle this?"

Rusty said, "Like Rangers always handle things: straight-ahead on."

Andy had no quarrel with that.

Andy pointed down the street toward the courthouse. "The jail is on the other side. Hard to see it from here." He drew his pistol to be certain it was fully loaded.

Rusty said, "I'd leave that thing in the holster, was I you. It's always better to try and talk your way through. There's time enough later to shoot your way out."

Andy holstered the weapon, but only after inserting a cartridge in the chamber he customarily left empty for safety.

Rusty warned, "Remember, we're here on our own. We don't have authorization from the captain, or even Sergeant Holloway."

"Any reason we have to tell anybody that?"

"None at all. We might even lie a little if it helps."

Andy could not see that they were attracting any particular attention as they rode down the hoof-scuffed street, stirring a little dust with their passage. The few people they encountered had no reason to know they were Rangers. Neither wore a badge, for the state had not yet adopted an official design. Some Rangers fashioned their own, most often from Mexican silver pesos. Neither Andy nor Rusty had chosen to do so. Silver was hard to come by.

The stable keeper stood outside the big doors of the livery barn. Recognition made his jaw sag. He started to raise his hand in greeting but withdrew the gesture before it was completed.

Rusty asked, "Friend of yours?"

Andy explained that the hostler seemed to be neutral in the Hopper-Landon feud, accepting business from both sides. "He was some help to me and Farley, but nobody saw it except us. I suspect he'd duck in his hole like a prairie dog if things started to pop around him."

"I notice a lot of the store signs have got the name Hopper on them. I haven't seen a one that said Landon."

"There's considerable more Hoppers than Landons. That's why the Hoppers have control of the county. Dick Landon was right to join the Rangers and get away from here. If I was a Landon I'd leave too."

"There's not much logical about a feud. Family pride gets tangled up in it, and hate twists people to where they can't see straight."

"I don't understand that. I guess it's because I don't belong to a family. Not a white family, anyway."

Rusty's face pinched with a momentary sadness. "Neither do I. But maybe that helps me understand it better. I'd give all I've got to be part of a family."

Andy knew Rusty was thinking of the Monahans, especially the lost Josie. He said, "We've got one another."

Rusty nodded. "Two orphans thrown together by the luck of the draw. That's not quite the same." He forced a half smile. "But it's the best we've got."

Andy tensed as the jail came into view. "How about we barge in there like we had the whole Ranger force behind us? Catch them standin' on their left foot."

Rusty made no argument. "You've been here before and know the layout. You do the talkin' and I'll follow your lead."

Andy had long been used to following Rusty. It struck him as strange now for Rusty to be the follower.

I can't keep leaning on Rusty all of my life, he thought. But there was still much he did not know. It would be easy to make a costly mistake. He had made several in the course of growing up, mistakes that had brought trouble to others as well as to himself.

Well, if I make a mistake again, it won't be for standing back.

He did not knock on the jail door. Finding it unlocked, he pushed it open and stepped inside. Sheriff Truscott sat at a desk. Startled, he dropped papers he had been reading and jumped to his feet. Andy made several strides, stopping so close that he could have reached across the desk and grabbed the sheriff by his shirt. Truscott was not wearing his pistol. It and its belt and holster lay at the edge of the desk. He made no move to reach them.

Andy summoned the strongest voice he had. "You don't need that gun. We're Rangers, and we're here on official business."

The lawman seemed slow to gather his wits. "I know you. You and your partner Brackett was the ones helped my prisoner get aloose."

"We had nothin' to do with that. I think you know it. Now you've got Farley Brackett locked up here on false charges. This is Rusty Shannon. Him and me, we've come to get Farley."

"That's easy said."

"Either we leave here with him or you'll have the state adjutant general and his headquarters Rangers down here. You'll feel like you been tromped by a buffalo herd."

Truscott's face reddened as he struggled for a reply. "Everybody and his damned dog has been tryin' to tell me what to do lately."

Andy had bitten off a big chunk with his bluff, but there was no backing down now. "What do you say, Sheriff? Do you turn him loose or do we go in and take him?"

Big'un Hopper walked in from the back room where the cells were. "What in the hell's goin' on out here?"

Truscott pointed his chin at Andy and Rusty. "These men are Rangers."

Big'un grunted. "I know them. That young one anyway." He pointed at Andy. "I can spot a Ranger half a mile away. Further sometimes."

Truscott said, "They've come for Brackett."

Big'un's jaw dropped. "You better not let them have him. Uncle Judd would bellow like a bull."

Judd. Andy remembered that was the judge's given name. Judd Hopper had survived the hazards of the vendetta to become patriarch of the clan.

Truscott turned on Big'un with sarcasm. "Maybe your Uncle Judd would like to come talk to these Rangers. They claim to have the state law behind them."

"Us Hoppers are the law here."

"Here, maybe, but nowheres else. You want Austin sendin' a force down here to poke around? Me and you and your uncle Judd would likely wind up in the penitentiary. And some of your other kin, besides."

"I say we ought to secede from the state of Texas like Texas done from the Union."

Truscott shook his head impatiently. "Big'un, I wish you was twice as smart and half as loud."

Rusty spoke for the first time. "You remember what happened to that other secession. Texas lost."

The deputy seemed to swell up to a couple of sizes larger. "I don't see but two of you."

Rusty said, "We're Rangers. Two is enough."

Truscott looked away from the big deputy. "I guess we can give up the Ranger. We still got Jayce's woman."

Big'un said, "And givin' her three meals a day at county expense. You know what I favor givin' her." He turned into the light. Andy noticed a ragged cut and discoloration around his right eye.

The sheriff snapped, "I told you to stay out of her cell. She gave you just what you had comin'."

"Yeah, but I'd have given her somethin' too if you hadn't come in there raisin' hell. I'd show her again why they call me Big'un."

Truscott's eyes betrayed concern as he glanced at Andy and Rusty. "Damn you, Big'un, keep talkin' and some folks in this town will peel your hide with a horsewhip. Won't matter if you *are* a Hopper."

Andy had an ugly mental image of Big'un forcing himself on Flora Landon, or trying to. Fighting down his anger, he demanded, "Now, what about Farley Brackett?"

The sheriff gave Hopper a go-to-hell look. "Go on, tattle to Uncle Judd, but I don't care to have the Texas Rangers on my neck. I'm givin' them Brackett."

Big'un scowled. "You'd better hold on to that woman. We ain't done with her."

"Don't you be tryin' to tell me what to do, even if you are the judge's pet nephew. Yes, we'll keep her for now. I'm spreadin' the word that I'm willin' to trade. If Jayce Landon will come and surrender himself, I'll let his wife go."

Big'un's square jaw dropped. "You wouldn't do that."

"Damn right I'd do it. We ain't all lost our sense of decency."

Big'un glared. "You're a poor excuse for a Hopper."

"I ain't a Hopper at all. I made the mistake of marryin' one, but my name is still Truscott. And I'm still the sheriff of this county."

"We'll fix that, come next election."

Andy told the sheriff, "Looks like you need to move to some county where there ain't any Hoppers."

"I've thought about it. A lot." Truscott jerked his head as a signal to Andy and Rusty. "Come on back."

A set of keys lay on top of the desk. Big'un grabbed them to keep them from Truscott. "If I was runnin' this office, a lot of things would be different."

Truscott jerked the keys from Big'un's hand. "You ain't, no matter how many times you kiss Uncle Judd's ass." He unlocked the door to the cell block. "Brackett, you got company."

A blanket hung in front of one cell. Andy realized it was a concession to

Flora Landon's privacy. The builders of the jail had not considered female prisoners. From behind the blanket came a woman's angry voice. "Oscar Truscott, if you let Big'un in this cell again I swear I'll kill him. Even if you hang me for it."

Truscott said, "I've told you I'm sorry, Flora. If he ever tries it again I'm liable to kill him myself."

Rusty vented his anger. "A man who would abuse a helpless woman ought to be shot. Or at least tarred, feathered, and run out of the county on a rail."

Andy suspected Rusty was thinking about Josie Monahan.

The sheriff said, "Whatever else you might say about Flora, you can't call her helpless. She fights like a cornered wildcat."

Rusty added, "Big'un ought to be *in* jail instead of helpin' run it. I don't see how you can keep him as a deputy."

"The judge don't give me no choice. I have to try and keep peace in the family. Most of the Hoppers think Flora deserves anything that happens to her. I've thought about shuckin' the whole business and leavin' here for good."

From inside another cell came Farley's grumpy voice: "I'd be willin' to pay for your train ticket."

Farley stood hunched, one hand gripping a bar to steady himself. He seemed not to see well. "Who's that out yonder? If it's Big'un come to beat on me again . . ."

Truscott said, "It's a couple of Rangers, fixin' to take you out of jail. And out of the county, I hope."

Farley squinted to recognize Andy and Rusty. "Badger Boy, you took your sweet time gettin' here."

Farley's face was bruised and skinned, one eye swollen almost shut. Andy turned angrily on the sheriff. "How could you let somebody do that to him?"

"Like I said, I don't call all the shots. I can't be here all the time."

Farley's good eye seemed afire. "You don't try any too hard. When that good woman was hollerin' her head off, you was awful slow in comin'."

"She took pretty good care of herself."

"But if she'd been a weaker woman, Big'un would've got what he went in there for."

Truscott unlocked Farley's cell and pulled the iron door open. Its hinges squealed. "Come on out. You're leavin'."

Farley was unsteady but waved off Andy's instinctive move to help him. "They ain't managed to cripple me yet." He held one hand to his ribs, where he had taken the bullet.

Andy demanded of Truscott, "Have you had a doctor come and look at him?"

"Once, when we first got him here. He gave old Doc such a cussin' that he won't come back."

Farley muttered, "Damned quack done me more harm than good. Like to've killed me, pokin' with his fingers. Then Big'un come and tried to finish the job."

In the outer office, Big'un watched darkly as the sheriff took Farley's belongings from a desk drawer. They amounted to little: a pocketknife, a few coins, a leather wallet. Farley looked in the wallet and grunted, "Empty."

Truscott shrugged. "There's people in and out of here all the time. I can't watch everybody."

Farley turned to Andy and Rusty. "Oscar stays out of the office a right smart, like he don't want to know everything that's goin' on. And what does go on around here would gag a buzzard." He gave Big'un a blistering look.

Big'un declared, "If it was up to me you'd stay in yonder and rot."

Farley pointedly ignored him. "I had a six-shooter. I ain't leavin' this place without it."

Reluctantly Truscott opened another drawer and withdrew a pistol, belt, and holster. "It's empty. Leave it that way as long as you're in this county."

Farley strapped the belt around his waist. He checked the pistol and found it empty of cartridges as the sheriff had said. He took a step toward Big'un. "If this was loaded I'd shoot you right now."

"You might try. Once."

"Even unloaded, it's heavy enough to make a hell of a weapon. If I wasn't inclined to be peaceful I'd hit you up beside the head with it, like this." He swung the pistol so quickly that Big'un had no time to dodge. The heavy barrel struck just behind the deputy's temple. Big'un went to his knees.

Farley said, "It's a good thing I'm of a forgivin' nature. If I wasn't, I'd hit you again, like this." He swung the pistol and knocked Big'un to the floor. He gave the sheriff a challenging look. "Any charges?"

Truscott made a poor effort to hide a smile. "I reckon not. But get out of here before he comes around."

Andy and Rusty hustled Farley outside. Rusty said, "If you'd hit him one more time you'd probably be up for murder."

"He deserved it. What a roastin' he's got comin' when the devil gets ahold of him. And the sooner the better."

Andy asked, "Do you think you're strong enough to ride?"

"I'm strong enough, but I ain't goin' nowhere. I'm stayin' right here till I see that poor woman set loose."

Andy said, "That 'poor woman' sounded pretty strong to me."

"Not strong enough to keep beatin' off the likes of Big'un. She took him by surprise the first time. Next time won't be as easy."

"I heard the sheriff tell him not to try it again."

"Oscar and Big'un hate one another's guts, but Oscar ain't goin' to stay and face him in a showdown. He'd leave town before he'd stand up to Judge Hopper and the rest of his kinfolks."

Andy said, "This Uncle Judd must be a ring-tailed panther."

Farley said, "He came into the jail once and looked me over like I was a beef bein' dragged to the slaughter. I could see why folks are scared of him. Even Big'un."

"But they're kin."

"Big'un has got plenty to be scared of besides Judd Hopper. When the Landons hear what he tried to do to Flora, he'll be lucky to see another sunrise. I'm stayin' here and make sure the word gets out."

Rusty said, "The Rangers aren't supposed to get tangled up in personal feuds unless there's a killin'."

Farley's lips pinched together. "There'll *be* a killin'. It'll be Big'un's."

They took their horses to the livery barn. The hostler seemed hesitant at first to accept them but softened when Rusty offered him money. "Havin' you-all in my wagon yard is like standin' in a storm with a lightnin' rod in my hand." He focused his interest on Farley. "I figured if you ever came out of that jail it'd be feet first. Big'un was braggin' that he'd see to it."

Farley said, "Big'un ain't seein' anything real clear right now."

The hostler seemed to pick up on Farley's implication. "The Landons would give you a medal if you was to put Big'un's lights out. Even a Hopper or two might chip in."

"I didn't put his lights out. I just turned the wick down a ways."

"That'll tickle a lot of people who ain't even kin to the Landons." The man paused, reflecting. "It ain't fair to put all the blame on Big'un, though. Jayce shot his brother Ned. You wouldn't believe it, lookin' at Big'un now, but as a young'un he was the runt of the litter. Other boys picked on him all the time. It's no wonder he got mean. Once he started comin' into his growth, he got over bein' a runt but he never got over bein' mean."

Andy said, "I suppose he paid back the boys that had picked on him?"

"He's still doin' it. One of them was Oscar Truscott."

Farley gave the hostler a minute's speculative study. "I don't suppose you're the type that spreads gossip."

"Not me. Gossip is a sin."

"If the Landons was to hear what I'm about to tell you, there's no tellin' what they might do." He proceeded to describe Big'un's attempted assault on Flora Landon.

The stableman listened with rapt interest, his eyes wide. He shook his head and clucked in sympathy for the woman. "Nobody likes Big'un very much, not even some of his kin. This would sure rip his britches if it was to get out."

"I'm tellin' you in strict confidence."

"It won't go no further."

The stableman led the horses away to turn them loose in a corral. Farley made a grim smile. "By sundown the story will be all over town and halfway across the county."

Andy said, "It's like you painted a target on Big'un."

"Right between his eyes."

CHAPTER
ELEVEN

ige Tennyson surveyed the small town from a bend in the road a quarter mile away. He looked as if he had ordered whiskey and been given milk. "I'm disappointed. I thought Hopper's Crossing would be a lot bigger than this."

Scooter echoed his misgivings. "Don't look like enough of a place for people to fight a feud over."

"They ain't fightin' it over just the town. Once there's been blood spilt, a feud don't have to be over anything else in particular, just blood. Other reasons don't count anymore."

"You really think they'll pay you to fight for one side or the other?"

"It's been nothin' but amateurs so far. I figured somebody'd be willin' to hire a professional. At least I thought so till I saw how puny a town they've got. Well, I'll ride on in and look things over. Worst come to worst, I can always visit the bank, if they've got one. But there may not be twenty dollars of real money in the whole shebang."

"Want me to come with you, Pa?"

"No, you shade up in them trees yonder and wait for me. The laws are still lookin' for a man and a boy travelin' together. It's better if you stay out here where it's safe and don't cause no notice."

Scooter accepted without argument. His father had demonstrated early on this trip how suddenly he could explode into a rage, though his temper usually cooled as rapidly as it flared.

Lige removed his feet from the stirrups and stretched his legs without dismounting. The long ride had stiffened him. "Be a good boy and maybe I can bring you some candy."

"I'd be tickled, Pa."

Lige looked back once and was pleased to see that Scooter had ridden that paddle-footed old horse into the shade and had dismounted to rest and wait, as he had been told. He smiled and thought how lucky he was to have such a good and obedient son. During his years of incarceration he had worried a lot about what would become of the motherless boy. He had not left him in the best of hands, letting him fall in with the no-accounts Arliss and Brewster, but he had had little choice. He had feared that the authorities would put Scooter into some bleak orphan's home if he stayed around where they would notice him.

That was the way with government, always messing in where nobody had invited it, he thought. Life would be a lot less complicated if there wasn't some law to get in a man's way every time he tried to turn a dollar or do something that pleasured him.

A good boy deserved a better horse. Lige had it in mind that when they left here and started up toward Indian territory he would watch for a better mount and do a little quiet trading. It was a father's duty to provide for his son. Nobody was apt to think enough of one horse to trail them all the way to Red River and beyond.

The town was as inconsequential close up as it had appeared from a distance. The residential area consisted of no more than a dozen houses, most built of rough-sawed pine lumber. The main street, actually only a wide wagon road, had a handful of business buildings: a general store, a cotton gin, a blacksmith shop, a church, a livery barn with several log corrals behind it. He noticed right away that there was no bank.

Scooter had been right. It was not worth fighting over.

He stopped in front of the general store and tied his horse to a hitching rail strung between two posts, its rawhide strips almost rotted through. A mongrel dog lying in the shade of the storefront made a halfhearted effort to get up and move out of the way, then settled back down. Lige had to step over him.

A couple of elderly loafers sat on a bench, watching him with a curiosity that told him the town did not have so many visitors that they went unnoticed.

He remarked, "Not too busy around here today. I thought Hopper's Crossing would be a livelier place."

An elderly man with a long gray beard and a cane said, "Hopper's Crossing is. But this is Landon's Flat. Hopper's Crossing is about six miles further up the road."

Lige felt relieved. Maybe the trip hadn't been a waste after all. "My mistake. I didn't know this place was here."

"Neither do many other people. That's the trouble. Now, if we'd won that fight over the courthouse . . ."

The other man looked as if he had just bitten down on a sour persimmon. "Spilt milk, Homer. No use hashin' over somethin' that happened a long time ago."

The man named Homer reacted with impatience. "There's plenty others still hashin' it over. That's what the feud is supposed to be about, even if most folks have forgot."

Mention of the feud brought Lige to full attention. "What do you mean?"

The sour-faced one said, "Been thirty-forty years ago. There was an election to decide which place was goin' to be the county seat. See that big empty lot over yonder?" He pointed an arthritis-twisted finger. "That was goin' to be our courthouse square. But them crooks over in Hopper's Crossing voted more than once and throwed in their horses and dogs. Stole the courthouse from us, is what they did. Us Landons put up a squawk, and the shootin' started. There's more of them Hoppers than there is of us, and they own most of the money."

Lige saw his chance. "Maybe what you-all need is a real gunfighter, somebody who knows what needs doin' and how to do it."

"A man like that would cost a lot. Like I told you, most of the money is over in Hopper's Crossing with their names on it. Bein' the county seat, their town prospered while ours . . . well, you can see for yourself."

Lige's first reaction was sympathy, but his practical side did not tolerate it for long. He hadn't come all this way to donate his services. He had come for the best reason he knew of: money.

He asked, "If you was to want to shoot the top man of that Hopper bunch, who would it be?"

The two old men looked at each other. The sour one said, "Judge Judd Hopper is the head of the clan. But if it was me doin' it, I think I'd shoot Big'un Hopper first. The judge runs the family, but Big'un is the one he sends out to do the dirty work. He enjoys his job."

"Where would a man find Big'un Hopper, if he was of a mind to look?"

"He's a deputy under Sheriff Oscar Truscott. He fiddles to the judge's tune, though. He don't pay much attention to Oscar, nor anybody else besides old Judd. Come to a showdown, he might not listen to Judd either. He's built like a bull and got a head like one."

Lige said, "Sounds to me like he'd be the one to kill, all right." But he was thinking Big'un would be the one to see about a gun-toting job. It was evident if he was to make any real money out of this situation, it would have to come from the Hoppers. Teaming up with the Landons would be like fishing in a dry hole.

He was about out of tobacco, and he had promised Scooter some candy. He remembered how much he had liked candy when he was a boy and how seldom he ever had any. Life was going to be better for his son than it had been for him, no matter what Lige had to do to make it happen.

Always in the back of his mind when he entered a place like this general store was the feasibility of emptying its cash box. He dismissed the idea in this case. From the looks of things he wouldn't get much more than tobacco money. He would stir up all the John Laws within a hundred miles and almost certainly spoil his chance of profiting from the Hopper-Landon feud. If prison had taught him nothing else, it had taught him patience.

The clerk seemed grateful for even so small a sale. Lige thanked him and turned back toward the door, thinking that Scooter was the only one who profited much from this trip. At least he would be getting some candy. On reflection Lige realized the knowledge he had picked up was likely to be of good use. At least he knew not to waste his time with the Landons. He would try the Hoppers instead. Failing that, the Hoppers' town must have a bank to hold all that money.

The two loafers had not moved from their place on the bench. Homer said, "Didn't take you long to do business."

Lige said, "Ain't much business to be done around here. That dog looks about as busy as anybody in town."

Like the old loafers, the dog had not moved.

Scooter waited in the shade of the trees as he had been told. Lige handed him the sack of candy. "Don't eat all of that at once. It'll make you sick at your stomach. Good things need to be stretched out so you enjoy them longer."

"Thanks, Pa." Scooter took a piece of hard candy from the sack. He held it up and stared appreciatively at it for a minute before he put it in his mouth. He talked around the candy. "I don't reckon you saw a bank?"

"Takes money for a place to have a bank. This wasn't the town I thought it was. We'll do better in the next one."

"We goin' there today?"

Lige looked up at the sun. "We still got some daylight ahead of us. Ain't no use wastin' it."

He set his horse into an easy trot. Scooter followed, crunching the candy with his teeth. The sound made Lige's skin tingle. His own tobacco-worn teeth would crumble if he put them through that torture.

He said, "I sure wish we could give these horses a good bait of oats. They've earned it, bringin' us this far."

The candy made Scooter's words sound garbled. "Oats cost money, don't they, Pa?"

"We'll have money when we get through with our business here. Them old fellers back yonder told me the Hoppers have done right good. I figure they'll be willin' to fork over for gettin' some of the Landons out of their way."

"You'd kill them people, Pa?"

"You've got to look at it from my side, son. Them people don't mean nothin' to us. They're goin' to kill one another anyway. I don't see nothin' wrong if I push things a little. I'm bettin' the Hoppers would be glad to keep their hands clean by turnin' their dirty washin' over to somebody else. Wouldn't be nothin' the law could do to them, and me and you would be long gone."

"Them Landons are liable to shoot back."

"The bigger the risk, the bigger the gain. Even marryin' an Indian woman and gettin' head-right land, we'll need some start-up money in the territory."

Scooter asked, "You reckon you'll make a good farmer, Pa? Been a long time since you done much of it."

"I growed up with my hands shaped like a plow handle. It's a good life."

He had not always thought so. Years ago he had decided that harvesting banks and prosperous storekeepers was better than picking cotton. Graying hair and arthritis now draped a nostalgic curtain over fading memories of a sore back and bleeding fingers.

They stopped in a stand of timber half a mile from Hopper's Crossing. "We'll make camp here. We've got the river for water and plenty of deadfall wood for a cook fire. Ain't nobody liable to pay us much mind."

Scooter asked uneasily, "You goin' to visit the bank, Pa?"

"Maybe later, when I'm done with the other business. Right now I'm goin' in to stable my horse awhile and get myself a haircut. I want to find out what direction the wind blows."

Scooter did not understand about the wind. It was coming out of the south. He could tell that without having to ask anybody.

Lige said, "Ain't no place better than a barbershop or a livery stable to find out what's goin' on in a town. I want to learn more about that feud and be sure who to talk to about offerin' my services."

Scooter seemed resigned to being left alone. "I'll keep out of sight, like before."

"I'm sorry, son, but once we get up into the territory, there won't be no need for you to hide anymore. There won't be no Texas law up there. We'll ride together, proud as two peacocks in the sunshine."

Lige sought out the livery barn first. The stable hand met him at the open doors of the barn.

"Want to put your horse up for the night?"

"I won't be stayin' that long, but I'd like him to have a bucket of oats. He's been rode a long ways, and he's kind of drawed."

"So are you," the stable hand said. "If you're hungry there's a pretty good eatin' place up the street yonder, toward the courthouse. How far have you come? Where'd you start from?"

"Over east." That was the opposite of the truth, but somebody toting a badge might come along and ask questions of the liveryman.

Lige figured he had come to the right place. This man looked like a talker, and Lige had come to listen.

Lige was fairly sure he recognized Big'un Hopper as the deputy sheriff walked out of the jailhouse. He had the stableman's description and his own memory of the lawman who visited the Ranger camp on the San Saba. Hopper was one of the largest men Lige had ever seen. He had a bandage wrapped around his head, a present from an angry Ranger, the stableman had said. Lige approached him warily, for he could not be sure how seriously Hopper took his responsibilities as a lawman.

"I expect you'd be Big'un Hopper."

From Lige's viewpoint the deputy towered like the cupola atop the courthouse. He outweighed Lige by at least a hundred pounds. Big'un took a belligerent stance. "I don't know you. Give me a reason why I ought to even talk to you."

"I think I could be of service."

"I don't need no ditches dug nor fields plowed, and we generally got a prisoner or two to sweep out the jailhouse."

"Them things ain't my specialty anyway. I do most of my work with this." He dropped a hand to the butt of his pistol. "I hear you Hoppers have got enemies."

Hopper showed a flicker of cautious interest. "Even if we do, what business is it of yours?"

"I could handle them for you at so much per head. All you'd have to do would be to point them out. I'd lay them out. Wouldn't be nothin' the law could hang on your family because I ain't no kin to any of you."

Hopper's interest grew. "Let's go in the jailhouse yonder and talk about it."

The thought of entering a jail gave Lige a chill. "If it's all the same to you, I'd rather we went someplace else. Someplace where nobody would see or hear us."

Hopper pointed to a small frame building with peeling red paint. "The blacksmith is shoein' horses out of town. His shop is private enough if you don't mind a horse or two."

The place smelled of iron and burned coal. Lige walked through it, checking the horse stalls, then peering out the back door to be sure no one was near enough to overhear the conversation.

Hopper asked, "Sayin' I was to agree to somethin', how do I know you could do the job? You don't look like no notorious gunfighter to me. I don't even know your name."

"For now, just call me Bill Smith."

Hopper seemed amused. "Smith? We've entertained a lot of your kin-folks in that jail yonder, one time and another."

"If I was to tell you my real name you'd recognize it. But I don't think I ought to, seein' that badge you're wearin'."

"This badge ain't tattooed on my skin. I know when to look the other way." Hopper's face twisted in a minute's silent study. "I'll give you a chance, but I don't want you seen with me or any other Hoppers. I don't want folks to make any connection."

"I don't care to have too many people see me anyway. I expect there's a reward out. They might get notions."

"I know an old farmhouse nobody is livin' in. You can stay there. When I've got somethin' lined up, I'll come and talk to you."

"I'll be needin' some supplies for me and my boy."

"Boy?" Hopper's eyebrows went up.

"My son. He's travelin' with me."

For a moment Hopper seemed to reconsider. "That's an extra witness. It's a complication I hadn't figured for." A calculating light came into his eyes. "Travelin' with a boy. Seems to me I've seen a flier." He snapped his fingers. "Timson. Wanted for bank robbery."

Lige corrected him. "Tennyson. At least you know a little about my reputation."

Hopper smiled as if he had just drawn four aces. "I believe you'll work out perfect." He drew some bills from his pocket. "This ought to tide you over for a week or two. Now here's how you get out to the place." He squatted on his heels and drew a map in the sandy floor.

Hopper left the shop first. Lige waited a bit so no casual observer was likely to realize they had been together. He moved to the shop door, then took two fast steps backward into the shadows. Surprise quickened his pulse. He could hardly believe what he saw: the two Rangers named Rusty and Andy and a third man who limped along, hunched over as if hurt.

Involuntarily he held his breath until the burning in his lungs forced him to expel it.

How in the hell could they have tracked us so far?

He felt trapped. He had been confident he had shaken off pursuit. Now here were these damned Rangers, so close he could hit them with a rock. He retreated to the back of the shop, where the shadows were darkest, and watched as the three passed the front door. He barely dared breathe. For a fleeting moment he entertained the notion of shooting them while they weren't looking. With a little luck he might get all three before they had time to realize what was happening.

But he dismissed the idea. Back-shooting had never been his style. Anyway, chances were that at least one would survive long enough to put a bullet in him. What would Scooter do then? The boy would be lost if his father failed to show up. Lige gradually calmed and tried to think rationally.

There was no question of staying in town to buy supplies. He had to get out of this place as quickly as he could without letting the Rangers see him. Perhaps they were not after him in the first place. Perhaps something else had brought them here, far from their camp on the San Saba. If that was the case, they would not be expecting to see him. He intended to make certain they did not.

He had tied his horse behind the bank. He did not know why he had chosen that spot except that something in his nature always seemed to draw him to banks. He eased back to the front door so he could watch the

Rangers. He saw them enter the livery stable and disappear into its dark-ness. He went out through the back door of the blacksmith shop and hur-ried to his horse. He left town in a slow trot to avoid attracting attention. He looked over his shoulder until Hopper's Crossing was well behind him, then set his horse into a lope.

It was a point of pride for Lige that his son watched his surroundings closely. He seemed to see everything that went on around him. Scooter walked out a little way to meet his father.

"Thought you was fixin' to get a haircut."

"Changed my mind. Didn't get supplies, either. I saw a couple of your Ranger friends, Andy and Rusty."

Scooter's eyes opened wide. "They after us?"

"Could be, or maybe we've just fallen into a run of bad luck. I didn't stay around to ask them."

"What'll we do, Pa?"

"We'll ride back to that last town and buy what we need. Then we'll go to a farm a feller told me about. He said it's a good place to stay out of sight till I'm called on to do a job."

The farmhouse was about as Big'un had described it, no better and no worse. It appeared not to have had permanent tenants for several years. Broken shingles on the roof would let water leak into the house when rain fell. A front window-pane was broken.

Scooter eyed the place with misgivings. "It'll take a week to clean this place up."

"We may not be here a week. At least this place is mostly in the open. We can see anybody who comes this way."

"You lookin' for somebody to come after us?"

"With the Rangers, you never know."

But Lige was worried not only about the Rangers. He did not entirely trust Big'un Hopper. The odds were that the man had been on the level about hiring him for a job. But after all, he *was* a deputy sheriff. He had rec-ognized Lige and remembered he was wanted for bank robbery. Perhaps he was simply setting Lige up so he could claim the reward, if any was offered.

Well, Lige Tennyson had not lived this long by trusting to luck. He had learned long ago that those who keep a hole card and watch out for them-selves are usually the luckiest.

"We'll fool them. They'll expect us to be in the house. But we'll camp in the barn back yonder. If the wrong people come, we can ride out the back and be in the timber before they know what happened."

CHAPTER

TWELVE

ndy thought the doctor was going to slam the door in their faces when he saw Farley Brackett. He stood with hands pressed against the jamb on both sides, blocking the doorway. He was a little gray-bearded man with rolled-up sleeves and an apron stained by old blood specks that never washed out. He looked as if he had just smelled a skunk.

He said, "Last time I treated that man he cussed me like a mule skinner. If he's not dying, take him to somebody else."

Andy said, "His wound is tryin' to heal, but we don't like the color around the edges. We'd take it as a favor if you'd look at him."

Reluctantly the doctor drew back from the door. "First cussword I hear out of him, I'll put a twitch on his nose the way I'd do an unruly horse."

Farley growled, "I told you he's just a horse doctor."

Andy said, "Be watchful what you say. He might decide he needs to cut on you, and I'll bet he could make it hurt."

The doctor said, "Your damned right I can. How did this disagreeable son of a bitch ever get to be a Ranger?"

Andy decided it might be wise to let Farley answer that for himself, but Farley had nothing to say except, "Let's get on with it."

He took off his shirt and shed the long underwear from his arms and shoulders. The doctor peered closely at the healing wound, then poked it with the tip of his finger. Farley shouted, and the doctor grinned.

"A little angry around the edges," he said, "but it's coming along. I wouldn't worry about it."

Farley said, "Of course you wouldn't. It ain't yours."

Andy asked, "Do you think he can ride?"

"He can if he's willing to put up with a lot of hurt and the risk of bleeding again. If it was me I'd wait a few days before I started off on any long trip back to wherever it is you-all come from."

Farley pulled up his underwear and put on his shirt. He moved gingerly, trying to minimize the pain.

Andy asked, "What do we owe you, Doctor?"

"I've got a special deal for Rangers since it's their duty to protect us even if they have to shoot us to do it. My services are free the first time. After that it's regular rates. A man dumb enough to get shot a second time doesn't deserve any favors from me."

"Thanks. Maybe we can send you some payin' customers."

"You already have, the night you two knuckleheads faced that mob in front of an empty jailhouse."

Andy tried to help Farley down the front step, but Farley motioned irritably for him to back off. "Don't treat me like I'm crippled. If whoever shot me is watchin', I want him to know that he didn't do but half a job."

"What if he tries to finish it?"

"I'm hopin' he does. I'd like to return the favor."

Rusty had not gone with them to the doctor's house. He had talked little during the time they had been in Hopper's Crossing. His gaze was often vacant, his thoughts seemingly far away. His concern over Farley's wound had been that of one Ranger for another, not one of personal friendship. His relationship with Farley had been uneasy since the time Farley's transgressions against Reconstruction authorities had brought trouble to Rusty's door.

He was brushing his horse when Andy and Farley entered the stable. He gave Farley only a fleeting glance, and he asked no questions. "I'm thinkin' about goin' on back to the San Saba," he said. "The captain's probably wonderin' what's become of us."

Andy said, "The doctor says it might be better if Farley doesn't ride just yet."

"He stands a good chance of gettin' shot again in this place. If he doesn't want to go stay with his mother and sister, he can batch at my farm till he's healed up better. I doubt that the Hoppers would want him bad enough to hunt him down over there."

Farley said, "I'm in no hurry to leave here. I want to see Big'un get what's comin' to him."

Rusty gave him a grim look. "Suit yourself, but it's time me and Andy was leavin'."

Farley lay down on a steel cot the liveryman had dragged out for him. "If the captain complains, tell him he can fire me."

Andy pointed out, "Without bein' a Ranger you'd have no authority to enforce the law."

"The law ain't enforced much here anyway."

Late in the afternoon the stableman came into the building and stopped to blink until his eyes adjusted to the dim light. He looked behind him before he approached the three Rangers. "I ain't gettin' myself mixed up in you-all's troubles, but I got a message for you."

Andy took the lead. "What about?"

The stableman looked back again. He lowered his voice. "Walter Landon came to my house. Said he was speakin' for his brother Jayce. He heard about the sheriff's promise to let Flora Landon go if Jayce would turn himself in."

Farley sat up on the edge of the cot. Pain from the quick movement made him wince. "Anything to get her out of that jail and away from Big'un."

Rusty asked, "What's this got to do with us?"

"You Rangers delivered Jayce here in the first place. He'd like you-all to be the ones to do it again."

Rusty said, "He wouldn't need us to deliver him. He could just deliver himself."

"He knows one or another of them Hoppers would kill him before he ever saw the inside of the jailhouse. But if you-all were guardin' him, they might not try."

Andy said, "Maybe they would and maybe they wouldn't. If they didn't, they'd just wait till he was in jail, then break in like they tried to do the last time."

"At least his wife would be free. If he got killed before he went into the jail, Oscar Truscott might not feel like he had to live up to his promise about Flora."

Andy frowned. "Jayce seems to've made up his mind he's goin' to get killed one way or another."

Rusty's eyes were cold. "After all, he committed murder." Since Josie's death he had lost sympathy for criminals who had blood on their hands. He had that much in common with Farley.

Andy argued, "In a way he's still our responsibility. It was Rangers who caught him and Rangers who brought him here."

Farley said, "He's set to hang anyway. A good, quick bullet would be better than chokin' at the end of a rope."

Andy turned back to the stableman. "How do we go about meetin' up with Jayce?"

"After dark a couple of his kinfolks will come in the back way lookin' for you. Be saddled and ready. They don't want you bringin' any guns."

Rusty said, "We're not goin' anyplace without guns."

"You'll have to talk that over with them, not me. I'm just deliverin' the message."

Andy looked at Rusty. "You and me. Farley's not in shape to be ridin' anywhere."

Farley said, "Like hell." He rose to his feet but sat down again, sucking in a sharp breath and bringing his hand up to the wound. "It's just as well. I don't want to look at Jayce, anyhow, after what he's put his good woman through."

Rusty asked, "Can we trust these Landons?"

The stableman considered. "Their word is good. Their only bad failin' is that they like to kill Hoppers. It's brought a right smart of grief down on them."

Rusty said, "It's our job to bring Jayce in, not make deals with him. But I suppose it won't do any harm to talk."

The stableman looked behind him. "If anybody asks, I had nothin' to do with this. Wouldn't be healthy for me to get on the Hoppers' bad side."

Andy and Rusty delayed saddling their horses until full dark in case some Hopper might be keeping an eye on them. They waited inside the barn's back door. After a time Andy heard a gate latch move. From outside, a voice spoke just above a whisper.

"Rangers? You-all in there?"

Andy looked to Rusty to answer, for he was senior. Rusty said, "We're here. Who are you?"

"Walter Landon, but that don't matter. Are you ready for a ride?"

"We've been waitin' for you." Rusty opened the back door and led his horse out. Andy followed. He saw two men, though in the darkness he could not make out their faces.

Rusty asked, "Where's Jayce Landon?"

Walter Landon's voice was young. "Not far. We'd rather you left those guns here."

"The guns go or we don't."

Landon yielded with a shrug. "Then give us your word you won't do anything against Jayce till he's had a chance to talk with you."

"That's fair enough. Lead out."

They rode about an hour. Andy realized the two men led them in a zigzag pattern to confuse them should they try to retrace their path in the daylight. But he had a good sense of direction. He knew they traveled generally northwestward.

A dark farmhouse loomed ahead. Landon hooted in the manner of an owl. From the house came an answer. No real owl would have been fooled, Andy thought. Nor would any Comanche, even given their dread of owls.

Landon warned, "Don't neither of you make any suspicious moves. Jayce is mighty edgy."

Andy did not doubt that Jayce had a rifle or six-shooter trained on them. It did not seem probable that he would have summoned Andy and Rusty out here only to kill them. Nevertheless, Andy felt cold.

He saw a movement on the dark porch and heard a voice he recognized as Jayce's. "Get down and tie your horses, Rangers. We'll parley out here. The house is hot and dark, and I don't favor lightin' no lamp. You sure none of the Hoppers followed you?"

Walter said, "We were careful."

Jayce asked Andy, "How's your head? Too bad I had to club you that time, but I needed to try and get away."

"The swellin's long gone."

"Where's the Ranger that gave me a beatin' for it?"

"Farley Brackett is laid up. Took a bullet tryin' to keep a mob from breakin' into jail and killin' you. We didn't know you'd already lit a shuck."

Jayce showed no sign that he felt any guilt, or any sympathy for Farley. He turned to Rusty. "Don't believe I know you. You *are* a Ranger, ain't you?"

Rusty made no effort at sounding friendly. "Name's Shannon. I've been a Ranger off and on since before the war. The *other* war."

"Damned poor way to make a livin', but I guess everybody has got to be somethin'."

"What do you consider yourself to be?"

"A Landon first, then a Texan. I shot Yankees durin' the war, but I was fightin' Hoppers when I was a kid."

"The last killin' you did wasn't any fair fight."

"We didn't always fight the Yankees fair, either. Main thing was to win. Polite gentlemen generally die first."

Andy could see the exchange drifting from the subject at hand. He said, "We didn't come here to talk about who's to blame. We're supposed to talk about you tradin' places with your wife in jail."

Jayce's voice hardened. "I heard about Big'un and her. I've got to get her out of there, whatever it costs."

Walter argued, "Givin' yourself up is an awful price to pay, even for Flora. You know how long you'll last in that jail. And even if you lived till the trial, Judge Hopper would see you hang before the sun went down."

Jayce shook his head. "I don't see no other way."

Rusty said, "There might be one. What do you-all think of Sheriff Truscott?"

Jayce's voice was sharp. "He's a Hopper-in-law, but he's a cut above the others. He's about as fair as you'll find amongst that tribe."

Rusty nodded. "That's the impression I got. On the way out here I've been thinkin' about a deal we might put to him. We'd turn you in to the law but in another county."

"This county or some other, it ain't apt to make a lot of difference in the long run."

"If we can get you a change of venue, you'll at least have a fair trial in some court besides Judge Hopper's."

"A change of venue won't save my neck. Ned Hopper was a son of a bitch, and I killed him. I ain't denyin' it. I'd holler it from the roof of the courthouse." Jayce stared off into the darkness, weighing Rusty's proposition. "You got a place in mind?"

"Sheriff Tom Blessing is a good friend of mine. Whatever the outcome, he'll see to it that you're dealt a square hand."

Jayce stared into the darkness while he considered the proposition. "At least it'd be somebody besides a Hopper who put the rope around my neck." Jayce beckoned his kinsmen into the house. Andy could hear the low murmur of voices but could not make out what they were saying. When they returned to the porch Jayce said, "Go talk to Oscar Truscott. If he says yes, I'll surrender. Not to anybody else, just to you Rangers."

Rusty told Truscott they needed to talk to him in private. Truscott called to the jailer. He was not the same man who had been on duty the night of

Jayce's escape. That unfortunate had prudently left town before daylight and had not been seen since. "Curly, go get yourself a drink. Maybe two of them. Don't be in a rush to come back."

The jailer gone, Truscott said, "I heard by the grapevine that you-all went out of town last night."

Rusty replied, "You must have eyes everywhere."

"I don't miss a lot."

"We had an interestin' visit with an acquaintance of yours."

"Jayce Landon? You didn't bring him in, though."

"No, but we worked out a deal for you." Rusty explained his idea about delivering Jayce to a more secure jail and seeking a change of venue.

Truscott frowned at first but gradually softened. "I know Tom Blessing. If he said it was fixin' to freeze on the Fourth of July, I'd carry my coat with me to the celebration."

"He'd take good care of your prisoner."

"I'm just wonderin' who'd take care of *me*. Things'd get ugly around here when Judge Hopper and Big'un and the rest got wind of what I'd done."

"If we handle it right, it'll be over with before they know."

"But I'd still be here afterward." Truscott mulled it over. His mustache began turning up in a tentative smile. "It'd probably lose me a wife, but she's took to sleepin' in another room anyhow, and her cookin' wouldn't tempt a hog." The smile broke into full bloom. "I'd love to see what it feels like to look the judge in the eye and tell him I'm through shinin' his boots. And I've wanted for a long time to poke Big'un in the eye with a sharp stick."

"When're you goin' to release Jayce's wife?"

"Right now, into your custody. She's been an albatross around my neck." Truscott reached into a drawer and withdrew a printed form. He dipped a pen into an inkwell and scribbled some lines. "Bring this back to me with Tom Blessing's signature on it, swearin' that he's got Jayce Landon locked up."

Rusty took the paper. "When it's all over you can catch up on your sleep."

"Not after the word gets out." Truscott led Rusty and Andy back to the cells. He said, "Gather your things, Flora. You're leavin'."

She remained hidden by the blanket that covered the front of her cell. Her voice was anxious. "What've you done to Jayce?"

"Ain't even seen him, but he's agreed to give himself up to these Rangers if I let you go."

She pulled the blanket aside, her eyes fearful. "You know he's got no chance if he comes back in here. I ain't lettin' you trade me for him."

Truscott told her that Jayce would be jailed in another county. She chewed her lip. "I'd rather see him run off to Mexico or someplace."

Rusty said, "He wouldn't do that, not and leave you in here. He's that much of a man, at least."

She declared, "He's a better man than any I see here."

Truscott said, "You better git while the gittin's good, Flora."

"I'll go, but if I get a chance to help Jayce get away I'll damned sure take it."

The sheriff grunted. "I don't doubt that." He unlocked the door. "I'll leave the blanket up. Likely nobody'll miss you before mornin'."

Flora came out carrying a small canvas bag. Her hair was disheveled, her dress wrinkled from sleeping in it. Truscott walked ahead of her and blew out the lamp in the front office. "You-all better go out the back door." He opened it cautiously and peered out into the night. "Looks clear."

Flora paused. "Oscar, for a Hopper-in-law, you're a better man than I thought." Then she was out the door.

The sheriff warned Rusty and Andy, "You-all better keep a close eye on her. She meant what she said about helpin' Jayce get away."

Rusty said, "You've got to respect a loyal wife."

"Jayce never deserved her. I can't see why she chose him over his brother Dick. There's no figurin' women."

Andy had not expected Truscott to release Flora so quickly, so they had not brought an extra horse for her. Andy put her up into his saddle. "I'll go back to the stable and get Farley's horse. He won't be needin' it for a while."

Rusty said, "While you do that I'll get her out of town, to where Walter Landon said he'd be waitin'."

"I'll find you."

In the stable, Farley arose stiffly and sat on the edge of his cot. He watched by lamplight while Andy saddled up. "You stealin' another horse from me, Badger Boy?"

Farley never would give up needling him about Long Red, Andy thought. "Call in the law if you want to."

Farley shook his head. "I can guess why you need him. Tell her not to use spurs. He's liable to throw her off."

———

At the edge of town Andy put Farley's horse into an easy lope. He caught up to Rusty and Flora before they reached the farmhouse where Jayce was supposed to be hiding.

Rusty asked, "Anybody see you?"

"Just Farley and the stable hand. They won't be talkin'."

Flora was still nervous about her husband. "This place where you're takin' Jayce, are you sure it's safe? Them Hoppers have got a long reach."

Rusty said, "If you're lookin' for an ironclad guarantee, there ain't any. But it'll be safer than that jail back yonder. There's not a better sheriff in Texas than Tom Blessing."

"From what I've seen of sheriffs, that ain't a strong recommendation."

"You've got to realize that savin' him from a lynchin' doesn't change things for him in the long run. He hasn't got much of a future either way."

She squared her shoulders. "Maybe. We'll see about that the first time somebody gets careless."

Walter and a couple of other men stepped down from the porch to meet them in the yard. The house was dark, but Andy could see a rifle in Walter's hands.

"That you, Flora?"

"It's me. Where's Jayce at?"

A figure stepped out from a black corner of the porch. "Right here, darlin' girl. Come see Papa."

Flora did not wait to be helped down from the horse. She slid out of the saddle and hurried to the porch as Jayce stepped to the ground. They embraced, then Jayce pushed her off to arm's length to look her over. "Are you all right?"

"Why wouldn't I be all right?"

"I heard about Big'un. I wanted to kill him."

"Him bein' bigger just makes it easier to hit him where it hurts the worst. I laid it on him good."

Andy grinned, remembering the bruises and cuts on Big'un's face. He was probably bruised in other places where it didn't show.

Rusty was impatient. "We better be movin'. No tellin' how soon before the Hoppers'll find out she's gone."

Jayce said, "I can't figure Oscar Truscott lettin' you go so easy."

"He trusted the Rangers. Bad as I hate to say it, you and me have got to do the same."

Jayce turned to Rusty. "You'll let her ride along with us, won't you?"

Rusty nodded. "It won't be safe for her here, at least till things cool off. Tom Blessing will see to it that nothin' happens to her."

Walter said, "Maybe some of us better ride along with you too."

Andy started to protest, but Rusty spoke up ahead of him. It seemed to Andy that he always did when something really important was at hand. "Andy and me are escort enough." Rusty's hand was on the butt of his six-shooter.

It would be easy for the Landons to overwhelm the two Rangers and set Jayce and Flora free. Andy suspected such a notion had prompted Landon's offer. Normal restrictions did not apply in family feuds. When survival was at stake, acts normally regarded as treachery were considered justified.

Flora told Walter, "I wish you'd let my daddy know that I've gone with Jayce."

"I'll see to it. We've got him hid. Big'un and his bunch might want to take it out on him when they see that they've lost you and Jayce both."

Andy saw no sign that any of the Landons followed as he and Rusty rode away with Jayce and Flora. But he slipped his pistol out of its holster and held it for the first couple of miles, just in case.

CHAPTER

THIRTEEN

The morning was far along when they rode up to the jail where Tom Blessing kept his office. Jayce surveyed the frame building with disapproval. "It don't look any stouter than the one over at Hopper's Crossing. At least that one's built of brick."

Rusty said, "They've talked for years about buildin' a better one, but the county's always short of money."

"Short or not, I'll bet the taxes ain't cheap."

"No, but there's still never enough money."

Andy looked toward the courthouse. It was his theory that the county's financial problems resulted mainly from leaky fingers. People normally tight with their own money were sometimes loose with other people's. In any case it made for interesting politics, each side promising to waste less than the other.

Tom looked up in surprise as Rusty and Andy ushered the Landons into his office. His expression showed that he recognized Jayce on sight.

Rusty said, "Brought you an early Christmas present. I know you didn't ask for it, but here it is."

Blessing studied Jayce with misgivings before looking back at Rusty. "You sure ain't Santy Claus. What do you want me to do with him?"

"Keep him away from the Hoppers till he can stand trial. And we'll need to get him a change of venue out of old Judge Hopper's jurisdiction."

"I guess I can take care of the first part. You'll need to talk to a lawyer about the other." He looked at Flora, a question in his eyes.

Rusty said, "This is Jayce's wife. We need a safe place for her too."

"This jail ain't really fixed up for a woman. Any charges against her?"

"Not unless she tries to help Jayce get away. Again."

Tom thought about it. "She'd be good company for my wife out at the farm."

Flora objected. "I want to stay in town, where I can be close to Jayce."

Tom shrugged. "You can put up at Mrs. Smith's boardin'-house. But if the Hoppers was to come lookin', it wouldn't be hard for them to find you there."

Flora's jaw set grimly. "It'll be their own fault if they do. They don't know how good a shot I am."

Andy wondered what she intended to shoot them with. She'd had no weapon when she left Truscott's custody, though one of the Landons could have slipped one to her later, in the darkness. Andy had checked Jayce to be sure he was unarmed, but he had not felt comfortable about putting hands on Flora. He did not intend to do it now. Some things had to be taken on faith, or at least on hope.

Tom said, "I'll need help guardin' Jayce. Can't be here twenty-four hours myself, and I've only got one deputy. If the Hoppers was to come down on us in force, one man couldn't stop them."

Rusty said, "Me and Andy. He's more our prisoner than he is yours anyway. I'll wire the captain for permission."

Tom nodded. "I'm obliged." He touched a finger to a marked calendar behind his desk. "District judge is due to hold court here next week. I'd like to get Jayce on the docket as quick as I can. The sooner he's out of this jail, the better I'll feel."

Flora said, "If you-all would turn your backs for a minute or two, you wouldn't have to worry about guardin' Jayce. Him and me would be on our way to Mexico."

Rusty said, "I halfway wish we could, but that'd break our agreement with Sheriff Truscott."

Andy said, "And our oath as Rangers."

Jayce said, "Don't worry about it, darlin' girl. I ain't been hung yet. A lot can happen."

Tom frowned. "Don't be gettin' notions. It's been a long time since I shot a prisoner tryin' to escape. I didn't sleep for a week afterwards, but I done what I had to. I'd do it again."

Jayce's voice was full of irony. "I sure wouldn't want to cost you any sleep." He took Flora into his arms. "Us Landons have died of everything else, but there ain't none of us ever been hung. If things go my way, I'll send for you from Mexico. Or maybe South America. I hear it's mighty pretty down there. They pull fruit right off of the trees, and nobody has to work if they don't want to."

To Andy that sounded more like Preacher Webb's version of heaven. It seemed unlikely that Jayce Landon was going to end up in heaven, or anywhere close to it.

Tom got his keys and motioned toward the back room where the cells were. "Like I said, Rusty, you sure ain't no Santy Claus."

Sheriff Truscott glanced up from a paper he had just signed as Big'un Hopper entered the office. The sun was already two hours high. In the past Big'un's perpetual tardiness had irritated Truscott, but this morning it was welcome. He would have been even happier if Big'un had not shown up at all. The two men tolerated each other only because Judge Hopper forced them to.

Big'un snapped, "Is that all you got to do, sit there writin' letters?"

"Writin' reports is part of the job. Austin always wants to know what's goin' on here."

"When I get to be the sheriff I'll tell Austin to go to hell."

"What makes you think you'll ever be sheriff?"

Big'un headed toward the cells in back. Truscott said, "I've told you to stay away from Flora unless I'm with you."

Big'un snickered. "Afraid I'm goin' to give her what she's been needin'? If I get a notion to do that, it'll take more than you to stop me. Hell, I got the notion right now." He resumed his march toward the cells. Truscott reached into a drawer and withdrew a set of brass knuckles he had taken from a Dallas footpad who had not been half so tough as he thought he was.

Big'un came roaring back, face splotched with anger. "What've you done with her? Where's she at?"

Truscott almost smiled. "I ain't got the faintest notion. I traded her for Jayce, like I said I would."

"You're lyin'. Jayce ain't there either."

"I turned him back over to the Rangers. They've taken him out of the county to get a change of venue."

Not quite believing, Big'un said, "Uncle Judd wouldn't give you permission to do that."

"I know he wouldn't. So I didn't ask him."

Big'un made two long, angry steps toward the sheriff's desk. Truscott raised his hands defensively, showing the brass knuckles. Big'un saw them and stopped, but his face kept getting redder. A wail of rage rose in his throat.

Truscott said, "Careful, you're fixin' to bust a blood vessel. That seems to be a Hopper family trait."

"You had no right."

"I'm the sheriff."

"You won't be sheriff long, not when I tell Uncle Judd about this."

"I'm sheriff till the next election. After that, you and the judge can go to hell for all I care. The Hoppers and the Landons and the whole damned county too."

Big'un's eyes narrowed. "You may not live till election." He stamped out the door.

It would not be long before Judd Hopper came boiling into the office just as Big'un had. Truscott found it odd that he felt relief rather than dread. In the past he had never been able to face down the judge. The man's overpowering presence had always cowed him. But now that the fat was in the fire, he almost looked forward to the confrontation. This time he had nothing to lose. He had already resolved to give up his office when his term was finished. The judge could do nothing to hurt him.

As he expected, Judd Hopper flung the door open and strode in, Big'un just behind him. The judge demanded, "Is it true what my nephew's been tellin' me?"

Truscott was surprised by how calm he felt. "Big'un has got a reputation for abusin' the truth, but in this case I expect he told you the straight of it. I let the Rangers have Jayce."

The judge placed his palms flat on the desktop and leaned across toward Truscott. His breath was hot on the sheriff's face and reeked of chewing tobacco. "You know I wanted to try him in my own court."

"I doubt that it'll make much difference where he's tried. He's guilty, and he'll be sentenced to hang."

"But his crime was committed here."

"Against your kin. Any normal judge would recuse himself from the case if it involved his own family."

"I wanted to personally have the pleasure of tellin' him he's fixin' to hang by the neck until dead, dead, dead."

"Big'un and his cronies would see to it that he was shot or hung before he ever got to trial. They tried it the last time, only the bird had already flown."

The judge sputtered, struggling to raise more argument but seeing the futility of it. His face was crimson, and veins stood out on his temples. "You're through in this county, Oscar. I'll see to it."

"Ain't much you can do till election. After that you can have the whole shebang."

The judge gave Truscott a look that would wilt cactus, then spun on his heel, starting toward the door. Big'un protested, "Ain't you goin' to do somethin', Uncle Judd?"

His uncle gave him no answer. Big'un followed him outside. Catching up, he said, "Looks to me like there ought to be somethin' you can do."

The judge's voice dripped sarcasm. "You want me to shoot him?"

"That ain't a bad idea. I've got half a mind to do it myself."

"If you do, you've got no mind at all. No Hopper can afford to shoot him. The state would have a dozen Rangers down here before you could spit."

Big'un thought about it. "What if somebody else done it, somebody who has nothin' to do with any of us Hoppers?"

The judge took a few more steps, then stopped, suddenly intrigued. "What do you mean, somebody else?"

"There was an old man—"

The judge raised a hand to stop him. "Don't tell me. I've got to stay clean. I don't want to know anything about it."

"All right. I'll wait a day or two till Oscar figures he's got us up a stump. Then don't be surprised at anything that happens."

The judge stared at him, torn between doubt and hope. "Nephew, you're not the brightest lamp in the window, but occasionally you think with your head instead of your fists. I hope this is one of those times."

"It is. You'll see."

Two days later Big'un made a show of rifling through the recent fugitive notices in the sheriff's office. He and Truscott had barely spoken since the confrontation with Judge Hopper. Now Truscott glanced up irritably from a report he was writing. "What're you lookin' for?"

"A telegram that came in here a while back. Described a man who robbed a bank out west."

"You think you've got a line on him?"

"Maybe. Feller told me about somebody he seen at the old Yancey farmhouse." He found the telegram and ran a stubby finger along the lines. "Sure enough sounds like the man, all right."

His interest piqued, Truscott took the telegram from Big'un's hand. "You certain this is him?"

"Can't be certain of nothin', but the description fits. The telegram mentions a reward. I thought I would ride out and at least take a look. I could use the money."

"If this is the right man, you'd probably get your head shot off. I'd best go with you."

Big'un feigned a protest. "I can handle it."

"Don't worry about the reward. It's all yours. But if this is the real bank robber it's liable to take two of us to bring him in."

"Suit yourself."

"I'll saddle up and meet you here in ten minutes. This report can wait till I get back."

Big'un smiled grimly as the sheriff walked outside.

"Hell, Oscar, you ain't comin' back."

Scooter Tennyson sat in a rickety chair leaned back against the barn door, dozing in the warmth of the early-fall sun. He dreamed he was fishing in the San Saba River and Bo brought an ax from behind the kitchen tent, telling him to cut more wood.

He awakened with a start, remembering that he was supposed to keep watch while his father slept inside. Blinking the sleep from his eyes, he saw two horsemen approaching. He froze in panic for a moment, then rushed into the barn.

"Pa, wake up. Somebody's comin'."

Lige Tennyson was quickly on his feet, grabbing for his pistol. He hurried to the barn door. "They're almost on us. You was supposed to keep watch."

"I'm sorry, Pa."

"Sorry don't fix it." Lige squinted, then relaxed. "One of them is that deputy I told you about, Big'un Hopper. Reckon he's come to give me a job like he promised. But I didn't figure on him bringin' anybody else." He started to put away the pistol, then thought better of it. "You stay back out of sight just in case."

"All right, Pa."

Lige walked out into the open. He kept the pistol in his hand but lowered it so it would not appear to offer a threat.

Big'un eyed the pistol with suspicion, but his voice sounded jovial enough. "Howdy."

"How do, yourself."

The other man spoke. "Do you go by the name of Tennyson?"

"Sometimes. Depends on where I'm at and who I'm talkin' to. And who *am* I talkin' to?"

So quickly that Lige missed the move, Oscar Truscott drew a pistol and pointed it at Lige's belly. "I am the sheriff of this county. I am placin' you under arrest for bank robbery and attempted murder. Drop that pistol."

Lige let the weapon fall to his feet. Confused, he looked at Big'un. "What kind of a trick is this?"

"Not quite the kind it looks like." Big'un drew his own pistol. Lige saw murder in the man's eyes and braced himself for a bullet.

Instead of aiming at Lige, Big'un pointed the pistol toward Truscott. The sheriff blinked in confusion.

Big'un said, "Looks like election is comin' sooner than you thought, Oscar." He squeezed the trigger. Truscott jerked. His horse jumped as the sheriff slid down over its left side.

Truscott looked up in mortal pain. "For God's sake, Big'un."

"God ain't watchin', Oscar." Big'un leaned from the saddle and fired again.

Observing from the barn, Scooter froze in shock.

Lige said, "God amighty. What did you do that for?"

Big'un smiled grimly. "The county is fixin' to get a new sheriff. A bank-robbin' fugitive just killed this one."

Shaken, Lige said, "Me? I ain't fired a shot."

"Nobody'll believe that. He came to arrest you, and you shot him."

"You bottom-dealin' son of a bitch."

"I found out a long time ago that you do what you have to if you want to win." He raised the pistol to fire.

Scooter hurled a rock almost the size of his fist. It struck Big'un's horse on the chest. The animal reared and whirled away. Big'un involuntarily squeezed the trigger. The bullet smacked against the side of the barn.

Lige scooped up his own pistol and fired as Big'un struggled to regain control of his mount. Big'un got off one more shot, then spurred hard to move out of range. Lige steadied his pistol and fired once more. He thought he might have grazed Big'un, but he was not certain.

Scooter stepped hesitantly toward the fallen sheriff. He wanted to throw up. The man's eyes were open. "I think he's alive, Pa. He's lookin' at me."

"No, son, he's halfway to either heaven or hell." Lige bent to close the lawman's eyes. "Like as not he was a good sheriff, but he sure picked a coyote for a deputy."

"What'll we do now, Pa?"

"Only one thing *to* do. We'll run like a rabbit."

"Where to?"

"There ain't nothin' but Texas all around us. Soon as that deputy gets to town and tells his story, every badge toter in the state will be huntin' for us. They'll shoot us down like hydrophoby dogs." For a moment Lige drifted toward despair. He blinked away tears. "They won't stop to ask your age."

Scooter's alarm intensified. He remembered seeing his father cry only once, when Scooter's mother had died.

Lige said, "I done you a bad wrong, son, bringin' you into this kind of a mess. Best thing I can do now is to send you back to your Ranger friends, where I found you."

"I don't know if I could find my way. I'm stayin' with you, Pa."

Lige's eyes were bleak. "When bullets get to flyin' they don't care who they hit. Man or boy, a bullet can't tell the difference."

"How far do you reckon it is up to the Cherokee country?"

"A long ways. There's probably fifty sheriffs between here and the Red River. That don't even count Rangers and town constables."

"We can travel in the dark of the night and hide durin' the daytime."

"That's the only thing to do. We'd better saddle up and get gone before that four-flusher comes back with a posse fired up to kill us both."

From the corner of his eye Scooter sensed a movement. Turning, he shouted, "Look out, Pa. He's comin' back."

A bullet thumped against the barn. Big'un had reversed direction and spurred toward them, firing as he came.

Cursing, Lige leveled his pistol. "Down, boy. Flat on the ground." He took two shots at the deputy.

Dropping to his knees, Scooter felt something strike his hip. It burned like a hot poker.

One of Lige's bullets grazed Big'un's horse. The animal squealed and broke into pitching. Big'un grabbed the saddlehorn and held on with both hands. He dropped the pistol. The bridle reins went flopping.

Lige tried to get him in his sights, but the horse's frenzied bucking made it impossible. Big'un managed to get hold of the reins and bring his mount under a measure of control. He turned toward town. The animal alternated between running and pitching. Lige took one more shot, but it was an empty gesture.

He said, "Get up, son. We got to go."

Scooter moaned. "Somethin's wrong, Pa. I can't get up."

Lige dropped to one knee, eyes fearful. "My God, he hit you."

Scooter looked down at his hip. He saw the blood and felt nausea wash over him. Though Lige was skinny as a log rail, he picked up his son and carried him to the old house's back porch as though he weighed nothing at all. "Slip them britches down, son. Let me take a look."

Scooter's hands were trembling. He could barely manipulate his belt buckle.

Lige asked, "Does it hurt bad?"

"It's startin' to. Mostly it burns."

Lige felt around the wound, then wiped his bloody fingers on one leg of his trousers. "Looks like the bullet went plumb through. Might've nicked the bone, though. I need to take you to a doctor."

"You can't go to town. Folks there would kill you in a minute."

"At least I've got to stop the bleedin'. Then we have to make a lot of tracks. You think you can ride?"

"I don't know. Maybe you ought to leave me here."

"And have that deputy kill you to shut your mouth? That's the reason he turned around and came back, hopin' to finish us both so we couldn't tell what we seen here."

"Would anybody believe us?"

"Not likely, but he can't take the chance. He's got to kill us."

He fetched a half-empty whiskey bottle from his blanket roll in the barn. "This is goin' to burn like the fires of hell. Holler if it helps."

Scooter hollered, but it did not help.

Misery in his eyes, Lige said, "Somewhere we'll find somebody who can help you. Till then, you've got to hang on, boy."

————

Big'un had a dozen men with him, all Hoppers or Hopper kin. Approaching the farmhouse, Deputy Harp asked, "Hadn't we better go in slow and careful?"

Big'un kept his horse in a stiff trot. "That outlaw will be miles away from here by now. But we'll pick up his trail and ride him down like a lobo wolf, soon as we do right by poor old Oscar."

A wagon trailed a couple of hundred yards behind. It would take the sheriff's body back to town for proper services and burial.

Old Oscar ought to be grateful to me, Big'un thought, rubbing his sore arm where Lige's bullet had grazed it. I've made a hero out of him. Every Hopper woman in town will cry at his funeral, and some that aren't even kin.

Harp said, "Reckon why that robber picked this place to hide out?"

Big'un replied, "Like as not them Landons put him up to it. Probably had him hired to kill some of us and keep their own hands clean. But me and Oscar flushed him before he had time to do any such of a thing."

"Damned shame your horse went to pitchin' when you tried to protect Oscar. You could've finished that killer then and there."

Nobody had questioned Big'un's account about Tennyson shooting Truscott in cold blood and about Big'un's horse going into a panic at a critical moment. Horses were like that. "Don't worry, we'll get him sooner or later. But everybody better remember, we're up against a murderer who won't stop at nothin'. He won't give any mercy, and he's got no mercy comin' to him. Shoot to kill."

"What about the boy?"

"Just remember that he put a bullet in Oscar too. He's already ruined for life, travelin' with an outlaw daddy. He's probably carryin' the trace of a noose around his neck." He had heard it said that anyone destined to hang bore a faint birthmark that foretold his fate. Perhaps it was the mark of Cain that Big'un had heard preachers talk about. He had looked for it on his own throat and had been relieved not to find it.

Truscott lay where Big'un had left him except that he had been rolled over onto his back, his arms folded across his chest and his hat covering his face.

Harp said, "Odd, ain't it, that an outlaw would do such a thing for a sheriff?" He lifted the hat to look at Truscott's face. "Looks natural, Oscar does, like he's just asleep. You reckon he felt any pain?"

Big'un remembered the pleading look in Truscott's eyes before the second shot. "I doubt he ever knew what hit him, it happened so fast."

Nevertheless, the memory made him shiver. He turned in the saddle to hide the emotion from the posse members. "Where the hell is that wagon?"

Harp stepped up close to the house. He said, "Did Oscar ever reach the porch?"

Big'un replied, "No, he fell right where he is now."

"Then you must've hit somebody. There's blood up here."

The stain had soaked into the dry old wood. Big'un studied it and felt a quick uplift. Maybe he had shot the old reprobate after all. He hoped it was a fatal wound. The boy would soon be caught, wandering around by himself. Given any kind of chance, Big'un would see to it that he did not live long enough to testify about what had really happened.

One of the men had circled the house. He shouted, "I've found their trail."

Big'un rode out to look. The tracks headed north. "Funny they'd go that way. Was I them, I'd head for Mexico."

Harp suggested, "Maybe they figure on some of the Landons helpin' them. We ought to wipe out the whole damned litter, or at least run them out of the county."

Big'un was surprised at how well this whole affair had played into his hands. "But the first thing we got to do is catch these killers. Afterward we can deal with Jayce Landon. We'll do what we had figured to do when we had him in our jail."

"We don't know where the Rangers took him."

"There's still one Ranger in town, the one called Brackett. He'll know."

"He won't tell."

"Yes, he will. One way or another, he will."

CHAPTER
FOURTEEN

ergeant Holloway had returned to the San Saba River camp. Rusty sent the captain a brief wire explaining the situation and requesting permission for him and Andy to guard Jayce until the circuit judge reached town. The captain wired back advising that additional ranger help would be sent if requested. Tom Blessing decided not to ask for it.

"Got to save the taxpayers' money where we can," he said. "Lots of them think we're stealin' it or throwin' it away on luxuries."

Andy smiled. If the courthouse or jail contained any luxuries, he had failed to see them. The place begged for a coat of paint, and a piece of cardboard had been tacked up where a windowpane was missing.

Flora was on her long daily visit to her husband. She responded to Tom's comment. "Jayce'd feel better if you would ask the captain to send brother Dick."

Rusty frowned. "Dick would take it hard, watchin' Jayce tried for murder. We all know what the outcome'll be."

She said, "Havin' him here would be a comfort to Jayce. I'd feel better too."

Rusty gave in. "It's against my better judgment, but I'll wire the captain."

When Flora left, Andy told Rusty, "Somebody said Jayce and Dick both courted Flora."

"It's a shame she made the wrong choice."

"When Jayce is gone she'll have a second chance. Maybe she'll take it."

Rusty observed him quizzically. "I knew that Farley Brackett was some taken with her, but I didn't know you were too. She's ten years too old for you."

Andy's face warmed. "It's not that way at all. It's just that she's got a lot of gumption. You have to admire that."

"You'd better admire her from a distance. She'd shoot you in a minute if it would save her husband."

"I'd call that gumption."

So far as Andy could tell, Rusty had shown no interest in Flora as a woman. He saw her only as a complication in his effort to guard Jayce, to keep him from escaping and at the same time to protect him from his Hopper enemies. Rusty seemed too tied up in his grief over Josie Monahan to involve himself with another woman. Andy's subtle and sometimes not so subtle efforts to arouse his interest in Josie's sister Alice had bumped against a stone wall of resistance.

Every time Andy went to the cells he felt Jayce's eyes watching him, calculating, ready to seize any opportunity for a break. Tom Blessing did not allow Flora direct contact with her husband. She did her visiting from a cell ten feet away from Jayce's. She could not even hand him tobacco. Either Tom or Rusty would examine it first, then pass it to Jayce.

Anyone who took a meal tray to Jayce had to leave his pistol in the front office and slide the tray through a wide slot in the cell door. Before anyone entered the cell to empty the slop jar or sweep out, Jayce had first to shove his arms out with a bar between them and submit to being handcuffed.

Andy said, "Tom's carryin' things to an extreme."

Rusty replied, "By the time you put in as many years as he has, you'll know not to get careless with the likes of Jayce Landon. He'll grab any chance, and he'll be willin' to kill anybody who stands in his way. So would Flora, I'm thinkin'."

Andy found it hard to imagine Flora killing anyone, even to save Jayce. But he took care not to get close enough that she might grab his pistol.

———

Farley Brackett's arrival took Andy by surprise. His face was bruised and swollen, cut in half a dozen places. He attempted to dismount by himself but fell to hands and knees. His startled horse jerked free and ran several yards before turning to look back.

Andy rushed to help. Though he had never liked the dour Ranger, he felt outrage at seeing him so badly battered. He lifted Farley to his feet and held him to keep him from falling again. He said, "You look like you've been drug at the end of a rope."

Farley's lips were swollen and cut. His speech was distorted. "Where's Rusty? Got to see Rusty."

"He's inside. Hang on to me. I'll get you there."

Farley had difficulty in keeping his legs under him. With Andy's support he labored up the step and through the door. Rusty sat at Tom's desk, writing a report for the captain. Tom lay napping on a cot, one arm over his face to shield his eyes from the light. He had stood watch for half the previous night. Awakening, he pushed up onto his elbow. "What in the world . . ."

Rusty strode across the room to help. Tom arose from the cot and motioned for them to place Farley on it.

Rusty demanded, "Who did this to you?"

Farley cursed under his breath as he stretched out on the cot. "Big'un. Who else? There's hell to pay over at Hopper's Crossing. The Hoppers are tied up in a manhunt. But when they get done with that they'll be comin' for Jayce."

Rusty said, "They know where we brought him?"

"They do now. Big'un had him a set of brass knuckles. I didn't have the strength to give him much of a fight."

"Nobody could blame you for tellin' him."

"I didn't tell him nothin', but the little feller that runs the livery stable spilled it all. He had heard you-all talk enough that he knew you brought Jayce over here."

"So you figure Big'un will be comin' after him?"

"As sure as New Year's follows Christmas. I ought to've killed him when I had the chance. I will yet."

"Better not. Remember, he's a deputy sheriff."

Farley cautiously ran his fingers over some of the angry cuts on his face. "Worse than that. He's the actin' sheriff now by order of Judge Hopper."

Farley explained about Truscott's murder. "Accordin' to Big'un, it was old man Tennyson and his boy that done it. He put out an order to kill them both on sight."

Andy felt his heart sink. "Scooter?"

"Big'un said him and the sheriff went out to make an arrest. The old man and his boy shot it out with them."

Andy declared, "Scooter wouldn't do such a thing."

"It don't matter whether he did or not. Big'un put out the word to take no chances, to shoot the both of them on sight."

Andy felt a chill. "He must be lyin'."

"Like as not, but most of Hopper's Crossing believes him. They're huntin' high and low, like a pack of coyotes. I wouldn't bet a Confederate dollar on the daddy or the boy either one livin' to get away."

Andy turned to Rusty in anguish. "We've got to do somethin'."

"Lige Tennyson picked his own road."

"I doubt that Scooter had any say in the matter."

"We wouldn't have any idea where to look for them. Anyway, it's our assignment to guard Jayce."

For the moment Andy hated Jayce Landon and Lige Tennyson both. Most of all he hated Big'un Hopper, responsible for their having to guard Jayce and for the shoot-to-kill admonition that put Scooter in jeopardy.

Flora called from the back room. "You-all come and let me out of this cell."

Farley pushed up onto his elbows. "You-all got that good woman under arrest?"

Rusty said, "We're tryin' to make sure she stays good." He explained the conditions under which she was allowed to visit her husband. "She passed a gun to him once. We don't want her doin' it again."

Farley eased. "I didn't know anybody figured that out besides me."

Andy said, "You think you're the only one around here that's got any brains?"

Tom released Flora from her cell and followed her out into the office. The sight of Farley's battered face stirred her to indignation. "I don't suppose he fell off of a horse."

Farley said, "It wasn't a horse that done this to me. It was a jackass."

"Turn Jayce loose for a few days, and I promise you Big'un won't trouble anybody again."

Rusty said, "I'm sore tempted, but how could we know Jayce wouldn't head south for Mexico?"

"You could hold me here in his place. He'd turn himself in again like he did before."

"Maybe. Maybe not. Jayce knows Tom Blessing wouldn't mistreat you like Big'un did. And Tom couldn't hold you for long since there's no charges against you."

She argued, "No tellin' who-all Big'un is liable to stomp on before he's through. What Hopper's Crossing needs is a few funerals, startin' with Big'un and his uncle Judd. Give Jayce a chance and he'll see to it."

Farley said, "Once I get my strength back, I'd be glad to see to it myself."

Scooter swayed from one side to the other in the saddle. Lige said, "Stay awake, son. You don't want to fall and start the bleedin' again. It's taken too long to get it stopped in the first place."

But he realized Scooter was not simply falling asleep. Fevering, he teetered along the brink of unconsciousness.

"I've got to find help for you, and damned soon."

Because the bullet had passed through, he had hoped his son would be able to keep riding until they put a lot more distance behind them. But instead of starting the healing process, the wound was getting uglier, and Scooter's fever was rising. Lige's hopes for escape had all but vanished. At first he had circled around a few farmhouses, fearing word had gone out that he had killed the sheriff. Now that he made up his mind to accept the risk, he had ridden for miles without seeing a house.

He had only a general idea where he and Scooter were. He hoped they had crossed into another county, where Big'un would have less influence. He had started north, hoping to throw off or at least delay pursuit, then had turned westward where there would be fewer settlements, fewer people to witness their flight. That, however, complicated his search for someone to help Scooter. He had given up the notion of riding only in the dark of night. He traveled boldly in the daylight.

At last he saw a small cabin. Smoke drifted from the chimney. "Hold on, son. Maybe these folks can help you."

He heard the sound of an ax, then saw an old black man chopping wood behind the cabin. Disappointment left a sour taste in his mouth. "Damned little help we'll get here."

The old man straightened and leaned on the ax while he rubbed his sleeve across his eyes in an effort to wipe away the sweat and sharpen his vision. Then he came limping out to meet Lige and the boy. "That young'un looks to be in a bad way."

"He's in need of help. Any white folks livin' close by?"

"Not close enough by the looks of him. There's the Shannon place over yonderway, but nobody's home. And there's Old Man Fowler Gaskin. You wouldn't take a stray dog to him."

"What about town?"

"It's a right smart of a ways. Too far for the boy to keep ridin' horse-back, I'm afraid, and I ain't got a wagon. Bring him in the house. I'll see if there's somethin' I can do for him."

Lige had always considered it gospel truth that black folks were supposed to be subservient. He took the old man's blackness as an indication that the cabin was probably filthy and infested with vermin. The thought of taking Scooter in there repelled him. Yet he saw no choice.

He said, "I'm goin' to need hot water to clean him up."

"That won't take long. I got plenty of firewood, and there's water in the well."

The cabin's single room was bedroom and kitchen all together. Lige was pleasantly surprised to see that the place was clean. He asked, "You got a woman, I suppose?"

"Never had no chance to get married."

"The place looks too neat not to have a woman in it."

"I used to belong to Mr. Isaac York. When he was sober he was particular about keepin' the place up. He wasn't sober much, but I got in the habit of sweepin' and scrubbin' for the times when he was."

Lige gave the cot a doubting look. He distrusted it but was in no position to be choosy. He gently placed Scooter on the top blanket and pulled down the bloody trousers. Sight of the wound made him sick to his stomach. "How about that hot water?"

"It'll be comin' in a minute. What happened to this boy?"

"It's best you don't know. Then you can't tell them anything."

"He's been shot, that's plain to see. And I'm guessin' you're the ones the Rangers told me about."

Lige's nerves tightened. "The Rangers? What did they tell you?"

"Told me about a man and a boy that robbed a bank out west some-place. I got no money in a bank here or anywheres else, so it don't scrape no skin off of my nose."

Defensively Lige said, "The boy had nothin' to do with it."

"It don't seem likely he would, him bein' so young."

"How often do the Rangers come by here?"

"Ain't seen one in a while. Rusty Shannon was the last to come by."

The name jarred Lige. "Rusty?"

"He's the neighbor I was tellin' you about. A hailstorm beat down his crops, so he's gone back to Rangerin' 'til spring-plantin' time."

Lige thought of his ride with Shannon and Andy to the San Saba River camp, where he'd picked up Scooter. The Ranger had seemed to be a man of dark moods. "I've met Shannon. He didn't have a whole lot to say."

"Hard times been doggin' his steps like a hungry wolf. He was all set on marryin', but his woman got shot and killed. He's a booger against men that breaks the law."

"And boys too?"

"He's got a soft spot for hard-luck boys. I mind the time he caught a white boy ridin' with the Comanches. They had stole him when he was little. Rusty taken him in and treated him like a brother. First time I seen Andy he was about the size of your boy here. Turned into a fine young man."

"Andy? Would his last name be Pickard?"

"Sure would."

"He was kind to my boy, Scooter."

"I ain't surprised. It would be his way of payin' back for what-all Rusty done to help him."

Lige tried washing away the blood, but his stomach turned over. He had seen lots of bloodshed in his day, but this time was different. This was his son.

The black man offered, "I'll clean him up for you." He took the wet cloth, rinsed it, and began washing around the wound. "This looks bad. I wisht I had whiskey to pour in that bullet hole."

Lige thought he could use some whiskey himself. "We need to cauterize that wound. Else it's apt to go to gangrene."

The black man's face twisted. "Old Shanty couldn't do that to this boy. I know how much it hurts. One time Mr. Isaac got drunk and taken a notion that I ought to be branded like he branded his critters. It was a long time before I could sit in a chair."

"I'm his daddy. It's my place to do it. You got a butcher knife I can heat?"

Reluctantly Shanty fetched a knife from his crude cabinet. "I'll hold him for you, but I'm shuttin' my eyes."

Scooter had been unconscious. He awakened screaming at the touch of the hot blade. With tears in his eyes Lige kept pressing against the wound until the smell of burning flesh became too much for him. He rushed out of the cabin and threw up.

He reentered after a few minutes. Shanty said, "The boy's unconscious again. He ain't feelin' nothin'. I rubbed some hog lard over the burn."

"Is there a doctor in town that we can trust?"

"Folks around here swear by Dr. Parsons."

"I'd be obliged if you would fetch him."

"Like as not I'll run into Sheriff Tom Blessing. What will I say?"

"I don't see why you'd have to say anything."

Shanty considered. "I never was no great shakes at lyin'. Folks see through me in a minute. But maybe Mr. Tom won't ask me nothin'."

"I hope not. Folks have already accused me of shootin' one sheriff. No tellin' how high they'd hang me if it was two."

The doctor spent an hour with Scooter. Lige watched him intently, looking for some sign of what he was thinking, but Parsons had the blank expression of an expert poker player. When Lige could stand the strain no longer, he demanded, "What's his chances?"

The doctor's eyes made a silent accusation. "They'd be better if somebody competent had seen him sooner. He lost a lot of blood, and what he didn't lose is in some danger of blood poisoning."

Lige's eyes burned. "You sayin' I'm fixin' to lose him?"

"I'd be lying if I told you he's going to be fine. But he's young and generally healthy. He's got that much on his side. I would caution you against moving him for a few days."

"This ain't no place for him." Lige gave Shanty an apologetic look. "Sorry, but that's the way I see it."

The doctor beckoned Lige outside and said, "There's not a kinder-hearted man in this county than Shanty York. You're letting his color cancel out your better judgment."

"I can't overlook it, though. It's the way I was raised."

"It got a lot of good men killed during the big war. For this boy's sake I hope you'll put those notions aside. At least for a few days, until he's stronger and better able to move."

"Looks like I ain't got much choice."

Back inside, Lige found Scooter half-awake. He placed a gentle hand on the boy's shoulder. He told the doctor, "There's people lookin' for us. I'd rather we wasn't found."

"I knew who you were as soon as Shanty told me about you. Lawmen over half of the state are on the hunt. The claim is that you two shot the sheriff over at Hopper's Crossing."

"But it ain't true. It was the sheriff's own deputy done the shootin', and he shot my boy too."

Lige could not tell whether Parsons believed or disbelieved him. That poker face gave nothing away.

The doctor shrugged. "It's been a long time since anything good came out of that county. Almost any funeral over there could be considered community improvement. Do you know I am obliged by law to report any treatment I do on gunshot wounds?"

"I remember when private matters stayed private."

"It seems that the government pokes its nose into just about everything these days. But I might get so busy that I don't turn in my report for a while. People my age are apt to be forgetful at times."

"What do I owe you, Doctor?"

A knowing smile crossed Parsons's face. "Did you come by the money honestly?"

"Some folks might argue either way about that."

"Just drop a couple of dollars in the plate the next time you go to church."

"If Scooter comes out of this, I'll let him do it."

Lige and Shanty stood on the narrow front porch, watching the doctor's buggy raise dust on the town road. Lige asked, "You a Bible-readin' man?"

"I don't read it, exactly, but I listen to the Word anytime I get the chance."

"Do you reckon the Lord allows for a righteous killin'?"

"You thinkin' about that deputy sheriff?"

"He does lay heavy on my mind."

CHAPTER

FIFTEEN

An hour past dark Big'un Hopper reluctantly rode into town with a volunteer posse of six men. Horses and riders were so weary that they seemed barely able to hold their heads up. It had been another hard day's ride, and a futile one. Big'un had mistakenly thought it would be easy to track the fugitives and put so many holes in them that their bodies would not float.

His cousin Harp said, "It's like angels lifted them up and carried them away. Or maybe it was the devil. Don't seem like the angels would help them that killed Oscar Truscott."

They had certainly not done anything to help Big'un. He had wanted to continue the chase if it killed half the horses, but the exhausted posse members had threatened to rebel. Even Harp had argued their side. If they couldn't find the trail in the daylight, they sure as sin wouldn't find it in the dark, he said.

Big'un knew they were right, though he had verbally chastised them and even threatened to beat up Cousin Wilbur, who had been a chronic bellyacher all his life. He knew the longer the fugitives remained at large, the less likely he was to find them. He hoped that Lige Tennyson's wound was serious enough to make him go to ground somewhere. After that, the boy would be easy. Sure, some people would balk at shooting him, but Big'un had told everyone who would listen that the boy had participated in the killing of Oscar Truscott. Once a young wolf got the taste of blood, he argued, he was beyond taming. Best thing was to shoot him at the first opportunity.

So far as he could tell, no one had doubted his story. Not even a Landon had spoken out against him. But if Lige and his boy had a chance to tell their version often enough, doubts might begin to surface.

It must have been the devil's doing that he had not been able to kill them at the farmhouse the way he had intended.

As the posse began to break up, Big'un declared loudly, "I'll expect every one of you to be here and ready with fresh horses at first light. Bring enough grub to last you for three or four days."

He heard a lot of groaning and knew that half of them would not show up. Things had come to a pretty pass when a man could no longer count on loyalty from his kin.

After the others pulled away, Harp said, "You never did like Oscar in the first place. Looks like we ought to be takin' care of Jayce Landon instead of chasin' over hell and half of Texas lookin' for that old man and his boy. The truth be told, they done you a favor. They made you the sheriff."

"You gettin' cold feet, Harp?"

"No, but I'm gettin' an awful sore butt. You have any idea how far we've ridden?"

"We'll ride a thousand miles if we have to. Jayce ain't goin' nowhere. We'll get around to him, but we've got this other business to finish first."

Harp accepted, but not with any grace. "If you say so, but was I you, I'd be givin' that Tennyson a medal."

"You've got no sense of justice."

Harp started to turn away but stopped, considering. "You sure you ain't just makin' a show for Oscar's widow?"

Big'un exploded into rage. "What kind of a man do you think I am? She's blood kin."

"She's good-lookin'. I ain't seen nothin' yet that would make you back away from a good-lookin' woman."

Big'un was tempted to lay the barrel of his new pistol against the side of Harp's head. But Harp was a better tracker than Big'un. He needed him. Someday when all of this was over, he would teach Harp a whole new code of conduct.

As he rode by the darkened courthouse a familiar, gruff voice hailed him. Judge Hopper walked out and jerked his head in silent command.

Big'un dismounted but had to hold on to his horse for a minute while his knees threatened to collapse from fatigue.

The judge's voice was impatient. "I gather that you had no luck."

"We had luck, all right. All bad."

"This is the third day you've been out on the chase. Don't you think that's enough?"

"It won't be enough till we get them."

"No tellin' how far they've traveled by now. Everybody in town knows you and Oscar didn't like one another. Some are beginnin' to ask why you've let yourself become obsessed with this hunt."

"I've got my reasons."

"And I can guess what they are. But if enough other people start to guess the same thing, you're liable to be in more trouble than you can handle."

"You sayin' I ought to quit the chase?"

"I'm sayin' they're probably in another jurisdiction by now. Let somebody else capture them."

"I can't. I've got to be the one that does it."

The judge stared solemnly at him. "I've seen some smart men convicted in my court, all because they got in too much of a hurry and were careless enough to leave witnesses behind. Good night, nephew."

Big'un watched his uncle walk away and become lost in the darkness. He gritted his teeth and slammed his palm against the seat of his saddle, startling the tired horse into jumping away from him.

At that moment he realized that his uncle had served notice in an oblique way. If Big'un got into trouble over Oscar Truscott, he was on his own. Judd Hopper's court would be of no help.

Damn you, Lige Tennyson, he thought. This is all your fault.

Lige stood in the middle of Shanty's garden, chopping weeds. He had been a little put off at first by the notion of doing chores for a black man, but it was better than sitting around fretting over Scooter's still-raw wound. That little cabin seemed to shrink a bit more every day.

Shanty rode up from the river on his mule. Lige straightened and wiped sweat from his face onto his sleeve. "Find your hogs all right?"

"Not all of them. I got a notion Mr. Fowler Gaskin has been over this way."

"Damn, but I hate a thief. Somebody ought to ride over to Mr. Gaskin's and plant a load of buckshot where it'll remind him what the Gospel says."

"It won't be me. Only reason I keep a shotgun is to kill varmints."

"From what you've told me, Gaskin is the biggest varmint around here."

"The Book says judge not if you don't want to be judged your own self. Now and then I get tempted, but I can't speak my mind free like if I was white."

Lige had never given thought to the fact that blacks had to be extra careful in expressing themselves lest they anger those whites who would not hesitate to inflict punishment. Lincoln's Emancipation Proclamation had granted them freedom on paper. It had not freed them from the invisible chains.

Shanty asked, "You looked in on the boy?"

"A while ago. He was asleep. That's what he needs the most, but I don't know how much more he can get."

"How come?"

"A couple of riders came by. I stayed in the cabin where they couldn't see me. I couldn't help thinkin' they're part of a posse, huntin' me and my boy. We need to be movin' along."

"Scooter's at a ticklish stage in his healin'. He oughtn't to be on his feet, much less in a saddle."

"If people keep comin' by, we may not have no choice."

"You're all right if you stay inside. Most white folks who pass by here wouldn't go in my cabin if you was to offer them twenty dollars."

"I expect the reward on me is a lot more than twenty dollars."

Shanty squinted against the sun, then lifted his hat to shade his eyes. "Looks to me like we're fixin' to have some more company, Mr. Lige."

Lige took only a fleeting look. "Good thing you seen him. I didn't." Bending over as if that would make him less visible, he retreated to the cabin. Shanty tied the mule, then picked up the hoe and continued the work Lige had begun.

Long before he could see the man's face, Shanty knew the visitor was Fowler Gaskin. Like Shanty, he rode a saddled mule, though a poor one that showed its ribs. Gaskin had a way of hunching over that identified him as far as a man could see him. Shanty forced a false smile. "How do, Mr. Gaskin."

Gaskin took a look around before he replied. "Anybody here besides you?"

"Ain't hardly anybody ever stops at my place."

"You heard what happened?"

"Ain't much to hear around this little old farm."

Fowler sat up straighter, enjoying the feeling of importance that came from being the bearer of news. "Been a killin' over yonder a ways. Seems like a man and a boy was wanted for robbin' a bank, and when the sheriff went to arrest them they shot him."

Shanty feigned surprise. "Wasn't Tom Blessing, was it? I sure would miss Mr. Tom."

"Naw, it was over the county line, by Hopper's Crossin'. Been a *re*ward posted. I wondered if you've seen anybody like that lately."

"Ain't seen hardly anybody at'all."

"I could sure use that *re*ward money." Gaskin looked hard at Shanty. "I seen a couple of strange horses grazin' out yonder a piece. Didn't know you had any horses."

Shanty began feeling nervous. He thought he saw suspicion in Gaskin's eyes. "Ain't mine. Strays followin' the river, I expect."

"If it was me, I wouldn't let nobody's strays be eatin' up my grass."

"Horses don't know nothin' about property lines. I figure somebody'll come along and claim them."

"Maybe so." Gaskin looked toward the cabin as if he expected to see someone. "Mind if I stop at your well and get a drink?" Normally he never asked; he just took.

"Help yourself." To refuse him would strengthen Gaskin's suspicion. Shanty had never refused him anything. He could only hope that Lige remained inside and kept quiet. He went on with his hoeing, but his worried gaze remained fixed on Gaskin.

Gaskin brought up a bucket of water on the windlass but took no more than a sip before dropping the bucket back into the well. He gave the cabin a long study. When he rode away he changed direction and kept looking back over his shoulder.

When he felt that Gaskin could no longer see him, Shanty laid down the hoe and went to the cabin, half trotting, half hopping on his arthritic legs. Lige came out onto the narrow porch to meet him. "Anybody we need to worry about?"

"It's past the worryin' part. That was Mr. Fowler Gaskin, and he looked like a dog that just found a bone."

Lige's eyes narrowed. "You didn't tell him nothin'?"

"Didn't have to. He seen your horses. I'm fair certain he figured it all out for hisself."

"That old mule of his don't look none too swift. I could catch up to him." Lige's eyes made Shanty feel cold.

Shanty said, "Ain't you already got trouble enough?"

Lige sobered. "Then me and my boy have got to get away from here before he comes back and brings some others with him."

"If you try to take Scooter very far, he ain't goin' to make it."

Lige's eyes showed fear. "I'm willin' to take my chances, but my boy . . ." The fear turned to anguish. "Ain't there no place safe for him?"

"The jail."

Lige stared as if he could not believe what he heard. "Jail?"

"Sheriff Tom Blessing's jail. Mr. Tom ain't goin' to let nobody touch Scooter or do him any hurt."

"My boy don't belong in jail. He ain't done nothin'. I'll admit I done the bank robbery like they said, but that was me, not him. He done his best to talk me out of it."

"I believe you, and I'll bet Mr. Tom will too. He'll see that Scooter gets the right doctorin'. He'll also see that nobody does him harm."

Lige wrestled with his doubts. "I've spent the biggest part of my life tryin' to stay out of jail. Puttin' that boy into one on purpose goes against everything I believe in."

"It'll be the savin' of him."

"You're probably right, bad as I hate to think so. But if I go with him I'll have gray whiskers down to my knees before I get out. If they don't hang me."

"I can take him. It'd be easier for you to keep hidin' out if you don't have the boy on your hands."

Lige nodded reluctantly. "I wouldn't go far. I'd want to be where I could sort of keep an eye on things."

Shanty considered. "Mr. Rusty's place. Him bein' a Ranger, I doubt as they'd do much lookin' around there. You could camp in the timber down on the river. If there was any news I could come and tell you."

Lige looked as if it would not take much to make him cry. "Ain't been but a little while since I got my boy back. It's a mean thing to think about us bein' apart again."

Shanty could only shrug. For this, he had no answer.

Scooter was too weak to get on his horse without help, and he bit his lip to keep from crying out in pain as his father lifted him into the saddle. Shanty said, "We'll stay in the timber as much as we can. It's a longer trip that way, but maybe we won't run into anybody."

Scooter's voice was almost too weak to be heard. "I'll be all right. Where are we goin'?"

Lige and Shanty had decided not to tell him until they had to. They knew he would resist the plan to separate him from his father. Shanty said, "To some good folks that'll take care of you."

It was dark by the time they reached the edge of town. Lige became agitated when he saw that a number of people were out on the street. "Why ain't they at home?" he demanded. "Even chickens know to go to roost come night."

Shanty said, "Maybe you better not go no further."

Lige turned to his son. "Shanty's takin' you on in. I'm goin' to have to quit you here."

Scooter was dismayed. "You're not stayin' with me?"

"It's for the best this way. But I ain't goin' far. Anything happens, I'll be here in a jiffy." He hugged his son, then looked away quickly, blinking. He cleared his throat and turned to Shanty. "I ain't never had much use for your people. Always thought they was shiftless and sticky-fingered. But you've done mighty fine by me and my boy. If there's ever anything you need . . ." He did not finish. He rode off into the darkness without looking back.

Scooter called after him, but his voice was soft and did not carry far.

Shanty said, "Hush, boy, you don't want the wrong people to hear you." He waited a minute, watching and listening. "Looks like there ain't nobody comin'. Let's go before somebody sees us."

"Where we goin'?"

"Told you while ago, to some good people who'll watch out for you."

As soon as he saw the jail, Scooter sensed the plan. He tried to turn his horse around, but Shanty caught the reins. "Hold on, boy. It's all right."

"You turnin' me in to the law?"

"Sheriff Tom Blessing ain't goin' to hurt you, and he ain't goin' to let nobody else do it. You can't keep runnin', the shape you're in."

"They'll try to make me tell where my daddy is at."

"You don't know, so you can't tell them much. Let me help you down. I'll take care of your horse later."

Though Scooter was not heavy, he was almost too much for Shanty. The old man sank halfway to his knees before setting the boy on the ground. "Hold on to me," he said. "I won't let you fall."

Shanty knocked on the door, then rubbed his knuckles, arthritis making them ache. In a minute someone opened the door slowly and cautiously. The muzzle of a pistol showed first. Then Andy Pickard poked a lamp out into the darkness.

"Shanty? What you doin' out this time of the night?"

"Brought you somebody."

Andy shouted, "Scooter!" He opened the door wide, looking past Shanty and the boy. "Got his daddy with you?"

"Just the boy. He's hurt."

Andy laid the lamp on the floor, then picked Scooter up and carried him inside. He laid him on a cot. "Better bar that door behind us, Shanty. Some folks from Hopper's Crossing have been hangin' around, lookin' for a chance to bust in."

"Nobody knew I was bringin' the boy here."

"It's not Scooter they've been after, not here at the jail." He explained that Jayce Landon was safely lodged in a cell.

Shanty said, "They're huntin' Scooter too. He witnessed a shootin'."

"So I've heard. They've got word out all over the country. They say his daddy murdered Sheriff Truscott."

"Scooter and his daddy tell it different. They say the sheriff's own deputy done it, then throwed the blame on Mr. Lige and the boy."

Andy absorbed that as he looked down at the youngster. "How'd Scooter get shot?"

"That deputy. He tried to kill the both of them so they couldn't tell what he'd done."

"Sounds like Big'un Hopper."

Scooter rasped, "That's him. That's what Pa called him."

Andy frowned. "If it was anybody else I'd find it hard to believe. But with Big'un, I'm not surprised at anything." He turned away. "I better go wake up Tom. He's been stayin' in the jail ever since we brought Jayce over here. Sleeps with one eye open."

Shanty said, "Come mornin' we better fetch the doctor. He treated the boy once, but he sure needs lookin' at again."

Andy blinked. "The doctor's already seen Scooter?"

"Once, out at my place."

"He didn't come and tell us about it."

Shanty headed off a smile. "I guess he ain't found the time. Doctors get awful busy."

"In some localities more than others."

Tom lay on a cot in an empty cell. He was already half awake when Andy went in to fetch him. He said, "I heard the door. I didn't hear any fight, so I supposed it wasn't any of the Hopper bunch bustin' in."

Andy explained about Scooter and his version of Truscott's death.

Tom said, "From what you-all have told me about this Big'un, maybe the boy's tellin' it straight. But we can't pass judgment. That's for a court to do."

"True enough, but we've got to give the boy protection."

"Sounds to me like he needed protection from his father."

"That's what I tried to tell the captain when he let Lige Tennyson take Scooter away with him."

"Where do you reckon the old man is now?"

"No tellin'."

"No matter. Our main job right now is to see that the Hoppers don't get to Jayce before he's had a chance to stand trial. If they want Lige Tennyson, they'll have to find him theirselves."

"From what Scooter and Shanty say, Big'un's liable to want Scooter as much as he wants Jayce."

"Let him come and try. Ain't nobody gettin' into my jail unless I put him there. Do you suppose anybody saw Shanty bring the boy in?"

"I think somebody is watchin' everything we do."

CHAPTER
SIXTEEN

Big'un Hopper was so tired that when he tried to pull the saddle and blanket from his horse's back he dropped them. He expelled a long breath and reached down, then straightened, pressing his hand against his back in a futile effort to ease the pain.

He muttered to himself, "The hell with it. Let them lay." He slipped the bridle over the horse's ears and watched the animal turn toward the water trough. He was eager for a drink himself. It would be a mix of coffee and whiskey, light on the coffee.

Carrying a lantern, Harp walked out to the corral. "It's been dark for two hours. I thought you never was goin' to give it up and come in."

The words were not exactly critical, but Big'un took them that way. Most of his kin had been walking the long way around him the last few days, afraid he might bite their heads off. Or worse, badger them into joining his posse to hunt for Lige Tennyson and his brat. He said, "If the rest of you won't go with me, I'll keep goin' by myself. I won't quit till I get them."

Harp hung the lantern on a nail. "You can quit huntin' for the boy, at least. We know where he's at."

Big'un stiffened. "Keep talkin'."

"He's over yonder in Tom Blessing's jailhouse."

Big'un swore. "How do you know?"

"You recollect that you put Cousin Bim to watchin' the jail so we'd know if they tried to smuggle Jayce out of there? He seen an old darky bring the boy in."

"How did he know it was the right boy?"

"He hung around close and listened to the talk. It was the Tennyson kid, all right, and he was wounded."

"Who would've wounded him?"

"I reckon you did. We found blood on the porch, remember? You thought you had shot the old man, but it looks like you hit the boy instead."

It took Big'un a minute to absorb that. He had aimed at Lige, but hitting a target from a running horse was always highly chancy. Until he saw the bloodstains he had not thought he'd hit anyone. "Anybody see anything of the boy's daddy?"

"No, but it ain't likely he'd go far without knowin' his son was goin' to be all right. I figure he's hidin' close by." Harp's voice dropped. "And he's apt to be killin' mad. Was I you I'd be keepin' four walls around me and no windows. That broad back of yours makes a good target."

Big'un shivered at the thought of a bullet smashing between his shoulder blades, severing his spine and setting him afire. It could happen if Tennyson was the crack shot he had claimed to be.

Harp said, "If we could just figure some way to smoke him out . . ."

Big'un said, "You told me an old darky brought the boy in. Know who he was?"

"Bim never heard his name, but I've been thinkin' about that old man Gaskin. He said he had a notion where Tennyson and the boy was at. Wondered how much we'd pay for the information and if we'd let him have some of it in advance."

"I remember. Everybody said he was just a lyin' old drunk always lookin' to get money without havin' to work for it. I gave him a cussin' and sent him on his way."

"Maybe you cussed him too soon. It just come to me that he said he thought they was hidin' out with a darky. Could've been the same one that brought the boy to town."

Big'un felt as if Harp had struck him. "You knew that and still you stood by and let me run Gaskin off?"

"Thinkin' ain't exactly my long suit. I leave most of that to you."

"Reckon you could find out where Gaskin lives? I'd get him to take us to that darky."

"He oughtn't to be hard to find. He's got a reputation."

"Then get at it. And next time somebody offers information, don't be so quick to run him off."

Fowler Gaskin's place looked about as Big'un expected. "I never could understand how some people can live in a pig sty. He ain't crippled, is he?"

Harp said, "From what I heard, the only thing crippled about him is his ambition."

Gaskin's garden was badly in need of attention. Big'un indulged in a moment's revulsion at the many signs of neglect. Not seeing the old man, he hollered in the direction of the leaning cabin, "Gaskin, come out here." In a lower voice he added, "Before the whole thing falls down around you."

Gaskin ventured as far as the doorway, peering at the visitors through pinched eyes. "Who's that hollerin'?"

"Come out here. I want to talk to you."

Gaskin reached back inside the door and brought out a shotgun. Big'un tensed, wondering if the old reprobate had the guts to fire it. Gaskin said, "I remember you. You talked awful mean to me. I got no business with you now."

Big'un pushed his horse forward and wrested the shotgun from Gaskin's weak and trembling hands. "Yes, you do. You said you knew where we could find Lige Tennyson."

"I said I *thought* I knew, and you cussed me out like I was a nigger. I don't let nobody treat me thataway."

Big'un asked, "How much would it take to make you change your mind?"

Gaskin's anger subsided. "A sight more than I asked you the last time."

"How do we know Tennyson is still there?"

"You don't. But if he's gone, I'll cut the price to half."

Big'un reached down and grabbed a handful of Gaskin's shirt. He yanked the old man up against the horse. "You greedy old robber, I'll pay you what I figure the information is worth, and not a dollar more."

Gaskin cried, "You wouldn't treat me thisaway if my boys was still here. They died fightin' for the South."

"That war is over, old man. We've got a new one now." He gave Gaskin a push that almost made him fall backward. "Go saddle your horse. You're takin' us to that darky."

Gaskin whined, "I ain't got a horse. All I got is a pokey old mule."

"That'll do. Saddle him or ride bareback, I don't care which."

Looking back in anxiety, Gaskin trotted awkwardly toward the barn. Big'un tossed the shotgun through the cabin's open door and heard it clatter on the floor. He said, "I ought to shoot the old rascal on general principles."

Harp said, "I doubt that many folks would show up for the funeral."

Gaskin led the saddled mule from the corral. He had regained a little of his bluster, but not much. "I'll be tellin' Tom Blessing about this. He don't let people come into his county and mistreat the voters."

"Stop talkin'. Get on that mule and ride."

Big'un was a little surprised by the neatness of Shanty's little farm. The garden and the field had been hoed. The crops looked healthy, in contrast to Gaskin's. He said, "I thought this place belonged to a darky."

Gaskin said, "It does. Mine used to look like this before I got down in my back."

He must have been down in his back for a long time, Big'un thought. It took years for a place to get as run down as Gaskin's.

Shanty was standing in front of a small frame shed, brushing a mule's back. He tried for a smile but could not mask his uneasiness.

Big'un asked Gaskin, "Is this the man who harbored Tennyson and the boy?"

"I'd bet a thousand dollars."

"You never saw a thousand dollars." Big'un turned to Shanty. "We know you took the Tennyson boy to town. Where's his daddy?"

Shanty considered a minute before he offered any reply. "I ain't got no idee."

Big'un assumed the old man was lying. He swung his quirt, striking Shanty across the shoulder. "I ain't got the patience to play games with you, boy. Where's he at?"

Shanty rubbed the burning shoulder. "I swear, mister, I don't know."

Big'un lashed him again. "That ain't the answer I want to hear. Try again."

Shanty's body shook, but he stood his ground. "I can't tell you what I don't know."

"He was with you. He's bound to've told you somethin'."

"He didn't tell me nothin'. Said it was better for me not to know."

Gaskin's courage had improved. He said, "These old darkys will lie to you every time. Give me that quirt and I'll put the fear of God into him."

Big'un suspected Gaskin was afraid he might not get his money if Shanty did not tell his tormentors what they wanted to hear. "Back away, Gaskin, before I use the quirt on *you*." He struck Shanty across the back. The old man flinched and choked off a cry.

Big'un said, "I'll bet you got aplenty of whip scars on you, old man. You'll have a bunch more if you don't talk."

Shanty drew up into a knot. "I been tellin' you the truth. That's all I can do."

Big'un raised the quirt again. Harp caught his arm. "You're fixin' to kill him. You don't want another killin' on your conscience."

Big'un's chin dropped. "What do you mean, *another* killin'?"

Harp's eyes narrowed. "I expect you know what I mean."

"Who you been listenin' to? Somebody been makin' talk?"

Harp's face twisted. "There's several wonderin' why you want that old man and his boy so bad, seein' as they eliminated Oscar Truscott and got you the sheriff's job."

Big'un's eyes smoldered. "Is that them talkin', or is it just you?"

Harp raised both hands in a gesture of surrender. "I ain't doubtin' you a particle. I'm with you all the way. I'm just tellin' you what some folks are sayin'."

"Don't you be listenin' to people who make idle talk. You just listen to me."

"I am, Big'un, I am."

Gaskin understood none of the conversation. He watched, frustrated. "Are you quittin'? You just fixin' to ride away without him tellin' you what you came to find out?"

Harp glared at him. "Looks to me like he's told all he knows. There's no use beatin' a dead horse."

Gaskin got down from his mule. "He ain't dead yet. I'll make him talk." Shanty drew his arms in tightly as Gaskin moved toward him.

Big'un pushed his horse between the two men. "I told you, Gaskin. Get back on your mule." He raised the quirt for emphasis.

Gaskin backed away. "I done my part. You owe me."

Big'un felt like quirting Gaskin, but instead, he dug a silver dollar from his pocket. He tossed it to the ground in front of the man.

Gaskin picked up the coin and flushed in anger. "A dollar? Is this all, just one dollar?"

"It's a dollar more than you're worth. If you don't want it, I'll take it back."

Gaskin put the coin in his pocket.

Big'un shook the quirt at him. "Now get away from here before I give you what you really got comin'." To Harp he said, "I hate a man who would betray his neighbor for money. Even a nigger neighbor."

Hunched in pain, Shanty watched as Gaskin got a handhold on the mule's ragged mane and pulled himself up. He said, "Mr. Fowler, my old dog died, but I'm fixin' to get me another one."

Gaskin snarled, "Your old dog was worthless. What you want another one for?"

"So that if you ever come messin' around my place again, I can sic him on you."

Gaskin's face colored. He turned to Big'un and Harp. "You-all goin' to let a nigger talk to a white man that way?"

Big'un said in disgust, "I don't see no white man."

In the midst of Big'un's frustration an idea began struggling to break free. *Smoke him out*, Harp had suggested. Harp was about to speak, but Big'un raised a hand to stop him, to keep him from interrupting his thoughts before the idea was fully hatched. He asked, "They still got the same old jailhouse?"

"Not much ever changes over there."

"I spent a night in that place once, years ago. They said I was drunk and disorderly."

Harp grinned. "Was you?"

"I expect so. Ain't been back in that town since. I decided not to give them any more of my business."

"It's their loss, then."

Big'un cast a glance over his shoulder to be sure Gaskin wasn't following to plead for more money. The old reprobate had put the reluctant mule into a long trot toward home. "How many people they got standin' guard at the jail durin' the night?"

"Generally a night watchman patrollin' the street outside. Three Rangers and the sheriff sleep inside. A deputy usually goes home."

Big'un rubbed his chin while he let his imagination run free. "Ought not to be hard to take care of the watchman. A couple of guns at the front door and one or two at the back could keep anybody who's inside from comin' out."

"What good will it do you if they stay inside? You couldn't get at them."

"That old jail is mostly built out of lumber. Say a fire was to start along the outside wall. That thing would go up fast, and if them on the inside couldn't get out—well, wouldn't that be a shame?"

Harp stared slack-jawed, awed by Big'un's audacity.

Big'un said, "First I'd like to know just what's goin' on in that place. I need a man to see inside. I want you to find me somebody who'll do anything for fifty dollars."

"There's aplenty of them around."

"This has to be somebody Jayce nor nobody else in that jail would recognize. Somebody who wouldn't mind gettin' a little drunk and disorderly and spendin' a night or two in the hoosegow. But somebody we can rely on."

"That's some combination."

"Find him."

"You're goin' to a lot of trouble just to get rid of Jayce Landon."

"That boy too. Let somethin' happen to him and like as not his old daddy would come runnin'. All I need is one clear shot. Now let's go where I can get me a bottle of whiskey. I got some thinkin' to do."

CHAPTER

SEVENTEEN

Used to being in Rusty Shannon's shadow, Andy was pleased at Rusty's attitude. He seemed to be leaning Andy's way in regard to Scooter.

Tom Blessing was still trying to make up his mind. He said, "The boy's fevered. Maybe he really saw what he says happened, or maybe it's the fever made him think he did. No jury is goin' to take his word against a lawman's."

Andy argued, "Even a *good* lawman goes bad once in a while, and Big'un's been a counterfeit from the start."

"I've known some lawmen who were bad to start with. Others learned it on their own. But I can't belive anything as cold-blooded as the boy tells about."

Rusty put in, "Whether it's real or he imagined it, Scooter's better off in here till everything settles into place. If Big'un did kill Truscott, he'll be lookin' to silence the boy. If it was Lige that did it, he'll probably stay around close so he can know what's happenin' to Scooter. That gives us a better chance to catch him."

Scooter lay on a steel cot in one of the cells. The iron-barred door was left open, for he was not technically a prisoner. Flora sat on the edge of the cot, keeping a damp cloth on the boy's head. She had all but adopted

Scooter as soon as she first saw him. She had never had a child of her own. Andy doubted that this was for lack of trying on Jayce's part.

Jayce feigned jealousy. From his cell he shouted, "Darlin' girl, you're payin' more attention to that boy than to your poor old neglected husband."

Flora tried to sound sarcastic. "He's younger, he's better-lookin', and he's got nothin' on his conscience."

"He will have by the time he gets a little older. Show me somebody who's got nothin' on his conscience and I'll show you somebody who's spent his life asleep."

Listening, Andy conceded to himself that his own conscience sometimes troubled him when he had time to pay attention to it. In his first years back in the white man's world after his time among the Comanches, he had given those who befriended him plenty of reason to wonder if they should have left him where he was. He had caused anxiety for Rusty in particular. Looking back, he could well understand how Rusty might have given up on him, especially when he threatened to run away and rejoin the Comanches. Instead, Rusty had taken him back to the Indians at considerable danger to himself. Andy had found it impossible to remain in that other world, though even now he still grieved over having lost his place in it. He sometimes questioned if he belonged in this one either.

The hard truth was that he did not fit comfortably in either world, white or red.

Jayce Landon had talked Tom into bringing a couple of forked tree branches to his cell so he could fashion a set of crutches for Scooter. He had promised, "I ain't fixin' to hit anybody over the head with them. The boy needs to be gettin' up and movin' around some. He'll need help with his walkin'."

Now he had a pile of wood shavings in the cell. He had trimmed away the bark and smoothed the surface with a pocketknife borrowed from Tom. He said, "These things'll need some cloth wrappin' to see that they don't rub sores under his arms. Otherwise, they're finished."

Tom said, "If they're finished, I'll thank you to give me back that knife." He extended his hand.

Jayce acted embarrassed. He handed the knife back through the bars. "Sorry. I almost forgot."

Andy knew Jayce had not forgotten anything, but he had hoped the sheriff would. Tom Blessing seldom forgot anything important.

Flora said, "I'll finish them up." She started back toward Jayce's cell, but Tom stopped her. He had never allowed her within reaching distance of her husband. He knew about her slipping a derringer to Jayce in the Hopper's Crossing jail.

He said, "I'll bring the crutches to you. Slide them out here, Jayce." Almost apologetically he added, "I appreciate what you two are doin' for the boy, but I can't afford much trust. Given the slightest chance I think you'd be out of here like a turpentined cat."

Jayce shrugged. "I told you that when I first came."

Flora wrapped cotton cloth around the top of the crutches as padding. "Feel like givin' them a try, Scooter?"

The boy turned himself around and cautiously put one foot on the floor. He had to use both hands to get the other leg into place. His face twisted with pain. Andy hurried to help him. "Does it hurt?"

Scooter grimaced. "Sure it hurts. But lift me up and see if I can fit them things under my arms." He was wobbly. Andy kept hold of him so he would not fall.

Scooter said, "I feel like I'm goin' down flat on my face. A little dizzy too."

"Don't be in a hurry. It'll take you a while to get the knack." He remembered a time long ago when a horse fall had left him with a broken leg. The crutches at first had seemed bent on bringing him down.

Tom asked, "Rusty, what did you find out about that bunch of riders who came to town this mornin'?"

Rusty said, "They were just Mexican traders bringin' a string of half-broke horses to sell to the farmers hereabouts. There wasn't a Hopper amongst them."

Tom said, "Strangers worry me, but the merchants wouldn't abide me turnin' them back at the edge of town. Visitors bring in money."

"It wouldn't be hard for a bunch of the Hoppers to slip into town at night. They'd love to get a clean shot at Jayce."

"That's why I put him in a cell that ain't got a window in it. As long as he stays there he's as safe as in church. Then after the judge gets here . . ." Tom did not finish. He did not have to.

Andy frowned. Flora did not deserve to be reminded constantly that her husband had an appointment with a rope. He said, "I need some fresh air. I think I'll go take me a little walk around town."

Rusty warned, "Keep watchin' over your shoulder. I wouldn't put it past the Hoppers to grab one of us and try to make a swap for Jayce."

Andy had not thought of that. He realized he should have. Rusty was usually a step ahead of him. Sometimes he despaired of ever catching up. He said, "If that happened, what would you do?"

Rusty said, "We're responsible for keepin' Jayce from harm till he's had his day in court. If it meant havin' to sacrifice one of us, that's what we're paid for. It's part of bein' a Ranger."

Tom nodded in silent agreement.

Their logic disturbed Andy. Jayce Landon was an admitted murderer. A death sentence was almost certain. To trade the life of a Ranger—any Ranger—to let Jayce live a couple of weeks longer seemed beyond reason. Andy deferred to the judgment of Rusty and Tom but retained his skepticism.

"I'll be careful," he promised.

Tom said, "Before you go, would you mind lettin' that drunk out of his cell? I expect two nights in there have sobered him up good."

The man had raised a ruckus in a saloon where things were usually so quiet the place could almost be taken for a Sunday school. Not wanting the burden of extra prisoners during this time of potential trouble, Tom had tried to let him off with a warning. At that point the drunk had thrown a chair through a glass window, and Tom no longer had a choice. Property must be respected, whether saloon or church house.

Andy unlocked the cell and beckoned with his thumb. "You've had enough free meals. Sheriff says he doesn't want to see anything but the backside of you leavin' town."

The man picked up his hat. He had brought nothing else in with him. He rubbed his chin. "I sure do need a shave."

"Go get it in some other town."

Andy followed him out into the sunshine. The former prisoner blinked against the brightness and looked up and down the street. "Where'd you-all put my horse?"

"In a corral at the wagon yard."

"Hope he got fed better than I did."

In a minute he was gone.

The weather was still warm, but with each passing day the sun edged a little farther to the south. The smell of fall was in the air for a while in early morning, though summer still ruled later in the day. Andy wondered how winter's cold would affect Scooter's healing.

Farley Brackett sat on the jail step, whittling a scrap piece of pine down to a pile of shavings that littered the ground at his feet. The cuts and bruises on his face were healing. "Where you headed, Badger Boy?"

"Just takin' a look around."

"What're you lookin' for?"

"I don't know, exactly."

"If you don't know what you're lookin' for, how you goin' to know it when you see it?"

Annoyed, Andy said, "Maybe you ought to go with me and help me look."

"Can't. I'm guardin' the front door. If you get yourself into any trouble, Badger Boy, you'll have to fight your own way out."

Andy could accept advice, even criticism, from Rusty or Tom, but he drew the line at Farley. "You just watch me."

"Oh, I'll be watchin' you, all right. But don't expect me to come runnin'. Last time I did that I got myself shot."

Andy never expected anything pleasant to come from Farley, and he was rarely disappointed. He wanted to think of a good retort, but none came, so he did not try for the last word. He walked through an open gate in the fence that surrounded the courthouse and jail. He stopped a minute to look up and down the dirt street. Before many more days it would be bustling as farmers in mule-drawn wagons began hauling the first of their cotton crop to town for ginning. Farm families with fresh money in their pockets would be crowding in to buy clothes and other necessities for the coming winter.

Right now the street was quiet. It looked about the same as he had known it during the years since his return from Comancheria except that the town had grown. He saw nothing to be concerned about.

He spotted a farmer he knew and walked over to talk with him. The farmer shook Andy's hand, then looked across toward the jail. He said, "I hear you-all have got a dangerous man locked up, and you're afraid somebody may come and try to bust him out."

"Some people would like to. We're prepared for them."

"Just the same, I ain't lettin' my family come to town till everything is over with. I wouldn't want them to get in the way of a shootin' scrape. Or maybe you can guarantee me that there won't be one."

"I can't even guarantee that the sun will rise and set tomorrow the same as it always has."

The farmer grunted. "I hope the judge shows up pretty soon and gets this mess over with. My wife is bustin' to come to town and see what's new over at the mercantile."

Andy admitted, "It won't be a bad idea to hold her at home a little while longer."

"Maybe you-all better send for some more Rangers."

"There's already three of us, and only one jailbreak to worry about. The head office in Austin figures three is probably two Rangers too many."

"You ought to take up farmin', Andy. All you got to worry about is drought, flood, hail, grasshoppers, and low prices."

Andy walked on down the street with no particular mission in mind except to look for something or somebody that seemed out of place. He peered into the mercantile store and saw no one except the storekeeper and a woman customer. He stepped through the door of a saloon and glanced over the half dozen men there. All the faces were familiar except one, and he looked like a drummer peddling his wares. The saloon was more than just a place for drinking. It was a public service of sorts, a social center where men could meet and swap news and views, a trading site for discussing deals and shaking hands on them. More horses and mules and cotton bales had been sold there than at the livery barn or the gin.

The barkeeper said, "Come on in. No use standin' there blockin' the door."

"Just lookin' for somebody." Andy went back outside, remembering what Farley had said. He did not know who he was looking for. How would he know him when he saw him?

Down at the livery stable, toward the end of the street, a man sat in a straight chair leaned back against the door. Andy at first took him to be the proprietor but after a closer look realized he did not know the man. Yet the face seemed vaguely familiar.

"Howdy," Andy said, trying to remember.

The man stared back, his eyes not friendly. He did not speak.

Andy said, "Seems like I ought to know you." He remembered now. "Your name would be Hopper, wouldn't it?"

"Might be."

"A while back me and Farley Brackett were on our way to deliver Jayce Landon to the sheriff at Hopper's Crossing. You were with a bunch that tried to stop us."

The man's tone was insolent. "That might be too."

"So what're you doin' here?"

"I've got to be somewhere."

"Not here unless you've got business. What's your business?"

"I've got a wife who bitches at me all the time. I come over here now and then to get drunk without her knowin' about it. Any law against that?"

He did not look drunk. Andy thought he could guess Hopper's real reason. He said, "I think you better move on out of town."

"Look, Ranger, I'm spendin' good money here, and I come by it honest. If I've broke any laws, tell me. If I ain't, then leave me the hell alone."

Andy was losing the argument and knew it. He had no grounds for running Hopper out of town. If he did so anyway, he might be subject to legal action. If he did not, and somebody got hurt, he would be blamed for not acting when he had the chance. It was enough to make him wonder why he had chosen to be a Ranger.

For a moment he considered going back to the jail and asking Rusty what he should do. But he had leaned on Rusty far too many times. Sooner or later he had to begin deciding such matters for himself.

He warned, "Watch yourself."

Hopper replied, "I always do. And them that's around me."

Andy returned to the jail. Farley still sat on the step. He had a new piece of wood to whittle on. The earlier one lay scattered in curled shavings on the ground.

Andy said, "I'll bet you didn't know we're bein' watched."

"I know. Bim Hopper's sittin' over yonder at the stable. He's spied on us for several days."

"You knew about him all that time?"

"Spotted him as soon as he showed up. I got to know Bim pretty good when Big'un and his bunch drug me away from my mother's place. He's got mean eyes, and fists hard as a pine knot."

"What are we goin' to do about him?" Andy instantly regretted asking advice, especially from Farley.

Farley said, "I'm waitin' for him to make a wrong move so I can shoot his ear off, or maybe his big toe. Somethin' he'll remember me by."

"He says he's in town to get drunk."

"He ain't been drunk since he came here. He's watchin' for us to let our guard down so him and his cousins can storm the jail and drag Jayce out."

Andy did not admit it, but his thinking ran the same as Farley's.

Farley said, "I hope they try. It'll be the best fight I've been in since I shot hell out of the state police."

Andy was disgusted. "This ain't some kind of entertainment show. There could be dead men layin' out in the street."

"The world could get along just fine without some of them Hoppers. They're a nest of vipers."

"They might not be the only ones killed."

"Have you taken a good look at that old jail? It ain't pretty, but it's bull stout. A whole regiment couldn't bust in without they had a cannon."

Andy was not pacified, but arguing with Farley was like trying to converse with a fence post. He went on up and entered the jail.

Rusty asked, "See anything?"

"There's a man watchin' us from over at the stable."

"Yeah, a cousin to Big'un Hopper. We've been keepin' an eye on him."

"How come you didn't tell me about it?"

Rusty smiled. "We thought we'd see how long it took you to spot him yourself."

Testing me, Andy thought, irritated. Like I was a new recruit.

After consideration he realized the description fit. He stood small against experienced lawmen like Rusty and Tom, even Farley. But he said, "Hadn't we ought to run him off?"

"It's better we leave him where we can watch what he's up to. The time to worry is when we *can't* see him."

Andy went to the window and looked up and down the street again. In a minute he said, "There's one thing you didn't know."

"What?" Rusty asked.

"That drunk we just let out of jail. He's over yonder talkin' to Bim Hopper."

Rusty and Tom both moved quickly to the window. Tom swore, "Well, I'll be damned. Looks like we've had a spy in our midst."

Rusty nodded. "Looks like."

CHAPTER

EIGHTEEN

Big'un Hopper looked back to be sure nobody had deserted him. He had twisted arms to the breaking point to get the six men who accompanied him on this punitive expedition. It would not take much of a scare to send most of them scurrying back to Hopper's Crossing. The only ones he felt he could depend upon were cousins Harp and Bim. Even those would bear some watching.

The wagon jolted along behind with several cans of coal oil he had brought. He could not afford to buy it locally because he would be remembered and the finger of blame would be pointed straight at him.

At dusk they were within half a mile of town. "Let's pull over into them trees yonder," he said. "We'll wait till the dark of the moon."

Cousin Wilbur pulled his horse in beside Big'un's. "The closer we get, the less I like this whole notion. I'm in favor of us gettin' Jayce, but there's other people in that jailhouse too. We could be charged with murderin' them all."

"Not unless we get caught. They can suspicion all they want, but suspicion don't hold no water in court. Anyway, I told all of you what we were goin' to do. I ain't lettin' you back out now."

"Accordin' to Bim there's a kid in that jail. What about him?"

"Remember, he's an outlaw's boy, and he was in on the killin' of Oscar Truscott. He's probably got the mark of a noose around his neck anyway."

"I still don't like it."

Big'un grabbed his cousin's shirt just below the throat and shook the man harshly. "Any more of that talk and I'll see that you walk all the way home."

He was much larger and stronger than his kinsmen. They might grumble, but when the voices quieted down Big'un was confident he would still prevail. He softened his tone. "Uncle Judd gave us a warrant for Jayce's arrest."

Harp asked, "Does Uncle Judd's jurisdiction reach over into another county's jailhouse?"

"He's a judge, ain't he?" Big'un trusted that none of them understood the limitations of Judd Hopper's jurisdiction. They knew all there was to know about mules and horses, cows and plows, but the intricacies of law were a mystery to them.

Wilbur frowned, considering the matter. "If Uncle Judd approves, I reckon it's all right."

Actually, Big'un had told his uncle only that they were going after Jayce. The judge had not let him explain. He had said, "I do not want to know anything about this. Then I can truthfully swear that I do not know what was done or who was responsible."

Big'un had thought it wise not to tell the judge that Jayce might be only one of the casualties, that others might include a couple or three Rangers and possibly even a sheriff. The old man could get downright unreasonable about anything that might bring state investigators in to snoop around. He had some skeletons of his own that were not buried deeply enough for comfort.

Big'un stretched out on the ground to rest while he waited for darkness. He tried not to sleep, fearing part of his crew might quietly slip away. He had some kinfolks who weren't worth killing, but now and then they were useful to him.

If all of the Confederate Army was like them, he thought, it's no wonder the damn Yankees whipped us.

He had not gone to war himself. The judge had pulled political strings to shield as many Hoppers as possible from conscription, arranging for Landon men to take up the slack. That served the demands of patriotism and reduced the enemy's numbers as well.

He waited until the stars were in full array, then prodded his kinsmen into reluctant motion. "The sooner we get the job done, the better chance we'll have to get out of this county before daylight. There won't be nobody able to identify us."

By the time they reached the first houses at the edge of town Big'un saw that he had lost two of his helpers in the darkness.

Harp said, "It's Wilbur and his no-account brother-in-law. We ought to've left them at home."

Big'un cursed. "When I get through with Wilbur..." He looked fiercely at those who remained. "If the rest of you have got any idea of quittin', put it out of your mind. I'll shoot the next man who turns back." He knew he would not, but it was important that they believed he would. When his temper was up, even the town dogs knew to slink away.

Only a few of the houses showed lamplight. Most folks had gone to bed. Things were working out according to plan. If he and his helpers got the job done quickly they should encounter little trouble from local citizens.

The courthouse and the adjoining old jail were like an island in the center of an open lot surrounded by a wooden fence that sagged in a couple of places. Big'un motioned for the driver to stop the wagon. They could carry the cans of coal oil from here. But first he had to locate and eliminate the watchman who patrolled the streets and periodically circled the courthouse. He waited a few minutes until he saw a man walking along the fronts of the buildings along the square, trying the doors to be certain they were locked.

Few people here were likely to recognize Big'un, but as a precaution he pulled his neckerchief up to cover his face. He stepped into the dark open space between two stores and flattened himself against a wall. He listened to the watchman's footsteps on the wooden sidewalk. As the shadowy figure crossed the opening, Big'un moved out behind him and clubbed him with the barrel of his six-shooter. He struck a second time to be sure the man remained out of action for a while. He dragged the limp body into the darkness between the buildings and left it.

He returned to where the others waited beside the wagon. "The watchman is out of the way. Now let's pull the wagon up to block the back door. Then their only way out is the front."

It took a little pushing and maneuvering to position the wagon over the single step so that the door could not be opened far enough for anyone to pass through.

A man stepped around the corner of the jail and stopped abruptly, drawing a pistol. "What're you-all up to?"

Before Big'un could think of a reply, a dark figure appeared behind the intruder and slugged him.

Big'un said, "Good work, Bim. He like to've caught us before we was ready." He unhitched the team and motioned for one of the others to lead the mules away. Big'un lifted a can from the bed of the wagon. "Let's give them walls a good dose of coal oil."

A cousin who went by the nickname Jaybo argued, "The thought of somebody burnin' up in a fire gives me the shakes. We could use a rail for a batterin' ram and bust the door down."

Big'un resisted an impulse to hit him in the mouth. "Would you want to be the first one to rush in there with three or four guns aimed straight at your gut?"

"If you look at it that way . . ."

Big'un assumed the argument was finished. "Bim, you watch the back door so no citizen comes and sets them free. The rest of us will take the front. If they try to bust out we'll shoot them. If they don't they'll know what hell is like before they get there."

Harp said, "Folks'll come runnin' to fight the fire."

"A shot or two in their direction will turn them back. This oughtn't to take long, dry as that lumber is."

Big'un tossed a match at the base of the jail's rear wall. The flames quickly licked their way up to consume the coal oil. He trotted around the side and lighted a couple of places. He motioned for his helpers to join him a few feet from the front door. He started a fire there, then drew his pistol and waited. "This'll be like pottin' fish in a water bucket."

Andy had turned in early, but he was not having a restful night. The folded quilt that served in lieu of a mattress did little to hide the fact that beneath it lay wooden slats that got no softer no matter how he turned. Farley Brackett occasionally broke into fits of loud snoring.

Rusty did not snore, but now and then he spoke a few words in his sleep. One word Andy recognized was "Josie." Though Rusty never spoke of her anymore, Andy sensed that she was still much on his mind. A couple of women here in town looked a little like her from across the street. Andy had noticed that Rusty seemed momentarily startled each time one of them appeared.

He managed to doze off and on, but the spells were shortlived. He worried about what was to become of Scooter. The boy was able to walk without the crutches Jayce had fashioned for him, though the effort was awkward and caused him considerable pain.

Scooter's father was hiding out there somewhere. Of that, Andy was sure. As soon as the boy healed enough to travel, Lige Tennyson was likely to steal him away. And to what? An outlaw life, probably, and most likely a short one. Andy had been considering the possibility of beating Lige to the punch, of taking Scooter where his father would never find him. Andy would have to resign as a Ranger, but he would be willing to pay that price. He would never be able to compensate Rusty directly. If he could do for Scooter what Rusty had done for him, however, that would be repayment of a sort.

And where could he take the boy? The Ranger camp had served as a temporary shelter, but it could not offer what he needed over the long term. The Monahan family kept coming to mind. They were generous, open-handed people who once had all but adopted Andy as one of their own. Surely they would do the same for another boy badly in need of a stable home and a sense of direction. And they lived far to the northwest, up in the Fort Belknap country of west-central Texas. Lige would have no idea where to begin looking.

It had been Flora's habit to spend most of the day at the jail, caring for Scooter and talking to her husband through two sets of bars. She would retreat to the boardinghouse at suppertime, not returning until morning. Tonight, however, she knocked urgently on the front door shortly after dark. "It's Flora," she said. "I've got somethin' to tell you-all."

Andy waited to see if someone else would get up and find out what she wanted. Farley grumbled, "Badger Boy, go let her in."

Andy's cot was farthest from the door, but he knew he could not out-wait Farley. He had gone to bed with his clothes on, all but his boots. He lifted the heavy crowbar that blocked the door. "Anybody out there besides you?" he asked Flora. He was mindful of the possibility that someone might use her to gain entry and free Jayce, or kill him.

"Nobody," she said. "But somebody may be comin'."

She stepped inside, and Andy closed and barred the door. She said, "Scooter's daddy just came to see me at the boardin'house."

"Old Lige? How did you come to know him?"

"He's never been far from town. He noticed me comin' and goin' from the jail, so he followed me to the boardin'house and introduced himself. Every day he comes and asks me about his boy. Tonight he saw somethin' he didn't like, and he asked me to give you-all a warnin'."

"About what?"

"He was camped in some timber just outside of town. A while before dark some men came with a wagon and stopped to rest awhile. Big'un Hopper was leadin' them. The old man doesn't know what they're up to, but it can't be anything good."

Rusty had left his cot and stood nearby, listening. "Where's Lige now?"

"Somewhere close, you can bet. He's worried on account of his boy."

One of Tom Blessing's temporary deputies had been sleeping in an open cell. He pulled on his boots and said, "I'll go take a look around."

Rusty said, "Much obliged. If you see or hear anything suspicious, give us a holler."

The deputy took a rifle from the office's gun rack. He said, "You-all want to bar the door behind me?"

Flora walked out with him. Andy set the crowbar in place.

Farley stretched out on his cot. "It'd take half the Yankee army to bust these heavy doors open. I'm goin' back to sleep."

Scooter had listened quietly. He said, "That's my daddy she was talkin' about. Did she say he's here?"

Andy said, "Somewhere around. He ain't forgot you."

He wished Lige would.

Andy had no intention of going back to sleep. Thinking he heard low voices outside, he left the cot and walked to the window. At first he saw nothing, for the night seemed pitch black. He stepped back and stumbled into a tin can filled with ashes, substituting for a cuspidor. It clattered and rolled across the floor.

Farley's gruff voice demanded, "Don't you know we're tryin' to sleep?"

"Sorry."

Farley recognized the voice. "I might've known it was you, Badger Boy. For God's sake, go back to bed."

Andy was about to when he saw a flickering light reflecting upon the ceiling. He swung back toward the window. "Fire!" he shouted. "There's a fire outside."

Farley said, "You're crazy." But he got up and looked for himself. "By God, Rusty, the place *is* on fire."

With that Rusty was on his feet too. He quickly pulled his boots on. Recognizing the possibility of trouble, he had been sleeping in his clothes, as had the others. Tom Blessing was also up from his cot.

Andy lifted the crowbar out of its brackets and dropped it to the floor. He pushed the front door partway open. Blistering flames leaped into his face, and he jerked back instinctively. A bullet struck the facing, followed by another, which thumped into the heaviest part of the door. He pulled the door shut.

Rusty said, "That Hopper bunch. They knew they couldn't break in. They're tryin' to burn us out."

Andy trotted to the back door. He could push it only a few inches before it bumped against something solid. The opening was too small to squeeze through. Someone outside fired a shot that splintered the frame. He said, "They got the back door blocked."

Farley strapped his gun belt around his waist. "Be damned if I'll stay here and burn."

Tom said, "The front door is the only way out, and they're waitin' for us there. But we've got no choice."

Rusty said, "Scooter can't make it on his own, and Jayce is locked in a cell. We can't leave him there to die."

Farley said, "They're goin' to hang him anyway."

Andy said, "I can carry Scooter."

Farley said, "If you let Jayce out he'll run like a scalded dog."

Rusty repeated, "We can't leave him to burn."

"He will anyway, soon as the devil gets ahold of him."

From behind his bars Jayce shouted, his voice on the edge of desperation, "Get me out of this trap."

Tom tossed his keys to Andy. "We'll take our chances on him. Turn him loose."

Eye-stinging smoke was already boiling up in the section that contained the cells. Jayce coughed heavily. Andy swung the cell door open and said, "You're on your honor."

Jayce made no response except to lower his head and cough into his hands. Once he was out of the cell area he said, "Let me defend myself. Give me a gun."

Tom Blessing said, "You know we can't do that."

"I ain't goin' out there empty-handed." Jayce stepped to Tom's desk and opened a drawer. He withdrew a pistol and spun the cylinder to see if it was loaded. "Now, are we goin' out there, or are we goin' to roast like a beef on a spit?"

Rusty accepted the situation without argument. "We'll go out shootin' and make them duck their heads. Andy, you follow close with Scooter. We'll be between you and them. Maybe they won't even see you."

Andy felt guilt about letting others stand the greater risk, but he knew if the boy tried to hobble out on his own, he would not get far past the door.

Farley gave a rebel yell and flung the door open. His pistol blazed. Tom and Rusty and Jayce burst out just behind him, firing at shadows. Andy crouched low, carrying Scooter in his arms.

Andy had heard Rusty say that rapid fire did not have to be accurate so long as it made the enemy keep their heads down. The Rangers and Jayce had cleared the door and were halfway to the fence before the Hoppers regained their wits enough to fire back.

An angry voice shouted, "Shoot, you cowardly sons of bitches. Shoot."

Andy would bet a month's pay the voice belonged to Big'un.

Someone in the Hopper line cried out like a hurt dog.

In the center of the yard was a well with a windlass and a circular stone wall three feet high. Andy dropped behind it. "Flatten out, Scooter, and pull your legs in."

He peered over the rim of the well, seeking a target. He fired once to no apparent effect.

He could hear excited shouts from over in town. Aroused citizens were beginning to respond to the fire and the shooting.

The Hoppers had lost their advantage. Now with the blazing building behind them, their silhouettes became targets. Rusty fired, and Andy saw a man fall. Then Rusty went down. Andy's heart jumped, and he fired at the spot where he had seen a pistol flash.

A rifle opened up from just beyond the perimeter fence. Someone had joined the Rangers in their fight.

Even with the light from the fire, Andy could see no faces he could swear to in court. A large figure arose from a squatting position and ran hard, disappearing around the corner while bullets whispered around him. Andy was almost certain he had seen Big'un Hopper.

A plaintive voice cried, "We give up. Don't shoot no more."

Andy sensed that Rusty was out of the fight. He took it upon himself to shout, "Everybody hold your fire. You Hoppers, raise your hands and stand up where we can see you."

The voice said, "I'm the only one still able to stand. Don't shoot."

The man who had fired from the other side of the fence climbed over, rifle in his hand. He had a shuffling gait. Andy recognized Lige Tennyson. Lige called anxiously, "Scooter! Where you at, boy?"

"Pa?" Scooter pushed to his feet and leaned against the well to steady himself. "Is that you, Pa?"

"It's me. Are you all right? They didn't hit you?"

"No, sir. Andy wouldn't let them." Scooter and his father hugged each other fiercely. Scooter cried, "What you doin' here, Pa? They'll put you in jail."

"I had to know if you're all right." A section of the jail wall fell inward. A shower of sparks lifted high into the air, then fell. "Don't look like they've got a jail to put me in."

Andy said, "You got here awful fast."

"I didn't have to come very far. Did Mrs. Landon deliver my message?"

"She did. But none of us expected fire."

The jail began caving in, sending waves of blistering heat rolling across the yard. The townspeople set up a bucket brigade. It was too late to save the jail, but they worked to keep the adjacent courthouse from catching fire.

Farley limped badly. In the flickering light of the flames Andy saw that one trousers leg was bloody. "Looks like you didn't dodge quick enough," he said.

"Like I keep tellin' you, Badger Boy, you're a damned jinx. Every time you're around, somethin' happens to me. You better take a look at Rusty. I think he's harder hit."

Rusty lay twisted on the ground, his right hand gripping a bleeding left shoulder. He swore under his breath, fighting against the pain.

Andy dropped to his knees beside him. "How bad is it?"

"Busted the shoulder, I think. Big'un done it before he turned and ran."

In a flash of anger Andy said, "I'll catch him. I'll make him wish he never got out of bed this mornin'."

"What about the Hoppers? Big'un was the only one I saw leave."

Andy made a quick survey. One Hopper was dead and one dying. Another had an arm bloody and dangling uselessly. The only one on his feet identified himself as Jaybo. The one with the bad arm refused to answer any questions beyond admitting that he was called Harp. He said, "I want a lawyer. And if I don't get a doctor, I'll bleed to death."

Andy knew that under these circumstances some Rangers would simply put another bullet into him. He was tempted. "The doctor'll see to Rusty first. He can look at you later if you're still alive."

"You'd let me sit here and die?"

Farley said angrily, "Why not? You'd've let us burn to death."

Jaybo whined, "I didn't want to come here in the first place, but Big'un—"

Harp hissed, "Shut up. Don't tell them a damned thing."

Andy said, "You're lucky you're not facin' a murder charge." He looked around. "Where's Jayce?" His eyes widened. "Anybody seen Jayce?"

His gaze swept the yard. For a moment he thought Jayce might have fallen to the Hoppers' guns.

Farley put the obvious truth into words. "I told you. He's took to the tulies, just like I said he would."

A woman's voice cried, "Jayce!" Flora Landon held her long skirt up clear of the ground as she ran across the yard to the Rangers. "Did Jayce get out?"

Andy said, "He got out, and then he lit out."

It took her a moment to absorb what Andy said. She began laughing and crying at the same time. "He got away?"

Farley said, "Slicker than a greased pig."

Solemnly Andy told her, "You know we'll have to go after him again. He's still got a murder to answer for."

"A justified killin'."

"Murder is never justified."

"A good killin' isn't always murder." Flora looked around to see who might be able to overhear. She lowered her voice. "You know what Big'un tried to do to me in Oscar Truscott's jail?"

"I heard. They said he didn't get it done."

"But he *did* get it done once before. Him and his brother Ned caught me alone at home. I couldn't fight off two of them." She looked at the ground. "I was too ashamed to tell about it, but I was so bruised up that Jayce knew by lookin' at me. That's why he killed Ned. He'd've killed Big'un too, but you Rangers never gave him the chance."

Andy thought about it. "Then it's more than just the feud. Big'un has had an extra reason for wantin' to see Jayce dead."

Flora nodded. "As long as Jayce is alive, Big'un has to be afraid he'll get the same thing Ned got."

Andy mused, "I wonder if Big'un knows Jayce is on the loose again, and it's his own doin'."

Farley pulled his trousers leg up to examine his wound. "We ought to stand back and let Jayce have him. We could arrest Jayce later and charge him for two killin's instead of one."

Andy shook his head. "That wouldn't be accordin' to law."

"Law ain't always justice. There's some things they never wrote in that book."

Andy rarely found himself agreeing with Farley, but in this instance he thought Farley made sense. The Comanches would never fret over piddling technicalities.

The doctor had come and was examining Rusty's wounded shoulder. "How does it feel?"

Rusty sucked in a painful breath. "It hurts, damn it! How do you think it feels?"

The doctor shouted, "Somebody bring a wagon. We've got to get this man over to my house."

The wounded Harp Hopper whimpered, "I'm bleedin' to death."

The doctor said without sympathy, "I'll probably have to take your arm off. Don't be in such a hurry to part with it."

Rusty looked up at Andy. "We have to see if we can find Big'un before Jayce does."

The doctor said, "You're not going to do anything, not for a while. That shoulder looks bad."

Rusty told Andy, "Then it's up to you and Farley."

"Farley's wounded too. Not as bad as you, but he won't be ridin' for a while."

Rusty fretted, "It's too much for you to handle by yourself."

Andy put on an air of confidence to cover his doubts. "I can do it. One thing bothers me, though. I can't charge him with murderin' Sheriff Truscott. The only witnesses were Scooter and his daddy. You've already said no court would take their testimony."

"But you can charge him with attempted murder of peace officers and with malicious destruction of this jailhouse. That should put him away for a few years."

Farley grunted. "Bury him six feet under and he'll never be a bother to anybody again."

Tom Blessing had been busy with the bucket brigade. The jail finally collapsed into a blistering-hot pile of charred wood and glowing coals. Only its two stone chimneys remained, standing like markers in a graveyard. When the courthouse was out of danger Tom walked over to join the Rangers. He checked on Rusty and Farley, then said, "Your prisoner sure made a mess out of my jail."

Rusty tried to smile but could not quite bring it off. "You've been wantin' a new one for a long time."

"I can already hear the taxpayers holler. They'll say the town is peaceful and we don't keep enough prisoners here to justify the cost."

"That'll change. The town's growin'."

Blessing mused, "It's just as well that Jayce got away. I have no jail to put him in now. The best I could do would be to chain him to a tree."

Flora protested, "He's a man, not an animal. He deserves a chance."

Andy said, "He had a chance, and he took it. You have any idea where he went?"

"I expect I do. Wherever Big'un goes, that's where Jayce'll go. If you want Big'un you'd better find him before Jayce does."

"I intend to try." Andy turned away from her. He found Lige standing beside the well, his arm around Scooter's shoulder. Andy said, "You know there's paper out on you."

"It'd be a wonder on earth if there wasn't. You fixin' to put me under arrest?"

Andy was aware that Lige's rifle had helped shorten the fight. "There's just one of me. I've got two wounded Rangers and two other fugitives to worry about. So far as I know the only legitimate charges against you are from Kerrville. Your take from that bank didn't amount to more than petty larceny."

"It sure wasn't what I expected. I never thought I'd be robbed by a bank teller."

"Do you suppose if I turned my back on you for a while you could disappear without causin' any commotion about it?"

"I'd bet you a hundred dollars on it, if I had that much."

"You have anyplace to go?"

"Maybe. Me and my boy talked about it some."

Scooter asked, "You takin' me with you, Pa?"

Lige bent down and hugged his son again. "I've done aplenty of thinkin'. You're a good boy. You've got a good future if you'll stay away from the likes of me. These Rangers can find a place for you where you'll grow up straight and strong and never see a jailhouse from the inside."

"Don't go without me, Pa."

"It's best this way. You may not see me again for a while, but if you ever need me I'll come runnin'. That's a promise."

Scooter cried, "I love you, Pa."

"And I . . . hell, son, you're a man almost. Men don't say things like that." He blinked a few times. "Men don't have to."

CHAPTER
NINETEEN

Walking toward the courthouse, Big'un tipped his hat to Aunt Maudie, mother of his cousin Wilbur. Her lips pinched, and her eyes flashed resentment. He wondered what kind of story her son must have told her. Damn Wilbur anyway, for deserting when he was needed most!

The reception from his aunt shook him a little. He sensed that the one awaiting him from Uncle Judd might be worse. He paused at the open door to the judge's office, summoning courage. He had imagined the scene over and over during the ride home alone. He and his cousins had managed to burn the jailhouse, but so far as he had been able to tell they had not even touched Jayce Landon or the Tennyson kid. He had seen a Ranger go down. He did not know if he was killed. The only casualties he could swear to had been on the Hopper side.

His uncle's attitude was every bit as blistering as Big'un had envisioned. Judd Hopper pushed up behind his desk and scowled like a screeching hawk about to attack. "So you're back. Why aren't you dead?"

Big'un hunched a little, bringing his arms up as if to defend himself. He was not accustomed to having to explain anything. "I done the best I could. Things just didn't work out."

"You ran off and left two cousins dead, another wounded, and one taken prisoner. If that's the best you can do, you're not worth hanging with a secondhand rope."

Big'un puzzled, "How come you already know about it?"

"The telegraph, for one thing. The word's already gone out to Rangers and local sheriffs. They'll be on the lookout for you."

"I didn't think anybody would recognize me."

"It appears they did. And by now the cousins they took prisoner have probably spilled everything they know."

"I'm not sure who they caught. I hope it's not Jaybo. He hasn't got the guts of a jackrabbit."

The judge's eyebrows arched. "Then you shouldn't have taken him along. And the others who deserted you before the fight started, they came dragging into town during the night with their tails between their legs."

"Damned cowards. I ain't real proud of this family right now."

"And most of this family is not proud of you, taking your kin out on a fool's mission. Do you know which one got killed?"

"I seen a couple of them go down. I couldn't tell which they was."

"So you ran off and left them."

"The Rangers came out shootin', and everybody ducked. They even gave Jayce Landon a gun. Can you imagine that, givin' a gun to that killer? And then some of the people from town joined in. Wasn't nothin' left but to get out of there."

"So you abandoned your kin to face it alone."

"They was of damned little use anyway. I could've done better by myself."

The judge bit the tip from a cigar and spat it halfway across the room. He lighted the cigar, his severe gaze never leaving Big'un's face. "There's one more thing I learned from the telegraph. During the excitement, Jayce got away."

Big'un was slow to grasp the significance. "Then maybe I'll get another shot at him."

"More likely he'll get one at you. You tried to burn him to death. My guess is that he's already back here among his kin. And he'll be comin' to get you if you don't get him first."

Big'un shrugged off the warning. "There's more of us Hoppers than there is of the Landons. My kinfolks won't let him come that close."

"Don't depend on your kin. You've lorded it over them for years. Now this last wild sashay . . . Everybody around here is sick and tired of that old feud. You're on your own, Big'un."

The impact began to soak in. Big'un protested, "Mostly I've just done what you told me to. You're the one who wanted me wearin' a badge in the first place."

"That was when you were useful. Lately you've been like an anvil strapped on my back."

"So you've turned against me too?"

"The stink of this will reach all the way to Austin. The Rangers will be down here like a plague of locusts, and there's no telling what they may turn up."

"I could tell them aplenty if I was of a mind to."

"You won't if you've got a brain cell still working. You'll turn tail and travel as far as you can get before the Rangers catch up with you, or Jayce does." A small knot of fear began stirring in Big'un's stomach. It burned like acid. He considered making himself scarce for a while, maybe taking a vacation in Mexico. But travel could be dangerous. The Landons would be keeping a watch on him. Jayce might catch him somewhere out in the open. Big'un was not sure he could beat him in a fair fight.

He argued, "Travelin' takes money. I ain't got any. How about openin' that safe yonder and gettin' me some, say a thousand dollars?"

Judd exploded. "A thousand dollars? You're not worth two bits." He stood up and pointed toward the door. "Get out of my office before I shoot you myself and save Jayce the trouble."

Big'un looked at the steel safe standing in the corner. Many times he had seen his uncle open it, yet he had never had reason to watch closely enough to learn the combination. Now he wished he had been more observant.

Anger churned his stomach as he moved toward the door. "You'll wish you'd done better by me."

"I wish your mother had drowned you like a sick kitten the day you were born."

Big'un was not sure what he would do. He was sure about one thing he would *not* do; he would not leave here dead broke. Uncle Judd owed him, and somehow he was going to pay. But as long as Big'un hung around here in the open, he was in jeopardy. The safest place in town would be the jail. He could bar its door from inside, and nobody would get in unless he allowed it. Unlike Tom Blessing's, this jail was of brick construction, not easy to burn down. Surely the Rangers would catch Jayce within a few days and remove him as a threat.

But what if a jury failed to convict him? Then Jayce could stalk him at leisure. Someday when Big'un did not expect it a bullet could come from nowhere and cut him down.

He had seen juries do the unthinkable, but surely they would not in this case. Murder was murder. They would see that Jayce was hanged. They had to.

Walking down the hall, he encountered several county employees, none of them kin. He saw or imagined condemnation in their eyes. Stung, he crossed the street to a small dining room where he often took his meals. The place was operated by the widow Jones, whose husband had fallen out of a wagon and broken his neck after emptying too many whiskey bottles. She looked at Big'un as if he were a stray dog bringing in fleas. Everybody in town must know what happened, he thought.

He trusted that she liked money more than she disliked him. He said, "I'd like you to deliver me my meals over at the jail for a day or two."

She arched an eyebrow. "You figure bein' in jail will save you from Jayce Landon?"

His temper flared. If a man had said that to him he would have bloodied his knuckles. "You just fetch my meals. I'm not payin' for your opinion."

"This is goin' to cost you extra. And it'll have to be payment on delivery."

He understood her implication, that Jayce might find a way to get to him. She did not want him to die owing her money.

He said, "I'll pay you, but don't send nobody else. I won't be openin' the door to just anybody."

Stung by the unfriendly receptions, Big'un went into the jail. He locked the door with a heavy key, then put an iron bar in place. Some of the fear left him, but not all.

To himself he said, "Damn you, Jayce Landon. This is all your fault."

He sat in a chair and leaned back against the jail's office wall, staring at nothing in particular, trying to come up with an idea. There was no telling how long it might take the Rangers to get Jayce. Being shut up in here for days, even weeks, was too bitter to contemplate. His thoughts kept going back to his uncle's safe. The old man always kept a substantial amount of money locked in it. It should be enough to keep him a long time in Mexico.

Gradually he came up with a plan. It was so simple he was surprised it had taken him so long.

———

Rusty lay in a bed in the doctor's house, his shoulder heavily wrapped. The doctor had drugged him to sleep. Standing over him, Andy thought he had never seen Rusty so pale, so helpless-looking. The doctor said, "He's one tough rooster. Others have tried to kill him, but they never got it done. He'll survive this time too."

"How many more can he take?"

"I hope he never takes any more. Every chance I get, I'm going to tell him to go home and stick to the plow."

Andy felt guilt. "I'm the one who talked him into goin' back to the Rangers after that hailstorm hit him. I wish I'd kept my mouth shut."

Farley sat in a chair across the room. His trousers leg had been cut away, and his wound wrapped almost as heavily as Rusty's. He said, "You never talked Rusty into anything he didn't want to do. He quit followin' advice a long time ago."

And *you* never started, Andy thought.

The doctor said, "Maybe when he's stronger you can take Rusty back to his farm."

"That's where he belongs."

"And maybe you can find a wife for him. He needs one."

"I've got one in mind," Andy said, thinking of Alice Monahan. "But Rusty will have to come around to it on his own." He straightened. "When he wakes up, tell him I'll be back soon as I can."

Farley said, "You're not very good at listenin' to advice either, but let me give you a little. Wire Austin to send you some help before you go pokin' around over in Hopper country."

"Can't lose the time. I expect Big'un has gone back over there, and Jayce is probably not far behind. May even be ahead of him."

"Wait awhile and you won't have to bring back but one. Or if you're really lucky they'll kill each other and you won't have to mess with either of them."

"That wouldn't be Rusty's way."

"It'd save the expense of one trial, maybe two. And it might keep us from havin' to bury an Indian kid who's got more nerve than good sense. Gravestones come high these days." Farley saw that his argument fell on deaf ears. "Wait a couple of days and I'll go with you."

The doctor said, "Forget it, Brackett. You couldn't straddle a horse if they gave you a thousand dollars."

Andy said, "I appreciate you makin' the offer. I'll swing around and let your mother and your sister know what's happened to you."

Farley protested, "They'll just fret over me for no reason. I've had a horse hurt me worse than this, steppin' on my foot."

"They deserve to know."

Andy did not allow Farley time for more argument. He walked out into the cool of the early morning. The smell of smoke was still heavy in the air, stinging his nostrils.

He met Flora Landon walking up the street from the direction of the boardinghouse where she stayed. She said, "I was on my way to see about Rusty and Farley. How do they look this mornin'?"

"They won't be runnin' footraces for a while, but they'll live."

"I want to tell them how much I appreciate what they did. They could've left Jayce to burn. Instead they gave him a gun."

Andy started to tell her Jayce got the pistol for himself, but she was in a grateful mood. He saw nothing to be gained by disillusioning her. He asked, "Is Scooter takin' to the boardin'house all right?"

"He's still hurtin' over his daddy goin' away without him, but otherwise he's all right. Been on his best behavior. If me and Jayce had ever had a boy I'd want him to be like Scooter."

"I appreciate you lookin' after him. When we've put this trouble behind us I'll take him to some folks who will make a good home for him."

"I'd take him in myself except they burned my house down, and my husband is on the dodge. I suppose you'll be goin' after him?"

"I have to, but I'm goin' for Big'un first. I hope I can get to him before Jayce does."

"Why don't you let Jayce take care of the job for you?"

"Then he'd have two murder charges on him."

"They can't hang him but once."

"With the right judge and jury he might not hang at all for one killin'. But two of them . . ." Andy shook his head.

She said, "Be careful, then. Remember that those Hoppers aren't lookin' to make new friends."

"They won't catch me asleep."

"You've got a good reason to take care of yourself. You may not realize it, but that Bethel girl is stuck on you. She'd take it hard if somethin' bad was to happen."

Andy tried to laugh away her concern. "So would I."

———

His courage almost left him as he approached the Brackett farm. For the tenth time since he had left town, he asked himself whether he should ride in or skirt around and proceed to Hopper's Crossing. His sense of duty prevailed. He owed it to Bethel and her mother to tell them what had happened to Farley.

It seemed that he never brought anything but bad news to this place. The women had good cause to dread seeing him. He squared his shoulders and rode straight to the house. A shrieking peacock announced his approach.

Bethel appeared on the front porch, one hand shading her eyes. She anxiously searched Andy's face for a clue and asked, "Is it about Farley again?"

It was unlikely she had already heard. He wished he did not have to be the bearer of the news. "He's been shot."

She swallowed. "How bad?"

"Not as bad as it could've been. He was strong enough to give me a cussin' when I told him I was comin' here."

"He'll be cussin' when he draws his last breath." She made an effort at a smile, but it was stillborn.

Bethel's mother stepped through the door and joined her daughter. "What is it? Farley again?"

Andy tried to ease her mind as quickly as he could. "He'll be all right, Mrs. Brackett." He dismounted and moved closer to the porch.

Bethel said, "He's been shot again, Mama. I swear, he draws trouble like a magnet."

Andy told them, "Wasn't none of it his fault. It happened in the line of duty." He explained about the burning of the jail and its occupants' escape under fire. "Farley took a bullet in his leg. He'll be limpin' around for a while. But Rusty's the one to worry about. He got hit pretty hard."

"Where is Farley now?" Mrs. Brackett asked.

"At the doctor's house. Doc was sayin' he'd probably let him go to a boardin'house by tomorrow or next day."

Mrs. Brackett said, "He doesn't need to go to a boardinghouse. Bethel and I will take a wagon and fetch him home."

"He didn't even want me to come and let you know what happened. Didn't want you frettin'. Said he'd ride over here and tell you himself as soon as he could get on a horse."

Bethel said, "I wouldn't bet two bits on that. As soon as he felt like he could travel, he'd leave without lettin' us know. He's taken a fool notion that nobody cares about him."

Andy doubted that anybody other than immediate family cared much for Farley. Even they found him a trial. He went out of his way to ruffle those who might try to get close to him. He seemed to distrust friendship as if he knew it would not last. During the war it had not. He had lost too many friends, too much family.

Bethel said, "We appreciate you coming out to tell us."

Andy said, "It wasn't much out of my way. I'm goin' to Hopper's Crossing."

"You're after Jayce Landon, I suppose."

"Him and Big'un Hopper both. I figure where I find one I'll likely find the other."

Her eyes widened. "You're goin' by yourself?"

"There ain't but two of them."

Bethel grimaced. "That's about what Farley would say."

"There probably won't be but one if I don't find them myself before they find one another."

"If they shot each other it would stop a lot of misery for both families."

"That's just what Farley said."

"But you're goin' anyway."

"It's my job."

She blinked away a tear. "Someday they'll be haulin' you here like Farley, wounded or worse. Is your job worth that?"

"The only thing I know for sure is that I have to do it. Else I couldn't look Rusty and the rest of them in the face."

"If you get killed, do you think they'll cry over you?"

"I won't know about it one way or the other."

This time she let the tear roll down her cheek, unchecked. "*I'd* cry for you, Andy."

He waited until dark before riding in to Hopper's Crossing. From across the street he surveyed the jail, remembering the night he and Farley had taken it upon themselves to guard it against a mob, needlessly, as it turned out. Through a barred window he saw a faint glow as if a lamp's wick was turned down low. Looking around to see if anyone was watching, he dismounted and walked over for a closer look. He found that cotton cloth had been tacked up on the inside. It was thin enough to allow lamplight to show but heavy enough that Andy could not see through it.

He stood awhile, watching and wondering until someone cautiously lifted a corner of the cloth. Andy saw little more than one eye, but he was almost certain: Big'un was behind that crude curtain.

He did not know what to make of it. It seemed unlikely that Big'un had come back and resumed his sheriff's duties as if nothing had happened. Yet there he was. Andy flirted for a moment with the idea of trying the door, but Big'un would be careful enough to have locked and barred it. He remembered that it was too strong for one man to break it down.

Hearing voices, he stepped into the darkness and flattened himself against the jail wall. Boots trod heavily upon the wooden sidewalk, stopping at the jail door. Someone demanded, "Big'un, open this door."

From inside came a familiar voice. "Who's out there?"

"Your uncle Judd. I want to talk to you."

"You already done more talkin' than I want to listen to. Unless you've brought me some money, that door stays shut."

"The jail is county property. As county judge I'm orderin' you to open up."

"For all I know, Jayce Landon is waitin' out there in the dark. All he needs is for me to open this door and give him a clean shot."

"Have you lost all your guts, boy?"

"Havin' guts is one thing. Bein' stupid is another. You know Jayce won't give me a fightin' chance."

"And I know why. Just about everybody in town knows." The judge cursed softly to the man who was with him. "On account of Big'un, the Hopper name doesn't mean what it used to around here. Before long every dog in town will be hiking its leg at us."

The two men walked away, the judge still grumbling.

If the situation had not been so serious Andy might have laughed at the irony of Big'un Hopper having made himself, in effect, a prisoner in his own jail.

Knowing the effort would probably be futile, he knocked on the door with the butt of his pistol. "Big'un, open up."

Big'un hollered, "I told you, Uncle, I'm done talkin' to you."

"This is Andy Pickard. Texas Ranger. You're under arrest."

Big'un did not answer for a moment. "Arrest? Are you crazy? I'm in here, and you're out there. You ain't comin' in, and I ain't comin' out."

"Give up to me and I'll take you somewhere that Jayce can't get to you."

"I ain't afraid of Jayce."

"Looks to me like you are. Else you wouldn't have locked yourself up in there."

"Go to hell."

"I'm just tryin' to give you a chance."

"I'll make my own chances. Now git!"

Andy had not expected Big'un to surrender, at least not right away, but maybe this would get him to thinking. "If you decide you want my protection, send somebody to find me. I'll be around."

Andy thought that Big'un was not likely to go anywhere for a while, not until he was sick and tired of self-imposed imprisonment. He rode down to the livery stable. The hostler showed surprise. "You all by yourself, Ranger?"

"There isn't anybody else. The other two Rangers got wounded."

"I heard about that. Good news is a long time comin', but bad news spreads in a hurry. Which one are you after, Jayce or Big'un?"

"Both. I know where Big'un is at, for now. Got any idea where Jayce might be?"

The hostler shook his head. "I've got to live with both sides. Wouldn't want anybody accusin' me of bein' a gossip. But if it was me lookin', I'd say go where the Landons are the thickest. Maybe out to Walter Landon's farm."

"Have you seen Jayce yourself?"

The hostler let the question die unanswered. "You want me to put your horse up?"

"That was my first intention, but now I think I'll go to Walter Landon's."

"You'd better either sing out loud or tiptoe like you was walkin' on eggs. Them Landons don't appreciate surprises, and they are uncommon good shots." He paused, staring at Andy with some apprehension. "They ain't the kind that forgives easy. I'd rather you never told them you even talked with me."

"I'm not a gossip either."

There was probably not a bigger gossip in town than the stableman, but in this instance Andy felt that he would keep his mouth shut. He could not mention having seen Andy without being asked what they talked about. Andy had rather his return to Hopper's Crossing not be noised around before he had time to size up his options. He had not seen many so far.

He knew the way to Walter Landon's farm, though he lost it in the moonlight a couple of times where lesser wagon roads split off from the main one. As he began to discern lamplight in the front windows he wondered which of the hostler's recommendations he should choose: to ride in announcing himself or to sneak in and observe quietly.

His first instinct was to see before being seen, but three hound dogs took the decision out of his hands. As they began barking and trotted to meet him, the lamplight winked out. He suspected that one or more rifles or shotguns were aimed in his general direction. He shouted, "Hello, the house."

No one immediately shot at him, so he felt hopeful.

A voice answered, "Who's that out yonder?"

"Andy Pickard, Ranger. You-all remember me."

"Are you by yourself?" The voice sounded familiar, though he could not identify it.

"There's nobody but me." He rode up almost to the front porch, hoping the moon provided enough light that they could see he was alone. He raised his hands.

A match flared, and the lamp burned again. A man stepped out onto the porch. The light was at his back so Andy could not see the face. He thought he knew the man by his shape and his stance.

He said, "Howdy, Jayce."

He heard a chuckle. "Sorry, Andy. Come closer and look again."

Moving up, he recognized Jayce's Ranger brother. "Dick?" He recalled how much the Landon brothers resembled one another. At a distance it would be difficult to tell which was which. "I thought you were still in camp on the San Saba."

"I took a leave of absence to be at my brother's trial. But it seems like you-all can't hold on to Jayce long enough for him to get a shave."

"He had a close shave at the jail. We all did."

"I know. I'm grateful that you-all got him out."

Andy suspected Dick had heard about it from Jayce. "He took care of himself. I've got no credit comin'."

"So now you're here hopin' to take him back."

Andy nodded. "Him and Big'un Hopper both."

"Just you?"

"I'm all there is."

"It might get you killed."

Andy suggested, "You're still a Ranger. You could help me."

"I already turned my brother in once. It's weighed on my conscience ever since. I wouldn't do it again for anybody." Dick jerked his head toward the door. "Tie your horse and come on in. We're all friends here."

For the moment perhaps, but Andy knew that attitudes would change in a hurry if he tried to take Jayce back to jail. He wrapped the reins around a post and went up onto the porch. He asked, "Can you look me square in the eye and tell me Jayce ain't here?"

Dick smiled. "If I tell you where he ain't, you might figure out where he *is*. My duty as a Ranger is on leave till I go back to camp."

Andy stopped abruptly in the open door. Flora stood in the front room with a couple of men, one of them Walter Landon, and a woman he guessed was Walter's wife.

Dick said, "You know Flora, of course."

Getting over his initial surprise, Andy told her, "I'm bettin' Jayce himself brought you here."

She said, "I didn't need Jayce to show me the way. My home is just over the hill, what's left of it." It was the kind of answer that said neither yes nor no.

He said, "I thought you were takin' care of Scooter."

"Tom Blessing's wife took him out to their farm. Big'un wouldn't dare do him harm out there, even if he could find the place."

Dick said to Andy, "I didn't know you-all had the boy. What're you goin' to do with him?"

"When Rusty is ready to travel we intend to take Scooter up north to the Monahan family."

"I couldn't think of a better place for him. I know you and Rusty have shared some hard times with the Monahans, and some good times too."

"I've seen them go down bruised and bloody, but they always got up and went on with their lives."

"That's like us Landons." Dick rolled and lighted a cigarette, his eyes narrowed in thought. "You're takin' on too much of a load to tote by yourself. You'd best forget about catchin' Jayce. I'd be tickled to help you with Big'un, though."

Andy wondered if anyone had told Dick of the outrage Big'un and his brother Ned had forced on Flora. It was not his place to do so. Gunning for Big'un would be legal for Dick so long as he did it within his duty as a

Ranger, but to do it for personal vengeance would outlaw him, as killing Ned Hopper had outlawed Jayce.

Dick asked, "Have you got a plan?"

"Not a trace. I'm hopin' somethin' will break in my direction."

Andy had a strong hunch Jayce was somewhere within shouting distance. He ventured a few probing questions that yielded him nothing. He realized that if he captured Jayce he would have to do it somewhere else. These people protected their own.

Dick said, "It's time to hit the soogans. I've been rollin' my blankets out here on the porch."

Andy took that as an oblique invitation to stay the night. It seemed a good idea if he was right about Jayce being near. Dick accompanied him to a corral, where he unsaddled his horse and turned him loose. He removed a blanket rolled and tied behind the cantle of his saddle. Back at the front porch he lay looking at the stars, crisp and sparkling in the chilled fall air. He caught the faint odor of Dick's cigarette.

He asked, "Why do you reckon it is that so many people can't find a way to live together? If they haven't got somethin' to fight about, they'll make up a reason. I'll bet you've got no notion how the feud started in the first place."

"I've always laid it on the stubbornness of the Hoppers, but I can't truthfully say they're more stubborn than us Landons. If one of us didn't start a fight, the other one would. I remember us young'uns jumpin' on the Hopper boys and fightin' when they hadn't even done anything to us."

"Maybe a Landon and a Hopper ought to marry one another. Things might get peaceful if everybody was kin."

Dick grunted dissent. "Things would just turn meaner. You ever watch a bunch of in-laws get together?"

Andy had never seen much of family life except among the Indians. There, just as in the white community, relationships could be fragile as glass. He said, "I get the idea that Big'un is the main one keepin' the feud stirred up."

"Him and his brother Ned. Ned's gone now, but Big'un is still a bad apple spoilin' the barrel. And behind Big'un is old Judge Hopper. He never gets his knuckles bloody, but he keeps stirrin' the pot. While everybody watches the fightin', he dips his hands into the county treasury."

"I'll bet if the Rangers got to lookin' around they could clean the judge's plow."

"Probably. But I can't put a halo around Jayce's head either. Even if he is my brother, I have to admit that he's done a lot to keep the fight goin'."

Andy thought before he asked, "Do you think Flora saw that side of him before she married?"

"I tried to tell her, but she wasn't ready to listen. After they went to the preacher it wasn't my place to tell her anything anymore. I tried to get Jayce to leave here when I did, to take her away from this part of the country and let the old fight die. But he didn't want to turn aloose. It had got in his blood like whiskey does for some people." He snubbed out his cigarette. "Flora deserves better than that."

Andy had guessed wrong. Big'un did not stay put.

Big'un was wary about going out the jail's front door, which faced the town's main business street. Even the back door could not be considered safe, but at least it was darker on that side of the courthouse square. Staying in the shadows as much as he could, he headed for the wagon yard. He had left his horse there in an open corral. He wished he could get his mount and go without the stableman seeing him, but that was not to be. The skinny hostler watched him saddling his horse and asked, "Where you goin' this time of the night, Big'un?"

"Vacation." Damn a man who asked personal questions, he thought. This nosy dickens's jaw would still be moving a week after they buried him.

"Ain't you afraid you'll run into a booger, travelin' in the dark?"

"The boogers we've got around here, they're even worse in the daylight."

Big'un tied his blankets and war bag on the saddle. As soon as he got his hands on a chunk of his uncle's money he would be gone. He was not sure how he would fit in Mexico, but if he liked it he might be a long time coming back. At least he wouldn't have to keep looking over his shoulder for that back-shooting Jayce Landon. And he would have a border between himself and the Rangers.

He reined his horse toward a quarry where workers cut building stones a few hundred yards from town. He had watched them use dynamite from a wooden shed. He had not learned much about handling dynamite beyond how to set a fuse and touch it off without blowing himself up. He figured that was enough in this case.

He had no idea how much he needed for the job, so he made a guess and tucked a box under his arm. It was about half full. He rode back to town and tied his horse to the fence behind the courthouse on the side opposite his uncle's office. Carrying the dynamite, he tried the back door and found it locked. He watched and listened before he drew his pistol and broke a pane. Reaching inside, he freed the lock. He waited and listened again until he was confident nobody had paid any attention to the sound of breaking glass.

The courthouse was almost pitch dark, but he had been to Uncle Judd's office so many times he could have found it in his sleep. He bumped into a desk on his way in, then felt his way along until he came to the safe. By feel more than by sight, he set the fuse and placed the stick back in the box with the others. He propped the box against the safe door, lighted the fuse, and moved out into the hallway to escape the blast.

The hallway was not far enough. The concussion lifted him off his feet and hurled him down the hall. His ears drummed with pain. Papers and pens and other small objects went flying. Windows shattered, and dust billowed like a dry fog.

Choking, he made his way back into what remained of his uncle's office. He saw a gaping hole in the outer wall. Glass crunching beneath his brogan shoes, he made his way to it and saw the safe lying outside. It was turned over, the door pressed against the ground. It would take several men to turn it.

Big'un did not know words strong enough to express his exasperation, but he tried all the ones he could think of. They didn't help. He could imagine his uncle Judd going into a mouth-foaming fit over this. Well, the money-grubbing old son of a bitch had it coming. It was his own fault.

Discretion told him he had better be moving before a curious crowd swarmed the damaged courthouse. He hurried out the back door and around the building. He feared the blast had frightened the horse into running away, but it was still straining against the tied reins. He patted it on the neck in an effort to calm it. As soon as he could get it to quit faunching around he mounted and set it into a long trot.

The stableman came running out through the barn's wide doors. He shouted, "What happened, Big'un?"

"Lightnin' strike." Big'un spurred his horse into a lope.

He had burned down a jailhouse and blown up a courthouse. Whatever might happen from now on, at least Hopper's Crossing would not soon forget him.

CHAPTER
TWENTY

Andy awakened from a cold half-sleep he had endured most of the night. A bloodred sun was just beginning to rise. His muscles ached from the discomfort of lying on the porch's hard floor. He felt around for his pistol but could not find it.

Dick Landon had already rolled his blanket and placed it against the wall. He said, "Don't you worry about that six-shooter. You'll get it back when we figure it's safe."

"Safe for who?"

"All of us, includin' you."

Andy sensed the reason it had been taken. "What time did Jayce get here?"

"He was here all the time. Him and Flora slept out in the barn. They're in the kitchen now havin' breakfast. You hungry?"

"Think Jayce will trust me?"

"No, but as long as you're not heeled there won't be any trouble."

Andy pulled his boots on. The air had the crisp smell of fall but not yet of frost. If Rusty had not suffered from that hailstorm he would be harvesting his fields, not lying in the doctor's house badly shot up. Andy wondered what Rusty would think of him now, about to share breakfast with a fugitive on the fugitive's terms.

Andy looked at the blazing sunrise. "I've heard them say that a red sky at sunup means there's a storm comin'."

"Only if you get reckless."

Jayce stood in the door, looking calm and friendly. "Come in, Ranger, and let Flora pour you some coffee. Eggs and biscuits are about ready. Walter's family has done et."

Andy followed Dick through the door. He sneaked Dick's pistol out of its holster and stuck it into his boot while all attention was on Flora at the woodstove. She poured coffee into an enameled cup for Andy. He thanked her and turned to Jayce. He said, "I was hopin' you'd be halfway to Mexico by now. I wouldn't have to take you in."

Smiling at Andy's show of confidence, Jayce poured coffee into a saucer and blew across to cool it. "Sorry about your friend Rusty. Hell, I'm even a little sorry about that ornery Farley Brackett."

Andy wrapped his stiff fingers around the cup, enjoying its warmth. "You got away from that jailhouse fire awful quick."

"I saw Big'un light out. Thought I could catch him, but I lost him in the dark. I didn't see any point in stayin' around, so I borrowed some citizen's horse. I wish you'd take it back to him with my thanks."

"You can ride it back yourself when I take you in."

"You don't ever give up, do you?"

Dick Landon spoke. "It's the Indian in him. Did you know he was raised by the Comanches?"

"I ought to've figured."

Flora said, "As soon as I saw that Rusty and Farley were not goin' to die and I put Scooter in good hands, I followed my husband."

Jayce said, "I'd already told her that if I ever had a chance to get away I'd head for home. She'd know where to find me."

Both Jayce and Flora looked sleepy-eyed. Andy remarked, "After so much travelin', you-all appear sort of worn out."

The two smiled at each other. Jayce reached out to touch Flora's hand. "I take it you're not a married man."

Andy said, "Never been asked."

"When the time comes, be sure you get a girl like Flora. But not Flora herself. She's mine."

"You and her could still get away from here. There's not much I could do to stop you so long as your family has got me a prisoner."

"There's one job I ain't finished yet."

"Big'un?"

"He's done a lot of dirt to us Landons." Jayce's face tightened as he looked at his wife. "What kind of man would I be if I just let it go?"

"A live one, and free."

Andy saw something in Flora's eyes. He saw that he had reached her whether he had reached Jayce or not. She told Jayce, "If we stay here you know what'll happen. Big'un will find a way to shoot you in the back if you don't get him first. And if you get him, the law will give you a quick trial and then hang you. Either way, I'll wind up bein' a widow. I want us to go somewhere and start fresh."

"I can't forget what Big'un done to you."

"I can. Revenge isn't worth it. I'd rather have my husband alive and at my side. The law will take care of Big'un, or the devil will."

Jayce argued, "Maybe you've forgot that murder charge against me, but the law hasn't."

Andy said, "That's Texas law. But you could go someplace like Colorado or maybe California. They never heard of Ned Hopper or you either."

He could see that Jayce was struggling. Jayce said, "Before I go anywhere I'd like to have the personal pleasure of sendin' Big'un to hell."

Andy had never quite grasped the concept of an eternal fiery hell for sinful souls. It was not part of the Comanche religion. "There's hell enough right here on earth, Jayce. At the least we can send Big'un to the penitentiary for a long stretch. At the best we might be able to hang him for killin' Sheriff Truscott."

"I got a little inklin' of the real hell before we got out of that burnin' jailhouse. That's the kind I favor sendin' him to."

Andy pushed his plate away with half the bacon and eggs uneaten. "Jayce, they'd drum me out of the Rangers if they heard me say this. What if I was to turn my back for a while, and you and Flora was to slip away real quiet? I'd be so busy huntin' for Big'un that I might not even miss you for three or four days."

Flora said, "He's offerin' us the best chance we'll ever have, Jayce. We can get away from this awful old feud, away from Big'un and all the other Hoppers."

Dick said, "Listen to her, Jayce. Her and Andy are givin' you the best advice you'll ever hear."

Jayce looked across the table at Andy. "If I go, I want everybody to understand that it's for Flora and not because I'm scared of Big'un. I'd gladly meet him face-to-face, but he'd never do that. He'd lay in wait somewhere and bushwhack me."

Andy replied, "That's the way I see it. The longer you stay around here, the less chance you've got of seein' Christmas. If I was you two, I'd saddle up and git while the gittin's good."

Jayce said, "I'm bein' ganged up on. I guess I can't outargue you all."

Flora nodded at Jayce. He pushed back from the table. "Ain't got much to pack." Flora started to follow him out the door but stopped long enough to lean down and kiss Andy on the cheek.

Andy saw a wistful look in Dick's eyes as his gaze followed Flora out the door.

Dick said, "Andy, you've just violated a basic Ranger regulation. You've let a prisoner go."

"I never really took him prisoner." Andy reached down to draw Dick's pistol from his boot. He laid it on the table in front of him. "You can have your six-shooter back."

Dick dropped his hand and felt of his empty holster. "Well, I'll be damned." His eyes narrowed. "Would you really have used this?"

"I don't know. I'm glad I didn't have to find out."

Andy finished his coffee then walked outside, where Dick watched his brother and Flora lead two horses out of the corral. Dick said, "You've got me beat. I never could talk Jayce into anything. All I could ever do was wish him luck and cover his back when I could. I got so tired of it that I had to leave."

Jayce pulled his saddle down from the plank fence. As he picked up his blanket, he dropped suddenly to one knee and grabbed his leg. Andy heard the crack of a rifle. He saw a wisp of smoke in a patch of timber a couple of hundred yards away.

Flora dropped her saddle and screamed, "He's shot."

Andy and Dick ran toward the couple. With a shout of rage Flora yanked a rifle from Jayce's saddle scabbard. She threw it to her shoulder and fired, then fired again.

Dick shouted, "Come on, Andy, let's catch the son of a bitch."

Andy paused for a swift look at Jayce. His trousers leg was bloody. The wound was far from any vital spot.

Dick grabbed Jayce's saddle and threw it on the horse Jayce had been about to ride. Andy quickly caught Flora's horse and put his own saddle on its back. Dick was fifty yards ahead of him as Andy mounted, but he soon caught up.

Big'un exulted for a moment when he saw Jayce go down. Then he felt the breath of the first bullet as it passed by his ear. He turned to grab his horse as the second bullet struck. It was as if a sledgehammer had hit him in the side. He went to his knees, almost losing his hold on the reins. The air was knocked out of his lungs. He gasped desperately for breath. Each try felt as if someone were jabbing a knife into his side.

For a moment he went into a blind panic. My God, they've killed me, he thought. Slowly he began breathing, but with breath came feeling. The wound in his side began to hurt like nothing he had ever felt in his life. He knew he had some broken ribs, probably a punctured lung. He exerted a heavy effort struggling to his feet and drawing himself up against his horse. He made several tries before he was able to lift his left foot into the stirrup, then pull himself into the saddle. He leaned far forward and came near to falling off.

He grabbed the horn of the saddle and beat his heels against the horse's ribs, putting it into a long trot, then a lope. He tried to turn his head and look back, but dizziness overtook him. It threatened to make him lose his seat. He reasoned that some of the Landons must be coming behind him. They would have started their pursuit as soon as they could grab horses.

This was going to be a ride for life.

He wished now he had followed his plan to quit the Colorado River country and immediately head for Mexico. But he had feared that Jayce would follow him no matter where and how far he went. He had to eliminate Jayce before he could feel safe anywhere.

Now he had failed in that as he had failed with the jailhouse fire and with his attempt to blow Judd Hopper's safe open. Seemed like he couldn't do anything right anymore.

He wondered when his luck had started to sour. Maybe it was when he and Ned found Flora Landon at home alone. They had grabbed the opportunity to drag her back to her bedroom. He had always thought her one of the most provocative women he had ever seen. Taking her as he had should have been pleasurable, especially considering that she was the wife of a lifelong antagonist and this represented a victory of sorts. Instead, it had left him strangely unsatisfied. It also left him with bruises and abrasions that lingered long after the fleeting moment of pleasure.

The world went by him in a blur as he rode. With each stride, pain drove through him like a lance. Tasting blood, he rubbed his mouth and saw red smeared across the palm of his hand. He knew coughing up blood was a sign that life was ebbing away. He was bleeding to death.

He felt his hand loosen on the horn despite his effort to tighten his grip. He was conscious of slipping from the saddle. Striking the ground set off an explosion of agony as shattered ribs punched into a lung. He tasted dirt and tried to spit it out. He lacked strength to raise his head. Face against the ground, he managed a few more breaths until the dirt he inhaled choked him.

His last conscious thought was, "Damn you, Flora, this is all your fault. And you wasn't worth it."

During the chase, Andy and Dick had never come close enough to catch more than a glimpse of Big'un. They had to follow tracks, which slowed them. Andy said, "We don't even know for sure that it *is* Big'un."

Dick said, "Who else would've shot at Jayce? He could be anyplace out yonder, settin' up an ambush for us."

"I don't think he's a good shot. He just nicked Jayce in the leg."

Andy was first to see the saddled bay horse grazing peacefully where the grass still contained some green. Dick said, "That's Big'un's, all right. I've seen him ridin' it around the country."

At first Andy thought Dick might be right about Big'un setting up an ambush. Then he saw the still form of a man stretched in the grass. Wind rolled Big'un's hat along the ground and picked at the loose tail of his shirt. "That'd be him, I suppose."

Dick said, "Flora must've hit him." She was the only one who had fired in Big'un's direction.

Andy drew his pistol in case Big'un might be playing possum. Riding up close, however, he could tell that Big'un was dead. He dismounted and turned Big'un over onto his back. Much of the man's clothing was soaked in blood.

He said, "That's the way the hide hunters like to hit a buffalo, in the lung. Looks to me like he bled to death."

Dick got down for a look. "The slower the better. I hope he had time to consider all his sins."

Andy closed Big'un's half-open eyes. "He's been worried that Jayce was out to kill him. I wonder if he had any idea it was Flora who brought him down."

"Seems like justice to me, seein' what he did to her."

"All the same, this could cause her some trouble if she stays around here in Hopper country."

Dick shrugged. "Nothin' we can do about that. We've got to go to town and report what happened."

Andy considered. "Maybe not. What if Big'un just disappeared and nobody ever knew what happened to him?"

Dick appeared intrigued.

Andy said, "We could tell them we lost his tracks. It should all seem natural enough. Big'un took his shot at Jayce and saw that it didn't kill him, so he quit the country. Lots of people drift away and are never heard from again. Everybody would figure after a while that he found him a safe place and decided to settle there for good."

"But what about his body?"

"All we need is a shovel."

Dick gave him a quizzical look. "That's crafty. Some of your Comanche raisin'?"

"I'm just thinkin' it would take care of several problems. If Jayce knew Big'un is dead he might decide not to leave. Then I'd have to arrest him and take him to trial. You know how that would likely come out, especially in this county."

Dick said, "I know a farmer who lives over the hill. He's not much for talkin', and he'd lend us a shovel without askin' questions. What about Big'un's horse?"

"We'll unsaddle him and turn him loose to find his way home. Folks'll figure Big'un caught a fresh horse and left for a better climate. With him and Jayce both gone, maybe the feud will die away."

They wrapped Big'un in his saddle blanket and buried him with his saddle and bridle. Andy watched the bay horse roll in the dirt then wander off, oblivious to the drama that had played out around him. Andy took a tree branch and smoothed the ground, hoping to hide the fact that it contained a grave. "It don't seem right without somebody sayin' some words over him."

Dick shook his head. "Wouldn't make any difference. He was beyond prayer a long time ago."

Scooter held the wagon team's reins, for his leg still pained him when he tried to sit on a horse. Rusty, his shoulder still bound, sat beside him on the wagon seat, restless eyes searching over the terrain. Andy rode horseback beside them, watching nervousness build in both Rusty and Scooter. The extra horses were tied on behind the wagon.

Rusty said, "The more I think about this, the more I get to wonderin' if it's right to burden the Monahans with me. I could heal all right in the Ranger camp."

Scooter asked, "What if they don't like me? And I don't know if I'll like them either." He still grieved over parting with his father.

Andy replied, "The Monahans wrote and told you-all to come, that they'd be glad to have you both. Anyway, Rusty, you've already been took off of the pay roster. Captain said anybody who's been shot up that much ought to retire before he gets himself killed. You've gotten to be a bad risk."

The captain had come near to taking Andy off of the roster too. "Look at your record," he had said. "You went off to transport a prisoner but lost him."

"It was the sheriff that lost him," Andy countered.

"Even so, he got caught a second time and you lost him again. Then there was the old bank robber, the boy's daddy. You had a chance to grab him but didn't. And that jailhouse arsonist—you ought to've caught him but let him slip through your fingers. Lord knows where any of them are now. That is not a good record for a Ranger, even a green recruit."

Andy had said, "I'll bet I can learn better, sir."

"From what I've been told you showed initiative on several occasions. That is a point in your favor even if the results were not as we might have wanted. I'll give you another chance, but you are on probation, Private Pickard."

Andy had thanked him for his generosity and then accepted leave to take Rusty and the boy to the Monahan family. Andy knew he had not followed the letter of the law, but he felt that he had served justice. That was the more important consideration.

A wheel dropped into a shallow hole and jolted the wagon. Scooter said, "Sorry, Rusty. I didn't see that one. I'll never make a teamster."

"You can make yourself into anything you want to be. You've just got to work hard at it."

"I'd like to be a Ranger someday, like you and Andy."

"You can do it if you want it bad enough. But by the time you get there things are liable to be considerable different. In my early days we mostly fought Indians. That's about come to an end. Now we're fightin' robbers and stock thieves, murderers, border jumpers, and the like. But we've got more to fight them with, like the telegraph. And they're startin' to build railroads across Texas. In a few years a Ranger will be able to put a horse on a train and take him halfway across the state in a day, then jump off ready for a chase. Show me the criminal who can beat that."

Andy said, "The way you talk, I think you'd still like to be a part of it."

Rusty shook his head. His hair that used to be red was rusty now, gray softening the color. "No, these last weeks convinced me it's time to hang up the six-shooter and take hold of a plow handle. This body has taken too many beatin's."

"The state will lose a good Ranger."

"But it'll gain a pretty good farmer."

A boy of about Scooter's size loped toward them on a paint horse, waving a misshapen felt hat over his head. He shouted, "Andy! Rusty!"

Andy pushed out a little in front to meet him. "Howdy, Billy. Still growin' too fast for your clothes, I see."

The boy rode up on Rusty's side of the wagon. "You been shot again? How many times does this make?"

"Too many," Rusty said, grinning. "How's all your folks?"

"Ready and anxious to see you."

Billy gave Scooter a critical scrutiny. "You the boy that's comin' to live with us?"

Scooter was ill at ease. "That's what everybody's tellin' me."

Billy considered for a bit. "I guess that'll be all right."

The Monahan homestead came into view. Billy said, "I'll lope on ahead and tell them to put supper in the stove."

Rusty leaned forward as if he could see the place better from the edge of his seat. "You'll like these folks when you get to know them, Scooter. They're the nearest thing to a family that I've got. I've seen happy days with them, and I've seen bitter tears."

"So I've heard," Scooter said.

Andy had told Scooter most of what he knew about the Monahans, about the tragedies they had suffered during the war because they had held to their Union sympathies, about their struggle to rebuild after the hostilities, about the loss of the patriarchs and the death of Josie Monahan, who was to have been Rusty's wife.

Rusty said, "The Monahans have been through more hell than most people ever ought to suffer. But they've always gotten up, squared their shoulders, and started again." His face went grim. "That's what we all have to do when trouble knocks us down. Else life will grind us into the ground."

"Like it did you when Josie was killed?"

Rusty looked at him sharply, then at Andy. "He told you about that, did he?"

Andy looked away, his face reddening. He had not considered that the guileless boy would say whatever popped into his mind.

Scooter said, "He told me Josie has a sister who's a lot like her."

Rusty's expression slowly mellowed. "Maybe a little bit."

The whole Monahan clan was waiting as the wagon pulled up to the house. Mother Clemmie, limping a little from lingering aftereffects of a stroke, led the greetings. She hugged Andy, then Rusty, taking care for the bandaged shoulder. She turned then to Scooter. "This is the boy you wrote about? I'm goin' to have to fatten him up some. Like he is, he won't hardly throw a shadow."

Andy shook hands with everybody who came up to greet him, then realized he had missed someone. Alice.

She and Rusty stood on the other side of the wagon. They had shaken hands, then neglected to turn loose.

Preacher Webb gave the blessing before supper, expressing special thanks for Rusty's survival and wishing a better future for the new boy who was to share the family's bed and board. Through supper Scooter and Billy kept eyeing each other nervously.

Afterward Webb sat down to read his Bible, though Andy was sure he already knew it by heart. Billy asked Scooter to go with him out to the barn. "We've got some new puppies. Maybe you can help me name them."

"I've never had a puppy," Scooter said.

"You can have one of these for your own if it likes you."

Andy stood at the window, watching the two boys start walking toward the barn, then break into a run. He turned back to help Clemmie and her married daughter Geneva clear the table. He said, "I'd best go look for Rusty."

Clemmie caught his arm. "I wouldn't disturb him right now, was I you."

Andy saw Rusty sitting on the front porch, talking to Alice. Clemmie smiled. So did Geneva. Clemmie asked, "How would you like some more of that cobbler pie, Andy?"

He said, "Sounds real good to me."

AFTERWORD

L ife in Texas was changing rapidly in the post–Civil War decade of
the 1870s, the setting of this story. The long and much-resented
federal occupation had ended. The disenfranchised former Confederates regained their vote, allowing them to elect state and local
governments of their own choosing. They adopted a new constitution guaranteeing their individual rights.

The Texas Rangers organization had disintegrated during the war years
and was abolished by the federally established postwar government. One of
the first acts of newly elected governor Richard Coke in 1874 was to reorganize this force, which had first been called into service by colonizer
Stephen F. Austin in 1823. Though a special frontier battalion stood watch
at the outer edges of settlement, guarding against Indian incursion, a majority of the state's Rangers now concentrated on suppression of crime and
violence.

A vigorous army campaign in the fall of 1874 drove most Comanches,
Kiowas, and other hostile Plains tribes to reservations. Buffalo hunters were
systematically annihilating the vast shaggy herds, forcing the Indians into
dependency on the government and opening the Plains for permanent
white settlement. Apart from relatively small outbreaks, Indian trouble was
over for most of the state. The Apaches continued to roam a few more years

in far West Texas, but settlement there was sparse and remained so until most of the more productive Texas land was taken.

Law enforcement was the Rangers' main concern now, and the challenge was formidable. The war had left Texas threadbare. Veterans returned to find their families in deplorable straits, often losing land and home to opportunists who flocked in to reap where they had not sown. The excesses of corrupt officials had bred a widespread contempt for law and an acceptance of violence as a means to accomplish what might otherwise not be possible.

From its beginnings, Texas had been subject to savage feuds. In one case Sam Houston felt obliged to call out the army to quell a particularly bitter fight. Other feuds flared in the combative postwar climate and required response by the Rangers to cool them down.

The border with Mexico had bred racial conflict almost constantly since the Texas revolution and would continue to do so well into the twentieth century. Border jumpers were a major problem for the Rangers in the 1870s. Captain Leander McNelly once stacked the bodies of a dozen bandits in Brownsville's town square as an object lesson. However, the Rangers had never forgotten the Alamo and were prone at times to administer punishment to Mexicans simply for being Mexicans without regard to guilt or innocence.

Cattle drives to the northern railroads were bringing fresh money into an impoverished state. They increased the value of range cattle and encouraged rustling, sometimes on a massive scale. Rustling required physical labor, however. Robbing banks was easier.

The banking industry grew in response to Texas's gradual economic recovery. Banks became a prime target for robbery by organized gangs as well as ambitious individual entrepreneurs who might rationalize that they were simply carrying on the Civil War against Northern interests.

The Rangers embraced new technology to help them meet these challenges. The spread of the telegraph meant that word of a crime could be flashed instantly across the state. Texas railroads, though few and of a limited regional nature, were beginning to plan expansions that would revolutionize travel by the early part of the next decade. That would allow Rangers and other law officers rapid transportation no outlaw's horse could outrun.

A few people were already experimenting with Alexander Graham Bell's new invention. Shortly telephone lines would be spreading across

Texas like spiderwebs. A Ranger in Fort Worth would soon be able to talk to one in El Paso and others in between. Such notable outlaws as Sam Bass and John Wesley Hardin, who earlier had been able to hit, then run for the brush, would soon find themselves hemmed in by wires and rails. They could still run, but it would be increasingly difficult to hide.

JERICHO'S
Road

For Jerry Hunt,
Art and Margie Hendrix,
avid collectors

CHAPTER ONE

After several years as a Texas Ranger, Andy Pickard concluded that the average criminal he dealt with was about as intelligent as a jackrabbit. That said, even a dullard could pull a trigger and hurt somebody. A case in point was the reluctant prisoner trudging along ten paces ahead of Andy, dragging his feet and wailing about the insensitivity of law enforcement.

"It ain't fair," the handcuffed man whined. "You're a young man, barely growed, but you're ridin' my horse and makin' me walk."

Andy said, "You shot mine."

"I didn't mean to."

"I know. You were shootin' at *me*."

The prisoner stumbled over his own feet and almost fell. "How much further we got to go?"

"A ways yet. It'll give you time to consider changin' your occupation."

Deuce Scoggins had earned a reputation as a second-rate horse thief who could not tell a mare from a gelding and knew no better than to peddle them in the first town he came to after he stole them. His trail had led Andy across several counties along the Colorado River, but a string of angry victims had made the path easy to follow. Confronted, Deuce had fired one shot in panic, killing Andy's horse, then had thrown up his hands and begged for mercy. Andy had made him strip the saddle, bridle, and blanket from the dead animal and transfer them to his own.

"Where'd you get this horse?" Andy asked him.

"Won him in a poker game."

Andy doubted that. Deuce was not smart enough to win a poker game. He had stolen this horse like he had stolen just about everything else he had. Deuce's sweat-streaked shirt was much too large, loosely draped over thin shoulders, the grime-edged cuffs almost covering his dirty hands. He had probably lifted it from somebody's clothesline.

Andy asked, "Did you ever think about gettin' a job and makin' an honest livin'?"

"Work? I tried once. Ain't much I can do good enough that anybody'll pay me for it."

"You're not very good at this, either."

Andy wondered if he was being fair, comparing Deuce's intelligence with that of a jackrabbit. He might not be giving the rabbit enough credit.

Deuce grumbled, "Even an Indian would treat a man better than this."

"You don't know Indians." Andy did. Through several of his boyhood years he had lived among the Comanches. "Be glad you *don't* know them. They'd make it a mighty short acquaintance."

The afternoon was almost done when they rounded a bend in the wagon road and saw the crossroads town ahead. Its largest buildings were a courthouse, a new jail, and a church.

Deuce brightened, seeing that his long walk was almost over. He said, "I heard their old jailhouse got burned down. It wasn't no nice place. I was in it once."

"Too bad you didn't go in the church instead."

"Can't you take these handcuffs off before we hit town? It's embarrassin' to let people see me this way."

"A little embarrassment might be good for you. There was a time when they would've necked you to a tree limb. As it is, they'll likely just send you to the penitentiary."

"I already been there. It ought to be against the law to put a man in a hellhole like that."

Sheriff Tom Blessing stood in the doorway of the redbrick jail. Recognizing Andy, he grinned broadly and raised his big right hand in greeting. He looked more like a farmer than a lawman, for indeed he was a farmer first. Despite his years he still had the muscled body of a blacksmith. "Bringin' me a guest, Andy?"

Andy grinned back at him. "I hated for your new jailhouse to stand empty. The taxpayers have put a big investment in it."

Andy dreaded the handshake because Tom could bend a horseshoe double, and he could break the bones in a man's hand. He had been sheriff here so long that many people in town could not remember anyone else serving in that office. He showed no sign that he was ready to yield any ground to his age. He said, "Come on in here, Deuce. I've got a nice cell with your name on it, all swept out and waitin' for you."

Deuce sounded like a lost soul crying in the wilderness. "I'm hungry and I'm thirsty, and this Ranger has wore my feet down plumb to the bone."

Tom offered no comfort. "Write a letter to the governor." He led Deuce past barred iron doors and pointed him to a cell. When Deuce was inside, Tom slammed the door hard. That reverberating impact always reminded Andy of a gallows trapdoor dropping. There was something coldly final about it.

Tom told Deuce, "I'll bring you a bucket of water directly. There's a slop jar under the cot. Make yourself at home." He winked at Andy.

Deuce was wanted in several counties, but Andy had brought him here because this was the nearest jail, and the sun was almost down. He did not care to risk camping with the prisoner on the trail. Here he could get a good night's sleep without worrying that Deuce might try to escape. Tom would keep the horse thief in custody until the several counties that wanted him sorted out their priorities.

Tom asked, "Did he give you any trouble?"

"Not after he shot my horse. He went to blubberin'. Thought I was fixin' to kill him. I let him keep on thinkin' so till I got the cuffs on him."

"Some Rangers *would've* shot him for killin' their horse. Whose is that you're ridin'?"

"No tellin'. Somebody's probably lookin' for him."

"I'll check my notices." Tom fingered through a stack of papers on his desk. "I got a message for you somewhere. Yeah, here it is." He handed a paper to Andy. "Your captain sent a wire to all the sheriffs around here, not knowin' just where you'd turn up. Wants you to report in to him."

Andy felt uneasy, wondering what the captain might want. Maybe the state's finances had turned tight again and the Ranger force was being trimmed. It had happened often before. His several years of service were no guarantee that he would escape the next cut.

He asked, "Reckon the telegraph office is still open?"

"I expect so. The operator's not anxious to go home of an evenin'. His wife's been burnin' the beans lately on account of him bein' a sorry poker player."

Andy mentally composed a brief message on his way down the street. In the telegraph office he wrote it out on paper, reporting the capture of Scoggins. He read it over and penciled out every word it could spare. The state disliked paying for long messages, so Ranger reports tended to be spare on detail. He remembered one Farley Brackett had sent: *Five fugitives met, three arrested, two buried.*

He told the telegraph operator, "If I get a reply, I'll be stayin' the night at the jail."

"I'll fetch it over soon as it comes."

Andy stayed to watch him tap out the message. He still marveled at the progress he had seen in just the few years he had been a member of the Rangers. It seemed unreal that he could write a few lines here and know they would be received miles away in an instant. The telegraph had done much to tighten up law enforcement across Texas. Word of a fugitive could race past him and alert officers to intercept him down the road.

Andy could not imagine how it might ever get much better than that.

Back at the jail he found Tom standing in front of the woodstove. The sheriff said, "I'm heatin' some leftover beans and corn bread for the prisoner, but I expect you'll want somethin' better. I'll go with you down to the eatin' joint soon as I get Deuce taken care of."

Tom had a farm a few miles out of town, but he often spent the night in the jail rather than make the ride twice, once out and then back in the morning.

Andy said, "If it wasn't already so late I'd ride out and pay a visit to Rusty Shannon. Maybe I'll do it tomorrow."

Tom smiled at the mention of the red-haired former Ranger. "I used to worry a right smart about Rusty. He pined away for a long time after Josie Monahan died. He's fared some better since he made up his mind to marry her sister Alice. She's been like a tonic to him."

"He deserves a run of good luck for a change. He had enough bad to do for a lifetime." Rusty had been like a brother to the orphaned Andy, teaching, counseling, providing a benchmark when Andy seemed about to lose his way. "If it wasn't for Rusty I don't know where I'd be now. In jail, like as not. Or dead."

Tom had a benevolent smile his prisoners seldom saw. "You never were that bad of a kid. All you needed was guidance."

Andy had been taken by Comanche raiders when he was a small boy. They raised him until he fell back into Texan hands at about the time his voice started to change. His reintroduction to the white man's world had exposed him to many pitfalls. Even now, in his midtwenties, he sometimes found himself facing situations where the choice was difficult to make. He had always leaned heavily on Rusty's advice. When Rusty was not around, he tried to visualize what Rusty would do.

He said, "Too bad Deuce Scoggins didn't have somebody like Rusty to point the way for him when he was young."

Tom shrugged. "Might not've made any difference. There's some people that nobody can help. They've got no skill and no trade. They're too shiftless for honest work, and every time they come to a fork in the road they turn the wrong direction. I've seen a lot like Deuce, driftin' to God knows where. I've got to watch myself so I don't get to thinkin' the whole world is that way." Tom's eyes narrowed. "You've been a Ranger for a good while now. You ever find yourself gettin' cynical?"

Andy had to think a minute before he remembered what *cynical* meant. "I still find there's more good folks than bad ones. If I try, I can even feel a little sorry for Deuce."

"Don't tell him so. It might encourage him to get worse."

The telegraph operator found Andy sitting with Tom at a table in the restaurant, hungrily emptying a bowl of thick beef stew. He waved a sheet of paper. "Got a reply to your message. Thought you'd want to see it right away."

Andy read it slowly, his finger tracing the lines. Rusty had been more successful in teaching him about farming and being a Ranger than about reading and writing.

"Any answer?" the operator asked.

"Just say, 'Will comply.'"

That ought to be short enough to satisfy the money counters, he thought.

The operator picked up a biscuit from the table and took a big bite of it as he went out the door. Tom asked, "New orders?"

Andy nodded. "Captain says our company is bein' cut again. Says headquarters in Austin wants to reassign me to the Mexican border."

Tom frowned. "If you've ever thought about resignin', this might be the time. A man can get killed down there."

"A man can get killed anywhere. Deuce might've shot me if he hadn't hit my horse instead."

"But it's like a holy war along the Rio Grande. Been that way since the battle of the Alamo and doesn't show any sign it's fixin' to change. You're automatically somebody's enemy on sight. It just depends on how light or dark your face is."

"Sounds like the Indian wars."

"The Indian wars are over with. This one's not. Do you speak any Mexican?"

Andy swallowed a mouthful of stew. "Just a few cusswords I've picked up."

"You'll have every chance to use them, and probably pick up a bunch more."

The captain had not given Andy a deadline for showing up in Austin. Because the horse he had taken from Deuce was undoubtedly stolen, he left it in Tom's custody and bought one at the livery barn. Rangers were obliged to furnish their own horses, but the state was supposed to pay for one killed in the line of duty. Andy trusted that he would be reimbursed. If not, he would still eat, though it might be a while before he could afford a new hat or a pair of boots.

Tom approved of the black horse. He rubbed his big hand down the back and the shoulder and finally patted the animal's neck. "Got long, strong legs. He'll serve you well in a chase."

"I hope I'm the one that does the chasin'."

"If not, you'll sure be glad for those good legs."

When Andy prepared to leave town the next morning, Tom said, "Sorry I couldn't provide you a featherbed."

The jail cot had been hard as a cement floor.

Andy smiled. "At least the price was right."

Tom said, "I'll ride with you as far as Shanty's farm. Then I'll be cuttin' off and goin' home."

"I'm glad for the company."

"If they send you by San Antonio, be sure to go and visit the Alamo. It'll help you understand the trouble you'll run into when you get to the Rio Grande."

Riding down the street, Andy saw two women pull a buggy up near a general store.

Tom said, "That's Bethel Brackett and her mother."

"I know." Andy hesitated, wondering if he should ride over and greet them. He realized they had seen him, so he had no choice. "Give me a minute, Tom."

Tom smiled. "Take all the time you want. If it was me and I was thirty years younger, I'd take the whole mornin'."

Dismounting, Andy extended his hands to help the older woman down. She said, "We had no idea you were in town, Andy."

"Passin' through on duty. You're lookin' fine, Mrs. Brackett."

He turned toward the younger woman, who had been driving the horses. Bethel seemed reluctant at first to accept his help. "Andy Pickard, I ought not to speak to you."

"What did I do?"

"It's what you don't do. You don't ever come to see a girl. You could be dead and I wouldn't know about it for six months."

He thought her pretty, even if at this moment she was being petulant. He said, "If I ever die, I'll write you a letter and let you know."

"You could've let me know you were here."

"Didn't get in till late yesterday. Can't stay. I've got orders to report to Austin."

She frowned. "Even my brother Farley breaks down and sends us a few lines every six months or so. I'd write to *you* if I knew where you'd be."

"Half the time I don't know that myself." Andy could not tell whether she was angry or just a bit hurt.

She turned at the door. "If you run into my brother somewhere, tell him Mother and I are all right." She went inside, leaving him embarrassed and not knowing what to do about it.

Tom had watched quietly. He drew in beside Andy and said, "That little girl thinks a lot of you."

"Hard to tell it, the way she acts."

"A woman likes to have some attention paid to her, and you ain't done it. She'd follow you in a minute if you was to just ask her."

"Follow me to what? A tent camp in the brush with a Ranger company? She was raised better than that."

"You won't be a Ranger forever. Sooner or later you'll get a bellyful of cold camps and short rations. You'll start lookin' for a place to light."

"I don't know as I could ever be a farmer like Rusty. Followin' a mule down a corn row is too slow a life for me."

"Lots of Rangers go in for sheriffin' when they get tired of the service.

They can uphold the law and still sleep in a decent bed most nights. If you was to decide to give it a try I'd hire you as a deputy."

"Much obliged, Tom, but so far I'm satisfied with what I'm doin'."

A former slave, Shanty York had inherited a small farm when his owner died. At first he had trouble keeping it because some neighbors objected to a black man's being a landowner. Several of them burned his cabin one night. Rusty and Tom and other friends rebuilt it and none too gently elevated Shanty's antagonists to a higher level of tolerance.

The old man looked frail. Nevertheless, he was working in his garden when Andy and Tom rode up. He seemed always to be busy so long as there was daylight to work by. Shanty took off an unraveling old straw hat and wiped a tattered sleeve across a black face shining with sweat. His broad smile displayed a solid row of white teeth. So far as Andy knew, he still had all the ones God had given him. "Mr. Tom! Andy! You-all git down and grab ahold of this hoe awhile."

He reached out his hand, and each man took it. For most people Shanty would precede their names with *Mr.*, as he did with Tom. But he had known Andy since the day Rusty had brought him home, a hurt and frightened boy who spoke only Comanche. Shanty had helped care for Andy's broken leg and patiently coached him word by word into remembering his forgotten English.

Tom exchanged a few pleasantries, then rode on toward his own farm. Shanty said, "You'll stay and eat with me, won't you, Andy?"

Andy said, "I wish I could, but I've got orders. Just want to drop by and see Rusty before I go."

Shanty kept smiling. "You don't need to worry none about Mr. Rusty. He's doin' fine, him and Miz Alice. I don't know as they've told anybody yet, but she's in a family way."

Andy chuckled. "The old rusty-haired son of a gun. I didn't know he still had it in him."

"It's in Miz Alice now. She glows like the sunrise."

It was useless to ask Shanty how *he* was doing. If he were on his deathbed he would declare that he was fine. His face gave little clue to his real age, but his short gray hair and the droop of his shoulders showed that he was getting old. Andy asked, "Anything I can send you from Mexico?"

"Any necessaries, I can get right here to home. Can't think of nothin' I'd want from way off yonder."

"The Rio Grande is pretty far, all right."

"Too far for these weary old bones. You be careful you don't come back speakin' Mexican. Took us long enough to get you over speakin' Comanche."

Andy reached into his saddlebag and lifted out a small sack. "Brought you some rock candy to sweeten your disposition." He knew the old man loved candy, but Shanty rarely splurged on such luxuries.

Shanty's eyes teared a little as he struggled for words. "I thank you mighty kindly."

Andy stalled, not wanting to leave. Every time he rode away he wondered if this might be the last time he saw the old man. He asked, "Would you like me to milk your cow for you before I go?"

"She's dried up for a little while. She's in a family way too." Shanty stared at him, his eyes serious. "You be careful, boy. They tell me there's lots of wicked goin's-on down along that river."

"There's wicked goin's-on everywhere." Andy reconsidered what he had said and wondered if his experience with lawbreakers *was* making him a little cynical. Tom Blessing had warned him about that.

He turned once in the saddle to wave at Shanty, then reined the black horse in the direction of Rusty Shannon's farm. The familiar terrain brought back memories, most of them pleasant, a few he did not want to dwell upon. Not far from here he had been part of an unlucky Comanche raiding party, come down from the high plains to steal horses. In a skirmish with Rangers and settlers his horse had fallen on him. Rusty had recognized that he was white and took him to his farm to heal. At first Andy had given him reason to regret his generosity, trying to escape back to his Comanche friends. He had eventually realized that the Indians had reached the end of their time as free-roaming horsemen of the plains. He had gradually accepted his place in the white world, though sometimes he still found himself thinking like a Comanche, feeling like a Comanche. He leaned heavily upon instincts that were sometimes so strong they puzzled him.

Like now, for instance. He sensed a horseman's approach before he saw him. As he crossed over a rise in the wagon road he saw a man on horseback, moving diagonally toward him. He recognized one of Tom Blessing's brothers. They stopped and visited a few minutes, but Andy did not mention what his instinct had told him. Most people did not know how to accept it.

Riding by Rusty's field, he saw that the corn was tall and green, promising a good yield. He remembered a time he had found the crops beaten into the ground by a hail so devastating that Rusty had reenlisted in the Rangers awhile to make up for the financial loss.

Alice stood in the cabin's open dog run, slicing a ham suspended from a rafter. She did not see him right away. She was a slender woman with light brown hair almost to her waist. He had always considered her handsome, though her sister Josie might have been prettier. Josie's death had dealt Rusty a blow that for a time threatened to break his spirit. Eventually he had worked his way up from the darkness and had come to accept Alice.

Andy had been pleased, though he had one reservation: he feared Rusty might regard her as second best, a substitute; that Josie still held first place in his heart. Alice deserved better than that.

She gave Andy a sisterly hug, then pushed him off at arm's length to look him over. "Don't the Rangers ever feed you? You look like you haven't eaten in a month."

He grinned. "I eat Indian style. When I can get it, I eat all I can hold. When I can't get it, I live off of what I ate before."

"I'll slice some more ham and see how much you can eat for supper. I've managed to put some weight on Rusty. If you'll stay around a week or so I'll fatten you up too."

"Can't. I've been ordered to Austin."

She appeared disappointed. "A few days of company would be good for Rusty. He hasn't been away from the farm much since plantin' time."

"I guess he figures he did enough travelin' when he was a Ranger. A man can get awfully tired of it."

"Don't you get tired of it, Andy?"

"Now and then. But soon as I rest up a little I'm ready to go again."

"There'll come a day when you'll decide it's been enough, like Rusty did. You'll want to settle down." Her eyebrows lifted. "Are you goin' to see Bethel Brackett before you leave?"

Andy looked down. "Already saw her, in town." He abruptly changed the subject. "Where's Rusty at?"

Her eyes told him she still wanted to talk about Bethel, but she said, "He went lookin' for a heifer. He thinks she's had her calf, and she's hidin' it out."

"Summer calves can be hard to raise."

"A farmer is ready to take a rain or a calf any time."

She went into the kitchen side of the cabin. "I'll start supper when I see Rusty come to the barn. How about some coffee while you wait?"

"I can get it myself."

Rusty had done his bachelor cooking at the fireplace, but Andy noted that a new iron stove had been installed. A shop-made table and sturdy wooden chairs replaced the crude homemade kitchen furniture that he remembered.

Coming up in the world, he thought.

He watched Alice, trying to discern sign of her pregnancy. All he saw was a brightness he had not found in her eyes before. He said, "Shanty tells me there'll be three of you by-and-by."

She looked startled. "How could he know? We haven't told anybody."

"Guess he saw it for himself. He said you glow like the sunrise." He studied her face. "I believe he was right."

"I have reason enough. I'm happy here. I couldn't ask for things to be any better."

Andy looked at the mantel. Always before, he had seen a picture of Josie there. It was gone now.

Alice turned to see where his gaze was directed. She said, "Lookin' for Josie's picture? Rusty took it down. He said he didn't need a picture to remember, or to keep pushin' the past into his face. Said yesterday's gone. Today is all we've got."

"You think he really sees it that way?"

He saw a flicker of doubt in her eyes. "Sometimes when he holds me I can't help feelin' that he's thinkin' of Josie." She blinked and turned away. "I've tried real hard to be a good wife to him. Lord knows he deserves it. I wouldn't ask him to forget Josie, ever. But maybe with time I can be as much a part of him as she ever was. Even more."

"Maybe you already are."

"No, not yet, but I will be. I'm a Monahan, and you've never seen a Monahan give up."

Andy heard a milk cow bawling. He walked to the door and saw that Rusty had ridden up to the log barn. He said, "I'll see if he needs any help."

"Tell him supper will be ready by the time he gets through with the milkin'."

Rusty pumped Andy's hand as if they had not seen each other in years. It had been only a few months since Andy had ridden by here on his way to an assignment. They exchanged small talk about crops and rain and local politics. Andy squinted. "I see a little more gray in your hair."

"You've got the sun in your eyes."

"Alice looks fine."

"She does, doesn't she?"

Andy pointed toward the milk cow. "You'll be needin' all the milk Old Boss can give. I understand you-all are expectin'."

Rusty was surprised. "Alice told you?"

"Shanty did. That old man sees things nobody else can."

"He ought to. He's been around since the Colorado River was just a creek. What brings you over this way?"

Andy told him he was due for reassignment to a company on the Rio Grande. That brought concern to Rusty's eyes. He repeated what Tom Blessing had said: "A man can get himself killed down there."

"A little risk never stopped *you*."

"It would now." Rusty glanced toward his cabin. "I've got responsibilities."

"I don't."

"You've got a responsibility to yourself. If you stay too long you're liable to get all shot up and have to quit anyway. Then you may be too crippled to do much of anything else."

"I'm doin' a job that needs to be done. When I stop feelin' that way I'll turn it back to them like you did."

CHAPTER
TWO

As cities went, Andy always found Austin agreeable provided he did not stay long. His first visit here had been with Rusty and Tom Blessing. He had spent his early years in Indian villages and later in the sparse farming community where Rusty lived. The size of this city had amazed him. It was the state capital, Texas's seat of power. That fact had been driven home to him by a tempest that boiled up in 1873 upon the transfer of the governorship from the state's reconstruction administration back to the Texans who had supported the Confederacy. Many former Rangers, cast adrift after the war, had participated in the forcible removal of a reluctant Unionist governor.

The place looked peaceable now after several years of stable and generally benevolent government. Andy rode up Congress Avenue toward the capitol building. The street was wide enough that several spans of mules or oxen could turn a wagon around without crunching its wheels against the wooden sidewalks. After seeing the town several times, Andy was still in awe of the wagon and carriage and horseback traffic and the busy-looking pedestrians along the street. It took a lot of people to govern the state, he thought. Or perhaps, as Tom had once suggested, it took one to do the work and two to watch him.

He paused in apprehension at the door of the Rangers' state office, wondering what was in store for him. He straightened his back and stepped inside, trying to look confident. A clerk sitting at a rolltop desk turned and viewed him over the rims of reading glasses set low on his nose. His annoyance over the interruption was but thinly veiled. "Yes?"

"I'm Private Andy Pickard. I was ordered to report here for reassignment."

The clerk did not recognize the name. His face was pale, the mark of a man who spent his days in an office rather than out in the field. Andy wondered if he knew which end of a gun the bullet came out of. After riffling through some papers he withdrew one and studied it. "Oh yes, Pickard. Do you know Major Jones?"

"Met him. He's visited camps where I've been." Major John Jones was well-known for spending a minimum of time in the office. He was usually on the trail in his buggy, inspecting the far-flung Ranger outposts that were his responsibility.

The clerk said, "Luckily you have chosen a day when the major is in. Unfortunately at this moment he has company. You may sit if you choose to wait."

Andy seated himself in an uncomfortable straight-backed wooden chair that he supposed was meant to discourage long visits. He became aware of loud and angry voices beyond the door of the major's office. He glanced at the clerk, asking a silent question. The clerk rolled his eyes. "The major is having a discussion with a representative of the treasurer's office. The gentleman is explaining why the Rangers must do more but do it with less money and fewer men."

Andy could not follow all that was being said, but he caught words like *stingy* and *waste* and *efficiency*. The latter seemed to receive special emphasis.

The door swung open. A man as pale-faced as the clerk strode out but turned to fling final words back at the major. "If it were up to me we would disband the Rangers. That would stop this needless drain on the state's resources."

Major Jones followed him, shaking his finger. "And I hope the next person to face a holdup man is yourself. I'd like to see how long it would take you to call for the Rangers."

A gust of hot wind seemed to follow the treasury representative's retreat.

Major Jones's fists were clenched. He said, "There goes a man who can make me forget the biblical injunctions against profanity."

As his anger subsided he became aware of Andy standing at attention. He said, "I remember your face, but your name is a puzzle to me."

"Private Andy Pickard, sir. I was ordered to report to you for reassignment."

"Oh yes." The clerk handed Jones a couple of sheets of paper. Jones glanced at them, then beckoned Andy into his office. He was known for quick perception and attention to detail. He could drop in on a camp unannounced and in a few minutes have a firm grasp on the situation there. If he found shortcomings he saw to it that they were being corrected before he left for the next place to be inspected. He believed in Ranger regulations, but his own conduct was based on higher rules. If he visited a camp on a Sunday, he personally conducted religious services.

The major was a small man, but he had a firm handshake and a strong, steady gaze that seemed to see into the hidden part of a man's mind. "Have a seat, Pickard."

Some officers might offer a man a drink at this point, but not Major Jones. He said, "As you may know, the legislature has seen fit to cut our budget again. Some from the settled parts of the state say we don't need Rangers now that the army has the Comanches and other hostiles safely tucked away on their reservations. I have argued to little avail that outlaws present as much of a challenge now as the Indians ever did. Would you not agree?"

Andy was inclined to defend the Indians, but he knew that was not what the major wanted to hear. "Yes, sir."

"I am keeping as many Rangers as I can, given the funds the state has allotted to me. Your record tells me you are one whose services I should retain. I am transferring you to a region that needs all the law enforcement it can get. Are you familiar with the Nueces Strip?"

"I've heard of it. Never been there."

The major turned to a map of Texas on the wall behind his desk and put his finger on the lower part. "It is that region between the Nueces River and the Rio Grande. Mexico still claims it in spite of the treaty Sam Houston won from Santa Anna. The scarcity of law has made it a gathering ground for robbers and cutthroats from both countries."

"I heard Captain McNelly whipped them a few years ago."

"Leander McNelly and his men put down much of the worst trouble, but fighting still goes on. Mostly it's between the races—white against Mexican, Mexican against white." He lowered his chin and stared hard at Andy. "How do you get along with Mexicans?"

Andy shrugged. "All right, I guess. Never knew very many. They haven't settled much where I come from." He had known a few Mexican boys among the Comanches. Like himself, they had been captured on raids and gradually assimilated into the tribe as potential hunters and warriors.

Jones said, "Mexicans dominate the Nueces Strip, at least in numbers. Some still consider themselves to be living in Mexico and not subject to American law. At the same time many Americans in that section do not recognize that Mexicans have legitimate rights, especially ownership of property. They drive them from their lands, or try to. They would like to see every Mexican banished to Mexico, or killed. It is not for us to choose sides. It is our responsibility to put down violence from whatever quarter it may arise."

"Sounds like that would take a lot of Rangers."

"Far more than we have, which sometimes drives us to actions we would not normally consider. Captain McNelly used extreme measures, but the situation called for them. He was up against desperate men."

"What do you mean, extreme measures?"

"At the worst, summary executions. We would prefer to observe all the niceties of the law, but outlaws respect only force. McNelly knew how to get their attention. He stacked the bodies of a dozen dead bandits in the town square in Brownsville. Afterward he conducted a raid across the river into Mexico and shot every suspect he came across. No doubt he killed some who did not deserve it. They were simply in the wrong place at the wrong time. This caused us no end of diplomatic trouble. It is easy to criticize him now from the comfort of an Austin office, but you have to give him credit. He put a damper on border jumping for a while."

Andy was troubled by the thought of shooting suspects. "It's been preached to me over and over that everybody has a right to be tried by a jury."

"No bandit summons a jury before he shoots someone. Mind you, I do not advocate summary justice. However, under extreme circumstances we may have little choice. Now, after what I have told you, do you think you can handle this assignment?"

Andy nodded. "I'll do my duty as I see it, sir."

"Your commanding officer may sometimes see it differently than you do. If so, will you obey him?"

"If I can't, I'll give him my resignation."

Jones mulled that over. "Well enough, but surely you would not desert him in a crisis."

"I won't quit in a fight, but I might resign afterward."

Jones dipped a pen in an inkwell and began to write an order. "How soon can you start?"

"Right now. I'm travelin' light."

"It is a long way to ride alone. I have assigned another Ranger of your acquaintance to the same place. Find him and you can travel together."

Andy thought of several he hoped it might be—Len Tanner or either of the Morris brothers.

Jones said, "His name is Farley Brackett."

Hearing that name was like biting into a sour apple. Andy and Farley had ridden together on several missions, but their relationship had always been prickly.

Jones said, "From all I know of him, Brackett is a good man to have at your side in a fight."

Andy knew that to be true but was tempted to tell Jones that Farley started some of those fights himself. The war had left a visible scar on his face and invisible scars on his soul. In the first years after the Confederate defeat he had been an unreconstructed rebel, a constant thorn in the side of Union authorities. He had brought trouble to Rusty Shannon's door and therefore to Andy as well.

The major handed Andy the order he had been writing. "Stop at Ranger headquarters in San Antonio as you pass through. They can tell you exactly how to find your camp on the Rio Grande. It is moved from time to time."

"Yes, sir." Andy sensed that the major was finished with him. He thought he should salute or something, but he simply backed to the door.

The clerk was waiting for him. He said, "I hope you've got a little money."

"A little. Not much."

"It'll have to stretch. We have no traveling money to give you."

"I don't eat much."

"That's good. You may have to live off of the land."

That was neither new nor news to Andy. "Any idea where I'll find Farley Brackett?"

"He put his horse in a stable down the street. Beyond that, I suggest you investigate all the dramshops."

Brackett did not have a reputation as a drinking man, but perhaps that was because he seldom had the opportunity, Andy thought. Whiling away the hours in Austin might tempt him to make up for time lost in dry and spartan Ranger camps.

Andy went to a livery barn where he and Rusty and Tom Blessing had stabled their horses on a visit several years ago. He recognized the proprietor as the same dried-up little man who had been there before, charging a shameless price for oats, hay, and corral space. Andy said, "I'm lookin' for a Ranger named Farley Brackett."

The hostler pointed to a stall. "His horse is here. I doubt Brackett has gone far afoot. Most of the Rangers I know had rather be whipped with a wet rope than to walk a hundred yards."

"If he comes in, tell him Andy Pickard is lookin' for him."

The hostler eyed him with curiosity. "You've got some older, but I believe I remember you. Ain't you the one that spiked them Union soldier boys' cannon so they couldn't use it to keep that Yankeefied governor in office?"

Andy suspected a lot of people in Austin remembered that incident. It had been a wonder someone was not killed. "I didn't spike the cannon, but I was with the ones that did."

"It was a hell of a show for a little while. Too bad it fizzled out before anybody got a chance to kill one of them damn Yankees."

Like many Texans, the hostler was still engaged in the war between the states, at least with words. Living among the Comanches at the time, Andy had been only dimly aware of the war. He knew a lot about its aftermath, however. To some degree it was still going on, just as the war between Texas and Mexico continued along the border years after it had been relegated to the past elsewhere.

He walked back over to Congress Avenue and entered the first bar he came to. It was moderately busy. He noted that most of the patrons wore suits. Men who wore suits in Austin were usually either lawyers or state employees. No wonder people complained about the waste of their tax money, he thought. This was a weekday. These men were supposed to be working.

Farley was not there. Andy waved off a bartender's question and returned to the street. A second barroom gave him no better result.

As he approached the third he heard a familiar voice raised in challenge: "I don't give a damn whether you like Rangers or not."

The reply came in an equally angry voice, though the words were muffled. Andy heard boots striking hard upon a wooden floor. A man hurtled out through the open door, speeded along by strong hands that gripped his collar and the seat of his britches. He sprawled on his stomach in the street. Farley Brackett stood in the doorway, making a show of dusting his hands. He said, "Come back in and I'll finish windin' your clock for you."

The man sat up but for the moment looked too confused to continue the contest.

Farley's eyes reflected surprise as he recognized Andy. "Badger Boy! What the hell you doin' here?" He did not appear pleased.

Badger Boy was an English version of the name by which Andy had been known among the Comanches. No one used it anymore except Farley, and he usually said it in a mocking way.

"Lookin' for you. I ought to've known to wait and listen for a fight."

"Wasn't no fight to it. I was just standin' there havin' me a peaceful drink when that gink asked me if I wasn't a Ranger. Don't know how he figured out I was. They never have got around to givin' us any badges."

"Some people claim they can tell a Ranger on sight, just by the way he walks and talks."

"I wasn't talkin' at all till that bird started to hooraw me. He said he never seen a Ranger that didn't smell like a skunk."

"If you try to whip everybody that doesn't like us, you'll be too busy to do anything else."

Farley transferred his irritation from the stranger to Andy. "You're a little young to be preachin' gospel to me, Badger Boy. I've been shot and shot at more times than you've had birthdays."

"A little preachin' might do you good, but I know you wouldn't listen to it."

"That, I wouldn't," Farley said, and went back into the bar. Andy remained on the sidewalk, debating with himself about following. He considered riding on alone and letting Farley follow in his own good time or not at all. He knew from past experience that Farley could be poor company, chronically dissatisfied and critical. But the major might not be pleased. He liked his Rangers to work together as a team, not pull against one another like stubborn mules.

He walked into the room and found Farley leaning against the bar, a drink in his hand. The war scar on the side of his face accentuated his frown. "You still here? I figured you left."

"The major says we're supposed to head south and report for duty on the border."

"I don't remember him sayin' I had to ride with *you*. Every time we work together somethin' bad happens to me. You're a damned jinx."

"I'm not crazy about the notion either, but if you don't like it you can resign."

"That'd make you happy, wouldn't it? Well, I'm not quittin'. Go find you a girl or somethin' and leave me in peace for what's left of the day. We can start the trip fresh in the mornin'."

Andy doubted how fresh Farley would be if he spent the evening in this bar or some other, but that was Farley's problem. "I've got my horse in the same stable as yours. I figure to leave soon after daylight."

Walking outside, he met the stranger Farley had thrown out. The man seemed to have gathered his wits, and his expression indicated that he did not consider the argument settled. Andy pointed his thumb at the door. "He's still in there," he said. He stood around a few minutes, listening to the sounds of a vigorous scuffle and the cheers of bystanders from inside.

Farley tumbled out the door and fell on his back on the sidewalk. Andy looked down at him and tried not to grin. "Enjoy yourself."

Farley rolled over and pushed to his feet, muttering under his breath. Face crimson and fists clenched, he stalked back into the barroom.

Andy's growling stomach reminded him that he had not eaten anything since breakfast. He had noticed a restaurant as he walked down the street. He met a policeman hurrying along the wooden sidewalk. The officer said, "Somebody told me there's a fight down thisaway."

Andy pointed. "You might look in that bar yonder. There's a right smart of noise comin' out of it."

By the time Farley got himself untangled from this mess he might be ready to travel, Andy thought.

Awake at daylight, Andy sat on the edge of the wagon-yard cot and looked at Farley, still sleeping, his blankets spread on a pile of hay. "Time to get movin'."

Farley did not respond. Andy had heard him come in during the night but had no idea what time it was. Farley had been talking to himself.

Andy said, "I'm fixin' to go get some breakfast. Then I'm hittin' the trail with or without you."

Farley still did not respond. Andy could see his chest rise and fall with his breathing, so he knew at least that Farley was not dead.

The hostler had a fire going in a small iron stove in the front office, a steaming pot on its top. He told Andy, "Got coffee here."

"Thanks, but I'm goin' for breakfast."

"You might want to take some coffee to your partner. By the looks of him as he staggered by here in the wee hours, he's liable to need it."

"His legs ain't broke. Let him come and get his own coffee."

The hostler seemed startled at Andy's lack of concern for Farley. "I thought you was Rangers together."

"Rangers, but not together any more than we have to be."

After breakfast Andy brushed the black horse, then saddled him. Farley was sitting up but still on his blankets. He appeared to have trouble focusing on Andy. "Where you goin' so early?"

"South, like we were ordered. You can catch up to me or not, that's up to you."

Farley rubbed a hand over his bruised and swollen face. His knuckles were red, the skin broken. "I must've had fun last night. I just can't remember much about it."

"Last time I saw you it looked like you were comin' out second best against a man who didn't like Rangers."

"It taken me a while, but I finally convinced him. It's what happened afterwards that I can't remember much about. The last I knew, him and me had a couple of drinks together, us and some policeman."

"A couple?"

"Maybe three. I never let myself get drunk."

Andy tied his blankets behind the saddle and started to lead the horse outside. Farley called, "Ain't you goin' to wait for me?"

"No." Andy mounted in the street and turned south to intersect the San Antonio road. He crossed the Colorado River on a wooden bridge and turned to look back northward toward the capitol building. Though he liked Austin, he never felt at ease in large cities. This one was home to maybe five or six thousand people.

He was a couple of hours down the trail when he heard a horse coming up behind him. "Badger Boy! Wait up."

Farley pulled in beside him. "Damn it, you'd make a man kill his horse tryin' to catch up with you."

"Told you I was leavin' soon after daylight."

"You could've waited. I was sick this mornin'."

"You look like a herd of cattle ran over you. For all I care you could've stayed in Austin."

"I was just havin' a little fun. Looks to me like I've earned it. Don't get much chance when we're out in the field."

"It's a good thing the major didn't see you."

"He knows that a man has to let off some steam now and again. Else he'll blow up like a boiler with the valve stuck."

Andy remembered how Farley had let off steam in the early years after the war, provoking the carpetbag state police into one fight after another. He had been like a wolf luring dogs into chasing him, then turning on them in a fury of slashing teeth. They had learned to pursue him only at a safe distance. Now he directed his belligerence at lawbreakers for the most part. That made him useful to the Rangers, though he tended to act first and plan later.

After a long, smoldering silence Farley remarked, "That's a good-lookin' black horse. Where did you steal him at?"

Farley had never gotten past a bone of contention involving a sorrel horse his father had given to Rusty Shannon and that Rusty had passed on to Andy. Farley always contended that the horse was his own and that his father had no right to give him away.

Andy said, "I always figured if you're goin' to steal a horse, you'd just as well steal a good one."

The wagon road south from Austin skirted the eastern edge of rough limestone hills where the Edwards escarpment rose out of the western portion of the coastal plain. To the east lay farming settlements along the Colorado and Brazos rivers. To the west, stock farmers and ranchers were freely expanding their operations now that they no longer slept with their guns, worrying about Indian raids. German enclaves such as Friedrichsburg and Neu Braunfels had sunk deep roots. The hill country had appealed to Andy from the first time he saw its long green valleys, its bubbling springs, its clear-running creeks and rivers. Someday, if he ever left the Rangers, he thought he could make a life for himself there.

Traveling at a pace that would not be hard on the horses, Andy and Farley took two days traveling from Austin to San Antonio. Farley said, "Last chance for a little relaxation. Ain't goin' to be much fun from here south."

"If you'd had much more fun in Austin you'd still be there."

"It'll be all business when we get to the border. Go on ahead if you want to, but whatever trouble they got down there can wait another night or two."

Andy did not feel like arguing. "We can tell them we needed to rest the horses." He would welcome the chance to look around the historic city. "We'll need to find Ranger headquarters."

"Tomorrow is soon enough. If they know we're here they'll want us to start south right away whether our horses are tired or not."

Andy had never been to San Antonio, though he had heard many stories about its turbulent past. The town had been a crossroads of early Texas history. Several pitched battles had been fought there, first for Mexico's freedom from Spain and later for Texas's freedom from Mexico. Though other cities in the state were rapidly gaining in importance, San Antonio remained the jewel in its crown—if a sprawl of picket *jacales* and single-story buildings of stone and adobe could be considered a jewel.

As soon as they found a convenient wagon yard and put their horses away, Farley disappeared. He had been to San Antonio in his hell-raising days after the war and knew where he wanted to go. Andy asked the stable's manager how to find the Ranger headquarters, then walked about, familiarizing himself with the center of town. Street traffic was heavy. A man had to look both ways before crossing over lest he be stepped on or rolled over by horses, wagons, and ox-drawn carts with high, solid wooden wheels that groaned and squealed on dry hubs.

He had known the population would be heavily Mexican, but seeing it for himself made him feel like an outsider. As a boy with the Comanches he had listened to Kiowas talking. He had felt helpless because he could not understand a word. He found himself just as lost trying to decipher some meaning from the Spanish he heard spoken all about him.

He had learned Comanche and relearned English. With time he should be able to pick up at least enough Spanish to get him by, he thought.

A strong German element was also evident, spilled over from early immigrant settlements founded in the 1840s. He despaired of ever learning to speak German. Spanish would be challenge enough.

He came unexpectedly upon what he recognized as the Alamo, at least the battle-scarred remains of the church that had been the center of the original mission complex. Much of the rest was gone, lost to new construction and bustling commercial uses. He was disappointed to find that even the old sanctuary had been turned into a warehouse. He thought it an undignified fate for a building where brave men had fought, bled, and died for Texas. Perhaps it would someday be turned into a shrine befitting the blood sacrifice that patriots of both Texas and Mexico had made there.

In the Ranger office Andy looked at a map that appeared to be the same as the one on Major Jones's Austin wall except that more trails had been added, some ranches and small towns penciled in. A lieutenant traced one of the trails with his finger. "With some exceptions, you'll find most white ranchers friendly to the Rangers. With some exceptions, you'll find most Mexicans distrustful and unfriendly. Both sides have cause." He turned back to face Andy. "Have you got anything against Mexicans?"

"Major Jones asked me the same question. No, I don't."

"Many people do, Rangers included. It's not onesided, though. Many Mexicans have a hard grudge against whites too. Especially Rangers. They say we use our authority and our guns to help the gringo ranchers run them out of the country."

Andy reflected a minute. "Do we?"

"We're not supposed to, but some take it to be their duty. Old wars don't die easy. They linger on like an incurable disease."

"I try to treat everybody just alike."

"That's a fine ideal. I hope you can live up to it when you've been on the river awhile. A man can lose his religion there if he doesn't get killed first."

Andy was not sure just what his religion was. Old Preacher Webb and others had counseled him about Christianity, but remnants of Comanche beliefs lingered as well. Sometimes the two seemed much the same. Other times they conflicted.

Andy asked, "When I get down there, what'll my duties be?"

"They'll be whatever Lieutenant Buckalew tells you to do. If he says ride, you'll ride. If he says shoot, you'll shoot. Don't waste his time or yours askin' questions."

"Yes, sir."

"When the lieutenant isn't around, you'll take orders from Sergeant Donahue. You may find that the lieutenant and the sergeant don't always see eye to eye."

"In that case, which one do I listen to?"

"The one who's there at the time." The officer turned toward a small safe. "How long since you've been paid?"

"I was out on assignment the last payday. And I had to buy a horse. About all I've got in my pocket is a whittlin' knife."

"I'll advance you a little travelin' money against your wages. We can't have a Ranger beggin' his way down the road. Keep account of your expenses. Maybe the state'll see fit to reimburse you. Or maybe not."

Andy normally wasted little time worrying about money, but once in a while the need could not be ignored. He had feared he would have to accept a wound to his pride by asking Farley to lend him a few dollars. But Farley might have no money left either after a couple of days and nights in

San Antonio. It would give Andy deep satisfaction if Farley had to touch *him* for a loan.

His stomach rumbled loudly enough that he was sure the officer must have heard. He asked, "Where can I get a decent meal cheap?"

The lieutenant seemed to approve of the word *cheap*. "There's a fair-to-middlin' chili joint down the street a couple of blocks and around the corner. It's not the Menger Hotel, but it's fillin'. And the cook washes his hands once a day whether they need it or not."

"Sounds like the place for me."

He started to leave, but the officer snapped his fingers and said, "Almost forgot. There's another Ranger who'll be headed the same way as you and Brackett. He came up to deliver a prisoner. Maybe you know him. Name's Len Tanner."

Andy grinned. "I've known him since I was this high." He held his hand flat at chest level. "I lost track after he got transferred away from my camp. Where do you reckon I'll find him?"

"Go where you hear the loudest talkin'."

Len had a reputation for a loose jaw. He could talk the bark off a live-oak tree. Andy had first gotten to know him when an accidental horse fall and broken leg took him out of Comanche hands and thrust him back into the life of a white boy. A jovial spirit who came and went as the mood struck him, Len had spun enticing tales of high adventure and eventually had talked Andy into joining the Rangers.

The café's proprietor had laughing eyes that offset the fierceness of his black beard. His body was shaped like a pickle barrel. He asked, "Cowboy?"

"Nope," Andy said. "Ranger."

"Ain't nothin' too good for a Ranger. I'll give you a choice: beefsteak or chili. Same price."

"That bein' the case, I'll take the beefsteak."

The man laughed. "Some of the biggest ranchers in South Texas come in here to eat. It's the only time a lot of them ever eat any of their own beef."

Andy took that to imply that most preferred to eat their neighbors' cattle. It also implied that the operator of the chili joint was not choosy about the source of his meat supply.

Andy said, "It doesn't sound like rightful ownership means much around here."

"Not unless a man is ready and willin' to fight for what belongs to him. There's people here who can steal your socks without takin' your boots off."

The cook poured a cup of coffee for Andy without being asked. A cast-iron skillet clanged as he placed it atop the stove. He plopped a huge spoonful of hog lard in it to heat and melt. He said, "The secret to a good steak is to fry it deep in plenty of hot grease."

Enough of it, Andy thought, and he could develop a belly like the cook's.

The cook said, "I ain't seen you before. Where are you stationed?"

Andy told him he was being reassigned to the border. The man's face went serious. "The trail down to the Rio Grande can be risky, especially the lower part. The more Rangers the better. You never know who's liable to pop out of the brush lookin' for somebody to shoot."

"I'll have another Ranger with me. Maybe two if I can find Len Tanner."

The name brought a flicker of recognition from the cook. "I believe that old boy was in here yesterday. He talked till my ears hurt."

"That's him."

The cook turned Andy's steak over in the skillet. "If I was you I wouldn't noise it around too much about bein' a Ranger. I rode awhile with McNelly's outfit. Down in that border country the Mexicans called us *rinches*, and they didn't say it sweet. I decided to move up here for my health."

Mention of Captain McNelly stirred Andy's curiosity. "What kind of a man was he?"

"As good a feller as I ever knew. He had a hard job to do, and he done it despite bein' sick most of the time. Some days he was almost too weak to stay in the saddle, but he wouldn't let go. He meant to clean up the border if he had to kill half the population. He *did* kill a lot of them. Some claim he went too far." The cook shrugged. "All I can say is that bandit raids tapered off right smartly by the time he got through."

Andy said, "From what I hear, they're back. Maybe not as strong as before McNelly, but bad enough."

The cook lifted the steak on a fork and dropped it onto a platter. "Want a little advice? No extra charge."

"Sure."

"Don't trust every smilin' face you see. You never know for sure who's your friend and who wants to see you dead. When in doubt, shoot first."

Andy asked, "What if I kill somebody innocent?"

"There's damned few innocent people down there. They might start that way, but they get over it."

Andy's back was to the door, but he sensed that someone had entered the room behind him. The voice was Farley's, and he sounded agitated. "Eat quick and let's get movin'."

"I thought you had some celebratin' to do."

"Done done it. I'm ready to go."

"What's the big hurry? It's already late in the day. We can't get far before dark."

"We can get far enough. I'll go fetch our horses while you finish your supper."

Farley left in a trot. The cook said, "Don't eat too fast. Ain't good for the digestion."

"I just hope he didn't kill somebody."

Before Andy had finished eating his steak and red beans, Farley was back and leading Andy's black horse. He shouted from outside, "Come on. Let's move."

Andy kept his seat until he had emptied the platter and finished his coffee. He paid the proprietor out of the money the lieutenant had advanced. The cook said, "Mind what I told you. They'll smile when you're lookin' and stab you when you turn your back."

Farley was fidgeting as if he had ants in his underwear. "You damned sure took your time."

"I don't see why we have to rush away from here like a couple of thieves."

Farley did not answer. He set his horse into a long trot. He did not bother to look back and see if Andy was following.

Andy caught up to him as they passed through the southern outskirts of town. "Who did you shoot?"

The question surprised Farley. "I never shot nobody."

"The way you left, I thought maybe you did."

Farley looked back. "It wasn't nothin' like that. I ran into an old friend of yours, and I was afraid he'd want to ride with us. I can't listen to Len Tanner all the way to the border. I might shoot him to shut him up."

Annoyed, Andy said, "All this rush was to get away from Len? Where did you find him?"

"I was visitin' a couple of ladies I know. He was there doin' the same thing. You're too young to understand."

"I'm old enough. Seems to me like you ought to find yourself a good woman and leave those other *ladies* alone."

"What woman would look twice at this scarred face unless she was paid to do it?"

"There's bound to be some. You've been searchin' in the wrong places."

"And you're stickin' your nose in where you've got no business."

Andy choked down his irritation. Though Len's chatter could be a trial, he would prefer it to riding with a morose Farley Brackett. "I've got half a mind to go back and find him."

"If you do, you'll go by yourself."

"That might be an improvement."

Farley grumped, "You're damned hard to get along with. Must be you ain't got all the Indian out of you."

CHAPTER

THREE

Andy looked back a couple of times as they put the historic old town behind them. He hoped he might see Len catching up. He said, "Len's a good Ranger, you can't take that away from him."

Farley said, "That don't mean I've got to appreciate his company. A man can put up with just so much jaw."

Andy knew of no one who disliked Len except some of the criminals he had sent away to board with the state. Farley was a good Ranger too, but Andy knew many people who did not care for much of his company, himself included.

He asked, "When are we goin' to stop and camp?" He hoped Len would catch up.

Farley said curtly, "You already had your supper, and I brought mine with me." He held up a pint bottle.

Andy had rarely seen him drunk, for Farley could hold a prodigious amount of whiskey without showing its effects. He had a stern will that did not permit interference with whatever he set his mind to do. Len, on the other hand, did not drink on duty or when he thought he might be called to duty. Even a modest amount of whiskey could start him to singing in a voice loud but seriously off-key.

At dusk Farley said, "We better call it a day. We been pushin' the horses pretty hard."

Farley had been pushing. Andy had just been trying to keep up.

Farley added, "We don't need no fire. It's warm enough, and we ain't cookin'. A fire just draws visitors."

Andy knew Farley was concerned about just one visitor, Len. They pulled off the trail a little way, unsaddled and hobbled their horses. Dragging one foot, Farley smoothed the rocks from a small patch of ground and spread his blankets. He hoisted the bottle without offering to share it. Andy would have refused it anyway. He had not developed a liking for whiskey and could not understand why others so readily did. It always burned his throat on the way down and kindled a fire in his stomach when it got there.

Farley said, "I don't suppose you seen my mother and sister before you left?"

"I did."

"How were they?"

"Fine. They're the *likeable* members of the Brackett family."

Farley accepted the implication without visible reaction. "You serious about Bethel?"

"I might be if I wasn't a Ranger."

"That's easy fixed. You could quit."

"If you don't like me ridin' with you as a Ranger, you sure wouldn't like havin' me for a brother-in-law."

"I'd seldom ever see you."

Andy said, "I guess that's right. You hardly ever visit your women-folks."

"It's better that way. All I ever brought them was trouble."

Andy kindled a small fire. Farley demanded, "What's that for?"

"I want to boil a little coffee after that ride."

"Never could see why some people got to have coffee all the time. It's too much trouble. With whiskey, all you have to do is pull the cork."

Andy heard the strike of a horse's hooves and saw a lanky rider approaching in the dusk. A familiar voice shouted, "Hello, the camp. You there, Andy?"

Farley groaned. "Oh hell."

Andy stood up and waved his arm. "Come on in, Len."

Len Tanner swung a spindly leg over his horse's rump and stepped to the ground. "I'd about give up on catchin' you fellers. I thought you'd wait for me in town."

Andy saw no need to explain and hurt Len's feelings. "Farley was in a hurry to leave. It's a right long trip to the river."

"I know. I had to deliver a prisoner all the way up to San Antonio. He was wanted for usin' his knife a little too free. That's a common failin' in this part of the country. Got some of that coffee left? I ain't had no supper."

Farley muttered, "I suppose after a few days in town you was too broke to feed yourself."

Andy figured Farley might be right about that. Wages slipped through Len's fingers like sand. He always said he could travel lighter without the weight of silver in his pockets. He was too skinny to carry much extra weight anyhow.

Len said, "I'll ride with you fellers if you'll have me. It always shortens the miles when I've got somebody to talk to."

Farley grunted and moved to where he had spread his blankets. "I'm hittin' the soogans. If you find me gone in the mornin' it'll be because I made an early start."

Len said, "Eager, ain't he? He wouldn't rush if he knew the border. It was easier fightin' Indians. At least when you saw one you knew he was your enemy. Down yonder you're never sure."

Andy asked, "How come you to transfer from the San Saba? That was a nice place to be stationed."

"The captain volunteered me. I guess they needed a man with experience."

More than likely the captain had heard Len's stories one time too many, Andy thought.

They set out the next morning soon after daybreak. Len began to tell about his experiences since he had been sent down to the border. Andy listened eagerly, but Farley quickly lost patience. He stopped and dismounted, lifting his mount's left forefoot and examining the shoe.

"I think there's a stone lodged in here," he said. "You-all go on. I'll catch up to you by-and-by."

Andy suspected Farley was trying to get out of earshot. He would probably drag along behind. Andy had rather listen to Len's stories than to Farley's grumbling anyway.

He had noticed a bright, shiny star on Len's shirt. Sometimes Rangers made their own badges. "Where did you get that?"

"A Mexican cut it for me out of a silver peso. Looks pretty good, don't it?"

"Looks like a target."

"Ain't nobody hit it yet. Been a couple tried."

"White or Mexican?"

"One of each. Most Mexicans don't like Rangers, and a lot of whites don't like Rangers gettin' in their way when they're tryin' to take what belongs to the Mexicans. We get shot at from both sides."

By noon Farley had not caught up. Andy could see him poking along a couple of hundred yards behind. Len asked, "Reckon we ought to stop and wait for him?"

"He likes his own company. Let him make the most of it."

"I figure he must've been born in the dark. Me, I was born in the daylight."

Andy enjoyed studying the changing landscape. It was gently rolling, mostly open except for watercourses lined with trees and many varieties of brush. Wide areas were flat enough for farming, though little had as yet been broken by the plow. Cattle of many hues grazed the tall, summer-curing grass. Some hoisted their tails and ran for the thickets. Others watched placidly as the riders passed, for this was a much-used public roadway. They were accustomed to wagon, cart, and horseback traffic.

He said, "Sure looks peaceful."

Len shook his head. "Wait till we get down into the brush country. Plant, animal, or human, everything there is lookin' for a chance to draw blood. They've all got stickers, horns, knives, or shootin' irons."

Farley grudgingly rejoined them as they stopped at an abandoned adobe hut from which windowsills and the roof had been removed. The mud walls were gradually disintegrating, most of their plaster covering gone.

Len said, "Sure feels good to sleep indoors now and again."

Farley spread his blankets outside, by himself.

As the next day waned toward dusk they began looking for a place to stop. They came upon a little creek that appeared to be a favored camping site. A half dozen Mexican ox carts were there. A couple of dark-skinned men walked out to meet the riders. They spoke in Spanish. Andy could not understand a word.

Len said, "I've picked up a little Mexican lingo. They're invitin' us to share the camp with them."

Andy asked, "They can see your badge. I thought all Mexicans hated Rangers."

"Just the same, they'd feel safer camped with us. There's gringos around who would be glad to do them harm."

Farley said, "They might wait till we're asleep, then carve their initials on our gizzards."

Len argued, "They're just freighters, haulin' goods from the Gulf of Mexico to San Antonio. They know if they hurt anybody they couldn't get away. An ox team travels awful slow."

"I don't trust anybody I can't understand. We need to find a place where we're by ourselves, or at least with people who talk our language."

Andy said, "The worst people I ever knew spoke our language real plain. They just didn't think the same way we do."

Farley snorted. "Stay here for all I care. I'm goin' on."

Andy glanced at Len and shrugged. They traveled a while longer. Farley turned from the road and followed a cow trail about a quarter mile. "Them people might come huntin' for us after dark. They'll play hell findin' us out here."

Andy was not keen on making a dry camp. He asked, "What have we got that they'd want?"

"Our horses. Our guns. We're gringos, and we're Rangers. That by itself might be enough."

Len said, "Can't fault anybody for bein' what they was born. The big dealer dealt us each a hand the day of our birth. It's up to us to play it out the best we can."

Farley said, "I was born cautious."

Not all that cautious. Andy remembered when Farley's reckless disregard for reconstruction law had made him a target of the carpetbag state police and brought bad trouble down upon his family. But Farley was selective in what he chose to be cautious about.

Len said, "If you-all are nervous about my badge, I'll take it off." He stuck it in his pocket. "If anybody jumps us now, it won't be because we're Rangers."

Toward noon the next day Andy began seeing dust rising in the south. It troubled him for a time because it was too localized to be a dust storm.

Len said, "It'll be a trail herd on its way north. Lots of them swing by San Antonio to supply their wagons."

The point man, riding at the front of the strung-out herd, was white. He gave the three Rangers a silent and distrustful study, then moved on past them. Len observed, "It's a steer herd bound for the Kansas railroad, I'd guess. Cow herds are generally headed farther north, like to Wyomin' and Montana."

Wyoming and Montana were exotic-sounding names to Andy. He said, "I wonder how it'd be to go up there ourselves."

Len shook his head. "The sight of a snowflake makes me shiver. Feller told me one time he was up in Wyomin' and seen a hat movin' along on top of the snow. When he went to look, he found a cowboy under the hat, and the cowboy was on horseback."

Andy grinned. Len declared, "It's the gospel truth. At least that's what the feller told me."

Farley's face was without expression. Andy could count on one hand the number of times he had ever seen Farley smile at a joke, or anything else. Farley nodded toward the cattle. "Notice how many different brands they've got on them?"

Len said, "A lot of those are Mexican brands." He pointed out that they were larger and more intricate than most of Texas origin.

Andy asked, "You think they're stolen?"

"Let's say they was got awful cheap. They swum the Rio Grande in the dark of the moon. Come daylight, they was citizens of Texas."

Andy said, "Maybe we ought to arrest this whole outfit."

Farley said, "Didn't the Comanches ever teach you how to count, Badger Boy? There's a dozen or fifteen of them and just three of us. I doubt you'd find a churchgoin' man amongst them."

Len said, "There's a chance these people bought the cattle in good faith from somebody else who brought them across the river. Anyway, the Mexicans they belonged to may have made up the loss already, swimmin' Texas cattle back in the other direction."

Farley said, "Sounds like everybody breaks even."

"Not everybody. There's losers, and they're generally the little fellers. Besides, it's bigger than just cattle. People get killed."

A swing rider approached. He had a sober bearing that indicated he might be the boss. He said, "I hope you-all ain't Rangers."

Andy said, "Why? What difference would it make?"

The drover spat. "The Rangers gave me trouble over the Mexicos in this herd. I had to pull strings in high places."

Farley said, "We're Rangers, but we ain't been given any orders yet. It's no hide off of our butt if you take these cattle to Timbuktu."

The trail man said, "Kansas is far enough. Time we get there they'll all be talkin' American."

The Rangers pulled away from the herd to get out of the dust. It struck Andy as curious that more than half the horsemen appeared to be Mexican. He said, "If these cattle were stolen from south of the river, the Mexicans with this outfit are robbin' their own countrymen."

Len said, "Some don't feel like they owe Mexico nothin', or Texas either. Santy Anna stabbed them in the back. After preachin' that his soldiers ought to be proud to die for Mexico, he gave away Texas to save his own hide. They don't see that anything is wrong if they can get away with it. That includes shootin' a Texas Ranger or a Mexican *rurale*. It's open season on anybody who gets in their way."

"Some of these drovers are gringos."

"Thieves don't pay much attention to each other's color as long as they're all fillin' their pockets. Afterwards they may try to cut each other's throats. Why, just last spring . . ." He started retelling a story he had already told twice on this trip.

Farley dropped back a hundred yards.

Len dismounted in front of an abandoned adobe house. He rubbed his mount's right foreleg. "Feels to me like my horse is comin' up lame."

Andy looked to the west, where the sun cast a rosy glow through low-hanging clouds. "He may just be gettin' tired. It's time we stopped for the day and gave the horses a rest."

Farley argued, "We've got an hour of daylight left."

Andy said, "You want Len to have to walk and lead his horse?"

"It wouldn't hurt him none. Might make him tired enough to quit talkin'."

Len said, "You go right on ahead if you want to. I ain't goin' to ruin a good horse."

Andy said, "I'm stayin' with Len."

Farley seemed about to argue the point but gave in. "You two need lookin' after. Anyway, they ain't goin' to pay us extra for reportin' in early."

Andy saw a well beside the house and led his black horse over to examine it. Looking down into the water, he saw no sign that it harbored any drowned rats or other small animals. Though the house appeared not to have been occupied in a long time, the windlass had a reasonably new rope. It was probably a gift from someone who passed this way often. Andy turned the handle and brought up a bucket of water. He poured it into a small wooden trough and brought up a second bucket so there would be enough for his horse. He cupped his hands and tentatively tasted the water to be sure it was good before he drank his fill.

Len started to walk through the door but stopped abruptly and stepped back. Andy heard a buzzing sound that he recognized instantly as a rattlesnake's warning. Len said, "I believe I'll sleep outdoors tonight." He handed his reins to Andy. "But I'll make sure this gentleman doesn't come out huntin' for me." As soon as Andy had led his and Len's horses away, Len shot the snake.

Holstering the pistol, he said, "Welcome to South Texas, where everything scratches, stings, or bites."

They searched around for sign of more snakes, then hobbled the horses. Andy built a small fire in a rock-lined hole that travelers had used before him. He let the fire burn down to red coals, then set a coffeepot on top of them.

He said, "Indians would make supper out of that snake. It tastes a little like chicken."

Len grimaced. "Help yourself. I've been hungry lots of times. I've eaten mesquite beans and jackrabbit. I've eaten horse and mule meat, but I ain't never been hungry enough to eat a rattler." He went on to describe at length a couple of times when he was desperate enough that he almost ate the tops from his boots.

Muttering to himself about liars and those who listened to them, Farley went out to gather some dry wood. He came back and dropped several dead mesquite limbs near the fire. "Riders comin'," he said. He went to his saddle lying on the ground and pulled his rifle from its scabbard.

Andy followed his lead by drawing his pistol. He counted seven horsemen, one a smooth-faced boy of fourteen or fifteen. The others were older and had not felt a razor in at least a couple of weeks, nor water either except to drink.

Farley said with some relief, "At least they're Americans."

Len's right hand rested on the butt of his pistol. "That don't guarantee nothin'. They may not like the law, so we better not tell them we're Rangers. They've got us outnumbered."

The riders stopped a respectful distance from the Rangers' camp. One rode forward with his right hand raised in a sign of peace. He slouched in the saddle. "Howdy. Looks like you-all have made yourselves to home."

Farley did not offer a welcome. "You got any quarrel with that?"

The rider shook his head. His whiskers were coal black, a sharp contrast to the washed-out gray of his eyes. "None at'all. We're just travelers like yourselves, lookin' to water our horses before we ride on a ways more."

Farley said, "The water's free for everybody."

The man said, "We come upon a bunch of Meskins back yonder. They eyed us like coyotes that found a mess of quail. I've got a hunch they been trailin', waitin' to hit us in the night when we're asleep. It'd ease our minds if we could camp with you-all."

Andy saw doubt in Len's and Farley's eyes.

The visitor said, "The more there is of us, the safer we'll all be."

Farley was slow to lower his rifle. "Maybe. What say you-all camp over on the other side of the house?"

The man waved his arm, and the other six rode in closer. He said, "My name is Burt Hatton. Me and the boys here, we just delivered a herd to San Antonio. There's people that'd gladly shoot us for the money them cattle brought. Failin' that, they'd at least try to take our horses."

Andy did not like the looks of the men. They reminded him of a wolf pack circling a small buffalo herd and looking to bring down a calf.

Len was uncharacteristically silent. As the men moved away, he said, "Andy, you look like you smelled a skunk."

"It's just a feelin' I've got."

"Me too. Seems to me like I've seen that hombre before. With all the whiskers it's hard to be sure."

The drovers made camp on the opposite side of the adobe ruin. Once their horses were unsaddled and hobbled, Hatton walked back over to the Rangers' campfire. He asked, "You-all headed for the border?"

Len was usually the first to speak, but he kept his silence. His badge remained in his pocket.

Farley said, "We thought we'd go down there and take a look around."

"I hope you've been told what kind of country you're gettin' into."

"We've got a pretty fair notion."

"You'll find more Meskins than white people. Damned shame, seein' as this country is supposed to be American. We've chased a lot of them across the river, but they keep birthin' more and more of them here. Seems like they're bound and determined to outbreed us. A white man has got to keep his guns strapped on all the time."

Andy was a little disturbed by Hatton's tone. "If a man owns his land, how can you run him off of it?"

"They'll sell out when you put the proposition to them right. A Meskin gets real agreeable if you stick a pistol up against his ear and cock the hammer back. Especially if you can bribe a couple of Rangers to stand behind you."

Andy saw anger rising in Len's eyes. He had seldom seen Len yield to ill humor. Len turned away from the campfire. "I'm goin' to see about the horses."

Andy followed him. He kept his voice low. "A Ranger wouldn't ever do that. Would he?"

Len frowned. "There's some that might. They think the border country would be a lot better off if all the Mexicans was moved to the other side."

"That's what they did to the Indians. They pushed them all north of the Red River." Resentment stirred when he thought about his Comanche friends forced into exile on a cramped reservation away from their former range. Yet he realized it had been the only way to curtail their raiding.

Len said, "The law says you can't put people off of their property, but some gringos ignore the law. They tell the Mexicans they can either leave or die. More often than not they sell out for whatever they can get. It usually ain't much."

"I wouldn't be a party to such as that."

"Me and you, we're just privates. We've got no say. If a sergeant says 'Fire,' all we can do is ask what at." Len looked worriedly back toward camp. "I'd swear that Hatton looks familiar."

"Maybe he's in your fugitive book."

Rangers carried a book with handwritten descriptions of fugitives. They consulted it often and kept it as up to date as possible. They took special pleasure in marking off a fugitive as captured or killed.

Len said, "Might be. I'll read it after a while when that bunch can't see me."

Andy returned to the campfire. He heard Hatton talking to Farley about border outlaws. "There's one in particular you better be on the *cuidado* for. Guadalupe Chavez has got a big ranch over yonder, stocked with good Texas cattle his bunch has stole. Used to have considerable land on this side of the river too, but Jericho Jackson ran him off of it."

Andy asked, "Who's Jericho Jackson?"

Hatton seemed surprised that Andy did not know. "Just about the biggest man on the Texas side of the border these days. Took over a large part of what Chavez claimed north of the river. He ain't a man to be crossed, not even by the likes of Guadalupe Chavez. They're blood enemies."

Andy said, "This Chavez, what kind of man is he?"

"A real bad hombre. His pistoleros come across the river lookin' for somethin' to steal and gringos to kill. He tells his people that someday he'll fly the Mexican flag again over everything from the Rio Grande to San Antonio."

Len said, "I hear that Jericho Jackson ain't no angel either. It's like he built a wall around his ranch and don't let anybody in that ain't an outlaw like he is."

Andy said, "I remember Preacher Webb talkin' about a place called Jericho. It had walls, but they fell down."

Len nodded. "That was on account of a soldier called Joshua, but I ain't met anybody around here by that name."

Hatton's eyes flashed in irritation. "I wouldn't go talkin' against Jericho. It can get a man hurt." He pushed to his feet. "Maybe the boys have got supper fixed." He stalked away.

Farley turned on Len. "What did you provoke him for? He was tellin' us things we need to know."

"I remember where I've seen him before. He was with a bunch we caught drivin' stolen horses. We got most of the horses back, but the ones they rode was faster than ours. We suspected they was workin' for Jericho Jackson, but it's hard to get anything on him. People like Hatton do his dirty work for him."

Farley chewed on what Len said. "You reckon there's paper out on Hatton?"

Len grunted. "There ought to be. I'd wager that the cattle they delivered to San Antonio still had Rio Grande mud on them. We better stand guard duty tonight, or we're liable to find ourselves dead in the mornin'. Or at least afoot. Notice the way he kept lookin' at our horses?"

Farley said, "I figured since the men was all white that we had no need to worry."

"White, Mexican, down in this country there's meanness enough to go around."

Andy asked, "So what do we do?"

Len made a wry smile. "What would your Comanche brothers do if they smelled Apaches?"

"They'd sleep with their eyes open and a war club in their hands."

Len said, "We'll do better than that. After good dark we'll move our horses, then we'll keep watch."

Andy half expected Farley to put up an argument because the idea was Len's, but he didn't. They made a show of stringing a rope between two trees and tying their horses and the pack mule to it. Before moonrise they quietly led the animals farther out into the brush and retied the picket line. They returned to camp but remained in the shadows beyond the campfire's dying light.

After a time Andy felt himself dozing off. Farley punched him with his elbow. He whispered, "Rub a little tobacco in your eyes. That'll keep you awake."

And maybe blind me, Andy thought. He declined the offer of Farley's tobacco.

He felt himself nodding again just before Len gently shook him. "They're comin'."

The fire had burned down to flickering coals that yielded little light. Andy could make out shadowy figures moving stealthily into the Rangers' camp.

He recognized Hatton's voice, raised in disappointment. "They're gone."

Someone else said, "They can't be gone far. Their camp stuff is here."

Farley raised up. "Yes, we're still here, and you sons of bitches ain't gettin' our horses."

Pistols blazed on both sides, and then a rifle. Men shouted and cursed. A youthful voice cried out in mortal pain. Hatton's men backed away, quickly lost in the darkness. Andy heard Hatton shout, "Pick him up and let's get out of here."

The smell of gun smoke was pungent. Andy heard horses moving away from the Hatton camp. His heart pumping with excitement, he said, "We must've hit somebody."

Farley said, "I thought they would just come after our horses. But they was after us too."

Andy said, "No witnesses, no charges."

Len said, "No use tryin' to follow them in the dark. I can't see that they done us any harm."

He was mistaken. At the picket line they found Farley's horse down. Andy knelt to examine it and found it was dead. "Stray bullet must've got him."

His first reaction was relief that his black horse had not been hit. But he realized that this would complicate the completion of their trip.

Farley declared, "Damned if I intend to walk all the way to the river."

Len said, "We can borrow a horse at the McCawley ranch, a little ways south. Till then we'll take turns walkin'."

Farley asked, "Who's McCawley?"

"Big Jim McCawley. He married into the Chavez family."

The name got Andy's attention. "Chavez?"

"He married Guadalupe Chavez's sister, but don't hold that against him. There was a time when even Lupe Chavez was considered good folks.

That was before Jericho and others tried to take everything away from him and his family."

Farley said, "I don't know as this is a good idea, havin' truck with Chavez's kinfolks."

Len shrugged off Farley's objection. "Big Jim's always been friendly to the Rangers. We've brought back stock of his that was run off by thieves."

"I'd be friendly too if they recovered my property."

"You'll be surprised how many *ain't* friendly." A smile spread across Len's face. "Once you see Big Jim's daughter Teresa, you'll be glad we went there."

Andy said, "You sayin' she's pretty?"

"Wait till you see her eyes. Dark as coffee beans. They melt me plumb down into my boots."

Farley said, "But she's Mexican, ain't she?"

"One look at her and you won't even think about that."

"Mexican is Mexican."

CHAPTER
FOUR

Hatton and his men had galloped more than a mile when Burt Hatton shouted for a stop and reined his horse around. "Let's see about that damned kid."

Jesse Wilkes held the wounded boy to prevent his falling from the saddle. "I'm afraid he ain't goin' to make it."

Hatton listened for sound of pursuit but heard none. He dismounted and raised his arms. "Lift him down to me." He lowered the groaning youngster to the ground. "I wish to hell you'd stayed home like you was told. Let's have a look at you."

He felt the warm stickiness of blood on his hands. He fished a match from his pocket and struck it for light. In the few seconds that it burned, he saw what he had feared. He heard a faint bubbling sound. "Of all the bad luck, they got him in the chest."

Wilkes said, "I'm afraid he's goin' to die."

Hatton made no comment.

The boy whimpered, "Where's Aunt Thelma? Take me to Aunt Thelma."

"You'll be all right," Hatton said, knowing he lied. "We'll carry you to a doctor."

"It hurts. Oh God, it hurts."

Wilkes was always finding fault. He said, "It was a mistake to let the boy come along. Jericho told us not to."

Hatton retorted, "We didn't let him come. He done that on his own."

The boy was a nephew of Jericho's wife. Given the responsibility of raising him, she had spoiled him so that he took advice from nobody except her. He had begged to help Hatton and his crew drive the cattle to San Antonio. It should not have been a dangerous trip. It became so only when Hatton took a notion to bushwhack three strangers for their horses and gear. It had looked easy.

Whose damn-fool idea was it in the first place? Hatton asked himself, though he knew it had been his own. He had not intended for Jericho to know about it. Hatton and the others would not have had to split their booty with him.

The boy cried, complaining about the pain until his voice began to fade.

Fearfully Wilkes said, "He's dyin', Burt. Do somethin'."

"Damn it, shut up."

In a few minutes the kid shuddered and was gone. Hatton shuddered too, and cursed under his breath. "Just my luck."

Wilkes said, "Better it had been one of us. It'll be hell to face Jericho. He's been known to kill a man for bringin' him bad news." He looked at Hatton, making it plain he expected Hatton to be the one to carry the message. "You know how he dotes on that woman of his, and she dotes on this boy."

Hatton frowned, considering his options. An idea took a little edge from his dark mood. "He don't have to know how the shootin' came about. We can tell him we got ambushed, and it wasn't our fault."

"Jericho'll see right through you. His eyes cut like a knife. Why would anybody pull an ambush on us?"

Hatton's spirits lifted a bit more. "Jericho hates Lupe Chavez like he was strychnine. He'll believe it if we tell him we ran into some Chavez bandits. We'll tell him they didn't give us a chance."

"*You* tell him. I wouldn't lie to him for a hundred dollars. What about the kid? We goin' to take him all the way home?"

"It's too far, and the weather is too warm. Come daylight we'll find a place to bury him. Jericho is goin' to ask a lot of questions. Everybody remember: Chavez's outfit ambushed us."

Wilkes grumbled, "I still say he won't believe it."

Hatton's voice was deep and dangerous. "You tell him different and I'll kill you."

Big Jim McCawley's place was not fancy, but it was large. A long Mexican-style rock house dominated a gentle knoll. It was surrounded by smaller, flat-topped buildings, mostly adobe, some of pickets, scattered haphazardly down the slope. Off to one side lay corrals with fences of stacked stones or upright tree branches bound tightly together with rawhide thongs dried to the hardness of steel. Everything appeared to have been built from raw materials close at hand.

Andy and Len walked their horses so Farley could keep pace afoot. He chose to lag behind a little so he did not have to listen to Len's long-running commentary on everything from the weather to the crowned heads of Europe, and now and then a detailed description of Teresa McCawley. Andy carried Farley's saddle and roll. Len carried his bridle and blanket.

Len said, "He ought to be gettin' in a little better humor now that he can see the ranch."

Though Farley had ridden for long stretches while Andy and Len took turns walking, Farley had been grouchy as an old badger awakened from sleep. He seemed somehow to blame Andy and Len for the loss of his horse, though Andy knew that was illogical.

Once while Len was taking his turn at walking they came upon a long-horned cow with her calf. Not accustomed to seeing a man afoot, she took Len for a threat to her offspring, lowered her head, and charged. Len's long legs carried her in a wide circle until she gave up and trotted away with her calf, wringing her tail in agitation.

Farley almost smiled.

Andy asked Len, "You sure McCawley will lend Farley a horse?"

"Better than that, I'll bet he'll give him one. He'd take the shirt off of his back for somebody in need. He was a Ranger himself once, long before the war."

Andy saw dust rising from behind a corral fence. As the breeze swung around from that direction he could hear men yelling encouragement. He saw a figure bobbing up and down, riding a pitching horse. He said, "Maybe Farley can have that one."

Len said, "It'd give him somethin' to cuss at besides us." His grin showed that the thought pleased him. He pointed his thumb toward a corner of the corral. "I see Big Jim over yonder."

A large man stood outside, watching the show from between the upright tree branches that constituted the fence. In size and stature he reminded Andy of Sheriff Tom Blessing. The rancher turned his head as the two riders approached. His big hand dropped quickly to a pistol on his hip, then eased away as he decided the visitors presented no threat.

Len raised his hand. "You know me, Mr. McCawley. Name's Len Tanner. I'm a Ranger."

McCawley's eyes lighted up. A pleasant grin spread across a face ruddy and deeply lined, seasoned by many years of sunshine and hard weather. Gray hair in need of a trimming curled over his ears. "Sure, I remember you." He shook Len's hand, then shifted his attention to Andy.

Len said, "This is Andy Pickard. The tired-lookin' bird draggin' his feet back yonder, that's Farley Brackett. Him and Andy are Rangers too."

McCawley looked at Farley's saddle, which Andy held in front of him. "A saddle by itself ain't worth much. How come your man ain't got a horse to go with it?"

Andy was content to let Len do the talking. Len explained that they had been set upon by outlaws. "There was one that called hisself Hatton. I'm pretty sure he was with a bunch of horse thieves that our scoutin' party jumped a while back on the river."

McCawley's eyes went grim. "Hatton. Yes, I know him. He runs with Jericho Jackson's coyote pack. I had him in my sights once, but my horse scotched and I missed."

"I heard somebody holler like he was hit, but I don't know if it was Hatton."

Andy rode up to the fence and looked over. The bronc had stopped pitching. It was circling the inside of the corral in a lope, its bay hide shining with sweat. A grinning Mexican cowboy held a hackamore rein high and tight. Three other cowboys stood inside the fence, watching, hollering for him to spur the bronc in the flanks. One was Mexican, two were white. Having heard so much about racial strife in the borderland, Andy was a little surprised at the camaraderie.

McCawley said, "That's Pedro Esquivel in the saddle. He's *puro jinete*, a natural bronc rider." He turned and saw Farley at last approaching the corral. "I suppose your man is hopin' for a horse?"

Andy said, "Yes, sir, but not that one."

McCawley smiled. "I've got several he can pick from. Nothin's too good for a Ranger."

Len said, "We'll see that Farley either pays you or brings your horse back."

"No need. It's a small thing against the debt I owe the Rangers. If the horse stayed here some thief would probably take it anyhow. We get hit by all kinds, Mexican and white."

Andy knew instinctively that he was going to like this man. The more he looked at him, the more he was reminded of Tom Blessing, solid as an oak, comfortable as a well-worn pair of handmade boots.

Farley trudged up to the corral, shoulders drooped in weariness. Sweat rolled down his face. Len introduced him to the rancher and said, "Mr. McCawley's goin' to fix it so you don't leave here afoot."

Farley always seemed to have trouble expressing gratitude. "I'll pay you when I can."

"I already told your friends that it's a gift."

Farley shook his head. "I'll pay you. I don't like leavin' debts behind me."

McCawley shrugged. "Whatever suits you." He looked at the western sky. "It'll be sundown directly. How about you-all comin' up to the big house with me? We'll have supper pretty soon."

What he called the big house was modest in size and far from new. The stones that constituted its walls were of varied sizes and hues. The building had been constructed for utility rather than for beauty. It reminded Andy of houses he had seen in San Antonio.

McCawley said, "I've promised my wife, Juana, a new house for years, but we're land-rich and cash-poor. If we could stop the raidin' and thievin', maybe I could lay aside enough money to build what she deserves."

The place might be old, but evidently McCawley's wife was making the best of it. A well-tended flower bed reached across the entire front, broken only by the doorway. It held roses, brilliant crepe myrtles, and several other colorful and eye-pleasing plants Andy could not identify.

The three Rangers removed their hats as they stepped over the threshold, past a heavy wooden door carved with cattle brands and horse figures. A heavyset, middle-aged Mexican woman spoke to them in Spanish, took their hats and placed them on a rack in the nearest corner. Andy assumed at first that she was McCawley's wife, then realized she was a servant.

McCawley said, "Juana's in the kitchen. You-all come on back." He led them into a room dominated by a large fireplace where the cooking was done. Andy remembered that Rusty Shannon had bought an iron stove for Alice. Maybe McCawley was waiting for that new house before he installed so modern a convenience. Through a window he saw an outdoor Mexican-style baking oven in an open patio.

The room smelled of fresh bread, reminding Andy that he had eaten nothing since breakfast but a strip of jerky.

A slender, black-haired woman was bent over a table, slicing strips from a hindquarter of beef. McCawley said, "Juana, we have company."

She turned. Andy saw that she was no longer young, but she still had smooth olive skin and large, expressive brown eyes so dark that they looked black. She smelled faintly of lilac perfume. Or maybe it was the flowers in pots scattered not only in the parlor but in the kitchen.

"My wife," McCawley said.

Andy felt awkward, not sure he should speak English to her. But he knew no Spanish. He bowed from the waist. "How do, ma'am? I'm pleased to make your acquaintance."

Len said, "Howdy, Miz McCawley."

Farley grunted something unintelligible.

She said, "Welcome to our home, gentlemen. If you would like to wash up, you will find water and soap and fresh towels in the patio. Supper will be ready in a little while."

McCawley said, "These men are Rangers."

She smiled, skin crinkling at the corners of her eyes. "Then you are doubly welcome. Our house is your house."

The Spanish-style patio sat in the center of the house. Flowers of many hues had survived summer's heat beneath the edge of the overhanging roof.

Len commented in a loud whisper, "She talks English purt near as good as me and you, don't she? I'll bet she was somethin' to look at when she was twenty years younger."

Andy said, "She still is." For a moment a vague image came into his mind's eye, a faint recollection of his mother. She had been killed by Indians when he was a small boy. He had no clear memory of her face, but sometimes he imagined he could hear her voice. He thought he heard an echo of it in Mrs. McCawley's. "She seems like a real pleasant woman."

Farley said, "But she's a Mexican."

Andy hoped McCawley had not overheard, but he had. The rancher said, "Yes, she's Mexican. There was a time when her family owned all this land." He made a sweeping motion with his hand. "Don Cipriano Chavez, her father, fought beside Sam Houston against Santa Anna. But that didn't help him when Americans decided they wanted his land. They killed him and Juana's first husband, and they tried to take away the property he had on this side of the river."

Len asked, "Then how come you to have this ranch?"

"After I married Juana, most of the land grabbers left this place alone. They knew I was a Texian, and I proved I would fight them. Some people called it a marriage of convenience, to save what her father left to her. But it was a lot more than that." McCawley looked back toward the door, his expression softening. "I was just a wanderer. I had no real aim in life except to survive. She gave me purpose. The land is in my name now, but it'll always be hers. And the children's."

Andy asked, "How many children?"

"I have a daughter and a stepson. Our daughter, Teresa, will be here in time for supper. She teaches the ranch children in a schoolhouse we built here."

"And the stepson?"

McCawley frowned. "Tony is away, with his uncle." His expression indicated that he did not want to dwell on this topic. Andy did not press him on it. He said, "You said bandits hit you pretty often."

"White renegades feel like this ranch is Mexican because of my wife. Mexican bandits feel like it's an American outfit because of me. We're fair game for all of them. Especially Jericho's bunch."

"Can't the Rangers stop him?"

Andy saw Len shake his head.

McCawley said, "Some of them don't want to. Jericho never lets himself get caught at anything he could go to jail for. He's like a general who runs an army from the rear and never goes out on the battlefield. And because he concentrates most of his attention on ranches in Mexico, a lot of the Rangers look the other way. They've never forgotten the Alamo and Goliad."

Andy said, "I thought McNelly stopped most of the bandits, white *and* Mexican."

"For a while. But he's gone."

Mrs. McCawley stepped out into the patio. "Teresa's here, and supper is ready."

McCawley motioned toward the door. "After you-all."

Andy waited for Len but not for Farley. His attention went immediately to a pretty girl with long black hair. McCawley introduced her as his daughter, but Andy had realized that the moment he saw her. She had the same dark brown eyes as her mother. They looked at Len and Andy, then dwelled for a moment on Farley before shyly cutting away. She waited for the men to sit. Farley did, but Andy and Len stood until she decided to seat herself. Andy was surprised at Len's sudden good manners.

Mrs. McCawley was last to the table. Light from the window revealed strands of gray hair that Andy had not noticed at first. She bowed her head and recited a prayer in Spanish. She crossed herself at the end of it, as did her daughter.

McCawley said, "Eat hearty. One thing we've got plenty of is beef. There ain't enough bandits to take it all."

Conversation lagged at first. Andy was too hungry to talk until he had emptied his plate. He was slower eating the second helping. He noticed that Teresa kept taking quick glances at Farley. He supposed she might be fascinated by his scar. It made him look a bit dangerous. Andy had been told that many women were drawn to men who looked dangerous.

To McCawley he said, "You've mentioned havin' trouble with Jericho. What about Guadalupe Chavez?"

A look passed between McCawley and his wife, and McCawley considered before he answered. "Some of Lupe's countrymen run off stock from time to time, but he leaves us alone."

Andy noticed that McCawley used the familiar form of the name, Lupe instead of Guadalupe.

Mrs. McCawley said, "My father was Cipriano Chavez. Lupe Chavez is my brother."

Andy stared at the girl. Her gaze was studiously fixed on her plate, though she had stopped eating. He thought she looked too innocent to be kin to a bandit whose name was known up and down the border. He remembered something the hole-in-the-wall cook in San Antonio had said, that very few innocent people lived on either side along the Rio Grande.

He remembered something else. McCawley had said his stepson was with an uncle. That uncle must be Guadalupe Chavez, Andy thought.

He had a feeling that whether or not his service on the river was pleasant, it should at least be almighty interesting.

After supper McCawley led the Rangers out onto the broad front porch, where he lighted a pipe while Len and Farley smoked cigarettes. He said, "You-all heard enough in there to raise a lot of questions. I feel like I owe you some answers."

Andy said, "You don't owe us nothin'."

"I want you to understand how things are. I was poor as a whip-poor-will when I first came to this part of the country. That was back in the fifties. Jobs were scarce. I served a little while with the Rangers, but half the time the state couldn't afford to pay me. Old Don Cipriano had land on both sides of the river, and he put me to work as a vaquero. By that time Americans were movin' into this part of the country in considerable numbers. They wanted land. They found that most of it was owned by Mexicans, so they started pushin' them out. The old man thought they'd leave him alone because he'd fought for Texas independence.

"Some of those Johnny-come-latelys hadn't fought for Texas, but they thought they had a right to whatever part of it they wanted. They took control of the courthouse and ruled that the old man's land grant wasn't legal anymore. When he fought back, they ambushed him and Juana's husband. Lupe hunted down the leaders and left them layin' dead as a skinned mule. Then he took a fast horse and went to Mexico."

Len said, "And after that you married Mrs. McCawley?"

"When a respectable time had passed. I was in love from the first time I saw her. Besides, I was grateful to the old man and wanted to save his land for her if I could. I had to face up to some hard men. I even had Jericho in my sights once. I ought to've killed him, but I let him go because there was a time when we used to be friends." McCawley looked regretful. "He's hated me ever since. I guess he figures he's beholden to me, and it grates on his soul to owe anybody."

Andy said, "At least you've given Lupe Chavez a reason to like you, marryin' his sister and savin' her land."

"No, Lupe doesn't like me. To him I'm just another gringo, and he hates them all. He'd be glad to come to my funeral if he didn't have to kill me himself. He leaves me alone on account of his sister."

Farley asked, "But you're American. Ain't it tough, standin' up against your own kind?"

"People like Jericho aren't my kind."

Andy thought he understood. "For a long time I thought of myself as Comanche. But there were some Comanches I had no use for." He explained to McCawley about the years he spent with the Indians.

McCawley said, "Then maybe you can understand the position I'm in. Sometimes I feel like I belong to both sides, and other times I don't belong to either one."

After dark the Rangers unrolled their blankets in the yard. Len lay on his back, looking up at the stars. He asked Andy, "What color would you say Teresa's eyes are?"

Andy said, "Brown. Dark brown."

"But they're not brown like anybody else's. They're different. They're . . ." He considered for a moment. "Damned if I can say just what color they are. But they're the prettiest eyes ever I seen."

Andy said, "Sounds to me like you're in love. But as I remember it, you've been in love lots of times before."

"Not like this."

Farley said, "She's Mexican."

Len's voice was defensive. "Half of her is white."

Farley gave the matter some thought. "I'll admit, I kind of liked lookin' at her."

After breakfast McCawley led them back out to the corrals. A dozen horses stirred in a single pen, warily watching the men who entered the gate. He said, "Take your pick, Farley."

Andy had always known that despite his faults Farley was a good judge of horses. He strode among them, making them walk, watching how they moved. He soon made his choice. "I like that stockin'-legged red." He had always shown a partiality to sorrels.

McCawley said, "You've got a good eye. He'll take you there and bring you back."

The Rangers saddled up. Andy shook McCawley's hand. "Please tell the womenfolks again how much we enjoyed their good cookin'."

"And you-all watch out that the next time you run into bandits, it's of your own choice and not theirs."

The Ranger camp was similar to one Andy had known on the San Saba River. It was a row of pyramid-shaped canvas tents and a set of crude but effective corrals built of tree branches tied together with rawhide. The tents could be moved on short notice as the need arose and the corrals quickly put together at the new site with whatever materials happened to be at hand.

A broad-shouldered man emerged from a tent and stood with big hands placed solidly on his hips as he watched the three riders approach. He gave Andy and Farley a critical study, then shifted his attention to Len. He said, "Look what the north wind just blowed in. I figured you liked San Antonio so much that you wasn't comin' back."

Andy could not be sure whether the man was joking or not. He sounded serious, even disappointed that Len *had* come back.

Len took no offense. "I left as quick as I could, Sergeant. Brought you two men."

"Prisoners?"

"No, Rangers."

The sergeant squinted, one eye almost closed. "It's hard to tell. They got an outlaw look about them."

This time Andy was seventy-five percent certain that the sergeant was not joking.

Len said, "Sergeant Donahue, this is Farley Brackett and Andy Pickard. They been transferred here from out in West Texas."

Donahue studied Farley with suspicious eyes. "Brackett? Seems to me like I've heard that name."

Len said, "He's got a considerable reputation up yonder where he comes from."

"Good or bad?"

"Depends on who you ask."

Farley gave Len a cautioning look.

Donahue nodded. "Well and good, but we judge men by what they do here and not by their reputation somewheres else." He spoke to Andy. "You appear too young to have much of a reputation as yet. Are you here lookin' to get one?"

"I'm just here to do my job, whatever that is."

"Well, boy, you better watch these border Meskins. They'll grind you up and make tamales out of you. I just got one rule when it comes to them. If you're in doubt, shoot." He punctuated that statement by jerking his head. "Come on, you'd best report to Lieutenant Buckalew and get on the pay roster. That don't guarantee you'll get any pay, of course." He did not look back. He had the air of a man who has no doubt that his order will be obeyed. The three Rangers followed him, leading their horses.

Entering the headquarters tent, the sergeant introduced Andy, Len, and Farley to the lieutenant. Buckalew welcomed the newcomers with more enthusiasm than Donahue had shown. He said, "You men are a welcome sight. As you will soon discover, this company is somewhat under strength. There's been a dearth of state appropriations. I see you brought your blankets. I hope you brought lanterns as well. You will have more use for them than for a bed."

Len put in, "They're good men, Lieutenant. You tell them what to do and they'll get it done or bust a gut."

The lieutenant smiled. "They don't have to go that far. All I'll ask is that they work thirty hours a day and eight days a week."

Len reported on their confrontation with Hatton and his bunch. The lieutenant listened intently, glancing at Andy and Farley from time to time for confirmation.

The sergeant demanded, "Are you sure they wasn't Meskins?"

Len said, "They was blue-eyed gringos, every one."

Andy had not noticed the color of their eyes, but he nodded agreement with Len. "They were white men."

The lieutenant said, "You think they were part of the Jericho outfit?"

Len said, "I can't say for sure that they belonged to Jericho, but I'm pretty certain they're part of a bunch we swapped shells with some time back. You was there that day, Lieutenant. Remember, they was tryin' to get away with some of Big Jim McCawley's horses."

"I remember. Think you killed anybody?" He asked the question hopefully.

"Somebody hollered like he was hurt."

"I wish we could shoot them all, Jericho's bunch and the Chavez gang too."

Sergeant Donahue interjected, "Or euchre them into shootin' one another without costin' us anything."

Once the formalities were taken care of, Len headed for the mess tent. A dark-faced Mexican cook used a wicked-looking butcher knife to cut a quarter of beef hanging from a tree branch. He dropped the slices one by one into a tin pan. Finishing, he chased the flies away and wrapped a blood-stained tarp around what remained.

Len said, "Pablo, we're hungry."

Pablo had a long, drooping mustache and a pitted face that showed he had survived a long-ago bout with smallpox. He looked westward to gauge the position of the afternoon sun. "Always, Tanner, you are hungry. You will wait like everybody."

Keeping an eye on the butcher knife, Len lifted the lid from a cold Dutch oven and found leftover flat-baked bread. He tore off a chunk. "Try it, Andy. It ain't bad when you get used to it. Mexicans don't know about bakin' biscuits."

Andy gave Pablo a questioning glance before accepting. He knew that getting crossways with the cook was about the worst mistake a man could make in camp. He saw that Pablo was awaiting his verdict on the bread. He took a bite and nodded. "Tastes mighty fine to me."

Pablo grinned. "Any time you are hungry, you come see me. We find you somethin' to eat." He shook the knife at Len. "You got enough. You wait for supper."

Len broke off another piece of bread. He said, "Another good thing about camp cooks is they've always got a givin' disposition."

The sergeant came looking for him. "Tanner, the lieutenant says we need to get the new men off to a quick start. In the mornin' you'll take Brackett and Pickard and patrol up the river. They need to get acquainted with the lay of the land."

Len asked, "We got to take Farley?"

"He needs to learn the country." Donahue frowned. "What's the matter? Don't you and Brackett get along?"

"I get along with Farley just fine. As long as I don't pay any attention to him."

Donahue grunted. "Just be damned sure you pay attention to *me*."

CHAPTER
FIVE

Burt Hatton came to a fork in the road and glanced with foreboding at a sign which stood on the left. It said: THIS IS JERICHO'S ROAD. TAKE THE OTHER.

He wished he could take the other and keep going. Facing Jericho was always unpleasant when things did not go as Jericho wanted. Hatton turned in the saddle and looked at the men who followed. One led a riderless horse. He said, "Don't none of you forget what we've agreed to say. We got jumped by Lupe Chavez's bandits. The kid got shot before we could reach cover."

He hoped Jericho would be mollified at least somewhat by the fact that they did not lose the cattle money.

Jesse Wilkes always looked as if he had sucked on a sour persimmon, and he had more complaints than a dissatisfied mother-in-law. He argued, "I still say you can't lie to Jericho. He reads faces like me and you read a paper."

"Let me do the tellin'. You-all just nod. Maybe he won't ask many questions. He'll be busy figurin' out some way to get even with Chavez."

"Whatever he comes up with, it'll be us that get sent to do the job. He don't do anything the law can grab him for."

Hatton's voice sharpened. "You've got nothin' to bellyache about. You get your share."

"Money's hard to spend in the graveyard."

"You can always leave if you're a mind to. Go back to East Texas. Maybe they've forgot about that murder charge they had out on you."

Wilkes seemed to shrivel. "They don't ever forget."

"And neither does Jericho, so keep your mouth shut and let me talk to him."

Wilkes went quiet, but his eyes still reflected his anxiety. Hatton had not chosen him as a member of the bunch; Jericho had done that. Hatton often found it hard to fathom Jericho's thinking. It was too bad Wilkes didn't catch that bullet instead of the kid. If it ever became necessary for Hatton to sacrifice somebody to save the rest, Wilkes would be his first pick.

Hatton's eyes kept searching the crooked wagon track ahead. Jericho kept a guard on this road in case some stranger came along who couldn't read the sign or chose not to heed it. The guard moved around often, so Hatton could never predict just where he would be. The regular guards knew Hatton and his riders, but sometimes Jericho put a new man on the job. Sooner or later he might assign somebody who was too slow on recognition and too fast on the trigger.

A horseman casually rode out from behind the leafy green cover of a mesquite tree and stopped in the center of the road, waiting. He had a rifle in a scabbard and a pistol on his hip but nothing in his hands except his bridle reins. A telescope hung from a leather string around his neck. He said, "Been watchin' you-all with the spyglass, so I knowed it was you. Been a long time on this trip, ain't you?"

Hatton wondered if the guard was being subtly critical. "It takes a while to drive a herd all the way up to San Antonio."

"Jericho's been gettin' a little nervous, wonderin' if maybe you-all decided to take the cattle money and look for greener slopes."

Curtly Hatton replied, "He knows me better than that." Should he ever succumb to that ambition he knew he had better travel a long way, for Jericho would send somebody to track him down. Jericho would not care how long it took. Forgiveness was alien to Jericho's nature. He never forgot, nor did he ever fully trust. Hatton harbored a suspicion that Jericho might have assigned one of the men riding with him to watch the rest. If there was such a spy in his midst—and Wilkes seemed the most likely candidate—Jericho would not be long in learning what really happened to his nephew.

Hatton tried to reason that he was wrong, that he was just being paranoid. A man was apt to get that way, working for Jericho.

The guard said, "I hope you'll tell him you saw me and that I was right on the job."

"Sure, I'll do that." But Hatton knew he would not. He had more important things on his mind than accommodating a lowly gun toter worried about staying on the payroll or hoping to be promoted to a more profitable position.

The nucleus of Jericho's headquarters had been built long ago in Spanish times when Indian raids were a periodic threat. The stone walls of the long main house were thick enough that no bullet would penetrate them. Narrow rifle ports allowed shooters inside to fire at an approaching enemy with minimum exposure. Beyond the outer walls that enclosed the major ranch buildings, the ground had been cleared of brush for two to three hundred yards to expose attackers as they came into good rifle range. The first brush removal had been done by the Spaniards. Jericho had maintained it for his own protection.

Most visitors were unwelcome, whether they were Mexican bandits or lawmen such as the Texas Rangers. He could stand them off if they ever came at him here in his stronghold. So far, none had tried. Even Guadalupe Chavez, who took pleasure in rustling the outfit's cattle, had never attempted to overrun the headquarters. Outlaws were welcome so long as they were white and were willing to operate under orders, though their stay was short unless they proved themselves.

Hatton hoped by riding directly to the barn that nobody would notice the riderless horse. That would give him time to present the money and put the boss in a good humor before delivering the bad news. But Jericho was at the barn, watching a hired hand shoe his favorite mount, a big gray capable of carrying a large rider. He watched the riders' approach, and his flinty gaze fastened hawklike on the lead horse.

Jericho stood more than six feet tall, broad-shouldered and muscular. Women were drawn to him and considered him handsome, but they didn't see him as Hatton saw him now, coiled tight and dangerous like the spring on a trigger. Hatton wondered if even Jericho's Missouri-raised wife had ever seen him that way.

Hatton tried to head off the question by dismounting and immediately unbuckling his saddlebags. "The cattle brought a little more than we expected, boss. Got the money right here. I think you'll be tickled."

The big man was not to be distracted. "Where's the boy?"

Hatton swallowed. "It's a long story."

"Give me the short of it. Where's he at?"

Hatton stammered. "It's like this . . . we run into some of them Chavez bandits . . ."

Jericho seemed to tower over Hatton, his eyes cutting like blades. "You tryin' to tell me you got him shot?"

"It was . . . there wasn't nothin' we could do. They was on us so fast . . . we tried to shield the boy . . . but he was hit before we could . . . honest to God."

"Damn you!" Jericho's hard fist struck so quickly that Hatton did not see it coming. He fell backward, dropping the saddlebags and startling his horse into breaking free. The animal ran off a little way and turned warily to watch. Hatton shook his head and raised one hand to his aching jaw. He felt as if a mule had kicked him.

Jericho stormed, "I told you I didn't want him goin'. I told you to leave him at home."

Hatton found it difficult to speak. He had bitten his tongue hard enough that he tasted blood. He wanted to explain that the boy had trailed after them and had not let himself be seen until the second day out on the trail. He had declared that he would continue to follow even if not given permission. A reluctant Hatton had told him, "All right, stay, but make a hand."

One of these days, he thought, his soft heart was going to get him killed.

Hatton had seen many times how mercurial Jericho's moods could be. He could laugh one moment and roar in anger the next. His initial rage slowly cooled, and he took on a look of genuine sorrow. "He was a good kid. Didn't listen to advice worth a damn, but he was my wife's only nephew. Like a son to her, he was."

"I'm sorry. I wish it had been me." That was an exaggeration. Hatton was glad it had not been him. He wished it might have been Wilkes. If not him, any of the others. He got up hesitantly, afraid he might get hit again.

Jericho said, "Why didn't you bring him home?"

"It was too far, and the weather was too warm. But we found a church-yard and buried him in hallowed ground. I just wisht we'd had a preacher to read over him."

"What kind of a church was it?"

"I don't know. Always thought one church was like another."

"They ain't. I'll bet you buried him in a Mexican graveyard."

Hatton could not look into Jericho's accusing eyes.

Jericho asked, "Can you find that church again? My wife'll want to go there and see where the boy is restin'. Maybe even bring him home. He don't belong amongst a bunch of Mexicans, especially seein' as it was Mexicans that killed him."

"Remember the village where that Ranger got killed a year or so back? He's buried in the same churchyard."

"Damned poor company for the boy. We'll move him."

Jericho looked toward the house, his visage grave. "I sure dread tellin' Thelma. This'll just about kill her."

His wife was the only person for whom Jericho showed any real affection. He catered to her as if he were deathly afraid she might leave him. Hatton could not understand how such a strong man could allow himself to be so much at the mercy of a woman, any woman. It was the only weakness he had ever seen Jericho display.

Hatton had seen very little of Thelma Jackson. Neither he nor any of the other hands were allowed in the big house except for Jericho's office, to which there was an outside door. To Hatton she was a shadowy figure, more mystery than reality. Jericho was strict about shielding her from the unpleasant aspects of his business and the men with whom he had to deal.

Jericho's grieving gave way to a dark and brooding anger that would simmer beneath the surface until some resolution was reached. "Chavez." He spoke the name as if it were a curse. "He'll pay if I have to follow him all the way into hell." His voice dropped so low that Hatton could barely hear it. "Has Chavez got any kids?"

Hatton felt a measure of relief. Maybe things were going to work out. "I never heard nobody say. I know he's got a woman or two. You know them Meskins . . . they shell out like rabbits. Stands to reason he's got kids."

"Even if he doesn't, that stepson of McCawley's is ridin' with him, ain't he?"

"So I hear."

"That boy is Lupe's nephew. You know what the Book says: an eye for an eye. A nephew for a nephew."

Hatton wondered where Jericho had learned about the Book. He had never seen him read from it.

Andy's horse lowered its head to drink from the Rio Grande. The other horses and the little pack mule followed suit. The river was less impressive than Andy had expected. It appeared no wider and certainly less deep than the Colorado or the Brazos. It had passed through a lot of desert country before it reached this point on its long journey to the Gulf.

Len said, "Depends on where you look at it from. Some places it gets wide and shallow. Mexicans can ride a burro across it. Other places it gets narrow and deep enough to drown an elephant. It's them wide, shallow places where we got to watch for signs of border jumpers. It's hard to hide tracks where a bunch of cattle or horses have crossed."

Andy asked, "If we find such a place, what're we supposed to do?"

"If they're headed south into Mexico, ain't much we can do. It's too late to help the owners. Their stock is gone unless they want to cross the border and try to take them back. The law don't allow us to do it for them. If the tracks head north, we may follow. Lieutenant Buckalew does. When Sergeant Donahue is in charge he usually tells us to leave well enough alone. He says Mexicans deserve to get robbed because they're all thieves anyway."

"Do we ever catch anybody?"

"Awful seldom."

"What could three of us do against a big bunch of bandits anyway?"

"Surround them. Give them to understand that we don't take kindly to their thievin' ways."

Ever since Andy had known him, Len had welcomed a vigorous scrap. He always maintained that an occasional good waking-up was healthful for the constitution, that it stirred the blood and loosened the bowels. As for Farley, he had been looking for a fight the first time Andy ever saw him, and he had not changed.

It could get dangerous, riding with two reckless companions.

Andy studied the land on the other side of the river. It looked no different from the north bank, though it was another nation. Over there he would be an alien and an enemy to most people. The thought was disquieting.

He had enjoyed the limestone hills and the fertile valleys of the San Saba River country. He found this region flatter and more desertlike, without the evident amenities he had found to the north. As someone had warned, most of the plants here had thorns, the animals had horns or tusks, and the insects had stingers. He remembered the homesickness that had afflicted him when he first fell back into the white man's world after his years with the Indians. Some of that emotion came over him now.

He supposed he might get used to it when he had been here awhile, but he was not sure he wanted to stay that long.

He expressed his feelings. Len said, "I felt the same way when they first sent me here, but you can find somethin' to like just about anyplace if you look for it. Else why would the devil live in hell?"

"I've never had a chance to ask him."

"You may run into him down here one of these days. He's got family by the name of Jericho and Chavez."

Farley growled, "This looks like the kind of country the devil would pick for his home. Anything you touch or that touches you is apt to bring blood."

Len said, "But there's pretty places too. I've been plumb out to where the Rio Grande pours into the Gulf. They got palm trees out there, just like in the Bible. I kept thinkin' I ought to see a camel someplace, but I didn't."

They came upon a small field irrigated by a ditch extending from the river. Up the slope stood a small picket house. A few spotted goats nibbled at brush and watched the Rangers approach. When the horsemen came close they clattered away, then turned to look again.

Len said, "These folks keep chickens. Sometimes when I come by here I buy a few eggs. Sure makes fat bacon taste better. Even beef jerky."

Andy saw a family working in a garden. At the Rangers' approach the woman shouted at two girls. All three retreated into the house. Andy heard a wooden bar dropped into place to secure the door. Len said, "They've had experience with gringos before."

The man stood at the brush fence, waiting to meet the riders alone. He bowed slightly and said a few Spanish words that Andy took to be a greeting, though his dark eyes conveyed a different message. He could not hide his dislike and his dread.

Len said, "Most of these people can tell a Ranger as far as they can see him. They don't like us and they don't trust us, but they'll accept our money." He spoke to the man. *"Huevos."*

"Tiene dinero?"

Len said, "He wants to see the money first."

Andy dug into his pocket and came up with two bits. "Reckon that's enough?"

"Two bits'll buy you the hen."

The man went into the house, returning shortly with several eggs in a small, crude basket woven of green willow stems. Len asked him something Andy did not understand. The man shook his head and replied with a shrug of his shoulders.

Len thanked him. "Says he ain't seen anybody cross the river in either direction except people who live close by. No bandits."

Farley said, "He wouldn't tell us anyway."

"If it's gringo bandits they'll tell you. If it's Mexicans they won't. Ask most white people along the river and they'll do the same except the opposite."

Riding away, Andy looked back. He saw the woman hastily hanging clothing on a line.

Len observed, "Them clothes ain't wet. That's a signal that Rangers are about. Anybody waitin' on the other side knows he'd best keep his feet dry."

Farley said, "I'll go back and yank them clothes down."

"No, folks behave better when they know we're around. The lieutenant had rather keep them out of mischief in the first place than to chase them afterwards."

At sunset they stopped to make camp. Andy removed the pack from the mule while Len scooped out a shallow hole in the dirt and filled it with dry leaves and small sticks. He lighted it with a match, blowing into the first weak, flickering flames to make them lick into the dry wood. He said, "We'll fix our supper, then we'll build this fire up to where they can see it. There won't be no cattle run across here tonight."

Andy pondered. "What's to stop them from goin' up the river to the next shallow place?"

"Us. This fire'll be here, but we'll be there. With another fire."

Farley argued, "Three of us can't be everywhere up and down the whole Rio Grande."

"No, but we can keep them wonderin' where we'll turn up next. It'll be as aggravatin' as a tick in the ear."

Farley dragged up more dry brush to keep the fire going. "I'd rather aggravate them with a bullet in the gut."

The fire went out during the night. Next morning after their meager breakfast Andy heard cattle bawling and determined that the sound came from the other side. Farley said, "Looks like somebody is fixin' to cross over."

Len agreed. "Let's ride to the bank of the river and show ourselves. It'll give them somethin' to fret about."

Len took a position at the edge of the water. Andy and Farley followed his lead. Andy asked, "How'll they know we're Rangers?"

"They won't know for sure, but they'll have to think hard about takin' the chance."

"Looks like they've got us considerable outnumbered."

"But they know they'd be easy targets in the water. Most of them would never make it all the way across if we set our minds to stoppin' them."

Andy could see the men milling about, several gathering as if in conference.

After a while he heard distant shots.

Len grinned. "Looks like they've got theirselves in a fix. Somebody's caught up with them."

The gunfire increased. Andy watched several riders plunge into the shallow water, making for the north bank. "They're leavin' the cattle behind."

"Wouldn't you?" Len slapped his leg and laughed. "Look at them run. If they could fly, they'd do it."

Andy saw a man fall from the saddle just as his horse entered the river. Another made it partway across before he slid into the water and began floundering. A companion grabbed him and pulled him against his horse's shoulder.

Farley drew his pistol. "They'll blame us for this."

Len drew his rifle from its scabbard and laid it across his lap. "Ain't it a shame." He appeared to welcome the prospect of a confrontation.

Andy cautioned, "Have you forgotten how to count?"

"They'll be stringin' out of the river one and two at a time. They're tired and pretty well boogered. Us three can take them all on."

Andy had his doubts but decided to put his faith in Len's prior experience and Farley's fighting nature. The Rangers met the riders as they straggled onto the bank, their horses dripping. Len pointed his rifle in their direction and ordered each in turn to shuck his weapons. Two seemed prepared to argue, but Farley cut them short: "Don't make us finish what them Mexicans started."

Andy had thought some of these might be men who had attacked him and Len and Farley several nights ago, but he recognized none of them.

Len said, "Well, looks like you boys bit off a bigger chunk than you could chew."

One growled, "All we done was buy a herd of cattle across the river. Bunch of Mexican bandits jumped us and took them over. You seen it yourselves, didn't you?"

Farley was openly skeptical. "How about showin' us a bill of sale?"

"Mexicans don't put much store in such as that. Most of them can't read or write."

"I'll bet they can read brands."

The raider complained, "We lost a man over on the other side, and we've got another with a slug in him."

Andy turned his attention southward. "Looks like those Mexicans are comin' across to finish the job."

The man's eyes widened as he saw riders moving into the river. "Let us have our guns back."

Len shook his head. "No, the best thing you-all can do is see if them horses of yours are faster than what the Mexicans are ridin'." He waved the muzzle of the rifle, pointing it northward.

The man protested, "Them guns cost us good money."

"If you don't hightail it you ain't goin' to have no use for money. And tell Jericho the Rangers said howdy."

The raiders' reluctance to leave without weapons was quickly surpassed by their fear of the angry-looking Mexicans coming across the river. Andy watched the men move away in a lope. He said, "We ought to've arrested them and taken them back to camp."

Len said, "We'd've lost half of them between here and there. Anyway, whatever they done on the other side, that's Mexico's business. They didn't break no Texas law. Wasn't nothin' we could charge them for."

Andy asked, "How do you know they're Jericho's men?"

"I'm just guessin'. Jericho runs most of the contraband business along this stretch of the river, just like Lupe Chavez runs it on the other side." Len dismounted and began picking up the weapons. "Let's wrap these in a blanket and tie them on the pack mule. Them Mexicans have got guns enough already."

Andy unrolled his blanket on the ground. "Do you think you can bluff them like you bluffed the others?"

"What makes you think I was bluffin'?"

Andy counted ten horsemen coming across the river. Several more had remained with the cattle. Len squinted, studying them. "I don't see Lupe Chavez, but you can lay odds that these are some of his men." He remounted and again brandished his rifle. Andy and Farley followed his example. As the riders came up to face them Len said, "You boys are on the wrong side of the river."

A lean young man pushed forward, a challenge in his dark eyes and the set of his shoulders. "There was a time when the river didn't mean nothin'. South side, north side, it was all part of Mexico." He was dressed like a

Mexican vaquero, but he spoke with little or no Mexican accent that Andy could discern.

Len said, "There's been two wars fought over that. If you ain't careful you'll start another." He softened. "I'm bettin'" you'd be Big Jim McCawley's boy Tony. I heard you was ridin' with Lupe Chavez. Where's he at?"

The young man ignored the question. "I'm Antonio Villarreal. I'm Lupe Chavez's nephew, but I'm not McCawley's boy. Who are you to be blockin' the way?"

"We're Rangers." Len pointed to the handmade badge on his shirt.

The young man's face twisted. "Damned *rinches*."

Andy had learned that *rinches* was a term the Mexicans applied to the Rangers, and not in a complimentary manner.

Villarreal said, "If you'll give us the road we'll take care of your job for you. We'll fix them so they'll never come again."

"Like you said, that's *our* job. You did yours when you saved your cattle."

"I know you Rangers won't do anything about those thieves. If *we* don't, they'll be back."

"Catch them on your side of the river and you can feel free to shoot them all."

The young man's voice bespoke contempt. "Maybe someday we'll catch you *rinches* on the other side."

Andy studied the face. He thought he saw some resemblance to Tony's mother and half sister. He said, "We met your folks."

That seemed to pique Tony's interest in a negative way. "I guess they told you all about me?"

"They said mighty little, just enough to give us a notion you jumped the traces."

"My stepfather is a gringo."

"Everybody says he is a good man."

"He is still a gringo. When I was a boy I had to accept him as a father. Now I am a man, and he is not my father anymore."

Andy did not know whether to feel sorry for the young rebel or to be angry at him. He said, "I'd give anything I own to have a father."

"You can have mine. And next time you side with Jericho's thieves we'll run over you like a freight train."

Farley spoke up. "You'll find the Rangers harder to bring down than that man you killed over there."

"He was a bandit. Anyway, he was just wounded. He's not dead yet."

Andy heard two shots echo from across the river. He winced. "I guess he is now."

Tony said coldly, "One less gringo bandit. The world is better off." He jerked his head as a signal and rode back into the river. The other men followed him.

Andy said, "He doesn't know how lucky he is. At least he's *got* a father. Stepfather, anyway."

Len said, "Too bad, but that's how it is down here. Most people choose sides accordin' to whether they're light-skinned or dark. That boy has set his eggs down on the Mexican side."

Andy pointed northward. The raiders had faded into the distance, swallowed up by the mesquite and other brush. "We could follow them and find out where they came from."

Len said, "They came from Jericho's little kingdom. Ain't much about about that."

Andy was intrigued. "Kingdom?"

"He runs it like he was a king. Nothin' happens in there without his say-so. Nobody pokes his nose onto Jericho's ranch unless he says it's all right."

"Not even the Rangers?"

"We go now and again, but he sees to it that we don't find anything or anybody we're lookin' for. If an outlaw needs a hidin' place, Jericho gives him one. They go out and do their devilment, then come back and give him a cut. He's built him a bank with stolen money, but he's managed to keep his hands clean. Even if the law was to bring him to trial, you couldn't gather up twelve men with guts enough to convict him."

Andy declared, "I'd like to see what he looks like. Have you ever met him?"

"Yep. And I'd pay money to buy back my introduction."

"What about that man they killed? Are we just goin' to go off and leave him over there?"

Farley said, "His friends did," and started north, following the raiders.

CHAPTER
SIX

ollowing the trail was easy. The raiders made no effort to hide it. Though crossing with Mexican cattle was illegal unless properly cleared through customs, they had returned without contraband. They had little reason to fear the law once they were north of the Rio Grande. Andy carried the blanket into which the men's weapons had been piled. He had to tie the ends together and lash the bundle onto the mule. It was an unwieldy load.

He said, "These guns may not ride this way very long."

Farley grabbed a handful of the blanket and tugged to get a sense of the weight. "I don't see where we owe it to them renegades to deliver their weaponry back to them. We ought to've thrown it all in the river."

Len said, "Jericho's got lawyers up in San Antonio that raise hell every time we even wink in his direction. There's a little store at the crossroads. We'll leave the guns there."

Andy asked, "You think they'll come back and get them?"

"I would if the guns was mine. A man appreciates things when he has to pay out his own good money for them."

They came to a plain-looking building, a nondescript mix of stone and picket construction. Len said, "That's the store. The owner sells stuff to Jericho's men and buys their stolen goods. He'll treat us friendly enough, but don't believe his smile. It's all show."

Farley said, "If he deals with Jericho's thieves, why don't we arrest him?"

"A jury that won't convict Jericho won't convict his friends either. I'd about as soon stand in front of a Mexican firin' squad as face Jericho's lawyers."

Andy grinned at a sudden thought. "If we can't put those border jumpers in jail, we can at least aggravate them a little."

Len brightened with curiosity. "How?"

"Let's stop in the shade of that tree yonder." Andy dismounted and lifted the heavy bundle from the mule. He laid it in the shade and untied the corners that held it together. The rifles and pistols slipped and slid, clattering against one another. "Let's take these guns apart. Puttin' them back together will give those boys somethin' to do besides play cards and drink whiskey."

Len was always enthusiastic over a chance for harmless mischief. "I'd love to stay and listen to them cuss a blue streak."

Farley was not smiling. "I still wish we'd dumped the whole shebang in the river and let them swim for it."

They removed barrels and cylinders from the pistols and field-stripped the rifles. It took a while, but Len never stopped talking, laughing as he pictured their reaction. When they were done Andy mixed the pieces as if he were shuffling dominoes.

Len said, "I'd give a pretty penny to watch them sort out all this mess. By the time they put everything back together, they'll be wantin' to use them on us."

Farley said, "Let them come."

Andy retied the bundle and attached it to his saddle horn. It still weighed the same but seemed less of a burden now. A middle-aged man came to the door, a smudged apron tied around his dough belly. He recognized Len. "Howdy, Ranger. Somethin' you-all need?"

"A little smokin' tobacco for me and Farley. Maybe a little *pan dulce* for the young'un here if you got any."

"Tobacco I got. He'll have to find the sweetenin' someplace else. I don't cater to the Mexican trade. Let them people in here and they'll be pilferin' stuff when I ain't watchin'."

Andy said, "Speakin' of pilferin', did you see a bunch of riders pass by a little while ago?"

The tracks indicated that the men had stopped here, but the storekeeper claimed no knowledge of them. "Ain't seen hardly anybody all day."

"They were tryin' to get away with some cattle on the other side of the river, but the owners caught up with them. They came back to this side in a considerable hurry."

"You don't say!"

Len said, "Anyhow, we've got some stuff that belongs to them. Reckon you can keep it till they come back?"

"Sure enough."

Andy brought the blanket inside and spilled its contents on the floor. A couple of cylinders rolled across the room. One disappeared behind some heavy-looking boxes. The storekeeper started to object but choked it off.

Andy said, "I hope you've got an empty box to put all this stuff in. I'll be needin' my blanket." He folded it and laid it across his arm.

The storekeeper grunted. "You won't want to be here when they see you've took their guns apart."

Cheerfully Len said, "They're welcome to come callin' at their convenience."

Farley said, "Tell them my name's Farley Brackett, and they can come see me if they ain't satisfied. I ain't had a decent fight since I left Austin."

The storekeeper gave Farley a quizzical look. "Brackett? Seems to me like I've heard that name."

"Lots of people have. Be sure you give it to them."

The three rode on. After a time Andy inquired, "Where does Jericho's land start?"

Len said, "We're already on it. He's got a six-shooter claim, at least. He says he bought out a bunch of Mexican owners. Ran them off is more like it, or he got a court to throw out the old grants like he tried to do with the Chavez family. Then he bought the land dirt cheap off of the county tax office."

The tracks led them eventually to a point where the trail forked. Andy saw a sign: THIS IS JERICHO'S ROAD. TAKE THE OTHER. "You ever been up this road?"

Len nodded. "Me and some other Rangers was trailin' stock headin' north. Jericho came out to meet us. Claimed the cattle belonged to him, and his men had just got them back from Lupe Chavez's ranch across the river. Even showed us some cattle with his brand on them. They wasn't the same ones we'd been followin', but we couldn't prove he'd pulled a switch on us. Sergeant Donahue wasn't anxious about it anyway. He said the more cattle that get stole out of Mexico, the better."

"In other words, just knowin' ain't enough. The only thing that counts is what you can prove."

Farley grumbled, "You get a little smarter every day, Badger Boy. But you still got a long ways to go."

Andy saw a dozen or so cattle grazing nearby. He rode over to look at them, moving slowly so they would not spook and run. "I see at least three different brands."

Len watched the cattle drift away. "And all Mexican. Most of Jericho's cattle are natural swimmers. Show them a river and they'll jump right in."

The horse tracks split at the fork. Some riders had gone on northward. Others had swung to the west, following the trail marked as Jericho's.

Len said, "I've already seen Jericho's headquarters. The outside of it, anyway. If we stay with the other bunch we might find a new hangout. Someday that could be a handy thing to know."

Farley said, "I'll follow that bunch west. I'd like to know what Jericho's place looks like."

Len cautioned, "You're liable to learn more than you intended to. But I don't reckon it's my place to try and tell you what to do."

"Wouldn't matter none if you did." Farley rode off.

Len hollered after him, "Chances are we won't find one another again. We'll meet back at the camp." In a quieter voice he said, "And that'll be plenty soon enough."

If Farley attempted an answer, Andy did not hear it.

Andy and Len followed the northbound tracks until eventually the trail split again. Len said, "Ain't but one thing to do. You take the right hand and I'll take the left. When we've seen whatever there is to see, we'll backtrack and meet right here."

Andy felt concern. "If you bump into somebody, you won't try to tackle them by yourself, will you?"

Len shook his head. "You know me. I ain't one to go lookin' for a fight."

"I don't remember you ever duckin' out on one."

"I'm just goin' to see what I can learn. I ain't got my fightin' britches on."

Andy knew Len's propensity for getting himself into trouble. He had that much in common with Farley. However, Farley met his challenges with a growl and Len met them with a laugh. Andy conceded that Len had a point. Sooner or later Jericho was likely to make a mistake, and it behooved the Rangers to know as much as possible about his ranch and what went on there.

He told Len, "You take the pack mule." The mule had more or less attached itself to Len's horse. It would not so readily follow Andy's.

Len said, "You won't have anything to eat."

"We'll be back together before time for that."

The sun bore heavily on Andy's shoulders. The back of his shirt and the underarms were soaked in sweat. Ahead he saw a windmill tower. That meant water. He was pleased that the tracks he followed veered in that direction.

Windmills were relatively new on Texas ranges. Railroads were first to try the idea, then farmers and ranchers had quickly adopted them to allow use of neglected lands that lacked living water in the form of springs, creeks, and rivers. Andy had seen a few windmills, but they remained strange and exotic to him. He was fascinated by the notion of a mechanical device that could harness the wind to pump water from unseen storage deep in the ground. He wondered how much longer people could keep coming up with such ingenious inventions. Surely they must be nearing their limit.

This mill had a tower built of lumber that still looked new except that it was already darkly stained by lubricating oil spilled from its gears. The cypress fan looked to be twelve or fourteen feet across. The sucker rod clanked as it rode up and down, striking the walls of the steel tube that enveloped it.

Water poured into a surface tank hollowed out of the level ground. A few cattle turned and warily trotted away as Andy approached. He imagined the pleasant taste of cool water gushing from the end of the outlet pipe.

He failed for a moment to recognize an angry buzzing sound. By the time he realized he had disturbed a nest of wasps, they were attacking him and the horse. He tried swatting them away but seemed to make them angrier. The black horse squealed and kicked, then broke into pitching. Already off balance from fighting the wasps, Andy lasted only two jumps before he was jolted out of the saddle. Instinctively he tried to break the fall by extending his arm. He hit the ground hard. The arm twisted beneath him.

His left boot was caught in the stirrup. He felt himself jerked violently, then dragged as the horse pitched, squealed, and broke wind. He bounced on the rough ground. He tried to shield his face, but one arm felt numb and useless. His foot pulled free of the boot. The dragging stopped. The horse continued to run and pitch without him. A few more wasps stung Andy before they began returning to the nest. They swarmed around it noisily as if awaiting another target.

Finding himself lying awkwardly on the arm that had taken the first impact, he rolled onto his back. The arm began to ache as feeling returned. He examined it gingerly, fearing it might be broken. He satisfied himself that it was not, though it was badly scratched and bruised. The sleeve hung in strips, as did the rest of his shirt.

His face and hands burned in more than a dozen places where the wasps had stung. He felt his cheeks beginning to puff. His eyes pinched. He tried to push to his feet, but his whole body hurt. He managed to sit up and take stock of his situation as the swelling almost closed his eyes.

It had not occurred to him that the windmill and open tank provided a hospitable breeding ground for wasps in a region where water was scarce.

He began feeling nauseated as the venom took hold. Vision blurring, he was unable to see his horse. He did not know how far the animal might have run. He crawled on hands and knees to where his boot had fallen from the stirrup. Painfully he pulled it on. Thirst began to plague him, but he did not want to try for the windmill again. He could still hear the angry wasps.

He wished he and Len had not split up. He had no idea how far Len might go in following those other tracks. When he returned to the rendezvous point Len was likely to wait awhile before deciding to follow Andy and see what had delayed him. By then it would probably be dark, and he would be unable to see tracks until daylight.

No telling how long I'll be here by myself, he thought.

His canteen was empty, and Len had the pack mule with all their provisions. At the moment Andy was too ill to eat, but sooner or later he would be hungry as well as thirsty.

Damn wasps, he thought. They say the Lord had a purpose for everything He made, but I don't see any reason for wasps.

He crawled into the thin shade of a mesquite tree and wished it were as solid as an oak.

Dusk came. He knew he would be by himself at least until morning. His blanket had been tied to his saddle, and the saddle was still on the horse. He resigned himself to sleeping on the bare ground, hungry and thirsty.

As darkness closed in, he heard something moving about. He paid little attention at first, for cattle had been coming up for water. Most seemed not to notice him. Those that saw or smelled him kept an uneasy distance. His blurry eyes made out the shape of a horse, his horse. It looked strange until he realized that the saddle had turned under its belly. He pushed himself to his feet, his legs aching. He spoke in a soft voice as he moved slowly and painfully toward the horse.

"Whoa, son. Gentle now. Whoa."

Grasping for the reins, he found one had broken off just below the bits. Holding the other, he patted the horse on the neck and rubbed his hand down its shoulder, then felt for the girth's buckle. The horse almost jerked away from him as the saddle dropped between its feet.

"Easy, boy. Ain't nothin' goin' to hurt you now."

Andy figured the wasps had become inactive for the night. Deciding to take a chance, he led the horse to the farthest end of the surface tank. There he let it drink. Hearing no buzzing, he took an even larger chance and walked to the end of the outlet pipe. Cupping his hand beneath the flow, he drank until his stomach ached.

He disliked tying the horse up short, but his rope had been lost. He had nothing to lengthen the one remaining rein. He tied it to a mesquite limb. He was disappointed to find that his blanket was gone. It had probably snagged on a bush and pulled loose.

He had already made up his mind he would be sleeping on the bare ground, so he was no worse off than before.

Andy spent a long and fitful night trying in vain to find a comfortable position. The itching was so intense that he could not help scratching the bites. That made them burn worse than before. He knew there were ointments that might help, but they had just as well be on the far side of the moon. He tried to remember if the Comanches had any remedy. Nothing came to mind.

Thirst told him he was running a slight fever. He drank his fill before dawn set the wasps to stirring again. He could see better than the evening before, but he still felt as if he were peering through a slit in a wall.

"Damn you, Len, hurry up."

Andy figured it must be around noon when Len finally appeared, following tracks from the south. He reined up and stared at Andy as if he were an apparition. He declared, "You look like wild horses have stomped on you."

Andy warned, "Don't get too close to that windmill. There's a jillion wasps in there, and every one of them is mad."

"You let a few little old wasps do all that to you?"

"When they hit you, you'll think they're the size of a cow." He told how his horse had thrown him and run away, losing his blanket and rope.

Len said, "I'll see if I can find them."

He came back in a while, carrying both items. The blanket was dirty and torn. He said, "Bet you ain't had nothin' to eat. I'll fix you some dinner."

Andy had begun to feel strong hunger pangs, a sign of improvement. Len roasted bacon on a stick. Andy eagerly bit in without waiting for it to cool.

Len said, "I'm fixin' to do somethin' about that wasps' nest." He pulled several handfuls of dry grass and wrapped them around the end of a thin dead branch from a mesquite. He dipped the grass into the fire, then carried the blazing stick to the windmill tower. He shoved it under the nest. A few wasps came buzzing out, but most were consumed by the fire.

Andy heard Len exclaim, "Uh-oh!" The flames licked upward along the tower's wooden leg, burning the oil spilled from the top. Len stepped back, swatting at a couple of wasps that had focused upon him as a target. "Looks like I've just played hell."

Andy said, "Throw some water on it."

"Too late for that, even if I had a bucket."

The flames intensified. Len backed away from the heat. "I think me and you had better mosey along. Jericho is apt to be a little put out about his windmill."

He saddled Andy's horse and shook out the dusty blanket, folded it, and tied it behind the cantle. Andy felt stiff. Swinging up onto the horse reawakened all of yesterday's soreness. The two horses and the mule danced uneasily, fearing the fire.

Len kicked sand over the small blaze on which he had fixed Andy's meager breakfast. "If they saw this," he said, "they'd know somebody camped here and set fire to the windmill."

"How else would it have burned?"

"Lightnin'."

Squinty-eyed, Andy looked up but saw no clouds. "Yeah, they'll sure be fooled, all right."

Riding south, Andy asked, "Did you find anything?"

"A few miles from where I left you, the bunch I followed stopped at an old Mexican ranch house. Jericho probably uses it as a line camp. Remind me to put it on the map when we get back to the company. What did you find?"

"A jillion wasps." Andy looked back. The fire had climbed up to the tower's platform. Once it burned all the wooden support and the cypress, the metal parts would crash to the ground. He said, "I'll bet that mill cost a hundred dollars."

"Jericho can afford it. His crew'll steal more than that between dinner and supper."

They had traveled a couple of miles when Len said, "Four riders comin' our way." Andy's vision had not improved enough for him to see them. Len said, "It's too late to hide. Let's just play innocent."

Len always had an innocent look about him, even when he was guiltiest.

As the horsemen came near enough for Andy to see them, he noted that a large man rode half a length ahead of the others. He said, "I'll bet that's Jericho."

"Yep, you're about to meet the big stud his own self. Don't act like you give a damn. He's built himself a little empire by makin' people afraid of him."

"From what I've heard, they've got a right to be afraid."

"Me and you can't afford to be. Show him the feather and he'll ride plumb over you."

Jericho Jackson looked to be more than six feet tall and stocky enough to weigh considerably over two hundred pounds. He was not fat, simply large. He rode a gray horse bigger than those of the three cowboys beside him. He had a reddish complexion and hair and beard of a strong rust color, not unlike Rusty Shannon's. His dark brown eyes fastened first on Andy, then on Len with a startling intensity. He recognized Len, though he probably could not have called him by name.

"Ranger, ain't you strayed a long ways from where you belong?"

"Rangers go anywhere they want to."

"Anyplace but my ranch. You lookin' for somebody?"

"Maybe. Who you got?" Len's voice had an insolent tone, one Andy was sure he had to work at. It was not his normal style. It would have been Farley's.

Andy recognized two of the riders. They had been with the men the Mexicans had chased back across the river. One leaned to Jericho and said something Andy could not hear.

Jericho said, "Seems like you've already made the acquaintance of my boys. They say you took somethin' that belongs to them."

Len said, "The guns? If they'll stop at that little gyp joint of a store they can get their property back."

Jericho switched his attention again to Andy. "You look like you been run through a coffee grinder, boy. You a Ranger too?"

"Private Andy Pickard. My horse drug me a ways."

"Probably because you took him where you and him wasn't supposed to be." Jericho leaned forward, his manner challenging. "You Rangers are always pokin' into my business, comin' on my land without so much as a by-your-leave. But when you're needed you ain't nowhere around."

Len said, "When did you ever need us?"

"Mexican outlaws murdered my wife's nephew. Never gave him a chance. It was one time we could've used your help, and you wasn't there."

Len and Andy looked at each other. Andy said, "That's the first we've heard about it."

"It won't be the last. I'm sendin' a protest to Austin."

Len said sarcastically, "They'll be tickled to hear from you."

"He was an orphan boy. My poor wife set a lot of store by him. I'll see that Lupe Chavez pays for what they done. When I do, you Rangers had better stay out of my way."

Andy said, "We can't, not if you break the law."

"It's a damned poor law that says you can't kill a Mexican when he needs it. As far as I'm concerned it's open season the year around on every saddle-colored son of a bitch this side of the river."

Jericho's red mustache seemed to bristle. Studying him, Andy was reminded of a book he had read about pirates. He seemed to remember that the character's name was Red Beard, or something like that. The longer Andy looked at Jericho, the larger he seemed to get. He doubted that he and Len could handle him in a fistfight even if the three cowboys stayed out of it.

Jericho's voice deepened. "You men are trespassin'. By rights I could shoot both of you."

Andy said, "Those who try to keep the Rangers away have usually got somethin' they don't want us to see."

Jericho glowered. "You-all are startin' to aggravate me. People with any sense are careful not to get my blood stirred up. Next time, stay off of Jericho's road." He looked past the two Rangers. "We been watchin' some smoke yonder. Know anything about it?"

Len turned to see. "We noticed it too. Grass fire, more than likely. You ought to caution your boys not to be careless with their smokin'. They could burn up the whole country."

Rusty had once said Len could talk the devil into joining the church.

Jericho pointed eastward. His manner was stern. "That's the shortest way off of my land."

Len pointed south. His manner was stubborn. "We're headed back to the river." He started, and Andy followed.

Jericho shouted after them, but Len did not acknowledge him. Softly he told Andy, "Act like you don't even hear him. He's a land grabber and a thief, but he's too much of a man to shoot us in the back."

They rode about a mile. Len abruptly turned to the east. Andy said, "Thought we were goin' to the river."

"That was just to show Jericho we wasn't afraid of him. It's a long way back to Ranger camp. You've got some bad cuts, and them wasp bites need attention. I'm takin' you over to the McCawleys'. Like Jericho said, you look like you been run through a coffee grinder."

CHAPTER
SEVEN

Andy was uneasy about baring his upper body to the McCawley women, but they brooked no argument. He had bathed in a stock tank to wash off the dirt, grass, and other debris left by the dragging. He had also rinsed his clothing. His shirt and the upper part of his long underwear had been shredded beyond repair, but they still covered enough to meet the requirements of modesty.

The older woman dug out several thorns with a needle, then rubbed him with alcohol that set him afire. He ground his teeth and tried not to groan.

She said, "The more it burns, the more good it does. You lost some hide."

Andy feared the alcohol was burning away whatever skin the dragging had left him. He drew his arms in tightly against his ribs and squeezed his eyes shut until the worst had passed.

Juana McCawley said, "You have more thorns, but they are in too deep. They'll have to fester out in their own good time."

He was glad she did not intend to poke around anymore with the needle. He said, "I'm obliged to you, ma'am."

The daughter, Teresa, rubbed a soothing salve over the wasp stings. He enjoyed the careful touch of her fingers, a contrast to her mother's less than gentle treatment with the needle and disinfectant.

Big Jim McCawley fetched him a shirt and a suit of underwear. "Our Tony left these behind. They'll fit you better than mine would."

"Many thanks."

McCawley said, "Len tells me you talked to Jericho."

"Mostly it was him that did the talkin'."

"That's his way. He's not interested in what anybody else says. He'll either scare you to death or make you mad enough to chew up a horseshoe and spit it at him."

Andy could understand that Jericho's physical size would intimidate many, but he doubted that McCawley had any fear of him. McCawley was about as large as Jericho, and like Jericho he was all muscle. Either man looked capable of wrestling a bull to a standstill. If they ever came to blows they might tear up enough ground to plant a garden.

From what he had heard of Lupe Chavez, Andy thought he must be a large man too. He had to be if he lived up to the stories.

Neither Andy nor Len mentioned seeing McCawley's stepson with the Mexicans who had crossed the river in hot pursuit of Jericho's raiders. They had decided it might upset his mother and sister to know he was putting himself in harm's way.

Teresa asked Andy, "Where is the other Ranger, the one who was with you last time?"

"Farley Brackett? He broke off from us to follow a different set of tracks."

Self-consciously she said, "He seemed rather nice."

Andy blinked. "You sure you haven't got him mixed up with somebody else?" *Nice* was not a term he had ever considered in relation to Farley.

She said, "He's not exactly handsome, but he's not ugly either, even with that scar on his face. How did he get it?"

"He brought it home from the war. Somebody told me it came from a Yankee saber. I never asked him." Farley would probably have turned on him like a biting dog and told him to mind his own business.

She said, "I think he is a lonely man."

For good reason, Andy thought. Farley never let anybody get close to him.

She asked, "Has he ever been married?"

"I doubt he ever considered it."

She suggested, "Maybe he never met the right woman. Or maybe he doesn't like women." She phrased that more like a question than a statement.

Andy knew Farley liked women, though on his own terms. He had bought and paid for commercial affection in San Antonio, but this was not something Teresa would want to hear. Andy said, "He's just been too busy bein' a Ranger."

"Most Rangers do not remain Rangers forever, do they?"

Sooner or later Farley was sure to provoke the wrath of some officer and find himself dismissed from the force. But she would not want to hear that either. "Who knows what any of us are liable to do?"

She said, "I've never seen a really *old* Ranger."

That would be easy to explain, though he did not. Most eventually became too stove up, or they wearied of endless horseback travel and wanted to settle in one place. Or, as occasionally happened, they died in the line of duty.

He said, "I'll tell him you asked about him."

She reddened. "Oh no. Please don't do that." She left her chair and hurried from the room.

Her mother watched her go, then said, "It is not seemly for a young lady to express interest in a man."

Embarrassed, Andy said, "I was just tryin' to help. Ain't had much experience in matters such as this." Perhaps a good woman might smooth Farley's rough edges and make him easier to get along with. The Lord knew he needed help of some kind. On the other hand, any woman who would give Farley more than a minute's consideration was probably not in her right mind.

Mrs. McCawley smiled. "Some things you must leave alone. They will work themselves out if the Lord wishes them to."

Because it was late in the day, the McCawleys had little difficulty in persuading Andy and Len to spend the night before they started back to camp. Andy looked forward to a couple of kitchen-cooked meals. And he found it easy to look at Teresa McCawley, though the memory of Farley's sister Bethel intruded, giving him a disquieting sense of guilt.

After supper the three men sat on the front porch of the rock house. McCawley smoked a pipe in silence. Silence was one thing Len could not long abide. He asked, "How come you and Jericho to get crossways in the first place?"

McCawley took the pipe from his mouth and stared at its glowing bowl. "There was a time long before the big war that me and him rode together. We didn't have nothin'. We were both ambitious, wantin' to make somethin' of ourselves. But Jericho had a different notion of how to go about it.

He saw people pushin' Mexicans off of their land and decided he could too. It was easy to say it was a patriotic thing to do since there'd been two wars with Mexico.

"I'd gone to work for Don Cipriano Chavez. He treated me good, and I took a likin' to him. Jericho tried to run him off and grab his property like he'd done with some others, but the old man fought back. So Jericho had him killed. Juana's first husband too. He hounded the son, Lupe, till Lupe took refuge in Mexico. That's when I married Juana. Puttin' an American name on the land kept Jericho from pullin' his shenanigans at the courthouse. He's been a thorn in my side ever since. And me in his."

Andy said, "Looks like the law ought to do somethin'."

McCawley nodded. "It does. For the most part it looks away, or it sides with Jericho and them that think like him. It doesn't pay to lose a war, and the Mexicans have lost two."

Andy asked, "What about the Mexicans that were livin' here in Texas? Did they take a hand in the wars?"

"Maybe not directly, but most of them sympathized with Mexico. A lot of Americans claim that justifies takin' away their property. Many Mexicans still claim that everything south of the Nueces River belongs to Mexico. That makes Americans and their property fair game. People like Lupe Chavez figure they're only takin' back what belonged to them in the first place. Both sides believe they're in the right. Those of us who try to sit on the fence take fire from both directions."

Andy asked, "Do you see any answer?"

"Maybe someday, but wars last a long time. They're not over just because the cannons quit. They're over when nobody is left who remembers what the trouble was all about."

The bullet sounded like an angry wasp as it passed between Andy and Len. The crack of a rifle shot followed in an instant. By instinct Andy ducked low on his horse's left side, opposite the source of the fire. Len shouted and set his mount into a hard run toward a little puff of white smoke rising behind a bush. Andy spurred hard to catch up with him.

They caught a Mexican trying desperately to reload a rifle. Andy leaped from the saddle and knocked him off his feet. The shooter fought, struggling to bring the rifle into position. Its bolt was jammed open. Andy wrested the weapon from his hands and hurled it away.

Mouth half full of dirt, the man shouted an angry string of muffled words. The only one Andy knew was *gringo*.

Len said, "Turn him over." He pulled the Mexican's hands together in front of him and snapped a pair of handcuffs on his wrists. The man saw the silver peso badge on Len's shirt and launched into another spasm of cursing. Andy caught the word *rinches*.

He asked, "Do you know what he's talkin' about?"

Len said, "Us, mainly. And he's upset over bein' a poor shot."

"What'll we do with him?"

"Take him to camp. The lieutenant'll have some questions for him."

"Reckon he's part of Lupe Chavez's bunch?"

"Could be. But there's oodles and gobs of bandits that don't belong to Lupe, just like there's a lot of Texas border jumpers that don't ride for Jericho. He may be one of those that got pushed off of their land. Killin' gringos helps them sleep better."

Andy looked around with some apprehension. "He might not be by himself."

Len said, "It's kind of like with rattlesnakes. Where there's one you'll sometimes find more."

Andy said, "I'll make a quick circle and find out." He rode out a little way while Len shouted at him to be careful. He saw no sign that anyone had been with the shooter, though he found the man's horse tied a short distance away. He led it back.

He motioned for the prisoner to mount. He cut a leather string from the man's saddle and tied the handcuffs to the big flat Mexican saddle horn. Anger in the prisoner's eyes began giving way to fear. He said something Andy did not understand.

Len said, "He's askin' what we're fixin' to do to him. I can't talk enough Mexican to give him an answer. About all I can say is '¿Quién sabe?' Who knows?"

Andy added that to his vocabulary. By now he had learned at least half a dozen usable words, not counting a few curses picked up here and there.

Riding alongside the Mexican, Andy was aware of the man's growing anxiety. His own initial resentment ebbed. He even began to feel a twinge of sympathy. "I believe he thinks we're goin' to shoot him."

Len said, "We ought to, but it's probably against some law or other. There's so many laws nowadays that a man can't do nothin', hardly."

By the time they approached the row of tents that made up the camp, the prisoner's head was bowed, his eyes closed. He mumbled to himself. Andy suspected he was saying a prayer.

They rode to the headquarters tent. The camp looked to be almost deserted except for the cook and a couple of Rangers standing at the mess tent. Sergeant Donahue emerged, gravely eyeing the prisoner. He asked, "What you got here?"

Len said, "He taken a shot at us. I swear I felt that bullet tickle the hairs growin' out of my ear."

Andy said, "We thought the lieutenant would have some questions for him."

"The lieutenant's been called to Austin. I'm in charge." Donahue motioned toward the headquarters tent. "Bring your prisoner in. I'll question him." The two Rangers had left the kitchen and ambled up to see what was going on. One of them was Mexican. The sergeant said, "Tanner, Pickard, you-all go on down to the mess and have Pablo fix you somethin' to eat. Me and Manuel will talk to your prisoner."

Manuel was the only Mexican Ranger in camp and one of only two or three Andy had seen anywhere. Manuel untied the leather string that bound the prisoner's handcuffs to the horn, then spoke sharply in Spanish. The man dismounted, casting a fearful look at the sergeant.

Donahue said, "I ain't real good at Mexican lingo. Manuel knows how to question a bandit."

It struck Andy that Manuel should have compassion because he and the prisoner were of the same blood, but Donahue dispelled that idea. He said, "Manuel hates bandits even worse than the rest of us do. He lost his family to them."

Andy turned that over in his mind. "Maybe he's *too* hostile."

"They may lie to him once, but they don't do it a second time. You-all go on like I said, and get you somethin' to eat. We'll take care of this, me and Manuel."

Manuel grasped the prisoner's shoulder and roughly pushed him into the tent. Donahue followed, closing the flap's opening behind him. Andy heard a clatter, then a solid thump, like a chair falling over and someone hitting the ground.

Len motioned. "It's none of our business from here on. Let's go eat."

"Sounds like they're knockin' him around."

"They're not treatin' him as rough as what he had in mind for us. He meant to see us both dead, remember?"

"I hate to see anybody mishandled."

"If you was to get caught by Mexican bandits, you figure they'd treat you like a pet? You know what your Comanche brothers did to people they captured. Like for instance your—"

Len broke off. Andy knew what he had been about to say—*like your mother.* The unexpected thought left him feeling cold.

He said, "I guess you're right. We'd better go eat." But he wondered if he would be able to.

Pablo saw them coming and lifted a blackened Dutch oven onto a bed of glowing coals. He dropped a generous quantity of lard in to melt as the bottom heated. "Pretty soon I fix you a good supper. You hungry, Andy?" He ignored Len.

Andy had lost his appetite, but it gradually returned as he smelled the aroma and listened to steaks sizzling in the boiling grease. Beef was plentiful. The Rangers had no compunctions about slaughtering cattle that strayed across the river from Mexico, even if sometimes they had to encourage the move.

Beans cooked for the noon meal had been reheated for supper and kept hot for anybody riding in late like Andy and Len. Andy sipped steaming coffee and tried to concentrate on the coming meal rather than what might be going on in the headquarters tent.

Len told Pablo about their trip, including their meeting with Jericho. He did not mention burning the windmill.

Pablo's mustache drooped more than usual. "That Jericho is *un mal hombre.* Very bad fellow."

Len shook his head. "I think me and Andy could've whipped him. But he ain't on the fugitive list, so there wasn't no use."

Andy pictured Jericho in his mind. "I'm not all that sure we could've done it. He looked as big as a horse."

Len said, "The big ones take longer but fall harder."

Pablo announced that the steaks were done. *"Comida."* Andy and Len each got tin plates and dipped the meat from the boiling lard. They added a generous helping of beans and broke off chunks of cold flat bread left from the company's supper. Pablo pointed to a can of molasses. "Got plenty lick. Good with the bread."

Len said, "We'll finish up with that for *dessert.*" He lit into his supper with a vengeance. "The Ranger service feeds good when you're in camp. The hell of it is that we're gone most of the time and have to fix our own. Old Pablo's hard to beat." He looked up at Pablo. "Where'd you learn to cook so good?"

Pablo wiped his dark hands on a cloth apron that once had been a sugar sack. "I was one time a soldier. The officer, he gives me a pot and says I must cook. I know nothing of such things, but when an officer says do, you do."

Len asked, "When was that?"

"In the war against the *americanos*. Once I fight you. Now I cook your supper. Pretty good joke."

"As long as you don't put rat poison in the beans."

"I would not do that for such a good boy as Andy. But you?" Pablo shrugged as if in some doubt.

Andy carried his plate and utensils to a washtub and dropped them in. He had just poured a fresh cup of coffee when he heard a shout from the direction of the headquarters tent. Turning, he saw the Mexican prisoner running. The interrogator Manuel calmly stepped outside, leveled a rifle, and fired. The prisoner staggered and pitched forward on his face.

Andy spilled most of his coffee. Len simply stared, his mouth open.

Pablo did not appear surprised. He said, "He was dead already when he came. When Manuel finishes with the talking, it is left only to bury them. It is an old Mexican way, the *ley de fuga*."

Andy had heard the expression. It referred to shooting a prisoner trying to escape.

Len broke his silence. "Lieutenant Buckalew don't hold with such as that."

Andy said, "But he's not here. I'm bettin' they pushed the prisoner out of the tent and told him to run."

Len frowned. "Whatever you think, you'd best keep it to yourself. Donahue can make life tougher than a boot for them that ask questions. Anyway, you didn't see the prisoner start. You just saw him fall."

"Call it a Comanche hunch."

"It ain't somethin' you could swear to in front of a jury."

Andy had seen death before, but it still shook him to look it in the face, especially when it was sudden and unexpected. He walked up as Donahue knelt beside the dead man and examined a blood-rimmed hole in the back of his shirt.

Donahue said, "Caught him right between the shoulder blades. Damned if I'd want Manuel aimin' at me."

Andy felt a troublesome responsibility inasmuch as he and Len had brought the prisoner in. "Did you-all have to kill him?"

Donahue was surprised at being challenged. "Look, Private, he was runnin' away. He was just another Mexican bandit. There's plenty of them left, so it's a small loss to the world." He started to leave but turned for a few more words. "Since you're so concerned, you can take a shovel and dig a hole for him. You and Tanner." He pointed. "He ain't the first. You'll find a bandit graveyard yonderway about a hundred yards."

"Anybody goin' to read over him?"

"Hell no. It was the devil that sent him. The Lord doesn't want him."

Andy wondered how so many people seemed to know what the Lord wanted.

Len walked up in time to hear most of it. When Donahue was gone he said, "Looks like you talked us into a diggin' job."

Andy knew who would do most of the work.

Mounds indicated half a dozen unmarked graves. Whoever was buried there had simply vanished from the earth. Andy guessed that friends and kin still wondered what had become of them. He and Len took turns with the shovel, though Len's turns were shorter than Andy's. When the hole was dug they buried the blanket-wrapped prisoner without witnesses and without ceremony. Andy doubted that a minister or priest had ever visited this burying place or given it the sanction of a church.

He said, "Wonder what his name was?"

Len wiped his dirty hands on his trousers. "You probably couldn't spell it even if you had a board to carve it on."

They returned to the mess tent for coffee. Manuel stood at the edge of camp, smoking a cigarette and staring off into the gloom. Pablo saw Andy looking in Manuel's direction. He said, "He has much hate in his heart."

"The sergeant said bandits killed his family."

"His papa had a farm. Not big, you know, just a little farm, but the Spanish king gave it to his great-papa long time ago. Banditos come. They shoot Manuel, they kill his papa, his mama, they carry his sister across the river. For a long time he looks, but never does he find her. So he kills bandits, and maybe sometimes he kills some who are not bandits. Many over there have tried to kill him, but some say he can never die. They say he is a son of the devil. The devil himself maybe."

Andy shivered. "Damned if he doesn't look like it."

Just before time for bed, Donahue came to the tent Andy shared with Len and others. He said, "Your horses need a day of rest. You and Tanner will stay around and stand horse guard tomorrow."

Andy noted that Donahue's concern was for the horses rather than the men. Guarding the company horses was usually easy duty but boresome. Most Rangers came to dread it. Andy had done his share on the San Saba.

Donahue added, "You can start tonight, Pickard. You'll stand the after-midnight watch."

"Yes, sir." Andy knew he would get little sleep before going on duty and none the rest of the night. He was paying for having questioned the sergeant.

Donahue gave Andy a long study, one eye almost closed. "I hear you was raised by the Indians."

Andy felt belligerence on the sergeant's part. "Till I was maybe eleven or twelve years old."

"I got no more use for Indians than I have for Meskins. I hope you ain't still got a bunch of Indian ideas in your head."

Defensively Andy said, "I don't scalp people, if that's what you mean. And I don't shoot them in the back."

"You better walk a real straight line, Pickard. I'll be watchin' you."

As Donahue walked away, Len said, "Talkin' too much can lead to trouble. You'd better learn to keep quiet, like me."

A raid was more likely here near the border than it had been on the San Saba, so Andy fought the sleepiness that kept tugging at his eyelids after he went on duty. Out west it might not have mattered if he gave in to it so long as an officer did not catch him. Here it could lead to deadly consequences if either Texan or Mexican raiders decided to make a try for the Rangers' remuda. A man could get killed before he came fully awake. The ugly image of the dead prisoner kept rising before him.

He pictured what Rusty Shannon's reaction might have been had he seen what Andy had witnessed.

A vague figure moved in the night. A man walked among the horses, bridling one and saddling it. Andy challenged him. "Who are you?"

A voice said, "Manuel."

"What're you doin' out here afoot in the middle of the night?"

"I have business across the river. Sergeant Donahue, he knows."

Andy thought on what Pablo had told him. He shivered. "You already killed one today. Isn't that enough?"

"It will be enough when they are all dead." Manuel rode toward the river, disappearing like a malevolent ghost into the darkness.

Andy began to wonder if he had made a mistake in agreeing to come to this part of the country. Rangers—some, anyway—had a different view of duty here than they had to the north and the west. In retrospect, Rusty's farm looked better than he had realized when he left there.

CHAPTER
EIGHT

Farley Brackett rode in about noon, hunched in weariness. Andy was standing horse guard. Farley reined in beside him and declared with a tone of accusation, "You-all didn't wait for me."

"We figured you'd come on back to camp."

"I might've needed you if I'd had a little bad luck."

Andy suspected Farley had not returned to the appointed place either. This was his way of grabbing the offensive and keeping it. Andy refused to take the bait. "We figured you're man enough to take care of yourself."

"I am. Many a state policeman found that out to his regret." Farley frowned. "I wish you and Tanner hadn't rode off with the pack mule. I ain't et in two days. Damn a country where you can't stir up at least a squirrel or a prairie chicken. I came near shootin' a javelina hog."

A little spell of hunger might teach Farley humility, Andy thought. Farley had ridden away in his own direction without even mentioning that he might want the pack mule or at least some of what it carried. Andy saw no gain in pointing this out. Farley would come up with an answer.

Farley gave Andy's face closer attention. "You been in a fight?"

"Wasps. I lost." Most of the swelling had gone down. Andy had thought it might no longer be noticeable, but Farley didn't miss much.

Farley snorted. "The country's full of bandits, and you waste time doin' battle with wasps."

Andy asked, "Where you been all this time?"

"I followed them cowboys plumb to Jericho's headquarters. That place is like a fort. The Spaniards that built it must've been awful scared of Indians."

"Len and me, we saw Jericho himself."

"So did I. He came in just before dark. He was damned mad about somethin'. I couldn't sneak up close enough to hear what his trouble was."

It might have been about a burned windmill. Andy chose not to tell about that. Farley would harp on it for a week. He said, "We got so close we could've counted his red whiskers if we'd wanted to."

Gruffly Farley said, "I got close enough to see what I went for, and I didn't let a few little wasps booger me away, neither." He shook his head. "Wasps! What are the Rangers comin' to?"

Andy flirted with the idea of putting a nest of wasps in Farley's bed, but he saw no way to do it without being stung again. He realized the notion was childish. Even so, it was pleasant to contemplate.

Farley turned toward camp. "I've been about to start gnawin' on my saddle strings. Has that Mexican Pablo called dinner yet?"

"Not that I've noticed." At mealtime the cook hammered on an iron rod bent into the shape of a triangle. The sound could reach for a mile.

Andy wanted to hear more about Jericho's headquarters, but asking questions would subject him to continued unpleasantness from Farley. He saw that a couple of the company horses had grazed far enough to be almost out of his sight. He trotted his mount around them, gently hazing them back toward the main remuda. The horses not in use were loosely herded during the day to allow them to graze freely but not to stray far enough that they could be picked off by an opportunistic thief. Every remuda seemed to have a few bunch quitters that preferred to be off by themselves. They had that in common with Farley Brackett.

Andy heard the dinner triangle, but he had to wait until someone came to relieve him. After a time Len showed up. He said, "Better go eat before Farley takes it all. Acts like it's the first meal he ever had."

Len could put away a prodigious amount of grub himself.

Most of the men had finished eating by the time Andy got there. Pablo stood at an iron stove. Its black smoke pipe extended out through a slit in the side of the tent. A young Mexican boy washed tin plates, cups, and utensils in a tub of soapy water. The boy was a prisoner being treated as a trusty. He had stolen a sack of sugar out of a Mexican store. Most border Rangers paid little attention to crimes by Mexicans against other Mexicans so long as they stopped short of murder. Even minor crimes against whites, by contrast, were treated as serious because it was thought they might lead to something worse if they were tolerated.

Sergeant Donahue's motto was, "Let them steal a chicken one day and they'll steal a cow the next."

Farley had finally eaten his fill. He sat facing Andy and cradled a cup of coffee in his hands. Sergeant Donahue was questioning him. "You say you saw Jericho's men brandin' cattle?"

"A steer herd, it was. Looked to me like they was puttin' a trail brand on them. Probably gettin' ready to drive them north to the railroad. I wasn't close enough to read the original brands."

Donahue nodded. "That connects with the report Manuel brought back from Mexico. Our spies told him Jericho is puttin' together a big trail herd, and the Chavez gang plans to capture it. They want to get even for that last sashay Jericho's men made across the river."

It was not a private's place to ask unnecessary questions. Andy assumed the sergeant intended for the Rangers to set up an unpleasant reception for Chavez's men.

Len was never bashful. If he wanted to know, he asked. "What's the chance we'll get Lupe Chavez hisself?"

Donahue seemed a little annoyed at Len's impertinence. Privates were supposed to listen, not speak. "Not good. We've never been able to catch him on this side of the river, just like we've never caught Jericho at anything that would stick against him."

Cutting off a chance for more questions, the sergeant strode toward the headquarters tent. He returned in a short time and said, "I'm takin' eight men with me on a special detail. We start in half an hour." He pointed to Andy and Len first, then nodded at Farley.

Len said, "I thought me and Andy was goin' to rest a little."

"You can rest when you get old. If you live that long. Now roll your blankets, then saddle up. I don't abide laggards."

Sergeant Donahue dropped the men off singly at intervals. He said, "You'll each patrol your section along the river. Watch for Meskin raiders, but don't challenge them. When they cross, get word to the men on either side of you. That word will work its way up to me. We'll all join together and quietly follow them to Jericho's herd."

Len asked, "Hadn't we ought to stop them before they get there?"

The sergeant cut him a hard look. "Damn it, Tanner, you ask more questions than an old maid schoolteacher. Can't you just follow orders?"

"Always did. I like to know the reasons, is all."

"We're not doin' this to save Jericho's cattle. We're doin' it to cripple Lupe Chavez. I figure Jericho's men will whittle them Meskins down a right smart before we have to step in and pick up the leavin's."

"Jericho's apt to lose some men."

"If so, we can mark them off of the wanted list."

Donahue dropped Andy a few miles after he dropped Len. He left Andy with an admonition: "You'll ride downriver far enough to meet Tanner, then you'll turn and go back upriver till you meet Brackett. The bandits'll likely cross over in the dark, so hit the saddle as soon as it's light enough to see tracks. And don't let Tanner drag you into any long-winded conversations, or you're liable to miss somethin'."

Donahue had said no bandits were likely to cross the river in daylight, so Andy saw no harm in resting awhile. The sergeant might not approve, but what he did not know would not hurt him. Andy had raw bacon and jerked beef as well as some of Pablo's leftover biscuits. He ate a little, then stretched out beneath a mesquite.

He awakened to see the sun going down. He chewed a little more tough jerky while he took his time saddling his horse. Watching the riverbank for tracks, he moved downriver in an easy trot. Eventually he met Len coming toward him. Len dismounted and stretched his long legs.

Andy said, "I see that no outlaws have shot you yet."

"It's so quiet I could hear the sun bump as it went down. I think Donahue saved the most likely stretch of the river for himself."

"Are you spoilin' for a fight?"

"Jericho's men may not leave enough of them to give us a decent scrap."

Andy said, "It doesn't matter who gets them so long as they're got. It'll be justice if some of Jericho's bunch are got too. There's no saints on either side."

Riding back the way he had come, Andy could see little by the scant light of a quarter moon. He wished for bright moonlight but knew this kind of night would be a border jumper's preference. The darker the better.

He heard water splash and stopped abruptly. He made out the vague form of a man riding a burro across a wide, shallow stretch of the river. He drew his rifle but soon slipped it back into its scabbard. One man on a burro hardly constituted a raiding party. He could imagine many reasons for the crossing. The rider could be going to or from a sweetheart. He could have family on both sides. Or maybe he was just stealing a burro. Whatever his mission, it was not likely to be of concern to the Rangers. But seeing the lone man reminded Andy how easy it was to pass between the two nations. The boundary was too flimsy to be a challenge to anyone determined to cross over.

He rested again. Just before daybreak he heard a horse walking toward him from the west. He stepped quickly to where he had his mount staked and put his hand over its nose to prevent it from nickering. Not until the rider was almost upon him did he see clearly enough to recognize Farley from the way he sat in the saddle.

Andy said, "You're awful early. See anything?"

Farley exclaimed, "Damn. I didn't even see *you*. Don't you know you could get shot, surprisin' a man that way?"

"Shootin' me would've pleasured you, wouldn't it?" The question was not entirely in jest.

"It'd cause me a lot of aggravation, talkin' to all them lawyers. I'd rather just ignore you." Farley rolled and lighted a cigarette. "I take it you ain't seen anything either."

"Nothin' but a Mexican on a burro awhile after dark. Probably visitin' a woman."

"A good time of night for it. You ever had a sweetheart, Badger Boy?"

"Always been too busy."

"For a long while I've known you're sweet on my little sister. She could do better for herself." Farley turned his horse around and started back upriver. He shouted over his shoulder, "Go on back to sleep."

In early daylight Andy built a small fire. He impaled a chunk of fat bacon on the end of a stick and propped it securely over the low flames. He fetched river water in a tin can and added ground coffee. That he set atop the coals. It was a poor substitute for Pablo's cooking, but it would sustain him. He doubted that the sergeant had anything better. Few Rangers ran to fat.

The sergeant showed up about the middle of the afternoon, checking each man's position. He said gruffly, "I hope you ain't been asleep and let somethin' go by you."

Andy's answer was curt. "I've had my eyes open."

"Some people have their eyes open and still don't see past their shadow."

"Nothin' has crossed over except a couple of buzzards and a man on a burro."

Donahue gave him a hard study. "Maybe. I suppose if that loudmouth Tanner had found anything he'd be up here by now to tell you about it."

"I expect so."

"Tonight'll be another dark one. Get an early start in the mornin'. If you find that they crossed in your sector, fetch Tanner, then send word up the line to me. Each man will relay the message and then ride down to where you're waitin'."

"You don't want me and Len to start followin' the tracks?"

"No. Tanner'd be faunchin' around wantin' to fight. He'd likely spring the trap too early."

Andy's impatience got the best of him. He declared, "I can see that you don't think me and Tanner can do the job. Why did you bring us with you?"

"I can't always have my pick. I make do with what I've got. Sometimes it ain't much."

Andy's face warmed. Watching the sergeant ride away, he began thinking of comments he should have made in rebuttal. Such ideas usually came too late.

He rode downriver toward Len's solitary camp. Len was at the halfway point, waiting. He lay in the meager shade of a mesquite. Andy told him what the sergeant had said. "He said me and you aren't supposed to follow the tracks, just wait till everybody else gets there. He doesn't want us gettin' in a fight till everybody's ready."

Len said, "He doesn't know how good a fight we can put up by ourselves, me and you. We're as good as any he's got."

Andy voiced his doubt. "Donahue doesn't seem to like me much. I don't know why. He makes me wonder if I ought to be a Ranger at all."

"Leavin' the Rangers wouldn't get you away from people like him. You'll run into his kind wherever you go."

"I guess. I remember a Comanche warrior—" Andy stopped himself before he spoke the name. He had never gotten past his Indian-taught reticence about using names of the deceased, at least those who were Comanche. For some reason that he did not understand, he had no such reservation in regard to white names.

Len asked, "You hungry?"

"I fixed a little breakfast, such as it was."

"I happened onto a fat young kid goat runnin' loose. He looked lost, so I declared him the property of the Rangers. Us two Rangers, anyway."

"Some people would call that stealin'."

"Looked like a stray to me. I didn't see nobody claimin' to own him. He probably swam across the river."

Andy doubted that. He also doubted that Len had made much of a search for the owner. But the goat had already been butchered. It hung by its hind legs from a tree limb. He said, "Whoever it belonged to, he'd probably call it a shameful waste to let that meat spoil."

After helping Len put away a good part of the kid, Andy made his way back to his own camp, then beyond to the point where he expected to meet Farley. Farley showed up after a time. He had a jug tied to the horn of his saddle. Andy asked him about it.

Farley said, "I found a Mexican comin' across the river with a mule load of this contraband. Ain't been no whiskey tax paid on it."

"Did you put him under arrest?"

"No, a workin' man has got to make a livin' whichever way he can. I just fined him one jug and let him go on his way."

"You're not a judge."

"He rode off happy as a pig in the sunshine. It was like I done him a favor by not shootin' him."

"Some favor. You swindled him out of that jug."

"He was breakin' the law. I had to do somethin'."

Trying to understand Farley's way of thinking could give Andy a headache. He said, "I'd best turn back. Sergeant says they're liable to come across tonight."

"See that you don't go to sleep in the saddle." Farley took a corncob stopper from the jug and tilted it over his arm without offering any to Andy.

Guadalupe Chavez took a long drink of pulque and wiped his bushy black mustache with the back of his hand. He passed the bottle to his nephew. He said, "It would be my wish that you not go tonight, nephew. I had a bad dream about this."

Tony Villarreal tipped the bottle upward and grimaced at the burn of the raw liquor. "I had a dream too, but it was a good one. I welcome a chance to poke Jericho in the eye. Besides, you are sending some good men with me. Why do you worry about me but not about them?"

"They are not of my flesh and blood. You are."

Tony stood nearly a head taller than his uncle. Despite his fierce reputation, Lupe Chavez was small in stature, not much over five feet tall but still as wiry as a half-grown boy. Some of his facial features resembled

Tony's mother's, though the harsh demands of an outlaw life made him look older than his actual years. His hair remained black as a crow's wing despite the furrows time and hardship had carved into his dark brown skin.

Tony said, "If God smiles on us I will bring you Jericho's ears."

"Be careful that you do not lose your own. Jericho may have the *rinches* on his side. They are gringos, but they can be terrible when their blood is hot."

"Their blood spills as easily as other men's."

"How would you know? How many have you killed?"

"None so far, but I look forward to the chance."

"You know that your stepfather is a friend to the *rinches*."

Tony's face darkened. "I do not acknowledge any stepfather."

"But he is your mother's husband, and half of your sister's blood is his. It is gringo blood."

"Hers, not mine. If it were mine I would be willing to see half of it spilled to rid me of the taint."

"That is easy to say when you have not bled. But I have, and I found no satisfaction in it. I am satisfied only when I see the gringo bleed. He has caused all the problems of our people. He has murdered our kin and stolen our land and raised his own flag over it. I wish we could call down a pestilence that would cause him and all his kind to die in slow agony. I thought we had it once, in the time of the rebel Cheno Cortina."

"Uncle, perhaps you are the new Cortina."

"I could not polish his boots, nor those of my father. But I do what I can."

"And it is my pleasure to help you."

Chavez smiled. "You are a good boy. We may yet see a day when not a gringo remains south of the Nueces. This country belongs to the Mexicans. We will take it back when the time is right. But not you, not today."

Tony did not answer. No matter what Tío Lupe said, he was going.

As the evening light faded, Jericho Jackson held his fidgeting horse outside the corral and watched more than a dozen men saddling mounts. All were armed with a pistol and either a rifle or a shotgun.

Burt Hatton looked up at him, for Jericho stood taller and broader in the shoulders than any man who worked for him. Hatton asked, "You think Chavez will come tonight?"

"Tonight, tomorrow night, it don't matter. Gonzales told me they'll be comin', and we'll be layin' for them when they do."

Gonzales was a spy, useful because he would do anything for money. He played the role of a harmless, poverty-stricken *curandero*, a faith healer, and moved freely wherever information was to be gathered. His information was always for sale.

"I never trusted that sneakin' Meskin. He may be lyin' to you."

"He likes my money too much to take that chance. Besides, he knows I'd gut him like a catfish."

Hatton worried, "What about the boys holdin' the herd? They could get killed."

Jericho shrugged. "I've told them to hightail it at the first sign of trouble. Let the raiders have the cattle. They won't take them very far. Just when they think they're gettin' away, we'll hit them like a hailstorm. There'll be dead Mexicans layin' all over the place."

"And maybe a few of our boys."

"They're bein' paid to take the chance. If any of them lets some Mexican kill them it'll be because they wasn't good enough to earn their wages."

Hatton suspected that Jericho considered him as expendable as any of the other men. He resented that, though his loyalty to Jericho was equally shallow. It was simply bought and paid for like any other kind of merchandise. He said, "Maybe we'll be lucky and get Lupe Chavez."

Jericho shook his head. "He's too cagey to go out on these forays himself. He sends other people to take the risks. But maybe we'll catch his nephew, Jim McCawley's stepson. If we do, I don't want anybody killin' him. That's a pleasure I want to save for myself."

Jericho's grim eyes made Hatton feel cold. Jericho wanted to take revenge on Tony Villarreal for the death of his wife's nephew. Nobody had dared tell him the truth, that the boy had died in an abortive raid on a travelers' camp and not at the hands of Chavez's men. Hellfire and brimstone would rain down if Jericho ever found out.

Hatton made up his mind that he would not stay to see that day. At the first good opportunity he would gather up whatever belonged to him, and whatever else he could easily lay his hands on, then leave this part of the country. He could not escape into Mexico, for too many people knew him there and had knives sharpened and waiting for his throat. The word *California* had a nice ring to it.

Jericho said, "Let's try not to let none of them get away. I'd like to take a dozen dead Mexicans and pile them up for everybody to see, like McNelly done that time in Brownsville. Them people have got no respect for us, but they do respect force. I don't see why the Lord don't send down a plague to kill every one of them north of the Rio Grande, and maybe south for a hundred miles."

"They must've done somethin' awful to make you hate them so bad."

"They made me an orphan when I was just a barefooted kid. Left me to root hog or die. Damn right I hate them. I been payin' them back ever since, and I ain't half done yet. I hope I can live to see the last of them gone."

CHAPTER
NINE

A distant crackle of gunfire made Andy's heartbeat quicken. It came from the north, but he was unable to judge how far. A Ranger named Bill Hewitt pushed his horse into a run. Sergeant Donahue called him back.

"Hold up there. Don't get in a rush."

Hewitt protested, "The fightin' has started and we ain't in it."

"We'll get there in our own good time. Let them have at one another awhile."

"There's white men in trouble up there."

"And not a Sunday school teacher amongst them. It's no great loss if some of Jericho's outfit get dirt shoveled in their faces. They ain't much better than Meskins."

Andy had found the tracks shortly after daybreak. A dozen or so horsemen had crossed the river in the night between Andy's station and Farley's. He had hurried to let Farley know, then had backtracked to fetch Len while Farley sent word up the line. It had taken a couple of hours for all the Rangers to gather. Donahue had led them in an easy trot, following a trail so plain that a tenderfoot could not have missed it.

Andy understood Donahue's lack of haste. The sergeant was letting Jericho's men administer the bulk of the punishment and take some themselves. The Rangers would arrive in time to sweep up any remnants of the raiding party. Jericho's losses would cause no regret except in Jericho's camp.

Farley said, "With any luck, the Rangers will get most of the credit without it costin' us anything except some shells."

Andy asked, "What does it matter who gets the credit?"

"Wake up and think, Badger Boy. Donahue would sell his mother to get promoted to lieutenant. If the papers in San Antonio and Galveston get wind of this, he's liable to make it. And I'd bet my saddle and fixin's that he'll make sure they hear about it."

Though Andy had reservations about Donahue, it had not occurred to him that the sergeant might have planned this little campaign more to advance his career than to punish outlaws.

Farley said, "There ain't many people do things just from the goodness of their heart. Most of them look out for theirselves first. You'd better learn to do the same if you don't want to set your boots under a poor man's table all your life."

If this was true, Andy thought, perhaps headquarters in Austin would assign Donahue to some post where he would consider the adversaries to be worthy of his attention. He had only contempt for Mexican border jumpers.

Hewitt kept pushing out in front, eager to get into the fight. Len was but little behind him, pistol already in his hand. A growing cloud of dust indicated that gunfire had spooked the cattle into a stampede. Through the swirling of hoof-stirred earth Andy began to see horsemen circling about. They were too busy firing at one another to try to control the herd.

Donahue shouted, "Spread out. Shoot every Meskin you see."

Andy followed Len, wanting to keep him in sight because he feared the excitement might make Len careless. But in the dust and confusion he lost him.

A Mexican appeared, a white horseman in close pursuit. The fugitive's horse fell, spilling its rider. The man jumped to his feet and raised his hands, pleading. The pursuer rode within point-blank range and shot him between the eyes.

Andy felt choked. He blamed it on the dust.

Two hundred yards away he saw a white rider slump from the saddle, then struggle to rise from the ground. A Mexican leaned over the fallen man and put two more bullets into him. Before the Mexican could pull away, a Ranger shot him down.

Andy's stomach turned. Both sides were turning this into an orgy of killing.

Donahue was chasing a fugitive but pointed at another who was spurring eastward. He shouted, "There goes a Meskin. Don't just sit there, Pickard. Get the son of a bitch."

By reflex Andy set off in a long lope. Sensing someone behind him, he looked back and saw Farley twenty yards in the rear, trying to catch up. The runner's bay horse was long-legged and strong of wind. For a while it lengthened its lead. The chase stretched to one mile, then two. Andy began to doubt that he could overtake the raider. But gradually the bay weakened, its hide glistening with sweat, its mouth white with foam.

Someone else appeared behind Farley. He was neither Mexican nor Ranger, so Andy figured he was a Jericho man. Farley pointed a pistol at him, and the rider turned back.

Andy tried to aim at the fugitive, but uneven ground made it impossible to hold the pistol steady. He shouted, "Stop or I'll shoot you."

The threat was hollow. Surely by this time the runner realized that if he was not shot now he would be shot soon after his capture. That was the fate of any raiders unfortunate enough to be run down.

The bay stumbled. Its rider tumbled to the ground, rolling up against a bush. Andy slid his horse to a stop and thrust the pistol toward the fugitive's face. "Raise your hands!"

He saw blood spread over the man's shirt front. As the raider looked toward him, recognition struck Andy like a fist to the jaw. This was Tony Villarreal.

The voice was weak but full of fight. "Go ahead, you damned *rinche*. If you're goin' to shoot me, do it."

Andy lowered the pistol, his mind in turmoil. He heard a horse coming up behind him. It was Farley's. He said, "Don't shoot him, Farley. This is Big Jim's stepson."

Farley said, "The hell you say. Looks to me like you've already shot him."

"Not me. Somebody did it before I saw him. How bad are you hit, Tony?"

Tony touched a hand to his ribs and drew it away, covered with blood. "What difference does it make? If you don't kill me, Jericho will. They're killin' everybody."

Dismounting, Andy turned to Farley. "Let's see what we can do for him. At least stop the bleedin'."

Farley did not leave the saddle immediately. "Ain't much we can do. He's a Mexican. Jericho's crowd'll finish him off."

"Not if we get him away from here."

"Where to? Not to the river. We'd run into some of Jericho's men as sure as you're born. They might shoot him *and* us."

Andy jerked his head, motioning to the east. "We could take him to his folks. I don't think Jericho's outfit is apt to try for him if we can get him to Big Jim."

"Maybe not, but Donahue'll raise hell. Fire us both, more than likely."

"After what I've seen this mornin', bein' a Ranger doesn't shine all that bright anyhow."

Tony's face was pale from shock, but his raspy voice was still defiant. "I don't need help from no *rinches*. Catch my horse for me and I'll take care of myself."

Andy said, "You'd fall out of the saddle before you went two hundred yards. We ain't doin' this for you. We're doin' it for your folks. I don't see where we owe you a damned thing." He took off his neckerchief and wadded it. Sharply he said, "Hold that against the wound. Maybe it'll slow the bleedin' till we can get you out of Jericho's reach." He looked back, fearing he might see someone coming.

Farley brought up Tony's bay. "I doubt this horse has got many miles left in him."

Andy said, "If he quits, we'll ride double." He helped Tony up into the saddle. "Hang tight to the horn. I'll ride close by and try to catch you if you start to fall off."

Tony muttered, "I can take care of myself."

"You've done right poorly at it so far."

As Andy mounted, Farley moved around to the other side. He cautioned, "You must like trouble, Badger Boy. You're fixin' to get us into a mess of it."

"If you want to leave, go ahead. I can manage alone."

Farley shrugged. "It's always pleasured me to aggravate people I don't like. I don't like Donahue much, and I got no use at all for Jericho. Let's move before him or some of his gun toters come lookin' for this hotheaded idiot."

Tony rasped, "Go to hell."

Farley growled, "Some people have got no appreciation. They'd complain if they was hung with a brand-new rope."

Despite the risk that Tony's tired horse would give out completely, Andy held to a brisk pace for the first couple of miles. Then he slowed, for Tony was barely able to grasp the horn and stay in the saddle.

He said, "Maybe we'd better tie him on."

Farley said, "He could fall and get tangled in the rope. I seen a man drug to death once. It was a gut-grabbin' sight."

The mental image was disturbing. Andy said, "Tony, you'll just have to grit your teeth and hang on."

The young man made no response. Andy was not sure he was still able to comprehend.

Farley turned in the saddle and swore aloud. "I knew our luck wouldn't hold. Somebody's catchin' up to us."

Andy looked back, holding his breath. He saw two horsemen. "They're not Rangers. Must be some of Jericho's people."

Farley squinted. "People, hell, one of them is Jericho hisself, big as a barn door."

Andy started looking for a defensive position but saw nothing except low thorny brush and almost flat ground. "Poor place to stop and put up a fight."

Farley grunted. "Most of the fights I ever had was in poor places. Best we get down and stand behind our horses."

Andy and Farley both struggled to get Tony to the ground without letting him fall. Andy drew his rifle and propped it across the saddle.

The red-bearded man seemed too large even for the tall horse he rode. Jericho and another rider reined their sweating mounts to a stop. The other man said, "Told you he looked like Big Jim McCawley's kid. We like to've lost him."

Jericho smiled coldly at the sight of Tony, leaning against his saddle and holding on to keep from falling. "Well, he's caught now." He seemed to recognize Andy. "Thanks for catchin' him for us. I'll take charge of him now."

Andy said, "No, you won't. We've got him under arrest."

"I don't see no badges on you."

"They never issued us any, but we're Rangers just the same."

Jericho's mouth twisted as he considered the situation. Andy watched him warily. Jericho outweighed him by fifty or seventy-five pounds. He had an air like a bull ready to charge. If he had been one he would be pawing the ground.

Jericho said, "You've done your job. You can turn this renegade over to me and go on about your business."

"He *is* our business. He's our prisoner."

"You're a long ways from a jailhouse. Give him to me and he won't get away again, not now and not ever."

Andy said, "We've seen how you handled the others you've caught."

"There's just one way to treat a bandit: kill him where you find him. No judge, no lawyers, no jury that might turn him loose and let him do it again."

"Do you know who he is?"

"He's a nephew of Lupe Chavez."

"And he's Big Jim McCawley's stepson."

"Makes no difference. He's a bandit. It's open season on all of his kind."

Andy's rifle had been pointed upward, toward the sky. He lowered the muzzle so Jericho could look directly into it. Instinctively Jericho tried to draw to one side, but Andy let the front sight follow him. The rancher made a big target.

Andy said, "Now, sir, if you'll back off, we'll be on our way."

Jericho showed no sign of retreat. He said, "I never seen a Ranger that had two dollars in his pocket. I'll pay you a good price for him. What'll you take?"

"They ain't buyin' and sellin' people anymore. Didn't you ever hear of Abraham Lincoln?"

Jericho glowered. "They shot *him*."

Andy held firm. "You ain't gettin' our prisoner."

Jericho's mouth made contortions without producing any sound. At last he said, "I don't know where you figure on takin' him, but wherever it is, I don't think you'll get there." He jerked his head. "Come on, Baldy, before I let my temper make me kill a couple of Rangers."

Nobody spoke until Jericho and his companion were a hundred yards away. Farley took a deep breath. "You sure put the Indian sign on him. I guess it's all that Comanche in you."

"You heard what he said. He ain't given up." Andy turned to Tony. "Let's move while he's tryin' to figure out what to do next."

Andy helped Tony into the saddle. Tony touched his hand against the wound in his side. It came away with fresh red color. Andy said, "Still bleedin' a little. Keep pressin' my neckerchief against it."

Farley remarked, "That dirty neckerchief is liable to kill him if the bullet don't."

As they rode, Tony asked, "What he said about you bein' part Indian . . . is that a fact?"

"Depends on how you look at it. My folks were white, but the Comanches took me when I was a boy. Kept me a long time. Some of their teachin' has stuck with me."

"I've been raised white and Mexican both. I guess me and you have got somethin' in common."

Andy shook his head. "Damned little. I've never swum the Rio Grande to raid somebody's cattle."

"It's not just somebody, and it's not really about cattle. It's about Jericho Jackson. Tío Lupe and me, we won't stop till we've settled our score with him."

"Looks like he stopped you today. Most of the men who came with you appear to've got themselves killed."

"Too bad, but there's plenty more ready to rise up against him. He's already dead. He just don't know it yet."

Andy touched spurs to his horse's ribs. "He's about the livest-lookin' dead man I ever saw. And I'm bettin' he's trailin' behind us, just out of sight." He pointed in a northeasterly direction. "Seems to me that ought to be the right direction to Big Jim McCawley's."

Tony protested, "It's not his place. It's my mother's and Tío Lupe's. I don't want to go there."

"It's our only chance, poor as it is. Jericho would never let us get you to the river."

They traveled slowly because Tony had trouble staying astride. Andy had to reach across at times and hold him in the saddle. He kept looking back.

Farley said, "Ain't no use lookin' behind us. They ain't there anymore." He pointed. "They're alongside us, and it looks like Jericho has picked up a couple more men."

Jericho and three others were two hundred yards to the left and working their way around in a slow lope to position themselves in front.

Farley spoke with a touch of sarcasm. "Well, Badger Boy, you got any ideas?"

"I can't think of a one."

Tony said, "Give me a gun. At least let me take him with me."

Farley said, "You bluffed him once, Andy. Maybe you can do it again."

"I wasn't bluffin'. I'd have shot him if I had to, and he knew it. I still will."

Jericho and his three riders stopped fifty yards away. They formed a line facing Andy, Farley, and Tony. Andy dismounted and helped Tony to the ground. He stood behind his horse, rifle again resting across the saddle.

Farley followed his lead. He said, "Maybe if we kill one or two, the others will figure out we're serious."

Andy said, "I don't like killin' a man if I don't have to." As the four began moving forward, he took careful aim and fired. A horse went down kicking.

Farley said ruefully, "But you've got no scruples against killin' a horse. I'd sooner kill a man."

"It's a poor choice either way." Andy levered another cartridge into the breech.

Jericho and his men stopped their advance. They appeared to be confused and quarreling. One rode away, his posture indicating that he had lost an argument. Jericho called after him angrily but to no avail. Jericho and the other remaining horseman dismounted.

Andy fired again, kicking up dirt between the two horses. Both jerked loose and ran. Farley took a shot, putting it just behind them. The horses broke into a full gallop, leaving the three men afoot. Andy could hear Jericho's voice, loud in rage.

He said, "They'll be a while runnin' those horses down. Let's circle around them and put some distance behind us."

Jericho fired a couple of futile shots as they cut to the south, then east again.

Farley muttered, "Keep shootin', Jericho. That'll just make the horses run faster."

Tony bent low over the saddle horn. Andy asked him, "You think you can make it the rest of the way?"

Tony ignored the question. He said accusingly, "You ought to've shot Jericho instead of the horse."

They had traveled most of a mile when Andy heard hoofbeats coming from the east. "Damn! I thought we'd left the trouble behind."

Shortly he saw two riders, one a large man on a big horse. Frustrated, he demanded, "How did Jericho get ahead of us again?"

Farley said, "Blink your eyes and take another look. That ain't Jericho, it's Big Jim McCawley."

Tony raised up, trying to see. "Tell that old gringo I don't need him."

Andy looked back. He saw Jericho and one horseman catching up but still three hundred yards away. "You'll never need him worse. Let's get to him before Jericho can get to us." He took hold of Tony's shoulder. "Hang on tight. We're goin' to lope up."

McCawley reached them first. He had already recognized his stepson. His eyes were wide with concern. "What's happened to Tony?"

Andy said, "He's got a bullet in him. If you hadn't come along, it was startin' to look like he might get some more. And us too."

Jericho paused to watch from fifty yards behind.

McCawley dismounted and stood beside Tony's horse. "Let's take a look at you, son." Tony tried to pull away from him, declaring, "Don't call me son."

McCawley tore the bloody shirt open. He did not like what he saw. "We'd better get him to the house as quick as we can."

Andy said, "That's where we were tryin' to take him. Jericho had it in mind to stop us."

Tony argued, "I ain't goin' with you. I'm goin' to Tío Lupe."

Jericho moved closer, his hired man following with obvious reluctance. The Mexican who had arrived with McCawley pointed his rifle toward them. Jericho made a show of keeping his hands high. He halted a few feet from McCawley and his stepson.

"Jim," he said, "you came near losin' this boy of yours. If it hadn't been for these Rangers . . . You better break him of runnin' with your brother-in-law's renegades, or he's in for a damned short life."

Andy felt hair rise on the back of his neck. Animosity passed between the two big men like lightning coursing through stretched wire.

Jim McCawley spoke in the voice of a judge pronouncing a death sentence. "If you ever hurt any of my family again, you'd better have a grave dug and waitin' for you."

"There ain't no grave deep enough to hold Jericho Jackson." Jericho pulled his reins, backing his horse a couple of steps. "You keep that chili-eatin' kid away from everything that's mine. Else when I've taken care of the son, I'll come lookin' for the daddy."

"You'd better hope to God you don't find me."

Tony knotted a fist and leaned forward. "Kill him! Kill him while you've got the chance." He lost his balance. His father caught him and pushed him back into the saddle. "Easy, son, or you're liable to kill *your-self.*"

Tony tried again to pull away. "I ain't your son. I don't have no gringo daddy."

The blood on his shirt had dried. Now it glistened again, fresh and red.

McCawley spoke in Spanish to the Mexican who had come with him. The Mexican rode in close to support Tony while McCawley remounted.

Jericho and his rider had pulled back but stopped thirty yards away. Andy could read Jericho's intentions from the way he sat, poised like a cat waiting to pounce. He said, "Might be a good idea if me and Farley was to ride with you, Mr. McCawley. Just in case."

"I'd be obliged. Even Jericho respects the Rangers."

"Not these Rangers, I'm afraid. But he'll respect the guns we're carryin'."

Tony still acted as if he might pull free and go his own way. His stepfather forcefully took hold of the reins and said, "It'll be good to get you away from your uncle Lupe for a while. Looks to me like he's poisoned your mind."

"Don't you say nothin' against Tío Lupe."

Farley told Andy, "I'm thinkin' Big Jim ought to've worn out a quirt on that boy's butt when he was young enough for it to've done some good. It's probably too late now."

Andy offered no argument.

CHAPTER

TEN

Only two men had returned so far to the stone house where Guadalupe Chavez waited south of the Rio Grande. They had come separately, one with a bullet in his shoulder, the other walking and leading a bleeding horse. Both said it was unlikely anyone else was coming.

"It was a trap, Don Lupe," the wounded man said. "We found but four men with the cattle. They ran away. But the Jericho, he had other men hidden. They came down on us like a whirlwind."

"What of my nephew?" Chavez demanded, eyes afire with accusation. "Did you run away and leave Antonio?"

"I did not see him, but the Jericho's men were everywhere. They were killing everybody. We had no chance."

Chavez was more inclined to shoot the wounded man than to treat him. "You should have watched out for him. He is but a boy."

"He is a man, a man who should not have gone with us." The black eyes held accusation of their own. Chavez flinched at a pang of guilt. He had tried to talk Antonio into staying behind but had yielded to the young man's insistence. He should have held tough.

Chavez pointed to a much larger stone house. "Go to the women. Let them tend your wound."

"Yes, *patrón*." The man hesitated, holding a hand to the bad shoulder. "Good men have died today. What do we do now?"

"I will tell you when the time comes. First I want to know what happened to my nephew. Send Gonzales to me."

Gonzales was an efficient spy. He could move about freely, appearing to be a ragged wood-gathering old peasant and no threat to anyone. To the contemptuous gringos he seemed beneath their notice, almost invisible. This worked to his advantage, for his ears were always open for information and his palms open for coin.

Gonzales appeared, his clothing tattered, his dusty feet protected only by *guaraches* so old that the leather was dry and twisted and black. His long gray mustache drooped like his shoulders. "You have work for me, *patrón?*"

"I want you to go across the river and see what has happened to my nephew. If he is dead, I want his body brought back here where he can be buried in hallowed ground with a priest to help his soul find its way to paradise. If he is alive I want to know where, so that I may send men to rescue him."

"This will be a dangerous business. The Jericho is killing every Mexican he sees."

"He will not waste a bullet on a worthless old man. He would not even stop to spit on you. I will pay well for the right information."

Gonzales nodded. Chavez had known he would respond to the prospect of liberal payment. His only concern was the man's greed. He suspected that Gonzales would be easily tempted. Should Chavez ever catch him dealing double, he would stake him down in an ant bed and let him consider the wages of perfidy while he died slowly, one bite at a time.

Gonzales said, "It is told on the other side that one of your men killed a nephew of the Jericho. For revenge he is resolved to kill a nephew of yours."

"Antonio?"

"Have you another?"

"Yes, but they are far away. Only Antonio has been with me. When were we said to have killed Jericho's nephew? I have heard nothing of this."

"I know nothing more, only what I have told you."

"Go then, and find Antonio. If he is alive, we must get him back. If he is dead . . . find out if Jericho has other nephews."

The lead slug clanked heavily as Farley dropped it into a tin pan. He pressed a clean, folded cloth over the wound. Bleeding had started afresh as he probed. "I've treated many a wound like this, a couple of them in myself. Now, let's hope he don't take blood poisonin'. Been as many died that way as of the bullet itself."

Andy asked McCawley, "Don't you think you'd better take him to a doctor now?"

"The nearest one is a two-day ride from here."

Tony's mother said, "He'll get better care from his own family than from a busy town doctor."

Few small towns had a hospital. A doctor might keep a patient or two in his own home. More likely he would lodge patients in a boardinghouse and visit them as necessary or as time permitted.

Teresa said, "You're tired, Farley. I'll bandage him for you."

Andy noticed her use of Farley's first name. Propriety would call for her to say *Mr. Brackett*. He was aware that Farley had been watching the girl, trying not to be obvious about it. And several times Andy had noticed her dark eyes fixed on Farley until he looked her way. She would quickly transfer her attention elsewhere.

Farley stepped out onto the back porch to wash his hands in a basin. McCawley and Andy followed. The big man said, "I'm much obliged to you both. If it hadn't been for you, Tony would be dead."

Farley only grunted. Andy said, "We did what we could. I only wish we'd got to him sooner, before he was shot."

"You've made an enemy. Jericho doesn't forget, and he doesn't forgive. You bein' Rangers, he probably won't shoot you himself, but he may hire somebody that can't be connected to him."

Andy said, "I'm not sure we'll still be Rangers when we report back in. Sergeant Donahue doesn't forgive or forget much either."

"I'll go over his head. I know people in the Austin office."

Tony had resisted Farley's initial effort to treat him. He had insisted, "Get Tío Lupe. I want him to do it."

McCawley had argued that by the time Lupe Chavez could reach here, Tony would be dead. And Chavez would probably not be able to come in any case. On the Texas side of the river he had a price on his head large enough to tempt even some who sympathized with him.

Now Tony lay half conscious, senses dulled by several liberal doses of whiskey before the surgery began. Andy knew it would be poor taste to ask McCawley why his stepson seemed to resent him so much.

Farley had no such inhibitions. He said, "There must've been a hell of a bust-up between him and you. What did you do to him?"

McCawley seemed jarred by the question. "Nothin' except to be white. We were havin' a right smart of trouble with bandits, so I sent my family down to his uncle. Figured they'd be safer at Lupe's place in Mexico. I didn't figure on Lupe fillin' his head with so much hate for everything gringo. Juana and Teresa came home after that spell of trouble died down, but Tony stayed."

Farley said, "Maybe you should've gone and brought him whether he wanted to come or not."

"I wouldn't have gotten back across the river alive." McCawley's eyes were sad. "Some folks complain about discrimination against Mexicans, but the knife cuts both ways. There's blind people aplenty on either side."

All the windows had shutters that could be closed and barred from the inside, a holdover from earlier Spanish times when Indian raids had been a recurring challenge. McCawley saw to it that the window in Tony's room was shuttered so no one could see in and perhaps get a shot at him. He said, "If Jericho's dead set on killin' him, an open window would be too much temptation."

Andy said, "Do you think he'd be bold enough to come here?"

"If Jericho sets his mind to somethin', he'll walk through hell's fire to get it done. I'll be puttin' men on guard tonight."

Andy said, "You can figure on me and Farley."

Farley gave Andy a cautioning look that said to speak only for himself, but he assured McCawley, "I'll stand my share."

McCawley said, "I'd be obliged if somebody would stay in Tony's room tonight and make sure nobody sneaks in."

Or out, Andy thought. He would not be surprised if, despite his wound, Tony took a notion to slip out of the house and make for the border. He probably would not get far, but it would not be for lack of trying.

Tony's sister sat at his bedside when Andy and Farley returned to the room. Tony appeared to be asleep but restless. Teresa said quietly, "He's running some fever."

Farley laid his palm against the boy's forehead. "At least he won't be runnin' for the border tonight."

She said, "He wouldn't do that. Would he?"

"He might. He's got guts. Meanin' no offense, but it's too bad he ain't got good sense to match."

She said, "I'll admit he's a trial sometimes. But he is my brother. I'd hate to see more harm come to him."

Farley placed a hand on her shoulder. "It won't. Me and Badger Boy will see to that."

She reached up and touched his hand. "Badger Boy?"

"It's a long story. If you've got time maybe I'll tell it to you."

She smiled. "I have plenty of time."

Andy left the pair and walked out to the kitchen to see about getting a cup of coffee. He doubted that Farley's story would paint him in a good light.

Someone shouted outside, "Mr. McCawley. Riders comin'."

McCawley flung the door open and stepped out into the night. He shouted, "Don't anybody shoot unless we're shot at."

Rifle in hand, Andy joined McCawley at the front of the house. Farley came hurrying, pausing to blow out the lamp in the parlor. Andy said, "Don't seem likely that it'd be Jericho. Not bold and open like this."

McCawley said, "Anybody who can outguess Jericho ought to be able to outguess the weather and the cattle market too. I'd put him on my payroll." He shouted to the oncoming horsemen, "Who are you?"

The answer came in a familiar voice. "Sergeant Donahue, Texas Rangers. Is that you, Jim McCawley?"

"It is. You-all come in slow so I can get a look at you." McCawley lowered his rifle once he was satisfied that the visitors were indeed Rangers.

Andy counted five men including the sergeant. He was pleased to see that Len Tanner was among them. He had been concerned that Len might have charged into the fray with his usual recklessness and gotten himself hurt.

Donahue gave Andy and Farley a critical look. "Figured you two would be here. I talked to Jericho."

Andy acknowledged him with a nod.

Farley said, "I'd guess he hollered murder."

"Somethin' like that. Said you-all took a prisoner away from him."

Andy said, "It wasn't quite that way. He tried to take a prisoner away from us. We didn't let him."

Donahue's frown deepened. "You exceeded your authority."

"I always thought a Ranger is supposed to protect a prisoner and not let anybody take one from him."

"Jericho claimed you threatened to kill him."

Farley said, "All we done was tell him that if he didn't back away from our prisoner, we'd shoot out his liver and lights."

"You meant it, of course."

Farley replied, "It ain't my way to say somethin' unless I mean it." He glanced at Andy. "This Indian boy's neither. Folks don't always agree with us, but they seldom misunderstand what we tell them."

"Why did you bring your prisoner here instead of deliverin' him to camp?"

Andy said, "That was too far. He could've bled to death. Besides, we figured Jericho would gather up more men and head us off. He had blood in his eye."

"It was still there when I talked to him." Donahue looked back at McCawley. "Jericho said it was your stepson. Have I your permission to go in and take a look at him?"

McCawley considered the question. "Just you. And understand that you're not takin' him when you go. He's too bad hurt to be moved."

Donahue stiffened. "I am an officer of the law. I do not accept conditions."

"You'll accept this one or you'll hear from my friends in Austin."

Donahue's mustache twitched in anger at this threat to go over his head. "Very well, but you should understand that I consider your boy a prisoner. I'll leave a guard. As soon as he's fit to travel, he'll be taken to jail."

McCawley yielded no ground. "We'll discuss that when the time comes." He motioned toward the door. "After you."

Len waited until Donahue and McCawley had gone inside. He moved up to Andy and said, "You-all have played hell with the sergeant's digestion. He wanted Jericho to get that boy. Said it would serve Big Jim McCawley right for marryin' a Mexican woman."

"I knew he had somethin' stuck in his craw."

"Ain't much he can do about the kid for now, but he'll chew on it. He'll have an awful stomachache by the time he gets back to camp."

Farley growled, "It'll be good for him."

Len shook his head. "But not for the rest of us."

Andy asked, "Were you with him when he talked to Jericho?"

"Yeah. Looks like Jericho's crew killed most of the Mexicans, but they took a pretty hard lickin' theirselves. He'll be shorthanded till he can rustle up some more men."

"So will Guadalupe Chavez. Maybe that'll put a stop to the raids around here for a while."

"Maybe." Len grinned. "But it was a pretty interestin' scrap while it lasted."

Donahue came out in no better mood than before. He was telling McCawley, "It wouldn't make no difference if you was the governor of Texas. An outlaw is an outlaw no matter who he belongs to."

McCawley asked, "Did anybody see him steal any cattle?"

"He was there."

"So were you. So were Jericho's men. Just bein' there doesn't prove anything."

"It'll be enough for a jury." Donahue jerked his bridle reins from the hands of a Ranger and jammed his foot into the stirrup. "I intend to see that he stands in front of a judge and jury that won't care about anything except him bein' Lupe Chavez's nephew."

Andy walked up as Donahue mounted. "Sergeant, you said you're leavin' a guard. Since he was our prisoner, I'd like to volunteer."

Donahue glared at him. "Permission denied. In fact, you and Brackett can consider yourselves unemployed. I am strikin' you from the roll as of now."

Farley protested. "On what grounds?"

"On the grounds that I don't trust either one of you any further than I can spit."

Farley said, "I got wages comin'."

"Take it up with Austin." Donahue pointed to the Ranger named Hewitt. "You'll stay here and be sure that boy doesn't set foot out of this house. Soon as he's able to ride, I'll send a detail to pick him up." Donahue looked back at Andy and Farley. "If you two have any belongings left in camp I'll send Private Tanner back here with them. If I ever see either of you again, I'll file charges on you for malfeasance."

Andy trembled with anger. He could not bring out the words he wanted to say.

Farley said them for him, a burst of profanity that would have done credit to a drunken mule skinner.

As the Rangers moved off, Len held back for a moment. "Sorry, Andy."

Andy shrugged. Nothing was left to say.

Farley grunted. "It may be a good thing anyhow. Have you ever seen an *old* Ranger?"

McCawley put his big hand on Andy's shoulder. It felt heavy as an anvil. "You've both got a job here with me if you want it. After a little coolin' off time . . . well, like I said, I've got friends in Austin."

———

Ranger Hewitt seemed unsure what his relationship with Andy and Farley should be, so he kept it formal. He said, "I'm sorry for what happened to you men, but I don't want it happenin' to me."

Andy tried to set him at ease. "We don't hold anything against you."

Farley added, "It ain't your fault you're workin' for a son of a bitch."

Hewitt said, "I'd ask for a transfer, but Donahue would probably fire me instead."

"You could hire out somewhere as a deputy sheriff. I hear most county deputies are paid better than Rangers," Andy suggested.

"But my daddy was a Ranger before the war. Died fightin' Indians. All I ever really wanted was to be a Ranger like him."

Farley said, "Then stay with it. Sooner or later Donahue is liable to bite himself like a rattlesnake. I don't see why the main office puts up with the likes of him."

Hewitt said, "You have to admit that he's pretty good at what he does. The trouble is that he knows it."

Andy nodded. "I can see why he's got his sights set on Lupe Chavez. I just can't see why he cozies up to the likes of Jericho Jackson."

Hewitt said, "You can't see it because you don't have a devious mind like his. He wanted Jericho to kill the McCawley boy because he knew it'd make Chavez mad enough to come shootin'. He wants Chavez and Jericho to hit like two freight trains rammin' together. With any luck they'd wipe each other out. Then Donahue would get credit for cleanin' up the border. He'd like to be known as another Leander McNelly."

Farley pointed out, "McNelly is dead, but Donahue looks so healthy it turns my stomach. I guess we shouldn't hope for too much in this world."

Next morning Andy watched as Jim McCawley prepared to walk out to the corrals. He said, "You haven't been in to see Tony this mornin'."

McCawley's expression was dark. "He talks to his mother and sister. He doesn't want to talk to me."

"I'm sorry."

"It's nothin' for you to trouble yourself about. It's between me and Tony . . . and Lupe Chavez."

Andy thought it best to change the subject. "I've been thinkin' about goin' back home to the Colorado River, but I'll stay awhile if you have a use for me. I don't know that I'm much of a cowboy, though. Never did much of that."

"I've already got enough cowboys. I'm afraid Jericho hasn't given up on the notion of killin' Tony. I'd like you to stay around close and help watch out for him. Farley too, if he's of a mind to stay."

"I don't think Farley is in any hurry to leave." Andy had seen Farley in intense conversation with Teresa after breakfast. He added, "Jericho might not stop with Tony if he saw a chance to get you too."

McCawley filled a pipe with tobacco, tamped and lighted it. "There's no enemy quite as bitter as a friend who's turned against you. Jericho wanted this ranch so bad he'd sell his soul to the devil to get it. Lupe Chavez couldn't stop him, but I did."

"What's to keep him from slippin' up and shootin' you while you're out on horseback, workin' cattle?"

"I have some good men with me, white and Mexican both. And I've got eyes in the back of my head when it comes to Jericho. You watch out for Tony. I can take care of myself."

Andy hoped he was right. He watched with admiration as McCawley walked out toward the corrals. The man's stern determination reminded him of Rusty Shannon and Sheriff Tom Blessing. He had seen both stand tall in the face of severe adversity.

Ranger Hewitt came out of Tony's room. Andy asked, "How's the patient?"

Hewitt shrugged. "I'd just as well find me a shade tree and sleep all day. He's not in shape to go anywhere."

"I'm not worryin' too much right now about him leavin'. I'm worried about somebody comin' in after him."

Andy entered Tony's room. The young man lay on a cot, his face toward the wall. He did not acknowledge Andy's presence. He had lost a considerable amount of blood, and he still suffered from shock. Andy could imagine how much he must be hurting. A wound was usually more painful the second day than the first. Andy said, "Are you hurtin' too much to talk to Big Jim?"

Tony offered no answer.

Andy said, "He's worried about you. You're not bein' fair to him."

Tony did not look at him, but he murmured, "What the hell would you know about it?"

"All I know is that you're bein' an ungrateful young whelp and your family is too good for you."

"My real family is south of the river. I wish you'd taken me there instead of bringin' me to this place."

"If we'd tried, your mother and sister would be cryin' over you this mornin'. You'd be dead."

"You figure I owe you somethin'?"

"Not a thing except maybe to act like a human bein'. I'd give everything I own to have a family like yours."

Tony cursed. "Take them and be damned. Soon as I can I'm goin' back where I belong."

"If you can get past Jericho, and the Rangers, and me."

CHAPTER

ELEVEN

e appeared to be a ragged old Mexican beggar, riding up to the ranch house on a tired-looking burro the third day after the battle. The ancient saddle with its wide, flat horn appeared almost as large as the animal itself. The man presented no evident threat, but Andy looked him over for sign of a weapon. He saw none. The man spoke in Spanish. Andy did not understand him, so he beckoned to the McCawleys' middle-aged maid. She had stepped outside to shake crumbs from a tablecloth.

He told her, "I don't know what he wants."

She spoke to the old man in Spanish and listened to his reply. "He asks whose hacienda this is. I told him Señor Jaime McCawley is the *patrón*. He says he has heard that Señor McCawley is a generous man and kind to poor Mexicans."

"Tell him that right now Mr. McCawley is also a very suspicious man when it comes to strangers."

She and the gray-whiskered oldster conversed a bit more. She said, "He says he means no one harm, that he is simply a poor man on his way to see his son in San Antonio. He is hungry and wishes only for a little food. In return he is a *curandero*, a healer. He would work his magic on any here who may be sick."

"I doubt as his magic would help much on a gunshot wound. And I wouldn't suppose he's got some kind of charm that would improve Tony's sour outlook."

"Many of our people put much faith in *curanderos*. They have powers no one else can understand."

Like Comanche medicine men, Andy thought. Logic told him the shamans' magic was useless, but he had seen strange things happen as a result of it. Sometimes logic did not work well either.

The maid said, "I will go and tell *la señora*."

"I wouldn't bother her." Andy found that he was talking to himself. The maid had hurried inside. Shortly, Juana and Teresa came out, the maid explaining to mother and daughter what the old man had said.

Big Jim's wife appeared intrigued. She asked something in Spanish. The man replied, *"Me llama Gonzales."*

Andy took that to be his name, though the rest of the conversation went past him.

Teresa said, "Mama, these *curanderos* are fakers. There's nothing he can do for Tony."

Her mother said, "There are many things we do not understand, child. What is to be harmed if he takes a look? Just a look, that is all."

"Papa may not be pleased."

"There are things your papa does not know either. We have never turned the hungry away from our door. I see no harm in feeding the old fellow."

Andy felt uneasy, but it was not his place to argue with Mrs. McCawley. He said, "It might be a good idea to search him and make sure he's not packin' any iron."

Teresa told the old man what Andy had said. The *curandero* made no protest. He lifted his arms to demonstrate that he carried no gun. He had a skinning knife at his waist. He removed it and its belt, hanging them over the horn of his old saddle.

Mrs. McCawley said, "He is a stranger. There is no reason he would want to hurt Antonio."

Andy replied, "Right now any stranger will bear watchin'."

The old man seemed a stranger to water. Mrs. McCawley and the maid brought him a plate of beef and beans and a cup of coffee on the patio. He sat in the shade and devoured the food quickly without availing himself of a chance to wash his face and hands.

Teresa frowned. Quietly she told Andy, "These beggars all have some kind of story. If he is a true *curandero*, why does he not heal himself?" The old man had a swollen cut on his hand that he had said resulted from letting his knife slip while he butchered a fat goat.

Andy said, "Maybe he expects the dirt to heal it."

Teresa said, "I have a bad feeling about this man. Would you watch him?"

"I will." Andy suspected she would probably rather have asked Farley, but Farley and Hewitt were out at the corrals looking over some brood mares a couple of vaqueros had brought in to mate with McCawley's best stallion.

When he had eaten his fill, Gonzales asked to see the sick man. Mrs. McCawley led him to the room where Tony lay. He said his medicine would work better if everyone left. The two women withdrew, though Teresa's eyes begged Andy not to go. The old man frowned at him. Andy sat in a chair and said firmly, "I'm stayin'."

Tony seemed to brighten a little as Gonzales spoke quietly. Andy strained to hear, but it was a lost effort because he could not understand the language. Gonzales laid his hands on Tony and said words that Andy took to be some sort of incantation. He had witnessed similar performances by Comanche medicine men.

Tony had spoken little to anyone in the family, but he talked at length to the *curandero*. Afterward, though he said nothing to Andy, he appeared to have a stronger light in his eyes.

Maybe there's more to this magic stuff than most of us can see, Andy thought.

He stood at the front door, watching as the old man rode northward on the overburdened burro. Teresa joined him, a question in her eyes.

Andy said, "I don't see as he hurt anything. Maybe he did Tony some good, even if it's only in his head."

She replied, "These are strange times. You never know for certain who are your friends and who are your enemies."

"I guess he's just a harmless old—" Andy caught himself. He had been about to say *harmless old Mexican*. She might have taken that as an affront to her mother's side of the family. It was the sort of thing he would expect from Sergeant Donahue, and perhaps Farley. He completed the sentence. "Harmless old beggar."

She said, "It will take him a long time to reach San Antonio on that poor burro."

"Time doesn't matter much to a burro."

The next time Andy looked in, Tony was sitting up, a pillow propped behind him. It was the first time Andy had seen him that way. Tony nodded, saying nothing though he appeared at least civil. His attitude changed when his stepfather came in hot and dusty from working cattle and stopped to ask how he was. Tony turned his face to the wall and made no comment. Big Jim looked dejected.

Andy followed him out into the parlor. He said, "If it's any comfort to you, a while ago he seemed like he was feelin' better."

"Seein' me spoiled it, I suppose." McCawley went into the kitchen. He poured a glass of raw tequila and drank half of it in one swallow. "His uncle convinced him that I married his mother just so I could steal this ranch. But it was the only way I could keep Jericho and some others of his kind from gettin' their hands on it. Once these border troubles are behind us, I plan to sign everything over to Tony and his sister."

"Maybe you ought to tell him that."

"He'd want me to do it now. I'm afraid it's too early. The courthouse crowd would find a way to take it away from him, like they took so much away from old Don Cipriano and Lupe."

"They might do it anyway if anything happens to you."

"That's why I keep a crew of good men around me, so nothin' does."

Farley and Hewitt remained at the horse corrals until nearly time for supper. They proceeded to the patio to wash their hands and faces. Drying himself with a towel, Farley said, "We seen an old Mexican stop at the house this afternoon. What was he after?"

Andy explained that he claimed to be a *curandero*, and that he spent some time with Tony. That quickly caught McCawley's interest. He said, "Nobody told me."

Andy said, "Guess nobody felt like it was important. Mainly he just wanted to beg a meal, then be on his way to San Antonio."

Farley said, "San Antonio's north."

"That's the way he went."

Farley and Hewitt exchanged looks. Farley said, "For a little while. But after he traveled north for a ways, he took a turn to the west. Me and Hewitt seen him."

McCawley's jaw dropped. "West, toward Jericho's?"

Andy felt a stab of conscience. He realized he should not have allowed Gonzales into the house. "You reckon he was here to spy for Jericho?"

McCawley mulled over the question. "He might've been, but what could he find out that Jericho doesn't already know? That Tony is here?

Jericho knows that. That we're keepin' a guard on him? Anybody with half a brain has to figure that we would."

Andy said, "He might've intended to do Tony harm, but I searched him for weapons before I let him come inside. I watched him all the time he was here."

"Did he say anything?"

"Not to where I could understand him. Most of it was sort of a chant."

"We could trail him," Farley offered.

McCawley shook his head. "We wouldn't likely catch up to him before dark. If he came here as a spy he probably won't stop till he gets to Jericho's place. Let's just be happy that there wasn't any harm done."

It nagged at Andy how the old man's visit had seemed to boost Tony's spirits. Maybe Tony believed in *curanderos*, or perhaps the old man had told him something. He returned to the door of Tony's room and looked inside. He wanted to ask what the visitor had said, but if it had been anything significant he knew Tony would not tell him. It was frustrating that he could not figure the old man's motives, though by now he was convinced that Gonzales had been up to no good.

Burt Hatton hesitantly entered the office that Jericho Jackson considered his private sanctuary from the frequent disturbances which plagued his life. He stood a moment, unsure of Jericho's reaction to the interruption, then tapped his knuckles against the doorjamb. He said, "That pet Mexican of yours is outside."

Jericho set down an account book he had been working on and flipped a stub pencil deep into the rolltop desk. It annoyed him that Hatton had entered unannounced and uninvited. "A little wait won't hurt him."

"He says he's just come from over at Big Jim's. Got word for you about that boy."

Jericho shoved the account book into a drawer and locked it. There was no telling when some of the help might decide to snoop, including Hatton. His finances were nobody's business but his own. "All right, damn it, I'll see him. But outside. I don't want him comin' in this house. He's liable to be carryin' lice."

It had been dark for an hour. Jericho lighted a lantern beneath the roof's narrow overhang and beckoned to Gonzales. The burro stood droop-headed where the old man had stopped him.

Jericho asked impatiently, "What you got for me, Gonzales?"

His knowledge of Spanish was limited. He knew Gonzales understood English, though the old man acknowledged it to few people. The appearance of ignorance served his purposes. Gonzales said, "I have done as you asked. I have seen the boy Antonio. He is in the house of his stepfather."

"Hell, I already knew that."

"He is stronger than his family thinks. He tells me he will soon get away. He wants to go back to his *tío* Guadalupe Chavez."

"I've figured he'd try. Him and Big Jim don't get along. When does he intend to go?"

"He says he thinks after two more days he is strong enough to ride. The McCawley and the women are to go to San Antonio. Among the vaqueros the boy has a friend who will bring his horse that night."

"Anybody watchin' him?"

Gonzales held up three twisted fingers. "*Rinches*. But they do not think he is strong enough to ride. He fools them. He has only to get out of the house while others sleep."

Jericho considered for a moment, then made a grim smile. "He won't go far. We'll get him as he leaves."

"It will be dark. He will be hard to see."

"Even if we lose him, he'll leave tracks. It's a long ways to the river. Come daylight we'll catch up to him."

"*Bueno.*" Gonzales extended his hand, palm up. Jericho dug several coins from his pocket. Gonzales counted them and looked pained. "What I have told you is worth much more."

"This is enough, you damned old bandit. You'll just get sloppy drunk on tequila. If I was you I'd buy me a young burro with it and feed that one to the hogs."

"But Señor Jericho . . ."

"Move along before I sic my dogs on you."

Looking as if he had bitten into a sour melon, Gonzales mounted the burro. His thin legs hung almost to the ground. He struck the burro across the hips with a rawhide quirt and cursed it as he rode southward.

Hatton said, "Kind of rough on the old reprobate, ain't you?"

"He'll take it. He likes my money too much not to. Anyway, I've got no respect for a man who betrays his own kind, even if his kind are Mexicans."

"How can you be sure he won't betray *you*?"

"He won't. He knows I'd skin him and nail his hide to the barn. I may do it anyway when I've finished with him. He leaves a stink wherever he goes."

The old burro was still wet from swimming the river when Gonzales quirted him up to the stone house. A man walked out and confronted him, holding a rifle.

"I am Fermín Gonzales. I have come with news for Don Guadalupe Chavez."

The rifleman studied him with distrust. "I know who you are. Get down. Let me see if you are carrying a weapon."

Gonzales said, "Only this poor knife. It is so dull it will not cut hog fat."

The guard looked him over carefully anyway. Gonzales said, "I am but a poor man doing a service for my good friend Lupe. Why would I wish to do him harm?"

"Perhaps someone has paid you to. We know you come from the Texas side. You have been watched since before you rode into the river."

"It is good to see everyone so careful. One can never be certain who are friends."

"Or enemies." The guard said, "Wait. I will tell Don Lupe." He walked into the stone house. Shortly he returned, followed by Guadalupe Chavez.

Chavez's eyes were as distrustful as the guard's. His voice was sharp and without friendliness. "What have you for me, Gonzales?"

Normally it would be custom to invite a guest into the house and offer him something to drink. Chavez did not. Gonzales was aware of the slight, but he hid his resentment. A wise man does not bite the hand that may soon offer him money.

"I have seen your nephew Antonio."

Chavez's attitude changed abruptly to one of eagerness. "Where is he? Is he well?"

"He is in the house of his mother. He is not well."

"But he is alive?"

"Yes. He was shot by the Jericho's men. Some *rinches* took him to the hacienda McCawley. But he gains in strength. It is his intention to slip away and come back here to you."

"When?"

"If all goes well, he will leave in two nights." He explained about his ruse to get into the McCawley house and speak to Tony. He told of Tony's intention to escape. He said nothing about Jericho, for that would risk revealing that he was working both sides.

Chavez frowned. "It will be a long ride to the river. Do you think he is strong enough to endure it?"

"He thinks he will be. I am not so sure. It would be well if you met him and made certain. The *rinches* are sure to follow him."

A disturbing thought came to Chavez. "Do you think Jericho knows where he is?"

"How could he know? Unless, of course, there is a traitor somewhere."

"I wish I could send word to Antonio that we are coming to meet him."

"I can go back. They accept me as a *curandero*. I can tell them I have come with medicine for the boy." That offer, and the risk inherent in it, should be worth a larger payment, he thought.

"Do that. Tell him to come to the old adobe camp. He knows where it is. We will meet him and see him safely to the river."

"It will be done." Gonzales hesitated, staring at the ground. "I have expenses, Don Lupe."

"Of course. Wait while I go into the house." Chavez came back in a few minutes with a small leather bag that clinked as he placed it in Gonzales's hand. "You have done me a service."

"*Gracias, patrón.* May you live well and die a very old man."

Gonzales hefted the bag. He knew without counting that it did not come up to his expectations. Disappointed, he started to complain but thought better of it and turned away. Chavez would probably chastise him for being greedy, as Jericho had done, and pay him no more. He reined the burro toward the river.

Chavez watched until Gonzales was a couple of hundred yards away, then crooked his finger and beckoned to one of the pistoleros who had fought the gringos with him.

He said, "I have no trust in Gonzales. It was he who told me Jericho was gathering a herd. It was a trap. He has promised to go to the hacienda of Jaime McCawley. Follow him. If he rides in any other direction he has lied to me. Kill him."

"*Sí, patrón.* It will be done." The pistolero went to catch his horse.

Gonzales crossed the river, but once out of sight he turned eastward. He had no intention of returning to the McCawley ranch and delivering Chavez's message. The risk was too great, the reward too small.

He saw some possibility that Chavez and Jericho might collide in their search for Tony. Perhaps if they had been more generous he would favor one or the other. As it was, beyond the loss of their meager bribes he would feel satisfaction rather than grief if either or both of them died. He was acutely aware that the two men held him in contempt, though they were not so contemptuous that they would not use him.

This was a game that more than two could play. It would serve them right if he were the instrument of their mutual destruction.

He would follow the river down to Matamoros, where a man with money in his pocket could debauch himself on the sweet fruit of the vine, dance with lissome señoritas, and be young again while the money lasted. He felt younger already. He could hear the music playing in his head. He hummed along with it and for a while did not notice the horseman rapidly catching up from behind.

Awareness brought alarm, and he quirted the burro vigorously across both hips. It was of no use. The horseman pulled up beside him, a pistol in his hand. His eyes were those of a hawk swooping in for the kill.

Gonzales tried to cry for mercy, but his mouth and throat were dry. He heard the shot. He felt nothing when he hit the ground.

CHAPTER
TWELVE

The sun broke over the eastern horizon as Big Jim McCawley helped his wife and daughter up into the buckboard. He turned back to Andy and said, "I hate to go, under the circumstances, but we've got to. I'm meetin' with a cattle buyer in San Antonio. Teresa needs books and things for teachin' when school takes up again. Tony seems to be comin' along all right. He just needs healin' time."

Andy said, "If anybody was fixin' to make a move against Tony, looks like they would've already done it. We'll keep a close watch over him."

Several of the ranch hands were going with the McCawleys to protect the family on the road. Travelers were beset from time to time by highwaymen who had no connection with either Jericho or Guadalupe Chavez. Andy, Farley, and Hewitt were staying.

Andy asked, "What do you want us to do if Sergeant Donahue sends for Tony?"

"How good are you at lyin'?"

"Never was much of a hand at it. The Comanches didn't have much use for a liar unless he was braggin' about a fight. They made allowances for that."

"Convince them that Tony is still too weak to be moved. We should be back in a few days. I know a good judge in San Antonio. I think I can get a court order to make Donahue leave him be."

That pleased Andy, though he wondered about the fairness of a legal system that would let a man of influence obtain favors unlikely to be available for the average poor citizen from the forks of the creek. He thought it probable that Donahue might know a judge or two himself.

The procession consisted of the buckboard, a wagon, and four horsemen. He watched it leave, then turned toward the house, where Farley and Hewitt stood beside the door.

In Andy's days at the ranch he had heard Tony say very little to anyone. He was surprised when Tony asked, "They gone?"

"They're just toppin' the hill. Why? Didn't they tell you good-bye?" He let a little sarcasm creep into his voice.

"I'm glad Farley Brackett didn't go along. I don't like the way he keeps lookin' at my sister."

"Farley's got his faults, but he wouldn't harm a woman."

"My sister is half Mexican. He doesn't have much respect for Mexicans."

"She's also half gringo. Does that make you have any less respect for her?"

"That's different."

"Not much." Andy looked at a small bedside table where a cup of coffee was going cold. "Need anything?"

"I wish you'd open the shutters and let some air in here. It was awful warm all night."

"We've kept the shutters closed so nobody can slip up in the dark and shoot you through the window."

"But it's not night anymore. Nobody's goin' to try it in broad daylight."

"I guess not." Andy swung the shutters back and opened the window. "Me and Hewitt will be close by. Holler if you need anything."

"I just need lettin' alone."

That suited Andy. He had had about enough of Tony's sour attitude. He was tempted to saddle up and ride away, but he had given his word to Big Jim. He might go, however, when the McCawley family returned. They had plenty of help. They didn't really need him. And he had no obligations to the Rangers anymore. Sergeant Donahue had taken care of that.

Lately Andy had given considerable thought to Rusty Shannon and Alice. And Bethel Brackett. He did not feel at home in this hot and brushy borderland, so different in people, climate, and terrain from what he had known. He had been revisiting his old dream of settling down in a pleasant valley, perhaps in the hill country, somewhere along the San Saba or Llano rivers.

Idling had never suited him for long. He had a sense that time was a gift not to be wasted. Through the day he pitched in with a couple of Big Jim's Mexican hands in digging postholes for a new corral. He could keep an eye on the house while doing that. Physical exertion helped him sweat off some of his frustrations. The fatigue that came upon him toward the end of the day gave him a satisfying sense of accomplishment.

Despite his reassurances to McCawley, he felt a vague uneasiness as night came on.

Farley said, "I can't see what you're worried about. Ain't nobody made a try for the kid yet."

"Dark always worries me. You never know who or what might be out there in it."

At dusk Andy and Farley made a wide circle around the house, walking to the edge of the brush and checking the outbuildings.

Farley said, "Like I told you, ain't nobody comin'. I'd bet my life on it."

"It's Tony's life we're bettin'."

Though he had seen nothing, Andy closed the shutters that covered Tony's window. Tony demanded, "Do you have to do that? I'll suffocate in here."

"Better than lettin' a Jericho man shoot you through the window. Maybe you'll think about this the next time you decide to pull a raid on somebody's cattle."

"I'll bet half of those cattle belonged to Tío Lupe in the first place."

"I'm not a judge. I'm just a Ranger. Or was. It's on account of you that I got fired."

Tony showed no remorse. "If you had any self-respect you wouldn't have been a Ranger anyway. The Rangers are a tool of the gringo land grabbers. They won't be satisfied till they've run all the Mexicans across the river." He scowled. "Who knows if they'll even stop there? I heard that to the day he died, Sam Houston was plottin' another invasion of Mexico."

"And I heard that the earth is flat, that if you go to the edge of it you'll fall off."

"Go ahead, make fun of what I'm tellin' you. You just haven't seen things from my side of the river. Someday some Mexican general will rise up and drive the gringos all the way north to San Antonio. Maybe farther."

Andy tried to think of an answer. "I guess you think that general might be your uncle Lupe?"

"Who knows? The strongest leaders we've ever had came up from the people. Like Father Hidalgo. He raised the cry for Mexican independence from Spain."

"As I heard it, they shot him."

"That was the Spanish. They were no better than the damned gringos. And we Mexicans beat them."

"And then the Texans beat you." Almost before Andy got it said, he wished he hadn't. He saw that he had touched a raw nerve.

Tony flushed. "You better watch out that when the stampede starts you don't get tromped in it." He turned his face toward the wall.

It was useless to argue with Tony. Andy felt foolish for trying. He went outside to be sure a proper guard had been set up. The face he saw at the front of the house was not the one he expected. He found a bronc rider whose name he remembered as Francisco.

Andy said, "I thought Toribio was standin' the first watch."

Francisco's grasp of English was tentative. He touched his hand to his stomach. "Toribio sick a little."

Andy remembered that Francisco had been in the house to visit Tony a couple or three times. Evidently their friendship went back a long way. "Well, you watch good. There may still be somebody lookin' to get at him."

"Good boy, Tony. I watch."

Andy had been sleeping on a cot in the hallway. An invader would have to go past him to get into Tony's room. Farley had spread his bedroll near the back door. Hewitt slept at the end of the hall nearest the front door. With guards inside and outside, Andy felt that Tony was well protected.

He did not remove his clothes, other than his boots. He would get up at least once in the night to check on the guards outside. The steady *tick-tock* of a tall grandfather clock in the nearby parlor slowly lulled him off to sleep.

He was jarred awake by gunshots from somewhere outside. Flinging off the light blanket that covered him, he dashed into Tony's room. Though it was dark he saw that the shutters were open. Tony was not in his bed. Andy rushed to the open window and tried to see out into the darkness. He heard a horse running. Somewhere out there a man shouted angrily. More shots echoed back from the brush.

He bumped into Hewitt as both tried to go out the front door at the same time. He saw the guard Francisco standing, looking off southward in the direction from which the shots had come.

Andy demanded, "What's happened?"

Francisco turned. To Andy's surprise he was smiling. "Antonio . . . he get away."

"But how?"

"I bring horse for him so he goes to his uncle. Men in the brush shoot, but I think they no hit Antonio. He is gone *por allá*, for the river."

Farley came running up. "Damn kid. I didn't think he was in shape to climb out the window, much less to ride a horse."

Andy said, "Looks like he fooled us."

Francisco chuckled. "Fool everybody."

Andy was tempted to hit him, but he saw no gain in it beyond possibly venting a little of his frustration.

"Looks like Jericho's men were layin' for him." He heard more shots, farther away. "Sounds like they haven't caught him."

Francisco said, "Fast horse. Nobody catch."

Andy said, "Come on, we'd better see if we can help him."

Hewitt said, "We couldn't find an elephant out there in the dark."

"But we know he's headed south. He won't stop till he gets to the river unless Jericho's men overtake him." He had no doubt that Jericho or his men had done the shooting. He would give odds that the angry voice he had heard belonged to Jericho himself. "Maybe we can cut his trail and catch up to him."

Andy went back for his boots. He trotted toward the barn, Hewitt and Farley close behind him. Hewitt fretted, "Donahue will have my hide for this."

Andy didn't give a damn about Donahue, but he felt that he had let Big Jim down.

They saddled and set out in a lope in the direction from which the last shots had come. The firing had stopped. That could mean Tony had eluded his enemies in the darkness, or it could mean . . . Andy did not want to think about that.

Hewitt said, "What I can't see is why Jericho is so hell-bent on gettin' that kid. It's not like he's Lupe Chavez's right-hand man."

Andy replied, "It's somethin' about Jericho losin' a nephew. Even a man like him can have feelin's for his kin. He blames Chavez. Got a grudge against Big Jim too. Killin' Tony would give both men a kick in the teeth."

Patches of thick brush forced them to slow down to prevent thorns from injuring the horses. The men were not immune to them either. Andy heard Farley curse as an unseen mesquite branch slapped him across the face. "Damn near put my eyes out," Farley complained. "Every time I go somewhere with you, Badger Boy, somethin' happens to me."

The only saving grace was that Jericho's men were probably having the same trouble.

In the darkness and the brush it would be easy to lose the way and begin traveling in circles. Andy picked out a star he judged to be more or less due south. Whenever they had to skirt around an obstacle he kept reining back in the direction of the star. He paused from time to time to listen, but he heard no more shots, no hoofbeats. He was fairly sure they had not gotten ahead of Jericho's men. He hoped they had not ridden past Tony.

"At least they ain't caught him," he said. "We'd hear shootin' if they did."

They continued riding through the night, though without any solid indication that they were on the right track. Andy began to be plagued by doubts, which he thought best not to confess to Farley or Hewitt.

Just at daybreak he heard desultory gunfire in the distance. He reined up to listen. "It's at least three or four different guns. Sounds to me like Tony is makin' a stand."

Farley said, "He won't hold out long if they've got him bottled up in the brush."

Hewitt pushed past Andy and Farley. "I've got to protect my prisoner."

The two quickly caught up with him. Andy said, "He's not anybody's prisoner, not till we pry him loose from the hole he's in."

They almost rode upon the Jericho men before they realized how close they had come. Andy heard the hiss of a bullet passing by his ear and clipping into a tangle of mesquite limbs behind him. He drew his pistol and fired a couple of shots. He had little expectation of hitting something he could not see, but it might give the pursuers something extra to worry about.

Farley said, "Let's surround them."

Another bullet sang as it passed by. Andy realized it did not come from the Jericho crew. "Look out. Tony can't tell us from them." He shouted, "It's Andy. We're comin'."

Jericho's men did not seem talented at hitting moving targets. They fired several ineffective shots as the three riders swung around them.

Andy saw that Tony's horse was down. Tony was lying behind it, pistol balanced across the saddle. Andy jumped to the ground. "Are you all right?"

Tony said crisply, "Hell no, I'm not all right. They shot my horse out from under me."

Andy saw blood on Tony's shirt and doubted it came from the horse. "Looks like they hit you."

Tony shook his head. "No, but the fall opened that wound up again. Been bleedin' some." His hand shook. "I can't hold my gun steady or I'd've gotten two or three of them by now."

"You ain't got a lick of sense or you wouldn't be out here in the first place. We're goin' to take you home."

"Like hell. You think you can get past them?" He nodded toward the Jericho men, less than a hundred yards away. "One of them rode off a while ago. I figure he went for reinforcements. The only direction we can go from here is south."

Andy realized he was right. They had caught Jericho's crew by surprise just now or they would not have gotten past them. They could not go back through or around them without heavy risk. He looked at Farley and Hewitt. "You-all ready for a swim?"

Hewitt said, "I'm still a Ranger. It's illegal for me to cross the river."

"Liable to be fatal if you don't."

"Since you put it that way . . ." Hewitt fired toward the men in the brush. "Just want them to know that we ain't gone to sleep."

Andy said, "Let's hoist Tony up into my saddle. I'll ride behind him."

Farley pointed out. "That means they'll have to shoot through you to get him. Are you sure he's worth it?"

"Probably not. But let's go."

Andy's horse fidgeted, made nervous by the shooting and the smell of blood. Tony was as weak as a sick colt. Andy and Hewitt struggled to get him into the saddle while Farley watched for the Jericho men to move. Andy swung up behind Tony. He said, "Hold tight to the horn so you don't slide off. One more fall just might put you under."

"It'll take more than that."

They moved into an easy lope. Shortly Farley shouted, "They're tryin' to go around us. We'd better whip up."

Andy looked back. He saw six riders, somewhat scattered but spurring hard. "How far is it to the river, Tony?"

"It's just ahead of us."

"Then we'd better give them a horse race. If they get in front of us, we'll never be able to go through them."

The ground seemed a blur as Andy and Farley and Hewitt pushed their mounts for all the speed they could get. But Andy's was handicapped by carrying the weight of two riders. Once the horse stumbled and went to its knees trying to jump over a bush. Andy almost lost his hold on Tony. The horse regained its feet, but it had lost some ground.

They hit the river still barely ahead of Jericho's men. Andy held tightly to Tony as the horse began thrashing, plunging through the water. This was not an ideal place to cross. The river had narrowed, but narrowing made it deeper.

The pursuers' aim was spoiled by the motion of their swimming horses.

Andy and the others broke out on the south bank and resumed running. But Andy's hopes began to sink as he saw that they were going to lose the race. Jericho's riders were gaining rapidly. Gradually they maneuvered around to the front, fifty yards ahead. They stopped and faced about.

Andy brought his horse to a stop and slid off, reaching up to help Tony down.

The riders began firing at them. A bullet thumped against the cantle of Andy's saddle.

"Get behind the horse," he told Tony. That was difficult because the horse kept dancing about, trying to jerk the reins from Andy's hand and run away. "Then drop down low where they can't see you through the brush."

Farley said, "They don't have to see us to hit us."

"We don't have to make it easy for them." Andy raised up, trying to see a target. He saw a man moving around to the left. "Tryin' to flank us," he said.

Tony tried to aim. Andy took the pistol from his hand. "You can't hold steady enough to hit the side of a barn. Don't be wastin' shells. We'll need all we've got."

He fired at the flanker. He saw the man drop, then rise again and go hopping back toward the others.

Farley said, "Aim higher, Badger Boy. His leg is too far from his heart." He had his rifle. He leveled it, squeezed the trigger, and the man fell.

Hewitt said, "Good shootin'."

"I got a lot of practice back in the days of the state police. They learned to keep their distance."

For a while Jericho's men seemed confused and uncertain, unnerved by Farley's accurate shot. Every so often they would send a bullet whispering harmlessly in the general direction of the fugitives, who for the most part kept low.

Farley raised up a little, as if inviting a bullet. "Look yonder, up the river."

Andy had been concentrating his attention on their adversaries and had not paid attention to what was going on to the west. He saw at least a dozen horsemen loping alongside the river toward them. He asked Tony, "Some of your friends?"

Tony seemed to pick up strength. "That old *curandero* must've told Tío Lupe that I'd be comin'."

Andy frowned. "But I'm thinkin' he told Jericho too. That's why they were waitin' for you soon as you left the house. Looks like he lit the candle from both ends."

Jericho's men exchanged a few shots with the oncoming riders, then broke and ran for the river.

Tony looked up at Hewitt. "You're still a Ranger. Tío Lupe had rather shoot a Ranger than eat. I don't know if I'll be able to stop him."

Hewitt seemed to be measuring the distance between him and the Mexicans. "I'd best go report to Sergeant Donahue that his prisoner got away. I'll be lucky if he doesn't fire me."

Andy said, "Tell him it was all my fault. He'll believe that."

Hewitt left in a lope, riding eastward to avoid contact with either Jericho's men or the Mexicans. Andy was relieved to see that no one from either group chased after him. He figured Hewitt would cross over at some shallow point. "He's a pretty good sort," he said.

Farley nodded. "At least he doesn't talk your ears off like Len Tanner. If I was to ever be a Ranger again, I wouldn't mind havin' him with me."

Farley must be mellowing, Andy thought. Usually he had rather have a boil on his butt than to pay anybody a compliment. First Teresa McCawley, now Ranger Hewitt. After this, Andy would not be surprised to see the sun rise in the west.

The first of the Mexican horsemen reined up. Andy was strongly aware of several pistols aimed at him. He raised his hands to shoulder level and tried not to betray any anxiety. Some people fed on others' fear.

He had never seen Guadalupe Chavez, but he thought he had heard enough to recognize him on sight. He would have picked almost any of the others before he would have chosen the one who turned out to be Chavez. To Andy's surprise, he was anything but imposing. He was a small, thin man, not much more than five feet tall and weighing perhaps a hundred thirty. His fierce eyes were so dark that they appeared black. A heavy mustache gave his face a fearsome look that belied his size.

He pointed to Jericho's fleeing men and shouted an order in a voice far stronger than his physical stature would indicate. Most of his men set out in pursuit, spurring into the river.

Only then did he kneel to look at his nephew's wound. Andy could not understand the conversation, but he sensed anxiety in the older man's voice. The only word he could pick out was *rinche.*

Tony explained, "He thought I was shot again. I told him I would've been if you hadn't come after me."

Andy saw no softening in Chavez's malevolent glare. Chavez shifted to English. "You would take my nephew to the Rangers?"

Andy said, "No, we intended to take him back to his mother and stepdaddy."

"But you are Rangers, no?"

Andy said, "We used to be. We lost our job."

"Not good enough even to be a Ranger? Tell me why I should not shoot you."

Tony spoke again in Spanish. Andy sensed that he was defending them. He thought it best to let Tony do the talking. Chavez seemed unlikely to listen with patience to a gringo, especially a used-to-be Ranger.

Chavez's grim countenance softened a little. "Antonio says you are friends of his. You are not friends of mine, but maybe I don't kill you for a while yet."

Andy hardly considered himself and Tony to be friends, but he was not about to argue the point. He said hopefully, "Since Tony is safe now, me and Farley will go back and tell his folks what's happened."

Chavez narrowed his eyes. "Or maybe go and bring the *rinches?* I think you may be spies for them. I must think on whether I will shoot you or let you go."

Tony spoke again in Spanish. Andy looked at Farley, who was equally at a loss with the language. A pleading tone indicated that Tony was trying to dissuade his uncle. Chavez did not appear to be yielding much.

Gradually Chavez's riders began trailing back. Two rode over to look at the man Farley had shot. The others had left him behind. One shouted something to Chavez, who responded by making a slicing motion across his throat. The man leaned down from the saddle and fired once.

Chavez said, "He was not sure the gringo was dead. Now he is sure."

Andy flinched despite himself.

Farley said, "They do take their politics serious down here."

CHAPTER THIRTEEN

C havez lighted a long black cheroot and stared up at Andy and Farley, his eyes unreadable. Though he was shorter than either man, he seemed taller to Andy. He held out his hand. "Your guns, please."

Farley hesitated. "I've got a sentimental attachment to my guns. I carried one of them all the way through the war. The other one I took off of a state policeman. He'd lost interest in it."

Andy cautioned, "You'd better give it to him, or he'll take it away from you the same way you got it." He forked over his own pistol to one of Chavez's lieutenants and nodded toward the rifle on his saddle. The man took it too. Farley then gave up. At Chavez's command a couple of his men helped Tony to his feet. Another led the unfortunate Jericho man's horse to Tony and carefully lifted him into the saddle. Chavez motioned for the Texans to get on their horses.

Tony slumped, weakened by the reopening of his wound, though the bleeding had stopped. He said, "Sorry, boys. When Tío Lupe gets his head set on somethin', it's hard to talk him out of it. But I'll keep workin' on him."

When Chavez was out of earshot Andy said, "From all the stories I've heard I thought he'd be a lot bigger, at least as large as Jericho or Jim McCawley. He reminds me of a banty rooster."

Farley replied, "A fightin' rooster. Santy Anna was a little man too, and look at all the hell he managed to cause."

The Chavez riders kept Andy and Farley hemmed up in the middle as they rode westward. It would have been foolhardy to try to run. They had nowhere to go except the river, and they would be cut down before their horses got their bellies wet. Andy tried to rationalize that Tony would soften his uncle's attitude, but he did not convince himself.

Farley muttered, "You've gotten us into a fix this time, Badger Boy."

"Me? I didn't do anything more than you did."

"But you're a jinx. Always was. Everything you get into causes me trouble. It's a wonder I'm not dead."

"You could've lit out with Hewitt."

"I wish I had. If we was still Rangers maybe Donahue would bring a rescue party and get us out of this. But as it is, I doubt he'll lift a finger. And it was you that got us fired."

Andy knew the futility of argument. For every answer he gave, Farley would come up with another complaint. He wondered how Teresa McCawley could see anything romantic about Farley. She would have a hard time gentling him if she managed to hook him, which she seemed to want to do. That was assuming he and Andy survived this scrape.

They came to a sprawling ranch headquarters, a mixture of stone and adobe buildings flanked by an expansive set of corrals built crudely but effectively of brush. It lay a mile or so south of the river. Smoke arose from several chimneys. The smell of burning wood reminded Andy that he had not eaten since last night's supper. He thought it best not to say anything that might be taken for complaint. He suspected that Chavez had a low tolerance for complaint, nor would he be hesitant in imposing a penalty. He had scarcely blinked when one of his riders had shot the fallen Jericho man.

Chavez barked a series of orders to his followers. Most dismounted and took up defensive positions while the others led their horses into a corral.

Chavez said, "One never knows what the Jericho may do. Come. We go to my house. I will tell the women it is time for *comida*."

Andy hoped that meant something to eat.

Chavez led them to a large stone house built along the same old Spanish lines as the home of Big Jim McCawley. He motioned for them to dismount and signaled one of his men to lead the horses away. He walked to the hand-hewn front door and beckoned the Texans and his nephew inside.

Farley muttered, "Like a fly into a spider's web."

Andy said, "You better do a lot of listenin' and damned little talkin'."

Two women came to meet them. Both were relatively young, and one was obviously pregnant. Chavez put his arm around her. The motions of his free hand told Andy he was talking to the women about the boy's wound.

Tony explained, "An old woman lives here, a *curandera*. She will make me well."

Andy said, "I hope she's cleaner than that old man who came to see you at McCawley's."

"That old man was no real *curandero*. He was a spy for my uncle. I told him when I would get away. Tío Lupe and his men waited for me at the river, but because of the Jerichos I could not cross where they expected me. That is why they were late."

Andy said, "They weren't the only ones who knew what you figured on doin'. Jericho's crew was layin' for you."

Chavez broke in. "The old man was two times a spy, sometimes for me and sometimes for the Jericho. He will not spy again."

Andy considered the implication and took no comfort in it. Death meant little to either Chavez or Jericho so long as it was not theirs.

Chavez went to a rustic old wooden cabinet and took out a bottle of some kind. He poured a drink for Tony and one for himself. He did not offer any to Andy or Farley. Instead he pointed to a pair of straight chairs. "You will sit. My men watch outside. If you try to go I will not have to concern myself with you anymore."

Chavez put his nephew's arm around his shoulder and took him down a long hall. The women followed. Farley continued to stand. Andy said, "He told us to sit."

Farley said, "I don't do somethin' just because some Mexican tells me to."

"Might be a good idea this time."

Farley sat.

Andy looked about the room. Instinctively he sought any opening that might offer escape, though he knew he would be caught and probably shot the moment he stepped outside. The furnishings were generally of fine quality but showed age and wear. He guessed most went back to Spanish colonial times. The house itself certainly did. It bespoke a more prosperous period, when a don could afford to buy luxuries from Mexico City and even Spain.

Farley said, "Livin' pretty high for Mexicans."

"The old don was a big landowner on both sides of the Rio Grande before the Americans came. I guess he believed in spendin' his money."

"I would too, if I had any."

"Your family still has a right smart of land. The carpetbaggers didn't steal all of it."

"It belongs to my mother and my sister, not to me." Farley's eyes widened a little. "Now that I think on it, the carpetbaggers did to us Bracketts what the Americans did to the Chavez family. But there were people here before the Chavezes. The Spanish did to the Indians what the Americans did to the Spanish and the Mexicans later. And what your Comanches did to the Apaches and any other Indians that got in their way. The same things keep happenin' over and over again. It's just the people that change."

Andy wanted to argue but recognized the truth in Farley's comment. "The trouble you stirred up with the carpetbaggers and the state police was like what Lupe Chavez does to Jericho and the other gringos."

"But I never hurt no honest citizens. Chavez don't make much distinction as long as they're gringo."

"He still looks on it like a war. Wars always hurt innocent people."

Farley frowned. "That ain't no reason to sympathize with him."

"But I do, sort of. It'd be simpler if I didn't. Then I wouldn't be pulled one way and another over what's right and what's wrong."

An old woman entered the house. She carried a small cotton bag. One of the younger women met her and escorted her down the hall. Andy reasoned that she was the *curandera* Tony had mentioned. He could hear a buzz of conversation from the direction of Tony's room.

Lupe Chavez returned, a satisfied look on his face. "All is well now. When the old woman speaks, heaven listens."

Andy said, "Wouldn't it be better to have a real doctor look at him?"

"Doña María is a doctor. She has not the papers from the university, but she knows things that are not written in the university's books."

Andy shrugged. He had little doubt that Tony would survive anyhow. He had been well on the way to healing before his fall reopened the wound. With a *curandera*'s attentions it might just take a little longer.

Chavez said, "You doubt, but there is much you gringos do not know."

Andy said, "I spent several years with the Comanches. They had their own version of the *curanderos*."

That piqued Chavez's interest. "You are not Indian."

"They tried to make one out of me. Came awful close."

Chavez demanded to know more. Andy told him how Comanche

raiders had killed his mother and father and taken him to raise as one of their own. He had been well on his way to becoming a warrior when he fell back into the white man's world.

Chavez became more animated. "There was a time we had to fight the Indians. In the days of my grandfather they drove many of our people off of their land. But not him. He built this house to be a fort. Never did they break in. Neither will the Jericho. Neither will the *rinches*."

"They tell me Jericho's house is a lot like this one."

"Because my grandfathers built it to stand against the Indians. But it could not stand against the lawyers and the Yankee land grabbers. They fight with paper, not with guns. So many lawyers, so many papers."

"Me and Farley, we're not lawyers. There ain't nothin' we can do to help you, and nothin' we can do to hurt you, either. I don't see any need in us stayin' here."

Chavez frowned. "I still do not know if you are spies for the *rinches*."

"We ain't. Even if we were, there's nothin' we could tell that would be of any use to them. They already know where this place is, and they'll pretty soon figure out that Tony is here. But they can't do anything about it. It's illegal for them to cross the border."

"It was illegal when the McNelly came with all his *rinches* across the river and invaded the Rancho Las Cuevas. He killed many men who were not bandits. He killed them only because they were Mexicans. Some were of my blood. My very own family."

Andy had heard stories about McNelly's bold raid in pursuit of bandits. It was claimed afterward that he hit the wrong ranch and killed several innocent men before he found his intended target. By then he was surrounded by Mexican soldiers and vaqueros. Only intervention by the U.S. Army extricated him and averted the annihilation of his command. Even so, he provoked an international incident that raised smoke all the way to Washington and Mexico City.

On the positive side, the border raids stopped for a while. Under the circumstances Andy did not think it prudent to mention that. All he said was, "I wasn't here. Neither was Farley."

"But you are *americanos*. You share the blame."

Andy was familiar with the concept of collective guilt, though he did not agree with it. To the Comanches, a wrong by one white was a wrong by all whites. Vengeance could be exacted upon any who came in handy.

Chavez said, "Poor Mexico. So far from God and so near to Texas."

The two younger women came up the hall. Chavez spoke, and both answered him at the same time. He turned to Andy and Farley. "We will eat now. Not even a gringo *rinche* is to be hungry in this house."

Andy took this as a hopeful sign that Chavez did not intend to shoot them, at least not for a while.

Chavez led them into a dining room, where the women began placing food on a large handmade table that had legs thick as fence posts. Its varnish had darkened with age and was worn through along the edges and much of the top. "You will sit."

He bowed his head and spoke a prayer. Andy found that inconsistent with the shooting of the wounded Jericho man, but he had never understood the flexible interpretations given religion by people who considered themselves civilized. It seemed they could find biblical justification for almost anything they chose to do.

Finished eating, Chavez said, "It is true that you wanted only to take Antonio back to his mother?"

Andy nodded. "And his stepfather. Big Jim has been awful worried about him."

"That man's name is not spoken in this house."

"Why? He's your sister's husband, and he raised Tony like he was his own."

"But he is not of our blood. The Jericho took our land with lawyers and a gun. The McCawley took it with a wedding. In the end it was all the same."

"You're wrong. Him and your sister love each other."

"That I do not believe. What he loves is the land. Our land."

Andy quit arguing. To anger Chavez might put Farley and himself in deeper jeopardy. He pushed his chair back from the table and said, "What now?"

"I am still thinking. You will stay while I decide." He walked to the door and shouted to a vaquero who stood outside, watching the trail. "You will follow Porfirio. He will see that you go nowhere."

Porfirio was tall and lanky with dark eyes cold as January. He carried two pistols and a rifle, which he politely but firmly pointed toward a small stone outbuilding that had a front door but no windows. He motioned for them to enter, then closed the door behind them. Andy heard the clatter of a bar dropped into place.

He said, "Pretty dark in here."

Farley replied, "Kind of like our future."

"Don't give up. I believe Tony'll keep talkin' in our favor."

"He's not much more than a kid. You think Chavez will pay any attention to him?"

"Seems to me like these Mexicans put a lot of store in blood relations."

"Especially when you hurt one of them."

Andy's eyes accustomed themselves to the dark interior. He found a goatskin and spread it on the dirt floor, then stretched out on it. "After ridin' all night and finally gettin' my stomach full, I'm tired out."

"You may be fixin' to get a lot longer sleep than you figured on." Farley found a piece of canvas and made a bed of sorts. "Every time I try to do a good deed for somebody, I find myself in trouble all the way up to my chin."

Cracks in the stone wall and around the door admitted just enough light that Andy could guess at the sun's position. Just at dusk he heard a commotion outside: dogs barking, a babble of voices, several shouts of warning. He sat up, wondering if Rancho Chavez was being invaded by Rangers or perhaps Jericho's outfit. He heard no shots, however.

Andy went to the door and tried to peer out through the narrow space at its edge. "Can't see a thing."

Farley said, "If it's good news we'll hear about it eventually. If it's bad we'll hear sooner."

After a while Andy heard the bar being removed. Porfirio swung the door open and beckoned, giving a curt command. Andy and Farley both blinked, for even at dusk the light seemed bright after their confinement in near darkness. Porfirio pointed toward the house. "*A la casa.*"

A buggy stood in front. Several vaqueros were gathered around it or were watching the front door. They appeared to be having a heated discussion.

One of Chavez's young women opened the door and motioned for Andy and Farley to enter.

Teresa McCawley shouted, "Farley! Are you all right?"

Teresa and her mother stood in the parlor. Teresa rushed to Farley and threw her arms around him. Farley looked surprised and confused, keeping his arms at his sides for a moment, then raising them to embrace the girl. "Ain't nothin' wrong with me," he said. "What's all the fuss about?"

For the first time Andy saw Big Jim McCawley over in a corner. He and Lupe Chavez were engaged in a silent staring match. It was not friendly.

McCawley asked, "You boys all right?"

Andy said, "We're fine. Been enjoyin' Mr. Chavez's hospitality. Kind of surprised to see you here."

"I'm surprised myself, but we had to come and see what happened to Tony. We had no idea we'd find you-all here too."

"Mr. Chavez insisted on us stayin'."

McCawley explained that one of the ranch hands had overtaken them on the San Antonio road with news of Tony's break. "Tony says he wouldn't have made it to the river if you-all hadn't come along at just the right time. I'm obliged to you. We all are."

Andy looked at Chavez, searching for any sign that he shared that gratitude. He said, "Me and Farley will escort you-all home when you're ready to go. You might run into some of the Jericho bunch." He looked to Chavez, half expecting to be contradicted.

In a cold manner Chavez told McCawley, "I offer you escort to the river. You will want to cross before dark. The women are welcome to stay as long as they wish."

Big Jim said stubbornly, "We'll all go together when my wife and daughter say so."

The two men stared hard at each other again until finally Chavez shrugged. "Naturally they will wish to stay with Antonio awhile. I do not like you, gringo, but you are safe under my roof."

"I've got a bedroll. I'll sleep outside and not contaminate your house."

Sternly Chavez said, "You stole our land by marrying my sister. So you will do the proper thing. You will sleep in a bed with the woman you married. She is your property now, just like our land."

Big Jim declared, "She's not property. Can't you get it through your wooden head that I married *her*, not your land?"

Juana McCawley's face flushed in anger. She lashed into her brother in rapid-fire Spanish that crackled like burning cedar. Andy did not understand the words, but their meaning was clear.

Chavez tried to stand up to her but finally slumped in surrender. He said, "I can defeat an army of *rinches* or the men of the Jericho. But I cannot stand against a determined woman."

Teresa held to Farley's arm. She launched a tirade of her own. Chavez shook his head sadly. "You also?"

"Yes, me too. Farley is my friend. You will not hold him any longer."

Chavez shrugged again. "You may all stay or you may all go. I wash my hands."

Andy spent two uneasy days until the two women were certain Tony would recover. They gave up hope that he would consent to leave his uncle and return home with them. Big Jim assured them, "He's probably safer here anyway, south of the river. Jericho might try for him again if Tony was at our place."

Juana and Teresa said their good-byes to Tony. Big Jim stood behind them, sadness in his eyes. Tony had spoken to him but little, and only in a formal, standoffish manner. He pointedly avoided addressing him either by name or by any version of the word *father*.

Farley muttered, "That boy needs a good whippin' with a wet rope."

Andy said, "He just ain't finished growin' up yet. Maybe he'll get better."

"If he don't get himself killed before that. I'll say this for him, though, he'd poke a bear in the eye with a willow switch and then try to skin him."

Teresa kissed her brother and told him, "We'll be back to see you real soon." She looked hopefully at Farley. "You're coming with us, aren't you?" She added as an afterthought, "You and Andy?"

Farley seemed a little flustered. "If you want us to."

"I do."

As he and Andy mounted their horses, Farley said, "You know how close we came to gettin' buried on this place?"

"The McCawleys saved our bacon. Them and Tony." He had to give Tony that much credit, at least.

Farley stole a glance at Teresa. "I swear that little girl gets to lookin' prettier all the time. If only she wasn't half Mexican."

"If it was me, I wouldn't let that make any difference."

"It oughtn't to, but it does."

Chavez sent an escort of vaqueros along to see the McCawley party safely to the river. None of the Chavez men would have dared molest them, but the region was infested by bandits over whom Chavez had no control. Several of McCawley's cowboys had camped on the north bank, waiting for their employer's return. They would pick up the escort duty. Andy and Farley were not really needed, but they had nowhere else in particular to go.

The procession crossed at a shallow ford. Chavez had sent a messenger to alert the McCawley crew, so the cowboys were waiting as the buggy and the horsemen pulled up out of the water. Andy's horse shook himself like a dog, startling the buggy team. McCawley had to draw hard on the lines.

Andy saw that the reception committee was more than the McCawley cowboys. Sergeant Donahue was there with several of his Rangers, including Hewitt. He touched the brim of his hat in deference to the women and told Big Jim, "From what folks say about you and Lupe Chavez, I wasn't sure you'd come back alive."

McCawley acknowledged him with a nod. "Folks say a lot of things that aren't true, Sergeant. Lupe and I are kinfolks, sort of."

"Some of the worst fights I ever saw was between kinfolks." Donahue turned a stern face toward Andy and Farley. "Don't you two know that you had no legal right to go into Mexico?"

Andy said, "That was when we were Rangers, but we're just citizens now. You fired us."

"I sometimes say things in the heat of the moment that I do not mean."

"You hirin' us back?"

"I never took you from the rolls. The company is too far under strength."

Farley's eyes took on a calculating look. "Maybe you could see clear to give us a raise in pay."

"The pay scale is set by the state. I have nothin' to do with it."

"It was worth a try." Farley glanced at Andy. "What say, Badger Boy? Want to give the Rangers another chance?"

Andy was not sure what his reaction should be. He said, "I don't see where I've got anything better to do."

Jericho Jackson brushed away the marks of the saddle from his favorite gray horse as it cooled down from the afternoon's riding. Working with his hands helped him relieve some of his tension. He fretted, "I don't know what's become of that old man Gonzales. I'd sure like him to tell me what's goin' on down at Chavez's."

Burt Hatton stuffed a wad of chewing tobacco into his mouth. "He probably took hisself up to Laredo and got drunk. You know these Meskins. Put a little money in their pocket and you won't see them again till they drink it all up. It takes twenty of them chili pickers to make a dozen."

"I'd give a thousand dollars to know what Chavez is up to."

Hatton said, "For a thousand dollars I'd go down there and ask him."

"Even if you got close enough to listen, you couldn't savvy what they said."

Jericho had not been among those who tried to ambush Tony as he left the McCawley house. Always leery of Big Jim McCawley, he had put Hatton in charge of that project. It had gone awry, as too often happened with Hatton. Jericho had come with the reinforcements who tried to stop Tony just short of the river, but he had been frustrated by the arrival of three Rangers.

For a time now Jericho had been on the lookout for a new lieutenant. When he found one he would send Hatton off on some mission likely to get him killed. The best thing to do with mistakes was to bury them.

Jericho said, "I can't help feelin' like that damned bandit is plottin' some kind of strike against me. He's bound to've figured out that we laid a trap for him with that herd of cattle. He'll be achin' to square up."

"Too bad we missed gettin' that nephew of his. At least we bloodied him up a little."

"All the more reason to wonder what Chavez may do next. I can't afford to leave here right now."

"Why would you want to?"

Jericho's eyes pinched. "That good woman of mine is still grievin' over her nephew. I been thinkin' about takin' her back to Missouri to spend some time amongst her kin. Maybe the change would ease her mind and set her to dwellin' on other things."

Jericho was about the strongest man Hatton had ever known, but he had one outstanding weakness in Hatton's view: he was excessively devoted to his wife. As unyielding as he might be to the men around him, he seemed almost subservient to her. Hatton believed women were emotionally unstable, so it was the man's responsibility to make the decisions. A woman's place was in the kitchen and the bedroom. She should keep her opinions to herself. That was little enough to ask if a man was expected to work and support her.

Hatton had been married once when he was young and foolish. He had left that nagging woman years ago and never looked back. He could not understand why Jericho bent backward to please his wife. Hatton would have told her to quit whining and get back to her knitting.

He knew that Jericho's fixation on avenging his nephew was prompted by his wife's grief even more than any of his own. Because of it, several Jericho men had died, and more might yet do so. Hatton would like to stop it, but he was boxed in. It might cost his life if he told Jericho who had really killed his nephew. He was not prepared to die for anybody, man or woman.

Jericho rubbed his red beard. "I've about made up my mind to hit Chavez before he can hit me again. I'll gather me a bunch of bold men, cross the river, and wipe out that Chavez outfit for good and all."

Hatton shook his head. "McNelly tried that once. Found himself up against a whole company of Meskin soldiers and come within an inch of gettin' slaughtered."

"Because he hit the wrong ranch and lost the element of surprise. By the time he got to where he meant to go in the first place, they were ready and waitin' for him. The way to handle Chavez would be to hit fast, hit hard, and leave nobody standin'."

Including some of us, Hatton thought. He did not relish being caught up in any such reckless venture. If need be, he could get along without Jericho. He had been skimming off some of the proceeds from cattle he had driven north for Jericho. He had a secret account salted away in a San Antonio bank. It would see him to a new life in some distant place beyond Jericho's reach.

He asked, "When you figure on doin' all this?"

"I don't see any reason to wait. Send out the word. We're hirin' fightin' men."

"Some of them will get theirselves killed."

"We won't have to pay the ones that don't come back."

CHAPTER
FOURTEEN

Andy was trying to decide if he had made a mistake, remaining a Ranger. Sergeant Donahue's attitude toward him seemed no better than before. He realized he would not have been retained had Donahue not been too shorthanded to patrol the river properly. He sent Andy the farthest of all the Rangers, way upriver from the base camp. Given a pack mule to carry supplies, he had to set up his own rude camp west of Len Tanner's appointed area of responsibility. Every second day he rode east until he encountered Len, then turned back to the west.

He had cooked for himself before, but it made eating more a chore than a pleasure. He lost weight. Only his coffee had any appealing flavor. After a few days he became acquainted with several Mexicans who lived near the river. He communicated mostly with an improvised sign language. What he recalled of plains-Indian hand talk was of little use, for the Mexicans did not understand it any better than they understood his English. In spite of the language barrier he managed to arrange for a couple of the women to cook a meal for him each time he passed by, though it was costing him most of his meager Ranger salary.

His assignment was to watch for sign of any major movements across the river from either direction. So far he had seen none. After a time he was just going through the motions, riding his appointed circuit as ordered but expecting to find nothing. In his loneliness he found himself spending more and more time visiting with residents who farmed along the Rio Grande. He began picking up fragments of Spanish. He found that some of these people worked hard to scratch out a living from a land that was grudging in yielding up its gifts. Others did only as much as they had to. Some were cheerful; some were moody, distrustful, and made little effort to communicate, especially with a Ranger. In short, they were much the same as people he had known elsewhere, white, red, or brown.

The one characteristic almost all had in common was that they considered themselves to be Mexicans rather than citizens of American Texas. To them the border was a political concept that they usually ignored. He was conscious of small-scale smuggling in both directions, mainly of liquor and tobacco, horses and cattle. He saw no significant harm in it so long as it did not involve raiding and violence. Some small farmers worked land and raised livestock on both sides of the river just as they had done when Texas was part of Mexico and the boundary was only an imaginary line.

So what, he asked himself, if Austin or Mexico City lost a little tariff revenue? Politicians could waste more in a day than penny-ante smugglers might cost in six months. If Donahue wanted such small-scale traffic stopped, he would have to send somebody else.

One day as he paused at the river's edge to let his black horse drink he saw two men approaching from the east, one riding, one walking and leading a horse that limped. He took them for local Mexicans until they came close enough that he could see they were Americans, one tall, one short. The tall one, on horseback, raised a hand in greeting. His round, sunburned face looked genial. Andy responded in kind.

"Hell of a thing," the man said, "havin' a horse come up lame way out in this nowhere country. My partner's gettin' footsore."

The shorter man was limping about as badly as his horse. His weary face was lined in misery.

The tall one said, "We been lookin' for somebody who might make a trade with us. A good horse for a lame one."

Andy replied, "Might be hard to come by without you're willin' to pay some boot."

The walker came up even with the man on horseback. He rubbed a dusty sleeve across his face and blinked the sting of sweat from his eyes. He had a scraggly beard of uncertain color, longer in some places than in others, like a garden with a spotty crop. He asked, "Do you know Jericho Jackson?"

Andy was instantly wary. "I've met the gentleman."

"Maybe you can tell us where his place is at. We're thinkin' we've come too far upriver."

Andy gave both men a long study. He saw nothing in their appearance that would brand them as criminals. Their clothing .was dusty and worn, holes unpatched at the knees. They looked like any number of working trail hands he had seen. Everything about them bespoke short rations and low pay. But he had to distrust anyone looking for Jericho. "You've come farther than you had to. From here you'd travel north and bear a bit to the east."

"How will we know when we're on his land?"

"You won't have to find him. He'll find you, or his men will."

The tall man in the saddle said, "Sounds like who we been lookin' for. Goin' to be hard to get there with a lame horse, though. I don't suppose you'd like to swap?"

"I don't suppose I would."

"You said we might need some boot. How's this?" So swiftly that Andy hardly saw the movement, the rider had a pistol in his hand. "Now, about that swap . . . we'd like it to be friendly."

His face no longer appeared genial.

Andy gauged his chances of successful resistance and knew they were next to none. Rusty had always told him there were times to fight and times to pull away. This was clearly no time to push his luck, not while he looked down the muzzle of a .44.

The man with the pistol said, "Before you get off, let's see you drop that six-shooter. Be real careful, or you could get a couple of holes in you that the good Lord didn't put there."

Andy considered warning them that he was a Ranger but thought better of it. The two might decide to take no chances with him if they knew. It would be easy to murder him and drag his body into the brush, where it might not be found for months, if at all. He eased the pistol from its holster and let it fall. The rifle was still in its scabbard, but he knew he had no chance to draw it. He dismounted and stepped away from the horse but held on to the reins. "It's not a good trade unless both parties are willin'."

"Me and Devlin are willin'. I reckon two out of three ought to be enough."

The limping man named Devlin removed the saddles from both horses and put his on Andy's mount. He took Andy's rifle and scabbard. "I wouldn't want you to back out on the deal and shoot us with this Winchester. Me and Barstow will cut cards later and see who gets it."

Barstow grinned. The genial look returned but seemed tainted now. "No hard feelin's, I hope. At least we're leavin' you your saddle and a horse to put it on. I hope you won't abuse him. He's gettin' some age on him, but that ankle will heal if you give it time."

The two men were laughing as they rode off to the north. Angry words welled up in Andy's throat and stayed there. He saw no use in saying them aloud when nobody could hear. He turned to examine the brown horse. He saw nothing special in its conformation to mark it as anything except a working ranch horse. The lameness was in the right leg. He lifted it, hoping the cause might be nothing more than a stone caught in the shoe. There was no stone. There was no shoe. The ankle appeared swollen.

"Looks like I'm not goin' to ride you anywhere," he said. He led the horse to the edge of the river to see if it would drink. It took several swallows, then raised its head, water dripping from chin and steel bits.

He was a couple of miles from his campsite. He had left the pack mule there, staked on a long rope to allow it to graze. He considered the mule, but it was not broken to ride. It would probably balk and refuse to move if he tried to get on it. Or else it would throw him off and kick him hard enough to break his ribs.

Perhaps when Andy did not meet Len at their usual rendezvous site he would come looking. Then again, he might decide Andy was simply late and get tired of waiting. Andy guessed that the sun was only a couple of hours short of setting. Chances were that the two horse thieves would stop and camp at dark, figuring they were safe. They might not appreciate how fast a determined man could walk.

They had not stripped his saddle of anything except the rifle, so he had his canteen and a chunk of bacon he had roasted but not finished at noon. He set off following the tracks. The thieves had taken the northeasterly direction he suggested. He was soon sweating. A southerly breeze found its way through his shirt and cooled him. At intervals he came across grazing cattle. Some shied away. Others, not used to seeing a man afoot, approached out of curiosity. A few even trotted alongside for short distances before they lost interest or he scared them off with a shout and a wave of his hat.

A coyote loped off a hundred yards, then turned to watch him. He had heard it said that coyotes could tell whether a man carried a firearm or not. He did not believe that, but he respected the Indian view of the coyote as trickster, a mischievous spirit always ready to foil the designs of men.

He stopped for short periods of rest, but impatience soon prodded him back to his feet. He wanted to go as far as possible before darkness. Though he intended to keep traveling after nightfall, following the tracks would be more difficult, perhaps impossible. Then he would have to depend upon his sense of direction. The two seemed to be traveling as straight a line as the uneven terrain allowed.

The stars indicated that it was somewhere around midnight when he spotted the faint glow of a dying campfire a little west of his line of travel. He indulged a moment in self-congratulation for managing to stay so close to the trail after darkness made him give up looking for it.

He hoped to catch the two asleep. He did not want to confront them in daylight with no weapon better than a mesquite club.

He moved carefully toward the glow, listening for any sound that might indicate someone was still awake. He heard nothing but distant night birds and the humming of nocturnal insects seeking to mate. He almost stumbled into the two horses. One snorted and pulled against the stake rope that held it. Andy sank to his knees and waited for a reaction from the sleeping men. He heard nothing.

He found the saddles. One of the thieves had buckled Andy's scabbard to his own rig. He quietly slid the rifle free. He tried not to look into the remnant of the fire because it compromised his vision in the darkness. He located the two men, both wrapped in their blankets asleep. He saw a gun belt rolled up and lying by one man's head. Gingerly he drew the pistol from it and stuck it in his own holster, which the thieves had not bothered to take. He moved to the side of the other man. He too had a pistol in a belt, and a second lying beside his head. Andy assumed that was his own. He retrieved both and retreated to the smoldering fire.

To one side of it he found a can in which the men had boiled coffee. Some of it remained, but it was cold. He set the can on the coals to reheat it.

He could have awakened the men then but preferred not to take a chance with them in the dark. He sat on the ground, sipping the bitterly strong coffee and waiting for daylight.

They might have been trail hands, but if so they had given up the drover's habit of rising before dawn. The sun was breaking free before Barstow yawned and laid his blanket aside. He blinked and stretched his arms, then became aware of Andy sitting there watching him. He froze.

Andy said, "Sleepin' kind of late, aren't you? I heard a rooster crow somewhere an hour ago."

Devlin flung his blanket aside and grabbed for his six-shooter. He came up with an empty holster. Andy waved a pistol at him. "It's over here."

Both men stared at him in shock. Barstow slowly raised his hands. Devlin followed, his jaw sagging.

Barstow turned angrily on his partner. "Told you we ought to've taken turns standin' watch last night."

Devlin's tone was accusatory. "Mister, I didn't believe you'd be so mean as to follow us on a lame horse."

"I didn't. I walked."

"Walked?" The two looked as if such a foreign idea had never entered their heads.

Andy said, "I get the notion you two ain't been at this outlaw business long. You're not very good at it."

Barstow said, "We got awful tired of herdin' cattle for beans and bacon. We thought there must be an easier way to make a livin'. We heard Jericho Jackson was lookin' for men who can handle theirselves and that he pays good."

"Whoever told you that should've also told you life can be short over at Jericho's. He's bad about gettin' men killed."

"Couldn't be any more dangerous than swimmin' cattle over a river when it's runnin' high."

"With Jericho you're liable to be crossin' stolen cattle over the Rio Grande with a bunch of mad Mexicans grabbin' at your shirttails. But I'm savin' you from that. I'm puttin' you under arrest."

"Arrest?" Barstow demanded.

"I forgot to tell you. I'm a Ranger."

Barstow turned on Devlin. "Damned if you ain't fooled around and got us in trouble again. It's easy, you said. Just swap horses, you said. If you hadn't been careless you never would've got yours lame in the first place."

"I couldn't help it. I didn't know he was so clumsy. He looked pretty good in the dark."

Andy surmised that Devlin had stolen that horse just as he had taken Andy's. He said, "I'm takin' mine back. You-all can switch around, one walkin' and one ridin'."

Devlin complained, "But I got blisters on my feet."

"The wages of sin. You-all get busy and fix us some breakfast. No use in startin' out on an empty stomach."

The meager meal consisted of coffee, bacon, and some dried-out bread the two had brought from somewhere. Done but hardly satisfied, Andy said, "Roll up your blankets and let's be movin'."

Devlin's stirrups were set a little short, but it would take time to unlace the leathers and retie them for Andy's longer legs. It was too far to go back for his own saddle. He hoped nobody would make off with it before he could get back to reclaim it.

Devlin complained constantly about his sore feet until Andy made Barstow change places with him. Then Devlin complained that Barstow's horse had a rough gait that shook his innards all the way up to his teeth. He reminded Andy a little of Farley Brackett.

Barstow trudged along, starting to sweat though the morning was only moderately warm. He argued, "Ranger, we ain't really done anybody harm. You got your horse back. We ain't robbed no bank or nothin'. Can't you see your way clear to just turn us loose? We'll take up our old jobs drivin' cattle and go to church every chance we get."

Andy said, "I know an old preacher man named Webb. He says that the church house is half empty as long as everything goes along smooth. But when there's trouble, people start comin' to meetin'. You two were all set to join Jericho's bunch of renegades. Now you're ready to sing in the choir."

"We'd been drinkin'. We're sober now, and things look different."

"Yeah. This time *I'm* holdin' the gun."

"I hear tell that the penitentiary is already overcrowded. I'd hate for us to make it worse."

Andy wondered how long the conversion would last when nobody was pointing a gun at the pair of would-be bad men. "It'll be up to a judge and jury to decide about that."

"Think how much a trial will cost the taxpayers."

Andy thought back on the prisoner he had seen shot in the Ranger camp. "Be glad it was me that caught you. Some Rangers wouldn't bother with a trial. Bullets come cheaper than lawyers."

Barstow shut up for a while, but Devlin kept whining.

Andy saw three horsemen approaching in a slow lope. He could not tell immediately whether they were Texan or Mexican, but instinct told him they were trouble. He drew his pistol and laid it across his lap.

Barstow said, "I hope them ain't some of your quick-trigger Rangers."

Devlin quit whining. His eyes were apprehensive. "We're your prisoners. You got to protect us."

Andy said, "They're not Rangers, at least none that I know. I'll bet they're Jericho hands."

The three reined up so close that Andy could have reached out and touched the one who by his manner appeared to be in charge. The leader demanded, "Who are you people? Don't you know you're on Jericho's road?"

It was not much of a road. It was more like a cow trail. Andy sized up the three and quickly decided they were not the kind he would lend money to. Like Andy, the leader held a pistol in his lap. The other two gripped rifles.

Andy said, "I'm Andy Pickard. I'm a Ranger. These men are my prisoners."

"I'm Orville Mapes, and your name don't mean a thing to me." He studied Barstow and Devlin. "These men ain't part of Jericho's outfit. What did they do?"

"They stole a horse. Mine."

Barstow spoke up with hope. "We was on our way to see Mr. Jericho Jackson about a job."

Mapes mused, "And you stole a Ranger's horse? Jericho ain't goin' to figure you're real smart."

"We didn't know he was a Ranger."

Devlin said, "If we had, we'd have shot him right off."

Mapes looked again at Andy. "Ranger or not, you've got no authority on Jericho's land without he gives you permission."

"Rangers don't have to ask for anybody's permission. They can go anywhere they decide to."

"Not on Jericho's property. I think you'd better hand me that six-shooter."

Andy knew he could not shoot his way out with three men at close range. He would be dead before the echo faded. He gave up the pistol and his rifle. They also confiscated the weapons he had taken from Barstow and Devlin.

Barstow asked, "What about us? You're goin' to turn us loose, ain't you?"

Mapes said, "I'm takin' you to Jericho. He'll decide what to do with you."

Barstow tried to speak with confidence. "He's just the man we wanted to see." A wavering in his voice betrayed doubt.

"Maybe. Then again, there's people who've seen him and wished they hadn't." Mapes jerked his head at Andy. "You-all seem to be short a horse. I don't suppose you'd object to this man ridin' double with you?"

His tone indicated that it was a command rather than a question. Andy saw no point in replying. He took his left foot out of the stirrup to allow Barstow to swing into position behind the saddle. The horse humped up a little, not liking the extra burden. Andy wished he would pitch Barstow off, but the horse settled down.

As they rode, Barstow continued pressing the case that he and Devlin could provide useful service on Jericho's crew. Mapes looked straight ahead and seemed to pay little attention.

Their conversion had been shorter than some of Preacher Webb's sermons, Andy thought.

At first he was surprised to see that Jericho's headquarters looked much like those of Lupe Chavez and Big Jim McCawley. On reflection he recalled that all had been built at about the same time and by the same people, the forebears of Don Cipriano Chavez. Designed for defense against hostile Indians, Jericho's place would still be a formidable fortress. Andy would not like to have to lead a charge against it.

Mapes pointed them toward an adobe barn backed by an extensive layout of corrals, much like Big Jim's. "We'll all wait out here till Jericho sees fit to come and look you over."

One of the men with him asked, "Why not take them up to the main house instead of troublin' Jericho to come to the barn?"

"Nobody goes up to the main house unless it's with Jericho's say-so," Mapes said. "He doesn't like his missus seein' the kind of men he associates with."

"You mean us?"

"If you was married to a pretty little woman from Kansas City, you wouldn't want her puttin' up with this grimy bunch."

Barstow asked anxiously, "What happens to us?"

"Who knows? He may decide to hire you, or he may decide to shoot you. With him you never know."

Devlin suggested, "Maybe we ought to've written him a letter before we came."

Andy wondered if he could write.

Mapes herded Andy and the two thieves into a corner of the barn. He said, "You-all had just as well sit. I'll go up and tell Jericho you're here. He'll get around to you in his own good time."

Andy sat on the dirt floor. Mapes left his two helpers to watch. One leaned against a saddle rack and spun the cylinder of his pistol. The other propped himself against the doorjamb and aimed his rifle casually at supposed targets outside. Andy compared their faces with those of Barstow and Devlin. They had a hard-bitten, determined look. They might at one time have been working cowhands, but now they fitted Andy's conception of hired pistoleros who would commit any crime if the pay was right.

He asked Barstow, "Think you-all have got it in you to qualify for a bunch like that?"

Barstow seemed too troubled to answer. Devlin stared apprehensively at the two Jericho men but tried to sound confident. "You're the one that needs to worry, Ranger. I doubt as they've got any patience for lawmen here. They're liable to cut off your ears and send them to Austin."

Barstow growled, "Shut up, Devlin. You may give them ideas about what to do with me and you."

Jericho seemed in no hurry to see his visitors. Andy waited in the barn for more than an hour before he saw a shadow fall across the threshold. Jericho's broad shoulders almost blocked the door. He walked halfway across the room and waited while his eyes adjusted to the poor light. Andy and the two thieves stood up. Jericho looked first at Barstow and Devlin, then at Andy. His eyes brightened with recognition.

"I've already made your acquaintance, Ranger. You had that boy Antonio. I wanted him, but you wouldn't let me have him."

He had seen Andy once before that, but Andy thought it prudent not to remind him of the day when one of his windmill towers had mysteriously burned down. Andy said, "It's against Ranger policy to turn a prisoner over for lynchin'."

"I wasn't goin' to lynch him. He'd have gotten a fair trial. We have our own court to try thieves and killers and trespassers."

"A kangaroo court."

"Nobody has ever appealed a rulin'."

"Maybe they haven't lived long enough."

Jericho's face darkened. "Don't be tryin' my patience. I don't have enough of it to waste."

As long as his blood was up, Andy decided to keep pushing. "They say you're runnin' a haven here for men in trouble with the law."

"Call it a sanctuary. The Mexicans hit somebody, then run to sanctuary on the other side of the river. You Rangers can't touch them there. I say if it works for them, it ought to work for me. I'm runnin' a sanctuary of my own here. I don't want the Rangers messin' with it."

"But you're in Texas. Lupe Chavez ain't."

"I'll say this for you, Ranger, you've got guts to come on my ranch and try to lecture me like that."

"I'm just sayin' what I think."

Jericho rubbed a big hand across his chin, squeezing his red-bearded face into a grotesque shape. "And most men in your place would've let me have that kid. Was you really prepared to die protectin' him?"

"I don't know. I never had to make that decision. Big Jim McCawley came along just in time."

The name brought a wistful look from Jericho. "Big Jim. You know, me and him used to be friends a long time ago, before he fell in with the Mexicans."

"But you still wanted to kill his son."

"Stepson. The boy ain't of his blood."

Jericho turned belligerently on Barstow and Devlin. "What about you two? What's your excuse for trespassin' where you wasn't asked?"

Devlin pleaded, "Me and Barstow came here hopin' we could work for you. We ain't got no truck with the Rangers."

"Work for me?" Jericho snorted. "What could you do?"

Devlin said eagerly, "We stole the Ranger's horse."

"And got caught. Damned little recommendation."

Barstow said, "We learn easy. Just tell us what to do and we'll do it."

Jericho beckoned to Mapes. "Take these two to Burt Hatton. If he can find a use for them, they can stay. If he can't . . ." He did not finish. Andy knew by the apprehension in the two men's faces that they were finishing the sentence for him in their minds.

Jericho turned his attention to Andy. "I've never been friends with the Rangers, but maybe it's time I tried to be. I can see where they might be of use to me."

"It's our job to enforce the law. We're not supposed to play favorites."

"I'd just ask you to lean a little in my direction in case a dispute was to come up. Most of my trouble has been with Mexican border jumpers, so that oughtn't to be hard for you to do. They're illegal anyway, the minute they set foot on the Texas side of the river."

"I'm just a private. Even the camp cook doesn't ask my opinion about anything."

Jericho asked Andy's name, and Andy told him. Jericho said, "I don't suppose you're a married man, Pickard?"

"I haven't had time for such as that."

"Any prospects?"

"Maybe, if I was to ask her. But it wouldn't be much of a life for her, bein' married to a Ranger who's always movin' around from one camp to another."

"You'll get tired of that sooner or later. Every man ought to get married. Havin' a wife gives you somethin' to come home for instead of spendin' all your time with the likes of the men you've seen around here."

Andy was surprised to hear that kind of talk from a man everyone branded as an unredeemed outlaw. It did not fit the image he had built in his mind. Lupe Chavez had not fit his preconceived notion, either. Both men aroused doubts about the validity of public opinion.

Jericho said, "Havin' a good woman can be the salvation of a man. I'd have you come down and meet mine, but she's not in a mood for company right now. She never could have any children herself, so she took her nephew under her wing after her sister died. Some of the Chavez gang killed him a while back."

"Sorry."

"I've had to watch that good woman grieve herself half to death. That's why I've wanted to get my hands on Chavez's nephew. I want Lupe to know how it feels."

"Would it make your wife feel better to know Tony's mother was grievin' the same way she does?"

"*I'd* feel better. Blood for blood. An eye for an eye."

Andy asked, "Is that why you're so dead set against Mexicans?"

"My feelin' about Mexicans goes back a lot further than that. It goes all the way back to when Texas fought for independence from Mexico."

"You're not old enough to've been in that fight."

"I'm old enough to remember it, though. I remember seein' my daddy take his rifle down from over the mantel and ride off to join the rebellion. Mexican soldiers caught him and stood him against a wall. Shot him down like a dog.

"My mother put me on a mule. We started runnin' for the Louisiana border to get away from Santy Anna's army. It was rainy and cold, and we bogged in mud plumb to our knees. She taken pneumonia and died. Left me all by myself, just a shirttail young'un. Damn near starved to death before I learned to take whatever I needed, however I had to. Lie, steal, whatever it took. I've been at war against Mexicans ever since."

Andy could think of a few arguments, but he knew they would not make a dent against so deep a hatred.

Jericho said, "I suppose you've got an old mother somewhere, puttin' a lamp in the window every night, waitin' for you to come home."

"Indians killed my mother. I was so little I can't hardly remember her."

He thought he saw a flicker of sympathy in Jericho's eyes, though it was gone as soon as the man blinked.

Jericho said, "Too bad. I still remember mine, twenty times a day. My wife looks a lot like her." He quickly changed the subject. "I suppose you're anxious to get back to your company."

"I was figurin' to turn in those two horse thieves, but I guess you're goin' to keep them and put them to work."

"I'll leave that up to my foreman, Burt Hatton. He'll escort you off of my ranch."

"I can find my own way."

"He'll see to it that nobody gives you any trouble. He'll have your horse waitin' for you at the corner corral." Jericho pointed. "And you tell your fellow Rangers that if I ever want any of you on my place again, I'll send for you."

Irony edged into Andy's voice. "Sergeant Donahue will appreciate hearin' that."

Jericho went out the door. Andy followed. After being in the dark barn so long, the bright sun hurt his eyes. When his vision cleared, he saw three men and four horses at the corner corral. Two of the men were Barstow and Devlin. Andy did not recognize the third until he reached the gate. Jericho had disappeared.

Andy said, "I know you."

Burt Hatton said, "And I know you."

This was the man who had led the nighttime attack on Andy, Len, and Farley as they rode south from San Antonio to join the Ranger company on the river.

Andy said, "The night you-all tried to hit us, we suspected you belonged to Jericho's outfit."

The man did not reply.

Andy said, "We heard somebody holler like he was shot. Was he?"

Hatton growled, "Get on your horse. We're takin' you away from here."

"I can go by myself."

"Jericho wants to be sure you're gone. You can go peaceful or we can tie you in the saddle." He poked the muzzle of a pistol in Andy's direction for emphasis.

Andy said, "I believe that six-shooter's mine."

"You'll get it when I'm ready. Or you'll get what's in it."

Devlin was holding a paint horse with a huge Mexican brand across most of its left hip. It had undoubtedly come from across the river, probably on some dark night. Though Indians fancied paints for their unusual coloring, Rusty had taught Andy to regard them with suspicion until they proved themselves. Andy said to Devlin, "Looks like they gave you a new saddle, and a horse to put under it."

Devlin said, "He ain't as good as your black. I'm thinkin' about another swap."

"You'd have to shoot me first."

"I've been thinkin' about that too."

Hatton snapped, "Come on, I got other things to do."

Andy followed him out the gate, the other men riding behind. They took a southeasterly course, in the general direction of the Ranger company's camp. Andy doubted that Hatton intended to go all the way there. He simply wanted to be sure Andy got off to a good start.

They rode for about an hour. Hatton pointed to a thicket of mesquite and catclaw. "Over there."

Andy saw no sense in riding into a thicket, but he looked into the muzzle of Hatton's pistol and decided against asking questions.

Hatton reined up just at the edge of the thicket. A javelina sow and four pigs snorted and went clattering into the brush. Their backs bristled and their short legs moved in a blur. Hatton beckoned for Barstow and Devlin to come closer. "Jericho left it up to me to decide if you boys have got a job. You want it bad enough to earn it?"

Both men nodded. Barstow said, "Just tell us what to do."

"I want you to prove yourselves. I want you to shoot this Ranger."

Barstow's mouth dropped open. Devlin looked as if he had just swallowed a scorpion. Barstow said, "You mean kill him?"

"Here and now."

Andy felt helpless and cold. Hatton's eyes were grim, leaving no doubt that he meant what he said. Barstow and Devlin appeared to be near panic. Barstow's voice was strained. "I ain't never shot a man. I can't do it in cold blood."

Hatton scowled. "I figured you two for counterfeit as soon as I saw you. You'll shoot him or I'll shoot all three of you. You'll make a good meal for those javelinas."

Hands trembling, Devlin drew his pistol.

Hatton said, "Steady down. You're as liable to hit your horse as to hit that Ranger."

Devlin held the pistol in both hands. It continued to waver.

Hatton cursed. "I told Jericho that neither one of you is worth the rope it'd take to hang you with."

Barstow bent down and came up with a rifle. "I reckon we rate a little higher than that." He swung the muzzle toward Andy.

Andy's mouth felt as if it were full of cotton.

Barstow moved the rifle a little farther. It pointed at Hatton.

Hatton demanded, "What're you doin'?"

Barstow was sweating as if it were the Fourth of July. "Never kill a Ranger. If you do, the rest of them will come after you. They never forget, and they won't give up till you're hangin' off of a tree limb or shot full of holes."

Hatton declared, "I'll have your heads on a pike."

Devlin trembled. "For God's sake, Barstow."

Andy took advantage of the moment to push his horse forward and grab Hatton's pistol with both hands. They wrestled. Hatton squeezed off one shot toward the thicket. A javelina squealed. Andy managed to twist the weapon free.

Hatton wheeled his horse around and spurred away, bent low over the horn of the saddle to present a poor target. Barstow took one shot but was too nervous to hit him.

Devlin complained, "You spilt it now, Barstow. We'll never get a job with Jericho."

"It's a damned poor job that says you got to kill somebody in cold blood, and him lookin' at you the whole time. There ain't enough money between here and San Antonio . . ."

Andy slowly regained his composure. "Thanks, Barstow. For a minute I felt like an angel landed on my shoulder."

Barstow was still sweating. He lowered the rifle. "If there's any angels around here, they're lost." He looked puzzled. "I was afraid Jericho wouldn't hire us, but I didn't expect he'd send his foreman out here to kill us."

Andy said, "I believe Hatton did that on his own." Killing Andy would have eliminated one witness to the attack on him, Len, and Farley. "And even if you had shot me, he'd have killed both of you and left us all lyin' here for the hogs. Dead men don't testify."

Barstow removed his hat and rubbed his sleeve over a face dripping with sweat. "Workin' cattle gets to lookin' better all the time. Maybe we can get our old jobs back."

Devlin said nothing. He was too busy losing his breakfast.

Barstow asked Andy, "You goin' to turn us in for stealin' your horse?"

"I would've, but you saved my life. I owe you a chance to get yours straightened out."

Barstow said, "Me and Devlin was just lookin' for a little more excitement than we been havin'. I think we've had enough of it to last us a long time."

"If I was you-all, I'd take a wide swing around Jericho's country, then head north . . . way north."

"That's what we'll do. And if I ever get arrested again it'll be for singin' too loud in church."

Andy watched them ride off in an easterly direction, then he turned southward. He wanted to recover his own saddle. This one, which had belonged to Devlin, could be traded to one of the poor Mexican farmers who had been selling him food down by the river. Devlin's horse, if it got over its lameness and didn't turn up on a list of stolen property, would give him an extra mount so he could alternate and always have one resting.

All in all, he had come out a little ahead on what had seemed to be a stroke of bad luck. He hoped that someday he might see Burt Hatton again under circumstances more in his own favor.

He had also seen another side of Jericho Jackson, a side that left him conflicted. Things had appeared much simpler when he'd seen Jericho simply as a cold and calculating land-grabbing outlaw. He did not know how to handle this unexpected complexity.

Burt Hatton entered the outside door to the room Jericho used as an office. He was seldom asked into the main part of the house. Jericho was strict about insulating his wife from the ranch help. Hatton's shirt was torn. A long red scratch marred his cheek.

Jericho looked up from his ledger book. "What happened to you?"

Hatton delayed his answer. "Mind if I get me a drink?" Jericho nodded, and Hatton went to a cabinet where he knew the whiskey was kept. He poured a small glass half full and swallowed it with a sense of urgency. "Horse cold-jawed on me. Ran through the brush."

Jericho often had a feeling that Hatton said only what he thought his boss wanted to hear, but the story was plausible enough. No man worth his salt worked in the brush country without taking scars and getting thorns imbedded in his hide. "Did you set the Ranger safely on his way?"

"Last I seen of him he was headed south."

"Good. I'd like to have a friend or two in the Ranger camp when the bullets fly again."

"I don't think you'd better count on him for a friend. We oughtn't to have let him get off of this place alive. We'll have trouble with him yet."

"Dead Rangers are bad for business. What about them two cowhands? Did you put them to work?"

Hatton frowned. "I sent them on their way. They didn't have enough sand in their craw for our kind of business."

"Too bad. We'll need all the help we can get when we make our big push on Lupe Chavez."

Hatton poured another drink. "And when is that to be?"

"I don't know yet, but it'll come. It'll be like the battle of the Alamo all over again, only this time it'll end different."

Hatton had a worried look. "Maybe we ought to leave Chavez alone. You've got more land already than you can rightly see after. What do you want with land in Mexico?"

"This is about more than land. It's an old fight that never got settled. And there's the business about my wife's nephew. Lupe has got to pay for that."

"Maybe I was wrong about them Meskin outlaws that killed him. Maybe they wasn't Lupe's men after all."

Jericho's brow furrowed. "You scared, Burt?"

"Not scared. Just thinkin' about the men that might get killed."

"They're bein' well paid for it."

"There's some things money ain't enough for."

"Money can buy anything. You just have to be willin' to pay the price."

CHAPTER

FIFTEEN

Len Tanner was at Andy's makeshift campsite when Andy rode in. "Where you been?" the lanky Ranger demanded. "I found your saddle where you left it. Been worried that some Mexican bandits might've drug you off and cut out your gizzard."

"I've been up to Jericho's."

"What in the hell for?"

"Gettin' another saddle." He waited for Len's puzzled expression to come to full flower, then explained about the horse thieves and Jericho's men taking the three of them to headquarters.

Len said, "It's a wonder Jericho didn't shoot you."

"The funny thing is that I got along right decent with him. He wasn't what I expected. I never once saw him breathe fire."

"You never saw no halo around his head, neither. He's a bad hombre."

"So everybody says. It's odd, but he reminded me of Lupe Chavez. Neither one of them has any idea how much they think alike. They just look at things from opposite sides of the river."

"They'd both cut your throat in a minute. But right now you'd better report to Sergeant Donahue before *he* cuts your throat. He suspicions that you swum the river to join up with Lupe Chavez."

"What would make him think that?"

"You took up for that boy Tony. You helped him get back to his uncle."

"I'd have done that for a lost pup. And I did it for the McCawleys, not for Lupe Chavez."

"Donahue ain't goin' to see the difference. As far as he's concerned they're all Mexicans, even Big Jim."

Andy said, "I'll go downriver and report to him. First, though, I'm hungry. Want to help me scare up some wood for a fire?"

While they ate, Len told Andy that the river had been quiet. "Ain't been sign of any raiders crossin' that we could see. Just the usual traffic. A few farmers, kinfolks passin' back and forth. I picked up a lame horse wanderin' around here. Don't know who he belongs to."

Andy said, "One of those horse thieves had him. I guess he's mine if we don't find out who he was stolen from."

They rode down the river past Len's camp. Halfway to the next Rangers' post they came upon Sergeant Donahue riding the line. Len said, "Here's your stray, Sergeant."

Donahue gave Andy a look that for a culprit would mean five years in prison. "Absent without leave. What's your excuse, Private Pickard?" He bore down on the word *private*.

"It wasn't by my choice," Andy said. He repeated what he had told Len about the horse thieves and being escorted to meet Jericho.

Curiosity erased Donahue's scowl. "I've never seen Jericho's headquarters. Not many Rangers have ever been there."

Andy gave him a rough description. "It looks a lot like the McCawley ranch, and Lupe Chavez's."

"I've never seen Chavez's either, but I'd sure like an excuse to go there and give them Meskins a good whippin', the way McNelly did." His eyes brightened at the thought. "By the way, what about them two horse thieves?"

Andy shrugged. "The last I saw of them they were headed in the direction of Canada." He thought it best not to divulge that he had made no effort to stop their going. He had probably broken some unbreakable Ranger rule.

Donahue said, "You should have pulled the trigger on them. Nothin' cures a thief better than a forty-five slug."

"I figured on bringin' them in as prisoners."

"Chances are fifty-fifty that some judge would turn them loose, and they'd go right back to what they were doin'. Death is pretty damned permanent."

"I'll try to remember that."

Donahue nodded, satisfied. "Since your goin' was not voluntary, I'll reconsider filin' charges. But consider yourself on probation."

Andy had considered himself on probation ever since Donahue took temporary command of the company. He asked hopefully, "Any word on when Lieutenant Buckalew will be back?"

"None. I think they may have found somethin' else for him to do. I'm lookin' to be advanced to lieutenant any time now. Maybe even captain."

"That'd be nice." Saying so put a sour taste in Andy's mouth.

Donahue said, "Go back to patrollin' your section of the river. I expect you're about out of supplies?"

"Pretty near."

"I'll send a pack mule out tomorrow with coffee and sugar and salt. As for meat, I see lots of cattle and hogs runnin' loose."

"They all belong to somebody."

"Meskins. If they holler, tell them this is a tax they owe for us keepin' them safe."

Safe. Andy considered the irony. These people along the river were subject not only to banditry from both sides but to harassment by those Rangers who considered every Mexican suspect. The few American settlers were not much better off, for they were particular targets of Mexican outlaws still trying to avenge Santa Anna's defeat.

At times Andy thought seriously about giving this part of Texas back to the horned toads, the scorpions, and the sharp-toothed javelinas. They had a prior claim.

Donahue turned downriver, and Andy proceeded upriver. He found the lame horse contentedly grazing in the river's grassy floodplain. The limp was less pronounced. Andy tossed a loop around the animal's neck and led him to his makeshift camp. He found his saddle hanging from a tree limb so wild animals would not gnaw on it. Len's work, he guessed. Now Andy had two horses and two saddles. He was coming up in the world.

An old man crossed at a shallow point, urging a burro along with a willow switch. He saw Andy and veered away. Andy had seen the old man and the burro before, and the old man knew Andy to be a Ranger. Everybody up and down this stretch of the Rio Grande did. It would be a long time before these river people trusted the Rangers, Andy thought. And some Rangers would never come to trust the people who lived along the river. The gulf between the two cultures was too wide to bridge, at least for now.

A trail led northward from this shallow crossing. Andy saw a procession coming from the north. He counted four men on horseback. A buggy trailed behind, carrying two women. As it came closer he saw that they were Juana and Teresa McCawley. One of the horsemen was Big Jim. The others were some of his cowboys.

Andy rode out to meet them. The riders drew guns, then put them away as they recognized him. He suspected he knew their mission before they told him. "Headin' down to see Tony?" he asked McCawley.

"We haven't heard a thing about him since we were down here the last time. The womenfolks are worried."

"I always figure if it's bad news you'll hear about it soon enough. Since I haven't heard anything, I'll bet Tony is all right." He tipped his hat to the two women.

Mrs. McCawley said, "You look thin, Andy."

"Eatin' my own fixin's, ma'am. Nobody would ever hire me as a cook."

"If you'll come up and spend a few days with us, we'll put some weight back on you."

"It'd pleasure me, ma'am, but I don't see as I can."

Teresa asked, "Have you seen Farley?"

"Now and again. He's closer to the main camp, so he slips down there and gets himself a decent meal when he knows the sergeant's not around."

Mrs. McCawley said, "It isn't far from here to my brother Lupe's ranch. He knows you now, so you could go over there when you get hungry."

"He might not like havin' a Ranger show up. Anyway, it's illegal for me to cross the river."

She frowned. "It's too bad people have to draw boundaries. There was a time when the river made no difference."

McCawley drew up beside Andy. "The trail has been unusually quiet. I've heard that Jericho has been hirin' a lot of men, but we didn't run into any. Not them or hardly anybody else. Makes me wonder."

"I had a visit with him. Maybe he's reformed."

"I wish I could believe that, but I know him too well. He has a hunger that can't be satisfied. Most people get drunk on whiskey. He gets drunk on acquisition."

Andy watched Big Jim and the buggy go into the river. The cowboys remained behind.

Andy asked one, "You-all aren't goin' to stay with them all the way?"

A cowboy replied, "Big Jim said we wouldn't be welcome down there. He feels like they'll be safe enough since the womenfolk are kin to Chavez."

Andy feared McCawley might be stretching his luck in view of

Chavez's dislike for him. Perhaps Chavez would not raise a hand against his sister's husband, but some of his followers might not be so reluctant. The McCawleys were almost out of sight when several riders came up from the south and met them. They halted briefly, then went on, escorted by what Andy assumed must be Chavez men. He saw no sign of hostility. Soon the procession moved beyond his view, hidden by the brush.

Andy asked the cowboy, "You-all goin' to stay and watch till they come back?"

"No, they figure to be there for several days. We'll come back to meet them when it's time."

Andy considered. "Maybe things'll stay quiet for a while. Chavez wouldn't seem likely to set up any raids while his kin are there. He wouldn't want his sister to see him as a bandit. She thinks of him as a hero."

The cowboy said, "I've got a cousin who steals horses, but I keep tellin' myself he's not a thief. He just knows how to get them cheap."

Len was waiting at the rendezvous point where he usually met Andy. He said, "Got orders from Sergeant Donahue. He says for everybody to gather their stuff and go back to the main camp."

"Does he think the raids are over with?"

"He ain't one to explain why he does things. He's generally got a reason whether it's a good one or not."

The change suited Andy. His stomach had complained for days about his shortcomings as a cook. Maybe now he could get a few solid meals. "I'll be along as soon as I can. Meet you at your camp."

"I'll see if I can catch a couple of fish while I'm waitin'." Len had grown up on a river. Fishing was second nature to him.

Andy said, "If a fat little shoat was to wander by with no earmarks on him, that'd suit me better than fish."

"I ain't even seen a javelina lately."

It was almost dark when they rode into the main camp. Len suggested they report to the camp cook first. The sergeant could wait. Pablo bade them welcome and gave Andy a pitying look. He said, "Pretty soon you get so thin the wind carries you away. You better take two plates."

When they carried their food to a wooden table, Farley came over. He said nothing in greeting but came right to the point. "Seen anything of the McCawleys?"

Andy knew which McCawley Farley was really interested in. "Several days ago. They went over to Lupe Chavez's to see about Tony."

"To Chavez's?" Farley looked as if Andy had struck him. "And they ain't come back?"

"Not unless it was today, after I left."

"From what I hear, there's fixin' to be bad trouble down there. They're liable to get caught in the middle of it."

Disturbed, Andy put down his fork. "What kind of trouble?"

"The sergeant ain't talkin' but some of the boys say he's pulled all of us back so we won't get in Jericho's way. His spies have told him Jericho's fixin' to hit Chavez like Sam Houston hit Santy Anna."

Andy found the idea hard to accept. "And Donahue figures to just let it happen? The Rangers are supposed to try and stop that kind of thing."

"Donahue's been chompin' at the bit, wantin' to go down there and do it hisself. But the law don't allow it, so he's standin' back and lettin' Jericho do it for him."

"Jericho's pulled raids over there before."

"Not like this. He's been hirin' men anywhere he can get them. They don't have to be cowboys. They've just got to be ready and willin' to use a gun."

Len listened gravely. "Maybe it's just as well to let the thing get settled for once and for all. It's been brewin' a long time."

Farley said, "But once the shootin' starts, a bullet won't care who's in the line of fire. Women, kids . . . that girl of McCawley's"

Andy tried to rationalize. "Chavez is nobody's fool. Maybe he's already got wind of what's comin'."

"He's not God. He can't know everything. His people will be outnumbered. They won't stand a snowball's chance in hell."

Andy wrestled with his conscience. The simplest course would be to remain neutral and let things play out on their own. The conflict was inevitable. The only question was when and where. It was not his business. He had no kin in the fight. Nobody could fault him if he could do nothing about it.

Well, there was one thing he could do. He could carry a warning to Chavez. At the least he could try to get the McCawleys out of harm's way before the attack. He felt he owed them that. But to do so would violate his orders and the prohibition against Rangers crossing the river.

He did not ponder long. He rose from the table, leaving his supper half eaten. "Tell the sergeant I've just resigned."

That would take care of the legalities.

Len spilled half a cup of coffee. "What're you fixin' to do?"

"If I don't tell you, you won't have to lie to him."

Farley smacked the palm of his hand upon the table. "You're thinkin' the same thing I am. I'm goin' with you."

"Every time we ride together, you get yourself hurt and then blame me for it. You'd risk it for Lupe Chavez?"

"To hell with Chavez. I'm thinkin' about the McCawleys."

"One McCawley, anyway. Are you forgettin' she's a Mexican?"

Farley said, "She's just half." He told Len, "Tell the sergeant I resigned too." He hurried to saddle his horse. Andy had to hustle to catch up with him.

Both horses had been ridden during the day, so Andy had to caution Farley to slow down. "We can't help anybody if we kill these horses."

Farley reluctantly pulled down to a brisk trot. "First shallow crossin' we come to, we better take it. The sergeant can't stop us if we're on the other side."

"Good idea," Andy said. Farley still had the wily instincts cultivated during his long hide-and-seek relationship with the state police after the war. They put the horses into the river half a mile farther on.

Stopping on the south bank to let the animals rest, Andy saw several riders moving at an easy lope on the other side. He sensed that they were Rangers. "Donahue didn't waste much time comin' after us."

"We've rained on his barbecue. He's figured on Jericho wipin' out Lupe Chavez and his whole outfit. The border would quieten down after that, and Donahue could claim the credit."

"And get a promotion."

Farley said, "I've got no use for Chavez, and Jericho ain't any better. The border would be better off without them. But I'd hate for somethin' to happen to the McCawleys."

"Especially Teresa."

Farley did not respond.

They skirted along the Rio Grande. The terrain and thorny vegetation were similar to that on the Texas side. The sandy soil was the same, the air the same, but Andy had an uneasy sense of being an unwelcome intruder, treading on forbidden ground. A couple of hundred yards made a tremendous difference.

Farley had the same reaction. He said, "I feel like a carpetbagger at a

Confederate reunion. We're a couple of gringos on the wrong side of the river. Targets for any Mexicans that come along."

Andy still saw Rangers riding along the northern bank. "Better here than over there. Donahue could probably chew up an iron bar and spit it at us."

He pondered the incongruity of his being on this mission with Farley. He had ridden with the dour Ranger before but always because he had been obliged to do so. Neither he nor Farley had ever pretended to like each other. At best their relationship had been one of forced tolerance.

He knew Farley was correct about the risk. The hostile feeling here against Americans in general and Texans in particular ran strong. A man could be killed for nothing more than being light-skinned and blue-eyed, just as on the other side some had been murdered for no better reason than that their faces were dark. Unreasoning hatred was not confined to one race.

Darkness overtook them. Farley said, "This part of the country ain't overrun with landmarks, even in the daylight. In the dark, how're we goin' to know when we reach the road to Chavez's place?"

"I think I'll recognize it."

"Think? Thinkin' ain't knowin'."

"If you've got a better idea, tell me about it."

They rode most of the night, stopping once to rest the horses. Andy tried to sleep but could not. His skin prickled with anxiety. For all he knew, this might be the day Jericho planned to attack. However, daylight brought no sign of invasion, no distant gunfire. He said, "Looks like we'll make it in time."

Five armed horsemen suddenly appeared like apparitions out of the brush and confronted them face to face. A strong voice demanded, *"Quién es?"*

Andy raised his hands. "Friends. *Amigos.*" He chilled at the sight of five guns pointed toward him and Farley. He hoped somebody spoke English, for under his current stress he could not muster a dozen words in Spanish. "We've got a message for Lupe Chavez."

One of the men demanded, "What message?"

Andy tried to think of the Spanish word for *danger.* *"Pel ... pel ..."* The rest would not come to him. "We've come to bring warnin'. Jericho's fixin' to invade him."

He feared the meaning was not getting across. The men talked quietly among themselves. Andy had a troubling sense that some advocated shooting him and Farley here and now. Their undisguised hostility told him it would take but little to tip the scales in that direction.

A tall, thin man began to dominate the conversation. Andy recognized him as Porfirio, who had held him and Farley at the Chavez place. So far as he remembered, Porfirio had not spoken English, but he seemed to be swaying the other four away from the notion of killing.

After several minutes of talk Porfirio motioned with the muzzle of his pistol. *"Vámanos."*

Andy said, "I suppose that means we're goin'."

Farley replied, "But where? To Chavez's, or to hell?"

They angled southwestward. In a while Andy saw the buildings he knew were the headquarters of the Chavez ranch. "I hope they'll believe us."

Farley said, "Even if they don't, Jericho's got to ride over me to get to the McCawleys. I ain't lettin' that girl and her mother be hurt because Lupe Chavez is too thickheaded to listen."

Andy thought Farley should know a lot about thickheadedness. He had about the hardest head of anyone Andy knew.

They rode up to the wide front door of the sprawling stone house. Porfirio dismounted and raised his hand. *"Esperen."*

He banged a heavy door knocker twice before a heavyset maid appeared, cautiously peering out through a narrow opening. He spoke quietly, and she admitted him inside. Andy looked at the other men who had brought him and Farley here. Their grim faces told him not to move.

Shortly Porfirio returned. Lupe Chavez stood in the open doorway, picking his teeth. They gleamed a brilliant white against the heavy black mustache and the dark brown of his face. Andy hoped for a sign of welcome but saw none. Chavez said, "You know *rinches* are not welcome. What brings you to my door?"

Andy said, "We've come to warn you about Jericho."

Farley put in, "He's fixin' to hit you like a hailstorm. If he can, he'll kill everybody here."

Chavez shrugged his thin shoulders. "He has come before. He has not found us easy to kill."

Andy argued, "From what we hear, he's raised enough fightin' men to do the job this time."

"He drove us out of Texas. Does he think now he can also drive us out of Mexico?" Chavez dismissed the notion with an oath that did not need translation. "He will leave here with his guts dragging on the ground, if he leaves here at all."

The mental image was graphic but not reassuring.

Farley asked, "Are the McCawleys still here?"

"They are."

"Do what you want to about Jericho, but I'm takin' those womenfolks away." Farley looked at Andy and corrected himself. "*We're* takin' them out, me and Andy."

Anger flared in Chavez's eyes. "You will not come to my house and tell me what I must do. It is for me to decide."

Farley flared back. "Then you'd better decide right."

Big Jim McCawley came out and stood a few feet away from Chavez. He reacted with surprise upon seeing Andy and Farley. "What's all this row? Aren't you-all too far south for Rangers?"

Andy said, "We're not Rangers now, we're just citizens. We're tryin' to tell Lupe Chavez that Jericho is comin' to settle old scores, and bringin' plenty of men with him. Things are fixin' to get woolly around here."

Farley interjected, "We come to tell you to gather up your womenfolks and take them away."

McCawley said, "I've never run from Jericho."

Andy said, "This is one time you'd better."

Chavez dismissed the idea with a wave of his hand. "We are not rabbits, to run from a pack of hounds."

"Even hounds run when somethin' bigger is after them."

Chavez asked McCawley, "Should I listen to these *rinches*? I do not want to look foolish."

Andy said, "Better to look foolish and alive than be layin' here dead."

No friendship existed between McCawley and Chavez, but they quickly came to a mutual agreement in the face of a common threat. Chavez said, "It is not that I have fear of Jericho, but I am a cautious man. I will send the women and children away." He gave an order to Porfirio. Porfirio relayed it to his companions, who quickly scattered.

Chavez turned back to Andy and Farley. His eyes narrowed in threat. "If you are playing me false and the Jericho does not come . . ."

Soon several wagons and a couple of buggies began picking up excited women and children at the clutter of stone and adobe houses that made up the Chavez headquarters. A vaquero drew McCawley's buggy up to the door of the Chavez home. The maid and two younger women came out, followed by McCawley's wife and daughter. Tony appeared, pale and thin, still hunched over from the effects of his wound.

Juana McCawley told her husband, "Tony says he will not go."

Tony said, "I want you to take my mother and sister away."

McCawley said, "We'll all go. You too."

"No, I will stay and stand beside my uncle. You and these Rangers do not belong. This is not a gringo fight."

Juana told her husband, "I will stay with my son, but I want you to take Teresa away from here."

McCawley held firm. "Go off and leave you? You know me better than that. I'll send Teresa with the other women, but I'm stayin' with you and Tony."

Teresa placed her hands on her hips. "My place is with family. If you stay, I stay." She looked at Farley. "You will be here, won't you? If you are here I will not be afraid."

Farley said, "I think you're all playin' the fool. I was figurin' on takin' you out of here."

"You would have to drag me."

Some of the wagons were already leaving, carrying refugees to a safer place. Andy made one more attempt to persuade the McCawley women. "We rode all this way to see that you get out of danger."

Juana said, "You brought warning. That is enough. Jericho will not take this place by surprise. Now you should go, the three of you." She touched her husband's hand. "As Tony said, this is not a gringo fight."

McCawley's face colored. "I've always hated that word *gringo*. I've never answered to it, and I don't now."

She retreated. "I say it only to make you go."

"Not without you two. And Tony." He bent forward and tapped a forefinger against Tony's chest. "Your uncle didn't raise you. I did. Like me or hate me, I'm the only father you've got."

Tony did not budge. "I'm stayin'."

McCawley shrugged. "Then I guess we all will."

Farley looked at Teresa. "I still think you ought to go. But if you don't, I don't either." He glanced back at Andy.

Andy said, "I'm not leavin' by myself."

After most of the women and children were gone, Chavez sent Porfirio to the river to watch for sign of Jericho. He sent other riders to rouse the neighbors. As the day wore on, men from nearby ranches drifted in to augment Chavez's limited force. Whatever endangered Chavez endangered them all.

Chavez was too busy to pay attention to Andy and Farley until far into the afternoon. He seemed then to notice them for the first time. "You are still here? I thought you *rinches* were long ago gone. I do not need you."

Andy said, "We're not here for you. We stayed because of the McCawleys."

"Then stay close to them. Let no harm come to my sister and her daughter and I will try to forget that you are gringos like the Jericho."

Late in the afternoon Big Jim McCawley came to sit beside Andy and Farley in front of the big house. He carried a rifle and wore a pistol on his hip. "I guess this outfit is as ready as it'll ever be. Lupe has set up a heavy ring for defense. He would've made a good general in the big war."

Andy said, "The trouble with defense is that you have to stand and take whatever comes at you. You don't carry the fight to the enemy."

"You see somethin' you'd change?"

"I might try a little Comanche strategy. They used to set up decoys to draw the enemy in. Then they'd swoop down from both sides."

"A flankin' maneuver?"

"I guess that's what you'd call it. Instead of lettin' the enemy surprise you, you surprise him."

McCawley thought it over. "I'll talk to Lupe. He might not like it if he knew you thought of it, so I won't tell him that."

McCawley returned after a time. Andy knew by the satisfied look on his face that he had been successful. McCawley said, "I just led him along a little at a time till he came up with the rest of it himself. Now he thinks it was his own idea."

Andy asked, "Did you ever think about goin' into politics?"

CHAPTER
SIXTEEN

Jericho heard a laugh from somewhere behind him in the blackness. He looked back angrily. "Burt, go tell them to keep quiet. This won't work worth a damn if we don't catch Chavez by surprise."

Hatton rode only as far as the first half dozen men behind him. He told them to pass the word back for silence. They were within half a mile of the river. Though predawn darkness and the brush still shielded them from view, sounds could carry to the other side.

Jericho had counted thirty-seven men when they left headquarters. So far as he knew none had had a change of heart and turned back. He had taken the precaution of telling the newly hired hands that they would be paid after the mission was completed, not before. He was by necessity dealing with a class of men in whom he felt little faith. Honor was a stranger to most of them. Some would accept his money, then disappear. He did not even trust Burt Hatton, his next in command. He had purposely delayed paying Hatton all the money due him. He had a strong feeling the man's loyalty was so shallow it had to be bought anew over and over in the form of wages.

Hatton returned, grumbling. "I got a bad feelin' about this."

Jericho was in no mood to listen to Hatton's recitation of misgivings. "You've had bad feelin's as long as I've known you. This'll be over so quick that we won't even break a sweat."

"You never know where the Meskin soldiers are at from one day to the next. Somebody's liable to fetch them, like they done that time to McNelly."

"We have to see to it that nobody gets away. Then they won't tell the soldiers anything."

Jericho could see that he had not calmed Hatton's fears, but it didn't matter much: Hatton had little choice but to go along. "Once this is over, Burt, we won't have to put up with Chavez anymore. Him and his bunch won't keep nippin' at us like a bunch of heel flies."

"You ever see a firin' squad, Jericho? I did once, down at Matamoros." He shivered. "Them soldiers stood two poor fellers up against a gate and shot them. The blood spilled like water."

"We'll finish up and be back across the river before they can even blow a bugle."

The sun dropped low, then set without sign of intruders. Porfirio sent back word from the river that he had seen no activity on the other side. Andy began to sense restlessness in the men stationed around the house. They had been primed for a fight, and no fight had come.

Farley expressed a thought that Andy had considered but rejected. "Reckon Sergeant Donahue's reports were exaggerated?"

"Nobody said exactly when Jericho was comin'. They just said that he would."

"If he don't pretty soon, you'll see things start comin' unraveled. A lot of the neighbors will start wantin' to go home and do their milkin'."

"Ain't likely he'd come in the night. Neither side could see their targets in the dark."

"When we fought the Yankees it seemed to me like the best time to attack was at first light. It generally caught them half asleep."

After dark Andy heard several men ride off to the west. Several more rode east.

Farley said, "They're desertin' already."

Andy said, "I don't think so. I believe Chavez has sent them off to wait out of sight. When Jericho strikes, they'll come in on the flanks."

"Sounds like Confederate military tactics."

"Or Comanche."

"Makes sense. Most of these Mexicans are more Indian than Spanish. If Lupe Chavez would shave off that mustache I'd take him for a Comanche."

The night was long and restless. Despite his fatigue from yesterday's ride, Andy found it difficult to sleep. He would doze, then awaken abruptly in a sweat, thinking the attack had begun. He realized he had been dreaming. He and Farley had taken a position behind a three-foot adobe wall that ran parallel to the front of the house.

Farley grumbled, "I don't see how you can sleep."

"I can't, much."

"I keep thinkin' about that little girl in there. If anything was to happen to her . . ."

"Those walls are thick. Ain't likely any bullets will go through."

"But what if Jericho managed to break into the house? The walls wouldn't help much."

"We have to stop him before he gets that far."

The stars began fading in the east, and several roosters crowed. Andy's nerves began to tingle. Farley had finally gone to sleep. Andy started to wake him, then changed his mind. Farley would wake up quickly enough if Jericho came.

Lupe Chavez emerged from the house and walked around his defense perimeter, cautioning the men to stay low and avoid being seen as the morning light improved. He came at length to Andy and Farley. "You are still here? I thought you might slip away in the night."

Andy said, "We told you we were stayin'." He repeated what he had told Chavez the day before: "We're not here for you. We're here for the McCawleys."

Chavez turned a disapproving gaze upon Farley. "Especially my niece, I think."

Farley said nothing.

Chavez sniffed. "Young women can be foolish. She should look to someone better than a gringo *rinche*."

Farley declared, "Show me somebody better."

Porfirio galloped in from the north and shouted for Chavez. Andy could not understand the words, but he understood the excited look and the way Porfirio pointed as he reported to his *jefe*.

Farley had dozed again. Andy shook him. The Ranger was suddenly awake and alert, his rifle ready.

Andy pulled the skin at the corners of his eyes, trying to sharpen the image. He thought he saw movement to the north, toward the river, but he could not be sure.

Farley thumbed back the hammer of his gun. To Andy the click sounded as loud as a gunshot.

McCawley came out of the house and took up a position beside them. Andy asked, "What about your womenfolks?"

"Tony's inside with them. He's standin' at a window."

Andy saw a rifle balanced upon a windowsill.

The sun had not yet broken over the horizon, but the predawn light was enough that now he could clearly see movement to the north. Jericho's horsemen had fanned out in a line over a space of more than a hundred yards.

Chavez gave an order in Spanish. McCawley said, "He's tellin' everybody to keep down. Let Jericho think he's caught us asleep. And he would have if you-all hadn't brought warnin'."

Andy rough-counted the riders. He saw around forty. "There's more of them than there is of us."

The Jericho men were within fifty yards of the Chavez defense line when a defender raised up. A Jericho rider fired at him. Andy heard Jericho shout, "Pour it on them."

The invaders spurred into a run, coming on like a whirlwind.

The defenders began rising, taking aim at the mass of horsemen coming at them. Gunfire crackled all around Andy. Riders pitched from their saddles. Horses fell, some struggling to regain their feet, some lying on the ground and kicking. To Andy's left a defender screamed and went down.

McCawley staggered backward, a bullet in his leg. Andy ran to help him, easing him to the ground.

He heard a curse. Farley held a hand to his side. Blood oozed out between his fingers. The impact had knocked the breath out of him. He gasped, trying to get air back into his lungs. Andy started toward him, but Farley waved him away and pointed in the direction of Jericho's men.

Powder smoke rose like a patchy fog, hiding many of the adversaries from one another. Andy was sparing with his ammunition. He fired only when he could see something to aim at. Bullets smacked into the adobe wall or whispered past his ears to sing off the stone wall of the house behind him. The incessant firing made his ears throb with pain.

The attackers came near breaching the defense line, then wavered. He heard a shout in a voice he thought was Jericho's. The invaders began pulling back, shocked and badly bruised by the determined defense.

About now, Andy thought, Jericho must be wondering what could have gone so wrong with his plan. Ordinarily so large a force should have overrun this ranch in a matter of minutes. They should have swept through the buildings with relative ease, cutting down the inhabitants before they had time to mount any creditable defense. Jericho was probably cursing, asking himself if he had a spy in his ranks.

The invaders took cover wherever they could find it, behind corrals, behind outbuildings, in the fringes of brush. They began a desultory firing. The defenders fired back. None of the shooting now was doing much damage to either side so far as Andy could see. He knelt over McCawley, pressing a handkerchief against the wound to slow the blood. He then went to Farley, but Farley refused help. He had regained enough breath to say, "It ain't that much."

Andy heard a drumming of hooves from the east, then from the west. The flankers were coming in, attacking Jericho's men from both sides. Many invaders hit the saddle and beat a fast retreat toward the river. Andy could hear Jericho's angry voice calling for them to come back and fight. Shortly he was left with only a handful of men unable or unwilling to quit the scene. They were well concealed but not in a position to carry the fight forward.

The shooting died away. Neither side offered many visible targets. An uneasy quiet fell over the contested ground.

Lupe Chavez raised up a little, looking over the wall. He cupped his hands around his mouth and shouted, "You, Jericho, you give up now? You bring with you too many cowards. They run like rabbits."

Jericho answered, "You don't see *me* runnin'. I come to settle things with you, Lupe. I ain't leavin' till I do."

"You are welcome to stay. I give you six feet of ground. It will be all your own."

"You damned chili picker, you ain't seen the day you can put me under."

The two men went quiet for a bit. Andy returned to McCawley. "I'll help you into the house."

McCawley put up no argument. Andy got the rancher's arm around his shoulder and boosted him up onto his feet. He half carried, half dragged him to the door. Juana opened it and cried out in alarm. The two women helped Andy bring McCawley into the house. They laid him upon the floor, well below the windows through which a bullet might reach him.

Tony looked down on his stepfather, his face softening. "He ain't goin' to die, is he?"

Juana said, "You have struck him in the heart, but the bullet did not. Do you just stand there, or do you help?"

Tony went to his knees. "I'll help." He ripped his stepfather's bloody pants leg open with a knife blade.

Andy went back outside, where only an occasional wild shot was being fired. Crouching, he returned to Farley, on his knees behind the wall, his shirt off and wadded up, pressed against his side. He did not give Andy time to ask questions. He said, "I told you, Badger Boy. This happens every time I'm with you."

"I'm not the one that shot you."

"No, but I'll bet they was aimin' at you instead of me. You're the damndest jinx I ever saw."

"I'll help you into the house."

"It ain't so much. Clipped my ribs is all. Might've cracked one, the way it feels."

Andy's patience was strained. "Don't be so stubborn. Teresa will patch you up, her and her mother."

Mention of Teresa had a positive effect on Farley. "All right, but soon as I can I'm goin' as far from you as I can get. A hundred, two hundred miles. Maybe more."

Teresa gasped as Andy brought Farley in. She appeared even more concerned over Farley than over her father. Andy tried to explain that the wound was not all that serious, but he saw that Farley was enjoying her attention. He went back outside.

For a while all was quiet. The shooting had stopped. Andy was sure the remnant of invaders remained, though they were well hidden.

He heard Jericho call again: "Chavez, you still there?"

"I am here, *diablo Tejano*. What you want now?"

"I got a proposition for you. We can make a deal."

"You came here to kill me, and now you want to deal? You got no cards."

"I have one. I'm bettin' I've got more guts than you do."

Indignant, Chavez stood up to his full height, just a little over five feet. He shook his fist. "I got plenty guts, gringo."

"Then let it come down to just me and you. We step out into the open, both of us. Best man wins. Either way, everybody else goes free."

"It would not be an even fight. You are a bigger target than me."

"Maybe I'm a better shot. It'll be easy to find out."

Chavez hesitated. "Why should I do this? You are in a trap. When you try to get away my men will kill you."

"I thought you wanted that pleasure for yourself. When it's over everybody will say you were too much of a coward to face me."

Chavez bristled. "I am not a coward."

"Then show me."

Chavez shouted in Spanish. Andy assumed it was an order for everyone to stay put, to take no part. Jericho shouted for his men to keep hands off. "This is between me and Chavez. Whichever way it goes, everybody else rides out of here peaceful. You hear me, Burt?" He paused, looking around. "Burt?"

Burt Hatton was not there. Andy wondered if he had been shot or if he had fled.

Jericho stepped out from behind a small shed, carrying a rifle. He walked toward the wall. Porfirio handed Chavez a rifle, then stood back as Chavez went out through an opening and stood waiting. Jericho walked to within twenty feet of him, then stopped.

Chavez said, "A long time we have been enemies, Jericho. But never did you come against me like this. For why now?"

"Some of your bandits murdered my wife's nephew. It was like she'd lost a son. I couldn't stand still for that."

"I know nothing of it."

"I had it in mind to kill your nephew in return, but it's better this way. I'd rather kill you."

"If you can, gringo. If you can."

For what seemed several minutes the two men stood glaring, taking each other's measure, each waiting for the other to move. When it happened it was so fast that Andy could not tell which man moved first. Two shots sounded as one. Chavez staggered, eyes stricken as he dropped his rifle and clasped both dark hands against his stomach. He tried to speak, but no sound came except a groan. His knees buckled. He went down on one shoulder.

Jericho's left arm hung at his side, shattered. Blood soaked a torn sleeve and dripped from his fingers. He swayed like a tree about to fall.

Porfirio moved toward him, fury in his eyes, but Chavez called to him in a weak voice. Porfirio dropped on his knees beside his fallen leader. The language was Spanish, but Andy surmised that Chavez was telling him to let Jericho go.

Tony hurried out and knelt beside his uncle. Quiet words passed between them. Tony looked at Jericho with hatred and seemed about to move against him. Chavez grasped Tony's sleeve and stopped him. A deal was a deal.

Chavez coughed and went limp. Tony folded his uncle's hands across his chest and pulled his fallen sombrero over the still face. He pushed to his feet, his eyes profoundly sad. "You'd better go, Jericho. I can't hold Uncle Lupe's people back very long. I may not be able to hold myself."

Jericho looked toward Andy. "What about you, Ranger? You got somethin' to say?"

"I ain't a Ranger anymore, but I expect there'll be Rangers waitin' for you at the river." He did not know what the Rangers could do about Jericho, however. His invasion of Mexico had not been a violation of Texas law.

One of Jericho's men took his boss's good arm and led him away.

Several of the Chavez men stood over their fallen *jefe* and removed their hats. One made the sign of the cross. Porfirio said something in a low voice. Three men carefully lifted Chavez and carried him toward the house.

Andy walked up to Tony. "I guess you're the boss here now. What comes next?"

The thought seemed to take Tony by surprise. "I don't know. I'll need time to think it through. I wish Uncle Lupe hadn't made that deal with Jericho. If we don't kill him now, we'll have to reckon with him sometime later on."

"He took a whippin' he won't get over any time soon. And that arm is bleedin' bad. He might not make it home."

"If he does, bein' crippled may just make him meaner."

Andy watched Jericho ride away with a few of his followers. The rancher was hunched over, in obvious pain.

Andy said, "This didn't have to be. It happened because of two hardheaded men. Either one of them could have stopped it years ago."

Tony said, "No, they couldn't. It wasn't just them. It was the Alamo and San Jacinto and the Mexican War. I was able to pick sides, but most people never got a choice. Their side was picked for them the day they were born—American or Mexican."

"You're some of both. Maybe you can help bring all this to some kind of settlement."

Tony shook his head. "It'll take a lot of time and a lot of funerals before that happens. I picked the Mexican side. I can't turn my back on it. I can't help my belly firin' up every time I see a gringo push some Mexican around. I want to kill him and all the blue-eyed gringos around him."

"What about Big Jim? He put up a good fight on your uncle's side, and he got himself bloodied for it."

"He's still a gringo. I'd like to forget that, but I can't. Every time I look at him, I'll remember what the gringos did to us."

"But a lot of Americans took abuse from Mexicans too. Remember Santa Anna? Remember the Alamo and Goliad?"

Tony looked at ground darkened by the blood of Guadalupe Chavez. "We remember what we want to remember, and we forget whatever makes us ashamed. There won't be peace on the river until no one is left who remembers these times."

Jericho Jackson's arm was afire. The pain brought blinding tears to his eyes. He turned his head, trying not to let Jesse Wilkes see them.

Wilkes said, "We better stop and do somethin'. You're bleedin' plumb to death."

Jericho felt drained of strength, but he did not want to stop before they crossed the river. He realized he stood a good chance of not reaching it at all. "Tie it off so it won't bleed so much," he said. "It's way too far to a doctor, but I know where there's a *curandero*. He'll fix me up till I can get to somebody better."

Wilkes tore a sleeve from his own shirt and wrapped it tightly above the wound. "Maybe that'll slow it down a little. In the war I seen doctors saw off arms that didn't look as bad as yours."

Jericho grunted. Wilkes was almost as pessimistic as Burt Hatton had always been. "Got any idea what happened to Burt?"

Jericho could see that Wilkes wanted to speak but was hesitant. He demanded, "Tell me somethin'."

Grudgingly Wilkes said, "I hate to say this, but I seen Burt turn his horse around and run for the river right after the first shots was fired. He wasn't in favor of this raid in the first place."

"Damned coward." Jericho tried to spit, but his mouth was too dry. "I've always suspicioned that he didn't put up much fight the time Lupe Chavez's bandits killed my wife's nephew. I wouldn't be surprised if he turned and ran then just like he did today."

Wilkes seemed to be summoning courage. Reluctantly he said, "Burt lied to you about that fight. He said he'd kill any of us who ever told you the straight of it."

"He ain't here now. Tell me."

Stumbling over the words, Wilkes managed to say, "It wasn't none of Chavez's men. What happened was, we came onto three travelers, and Burt wanted their horses. Thought they might be carryin' money too. Said we could rob them on the quiet and lay the blame on Mexican bandits. And we wouldn't have to divvy up any of it with you. He figured on jumpin' them after dark and takin' them by surprise. They surprised us instead. We didn't know it then, but it turned out they was Rangers."

A building anger almost made Jericho forget the pain. "He told it a lot different."

"He didn't know but what you might shoot him—and maybe us too—if you found out he got the boy killed on a fool stunt like that. It was a lot easier to drop the blame on Lupe Chavez."

Jericho slammed the palm of his good hand against his leg. "The lyin' son of a bitch! The main reason for this raid was to get even with Lupe for killin' that boy. And now you tell me it wasn't even his bunch that done it."

Wilkes hung his head. "I ought to've told you a long time ago."

"Yes, you should. But get me back to the ranch. If Burt is there, it'll pleasure me to shoot him between the eyes."

Approaching the river, he saw strangers waiting on the north bank. They were Rangers, he guessed, and they appeared to have taken several of his men into custody.

Jericho said, "I can't see clear enough to tell if Burt Hatton is amongst them."

"I don't think he is."

"Maybe he went upriver and crossed where there ain't no Rangers. We'll do the same."

Wilkes argued, "Them Rangers might be able to do somethin' about your bad arm."

"To hell with the arm. We're goin' after Burt. If I start to fall off, you grab me. I ain't stoppin' till I catch him."

Burt Hatton reined up and studied the Jericho headquarters. The place looked deserted. All able-bodied men who could handle a gun had gone on the raid. He had known as soon as the opening volleys were fired that the expedition was a failure. The surprise Jericho had counted on had gone sour somehow. Chavez had been ready with a lethal defense.

The early fire cut down several men on either side of him. Hatton quickly decided he did not intend to join them and die for someone else's folly. Jericho had allowed his hatred for Chavez to trump his judgment. Hatton had turned his horse around and quirted it most of the way through the brush and the sand to the river. Just in time he spotted a party of men waiting on the other side and guessed that they were Rangers. He rode farther west and crossed at another shallow point.

Now he surveyed the Jericho headquarters. He did not know if Jericho had survived, but chances were that he had. The boss had always enjoyed better luck than any two men were entitled to. Hatton sometimes suspected he had made a pact with the devil.

Well, Jericho would not put Burt Hatton in harm's way ever again. Hatton intended to gather up what belonged to him, plus some that didn't but should, and hunt for greener grass. The farther from Jericho, the better.

If he was lucky, he thought, no one would be in the house except Jericho's citified wife. Hatton had always resented her because Jericho thought she was too good to associate with the common hands. That old black maid of hers would probably be there too, but she was harmless. She was likely to do nothing except holler. The two might give him a little sass, but he did not expect them to offer any physical resistance. Chances were they would cower in a corner and cry.

He tied his horse outside. He started to push through the outside door into Jericho's office, but he changed his mind. That was the way he had always entered because Jericho did not want him venturing into the rest of the house where that pampered woman might have to look at him. This time Jericho was not here to make him go in like a servant. By God, he would go in the front like white folks should.

He shoved the door open and waited a moment, letting his eyes adjust from sunlight to the darkened interior. Hearing a gasp, he turned. Jericho's wife stared at him, her mouth open in surprise. Hatton had never studied her closely before. He found her skinny and frail-looking. He wondered what Jericho had ever seen in her. He could buy the favors of better-looking women in any town for the change in his pocket.

She demanded, "What are you doing here? Where is my husband?"

"Maybe in heaven, maybe in hell."

Her hands were clasped at her flat breasts. "He's dead?"

"A bunch of them are. I don't know about him. Things was a lot worse than we expected, so I lit a shuck."

Her face tightened in anger. "You are a coward, sir."

"If I wasn't, I'd be gettin' dirt shoveled in my face. Them Meskins are damned good shots." He made his way from the parlor to Jericho's office at the end of a corridor. He knelt in front of the safe and exercised his fingers.

He had never opened the safe before. Jericho allowed no one to touch it. But he had watched Jericho many times, and he had made a mental note of the combination in case a situation like this might arise.

Mrs. Jackson followed him, the black maid just behind her. She demanded, "What are you doing at that safe?"

"I'm fixin' to open it."

"Why?"

"It's got money in it. I ain't leavin' here with my pockets empty. I've spent too much of my life that way."

He turned the knob one way and the other, trying to remember the sequence of numbers. He missed once, but on his second try he swung the door open. Inside was a metal box in which he had watched Jericho place large sums of money from time to time. He did not bother to count. He could do that later, when he was well away from here. He rifled through the papers and ledgers to be sure he was not overlooking any currency. Satisfied, he tucked the box under his arm and rose to his feet.

Mrs. Jackson gripped a pistol with both hands. It was a big Navy Colt, heavy enough that she had trouble holding it steady. "You are not going to rob my husband," she said. "Put that back."

Instead, he threw the box at her and jumped aside as she pulled the trigger. The explosion shook the room. Smoke blossomed around her. Before she could thumb the hammer back he grabbed the warm barrel and twisted the weapon from her small hands. He raised it and swung it down hard, striking the top of her head and slanting down the side of her face. She dropped like a sack of corn.

The black woman screamed and came at him with a poker from the fireplace. He deflected the blow with his left arm and pointed the pistol into her face. "Back away, Mammy, or you'll be a dead nigger."

The maid dropped to her knees beside the unconscious woman. "Miz Jackson. Wake up, Miz Jackson."

Hatton retrieved the metal box and backed toward the door, still carrying the Navy Colt. He said, "When she wakes up, tell her I didn't come here to do that. But I don't stand for anybody pointin' a gun at me—man, woman, or child."

He tied the box to his saddle, patted it as he might a dog, then mounted and rode north in an easy trot. He whistled an old tune he had heard in a San Antonio dance hall.

A day that had gotten off to a miserable start had completely changed complexion. It looked now like a sunny day in spring. All it needed was a rainbow.

Jericho's arm hung stiffly at his side. Every heartbeat sent pain drumming through his body as he rode up to his stone house. Jesse Wilkes had been obliged several times to hold him and keep him from falling. His head ached, and he felt fever rising. Before long he was going to be sick as a calf with the yellow scours.

"Help me into the house, Jesse. I don't want to fall down in front of her."

He had always tried to let his wife see nothing but strength and purpose from him. He hated the thought of her seeing him in this deplorable condition. He had sent one of his riders to fetch a *curandero*, but it would be a couple of hours at best before the healer could get here. Tomorrow he would have Wilkes start with him to San Antonio, where an honest-to-God medical doctor could tend to that arm.

Wilkes opened the door, then supported Jericho as he crossed the threshold. They stopped abruptly just inside. Jericho's wife lay on a divan. A cloth covered most of her face, but not so completely that he did not see a deep bruise across her jaw.

"What the hell? Did she fall?"

The maid burst into tears. "It was a man done it, that man you call Hatton. He was takin' money out of your safe, and she tried to stop him."

Staggering, Jericho made his way to his wife's side. She appeared to be only half conscious, but she recognized his voice. Her fingers closed weakly over his hand. She murmured, "Jericho? Is that you, Jericho?"

"It's me. I'm home." Jericho lifted her hand and kissed it, then turned back to the maid. "How long since Burt left here?"

"Not long. I ain't kept track of the time."

"Which direction did he go?"

"I was too busy to watch him leave, but it sounded like he went north."

Jericho said, "Wilkes, help me back to my horse. We'll catch him if we have to trail him plumb to San Antonio."

"Jericho, you ain't in no condition. If you don't take care of that arm, it's liable to kill you."

"Damn it, I didn't ask you, I *told* you. If the Lord decides to take me, that's all right. We all got to go sometime. But I want to see Burt Hatton go ahead of me. Hand me that shotgun from over the mantel."

"Like as not he's got a rifle. He may not let you get close enough to use a shotgun."

"I'll get close. I don't think I can hold a rifle steady, but that scattergun will get him."

"You may not live that long."

"Ain't nobody ever killed me yet. It'll take a better man than Burt Hatton to do it."

Hatton had put several miles behind him. The day's excitement had drained him. He knew he had to keep going, because if Jericho had survived the shooting at the Chavez ranch he might have reached home by now. Hatton wondered which would anger Jericho more, his wife's injury or the safe with its money box gone. It was a cinch that if Jericho was alive and on his feet he would sooner or later follow Hatton's trail.

But Hatton was in dire need of a drink. He could have taken a bottle from Jericho's house if he had thought of it, but his mind had been too involved with grabbing the money and getting away. His path would carry him by a crossroads general store that dealt in groceries, cheap whiskey, and sometimes destitute young Mexican women desperate to make a living any way they could. He saw the place ahead, a flat and ugly structure built of pickets and plastered to keep the wind and rain out.

It was his intention simply to buy a bottle and drink while he rode. But once he was inside, the metal box pressed firmly under his left arm, he decided to linger long enough to savor one drink at leisure. Then he could ride on. The first drink led to a second. By that time a slender young woman had sidled up to him at the rough plank bar and put an arm around his waist. He did not understand much she said, but imagination filled in the gaps. He poured a drink for her and another for himself. His fear of Jericho began to fade as the whiskey and the woman's big brown eyes warmed his blood. The bottle was more than half empty when he grabbed it by the neck and followed her through the rear of the store. She led him into a small picket shack in the back.

He lost sense of time. He swung his legs down from the bed and knocked over the empty bottle. His head felt light, and the room did slow circles around him. He tried to pull his britches on but had trouble keeping both feet from going into the same pants leg. The woman had to help him. He knew she had dipped into the metal box. He did not know how much she took out of it, and at the moment that did not matter. It came back to him that the box was Jericho's, and that Jericho was sure to come looking for it. He buttoned his shirt wrong but left it that way. He strapped his gun belt around his waist, part of the shirttail hanging over it.

The woman was rubbing against him and making what he surmised was love talk in Spanish, but he was feeling an urgency to move on. His fear of Jericho began to penetrate the fog raised by whiskey and lust.

He said, "*Adiós*, sweet thing," and staggered out the door into the daylight. His heart took a leap as his bleary eyes discovered two men standing there. They were Jericho and Jesse Wilkes. The metal box fell from his hands and burst open on the ground. Paper currency began blowing away.

Jericho carried a shotgun under his right arm. His left arm hung stiffly at his side. The sleeve was the rusty red of dried blood, and in the center it glistened with blood still fresh. The voice was not what he was accustomed to from Jericho. It was a little man's voice, strained and weak, but the words crackled with hate. "Burt Hatton, you are a woman beater, a thief, and a liar."

Hatton saw the muzzle of the shotgun coming up. He drew his pistol and squeezed off one shot before the blast slammed him back against the picket wall. As he slumped to the ground he heard a woman's scream from inside the shack. A green bill drifted in front of him. By reflex he reached out, but his fingers were too weak to grasp it. The wind carried it away.

CHAPTER
SEVENTEEN

Andy stood beside his horse and looked back toward the Chavez house. He had tried to help Farley saddle up, but Farley had stubbornly waved him away though his face was twisted in pain. He managed to saddle his horse by himself.

Teresa stood just outside the front door, watching.

Andy said, "She doesn't want you to go."

Farley did not reply. He went about tightening the cinch, mumbling under his breath.

Andy said, "That wound is liable to get infected. Why don't you stay here and let them take care of it for you till you're sure it's goin' to heal all right?"

"Why don't you mind your own business, Badger Boy?"

"Personally, I don't care one way or the other. But that girl has got feelin's for you, and it's hurtin' her to see you go. I think you've got the same feelin's for her."

"What if I do? What kind of life would people let us have together, me white, her Mexican? Half, anyway."

"I'll bet Big Jim and his wife had some doubts too, at first. But it looks to me like they've done pretty good together."

"I ain't Big Jim."

"No, you sure ain't." Andy felt a flicker of resentment, seeing the sad-eyed girl watching from the house. "If you was, you wouldn't worry about what other people say. You'd only think about what *you* want, you and her."

Farley groaned as he pulled himself into the saddle. His hand went to his side, pressing against the wrapping that bound his ribs. "If we hurry up, maybe we can catch Jericho before he crosses the river."

"What for? We're not Rangers anymore. What Jericho does is none of our business."

Farley grimaced. "It just rubs me raw thinkin' about what he done here today. There's been people killed and a good many more shot up on his account. He ought to be called to answer for it."

"He took a bullet. Wouldn't surprise me if he loses that arm."

"It ain't that I got any sympathy for Lupe Chavez. I don't. But he's dead, and Jericho's still alive. Everybody would be better off if they was both dead. Maybe the border would finally settle down."

The border would not settle that easily, Andy thought. Two people, even those as powerful as Jericho and Chavez, would not make that much difference.

Andy had seen Jericho ride away with one of his men. Jericho had appeared to be in a bad way. He said, "Like as not the Rangers will pick him up as soon as he crosses the river."

"What can they do to him? Any law he broke was on this side of the river, not in Texas."

Andy admitted with regret, "You're probably right."

Before the house faded from sight, Farley shifted in the saddle and looked back. Andy suggested, "It's not very far. You could still turn around."

"I've made up my mind."

They rode in silence most of the way to the river. As they approached it Andy could see horsemen on the far side. He guessed there might be thirty or more. "Some of them are Rangers. Looks like they've been pickin' up Jericho's men as they cross over."

Farley drew rein. "I expect Sergeant Donahue is with them. Looks like we're in trouble, me and you."

"Might be. We left word that we'd resigned before we went over, but he didn't accept that the last time I did it."

Farley appeared to wrestle with his conscience. Finally he said, "Go on by yourself if you want to. I'm turnin' back."

"Thought you'd made up your mind."

"It's *my* mind. I can change it if I want to."

Andy smiled. "Just be sure you don't ever say or do anything to hurt her, even if she is a Mexican."

"Just half," Farley said. He turned and started back toward the Chavez headquarters.

Andy watched until Farley was out of sight, then put his horse into the river. Len Tanner rode to the water's edge to meet him as he came out. "Awful glad to see you, Andy. I was afraid you might've got yourself shot in the big doin's over there."

"They tried, but they missed."

"Was it Farley that I seen turn back? I hope he didn't get his grouchy self wounded." His tone of voice indicated that he wished otherwise.

"Once in the side and once in the heart. The one in the heart is a wound he's apt to carry the rest of his life."

Len understood and shook his head in disbelief. "Well, I'll swun. After all the things he said."

Andy saw Sergeant Donahue riding toward them. "What has Donahue been sayin'?"

"About you, nothin' that falls easy on the ears. But about today, he's grinnin' like a possum. He's sure this is fixin' to earn him a promotion."

"I don't see Jericho in that bunch."

"Ain't much he can do about Jericho anyway, seein' as everything he done was in Mexico. But he's got most of Jericho's men, the ones that made it back across the river. He's holdin' them till we can check all of them against the fugitive list. The ones Jericho didn't lose on the other side of the river, he's apt to lose over here."

Donahue stopped his horse and gave Andy a hostile study. "You're under arrest, Private Pickard. In goin' across the river you violated a direct order."

"I resigned before I went."

"That resignation was not delivered directly to me. I do not recognize it." He looked past Andy. "Where is Private Brackett?"

"He's stayin' over there for a while. He got himself wounded."

Donahue said, "Serves him right. What about Jericho? He has not crossed."

"He left before we did. Had a few men with him. They probably saw the Rangers waitin' and decided to find a quiet place farther up the river."

Donahue frowned. "Then he's probably on his way back to his stronghold."

"He looked like one arm was shot to pieces. I'm guessin' he headed for home to get it taken care of."

"You've been to his headquarters before. I want you to guide me there."

"But I'm under arrest. And I'm not a Ranger anymore."

Donahue snorted impatiently. "I told you I do not accept your resignation. But take me to Jericho's and I will consider you no longer a Ranger."

"What about that arrest business?"

"I'll drop the charges."

"If we find Jericho I don't see much you can do about him. Not legally."

"I just want him to know that he's not the cock of the walk around here anymore. I'm goin' to tell him the Rangers can go anywhere they want to. From now on Jericho's road is open to the public."

Donahue did not wait to see if Andy would accept. He called, "Tanner, I want you and Bill Hewitt. You are goin' with me and Pickard."

It struck Andy again how similar Jericho's stone house was to those of Lupe Chavez and Big Jim McCawley. He saw a man sitting on a bench at the edge of a colorful flower bed, just to the right of the front door. The man watched the Rangers' approach but made no move to get away. He sat until they were within stone-throwing distance, then stood up to wait for them.

Donahue demanded, "Who are you?"

"Name's Jesse Wilkes."

"We've come to see Jericho Jackson."

Wilkes jerked his thumb toward the door. "Inside."

Donahue dismounted and said, "Hewitt, disarm him, then stay out here and watch him. We do not want any interference."

Wilkes said with glum resignation, "Ain't nobody fixin' to interfere with you. Just go ahead in."

Pistol in hand, Donahue motioned for Andy to open the door. "I'll be right behind you."

Andy felt a momentary queasiness about going in first. If Jericho was waiting with a drawn weapon, Andy would take the first bullet. Donahue was using him for a shield.

He blinked, for coming in from the sunshine made the room appear dark the first moment. He saw two women standing in the parlor, facing him. One was black. The other was white, a tall, thin woman Andy knew must be Jericho's wife. He saw a deep bruise on her swollen face.

Donahue stepped out from behind him. "We've come to talk to Jericho Jackson. Where's he at?"

Mrs. Jackson remained silent but pointed down a dark hall. She led the way. Donahue said, "Pickard, Tanner, you-all stick close to me. No tellin' what Jericho's reaction may be."

Mrs. Jackson stopped at an open door and motioned for the Rangers to go inside. Andy saw Jericho Jackson lying on a bed. A candle burned on a stand beside him. Beside the candle lay a Bible.

Andy did not have to move closer to see that Jericho was dead. He turned toward the woman. The grief in her eyes told him to ask her no questions.

Donahue's eagerness was gone. Soberly he said, "You men can bear witness that the fugitive is deceased." He puzzled, "But how could a wounded arm have killed him?"

Mrs. Jackson summoned enough voice to say, "Ask Wilkes."

Outside, Wilkes explained that he and Jericho had followed a man named Burt Hatton. Andy recognized the name. Though Jericho had blasted Hatton with a shotgun, Hatton had managed to put a bullet through Jericho's lung.

Wilkes said, "Wasn't nothin' anybody could do for him except bring him home to his woman. I done that. Now, if you-all have got no further business with me, I'll see to his buryin'."

Donahue said, "Somebody else will have to do that. You'll be goin' with us. We'll want to check you against our fugitive list."

Mrs. Jackson had come out to stand beside the door. Andy asked her, "You goin' to be all right, ma'am?"

She shook her head. "No, but I'll get by. I still have a home back in Missouri."

Donahue asked, "What do you figure to do with this ranch and everything that belonged to your husband?"

"I've not had time to give it thought. I'll probably sell what was legally his. As for that which was not, I'll try to find who rightfully owns it."

Donahue frowned. "Be careful who you let have it. This is a white man's country now."

She stiffened. "The kind of outlaw white trash my husband surrounded himself with? He tried to shield me, but I am not blind. I was always aware of his shortcomings. Where I can, I'll make amends."

Donahue warned, "You could be askin' for trouble."

"If trouble comes, I'll call on the Rangers." She went into the house and closed the door.

Donahue cursed under his breath. "She'd better not call on *me*. Be damned if I'll answer."

Andy said, "If you don't, you may have to hunt for honest work."

They returned to the main camp, where the Jericho men had been escorted for screening to determine which of them might be wanted somewhere. Len had searched his fugitive list and found Jesse Wilkes was sought on a murder charge. Several others held in the camp had already been identified as well.

Sergeant Donahue was jubilant. "This will look great in the newspapers. I can see the headline: BIG CLEANUP ON THE BORDER."

Then he saw something else, and he froze to attention. Major Jones of Austin walked out of the headquarters tent and beckoned. "Sergeant, I want to see you."

Flustered, Donahue made a halfhearted salute. "You've come just in time, Major. We've done a good piece of work here."

"So I see."

"We've broken up two of the worst bandit gangs on the border, one on each side of the river. The people of Texas can be proud of my Rangers."

"Well and good, but I think the adjutant general will want to know why you didn't do it sooner."

Donahue blinked. "What do you mean?"

"I am given to understand you had advance word that Jericho was gathering a hard crew for that invasion. You stood by without making any effort to interfere. If these men are wanted today, they were wanted then. Why didn't you round them up before they went into Mexico?"

"Nobody's ever invaded Jericho's little kingdom."

"You had good reason to do so. All you lacked was the will."

Donahue slumped. "At least Chavez and Jericho are both dead. The country is well rid of them."

Jones nodded. "True. But many others are dead too, white men and Mexicans both. You will have a chance to explain all that in Austin. Perhaps the adjutant general will see fit to keep you in the rank of sergeant. Or he may suggest that you seek employment elsewhere."

The major turned and walked away, leaving Donahue standing with his head down.

Andy waited until the major went back into the tent, then followed him. He said, "Sir, I've already tried twice to turn in my resignation. What do I have to do to get it accepted?"

The major stared in surprise. "You can't mean you want to leave the force."

"I think I've been a Ranger about long enough. The time has come for me to try my hand at somethin' else."

Jones's voice was regretful. "I can handle the resignation for you. But are you sure?"

"I've thought on it a lot. I'm sure."

Outside, Len Tanner put his hand on Andy's shoulder. "I'm goin' to miss you."

"And I'll miss you. Don't you ever consider quittin' too?"

"Nope. Never had so much fun in my life." He gripped Andy's hand so hard that it hurt. "Tell Rusty and them I said howdy."

Andy's heartbeat picked up as he saw Rusty Shannon's double cabin ahead. He had grown to manhood here. He felt that he was home, though he knew he would not stay for long. He looked over the fields, expecting to see Rusty working there, but in this he was disappointed. He rode up to the cabin, dismounted, and shouted, "Anybody home?"

Alice Shannon stepped out onto the dog run that separated the two sections of the cabin. She shaded her eyes and called, "Andy? Can that be you?"

"Sure is. You got anything to eat?"

"If I don't, I'll fix somethin'." She hurried out to meet him. As her apron flared in the wind he noticed that her stomach was extended. He hugged her but took care not to squeeze too hard.

He said, "Looks like pretty soon there's goin' to be another mouth to feed around here."

"Two of them if you're stayin'."

"I just came for a little visit. Wanted to be sure the two of you are all right. I can see that *you* are. How's Rusty?"

"Fine. He's tickled over the prospect of bein' a daddy. He went over to Shanty's. Ought to be home pretty soon. Come in and have some coffee. We'll eat supper when Rusty gets back."

Andy heard a rattle of trace chains and looked toward the road. He saw Rusty's wagon. "I'll wait out here for Rusty." He frowned, trying to think of a delicate way to ask her. Finding none, he blurted, "Last time I was here you were still wonderin' if the reason Rusty married you was because you reminded him of Josie."

"Josie will always be with him. I don't try to take her place. But I've made my own place with him now." She touched her stomach and smiled. "The baby and me." She went back into the cabin.

Rusty hauled the mule team to a stop and jumped down from the wagon, wrapping the reins around the brake. He rushed up to pump Andy's hand. "Thought you were way down on the border. Are you on leave?"

"No, I'm not a Ranger anymore. I decided it's time to find out just where I belong."

"You've got a place right here as long as you want it."

"No, this is yours and Alice's. And however many little Shannons may come along. I've thought a lot about that country out west, along the Llano and the San Saba. I took a likin' to it while I was stationed there."

"It's a pretty country. But it's a long ways from here."

"Everything around here is settled up. That's a new country. Lots of room to grow in."

"Not by yourself. You'll need somebody to help you, somebody to come home to of a night. It took me a while to realize that myself, but I know it now." He looked toward the house, where smoke rose from the kitchen chimney. "I didn't realize how lonesome this place used to be till I brought Alice to share it with me."

Andy looked at the ground. "Seen Bethel Brackett lately?"

"Saw her in town a few days ago. She's prettier than ever."

"Anybody courtin' her?"

"If they're tryin', they're not gettin' anywhere. First thing she did was ask me all about you. She hadn't heard from you in a long time."

"I ain't much hand at writin' letters." He glanced at the house. "Reckon Alice would take it badly of me if I was to skip supper and go on over to see Bethel?"

Rusty grinned. "She'd think it's the smartest thing you've ever done."

Andy moved quickly into the saddle. "I may not be back tonight." He spurred the horse into a long trot. He looked behind him once. Rusty and Alice stood in the yard, arms around each other. Alice waved.

Andy put the horse into a gallop.

The sun was going down as he reined up in front of the Brackett house. He yelled, "Bethel! Are you in there?"

He heard a cry from inside. She stepped out onto the porch, then hurried down the steps. She skipped toward him with outstretched arms as he swung from the saddle. When they broke apart he asked, "Ever been out west to the hill country?"

"Never have."

"How would you like to go?"

She hugged him again, hard. "Just tell me when we're leavin'."